Also by Stephen Swartz

A Girl Called Wolf

A Dry Patch of Skin

A Beautiful Chill

After Ilium

Aiko

The Dream Land Trilogy
I. Long Distance Voyager
II. Dreams of Future's Past
III. Diaspora

EPIC

FANTASY

*WITH DRAGONS

AN EPIC NOVEL

STEPHEN SWARTZ

MYRDDIN PUBLISHING GROUP

UNITED STATES · UNITED KINGDOM · AUSTRALIA

ISBN-13: 978-1-68063-025-1

ISBN-10: 1-68063-025-3

unique electronic & print books

www.myrddinpublishing.com

Cover Design by Iris Schaeffer

(Theodor Severin Kittelsen [1857–1914], *The Dragon Awakens*)

EPIC FANTASY*
*WITH DRAGONS

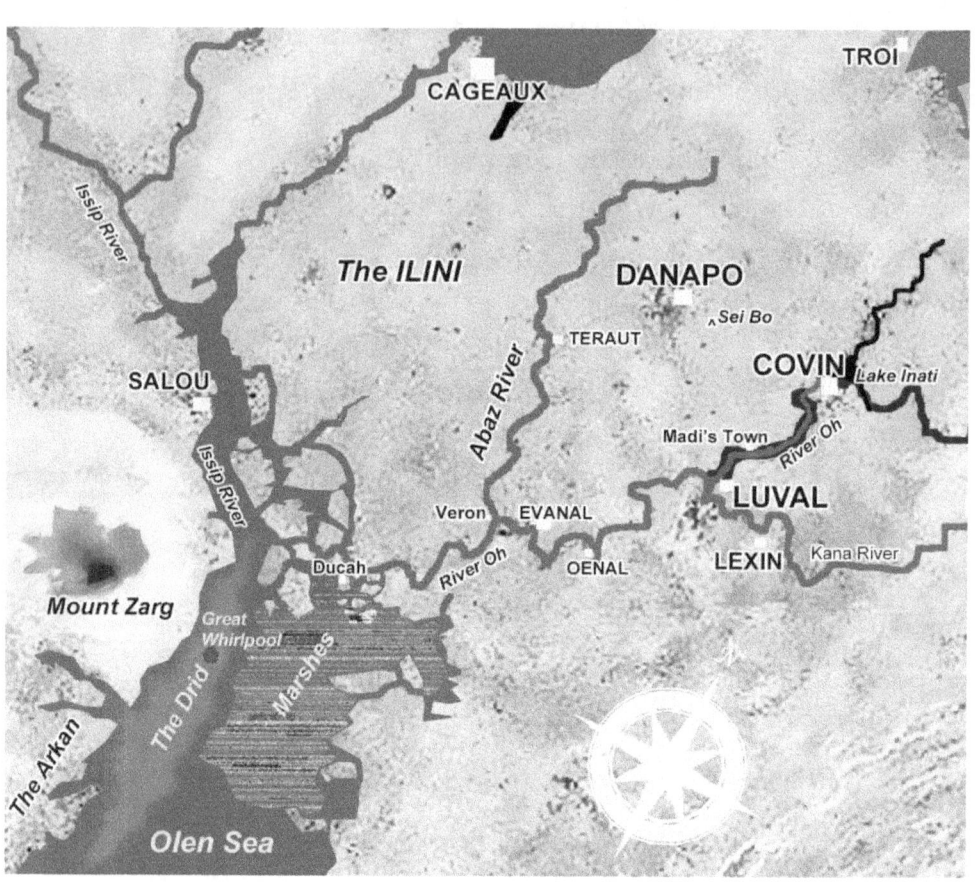

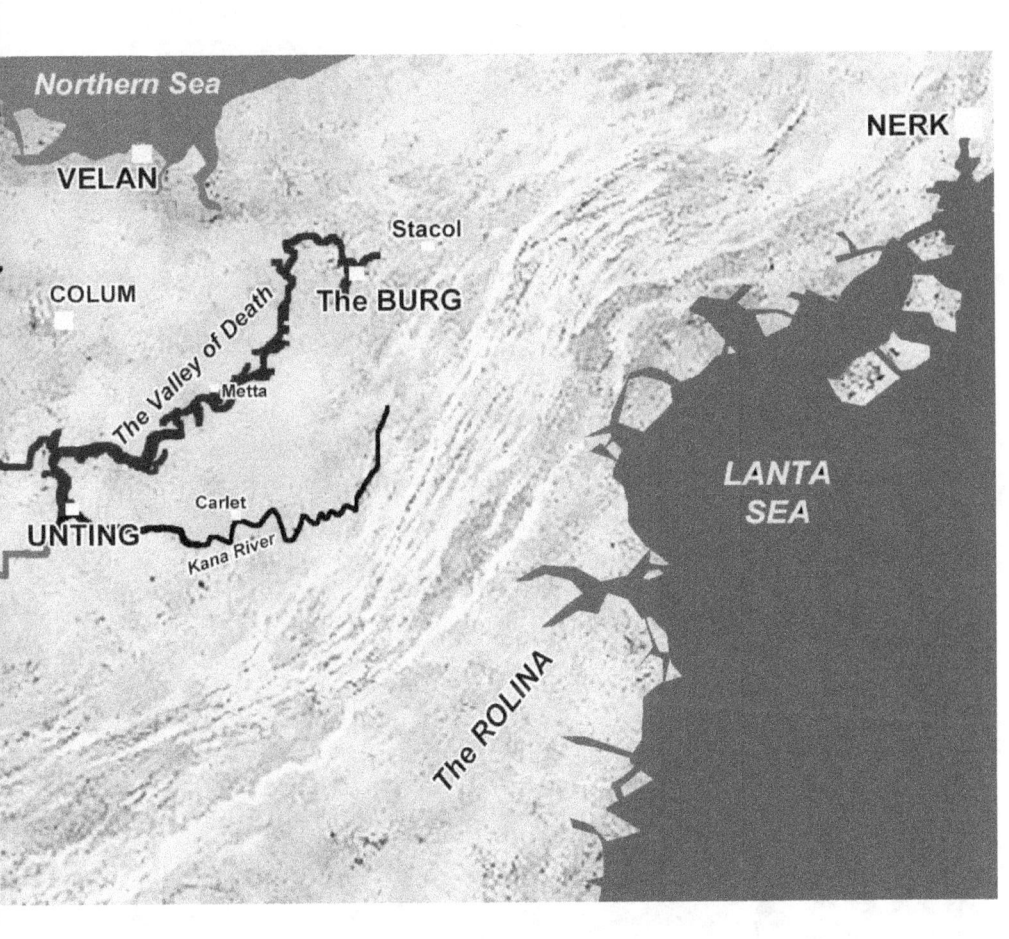

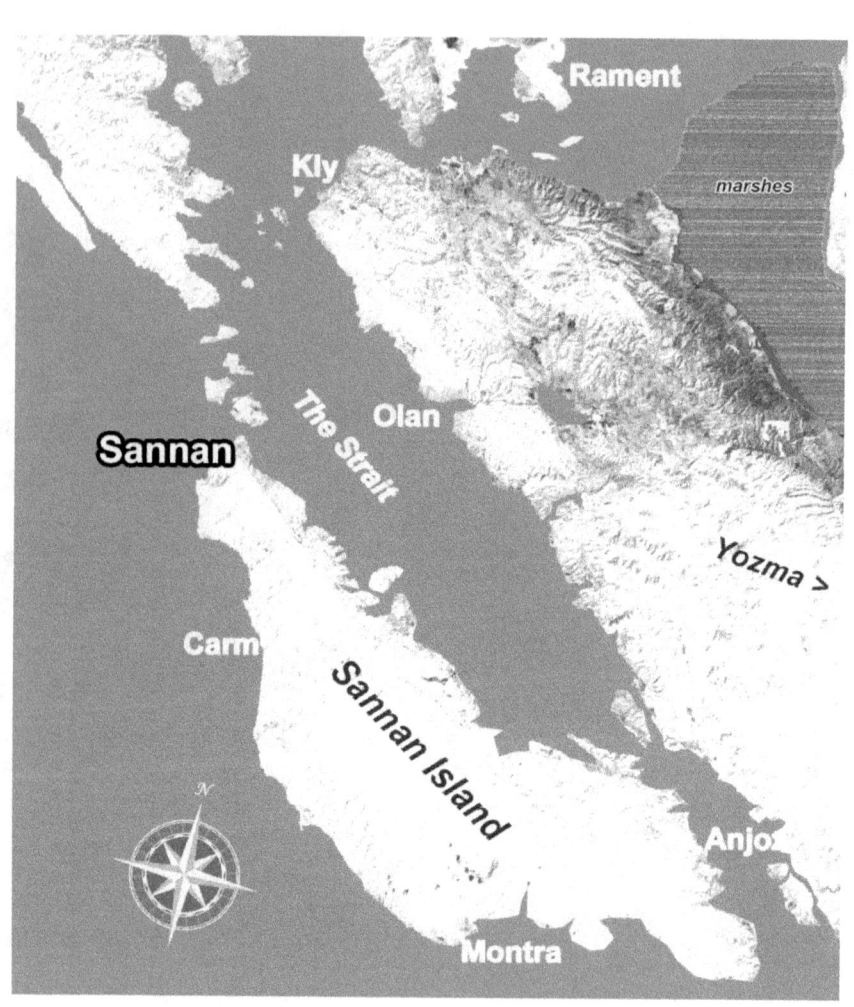

Perhaps all the dragons of our lives are princesses who are only waiting to see us once beautiful and brave.

Rainer Maria Rilke

1

The Beasts Above

ONE SUMMER DAY, WELL PAST THE NOONTIDE, CORLAN was riding his mount up the side of a mountain, the trail along the cliff barely wide enough for them to pass, when he heard a familiar screech echoing through the desert canyon. He turned in the saddle, glancing back over his brawny shoulder, whiskered chin brushing his sweaty shirt. His eyes brightened as he gazed down the long, ancient riverbed, searching for targets at the extreme range of his vision. He examined the crest of the jagged hills there, then surveyed the bronze sky just above them. With a scratch of his whiskers, he grinned.

A dragon clan was approaching. He counted again. Eleven of them in a loose V formation. Just when he believed he would never fill his quota, there they were! It would be a good day, after all.

Corlan pulled rein on his mount. Brushing his wind-swept hair out of his face and keeping his eyes fixed on the clan, he reached behind the saddle for the dragonslinger. Pulling the tubular weapon around to his lap, he next grabbed an iron bolt, wrenching it from one of two quivers that hung from each side of his mount. He loaded the bolt into the weapon's barrel and screwed back the spring lever to the third mark.

Squeezed against the cliffs overlooking the barren canyon was not the best location, Corlan knew. He had been heading for higher ground, to his usual place which had better cover. Yet the dragons were already coming. Even so, he decided, from this cliff he could easily pick a few of the aerial beasts out of the sky. He could fill his monthly quota and be heading back to the city for a stout brew and a good woman. After enough days of relaxation, he would return to the Valley of Death once more.

He set the weapon's mark on the first dragon, a large gray-belly, and released the spring. The iron bolt shot out into the canyon and struck the nearest winger behind the base of the jaw, a weak point, ripping the beast out of the formation.

As he watched the dragon fall to the valley floor, a puff of dust forming when it crashed, he smiled. No soft heart for Corlan; he was only doing his job: saving the realm from the scourge of dragons. That's what he always told people. It wasn't that he enjoyed culling the herd. Yet he had admitted a few times, usually while drinking, that the work was pleasant enough. He had a lot of time to think, sitting on the canyon's edge, waiting for dragons to fly past.

He was less interested in explaining how he happened into this risky occupation. "Politics," he snarled at those who asked. "Mere social squabbling, all it was. Not at all what people might assume." What they might have assumed was that sometime in the darker days of childhood he'd had an unpleasant encounter with a dragon, even a small one. Thus, hatred for them would boil throughout his life until he could resist no more and marched out to battle them. People would understand that; most members of the Dragonslayer Guild told similar tales.

No, for Corlan, it was different. He was new to the occupation. One day he had been the grandson of a king, the next day an outcast making his way across the battlefields of the realm. His father had taught him well the military arts. So he had served any lord who offered him enough coin. He trained soldiers to fight, then watched them die—thought Corlan, marking the next aerial beast.

As a field captain, he had garnered some fame: the second Battle of Green Mountain was a decisive victory. And the Battle of the Two Rivers, north of Bany, decided a crucial border. For that, he had been handsomely rewarded by the Prince of Nerk. The next war, however, did not go as well—

The dragon's scream shook him from his thoughts. Ripping the lead winger out of the formation compelled its lieutenants to turn upon him with their full fury. Corlan was ready, of course. Few men could keep their fear in check when dragons swooped down. In fact, many a loincloth was soiled by the first encounter. Their lives were measured in minutes—with a toasty end to regrets imagined and loves unfulfilled. And yet, he often realized, he hadn't much to live for anyway. He'd wasted most of his thirty-eight years and saw nothing in his future, so he relished the fight.

He loaded the dragonslinger with a fresh bolt, ignoring how unprotected his location was. The metal dart was the length of his arm and tipped with a trident of barbs. For good measure, between the barbs was a capsule holding the best poisons the wizards could create. Upon impact, the barbs cutting into the flesh of the dragon, the capsule would burst and spill its toxin into the body of the beast—in case the wound itself did not take down the creature.

As he prepared to fire the weapon again, Corlan kneed his broad, muscular mount, the ungainly *hippor*, into the shadows of the cliffs where they would be safe a moment longer than if they were in full view. The hippor grunted disagreement but complied. The quivers of iron bolts that hung from each side clanged.

"Come on, beasty! I've a gift for you!" he shouted at the next dragon trying to locate him on the mountainside before giving a vain cry and turning away.

Corlan scanned the clear sky, bronze sun nailed to the zenith. He measured the distance with his trained eyes. He could rip a few more, he decided, thinking of children that had been carried away and farmsteads burnt. The more dragons dropping from the sky, the better. The better the ground, he thought. He loathed stepping in dragon waste.

Pressing his boot against the side of the cliff, Corlan dismounted, dropping to the dirt beside the reddish-brown hippor, raising a reddish-brown cloud of dust. The hippor yawned. Its broad throat opened for a moment, flashing its tusks before closing. A snort from its nostrils sprayed the ground.

"You keep doing that, Chug, and I'll trade you for another!"

He kicked some dirt over the toes of his boots to dry the mucus sprayed from the hippor's nose. Pulling a cloth from the saddlebag, he wiped his leg from knee to hip and tossed the rag over the edge of the cliff. The wind blew it back at him. He slapped the cloth down and trained his eyes again on the approaching dragons.

Corlan expelled a hard breath as he screwed back the spring lever. He was tired of the hippor. If only *horses* still existed. But the last horse was dead more than a hundred years already. It had been kept in a small pen on the palace grounds where the king thought it would be safe from a starving citizenry. In the end, it was not safe. So the wizards used old magic to create this new riding beast.

Three of the dragons were circling overhead, locating their prey against the mountainside. Corlan's red and brown clothing merged into the reddish-brown cliffs. Even his auburn hair helped him blend in. Yet their eyes were sharp. He wished then that he'd reached his usual hunting spot where the overhanging rock protected him.

The beasts screeched their displeasure. With boots planted in the dirt, he leaned back against the hippor, urging it tighter against the cliff. He took his stance, checking the bolt in the dragonslinger. He had another bolt leaning against his knee, ready to load next.

The grey-belly with teal throat stripes came in screaming, wings wide and talons drawn, making a ridiculous spectacle—as though it was trying to frighten children all the way in the city.

Corlan sent the iron bolt through the dragon's throat. The beast dropped from the sky, falling past him and down to the valley floor. The iron bolt had cut clean through the dragon's neck and continued arching into the sky. Teal clouds of glandular fluid from the dragon's throat dissipated in the hot, dry air.

In went the next iron bolt, the spring set, weapon aimed.

The second dragon, a female grey-belly with splashes of orange on the tips of her pale wings, came straight at him, likely upset about loosing her mate. He saw the fluttering throat skin, heard the high-pitched cry before she expelled a burst of noxious gas which, with a deliberate hiccup, ignited. The dragon's subsequent breath sent the fireball blazing at the cliff.

Corlan crouched under the hippor's large head. Flames exploded around him, splattering against the cliff.

"Chug!"

Squealing, the hippor bumbled forward, almost trampling him. Its bulbous rump and hairless tail were aflame. Corlan swatted at the flames. There was nothing more he could do. A canteen of water would not be enough and he needed the water for the journey home.

"Now do you hate dragons?"

Before he could decide what else to do, the dragon charged the cliff again after making an arc through the sky.

Corlan shoved another iron bolt into the dragonslinger. His hands worked without thought, pulling back the launch spring to its tightest mark. He raised the weapon, aimed, and released the bolt, striking the dragon under its lower jaw, close to the sweet spot.

Momentarily distracted, the aerial beast crashed into the cliff, one sharp wingtip scraping along the trail that hugged the rocks, nearly catching his boot.

Corlan dove aside—as he glimpsed the hippor disappearing over the edge of the cliff, its rear end burnt and smoldering.

In the next instant, a large red-bull swooped up from below and snatched the fat animal in its maw. The dragon sailed high into the sky with its treasure. With a quick toss, the dragon caught the hippor in its mouth and bit off half, letting the other half fall. Then the dragon dove and caught the second half, and downed it in another gulp. Taking on the extra weight forced the dragon into a lower course and it struggled to rise. The other dragons screamed but the red-bull only belched in response.

The formation turned away, continuing along the valley. They would not spare more time or effort dealing with another pesky gamekeeper. Three already were lost on this passage through the valley. Count yourselves lucky, thought Corlan, breathing hard despite the reddish dust blowing off the cliffs.

"I got greedy," he mumbled, kneeling on the trail. He placed his hand inside one of the footprints left by the hippor.

He scanned the valley below for other dragons and thought of the stories he'd heard in this tavern or that one. Travelers reported that beyond the mountains, at the far end of the Valley of Death, long after it turned to the southwest, lay the dragon nesting ground. A vast marsh, a sea of grass spotted with low isles. On those isles dragons would settle during the cold season and mate. After the cold season, their nests would be full of eggs. In the spring, they would hatch. And he would meet them later in the Valley of Death.

If only he could make his way there to the nesting ground and destroy their eggs before they hatched. Then the entire realm would be safe for humankind—even for the well-ensconced prince and his fashionable court. Certainly he would be rewarded by the prince. Besides, the less Corlan had to step around dragon waste, the better. He was already into his third pair of boots this year.

He realized he had no beast to carry him and the remaining iron bolts down through the mountains and back to the city. One quiver of bolts had fallen with the hippor and the other had only three bolts remaining. He was done with hunting.

"Should've waited," he cursed.

He was glad he was not any farther from the city. It would still be a hard journey by foot.

"No more Chug." He clapped his hands to clear the dust.

After brushing his sleeves, he blithely ran his fingers through his long, tangled hair—almost as though he were about to step into the private chamber of a lady of the Court whose attentions he had garnered in recent weeks. The lovely, blond Petula, he sighed. Instead, he was only setting himself for the road home. It seemed his life was nothing but roads: always going somewhere but never arriving.

His boots had gotten scuffed and the snot of the hippor made every particle of dust cling to them. He sat on a rock and pulled off his boots to clean them properly. As he worked, he could hear the fading cries of the dragon clan winging down the valley. The clans seemed smaller than usual this expedition, so perhaps the efforts of the Guild were actually reducing their number.

When the dragons were gone, he thought, he and his fellow guild members would be out of employ. No more enjoying the prince's favor. That mattered little. But no more the admiration of the ladies at Court, either. That did matter. The ladies loved bedding a dragonslayer. After all, he was the only true man at any Court gathering.

"Pity," he grunted, examining the results of his cleaning.

Rebooted, Corlan set out at a brisk pace, the heavy dragonslinger resting against his shoulder. The quiver of three bolts hung from his other shoulder. They would become heavier the more he hiked, so he whistled a bawdy tune as he hiked the trail, eager to return to the Burg once more.

Corlan's hike took two full days along the narrow, dangerous trails to arrive down to the valley floor. He *tsk*ed, kicking dirt from his boots, daring to stride in the open with his dragonslinger held at the ready.

No secret to the name of this valley, once flowing with a mighty river. Over time the empty canyon had widened further, filled only with rock and dirt and dragon waste. After the river ceased to flow, it seemed as though all life in the valley had been scraped away, leaving a long desert canyon. Nothing grew in the valley and anyone who ventured into it often left in the maw of a passing dragon.

He breathed deeply, sucking in the coarse red dust of the valley, scanning the skies. Ahead, a beam of light broke through the hazy sky like a waterfall and showed him the way home.

And the hippor lost! He wondered how to explain to the prince. How could he meet the cost? Not even a record slaughter would likely keep the prince from expressing his anger. Hippors were not easy to come by, after all.

Corlan chuckled, stepping around a low flat rock that threatened to introduce itself to his toe.

At the end of the Valley of Death, he saw the spires of the palace rising above the encompassing stone walls, yellow in the sunshine. With his feet aching, a pang of joy flickered through him.

He made his way past the crumbling cliffs and located the device that people once used to go foraging in the valley. Long ago, when crops grew there, people would harvest them. They called the device a *lifter*. However, now there was no spark in the magical cords, so he was forced to pull himself up, hand over hand, grabbing hold of the cord himself.

Finally Corlan stood on the wide veranda that members of the Court used for evening gatherings. There, the rich folk laughed and sang, drank and ate, danced and exchanged acts of affection — while he stood watch bearing his dragonslinger, ready to knock any curious beast from the sky if it should come too close. He stood watch over the courtesans who thought they lorded over him. The prince was by far the worst of that ilk; who was more important, Corlan considered, the prince or the man protecting the prince?

He went through the palace gardens, stepping around long beds of pink and purple flowers, ducking under low-hanging branches. Maneuvering the unwieldy dragonslinger through the lush flora was aggravating. Then he broke free and strolled across a small yard and passed under an arched gate of yellow stones. He slipped out along the west side of the palace, emerging straight into the market square full of merchant stands. Dozens of citizens went about their business with no thought or care, it seemed to Corlan, not to the dragons that would return tomorrow or the next day, as certain as the sunrise.

He threw a cowl over his head, not wanting to be engaged by anyone who might recognize him. He was much too tired for polite conversation. He would go straight to a bath house.

Despite his attempt at disguise, Corlan was not three blocks down the lane before a young man wearing a scriber's brown robe with a red flower stitched over the right breast stalked up to him, hand outstretched to halt his progress.

"Sir Corlan," the young man spoke, "you are requested to attend the chamber of Sir Urix."

Corlan scowled. "He's still alive? I've thought him passed three times already this year."

"Yes, sir. He is alive yet."

"And I'm no *sir*. Not for many years now."

"I apologize."

"What's the trouble?" asked Corlan. "I can't be rushing to visit an old man every time he coughs. Let the staff attend him."

"Sir Urix requests to see you. That's all."

"How does he know I've returned? I only this hour arrived."

"As soon as you return is what he commanded."

"So you've been waiting for me?"

"Yes. For fifteen days."

"Indeed." Corlan nodded in appreciation. "Then you likely want some coin." He pulled a silver disk from his trouser pouch, flipped it to the youth, who fumbled it.

"Yes, sir," said the scriber, picking the coin from off the ground. "Thank you, sir." The young man frowned, seeing Corlan's sour face. "Not sir. Uh, how shall I address you?"

"My name is Corlan. You can call me by that name." He glared at the scriber; he seemed puzzled. "Or call me dragonslayer."

"Yes, sir—er, uh, mister...uh, Dragonslayer Corlan."

"A bit better. Now let's attend an old man." With a quick wave of his hand, Corlan sent the young man ahead.

He followed the scriber back to the market square and up to the front gate of the palace. Instead of confronting the guards there and entering, they turned sharply to the left and went down a narrow lane. They stopped before the Legany Lodge, a home for the infirm.

"Here?" growled Corlan, staring up at the shabby sign over the weathered door. "What's this? My grandfather doesn't belong here. He belongs in the palace!"

2

Trouble in the Burg

THE OLD MAN BLINKED, showing a sign of life as he rested like a statue on the wooden bench, covered with a thread-bare blanket. Light from a window struck his throat and chin, the remainder of his face and body left in shadow.

"So this is what you're worth these days." said Corlan, taking in the spare, dingy room and frowning at the caretaker. "How is it you've come to such a place?"

"It is by order of the prince." The caretaker, in white apron and cap, bowed his head. "Sir Urix is in his final days, said the prince."

"But here?" Corlan stared down at the old man on the bench. "Not even a soft mat for him? Do you know who this is? The prince is a superstitious fool. No harm will come to the living if a man dies under the same roof."

"But he—"

"I'll complain to him later," Corlan snapped. He set down the dragonslinger, leaning the tall weapon in the corner of the room. He dropped the quiver with its three iron bolts beside the long tube, rubbed his aching shoulder where the quiver had hung, realizing the old man had already begun speaking.

". . . to welcome you to my humble abode," he was saying.

Corlan watched the jiggling of wattle as the old man spoke.

"It's not like it used to be," said the old man in a gravelly voice, as though the words might be his last. His long white moustache, almost covering his mouth, shook as he spoke, then spilled down each shoulder. "Not like in the olden days."

"When you were young?" Corlan asked, his voice weary. It had already been a long day and he wished only to bathe and sleep. He clapped his hands, shaking off the dust, and dropped loudly onto the empty bench across the room. With a moment to close his eyes, he could easily become the next tenant of this hospice.

"Yes! By the gods!" the old man snorted. "When I was half your age. When the great princes ruled the five kingdoms."

"Old man, you are lame in the head," said Corlan. "Don't recite to me the Book of the Princes. I had too much of that in my schooling days."

"Then you learned it."

"And you are not nearly as old as you claim to be."

The old man shifted his body upon the bench, trying to roll onto a shoulder to better regard his visitor.

"Corlan, my boy," he said with gnarled fingers pointing, "you are as old now as I was when I took ill. Still it's a useful length of time. No need for you to speak further, Corlan, for surely you have spoken to the limits of your brain."

Corlan laughed. "Grandfather, you are the one who's lame in the head. Because you're lame you don't know you're lame."

"Don't let your mother hear you say that...especially now, in my dying days. She will never forgive you."

"Grandfather, she—"

Corlan turned away, coughing like he had swallowed the wrong words. Outside the window, the sky was black with smoke, dragons tussling once more, dueling above the city.

"Tell me of your mother. How is she?" The old man grinned, his eyes full of hope. "I want to know everything about my daughter. Is she still a lovely lass, a mild maiden traipsing barefoot through the daffodil meadows under a pale blue sky? Are her cheeks rosy? Is her red hair tied back like a horse's tail? Does she still bathe in the clear stream running from the eastern hills? Tell me of my Merilla."

Corlan nodded slowly, trying to recall the face of the woman who had pushed him out from between her legs. She must have nursed him, too, at least in those first hours. Perhaps at other times. There were flashes in his mind of a red-haired woman patting his head, fingers tossing his auburn hair, or giving a slap to his backside, or sometimes setting him on the floor like a pet puppy while she ate her dinner. There was also a man intruding on his memories. The woman told him to call the man *Papa*. He was big and burly, had a coal-black beard that seemed to always touch the floor. He had large hands that swatted him often, and the man would ignore his cries. Then a cold darkness would fill his head.

He stared at the old man on the bench: his *papa*'s father. How different the two men were. How different they both were from him, Corlan decided, brushing his auburn hair out of his face.

"Grandfather, it has been many years. Too many, and she has now passed on to the dark world. You know that. Have you forgotten her? Perhaps you confuse Merilla with your wife? Damia, also, has long passed."

"Merilla lives on, you know, in my brain. Damia...? You say she was my wife?"

"Yes, your wife — my grandmother. Merilla's mother."

"I cannot recall Damia."

"Search your brain, old man. That's all you have of them. Hold fast to it, if you wish. I assure you Merilla is dead. Dead and burned. I watched the smoke rise to the heavens myself. Even a few dragons came to suck up the smoke, infernal demons!"

"Such small talk!"

The old man chuckled, broke into a coughing fit.

Corlan waited. He wondered if he should slap the old man's back. Before he could act, the coughing cleared.

"You've a gift for it," the old man finished.

Corlan stood, brushed off his jerkin, and moved to the side of the bed, gazing down at his grandfather.

"Not much time remains for you, Grandfather."

The old man's eyes widened. "Are you the one come to end me? Is that the reason you've come to see me? How cruel to send my own kin to do the deed."

"No, Grandfather. It's not me."

"Then you came seeking amusement of me?"

"Neither that."

"State your business with an old man then!"

"You sent this lad to gather me. Have you forgot? I thought it might be important. Otherwise I'd be seeking a bath now."

"Yes...important."

"Since I've come at your request, now may be a good moment for you to give me your secrets."

The old man blinked. "Secrets...?"

"Yes, the location of your treasure, for one. The trick of slaying dragons, for another. The message to take to the next generation. I'd ask for words of wisdom if I believed any of them existed."

"Yes, I see. You wish to honor my ghost by stealing the only thing I have left: my secrets."

"And words of wisdom, if you have them."

"Words of wisdom, eh? That's what you want? I'll give you words of wisdom! Don't ask people to tell their secrets! How's that?"

"We are kin in flesh and blood. Both from the farmstead at Stacol. I recall your visits, telling my father to treat me right. And we both have been in battles. We both took employ as dragonslayers, you only for a brief time, me forever. So you should want to help me. And I shall pass on your wisdom to my sons. Secrets, indeed!"

"You have sons?" He laughed and spittle ran from the corner of his mouth. "I don't believe you. What're their names? Their ages? The color of their eyes?"

"It's true. Yet I haven't seen them for many years. I'm sure they are well-fed and brought up finely by their mothers."

"Mothers? How much of a bed-stormer have you been?"

"I've met a few ladies, it's not a lie. Nor a secret. And with them a few sons were made. Maybe daughters, as well. I'm not caught up on all that. It's not a foul thing to do, Grandfather. You did that, too."

"So tell me of them."

"The first, the eldest, Harral, likely has twenty years by now, and dark eyes like his mother. Oring has likely sixteen, with brown eyes. Young Tevar is yellow-haired with green eyes, perhaps twelve. I'm unsure. The eight-year-old red-head is called Urix, having blue eyes. The daughters—"

"You named your son after me?"

"Yes, Grandfather. His name is Urix. As though he might be some kind of a king one day. Poor lad. That's a dim fate."

"Is that for my honor or for a favor you'll be asking?"

"'Twas to humor the mother."

"And was she humored?"

Corlan shook his head. "After three sons I could think of no more names. That's the truth of it. Yet if you wish to believe I honor you with the name, I bow to your claim. Young Urix has the look of you and the strength of me, the wisdom of his mother, and the toughness of the mountains where he was born, under the dragon-thick sky!"

"He is my great-grandson! I bless him!"

"Thank you, grandfather. I'll tell him someday."

"It's not only me. I was named after my grandfather, too, and he was named after his grandfather. We go back many generations."

"Yes, I know. You never forget to remind me of your heritage."

"Your heritage, too!"

The caretaker straightened, raised a hand. "Be easy on him, sir."

Corlan nodded, let a grin slip upon his face. "I am." He turned his attention back to the old man. "So you are named—all of your line are named—for Prince Urix, the Great Loser."

"He was not! How dare you!"

"He was, Grandfather. It's so long ago you've forgotten. He died during the War of the Five Princes. He was killed by his own hand. He was the weakest of them."

"No, you take it back! Cut your words!"

"It's true. Ancient history now. Everyone knows it. And the other brother was executed. Another killed in the final siege. The last had a mournful reign full of torment. I cannot recall the fate of the other remaining brother. He went east, I think. Became a religious fanatic. Ancient history, as I said. Not today's news."

The old man coughed, waited to see if Corlan would be a dear and catch his spittle, perhaps slap his back. Corlan remained stiffly at attention, unmoving.

"Now I've need of expense," said Corlan in a softer voice. "A pouch of coin would do nicely."

"Whoring again?"

"Neither that." He cleared his throat. "I mean, the expense is not for that business."

"State it then."

"At the top of each month, I venture into the Valley of Death on a dragonslaying expedition. The prince employs me. And he provided a hippor to carry me yonder. As you might guess, a dragon got to the hippor and it was lost."

"The prince will punish you?"

"I should be prepared to pay the prince if he insists."

"What punishment might he lay upon you?"

"Slaying dragons is all I'm good for, so he might cut short my employ."

"So you would be left to rummage through the trash heaps. Is that your fear?" The old man tried to chuckle, couldn't.

"We have many fears among us."

The old man grunted. "And yet we do not have much coin among us."

"I thought you had wealth hidden away," said Corlan, lowering his voice. "Mother always said so."

"Merilla needed to believe we were a good family, a clan worthy of marriage, her dowry secure. The truth is much different."

"There is no wealth? No treasure hidden away?"

"What would you call treasure?" asked the old man.

"Coin, gold, jewels — the usual items people value and trade."

"Not food? Not drink?"

"Those are easy to obtain."

"Are they?" He blinked as if opening a new set of eyes, a pair that were designed for serious staring. "You forgot that vital part of your studies: the generations of famine following the great plague."

"You are full of stories today."

"Not stories, it's truth! Man killed man, and the lonely few remained. The story is oft repeated, with different colors, different textures, and scents."

"Yes, yes, we progeny of the survivors. A sad tale of woe, made more pathetic by your wagging tongue. Tell it to your jailors here, not me. An old man has only stories to offer from his death bed. That's what is sad. Yes, better you'd died younger, in a battle, and we'd sing praises today. Now, though, I need to know where you have hidden your wealth. The prince will certainly demand coin. Without a hippor I cannot continue my employ. Then you'll have no one to visit you."

"There is treasure," said the old man, coughing. "You may not think about it the same as do I. It is...a secret."

"I know. It's hidden, as you say, though you deny it."

"Not hidden. Not as a box of jewels might be buried in a desert. Yet hidden, as you seem to believe, in a place where none may access it. That is the secret."

Corlan frowned. "You're teasing me."

"You are the teaser."

"What is it and where is it?" Corlan's voice was stern.

"It is a secret." The old man tapped his temple twice. "It is hidden in here." He tried to chuckle but broke into coughing.

"Then none will find it," said Corlan, gruffly.

"Do you want it?"

"What value does a secret have for me this week?"

"Perhaps not this week, yet it could pay you well in time."

Corlan shook his head. "What is the secret?"

"You cannot guess?"

"By the gods, do not make me guess! I haven't the time."

The old man glared at him. "I'm he who has no time."

"Come, tell it, then," insisted Corlan.

"Very well, I shall."

Corlan waited. A few minutes passed. The air hardened. Hearts slowed. His eyes fought against his grandfather's sharp stare.

The old man opened his mouth: "It is the secret of dragons."

Corlan rolled his eyes against his will, and noticed the caretaker grinning in the corner of the room.

"Grandfather, why have you withheld such a secret if you knew I needed it? Are you lame in the head, as I well suspect?"

The old man pursed his lips, as though he was considering a more worthy answer, then uttered: "No."

"Then tell it."

The old man grunted, wagging his gnarled finger. "You must do something for me first."

Corlan nodded. "Of course there must be some condition!"

"First you must refill my medicine. I've been without for nearly a week. Without makes my heart grow cold."

"So your heart is cold from lack of medicine?"

"You judge me harshly. The winter hags torment me."

"It is late summer now."

"Yet these winter hags chill me."

Corlan threw his hand in the direction of the boy standing quietly by the wary caretaker. "Send the boy to fetch the medicine. I've more important tasks to tend to. I'm a dragonslayer, after all. Not a nanny."

"The boy wouldn't know where to go. He wouldn't stand watch to be sure it is made properly. He wouldn't be able to assure payment was not inflated by the apothecary."

"Truth," Corlan said with a quick nod. "Very well, Grandfather. I'll fetch your damnable medicine. Then you must tell me that precious secret you hang over my head like dragon claws."

"I knew you would understand."

Corlan waved at the boy. "Come, we have a mission."

"Make it soon," said the old man.

"Certainly." Corlan turned to the boy. "I'll show you where to go and you bring it back here and give it to him."

The old man pouted. The boy nodded, his face unsure what he was being asked to do.

"You're able to assist?" Corlan asked the boy, who turned and gave the caretaker a look. The caretaker nodded.

The boy nodded, too. "Yes, sir." He caught his word and froze.

"Then let us be away," said Corlan, ignoring the boy's *sir*, already taking a step toward the door. He glanced back. "I shall expect your great secret upon my return, Grandfather. Find the words. All of them." He pointed to the corner. "I'm leaving my dragonslinger here. I trust you won't be using it in my absence."

"I doubt I could lift it at my ripe age."

"Then I'll trust you."

And there was Bratiste!

Stepping away from the lodge, Corlan spied his arch-rival. Tall and thin, the man always went out ensconced in his usual all-black garments, elaborately embroidered with dragon motifs, flashing his signature scarlet cape.

Today Bratiste escorted a pair of tandem wagons heaped with the steaming carcass of a featherback dragon, plumage mostly crimson and teal with orange down the tail. A small army of assistants made sure it did not fall off the wagon as they maneuvered it around a turn and onto the main avenue much to the uproar of impoverished citizens hoping for a slice. The meat was thought to be poisonous yet with the proper cooking methods, portions were able to be made palatable. It was still a painstaking process but if one were famished, one would endure the details — and the bitter flavor.

Corlan stared hard at his rival, hating the boisterous crowd that paraded along with the dandy.

"Likely he purchased this one from the animal park in Ladelf," he muttered to the boy who had followed him out of the lodge.

The boy, wearing the emerald leggings and copper tunic of a lodge servant, seemed in awe. He seemed afraid to be out of place, free from his normal duties at Corlan's urging.

"There are dragons in animal parks?" asked the boy.

"It's likely." Corlan snorted, turned to go. "Ladelf had the largest, as I recall —"

"Master Corlan!" called Bratiste, seeing him.

Corlan grunted. *Master indeed! You're the stage boy of the city! The pretender!* "Bratiste," he acknowledged with a frown.

The man had no aura of menace about him, no scent of effort, no scowl from facing death day by day. The least likely dragonslayer in the realm, thought Corlan, jutting his chin out.

"So you've brought home your dinner."

The finely-dressed, willowy man stood before him, gazing back over his shoulder at his prize as the wagons rolled heavily past them.

"Not dinner, old fellow, but certainly a worthy prize, eh?"

"Prize?" Corlan feigned amusement. "What does this one pay? Is there a contest which I'm unaware? I've not seen banners."

"Figure of speech," said Bratiste with a playful slap to Corlan's shoulder. "You shall catch on eventually. Left school early, didn't you? I keep forgetting. Must make amends for that."

Corlan made a fist, ready to ram it into the man's belly if he dared touch him again.

Bratiste looked him over. "Rough rags! The old leather suits you. Although one might easily mistake you for a vagabond, begging for favors, secrets and all. You have an odor about you—"

"I am this day returned from the valley. No chance yet to wash. Yet you seem as fresh as church day."

"The valley? That's daring! Why there? Hiding from something? From someone, perhaps? I hear the iron coin ladies clamor for you. Bold on them, after you've been in that desolate locale. Such a filthy venue for a killing."

"Because dragons fly there," Corlan answered, struggling to hold back his anger and his fist. It would not do to launch into a public fight, no matter how much he wished to. The civil patrols were quick to lock up anyone who dared fight.

"So what do you think of this one?" asked Bratiste.

"It's good size for a featherback." Corlan squinted at the beast on the wagons. "Sky kill?" He coughed deliberately. "Or sleep kill?"

"I took this one in-nest, if you must know." He twirled his long waxed moustache. "A dead dragon counts the same, no matter how you kill it."

"Dragonslinger?"

"By the gods, no!" the man laughed, a sharp whiny noise that aggravated Corlan's ears. "That's a device only for a fellow of your impressive dimensions. No, 'twas poison for this one."

Bratiste proceeded to explain how he mixed potions into a large meat pie, delivering it to the maw of the great beast. Upon waking, the dragon swallowed the pie, thereafter becoming ill and soon died. One of his assistants was chosen to slam home a favorite lance as an honor.

"And then my assistants collected the body. Now we parade it through the streets to let the citizenry know to be unafraid! And you, Master Corlan, also be unafraid."

Corlan cleared his throat, spit loudly to the ground, just missing the polished black boot of his rival. Bratiste hopped back, frowning.

"You are jealous, perhaps. It does seem so."

"Not of you," growled Corlan.

"I believe you are. Happily, it's no concern of mine."

Corlan narrowed his eyes. "I hunt in the Valley of Death. I rip dragons out of the sky. I face their wrath. I don't bother to haul the stinking carcass back here to show it to everyone. It's not a street spectacle."

"Ah, but it should be!" exclaimed Bratiste, wagging a finger.

Corlan snorted. "I thought you intended it for the public dining hall. Poor folks would eat it, I suppose. They'll eat anything. Besides, everyone knows you can't eat dragonflesh."

It was Bratiste's turn to snort, although in a dainty manner that offended no one. He produced a lacey crimson handkerchief from a chest pocket and dabbed at his nostrils.

"Incorrect," said Bratiste. "The tail and haunches are quite edible if prepared properly. A thick sauce with peppers will mask the bitter flavor. Any other parts are likely too infected with toxins to be safe to eat. One would face a serious result, possibly death by belly rupture. The featherbacks are the safest. They taste rather like burnt *chickor*. And the feathers can be used for decorating the palace and high-class ladies' finery."

"I see...."

"That one will feed a hundred people, I'd wager. Give them roots and greens, a portion of stale bread, and it is a full meal. They can live on another day, do their tasks. You see? I provide a service."

"You do provide a service," Corlan chuckled, glancing at the boy.

The boy pinched his eyebrows, shifting his gaze from Corlan to the man dressed in black, then back to Corlan.

"Ever the trickster, Master Corlan. How's your grandfather these days? Mindful still?"

"Ever the dragon's breath, Bratiste—Braden Batiste, provocateur, I should say. Let us not cross paths again. At least not this week."

26

"Truly. I've had enough engagement with you, as well."

"Then it's settled."

Bratiste offered his black gloved hand to shake.

Corlan stared unwelcomingly at it.

"So generous!" sneered Bratiste, dropping his hand.

And Bratiste spun on his heel and stalked off, joining the parade, wading into the cheering crowd.

"I'll pay someone to pray for you, Master Corlan!" he called back over the crowd noise. "It won't cost much, I'm certain!"

Corlan waved him off, showed him his raised thumb as an insult, and turned to depart.

"You are not friends with Sir Braden?" asked the boy.

"Never." He glanced at the boy. "And neither should you."

"Is there a reason?"

Corlan stopped, took a deep breath.

"That, young man, is a first-class deceiver. An interloper. The evil afoot. Churchmen speak of him by other names, yet there he is. There he goes. Avoid him."

"Yes, Master."

"I am not your master."

"He called you master."

"Yes, well...a poor humor runs through him."

"Oh—"

"Come, boy, we have work to do."

Not one full day returned, not even a single step inside his own bare apartment above the tavern, unable to wash off the valley's dirt, and his day was one petty task after another! First his cantankerous grandfather, the snooty Bratiste next, then running an old woman's errand fetching medicine!

"Here's the shop," grunted Corlan to the boy hurrying to keep up with his long strides.

Inside stood two well-fed women and an old man. They glanced at Corlan as he blocked the doorway, cutting off the afternoon light. The shadow he formed there was ominous.

"I shall attend to you forthwith, sir," called the hunched man wearing the apron behind the wire screen.

With a sword hanging on his hip, Corlan felt foolish among them. He wasn't a man who frequented such shops. Only once had he been inside one like this and that was to get a poultice for a talon wound he'd received on an expedition. The poultice killed the infection yet he retained the scar across his chest.

He turned to the boy beside him. *Why couldn't he run this errand for the old man?*

"When I get the medicine," Corlan said to the boy, "I'm sending you back with it. I have other business to attend. You understand?"

The boy nodded hesitantly.

"You know the way back, don't you?"

Again the boy nodded.

"Then you take this medicine and give it to my grandfather —"

"How may I be of assistance?" asked the apothecary.

Corlan explained what was needed and the aproned man assured him it could be easily manufactured. The process would take a while, however, perhaps an hour *if* he had all the ingredients in stock. He thought there might not be enough of one ingredient so he would send for more from another apothecary.

"Blackbane is hard to get these days," said the aproned man. "Or I could substitute other ingredients which would provide the same effect. It all depends on circumstances."

"Do the best you can, as quickly as you can," said Corlan.

"You wish which method?"

"Just make it quick."

"Then I'll use substitutes."

Corlan turned and whisked the boy out of the shop. An hour! That would feel like a full day in the valley. What to do?

He needed a drink, he realized. Plenty of dust still in his throat. Down the lane was a tavern. He ushered the boy through the front door. All eyes turned to them.

"Corlan the dragonkisser!" the barkeep announced.

"How do you know me?" growled Corlan, his hand on the hilt of his sideblade.

"Everyone knows you. Famous lover of dragons. Never brings any dragonware back. Who knows how many aerials he kills?"

A few men in the tavern laughed.

"Aye, he loves them so much!" a man at the bar sang out.

Corlan spun around.

"Vacation on the prince's coin!" said another man.

"You're ones to talk!" Corlan barked.

He decided a quick drink was necessary enough at this point that he would endure the insults. He ordered a cheap lager. He asked the boy what he wanted. All right, soda water for the boy, with a fruit wash, something mild for a young assistant.

"Thank you, sir," said the boy.

A mug and a small glass were set on the bar. Corlan sat, drank.

The boy stood beside him, then reached for the glass.

"How's it you've come to my establishment today?" asked the barkeep. "Were you kicked out of the Guild meeting already?"

Corlan looked up, eyes narrowed. "Guild meeting?"

The barkeep laughed. "Many of your fellow guildmen stopped in here on their way to the meeting. You just missed them. That's how I could recognized you: always the last one to show."

"There's a meeting today?"

"That's what they were complaining about. Big stuff, they said. Important news. Lots of grumbling."

"Grumbling on what?"

"You haven't heard?"

"I returned from my expedition only today. I've not even been to my home yet. How am I to know?" Corlan tossed down his lager, turned to the boy. "Come!"

3

The Tally and the Toll

ON THE GUILD HALL'S FAÇADE two wooden dragon heads twice the height of the hall's roof rose starkly into the sky, facing each other, their forked wrought-iron tongues curling outward, their hammered copper wings bracing the entrance. More than a dozen rough-looking men stood outside the open doorway, listening.

Corlan pushed his way through them.

Inside the hall, a hundred dragonslayers stood before a small dais. On the dais stood Jugor Mal Vé, the guild master, as ancient as the world, dressed in his finest gold-trimmed black leather jerkin and dragonscale trousers. The man's waist-length red beard fluttered in the breeze created by his boisterous ranting, like a trumpet calling all of them to battle. He stormed across the dais, then spun and reversed his direction, his arms in winged-sleeves waving wildly, voice rising and falling, booming on the important words.

"What is the complaint?" asked Corlan of the man next to him.

The man recognized Corlan, offered his hand. Corlan shook it.

"Loovis, correct?"

"Yes, Corlan. I apprenticed with Pellar."

"Me, too."

"He died last week. On a poorhouse bench."

"He did?"

"You missed his burning."

"Pity, that. I was hunting. He would've respected that."

Loovis jutted his chin toward the dais. "Jugor complains of our quotas being down. The prince is angry."

"That's typical. Why the rant then? Jugor hates the prince."

"The prince threatens to dismiss half us. Says there's not enough coin for all us."

"That's foolish. Then how will the dragons be controlled?"

"Agreed."

They listened to the guild master rant for a while, the old man's voice never diminishing its ferocity.

Soon Jugor paused and members of the Guild immediately voiced their concerns and asked questions. For men bearing weapons, it was a civil gathering. A dragonslinger resting against the shoulder was a mark of rank, enticement to ladies eager to bear the next generation of dragonslayers. None of the men had any interest in fighting another member, not in the Guild Hall. They were united in their single task: eliminating dragons from the realm.

Finally, Corlan had heard enough.

"Indeed, we need to confirm our kills," Corlan called out above the din, "yet in some way other than dragging back a stinking corpse for the poor to eat."

Some of the men—and the three women dragonslayers—shouted their agreement.

"We are progressing! We are eliminating the horde. It takes time, but we are winning this war. The fact the prince doesn't see all the rotting bodies should not give him the right to say we slack!"

"Aye, we're dragonslayers, not dragonslackers!" shouted a man.

"It isn't always easy to snatch off a talon or cut a tongue out just to haul it back to prove our success!"

Corlan pushed his way forward to the dais, climbed onto it.

"It is enough burden to haul the iron bolts on the back of a poor hippor! I am returned today from the Valley where I did slay fifteen dragons! Three in my last day there. I met the quote plus three. I know where they live, heard where they hatch! Yet I'll not burden myself hauling back souvenirs!"

Many of the members cheered.

"You survived the Valley of Death?" someone called over the din.

"It is a valley of death for the *dragons*—those that dare fly the course!" Corlan added a chuckle. "Where do you hunt?"

The answers varied but all were locations to the north or east of the city, the fertile lands of humans, farmsteads and villages, where Corlan was born and raised. A few hunted to the south among the tall trees or over the snowfields atop the mountains. Some ventured as far as the eastern coast to pursue sea-serpents even though they did not count in the quotas set by the prince.

"None of you dare enter the Valley of Death?" asked Corlan. He felt both powerful and puzzled standing before them.

"Corlan is a braggart!" someone called.

"It's called the Valley of Death for a reason," shouted Corlan.

"Nothing lives that way since the river flowed away."

"Dragons seldom are sighted there."

"It is a wasteland."

"Who can say what Corlan does on his sojourns?"

"Any dragons found in the valley would be corpses already."

"Untrue!" Corlan waved his arms, signaling for quiet. "That is the main road for dragons flying between their hunting grounds — here where we live — and their nesting grounds in the western marshes."

There was stunned silence. Hadn't any of them considered where the dragons actually lived? Where they mated? Corlan frowned. They only cared about making their quota and drinking away their coin.

"They have nesting grounds?" someone in the back asked.

Corlan pressed his hands into his hips. "None of you have gone to the west?"

Shaking of heads, a host of befuddled grumbles, assorted coughs and spitting.

"Nesting grounds, yes!" said Corlan. "Where dragons are born. Rather, where they hatch."

"You seen them?" called someone.

Corlan shook his head but maintained his sharp glare. "I have met travelers come from the west. They state the truth. In the west are vast marshes where dragons nest, where their eggs are laid, where the draglings hatch."

"It's all myth! Dragons are born from black magic!"

"Mountain caves are their homes."

"The sins of mankind created dragons!"

"Pray to the gods and carry your dragonslinger!"

Again Corlan waved his arms. "Hear me!" He waited for the din to lessen. "Listen to me!"

The din dropped to nothing but the shuffling of a hundred pairs of boots against the wooden floor.

"Travelers from the west say it's so. Where the Valley of Death ends in the far west, the land falls into marsh. A hundred miles of wetlands. The marshes slip into open sea. Below the heights of Salou!

The citizens there have dragon troubles worse than ours."

"Everyone's got dragon troubles!" someone shouted.

A black-clothed man burst from the crowd and mounted the dais.

"Are you proposing a trek to Salou?" asked the new speaker. It was Corlan's rival, Bratiste. "Salou is only a myth, an ancient city destroyed by dragons quite long ago. How can you propose going to Salou?"

"If that's what it will require," said Corlan. He was not afraid of Braden Batiste, but he knew the man had connections and had the favor of the prince. Many members of the Guild followed the man's lead so Corlan could not oppose him before the members. "Salou does exist. I've met travelers who met travelers from Salou. Yet my destination is the marshes, not Salou."

"Gather a brigade of dragonslayers for a foolhardy journey down the Valley of Death?" Bratiste grinned. "Then who shall guard the skies over the Burg? A classroom of children? And poor widowed mothers?"

Corlan stepped toward Bratiste, poised at the end of the dais, his chest puffed out.

"You have shown your willingness to avoid danger for the whole period of your Guild membership," said Corlan. "You are not afraid of such a trek, are you?"

Bratiste took a firm step toward Corlan.

"Everyone saw that magnificent featherback I brought in today. Everyone knows I can bring home the dragon. I have nothing to fear from dragonslackers such as you." He offered a fake laugh. "You say you killed fifteen? Where are they?"

"I leave them where they fall," Corlan growled. "To anoint the earth, to make the soil fertile for tiny plants and the bugs that feed on them. I provide a service, you see."

"Wasteful." Bratiste flung his arms out. "You see how this lowly dragonkisser cares for our citizens' needs? Even dragonflesh will feed some of us. The poor folks know how to cook dra—"

"It's not for wastefulness. How do you expect one man to carry back even a few souvenirs of fifteen slain dragons?"

"Ah! Master Corlan prefers to hunt alone. Better to avoid all these uncomfortable questions upon his return. No one presses him. No one queries." Bratiste turned to the crowd, hands raised high. "Are there enough votes here today to oust this imposter?"

"Now hold a moment!" Corlan rushed to Bratiste, who stepped back so that Corlan stumbled to his knees.

"Excellent! Clumsy, as well."

Corlan stood, felt his knee aching from the crush against the dais wood. "You are the oaf in this hall."

The crowd began jeering and Corlan took it as a sign that he had no backing to pursue his counterattack. If the two of them were alone in an alley, then....

"At issue is a trek to the nesting ground," Corlan cried out, trying to salvage his dignity.

"None here wish to abandon our city for your escapades," said Bratiste. "None here are so disloyal as to walk away, leaving the city defenseless."

"I'm only suggesting a solution to our problem."

"Then take volunteers. A few apprentices may follow. They need some experience...or amusement. However, the better of us should remain at the ready, serve the prince, protect our city. You may leave at any time, Corlan. Gather your slim belongings and fare thee well, dragonslacker first-class!"

He watched the members' faces flicker with understanding. He knew his face was red, his fists ready to swing hard at the whiny rapscallion who insulted him before his Guild brethren. Yet the crowd stood opposed to him.

Patience, he told himself. *The victory will be yours in the end. When you return with broken egg shells and no more the dragons fill the skies. Then you will be hailed far and wide as the supreme dragonslayer! Perhaps you'll become the next guild master!*

"What say you to the trek?" Jugor Mal Vé called out, loud enough to be heard over the excited cacophony of dragonslayers.

A few hands rose from the crowd. Three. Five. Eight. One hand lowered. Seven held fast.

"Very well," said Jugor. "Corlan may lead these seven to the west and destroy the nesting ground and what manner of dragonkin they may find there. It will be to our benefit. Let us approve the trek."

"It is a long journey," Corlan spoke up, "yet that is what we must do to eliminate the dragons that besiege our lands. Kill them in their nests. Kill the draglings before they hatch. Wipe them away!"

The crowd cheered as only a hundred snarly and dangerous men could, thundering like the skies had been cleaved by fire.

"You cheer this foolish idea?" Bratiste asked the membership, screwing his face around and slapping his leg.

"Not even you, Braden, have a plan to rid us of all the dragons," said Jugor. "If Corlan succeeds, we all win. If not, it is no loss to us, only to him. And those who accompany him."

"There is a great harm to his success," said Bratiste with a slow swing of his arm out to the crowd. "Have you not considered?"

"What is it?" asked Jugor.

"If Master Corlan succeeds—no doubt through some assistance from the gods, for no other method shall win him any decent portion of success—then dragons will wing their way never more."

"Yes, that is the plan," said Jugor. "We all agree."

"And we shall have no occupation!"

The Guild members fell silent. In a heartbeat a fresh roaring from them threatened to raise the roof of the Guild Hall off its rafters.

"I declare Master Corlan's plan a ruse intended to put us out of employ," cried Bratiste, facing the crowd, his hands out as if he were pleading. "And then what shall we do? Cut the earth and toss seeds? Wash the smelly chamber pots of grandmothers? Learn to read the sacred scrolls? Squeeze the milk of the hoven?"

The Guild Hall was quiet.

"While I personally have no need of employ, many thanks to the generosity of my father and his father before him, yet I understand these men need such employ. They provide a service."

"Then you should quit." Corlan grunted. "Let another take your place, to have such employ. Return to your fine house and sew your fine garments!"

Bratiste glared at Corlan, pointed at him.

"This man is not our friend. Send him out at once! Send him into the Valley of Death and wish him a fair journey. Let him mate with dragons. Who should care? Let him be their snack. Who should care? He is no friend of us!"

Corlan felt all eyes on him. His hand went to his sword hilt.

"Dare not raise a blade in this hall," Jugor cautioned.

"I prepare my defense. If none attack, I have no need to release my blade upon them."

Jugor nodded, clapped his hands.

"Then go safely from this hall, Corlan."

"Get thee out to the street," Bratiste said, followed by a chuckle. "Yes, get thee to the chamber pots, and clean some of them. We have much waste to heap upon thee. Learn a new trade, Master Corlan."

"I must agree," said Jugor. "It's best you leave now."

Corlan stepped backward, almost tripped coming off the dais. He spun around to check possible attackers, keeping his hand on the hilt of his sideblade. He pushed through the crowd, out the doorway, the last men jostling him as further obstacle.

Gefgar the giant gave him a hard shove and Corlan straightened himself with fists raised. "You want a punch in the face?"

"From you it would be a mere kiss," the burly man responded.

"I have no time for idiots like you today!"

Gefgar roared in laughter, crossed his arms over his broad chest.

The men outside had heard enough. They gave Corlan scowls and one spit at his boots.

"May you all feel the dragon's breath!" Corlan cursed at them, then hurried away. It was not in fear but in his eagerness to remove himself from any action that may further ruin his day.

He was past the second block when he remembered the boy he'd brought with him from the lodge.

And he needed to return to the damnable apothecary to fetch his grandfather's medicine—like some old maid between her cleaning of the chamber pots!

To return to the Guild Hall or go on to the apothecary? Would the boy have waited at the Guild Hall? Did something happen to him?

He made his way back to the Guild Hall, where he almost tripped over the boy.

"There you are!" cried Corlan.

"Yes, sir."

"I thought surely you might've been done in, made to serve, by one of those vagabonds."

"I tried to wait, sir—"

"No *sir*. Understand?"

"—yet it seemed you wouldn't be coming out soon, so I thought to wander a bit."

"Good boy." Corlan patted his shoulder. "There was indeed a fair degree of nastiness inside. It's good you did not stay."

"The men outside looked at me with strange eyes," said the boy.

"They didn't touch you, did they?"

"No, yet they looked as though they might."

Corlan grunted. "Dragonslayers are often foul men."

"Yes, sir."

"Not me. I've got a woman, a lovely lady." He smiled to himself, then turned to the boy. "Come now! To the medicine shop!"

The small chamber in the Legany Lodge was full of men dressed in dark brown robes when Corlan and the boy returned with the pouch of medicine. The robed men huddled around the bench, regarding the old man, his eyes closed. One of the robed men hummed a dirge.

"The hour is late," spoke another one of the robed men, seeing Corlan gazing at the man on the bench. "Time for Sir Urix to climb into his boat and set sail. The horizon calls."

The other men gathered around the bench chanted in low voices, causing the walls to vibrate with them.

Corlan broke into the circle and stared down at his grandfather.

"He was alive a few hours ago. He sent me to fetch medicine."

"And fetch it you did," said the leader, dressed in a less ragged robe than the others. He also wore a dingy yellow hat. "Too late to do him any good, it seems. Still, you did the final deed for him. The gods will not judge you harshly, I pray."

Corlan dropped the medicine pouch on the old man's belly. He listened to the chanting. The leader of the group placed his gaunt hand on Corlan's muscular shoulder. He guessed the men in robes were magi. Perhaps they were the Order of Draconus, who always attended dragonslayers. The Order accepted dragons as retribution sent by the gods for the evil committed by humans. Yet Corlan had never attended any prayer festival or offered donations in the charity boxes. His mother had shunned them, too, so he felt no guilt. Yet he was never a rude fellow.

"He promised me...."

The chanting continued.

"He said he would tell me a secret...when I returned with this medicine."

The chanting ended.

"What secrets he had are locked within him now," said the magus leading the gathering.

Corlan expelled a great sigh, as though everything happening to him had gathered all at once and attacked him full on. The strength in his muscles bled out. The tautness of his sinews went slack. The blood pumping furiously became thin and flowed like the final rivulet of a once great river withered to a gurgle in a ditch. His eyes fell shut.

"I am certain you tried with all your heart's melody to abide your grandfather's wishes," spoke the magus, "yet in the end you were, as we all are for many of our allotment of days on this world, a moment too early or too late."

The magus gazed at Corlan, who had bowed his head.

"Did you say your final words to him? Did he know how much you loved him? Did you wish him a comfortable journey across the sunset sea?"

After a moment of silence, the boy stepped forward. "I was here. He said the words. I heard him."

Corlan looked up, surprised, then turned to glance at the boy who stood behind him.

"It's true," the boy repeated. "He said them."

"The gods are pleased," said the magus, nodding his head and stroking his fluffy gray beard. "He shall have a comfortable journey, after all. And in the next world he will not want for vengeance upon his kin. He shall have maidens tending him and sweet bread served four times each day. The sun shall always shine and the breezes shall cool his body. He shall dance and drink and sing and sex—all the pleasures he deserves for a life endured in this realm."

Corlan let the words flow through him. It was truly a nasty world they lived in, he realized. And if his grandfather had endured it, he would also. After all, it seemed there would be enough reward in the dark world. And no dragons. He envied the man.

He recalled his mother, that red-haired woman who was a ghost in his mind, telling him almost the same words when he heard that his father had been killed in battle. He had pushed all that business to the back of his head. Now it crashed through his head like a deluge. His grandfather's son, Corlan's own father, led the army to battle as his elder son sat on the throne watching half-naked girls dance in the Great Hall of the palace. With his father's death, his uncle became the next king. And it was this old man, this grandfather, who had sent out his father, and not his uncle, to lead the army!

What did he know? What had he planned?

In the end, this grandfather was relegated to a hospice rather than comfortable quarters in the palace. The prince ordered it. That was unkind, certainly. Yet Corlan suddenly hated this man who lay dead before him.

"May peace lay upon Sir Urix," the robed men chanted in unison over and over.

"May peace lay upon Sir Urix," repeated Corlan, "of the Burg."

"...of the Burg," the boy's thin voice trailed.

Enough torchlight shone to blot out most of the stars yet the brightest sight in the sky that eventide was a pair of dragons dueling between the drifting clouds. First one spit fire, then the other. They took turns grappling with each other, locking talons onto ribs or snapping teeth on tails. They gave such great cries that children were kept from sleep as the night slipped away.

The magus, and anyone associated with the Order of Draconus, would likely mark the spectacle as an omen. Whenever dragons fight each other in the night sky on the day an old king dies, it has to mean something. Perhaps it was a sign that his grandfather's spirit would be accepted into the dark world without excessive fee. Or, perhaps, it meant his spirit would be refused and left to wander about the living world. Such a spirit might counsel the living—or, as likely, harass them. Existence in the world of the living came with no rewards or carnal pleasures. The only way to pass the centuries was to fashion tricks to play upon the living. To ward off such trickery, religious folk designed countless prayers and magic spells, made talismans and kept out of certain areas of the realm.

Corlan wondered if his grandfather might still be floating around the streets of the Burg, lost and hoping for a pair of dragons fighting in the night sky to consume him and put him out of his pain. That is what he wished for his grandfather, even though he was the man who sent his father to certain death. Somehow the distant past did not hurt him any longer.

"You see how they treated you when you got old?" he muttered, wondering if his grandfather's spirit heard him. "There's no loyalty for family. Not our family. I should call upon the king and demand redress." He wondered if the equally aged King Belgar, ensconced in his high fortress in Alto, would listen to a dragonslayer's complaint about his sniveling cousin, Prince Vilmer. Not very likely.

Corlan watched the dragon fight from the tiny balcony hanging off his apartment above the tavern. The owner of the Fang & Claw let him use a storage room in exchange for assorted dragon parts Mux Posen, the owner, might sell in the tavern. When he could, Corlan cut off talons, dug out fangs, shaved off scales, and brought them home as souvenirs. He could not get to the fallen bodies of every dragon he slew, of course, so he could not prove his tally to an official counter's satisfaction.

"Our days are numbered," he mumbled as he leaned against the railing, feeling it give a little. He sat down, pushed his legs between the slats of the railing, letting them dangle over the edge, his bare feet welcoming the night air. His back pressed against the plaster wall.

With his dragonslinger leaning in the corner of the room and the pouch of his grandfather's medicine tossed upon the cot, he finally could wash off the weeks of dirt. Scooping water up from the basin on the floor, he had dabbed rags over his body. He dipped his head into the water and rubbed a bar of soap from ear to ear, and chin to toes. He took pains to clean the difficult areas, ready for a companion to soothe his broken spirit and aching body. By the time he felt fresh enough for a lover, he was too filled with sorrow to go on with his plan.

"A plan!" he snapped loud enough the balcony under him shook. "Another damnable plan...."

His sigh was rough, like the death-throes of a dying dragon.

In the sky the duel had ended. Trailing fire streaked the clouds and the victory cry lingered. Somewhere in the north a dragon had fallen. He was tempted to go claim it but expected that others would arrive before him. He had no hippor anyway to drag the carcass back into the city.

He would soon need to report on his expedition—and the loss of the expensive hippor.

"A new batch of *girafors* are ready to hatch, I heard," Mux Posen had told him when he mentioned losing the hippor.

"Always it's wizards that save the day," Corlan had mumbled, then raised his stein and downed another swallow of ale. "That'll be the day. Dragonslayers riding girafors." He cocked his head. "If they can carry a quiver of bolts...it could work. It might work."

He picked at a scar that stretched across his shoulder, a gift from a dragon he laid low a year before. He applied the usual salve and it seemed to be healing well. He examined the calluses on his feet. Good boots were hard to come by; he thought he might need a new pair but he realized he had no coin for such a purchase.

"No dragon remnants, no coin, no hippor, no bedmate." He gazed up at the stars. "At least I've a cot for the night. And a stein of ale. Everything else can wait till the morrow. What harm could befall me as I sleep?"

He pulled himself up, crawled off the balcony, stepping down into the room. Stretching his arms and legs, he felt just how sore his muscles were, something he hadn't noticed in the busy hours of his return to the city. His shoulders and back were tight, his legs unable to carry him. He wondered if he was getting too old for the tasks of his profession. He untied the loincloth, let it fall to the floor and kicked it into the pile of clothing bound for the laundry. The tavern owner's daughter would wash them, he knew.

Flopping on the cot, he bent an arm back under his head, stared at the beams overhead and thought of the view his grandfather must have had in his final breaths. And then Corlan closed his eyes, at the last instance fearing death, imagining he would never again awaken. Or worse: awaken surrounded by a horde of dragons.

Yet awaken he did—at the banging on the door just before the sun could cut the horizon outside his window.

He was groggy as he stumbled up from the cot, pinching his eyes with one hand. He reached for the door handle just as the door burst open and four uniformed men with lances forced their way into the small room.

Corlan fell back, unsure whether to throw on some clothes or to demand to know the reason for the intrusion.

He grabbed the blanket from the cot, wrapped it around his hips.

"What business have you?" he growled.

The four lancers took positions on either side of the open door. A man dressed in palace garb, blue jerkin and red trousers, red hat and white gloves entered: a palace crier.

The man opened a scroll, held it up, and read in a voice much too official for the poor room.

"Corlan of the Burg, dragonslayer *former*, Dragonslayers' Guild, removed by unanimous vote of members present, is hereby required to address his position to the Court of Prince Vilmer of the Burg. Under penalty of public pain, the captive today must make amends to all who have claim against him, beginning with His Majesty, the Prince, next to the Guild, then to citizens seeking redress of actions both professional and civil to include but not limited to drunkenness, thieving, whoring, fighting, and various offenses to the sensibilities of all who reside in the city."

The crier paused to examine Corlan's reaction: he seemed too sleepy to comprehend his troubles.

"This day we come to fetch you and remove you to the Court of the Prince, where you shall speak about your shortcomings!"

Another stare at the muscled man in the blanket.

"Prepare yourself or be dragged through the streets as you are!"

Corlan sleepily waved them off.

"Yes, yes, everyone knows! Corlan, the greatest dragonslayer the Burg has ever known, cast out of his own Guild for daring to suggest a proper way to rid the realm of dragons! Because they — the *fools!* — fear losing their employ! Then they'll be street beggars."

"Ready yourself," spoke the crier.

Corlan reached for the fresh garments hanging on the wall hooks, left for him by the laundry girl when he began his expedition. He dressed in the tan leather trousers, dark green shirt which laced at the throat and a brown doe-skin vest, deciding the dark blue cloak might make him look a bit more regal. He grinned at the crier.

"I might take up that occupation...street beggar. Such freedom! What say you to that? Would you give me coin?"

Corlan sat on the cot and pulled on his boots, still scuffed and dirty from the previous day and the weeks before he returned to the city. He took a rag to the toes and gave a quick brush up the ankles.

"That is, *if* the prince will allow me and my rattle cup to inhabit the lanes and the market. That would be fair, eh? Do you think I might gather enough coin to purchase even a small fruit that has lain too long at the bottom of a lady of the Court's golden toilet basin? Am I worthy enough for that?"

The crier gave a smirk. "It is for the prince to say."

"Yes, yes, the prince! May the gods have mercy on his spirit, he will surely say — say a lot, in fact! The man never shuts his mouth."

Corlan began laughing.

"Are you ready?" asked the crier.

"If you think I am fit for public display."

"Better than we had any right to expect," said the crier, adding a sharp nod. "We go now."

Corlan stepped out of the apartment, followed by the quartet of guards and the crier last of all. At that moment he considered dashing down the stairs and out of the tavern, escaping through the city and out to the wasteland in the west. The guards were behind him; he could run off easily. Yet, would he be able to make his way through the streets without others hindering his passage? It already seemed the entire city knew he was in trouble. Perhaps it actually would be better — a better chance to argue his case, disposition of one hippor — if he did face the prince.

At the bottom of the stairs, he paused and regarded his escorts.

"Keep moving!" snarled the crier.

One guard gave him a shove from behind.

"I was about to run away," said Corlan with a chuckle. "Then, oddly, I decided I must argue my side of the issues to the prince. I'm bound to be set free."

"Or just bound," said the crier.

Corlan sneered at him. "You obviously slept alone last night."

The crier gave a smirk. "As did you."

As they marched on down the lane and turned into the market square, the quartet of lancers drew the attention of passersby. Some stood in awe that someone was actually being held captive in their free city. Some called to Corlan, teasing him or cursing him. He did not lower his head and he met the eyes of anyone staring at him.

The group turned onto the main avenue that led straight up to the front gate of the palace. There, a larger contingent of guards blocked their way. The crier announced their official business and the gates were opened for them.

Corlan had been in the palace previously. Several times, in fact, although none of them gave him pleasant memories. He was only a boy, then an impatient youth, then a full grown man. The visits had seemed like bouts of bad humor. Except for the feasts of the past year or two and the ladies he met who admired his scars.

The Great Hall was as he remembered it: streamers falling from the high vaulted ceiling to the slick gold and white marbled floor. Golden cloth draped the mighty bannisters. Gold and brass reigned everywhere. The elevated floor where the giant chairs stood was lain with gold carpets. The great thrones were also trimmed with gold. Each was large enough to comfortably hold a full-grown god. The prince could stretch out, leaning into a corner with his feet almost at the edge of the cushion. The back rose high enough that the prince could stand up tall on the seat and not meet the top of the headboard with the tip of his crown. In ancient days, went the tale, the kings were taller. Either that or whoever designed the massive thrones intended the chief and chieftess of the gods to come for a visit one day. If they did visit, they would be able to sit comfortably with their proper ranks faithfully honored.

"And the people would bow low, chins on the floor, noses at the backsides of those in front," muttered Corlan as he was led over to the center of the Great Hall and urged to kneel.

The quartet stepped away from the spot Corlan occupied in the center of the floor yet remained close, standing watch at each corner of his imaginary cage. The crier stood before Corlan, holding the scroll. Around the perimeter of the hall stood members of the Court, ladies and gentlemen, with a cluster of servants ready to serve them once the official business was concluded. It seemed to Corlan that he was to be the designated entertainment of the day.

An hour passed and still he knelt on the hard marble floor, his knees growing numb.

Members of the Court milled about, chatting casually with each other, never straying too far from the walls.

Finally a trumpet sounded and everyone settled into their places.

4

Trial by Prince

PRINCE VILMER SAUNTERED into the Great Hall as though it was merely an extension of his private sleeping chamber. He seemed surprised to find so many people standing about. Of course he was prepared by a staff of clothiers to step into the public area. He was garbed in the finest fabrics the realm could produce, all gold and glittery, further embellished with more gold and, for contrast, crimson streamers at each arm and leg joint and around the collar of his gold-on-gold coat and trousers. His palace slippers were golden yet his stockings were the same bold crimson. The blood and gold look he relished, all the better to impress the Court that he was just as battle-tested as his army and as fabulously wealthy as the gods. To add to the effect, a tasseled golden train fell down his back and out across the floor, as though he was the Great Hall's bride. His head was crowned with a fluffy golden hat as large and bulbous as —

As the backside of a hippor, thought Corlan.

All those in audience *oo*ed, *aw*ed, and swooned at the glorious appearance of their gilded lord, the youthful Prince Vilmer.

Except for Corlan, who stared at the opulent figure more from curiosity, not admiration. He knew he could best the slim simpleton with one arm tied behind his back while hopping on one foot. The boy-king was a head shorter and a few years younger than Corlan. Yet the prince had regal power over him, a quirk of inheritance supported by gifts to the right families of the city. And a well-trained militia. So a twitch or a word from the boy-king and guards would quickly dispatch him with their lances and swords.

He was made to stand, now that the prince was present.

"Greetings to all," Prince Vilmer called when at last he had settled on one of several dignified poses, sampling each in front of the giant throne. He held his left arm outstretched as if to welcome everyone.

The members of the Court bowed, straightened up in unison.

"I have no doubt that all of you welcome the opportunity to come to Court this fine summer morning. Summer? It seems autumn is about to begin! So I am grateful for your indulgence. I have need of primary witnesses. Today should be an invigorating interrogation of our favorite vagabond. Surely we shall be quite entertained."

Some of the audience chuckled at the prince's sharp wit; most simply nodded their understanding. When the prince summons you to Court, you go, and you smile and follow the customs.

The prince dipped his head slightly in response then recast his stance on the wide stage.

"Corlan, my dear boy!" The prince beamed. "My, how you have grown!"

Corlan remained upright, eyes focused on the prince.

"You do not bow?" spoke the prince in his rather high voice. "Do you intend to insult me?"

"No intention at all," Corlan replied without any arrogant tone in his voice. "I was roused out of a sound sleep this morning by your errand boys and I'm simply too tired at this moment to remember all the rules."

The prince mugged, unsure how to respond.

The audience waited.

"That is understandable," the prince said after a moment. "Now that you are fully awake, you should follow the protocols. Or shall we introduce you to the protocol of re-education?"

Corlan remained at attention.

"So then you will follow the protocol...."

Two guards stepped toward Corlan.

"You will follow the protocol!" shouted the prince.

Corlan nodded. The nod became a head bow.

"Lower...."

The head bow became a bend at the waist, a moment's pause, and a return to upright form.

"The protocol has been followed," announced the prince.

The guards stepped back.

The prince cleared his throat in a loud, vulgar manner. A basin-bearing boy rushed to his side to catch the royal phlegm and hurried away, behind the stage curtain.

"Now then...."

The prince resumed his haughty posturing, full of frivolous arm gestures and a generally upturned chin. After all, before being thrust into the glamour of royalty, he had aspired to the theater, playing the roles of the Five Princes, each in turn, in several productions. Most members of the Court knew that fact and enjoyed his antics on stage; they were a captive audience.

"It has come to my attention," the prince continued, "that you have some explaining to do. This is the reason you were roused, as you insist, from a sound sleep. The day begins early, you know, as soon as the sun cuts the horizon. Only criminals and drunkards sleep later." He struck a new pose. "Which are you?"

Corlan breathed several steady draws, exhaled.

"I am neither."

"...Your Majesty," the prince added.

Two guards raised their lances, expecting a command.

Corlan bowed his head. "Not either one, Your Majesty."

"Then how is it that you attend our audience this morning in such a dire situation?"

"Dire? ...Situation? ...Your Majesty?"

A half-dance by the prince to the far end of the stage, a spin on the heel, train tangling around his legs in a strikingly original pose, again facing Corlan.

"Why, yes," said the prince. "One has heard tales concerning your many grievous activities during your brief return. First, one hears you have returned on foot. That is to say, without the *hippor* the Court had lent to you for official use. They are rather rare, you understand."

"Unfortunately, it was lost during the expedition."

"Lost? Do you mean to say you misplaced a hippor?" The prince practically slid to the center of the stage, struck a fresh pose for his audience. "You hear this, good members of the Court? A hippor...misplaced." He laughed, returning to Corlan: "Or did the hippor simply run away? Is that what you mean to say?"

It was hard for Corlan to keep his anger in check.

"I mean to say it was killed."

The prince feigned shock. "Killed? How so?"

"I was in the Valley of Death. I was hunting dragons. That is my occupation.... Your Majesty."

"Can it be true? I've not heard of dragonslayers venturing in that direction."

"It is true. I go there because that is the route many dragons take between their nesting grounds and their feeding grounds. Which are our farmsteads. They fly overhead nearly every day."

Almost as one, the audience looked out the tall windows on the side of the Great Hall or otherwise cocked their ears upward to listen for the approach of dragons overhead.

Corlan noticed their fear. "You see how the Court is afraid?"

"We have good people to watch the skies for them, for all of us," the prince said to reassure the audience. "I do not need to personally stand outdoors with my eyes turned skyward."

"Of course, not.... Your Majesty."

"Then explain the hippor. How could you lose a hippor? They are so large...not easy to lose." He turned with a sly grin to the elderly magister in long purple robe standing off to the side of the stage, a bundle of scrolls on the high desk there, expecting at least a knowing chuckle but getting none.

"The hippor was burned by the breath of an attacking dragon," said Corlan. "Then it fell off the cliff and was snatched by a different dragon. As dinner."

The crowd in the Great Hall burst into a nervous, fearful din.

"I couldn't save the animal although I did rip three of the dragons from the sky that day."

The prince seemed perturbed by the revelation.

"So you admit you put the hippor in harm's way?"

"In harm's way? I was hunting dragons! Everywhere out there in the Valley of Death is harm's way!"

The crowd became talkative.

"Calm yourselves or fear the lance!" the prince cried out.

The magister stepped forward, waist-length beard swinging back and forth. He pounded his wooden staff against the marble floor three times and the crowd gradually fell silent. The magister stepped back. The prince held up his hand as if to forgive the audience.

"Do you know the cost of producing a hippor?" asked the prince, lowering his hand. "It takes years to produce one. The cost of making one hippor is seven thousand *regals*."

The magister stepped over to the prince, spoke softly.

"The cost of a hippor is actually *seventy* thousand *regals*, so say my bookkeepers." He focused again on Corlan. "Seventy thousand! The wage of a thousand skilled workers laboring for seventy months. For half our citizenry, it is nearly the same as a lifetime's wages. I dare say: it is a *princely* sum!" He waited for indications of amusement from the audience. None came. "Have you sufficient coin to balance that debt?"

Corlan wanted to grin but held his face frozen. "I seem to be out of coin today."

"That is no surprise to us," the prince declared with a laugh that rang hollow.

He stepped down to the marbled floor of the Great Hall. A pair of lance-wielding guards rushed to each side of the prince.

"Listen, all! My father's brutish nephew here has had a wild time since his return to the city yesterday. With no material claim to the dragons he killed, we can only believe he sojourned in some paradise he located there in the valley—wasting our resources, perhaps dining on the hippor when the poor folk of our city are forced to beg for scraps of dragontail from the other, more worthy, more productive of our dragonslayers." He turned to the audience, arms raised. "Is that what we want? Is that what we expect from our hired men?"

"I was not on any sojourn—"

"And this one attempts to hide among the merchants upon his return, clearly ashamed of his inability to produce evidence of *all* the dragons he claims to have killed."

"I slew fifteen dragons on this latest hunt. More than one hundred for the year."

"Where is proof?"

"I can't be expected to haul back wares from fifteen dragons. And many were not easy to get to after they crashed. I leave them where they fall."

"Your colleague, Braden Batiste, returned with a whole carcass to be shared with the poor. That is a worthy dragonslayer!"

"He has a squad of assistants. He has runners locate dragon lairs for him. Then he uses poison, never the dragonslinger, as I do. In fact, he often uses an orphan boy as bait. That's a cowardly method."

"Results, my boy! That is all that matters."

Corlan scowled. *Boy? He's never even stepped on a garden lizard!* "Perhaps you should join me on a hunt, then, and see for yourself. You could mark a tally on a scroll and later show it to everyone here at Court. You could see how sweat appears."

The prince threw his arms up. "You mock me? Do you?"

"It is a humble suggestion."

"...Your Majesty! Say *Your Majesty!*"

"Your Majesty."

"Never forget," said the prince in a voice soft yet menacing, "I am the majesty to which you owe a debt. And now...it is time for me to collect it."

Corlan cleared his throat, which had become dry with nothing to drink since the previous evening.

"I was going to deal with that business. I only wanted to refresh myself first. To be presentable. That's the reason I did not go directly to the guild master."

"Or to this Court?"

"Same reason."

"No, instead of settling your business affairs, you went straight to see your grandfather, a worthless old man."

Corlan scoffed and the prince showed anger on his face.

"A boy was waiting to take me to him," said Corlan. "I returned to the city as usual and before I got any distance from the palace, the boy stopped me and led me to the lodge. I had no idea Grandfather was in such a grave condition. Nor that you are so suspicious of the dead haunting your halls."

"Grave condition? Such wordplay! Perhaps you secretly wished him quickly into the grave?"

"Not true!"

"Are you not after an inheritance?"

Corlan looked at his boots, thinking.

"The old man has nothing. You should know that—Your Majesty! I wanted nothing from him, never have. The boy took me to the lodge where he has spent his final months. I was surprised he had been put there instead of quarters befitting his noble life. Only arriving in that squalid room did I realize his true state of health. Were you aware? He bid me fetch his medicine. It seemed he'd not had it for some time, once it was empty." He glared at the prince. "I wonder whose work that may have been!"

"You make accusations? Threats? To me?" The prince's voice was as high as the ceiling of the Great Hall.

Corlan held himself steady despite his thumping heart.

"I state facts. Only facts."

"Then state more. How did you come to such a poor condition? I would have thought you were quite happy to follow in your father's weighty steps."

"Not at all. He had no direction."

"As everyone knows!" The prince grinned.

"He died in battle." Corlan's voice strengthened. "That is a noble death, is it not?"

"Noble if on the winning side!"

"He couldn't choose the side he was on. Your father sent him to fight. And fight he did—without enough soldiers!"

"There is no need to beleaguer ancient history here today—"

"It is far from ancient!"

"Ancient compared to today. There are no wars in the realm, not like those of old. Must we recall the War of the Five Princes? You know I have played each of them on stage. We have learned much about humanity from those cruel days of yore. The scrolls teach us much. There are no more wars. There are only dragons."

"It needs to be made clear," Corlan spoke out. "Your father sent his younger brother to battle in a losing cause, undersupplied and undersubscribed, with his ranks mostly filled with untrained youth, the sacrificed sons of poor families your father wished to punish. Meanwhile, your father sat on that throne behind you there and passed gas all day! While my father died fighting for our city! And our grandfather, Urix! Your father had him locked up until he was sick enough to be set free, and then sent to a cheap hospice!"

"How dare you!" shouted the prince.

"I dare." Corlan raised his arms to shoulder height, turning in place as he beseeched the audience. "Now you understand how he treats his own kin!"

The prince waved his arms frantically to recollect the audience.

"My father did not command him to lead the army into battle. It was Sir Urix who commanded Faltor to go, for your father had the skills to lead an army. My father, Sir Belgar, was better at this civic administration—which is what people need most after the battle is fought."

"And lost!"

"Faltor should have been stronger, should have fought harder."

"No general can win fielding an army of children."

"It was Urix who suggested that Faltor lead them into battle," said the prince in a calmer voice. "That is the truth of it. You and I had nothing to do with that event. We were children. Now it is in the past. You went into your Valley of Death and I took the scepter of this wayward city, and made it into the envy of the realm; indeed, doing what I am good at. King Belgar in Alto is pleased."

The audience gave a cheer.

"The Court needs to know!" The prince stared at his Court. "They need to know who you and I truly are: *cousins* at opposite ends of this city."

"Opposite ends? I should say opposite points of a tower, or of a flag pole: me at the top, glorious and free, and you at the base."

The prince stepped forward, raised his arm up and let it fall to his side. Corlan lowered his arms, his turn finished.

"Know you all here assembled today," the prince spoke, "that my cousin, Corlan, is at the *base*. I mean that as more than a joke. He is not only at the base, he *is* base. That being the lowest of the low."

He gave Corlan a knowing smirk. They had played together as boys and one time Corlan had hit him for some reason. Vilmer ran to Corlan's mother to complain. To make it worse, his own mother had spanked his bottom as Vilmer gleefully watched.

"There is nothing lower, true? than a man who hunts dragons. A man who traipses through the defecation of dragons. A man who shares their vile, filthy breath. A man who loves all there is about the dragon business!"

"We dragonslayers protect the city!"

"So you say...yet at what cost?"

The prince paced left, returned to his right, nodding pensively.

"I have knowledge of the Guild Hall incident of yesterday. You stood and proclaimed blasphemy. Many witnesses there. You were shouted down. You were removed from the Guild Hall. I believe you were also voted out. True?"

Corlan did not know how to respond. His mouth fell agape, then closed tightly, jaw clenched.

"Is it true? You are no longer a member of the Dragonslayers' Guild?"

Corlan looked down at the floor, saw a faint reflection there in the polished tiles of his enemy, the prince. He stepped forward to place his boot on the face he saw.

"That is what happened. Such a small matter. An administrative notation all it was. They will welcome me back when I bring them dragon remnants, what you call souvenirs. That is the protocol. Proof enough of one's slaying skill and daring, then I'm a member again."

"Yet how shall you demonstrate your skill and daring when you have nothing? No hippor to take you out. No dragonslinger to kill an aerial? Oh—yes, we claimed your dragonslinger as partial payment for expenses extended to you by the Court and not repaid."

"But I've only returned since yesterday! How can I be expected to make payment so soon? I would need to convert assets into coin. That would require selling dragon parts to merchants, a few days work at best. Then—"

"You've been seen hiding from us. Spending coin on medicine for a dead man. Drinks for yourself. Pleasures with a young boy. Wage for a whore or two—"

"Your Ma-jes-ty!" Corlan exclaimed.

The audience gasped, certain the guards were about to strike the insulant man.

"You are quite mistaken—or your spies are," Corlan continued in a louder voice. "The boy was a caretaker at the lodge where our grandfather rested. I only took him with me to the apothecary to fetch the medicine. The boy was supposed to take the medicine back to him while I attended the Guild meeting."

"Yet you took him to the Guild Hall. A violation of the protection of juveniles law. The boy might have been taken under by one of the dragonslayers there. Or you. We know how dragonslayers can be."

"Dragonslayers aren't that sort. He was in no harm and joined me as I left the Guild Hall to return to the apothecary."

"A clever story!"

"And there was no whore or two, as you say. After all that hassle, I was much too tired for any sort of amorous activity."

"So *you* say!"

"It is all true!"

"Calm yourself, cousin, lest you unleash my rage."

The audience seemed satisfied with the regal retort so the prince enjoyed the moment.

"You know how loud, how...*hurtful* your voice can become."

Corlan punched his fists to his hips. "I speak only to answer your questions. I speak to defend myself."

"A good man has no need of defense."

"An evil man will quickly slay a good man who fails to defend himself."

"Ah, you're a quick one!" The prince raised his chin as though he was speaking over the heads of the guards and Corlan, directly to the audience. "You see how he insults the Court? Insults me to my regal face? Being cousins does not give him standing."

The prince waved his hand at the quartet of guards boxing Corlan in and they stepped closer to him, lances at the ready, metal tips aimed at his waist and chest.

"Is this necessary?" called Corlan. "I believe I have answered your questions truthfully and completely. You should allow me to return to my apartment, nap until I am fully rested, and then I shall get to work making amends to you and the Court, whatever it takes, no matter how long. Grandfather would want it that way."

The prince grinned like he had a delightfully different idea.

"Make amends you shall. We would prefer such to throwing you into the dungeon for a lengthy sojourn. What do you recommend?"

"Recommend? ...Your Majesty?"

"Your sentence."

"I thought I explained everything already. Why does there need to be a sentence?"

"What will you do to make amends?"

Corlan breathed deeply, turning in place, eyeing the four guards around him. They took a step back, keeping their lances ready. He could probably defeat them, yet not without some injury to himself. He might get through the crowd and escape into the palace, find some hiding place, wait out the search.

And flee to the Valley of Death without provisions....

He shook his head slowly, forming the words.

"Here is what I propose: Let me return to the Valley of Death, fully supplied, and I will not only make the quota of dragon kills, I will exceed the quota, double it or better. I will be certain to collect plenty of remnants to present to you and the Court. Furthermore, I will trek onward to the nesting grounds in the far west and there I will destroy them all."

"Destroy them? How is that possible?"

"As I told my fellow dragonslayers in the Guild Hall, the nesting grounds are where dragons are born. Smash their eggs and there will be no more dragons."

The Great Hall fell silent. Then murmurs arose. The audience was eager to know more, it seemed. The prince had no response, pacing the stage.

"Can you do this thing?" asked the prince after a moment, almost to himself. Then, with bolder voice: "Or is it merely a ruse to escape the city and avoid your sentence?"

Corlan shook his head. "On what basis am I given a sentence?"

"On the basis that I am the prince of this city and you are not. And that you have offended us. That you are in debt to us. That you have acted badly, against royal decree in numerous ways, avoided your civic responsibilities in the short time since you have returned. That you have...."

The prince trailed off, seemingly unwilling to mention the next.

"That I have what? ...Your Majesty?"

The prince waved his hand at the magister standing to the side of the stage. The magister stepped behind the drapery and returned a moment later with a scroll, handing it to the prince with ceremonial formality.

"I have here," said the prince as he unfurled the scroll, "a report on various immoral behavior perpetrated by my brutish cousin."

Corlan cocked his head to the right, rolled his eyes. "There is a scroll for everything, it seems."

"There is! This scroll is a report on your dalliance with a lady of the Court."

Corlan reddened, took half a step forward. "What?"

"Yes, a lady of the Court!"

He dared take another step and the guards raised their lances.

"Don't say the name!" Corlan shouted. "Protect her name. Save her reputation. I'll confess to dalliance yet I assure you our acts were mutual. I ask that she be spared from ridicule. Let it fall upon me alone." He bowed his head. "Your Majesty! And I shall go forth as I have offered. I shall slay many dragons for the good of the city and not bother any member of the Court from this day forward...to the end of my days."

"Ah hah!" The prince paced back and forth, hands clasped behind his back. "A fair deal! You must care for her indeed. I have the name here, of course. And I shall say the name."

"Don't!" cried Corlan.

"Don't...?"

"Your Majesty."

"You do not say 'please'?"

"Please do not say her name...Your Majesty."

The prince paced across the stage but screwed his face up as if deciding what to do next.

Corlan watched, waited, wondering if the name on the scroll was

Petula. However, she was not a lady of the Court. She only served during feasts. He tried to think back a few months. Triza—was that her name? It was only a couple of nights they were together. Perhaps Mauvel? That was more than a year past and didn't involve much. It could be some other lady of the Court whom he had not shown sufficient interest in, causing the lady to accuse him simply out of vengeance. What did his cousin really know? Perhaps it was a bluff. He had dallied with several ladies of the Court, true, yet none kept his heart so warm as did Petula.

"This brute," the prince declared theatrically, "has dallied with his own dear cousin!" He regarded the audience, seeking their abject disapproval. "Oh, not me, naturally. She is, however, my sister!"

"Vorinna...?" asked Corlan. "Why, I wouldn't touch her with a twenty-foot pole!"

"You dare speak that way of my sister?"

In all honesty, Corlan had never had any interest in Vorinna, a tall and gangly woman with poor skin and odd facial features. Her mouth never closed, supported by two long front teeth. Her ears flapped like the gills of a fish and her hair was known for dropping in bunches whenever she suffered a bout of anxiety—which happened regularly, as shy as she was. At least that was how she had appeared the last time he saw her. That was several months past. Corlan felt pity for her, but he would never have chosen her for any dalliance—*gods, no!*

Corlan's heart felt relief that it was not Petula who was called out by the prince.

"My dear cousin is a fine maiden," said Corlan calmly. "I do care for her as a member of the royal family, which is the reason I could never enter into that sort of relationship."

"Then how is it she is now with child?"

A shriek erupted behind the curtains, followed by a loud thump against the wooden floor there. Court assistants ran out of the Great Hall.

"With child?" Corlan was shocked. What manner of man would lay with such a woman? She was so...*ugly!*

"Someone has been with her, no doubt against her will—forcefully, violently—and we know you to be unforgiving when it comes to your own whoring."

"I swear I have never touched that woman!"

The prince turned to the audience, pinching his eyebrows.

"Then someone here is the culprit! One of you is the dallier! Come forth! You must wed this maiden to save yourself from never-ending pain! Yet you shall never be a member of the royal family, of course, as a result of your deceit."

The magister lumbered over to the prince, handed him another scroll.

One scroll after another, thought Corlan. His knees were getting tired standing so long.

"Now hear this!" the prince called out. He read out the names of eleven men. Guards broke into the crowd to apprehend each of them. Some of the men had their wives grabbing at them, unable to believe they would be so accused. The men were brought to the front of the Great Hall and lined up before the prince—between the prince and Corlan. All of the eleven except for...

"Braden Batiste!"

Corlan's head snapped around, searching for his arch rival among the audience behind him.

"Is Batiste not among us?" asked the prince.

There are *gods in the heavens!* Corlan grinned, tried to hide it.

The prince turned to the magister: "Find him at once!"

The line-up was led away by a squad of guards, and Corlan once again stood alone in the center of the Great Hall with the members of the Court behind him and to either side along the walls.

The prince centered himself on the stage, handing off the scroll to a boy, then wringing his hands as though flinging water, done with the matter.

"I believe you, Corlan. This time only. This dalliance only. Yet you and I know the truth: you will dally with any maiden you find and only for your moment's pleasure, with no foresight of proper union under the supervision of the gods or our magi. Someday you will, I know. When you are old and gray, quite unable to father another generation, then you'll die of regret."

Corlan smiled against his will. He'd had no concern for a proper union until recently, when he met Petula, yet the idea now seemed inviting.

The prince stood tall, bounced a bit on his heels to seem taller.

"So be it." *Dramatic pause.....* "I accept your proposal."

Corlan blinked. "That being...?"

"What you said. You go off to the Valley of Death and we never hear from you again. Unless you happened to achieve the goals you stated, killing all the dragons and returning with proof of it. Then we may yet reconsider your banishment from the city."

"Banishment...?"

The prince turned to the guard captain, waved for him to remove the prisoner. The guards moved against Corlan.

"By dawn tomorrow, you shall exit the city," the prince declared. "And we shall expect to not be bothered by you for a very long time. You have the remainder of today to settle your affairs."

"Will I receive provisions?" he asked, gazing up at the prince.

The prince seemed to think about the idea a moment. The guard squad halted, Corlan in the middle of them.

"It seems only fair. The usual expedition supplies."

"And a mount?"

"We have no more hippors. You may have to try a *girafor*, if you don't mind the long necks. The saddles are a bit uncomfortable."

"I only need it to carry supplies, especially the iron bolts for my dragonslinger—"

"Your dragonslinger? Did you not offer it as partial payment."

"I need it to achieve my goals. To shoot down dragons. Bow and arrow will not suffice."

"Very well, take it. Be gone now!"

The guards hesitated, uncertain whether the prince was finished or simply caught in another dramatic pause.

"Be gone, I said! Remove this brute from my sight!"

The guards moved off with Corlan.

"Tomorrow's dawn and you are gone!" the prince called after them. "Ah, I made a rhyme. Clever."

The audience began to mill about, their chatter rising.

"I did not dismiss you!" called the prince. "We have other matters to discuss. It is near the time of the Dragon Festival and we should make arrangements for music, food, drink, decorations, and costumes, decide the rules, the guest list—the palace and members of the Court, except if you wish to invite a unique individual who might make our Festival more endearing, that sort of person—and the venue must be prepared, inspected. It is the most important event of the year, so great care must be taken to the details. I shall expect a detailed report of the arrangements by tomorrow afternoon. Enjoy the remainder of your day!"

Escorted back to his apartment by a quartet of palace lancers and the captain, Corlan thanked them in a mocking tone.

"You heard the prince," said the captain with a hint of delight. "At dawn, you are to be gone. Start packing."

Corlan swung his arm around the room. "Won't take long."

He began undressing.

"What are you doing? You must pack."

"I'm going to finish my sleep first."

"You must pack!"

Corlan glared at the captain.

The captain glared back. There would be no peace until he had packed. So Corlan went about the room, shirtless and barefoot, stuffing clothing and a few other items into a cloth sack. He tossed the sack on the cot.

"Done."

The captain ordered the lancers out, then paused. "We return early," he said with a sneer. "Be ready."

Corlan flopped on the cot, grabbed the blanket and pulled it over himself and was soon snoring loud enough to be heard in the tavern below. Mux Posen was opening it for the noontide drinkers.

A couple hours later, tapping on the door nudged Corlan enough that he opened an eye, turned his head toward the door and grinned. He sat up, awake but not yet recovered. He sniffed himself, took a swig of water left in a cup, and ran his fingers through his mussed hair.

He stood and stepped to the door, wondering if he should put on more than the loincloth he was wearing. He had a hunch who might be tapping rather than knocking or pounding on the door.

"Oh, Corlan, my darling!" exclaimed the buxom blond woman leaning against the frame when he swung the door open.

Petula pushed her way into the room, sweeping her arms around his shoulders, planting her lips on his cheeks then his mouth. He wrapped his big arms around her waist, pulling her close. As they kissed, he turned them around and kicked the door closed.

"Petti," he said with a welcoming sigh when their lips parted.

She playfully pinched his cheeks. He grinned.

"I heard what they did to you."

"Yes, terrible things. I need some comfort now."

She released his cheeks, hugged him tightly. "That's the reason I hurried here."

"You're always welcome, Petti."

His fingers unbuttoned the back of her pale blue dress, the one she wore while at tasks in the palace. The white collar framed her pale throat. As she breathed quicker, he let the dress slip off her shoulders and her bosom fell against his chest. The dress dropped, caught on her hips. She wiggled to make it drop further, down to her ankles, then stepped out of it. The private garments were no match for Corlan's hands and soon they were on the floor, too. His loincloth followed.

They stretched across the cot and worked hard to make the floor shake, the walls lean in, and the thin down mattress push vigorously against the frame, squeaking and clanging until the complaining thumps from the tavern below were the only sounds that seemed out of place. Finally, they collapsed on the cot. It had held together.

"Corlan, my darling," Petula said, breathing heavily, her chest rising and falling beside him. "It's one month already since we've been together...."

Despite her tanned cheeks, her skin was pale where it had been covered and shielded from the sun. Corlan loved the twilights of her body. He walked his fingers along the borders, tracing them. She walked her fingers over his chest. He chuckled as she toyed with him, rubbing a raised scar there. Her blue eyes blinked.

"I hadn't noticed," he grunted. "Too busy slaying all the dragons, don't you know?"

"Don't I know it!" She slapped his shoulder. "I waited each day by the west gate from the end of dinner service to the first star, just hoping for the sight of you returning. I hugged that oakwood that overhangs the balcony, pretending it was you. You know the one."

"Where we first made joy together?"

"Yes, our first joy — there in the midnight dark, under the vault of heaven. You know the gods were jealous of us that night."

"Let them be jealous!"

"We will," said Petula with a twist of her lips, "we surely will, my darling."

"When I return...."

She pushed herself up on an elbow. "Then it's true?"

"Indeed. Words all told, now I'm banished from the city." Their eyes met. "For as long as takes to gather enough dragon memorabilia to satisfy my debt to the prince. Then I may be let in."

Petula sniffled. "I can give you some coin."

"No, Petti. It's not your debt. You haven't but a small portion of it. I will manage it. Besides, I swore to go to the far end of the valley, all the way to their nesting ground and slay them in their eggshells."

"Can you do that? It is so far...."

"A long journey, yes."

"When will you return?"

He gazed up at the beams of the ceiling, firm wood that seemed forever strong. His heart beat quicker.

"Likely years hence." He settled his gaze upon her. "Many long years. I cannot say."

"Oh, my darling, Corlan...."

He curled an arm around her shoulders and she snuggled against his chest. Their breathing soon matched and their hearts fell into the same rhythm. His fingers stroked her blonde locks as her hand tickled his chest. There was solace in the touching of two spirits, reaching for each other through flesh. They understood.

"I will remember you," Corlan whispered, "but I will understand if you do not wish to wait so long for me to return."

She kissed his rough shoulder. "I will wait...." She made a line to his whiskered throat and kissed there. "...as long as it takes."

"You do not need to make such a promise."

She rubbed her fingertip along the scar across his chest. He had told her the story of how the dragon talon had cut him. "I do make it." She kissed the raised scar, a scimitar shaped beauty mark.

"No, you would throw away your life on a dream," he said.

"It is our dream."

"A dream is something to awaken from. Then it no longer exists."

"Our dream will exist forever."

"Petti, there are many chances for death on this journey. I might never return. That's a possibility. We dragonslayers live a dangerous life and nothing is certain."

She pushed herself up, laying over him, holding his face between her hands, staring into his eyes.

"I know you, Corlan of the Burg. Better than most people. I know you will survive. I know it. Do you hear me? And you'll return to me. I know that, too. No matter how many years it'll require, you'll find my face smiling at you, and my heart beating strong for you, my body always for your comfort—on the day I see you again and for all the days after. I'm always yours."

"You warm my spirit, Petti. You're so unlike other whores."

She pouted. "Because with you, I'm not a whore. I'm a maid—an old maid, yes, but a maid who wants a man to hold me at night. A man to hold me right. I'm passing the age—"

"I'll hold you all night. Or all afternoon, as it is today."

"You are the only man for me, Corlan of the Burg."

"And you are the woman for me."

"The only woman?" she asked with a posed frown.

He grinned. "I promise you."

"I know the journey will be hard." She gave him a quick kiss. "If you ever find a princess somewhere along the way, and she beguiles you so...and the only way for you to regain freedom is to make joy with her, then do it. I give permission. Then you'd better rush right home to me!"

"So you'll forgive me?"

"I will. Yet you'll have to ask me for forgiveness first."

He laughed and she seemed hurt by it.

"Do you take this seriously?"

"I do, Petti."

"Then your promise is true?"

"As true as the joy we make together."

With a rain of kisses, they swung themselves into another circus of animal passion, each the artist of the other, until the day darkened and the breeze through the window was no longer warm. No words were spoken because they both understood. Except one thing. Petula patted her bare belly yet her tired lover did not get the hint.

Sometime after the lights of the city had been extinguished, after even the tavern regulars had departed drunkenly, the buxom blonde Petula slipped quietly out of the Fang & Claw and disappeared into the night.

INTERLUDE

The Ancient Ritual

INTO THE GREAT SLUMBER CHAMBER of the queen ran the little
girl they all adored so very much. The nine year old princess could
do no wrong. With rosy cheeks and a button nose, her amber hair
usually gathered into three braids down her back, she delighted
everyone each day with the sweet sounds of her voice. Servants and
staff welcomed her playful antics. One day she might be dancing on
the staircase to a tune only playing in her head. Another day she
would sing to herself or to the birds in the palace gardens who
would cease their own songs to listen to hers. Other days she might
build a tiny house for a furry dabbler, putting together pieces of
wood that the carpenters left while constructing the great bed upon
which her dear mother would rest for the next several months of her
laboring.

"Is it time? Is it time yet?" the little girl would ask members of
the staff as she skipped through the palace each day. "I've been
waiting since forever!"

They would cheerfully praise her concern, as any daughter
would have for her mother.

"Where's Mama?" The little girl gasped. "I mean, the queen."

Queen Dorothea needed a new slumber seat for the new birthing
period. Custom declared that the same bed could not be used both
for the conception and the birthing. The previous slumber seat, she
had loudly complained, had been soiled by the rough scent of a man
and she dared not endure it any longer. However, that was merely
polite prattle. The custom simply required a new bed for the
birthing. The man, nameless after the deed, had been sent quickly
away.

The queen knew it was a function of nature that she lower herself to the level of the beasts for these common grapplings. It was hardly different from when she lumbered daily over to the big drop and let loose her meal waste. The unpleasant task was made tolerable by a quartet of musicians and a duo of perfume-squirting maidens. A team of wipers made certain none of that function followed her out of the chamber to haunt her through the day. Whenever the function might be particularly acute, she would be served a dessert cake with cream sauce while carefully braced over the big drop, although she found it disgusting to take in while putting out; however, the hours required of the effort demanded she take sustenance there lest she succumb to the strain.

"Her Majesty has dropped!" the court crier would call out when the act had been completed. "Court physicians have deemed the royal output normal!" Then all would know the queen was ready for a new day of regal routines, whether they be court duties or more personal pleasures. "Make way for Queen Dorothea!"

It was for the good of Sannan, of course, that she lay with a chosen man for a few hours once in a while, that occasion being two instances each year. Her mother had taught her about the duties of a queen, and one of the most sacred was to produce an heir. When the day came, a team of assistants made sure the act was performed with a minimum of imposition and inconvenience.

No one could say what became of the sire after the final night of exhausting exuberance. After all, men were of no concern to anyone in Sannan. A few men worked the vineyards and farms of Sannan Island, far away from the city, or herded animals farther from the city, but they mattered not.

"I shall have a new slumber seat," ordered the queen as her first words the following morning.

Carpenters were assembled, craftsmen came to her chamber, and a new bed was designed and constructed, larger than the previous — for the birthing was more important than the conceiving. None of the artisans paused to consider that the queen also was now larger.

The new slumber seat stood tall at the head and nearly as wide as the chamber, as though the entire purpose of the room was absorbed by the slumber seat. Atop the hearty furniture boards were set six mattresses, covered in the softest fabric, laden with the finest of accessories: three exotic duvets, two thick quilts, bright coverlets, frilly bolsters, woolen blankets, smooth sheets, and pleated skirts, with a carefully arranged collection of pillows representing every degree of softness, placed from largest to smallest, from firmest to softest, stacked high against the headboard and continuing up the wall above the headboard.

"My Queen," the head nursing maid dared speak, "would not the tower of pillows, upon some distant morn, perchance collapse down upon you? Dare we believe the tower of pillows may collapse upon the babe?"

The queen waved her meaty hand, dismissing the nursing maid.

"I will catch any pillow that falls, although that function is not part of my contract. I will consider that function, if it occurs, to be due extra weight in fees. I shall have the fees sent to my vault forthwith."

"As you command, Your Majesty."

Dorothea was the queen, after all, and her mother, grandmother, and great-grandmother had been queens, as well. She came to believe she had power over absolutely everything within the boundaries of the realm, from the sky-scraping peaks far to the east to the steaming swamps in the south, from the vast white way of the north to the dry sands of the western shores. She claimed the deep blue strait, as well, though no one made that fact known to the people of the mainland.

In truth, she reigned only over the island of Sannan, which was much smaller than a realm. None dared point out the difference. The palace rose from the port town of Sannan on the northern tip, facing the strait. All of it, the true portion, belonged to her from the day and hour she accepted the appointment from her mother, Queen Marvala, who lived for one hundred forty-four years sixteen days and twenty-two hours. Dorothea was deemed the best choice among Marvala's six daughters and given the official appointment at the age of twenty-five.

And then Princess Adora was born!

A palace guard captain bearing the name Yvik stood tall and straight one day a little past the mid-day meal, checking the correctness of her charges. In her bright yellow uniform, crimson epaulets and trouser stripes, wearing a tall crimson cap with yellow foreshield, the woman made a wonderful sight when Queen Dorothea rounded the turn in the palace corridor, the passage between the Great Hall of Talk and the smaller Hall of Show.

Yvik was fair and square, and sported very yellow hair, her jaw in alignment with the latitudes of the world. When the queen appeared in the corridor, Yvik had swung her sword up in salute, blunt edge against her shoulder. Her mistake was to allow her lips to part and her gleaming teeth to show, what some might call a grin.

The queen halted, and her procession crashed against themselves behind her in the corridor.

"What is your name?" asked the queen of the captain.

"Your Majesty, I am Yvik, captain second-class, first of the fifth, of the palace guards." She remained tall and rigid.

"I dislike the name yet your face pleases me," said the queen with a flick of her fan. "You shall arrive at my slumber chamber at the edge of night."

"Tonight, Your Majesty?" she asked, sounding overwhelmed.

"Did I fall over my words?" the queen retorted. Her nervous staff chuckled for her. She turned to her notetaker. "See that this one is properly attired. And do give her a better name. I won't be calling my painful delights to such a name as Yvik!" Her eyes returned to Yvik. "Oh. And bring your pet."

"Pet, Your Majesty?"

"You do have a pet, don't you? Most upper level staff have one, I hear. I'd think a guard captain, even second-class, would be able to afford one. If not, I'll need to raise your wage."

"Yes, Your Majesty, I do have a pet."

"Then bring it!"

"Yes, Your Majesty."

So at the designated evening hour, Yvik arrived—briefly renamed Destina. She arrived dressed in a floor-swishing crimson velvet robe with golden flourishes provided by the queen's staff and smelling of the spice-laden perfumes and the musk of wild, rutting beasts which, the queen's body maid knew, never failed to excite Her Majesty and made her body quiver, respond in heavenly fashion, and in the end assured that she would achieve success in the ancient ritual.

Destina was let into the chamber, taken to the slumber seat, and ceremoniously unrobed. Beside the woman knelt her pet, naked but for a narrow cloth wrapped around the dirty parts.

"There's my lover!" cried the queen from atop the stack of six mattresses she pressed down to the height of four.

A single gold-spun sheet covered the queen save for her rounded head and coiled hair and the tops of her thick shoulders. Her chubby hands and rotund arms rose and clapped the air above her chest, the signal to begin the ritual.

Her body maids assisted in maneuvering Destina and her pet into the proper positions, her perfect un-uniformed body aligned over Her Majesty's great wealth of flesh.

Beside Destina crouched her pet, a short, thin *man* formerly of the stables, having the name Gup or Gunt, not that it mattered. She had bought him from the stablekeep not quite a year before, when she believed she owed herself a small measure of enjoyment at the end of her duties each day. Fortunately, he had proven worthy of her choice. Now she must give him up. Indeed, when Her Majesty invites you to visit her slumber seat, you do not arrive without a pet to share.

As everyone assembled in the queen's slumber chamber knew, it was the time of the great mating, when a woman chooses a pet for her slumber seat. Twice each year a festival was held on Sannan and men were let into the city. Much mating occurred during the festival weeks. The remainder of the year, many of the high-born ladies kept a pet for an occasional evening's dalliance. Her Majesty, however, could not abide such a poor, dirty thing being in the palace anymore than absolutely necessary for nature's briefest call.

Thus, ointments and oils were applied by the queen's body maids, and after some time a union was made. The pet grunted and the exuberance of its actions delighted the queen. The queen likewise squealed in something between a cry of pain and a plea for mercy. The strained voice Destina shared with the queen when the peak rolled over her was similarly a combination of animal noises. And a strange, annoying whistle.

The women shared a gasp.

"What is that?" the queen asked, huffing and puffing.

"My pet has made a noise, Your Majesty. My greatest apologies!"

"It smells so foul!"

"A thousand pardons, Your Majesty!" cried Destina.

"Only a thousand? I would think a million might get you closer to saving your position in the palace guards." The queen regarded her body maid. "Remove the dirty thing this instant!"

Two beefy women grabbed hold of Destina's pet, pulling it off the queen's wide body.

"Ooo, it drips!" cried the queen with a hiss.

"That is the final act, Your Majesty. It is common. It proves the ritual was a success," said the body maid. "The pet is done."

"Then we have finished? It is done?"

"Yes, Your Majesty."

"Thank the goddesses! I don't know how much more I could have taken. All that pushing and grunting! Terrible!"

The pet was promptly pulled from the slumber chamber and no one knew or cared what became of it.

Destina was wiped clean, put back into the robe, and dismissed to some new location where she was unknown yet again called Yvik.

The queen's body maids tended to her prodigious skin, washed the inward places, then set about testing the success of the ritual.

After several hours in which the nursing staff pushed a long, thin tube up and inside the queen, measuring the dripping at the top of each hour, listening for just the right gurgle, just the right pop, just the right hiss, the chief nursing maid finally pronounced success.

"Thank the goddesses!" the queen repeated at the bottom of each hour. She hated the testing but knew it was necessary. Better that than the need for a repeat performance. Pets could be so disgusting. Palace guards could be so quirky. If only the goddesses could flick their holy fingers and make a child appear fully formed.

On the seventh day following the ancient ritual, a royal announcement was made, stating to the people in Sannan that the queen had in this time of union achieved royal success. A great cheer arose throughout the city. At last, their queen would bear a royal heir.

And so, after some time, like in stories big and small, whatever was required for the goddesses to mix together the perfect specimen of ladyhood, it was Queen Dorothea who opened her mighty thighs and with great effort and pain pushed out the perfect babe.

The fleshy thing was immediately identified as a lady and given straight into the arms of Her Majesty.

"She looks so adorable!" the queen was heard to say. "I shall call her Adora."

"Hail Princess Adora!" the nursing staff cheered.

As was the custom, lost in the eternal fog of ancient ritual, if the thing produced from the loins of woman had been a male, it would have been quickly removed from the chamber as though it had never been created. No mourning would occur and no announcement of the failure would be made. A female child, however, was placed into the breast cradle immediately and offered a nipple to suck, encouraged to dine with great passion from that first day forward and for as long as the teats gave milk.

Adora, the little princess, noted the arrangement, standing quietly beside the nursing lounger, watching her mother lovingly press the new babe against her large breast.

"What words have you to say to your new sister?" asked Queen Dorothea, nine years after birthing little Adora.

"I suppose I will say to her 'Welcome to Sannan.'" The pretty girl thought for a moment. "What shall I call her?"

The queen smiled, her chubby cheeks flushing as they often did when she was delighted.

"Let's call her...Lumina. She is so bright. She lights up my life. How is that?"

"Lu-mi-na. Yes! I like it!" exclaimed the girl.

"So it is done. The naming. A lovely name for a queen. Almost as great as Adora. Now let the realm know my second daughter is to be called Lumina—Princess Lumina."

The chief maid exited the slumber chamber to pass the news to the court crier who would make the official announcement.

"What will happen to the other babe?" asked Adora.

The nursing maids chuckled. Such a beautiful, naïve child, they seemed to suggest. Once she returns to her tutors, she will learn more of the customs of Sannan.

"It's none of your concern. Go and make play for yourself."

Adora turned to the basket on the floor beside the great slumber seat. In the basket the babe gurgled, threatening to cry, its tiny feet wriggling above the basket's rim. She wanted to step closer and get a better look, to see if this one was as cute as the babe resting on her mother's chest sucking the nipple.

"Sometimes the goddesses may bless us with extra measure," the queen spoke in a soothing voice. "As always, we must dispense with males, all the sons and brothers, fathers and uncles, lest they return our great realm to ancient depravity and ring loud the bellicose bell. You must remember the history of wombkind."

"I do," said Adora. "I listen to my tutors always."

"As you should." The queen spoke to her maids a moment. When she turned to Adora, she said: "I pay much to hire only the best tutors for you, so you should trust what they tell you."

Adora stared at the babe in the basket. The queen saw her abject attention and waved at one of the nursing maids.

"Remove the waste," commanded the queen.

When the basket was taken out, Her Majesty turned as best she could, rolling on her side upon the slumber seat, and gazed at her elder daughter.

"When your time comes, little one, a suitable sire will be arranged for you. You need not trouble yourself until then. After the coupling, you need never have to see that beast again. Until then, you have plenty of lovely girls to play with. So go on and make play. Those twins that Countess Nadal has...you always get on with them, do you not? Delightful girls."

Adora pouted.

"Do not show a sour face. The maids will think you have erred in some way. And we shan't call you Adora any longer, for you won't be adorable any longer."

"But, Mama, I want—"

"Adora!"

"I'm sorry, Mama."

"Mama? You forget who you are, child!"

The girl bowed her head. "Yes, Your Majesty. Forgive me, Queen Dorothea. I'm only a child."

"Very well, forgiven you are."

After a moment, Adora raised her eyes to her mother.

"May I keep it for a pet?"

The queen stared at the child, then shifted her weight upon the great slumber seat, tucking the newborn daughter into the cleft of her elbow with a warm smile. The nursing maids gasped, fearing that the newborn would be crushed.

"A pet?"

"Yes, Your Majesty."

"Already you fancy a pet? You're not yet of the age for that."

The girl lowered her eyes. "I just want to play with it."

"You must know such creatures will grow into adulthood, just as you shall. It is not a good thing. Not much of a pet then. By such an age it will be dangerous. They surely will be violent."

"I only wish a pet for now," said Adora, looking up. "If it please Your Majesty. Caring for a pet will teach me many responsibilities."

"Responsibilities!"

The queen chuckled. She rolled over onto her back once more to hand off the newborn babe to a nursing maid.

"Better you had a canine or feline for that kind of lesson, or even a small dragon would do as well. Not a male babe."

"I beg you, Mama — Your Majesty!"

"Begging? That's not very becoming of a princess."

The queen thought for a moment, her chubby fingers stroking her daughter's soft cheek.

"As you wish, child. You shall have the male babe as your pet. Yet only until it reaches the size you are now. Then it must be set aside as the others are. Before it can do any harm."

"What will become of the babe then?"

"Sent to the workhouse for training. All males we keep become either warriors or laborers, as you should know. Ask your tutor the lesson about males. Only the tests will determine which path it goes. If a warrior, then we may need a few battles to be able to determine who of them is worthy of service for our women." She raised her voice for the notetaker's benefit: "We owe a battle to Anjoz, don't we? They dare encroach upon our south shore." Regarding the princess, "Those warriors who are victorious will serve us. Those who do not pass will become common laborers."

The girl gasped, as though expecting a pinch of pain.

"And laborers do not touch maidens."

"Correct, child. Your tutors have taught you well. I shall add to their wages."

"Will there be a battle soon?" asked Adora.

The queen chuckled. "Why soon?"

"I wish to know if my pet will stay or go before I devote my time to caring for it."

The queen patted the girl's head. "Spoken well! You will make a fine queen some day, Princess Adora. You are always planning for the future and wanting it now. Such a delight!"

The queen gave the command and the basket was retrieved with some effort, already more than halfway across the courtyard, close to the disposal bin, and promptly returned to the slumber chamber.

On the floor at Adora's feet, the male babe wriggled and cooed contentedly in the basket as though nothing awful had happened or was about to happen. That was as it should be, thought Adora as she gazed down upon her baby brother.

5

The Fortunes of Many

TWO DOZEN STEPS BEHIND Petula's departure, hidden in the pre-dawn shadows, marched the squad of six civil patrol men sent to deliver Corlan to the palace.

"It is time to rise," grunted the captain outside the door. "Come out or we will drag you out."

Corlan arose, weary and sore. He stumbled to the door, hung on the handle a few breaths, and realized as he opened the door that he was still naked. After the hours with Petula, he cared not. He simply wanted to keep that memory fixed in his mind, playing the afternoon tryst over and over.

"You're not ready?" asked the captain, dressed in palace garb.

"Give me a minute," Corlan said softly, as though he had not the energy needed to raise his voice.

He picked up the strip of cloth from the floor at the foot of the bed and wrapped it around his loins, then dug some clothes out of the sack he had gathered them into the previous day, and dressed in tan corduroy trousers and white linen shirt, pulled on a dun leather vest and thick gray stockings. He sat on the cot to pull on his black boots. A blue jacket hung from a hook on the wall. He didn't remember it being there before but he thought the tavern owner or even Petula might have left it for him. So he took the jacket, folded it and stuffed it in his bag. The day was too warm to wear it but he knew someday he would need it.

"Ready," he spoke, slinging the sack over his shoulder.

"That's all of six minutes," snorted the captain, frowning. "We're behind schedule now."

The group paused in the tavern below, too early for a final drink. Corlan reminded Haret, the tavern owner's grown son, that he was leaving for a long time and the room could be rented again.

"And if you wouldn't mind, gather the rest of my things and store them for me," he added. "Someday I'll collect them."

"Best o' ever'thin', Corlan," sang Haret, preparing for the day.

"I'll bring you a dragon tongue. You can hang it over the bar."

"I look forward to hangin' it."

As the group exited, the streets were dark and shopkeepers were lighting their dragon lamps. A cube of burnt dragon flesh, a charcoal brick called *dragonfire*, would provide hours of light, the higher grade residue could burn a full day and night.

Corlan was led through the main gate, where the civil patrol was exchanged for palace guards. They escorted him past the principal fortress where the Great Hall and the royal chambers stood, and on to the outer precincts. He was shown through a stone arch and down a walk leading to what he saw was the armory, lit by the forge.

Two men waited for the group: a small, elderly man dressed in a white wizard's robe and a muscle-bound giant wearing only leather straps across his chest and around his waist and hips, bronze skin slick with his effort. The giant was pounding the anvil with a hammer and his sweat glowed in the lamplight. He held up what looked like an iron bolt intended for the dragonslinger weapon.

"This is he?" asked the wizard, turning to greet them.

"Corlan, citizen of the Burg, sentenced to banishment, days unnumbered, by order of Prince Vilmer," said the captain.

"For crimes I did not commit," Corlan added.

"It is not too late to send you off to the dungeon," the captain snarled, slapping Corlan's shoulder with the flat of his sword. The captain turned to the wizard. "He's to be outfitted for a lengthy expedition, plus double rations. The order allots him two beasts."

"Here," grunted the giant smith. He lifted a long leather quiver of iron bolts, trident tipped as Corlan was used to, and set them against the wall by the entrance. Each iron bolt stood as tall as Corlan's full leg, heel to hip — a bit shorter than he preferred. The smith brought over a second quiver and set it beside the first one. Each quiver held twenty of the iron bolts, the maximum a strong man could lift. "Only got twenty with poison, others no poison."

Corlan nodded. "And the dragonslinger?"

Without a word, the blacksmith brought out the weapon. Corlan smiled, recognizing his slinger. Now he felt much better about going on a hunting expedition.

"And the rest?" asked the captain loudly.

"Come with me," said the wizard.

The white-robed man led the group out of the armory and down a slope, through another set of arches, then along a stone path. They turned into a fenced yard where several animals had been sleeping but awoke with the arrival of the men.

The animals stood tall, their necks reaching into the sky, long legs thin and spotted. The bodies sloped from the base of the long necks down to the rump and its tufted tail. Their small heads had two horns above their beady eyes and long snouts. Long, gray tongues flicked in and out of wide mouths.

"These?" asked Corlan, surprised. "These are what I get?"

The wizard stroked his beard. "These are all we have. No more the hippor to bear you onward. I hear you killed the one lent you."

"A dragon killed it, not me."

"Nevertheless. We have no others ready to ride yet. Give us six months and we will have one for you."

"He won't be here in six months," growled the captain. "He's to begin the banishment today."

"Then you must make do with these girafors," said the wizard. "The order is for two beasts of burden, as this captain states. So we give you these animals. That leaves three. We have four others in process, ready in two months."

"These are no suitable mount," said Corlan. "Certainly not for a journey through the Valley of Death."

"Silence, vagabond! You take what is offered or do without." The captain studied the girafors. "Either way, you depart before the sun cracks the horizon."

Corlan rubbed his chin. "I suppose I could eat one far down the trail, if needed. The other will carry the quivers and the slinger."

"Then you are ready," said the captain, gazing long at the eastern horizon, starting to burn orange.

The wizard called to the boys tending the girafors. Each boy took hold of the harness around his animal's shoulders and pulled the reins drooping from the head. The boys led the girafors over to where the wizard stood.

"The Clona arts have a long history," the wizard spoke, admiring the girafors. He raised his hand and petted the nearest one. "Long ago there existed giraffe and hippo and elefans and many other animals, all rare species. So rare that their essence was kept in special jars for the future. People expected they would die out completely someday. Not so with our everyday beasts such as the horse, the swine, the cow, the chicken and goose. None thought to save their powders in jars. They died out. Not so the dog and the cat, of course, nor the rat and rabbit. Always with us! So when these rarer animals left us, we used the powders that had been saved to remake them."

The wizard stepped around the first girafor and ran his hand along the long neck of the second girafor.

"The first of these were so delightful the wizards of those days gave them new names: *Giraffe Operandi Redux* — that is, Giraf-O-R or *girafor*. The remade version. And the same with the hippo: Hipp-O-R or *hippor*. And the alpaca became Alp-O-R or *alpor*. The elk became *elkor*. You see?"

"I see," said Corlan, fidgeting.

"Here we have the happy couple, male and female," explained the wizard. "Male and female, yet unable to mate and bear offspring. We must remake each one separately." He patted the rump of the girafor that had a mostly beige coat with large tan spots on its backside. "We call this one, the female, Elo. The other girafor, the male, is Pex. They are learning to respond to the sound of their names."

"Do they?" Corlan was skeptical of trying to make a long journey with these two as pack animals.

"Try it. Call them."

Corlan nodded, willing to play along. He cupped a hand to the side of his mouth. "Elo!"

The girafor turned its head, looking for the owner of the voice that called its name.

"Elo! Here, Elo," called Corlan. "Come to me, Elo."

The girafor took a few uncertain steps forward, located the voice and lowered its long neck, pushing her head up against the wizard.

"You are their master, it seems," Corlan said with a laugh.

"They will learn soon enough it is you who calls them."

"Pex!" Corlan called out. "Come here, Pex."

The second girafor, with dark brown tufts of hair running down the length of its long neck and continuing along its spine, took a step. Its flanks were covered in dark brown spots, smaller marks on its throat and belly. It stepped ungainly over to Corlan and lowered its neck, flicked out its gray tongue and swiped at Corlan's cheek.

"Back now!" Corlan said, tripping. He wiped his cheek. "These are magical creatures?"

"We have limited resources. When the Great Fire came to the city, only a few animals could be saved from the royal park. Not all were suitable for Clona magic. We did not have the dust of every beast."

"And yet there was dust of dragons," Corlan growled.

"Not true. It is only gossip. We were not part of that guild. And I was never in that line of wizards. My work is clean—wholly natural—not to be confused with dragon conjuring. They are a dirty bunch of thieves."

"I believe you, Wizard."

"Call me Nilas." He held up his left hand, palm open. On his palm was a red five-pointed star, the mark of his guild.

"Thank you, Nilas." Corlan slapped the wizard's open palm with his own palm, an ancient ritual of trust. "I will take good care of these strange beasts you've given me."

"May they serve you well in the desert wastes to the west, and to whatever lands are your destination."

"Thank you."

"One caution: Mind they don't bump their heads on low-hanging objects. Like these stone arches."

"I will remember."

The captain gestured to the palace guards, who lined up around Corlan and the girafors.

"Let's be off now! Time is crumbling away. The sun is almost over the eastern hills."

Corlan saw the east was lit by the sunrise although the sun was not yet visible. He wondered how strict the prince would be, counting down to the final second whether or not he had been lowered to the valley floor. He would consider his banishment to have begun when he stepped onto the lifter, for then he would no longer be on palace grounds.

The captain seemed concerned with the time, ordered him to march back across the outer precincts, over to the far end of the gardens, past the wide veranda overlooking the valley. If one stood in the right spot, one might gaze down the valley for many miles, until it bent and was lost to its destiny.

Corlan recalled those moments with Petula, hiding among the flora of the garden, wary of palace guards discovering them. They never did get caught. And now, he sighed, now they never would.

"Down you go," the captain ordered.

The first to descend was the male girafor named Pex, escorted by the boy who was its handler. The others waited at the top. Once off the lifter, the platform rose and they loaded the second girafor on it with the second boy. When the lifter returned, the guards set the bags of supplies on the lifter. Then Corlan stepped on it.

"Now it is time for the orders to be carried out to the end," the captain spoke as if it were a memorized speech. "You shall not return to the Burg without permission of His Majesty, the Prince. Permission depends on proof of your high quota of dragon materials salvaged from the kills you make. Return no less than one year hence and with sufficient supply about you and the Prince may grant you residence in the city once more. Return without sufficient materials, or return within one year, and the Prince, at His Majesty's discretion, shall command the active guard contingent to execute you, or again banish you into the wastelands. Understand the terms?"

Corlan glanced at Nilas, then back at the captain. "I do."

A lit window caught his attention, high on the tower of the main keep. Although the window was too small and too far away for him to know for certain, he suspected it was the prince's chamber. He had no doubt his cousin would wish to watch his departure. Vilmer could never let it happen without seeing it for himself, even secretly.

Corlan lifted his arm stiffly, feigned a salute to the lit window.

The captain turned to see where Corlan was gazing, turned back to order him onto the lifter.

"Fare you well," said Nilas. "The fortunes of many ride on your fine shoulders."

"I feel the weight already."

And the crest of the sun broke over the eastern hills, striking the stones framing the lifter bay. The entrance where they stood blazed in orange, like the flame of a dragon's breath. Corlan raised his hand to shield his eyes. With his boots planted among the supply bags, he gathered up the dragonslinger, leaned it against himself, one arm wrapped around it.

At the jut of his chin, the lifter jerked and began the trip down to the valley floor.

At the bottom, he stepped off and unloaded his supplies.

"Your turn," he called to the boys, standing a short distance away, keeping the girafors calm. "You must go back up now. Hurry, before they forget you and close the lifter."

One boy took the reins of the second girafor and the first boy went alone to the lifter and stepped onto it.

Corlan signaled for them to raise it.

As soon as the lifter rose above Corlan's head, moving slowly along the track, he heard the boy who had remained below shouting.

Corlan spun around to see one girafor running away and the boy chasing after it. The second girafor was nervous, trotted in the same direction for a bit yet did not run away.

Corlan hurried and grabbed the reins of the female. He looked underneath the belly: *Yes, female.* "Easy, Elo, easy."

He glanced at the lifter, saw it nearing the top. He swung his head around to see the other girafor trotting away with the boy frantically chasing after it. They were about fifty yards down the valley. The boy had halted the girafor's escape, taking hold of its reins, but he seemed to be having trouble calming the beast.

A loud clanging noise startled Corlan and he stared at the lifter. It was hung up near the top. The metal cords had tangled, he guessed. He tried to see what was happening. Through the vegetation along the top edge of the cliff he saw guards trying to pull the boy up from the cage of the lifter. As soon as they got the boy free, the lifter made a metallic grunt and halted. Attempts to make it finish the trip did not work. Lowering it did not work, either.

Corlan watched them working on it, heard them complaining.

"You'll have to take that boy with you," someone shouted from the top, leaning over the veranda railing. "The lifter is broken. Can't lower it."

"Can you repair it?" Corlan shouted up at them.

"How long to do that? Days? Weeks?"

"I cannot take a boy with me on this journey!"

"There's no choice."

Corlan shook his head. Just one more trouble in a pair of days he wished he could live over again.

"Think of him as your apprentice," someone called down with a laugh. "He's an orphan, so no matter."

"No, I can't do that. It's too dangerous."

"We can't bring him up."

Corlan cursed, scratched his whiskers, feeling the sun on his face. He paced around the stack of supplies. He looked back over his shoulder at the girafor caught by the boy, the two of them returning to where he stood before the bottom lifter bay.

The boy arrived beside him, the male girafor in tow. The female seemed content to graze on a few tufts of foliage that still struggled to grow in the red dirt of the valley floor.

"Are you ready to go?" the boy asked him, a little out of breath.

Corlan turned to the boy. "There's a problem."

"What is it?"

"The lifter is broken." Corlan pointed to the top of the cliff. "No way to fix it for a few days or weeks."

"Oh." The boy did not seem upset by the news.

"You understand? You can't go home."

The boy smiled, brushing dust off his red-brown shirt. "So I will go with you?"

Corlan wanted to spit but for the sake of the boy did not.

"You understand why I'm down here? Why I'm sent out into the valley? It's because I'm banished. I can't return to the city, not for one year. It's the punishment assigned by the prince. I might never return. It's dangerous out there. You don't want to be part of it."

The boy seemed to listen yet his face did not change.

"Dragons fly this valley," said Corlan, gruffly. "It's likely you'll be eaten by one of them. Maybe two of them, and they'll fight over you, tear you apart. Is that what you want?"

The boy shook his head, the head full of black curls flickering in the dry breeze. "No, sir."

Corlan gazed up the cliff. "Can you climb up there?"

The boy followed Corlan's gaze. "Up there?"

"It is too high. Not much to grab hold of. Maybe they have long enough rope.... We could tie you and they could pull you...."

"Please, sir," said the boy in a sad voice while Corlan continued visually measuring the distance up the cliff. "Let me go with you, sir. I won't be any bother."

Corlan slapped his fists to his hips, staring at the boy.

"That's what you want?"

"Yes, sir. I haven't much prospects in the city."

"You're just a boy. You shouldn't be worrying about prospects just yet, anyway."

"I don't have a home, sir." The boy's eyes produced tears. "I only live in the palace and work in the kitchen."

Corlan cursed. He couldn't keep the words back.

"The cook speaks worse than you. He always says those words. Please don't send me back to him."

Corlan kicked the dirt, gazed up at the broken lifter, then back at the boy. With his hand to the side of his mouth, Corlan called up to the men at the top of the cliff.

"How much time to repair it?"

"It could be a week or more," came the answer, shouted down.

Corlan nodded, realizing the only solution. He called up to them: "I will explore up the valley a while, and then return the boy in one week or so. Enough time for repair?"

"We cannot know that today."

"You better find someone to fix it!"

"And you better not harm that boy!" came the echo.

"It won't be me returning with dragon materials in two weeks, just me returning the boy. Then you bring him up. I'll also need more rations by then if he is sharing mine."

"Thank you, sir," said the boy.

With a wave of his hand, Corlan confirmed the arrangement: "One or two weeks then...."

He turned to the boy. "Now you're on the expedition. You do as I say. Be careful not to get killed."

The boy smiled. "Thank you, sir."

"Don't call me *sir*. My name is Corlan."

"Yes, sir — I mean, yes, Corlan. Sir."

Corlan's frown froze the boy.

"You have a name?"

The boy bowed his head. "They call me Tam."

"Very well, Tam. You're my apprentice."

For about ten miles from the base of the cliff that fronted the palace grounds at the west end of the city, the valley turned sharply to the northwest, keeping to a narrow canyon for the first few miles, then gradually widening and its sides lowering to become a true valley. The ancient river plain spreading from that point onward was dry now and dirt, sand, and gravel covered the riverbed. Little vegetation grew in the valley, even less as the valley went west, one reason the people of the Burg called it the Valley of Death. They also might come under fire by hungry dragons winging their way to the northeast or, after their hunting, to the southwest. That was the true reason for the name, as far as Corlan was concerned.

After three days of steady march to the north, with the girafors bearing the heavy supplies, Corlan and the boy finally turned west, walking for most of a day. They followed the valley as it turned to the southwest. All the way, the sun blazed upon them and the dry breeze from the south parched them. The expedition stopped frequently for refreshment from water sacks they carried. The boy did not complain even once and that impressed Corlan.

There was not much in the valley to excite the boy. For the first five days they had seen no dragons winging overhead.

"Will there be dragons?" asked Tam in a worried tone.

"There should be some of them flying the valley by now," Corlan replied. "Five days with no sighting...."

They had camped on the higher ground, toward the south edge of the valley where rock outcroppings shielded them from view if any dragons were to fly over. The rock outcroppings were dangerous by themselves, subject to cracking and falling at any moment, especially if an earth-wyrm felt like scratching an old itch and chose to roll over in the ground beneath them.

"Is it true?" asked Tam.

Regarding the boy, Corlan remembered his little brother, Damus, lost to a dragon attack when he was about Tam's age. Corlan had been too young for dragonslayer training, but the sight of his brother running as fast as he could across the fallow field outside the family's farmstead still haunted him. Damus was not fast enough to escape the fireball tumbling after him, catching him and consuming him.

"The ground shakes," said Corlan, chewing the dried meat of an animal he did not recognize. He reached for another from the ration pouch, kicking the embers back into the fire with the toe of his boot. "People invent stories to explain everything, I suppose. We have plenty of dragons to make our lives miserable, so why not a tale of a dragon hiding under the ground? It turns in its sleep, scratches an itch, and the ground shakes."

The boy nodded. "So not true?"

"I don't wish to test that."

In the morning they packed the tarp and continued the trek.

The next day the familiar shadows once again striped the valley floor and Corlan gazed skyward, spied the quartet of beasts bearing down on them from the southwest, their wide wings flapping lazily.

He pushed the boy into the shadows of the cliffsides, tugging the girafors after them. It was mid-afternoon and the bright sun cast long shadows across the dry riverbed. They pressed up against the cliffs as Corlan prepared the dragonslinger.

"I will let these pass," he said, "yet should they attack, I want to be ready."

The boy finally lost his bravura, cringed between the girafors.

"They likely would go for the girafors first, so better you not hide there."

The boy moved stealthily against the cliffside and found a small indentation to squeeze into.

The dragons flew in formation—all green-horns, the large male in the lead, three females following. The prominent horns sprouted from their foreheads were dark green, the remainder of their bodies brown or dark gray, the folds of their open wings a pale lime-green.

"Green-horns," he said to the boy. "They will smell us."

Corlan lifted the dragonslinger to his hip, pulled back the launch spring, inserted the iron bolt he pulled from the quiver hanging over the male girafor's back.

The formation swung low as they got closer, seemingly following a scent. The lead dragon, the male, turned its head back and forth as if searching for whatever it smelled. The females seemed not to notice. They slowed only in response to the male's pause.

Suddenly the male spun around, its huge ungainly wings flapping vigorously to right himself. Talons drawn, it hovered in the air a few yards above the ground, head reared back, forked tongue extended, flicking the air. A cry erupted, calling the females to land.

"This may be the end of the expedition, Tam."

Corlan waited in silence, pressed against the cliffs.

"I'm sorry your career is so short."

He heard the boy whimpering but couldn't see him, hiding in the space between the rock walls.

The male green-horn alighted among the sand and gravel of the riverbed, a cloud of dust forming around its feet. It reared its head back as if to prepare a burst of fire. Instead, there was a cough and something oblong was expelled from its mouth, falling to the ground. Covered in thick green mucus, it was impossible to determine what creature the dragon had tried to swallow.

The females gathered around the foul bundle, began snipping at it. The male tried to push them away with its head. The females squawked, strutting around the male. Threatened, the male hopped away, unfolding its wings. The females divided the carcass, raised their heads and stretched their necks as they each snatched away and swallowed equal portions.

Suddenly, the male extended its mighty wings fully and turned in the direction of Corlan and the girafors hidden in the shadows of the cliffs. Its eyes burned yellow. Its fangs dripped with saliva. It seemed to be deciding if there was anything in those shadows that might be worth investigating.

Here it comes, thought Corlan, his finger against the launch pin of the dragonslinger.

The male took a lumbering step, tail wrapping around its hind legs, wings remaining extended.

Corlan knew the beast was not ready to attack, not with its wings extended. It was a way to cool itself. Yet it continued to stare into the shadows and Corlan hoped the girafors would not spook and the boy would not think to run.

Then he heard the sound he feared: a rough gurgle followed by a harsh scraping noise, like stones tossed into a gristmill to break up the grain. Fire was being created deep in its belly.

Had the dragon located them? Had it smelled them?

The male slowly raised its head but kept its chin level, puffing out its chest and closing its wings, preparing to let loose its breath.

One of the females shrieked, then launched into the air, ready to continue the journey, it seemed. The male turned its angry head to follow the movement, then turned its entire body in one great heave in the direction of the female winging upward to catch the wind.

The other two females cried after the first and the male grunted, swallowed its fire, and jumped into the air, flapping its heavy wings like a pair of mountain peaks.

As they gained altitude, the male spit out globs of *dragonfire*, yellow-orange gaseous orbs the size of human heads that fell to the ground. When they hit, the membranes ruptured, releasing noxious gas, an orange-crème haze which the breeze drew out in long misty streams that were long to dissipate or settle.

Corlan watched as the four dragons faded into the eastern sky, holding his breath, then taking a few more minutes to breathe with his nose against his sleeve. The girafors snorted, tried to prance away their anxiety. The boy appeared from the cleft and immediately went to calm the girafors.

Corlan pulled the iron bolt from the dragonslinger and eased back the spring.

"And that is what dragons are all about," he said in response to the boy's wide eyes. "We were lucky. That female was in too much hurry to be on her way to the hunting grounds beyond the city. Else that male was ready to fire us."

He noticed the boy's trousers were wet.

"Congratulations, Tam." He gave a quick salute. "Today you are initiated into the dragonslayer's guild. You've passed the first level. Every apprentice I've known wet himself the first time he got close to dragons."

6

The Beasts Ahead

"MOST DRAGONS ORGANIZE into harems," Corlan explained as they hiked through the valley. "You know what a harem is, boy? It's when a man has several wives. The man is in charge and the wives take care of him. Like that. I hear it's the way of life on the eastern shore. Far south of Nerk, I mean. A place called Rolina."

"It's like mama takes care of me...er, uh...*took* care of me."

"You saw those green-horns, right? The male is larger but three females can overpower him." He shook his head. "Must've been sick, I think. The male. It had good form yet its behavior was strange." He laughed. "Something he ate perhaps?"

Tam joined the laughter, hiking up the hem of the shirt Corlan gave him to wear until his trousers could be washed.

"Still not sure what sort of thing it spit up," said Corlan. "Looked like a farm animal, all wrapped in hair, fur, and whatever was on the ground with it."

"You mean a hoven?" asked Tam.

"Most likely. Yet why couldn't it keep the carcass down?"

"It could be a bad hoven. Beasts like them eat all sorts of bad fodder, Chef said. They get ill, and people sicken from eating a fine steak. I had to sniff each slice of meat."

"Diseased, eh?" He considered it a moment. "Could be."

"The others didn't mind eating it."

"No, they didn't."

Corlan had to think about it. Strange behavior. He had never seen a dragon spit up a whole animal as though it tasted bad. He had witnessed dragons blasting a stubborn meal with fire, reducing it to charred bones—and then swallow it. Perhaps it was the dragon that was ill, and couldn't stomach the hoven.

He thought of Bratiste, the way he used poisons to kill dragons. Corlan could see the benefit in that trick. No risk to the dragonslayer, just offer a poison-filled sacrificial animal to the dragon, then wait. The poisoned ox as appetizer.

And he gets all the glory! He spit into the red dirt.

The next day, Corlan halted the group and pointed at some white things rising from the brown dirt and gravel ahead.

"What is it?" asked Tam.

"This is the place. I shot three out of the sky there." Corlan turned and gazed up at the cliffs on the mountainside, confirming with a nod that he was back in the same spot. "I shot them from up there, on the cliff. Only the bones remain. See them? Come on."

They hurried to where the bones curled out of the dirt, a few ribs, scraped clean by whatever animals or insects ate the meat off them. The blazing sun did the rest, turning it into polished ivory. If he could haul it back, it would bring some good coin.

Tam ran up to the encircling hoop of ribs, ducked inside them, and stood up fully without his head touching the upper curve of the rib cage. He held his arms out.

"Yes, that one would fit you whole in its belly," said Corlan with a chuckle. He glanced around, checking for any uninvited guests. "Probably other dragons fed off the carcass, then dispersed, leaving only this portion."

"Dragons eat dragons?" asked the boy.

"Dragons eat anything."

Tam stepped out of the rib cage. He stood close, leaning down to inspect the bones.

"They got holes in them," he said.

"Like combs of honey bees," said Corlan. "There should be bones of two other dragons around here. Or one of them flew on before crashing. Either way, another beast killed."

Tam was amazed. "This bone seems brittle." He scratched it and it flaked apart, fell to the dirt.

"Of course it does. In order to fly they must have light bones."

"Oh."

"Not so solid. Hollow. Strong yet light."

"Oh."

"You've much to learn about dragons...."

Corlan shielded his eyes with his hand as he gazed ahead. "I see more bones, gleaming in the sunshine. Come."

A few minutes' walk and they arrived at another set of bones, scattered along the shore of the riverbed. Several thick vertebrae and a huge pelvis broken into four pieces were all that remained. Tam stood next to the largest piece of pelvis, resting his elbow on top.

"Chug...." Corlan sighed, gazing up at the mountain. His eyes searched for the path along the edge of the cliff where he had stood. He could barely detect it, the red-brown rocks so evenly colored. It had to be the same place where he had fired the dragonslinger upon a clan of dragons winging past.

"Is it dragon bones?" asked Tam, squatting to examine them. The bones were clean. He poked them with a long stick he had found.

"No, it's not," Corlan answered. "It's my hippor. The one I rode. The one the dragons tore apart."

Corlan studied the boy.

"It's what dragons do," he muttered, thinking about what the boy had told him of his childhood while they hiked. "A dragon bit it in two, ate it, then dropped the bones here."

"Did you kill the dragon that ate it?"

Corlan shook his head. "I killed others, but not that one."

The boy stared hard at the bones, poked the vertebrae with the stick, pretending it was a sword.

He stared at the boy. When they camped the first night, Corlan had asked Tam to tell his history. Corlan merely wished for a tale to listen to as he relaxed. Instead, the boy told him a lot.

"She was a washer woman," he had said.

Corlan knew what the boy meant. His mother offered a bath to dirty, dusty strangers who arrived in town. For a few coins she would bathe them. For more coins she would wash their clothes. And for a few coins more she would provide other services.

"And then she died," he told Corlan.

"Got a disease, eh?"

"She got smashed. She was working and the house fell on her."

That sparked images in Corlan's head. He recalled the incident a few years back. A quartet of dragons had chosen a path over the city and became startled when some dragonslayers decided to take them down. The four dragons were hit easily enough with iron bolts. They dropped immediately—and crushed several people and smashed a few buildings. The boy's mother was among the dead there in the bath house, crushed with a dozen others.

"And your father?" asked Corlan, realizing the answer as soon as

91

he spoke the question.

"I don't know who he is."

Certainly a stranger who arrived in the city one day and needed a bath, needed some relaxation, and had enough coin.

"I didn't have nobody to care for me," said Tam.

"No brothers or sisters? No aunts or uncles?"

He shook his head. "I had to beg for food."

Corlan nodded, understanding. He often saw the street children, filthy and dressed in rags, bothering the citizens. He never paid much attention to them, believing the citizens would give them some scraps of food eventually.

"I followed a path to the palace," Tam had continued, "through the gardens. I smelled a great and wonderful smell. It was the kitchen and the cook saw me. He set out a plate of food for me—just like the royal family eats!"

Eventually the cook kept the boy on, had him help in the kitchen.

"He said he found it funny to serve a street boy the same food as to the prince."

"So you and I both have a connection to the prince," Corlan had snickered.

"Truly?" The boy was surprised. "What's your connection?"

Corlan broke into laughter that shook the valley, made the two girafors startle and strain at the ropes.

"Prince Vilmer is my cousin. Our fathers were brothers. We have the same grandfather. Yet he got the throne. Palace politics, that's all. Social squabbling. I'm much more happy slaying dragons."

"Then you are...you're Prince Corlan!"

Corlan grimaced. "Let's have none of that now. I'm just Corlan. Corlan of the Burg."

"But, sir...you are—"

"Stop your tongue!"

The boy hesitated, then spoke: "You are from the Tang family?"

Corlan spit, rubbed the glob into the dirt with the toe of his boot.

"I told you not to say it." He shook his head, not believing the boy would be so bold.

Tam grinned. "You are a prince."

"Very well, since it is only you and me here in the valley...."

"Prince Corlan!" the boy sang.

Corlan grabbed a bunch of his long auburn hair, flowing in the hot breeze. "See this? This hair is from my mother. She was a red-haired lady, so most people don't think I'm a member of the Tang clan. Not like my cousin who has the black hair. It's the way people are: you take up with whoever makes you feel warm, whoever pleases you—not just the person you're told to take up with." He gazed up at the stars. "So I took up with a blond-haired woman. Or, I should say she took up with me. Her name's Petula. Now that I'm banished I may never see her again."

He let go his hair and a sudden breeze threw it all into his face. He brushed it back.

"You don't want to be Tang?" asked the boy after a long silence.

"It doesn't matter what family you're from, boy. All that matters is what you do. You have to stand up by yourself—drop your name, the name of your family, and stand on your own feet without any name. That is all anybody will respect."

The boy gave him a respectful silence.

Corlan hated being reminded of his heritage. At first, he wanted to make the boy stay quiet, perhaps strangle him. But he thought of his own words: *what you do, not who you are; who you are is what you do*—and he could not harm the boy.

But for a small trick of the gods several generations past, he might have had a poor life like this boy. Instead, when the city needed a new lord-mayor long ago, it was Daltin Tang who was chosen—according to the scrolls his great-grandmother had; growing up in a brownstone house on Grant Street, as it was called before the city was destroyed and the present one rebuilt further down the river valley. He became a community organizer, known for his fair treatment of everyone who came to him with problems. People respected him, then feared him. In time, members of his family ruled the city.

Daltin was a natural leader, his grandfather had told him every time the old man took to reciting the family lineage when Corlan was a boy. But Daltin's descendants became despots, and engaged in petty bickering, started battles with neighboring states—until his father was sent out to settle the conflict they had with Falo to the north. That was the battle where he was killed. The Plains of Olea would forever be hallowed ground.

"Sir?"

The boy's voice brought him back to the present, to the campsite in the barren Valley of Death—because he'd been banished, Corlan remembered as though it was last night's dream.

"Don't call me *sir*," he grumbled.

"I'm sorry...Corlan." The boy waited. "Corlan Tang."

"Stop it!"

The boy laughed. "Prince Corlan Tang!"

"It's Corlan of the Burg. Everyone knows me by that name. I'm just an ordinary citizen."

To break the spell, Corlan pressed Tam to tell more of *his* story. He had watched the boy, noting his black curly hair and tan skin, his wide inquisitive eyes and smallish nose, with a boy's thin frame and gangly legs.

He was a quick learner, the cook discovered, so he treated him like a son. He got the easy assignments, which led to the other kitchen boys teasing him, bullying him. After some time, he had enough and plotted his escape. A random encounter with a stable boy provided a way.

"I knew they would do that," said Tam as they finished dinner beneath the stars. "I mean, leave me. Try to send me away. The cook always beats me. He wants me to go away."

"Does he?"

"And the other boys trick me."

"Do they?"

"So I switched with another boy, a stable boy. I always told him the food's better for kitchen boys." He bowed his head, then looked at Corlan with sad eyes. "No more will I be a kitchen boy. I'm ready to learn to kill dragons, sir."

"You're anxious to kill a dragon, eh?" asked Corlan, amused.

"Oh, yes!"

So they had talked about dragons late into the night and the sun struggled to rouse them from their slumber.

As they left the hippor bones and traveled on, Corlan swung his arm out along the riverbed. "Long ago a great river ran here." He pointed to the far distant side of the valley. "This is the widest it ever was, at least in the area I've seen. From that side all the way to this side. About five miles." He swung his arm in the opposite direction. "Farther to the southwest, it'll likely be ten miles across."

Tam was in awe, gazing back and forth at the opposing shores.

"What if all the water of the river suddenly comes washing down the valley?" he asked.

"How could that be? It's been dried up for centuries."

Tam frowned. "I was just wondering."

Corlan grinned, surprised at his patience. Maybe it was good to have a companion on this trek. It was destined to last a long time, after all. Having someone to talk with, even a boy, would make the time pass quicker.

"We'd have to make a run for the shore." Corlan squinted toward the south shore. "This one is closer."

"I can run very fast," said Tam.

"Let's hope we never need to run fast."

"If dragons come, we have to run. Right?"

"I would, yes."

"You have the weapon to kill them."

"I do. So perhaps I would stand and fight. I'd pull the slinger to my hip and load a bolt and launch it at the beast."

"And down it crashes!" Tam was excited.

"Let's hope so."

"Will I ever get to launch the iron bolt at a dragon?"

Corlan thought a moment. "I'm sure the day will come for you."

Leaving the hippor bones, they had marched farther through the Valley of Death, mostly heading southwest. On each side of the wide riverbed rose sheer cliffs, with some mountains of significant height. A few were high enough they had flora on their slopes, something Corlan remarked on.

Tam continued asking questions about dragons, about the weapon called dragonslinger, and about Corlan's history. Corlan responded with as few words as necessary. He had said too much already. The valley was dry and he wanted to save his breath and his saliva. He told Tam that very fact several times, yet the boy kept talking. Then he was thirsty from all of his talking.

They stopped for the night when the sun finally dropped below the horizon. A range of jagged hills lay ahead.

Corlan set up the tarp while Tam cared for the girafors, then they made dinner.

"Now featherbacks are a rare breed," said Corlan, sitting against the rock wall and wishing he had a stein of ale instead of just tepid water. "They have the same wings as most dragons but their body is covered with small feathers. Usually red or pink, and green, blue, yellow. They can be plucked and used for decoration. Plenty of them around the palace. The meat is mild compared to most dragons and if prepared in a certain way it can be eaten without any harm. Tastes like burnt chicken. And the spines, the head horns, and the talons make good weapons. It's the best of the dragons to capture whole. I saw one rolled through the streets on two wagons the day I returned to the city. Seems so long ago now."

Tam was attentive, amazed at the lessons Corlan gave him.

"Which dragon do you like killing most?" asked the boy.

Corlan grinned, enjoying having an admirer.

"Whatever dragon is attacking me gets my attention first." He laughed. "If they were lined up and I have my choice of any of them, I'd probably kill the mountain-master first. They are the ugliest, and because they tend to make mountain tops their homes it is difficult to climb high enough to kill them. I've seen some that lower their great wings and cover the whole mountaintop. I've only killed one, though. I was on an expedition. I camped one night and when I awoke it was standing over me. It was as big as the sky. I had to run for my battle axe, no time for the slinger."

The boy shuddered. "How'd you kill it?"

"I took the axe and ran up its long tail, like it was a staircase in a palace, straight up to its back, stepping around the spines. It tried to reach for me, there on its back, with its ugly head and its fangs. Then I started hacking away with my axe. I cut a hole in its side, between the ribs, and I jumped down between the ribs, like I was going down into a cavern. I whacked my way inside it, into all the guts, and I kept swinging my axe. Stomach, liver, entrails! I cut my way out of the beast with the axe, too, right out its big belly. I sure was a mess, of course, covered in dragon guts, but that monster was dead."

Tam's eyes were wide open. "Wow...."

"Next, I'd kill the red-bulls. They're dangerous, too, prone to fire at the least distraction, so they need to be killed fast. I've knocked many of them from the sky. They have a weak point behind the head, a soft spot at the base of the skull. If you can get a bolt there, they die instantly and fall from the sky like big sacks of dung."

"I want to see that!"

"Remember, when it comes to dragonslaying, you'd better see them first and kill them before they see you. Once they sight you, it's almost impossible to escape their wrath. If you shoot at them, they become especially hateful."

"I saw a fang-master once," said Tam. "It swooped down and it snatched a man up in its fangs."

"Yes, fang-masters have unusually long fangs. That's because they chiefly hunt other dragons. They need big teeth to grab hold of a big dragon. And the drapers...designed perfectly for scavenging with that long lower jaw. Of course, they're all dangerous. Even the ones that look pretty, full of colors, or, like the grey-bellies, seem timid — they all will turn on you if you show any fear."

"You ever see a two-feet?"

"A few times. Up north, mostly. They hardly seem like dragons with only two feet and two wings. Some people call them *wyverns*, you know? But that's an ancient name."

"What kinds fly this valley?"

"You saw that quartet of green-horns. Besides them, mainly red-bulls, grey-bellies, hornchins.... The ones I killed here when I came out with the hippor, they were grey-bellies. They can be nasty. I mean temperament. No need to threaten them for them to go after you. As it was, I climbed up the mountains on the south shore to be at their height as they winged past me. Dropped three of them."

"But you lost the hippor."

"And I walked back to the city."

"You must feel sad."

"Sad? That's an odd thing to say. Why?"

"You lost the hippor. Didn't you like the hippor?"

"It's a mount. Something to carry the supplies. Not my friend. A colleague. We worked together."

"Oh."

Corlan coughed, cleared his throat, spit far into the riverbed.

"We can't get sentimental over mere things. Beasts, animals, the tools and other work things we use. I don't love my dragonslinger. It works for me. I treat it good so it works good. It's about life or death that way."

Tam understood.

"The farther we travel," said Corlan before he extinguished the dragonfire in the lamp, "the hotter it will get. We will need to switch over to traveling at night to avoid the sun."

"How will we see the road?" asked the boy, looking up from his bedroll.

"There is no road," Corlan said with a chuckle. "As for light, there are stars. And sometimes dragons will hiccup or fart as they fly over us, and there's the light we need."

"They fart?"

"Like all beasts. Smells like sulfur."

Tam let out some gas and smiled, then closed his eyes.

"Not like boiled beans," muttered Corlan.

As the dawn painted the far shore of the dry riverbed, they packed up the camp and began their march southwest, tugging the girafors after them. The valley bent more west before the sun cut the horizon.

There were only a few scrub plants here and there as they trekked, so Corlan let the girafors graze. Some cactus, too. An occasional tumbling bush. A snake slithered in front of them and the girafors panicked. Tam calmed them.

"You've a way with the beasts," said Corlan.

"The stable boy showed me."

After another three days of marching, no more signs of life could be seen. No vegetation. No animal footprints. On the slopes along the shoreline the vegetation had turned brown. The river basin remained wide, the same clay and sand surface. There were no convenient rock outcroppings to hide under and Corlan felt vulnerable. He knew the area, and he knew there was not much beyond the next bend of the valley. They were closing on the furthest extent of his travels.

Yet Corlan knew the nesting grounds were much farther. In fact, the travelers from the west he'd met had spoken of the ruins of great cities along the valley. Corlan could not confirm all he'd heard but the way the stories were told made him believe them. *Is there any reason a weary traveler would think to tell false tales of dragons in the far western realm? To what purpose?* It had to be true. His observation of the migration routes seemed to back the travelers' stories.

It didn't matter now. He had been sent away; he could only travel southwest as the valley turned, no matter what he might find there. He might find death. It would arrive quickly and with much pain. One slip of attention, one careless movement, one instance of hesitation and he would be dead. And with his death, there would be no one to know his fate or write the history of his life. And Petula would wonder what became of him.

Corlan turned to regard the boy, finishing the dinner.

"You know we'll have to go back soon. I told them we'd return. The lifter should be repaired by now."

"Maybe it won't be fixed," said Tam anxiously.

"Why not? It seemed a simple thing, just needed time."

"I want to continue with you, sir."

Corlan shook his head. "This is no place for a boy."

"It's not what I want," Tam snapped, jumping up. He kicked at a stone which skipped up and fell a short distance away.

"The valley is worse from here on to the west. Even I do not know what we might find there. I promised them I would go all the way to the end of the valley, to the nesting grounds of the dragons. That's no place for a boy."

"You said it before. And I want to go with you. Even so."

"I promised them I'd return you in two weeks. It's been that now already."

Tam turned away from Corlan. "No, it's not."

"It is."

"I don't wanna go back!"

"You've had your adventure. Now it's time we head back. I will return you to a safe place and I will start my journey again. Maybe get more supplies."

"No!"

"That was the plan. You wouldn't even be with me if it weren't for the lifter breaking. You've gotten your taste of a dragonslayer's life. It's not so comfortable, as you can see."

"I can't go back there, not to the kitchen, not to those bully boys—and the cook hates me!"

"You said he took you in as his own son."

Tam dropped his head to his chest. "I lied. He took me in but only so I could work. He makes me work hard, all day and all night."

"You're changing your story?"

"Not changing it. Correcting." The boy pouted, sniffled like an actor. "He thought I would work for nothing. For food, I mean. A bed shared with other boys. A bath shared with other boys. Everything is shared. I also got shared with—"

Tam was crying and Corlan, unaccustomed to such a situation, did not know what to do. The tears looked real.

"It's not good." Corlan shook his head.

Corlan felt a memory pushing its way into his forehead, images of nights in a forest and beasts chasing him. He was not sure where the images originated. Perhaps his mind was playing tricks on him.

"Men can be cruel," said Corlan, picking at his nose.

The more images flickered through his head, the more he knew how corrupt the city had become. The basic idea of a city as a place of common purpose had been corrupted. Now every citizen sought after whatever he could get from others, whether by force or by guile. It was not the city he would have if he were thrust into the role of administrator.

No, that was a job for a scriber — someone who knew history and could see all ages in a glance, then establish measurements, weights and balances, for the people, and convince them to follow a common plan. That would be ideal. Not the tyranny his cousin had in place.

Yet it had not come to be, not even by the power of the sword, in all the years he had been taught about. Of course, his father had used a sword to little success, and his father before him —

"So let me stay with you."

"Huh?" Corlan was drawn back to his true time and place, a bit surprised to find himself where he was. "What's this?"

He looked the boy over. Real tears. True fear in his face.

"This could last the rest of your life, you know. What I'm saying is your life might be unnaturally shortened on a journey like this." He rubbed his chin, scratched whiskers on his throat. "Yet, maybe it's a better life here in the wastes than back in the palace. The gods know I wouldn't want such a life there for myself."

Tam grinned, reached for Corlan. "Thank you, sir! Thank you —"

"I am no *sir*," Corlan said with a grunt, leaning away from the hug. "How many times need I remind you?"

7

The Valley of Death

CORLAN COUGHED A FEW TIMES to clear the accumulation of dust he had breathed in. He spit a mighty glob far out across the river bed.

"I've walked this path fifty-eight times," he spoke to the stars. He knew the boy would be listening. "I've killed probably two hundred and twenty dragons in this valley. Three hundred overall, counting other places across the realm. More than any other dragonslayer in the Burg, I'd wager. Maybe not the most of any dragonslayer ever, mind you, but I started late. Jugor Mal Vé, our current guild master, counted two thousand before he was forced by his wounds to do battle with retirement."

He looked over at Tam, saw the boy had fallen asleep.

"It never gets old. Relaxing under the stars.... Sometimes you see dragons battle each other, lighting up the whole sky. Other than that fury, it's a peaceful life. On your own, no one to squabble with, do as you like. The only regret is being away from a few hours of joy. And some good brew. I make up for regrets when I'm back in the Burg."

He studied the boy. How calm he seemed, probably dreaming of something pleasant. Maybe memories of his mother. Corlan could not remember his. The farmstead near Stacol—that, he remembered.

"And then," said Corlan, "thinking long about the possibilities, I turned in, myself, wishing for a few happy dreams, as always, and being prepared for the worst of them. You usually get what you ask for, boy, just never in the way you expect."

He set the dragonfire's glow to a lower level, dimming the light, and stretched out on his bedroll. Sleep came within minutes.

Then the unexpected noise shook him awake.

He remained still, feigning sleep, his eyes scanning the darkened landscape. He sensed movement out on the riverbed and turned his eyes toward it.

Squatting there in the middle of the riverbed, foot claws digging into the red dirt was a huge blue-lightning, hissing and grumbling, in search of something. Most likely food. Its wings beat slowly in the air as it lowered its head, the prominent blue stripes along its head and neck almost glowing in the moon's half-light. With mouth agape, it coughed up a vile bundle of something, the steaming mass plopping hard on the rocks there.

Corlan slowly bent his body toward the dragon, careful not to let his motion catch the beast's attention. At the same time, his right hand reached for the dragonslinger always at his side when he slept, loaded and ready. He checked the boy: asleep, and unaware of the danger that had landed nearby. The cliff overhang provided some shadow to hide under.

The blue-lightning shook its head back and forth, seemed to gag on something, then erupted a fire-breath that lit up the valley.

"What's happening?" Tam suddenly called.

Corlan shhhed him, pointing out at the dragon.

The fire-breath was weaker than normal, Corlan saw, yet it would still roast a man alive if it struck him. As it was, the thing that had been coughed-up was the target. It burned, low flames rising from it. The dragon turned it using the stubby black horn on its nose. When the thing seemed to be cooked properly, the dragon proceeded to pick it up with its fore-fangs and toss it into the air, gulping it all at once.

The dragon had not noticed them, focused as it was on consuming whatever didn't taste right. With the meal reheated and swallowed, the blue-lightning danced circles in place, flapping its wings, its wing-talons wriggling. It squawked loudly several times, an unhappy sound to Corlan's trained ears.

The noise confused the girafors, caused them to stir, jerking against their ropes. The animals were mute yet the noise of hooves crunching the sand made enough sound. Corlan cursed.

The blue-lightning turned in the direction of the campsite. Its teal eyes brightened at the sight of more tasty morsels against the cliffs.

In one instant, Corlan rose on his knees and pulled the slinger to his hip, screwing back the launch spring—as the dragon lumbered two and a half steps toward them, mouth open, fangs dripping, hot breath seething, conjuring another stream of fire—and launched the iron bolt straight into the gullet of the dragon.

The boy cheered behind him but Corlan dared not glance back.

Feeling the invasion, the blue-lightning turned its body, shaking its head, coughing, trying to get the iron bolt out.

Corlan reloaded, launched another that struck the dragon on the throat, cutting into the hardened scales just below the jaw where it was weakest. Corlan knew dragon anatomy. He loaded another bolt and waited.

The dragon swayed, pointed its face skyward and attempted to cry out. The sound was a rough, anguished groan. Likely the poison in the capsule on the first iron bolt had erupted and spilled down the throat of the beast.

Corlan stood, holding the dragonslinger against his hip.

Tam hid behind him, peering around him, muttering to himself his excitement.

"He's done for," said Corlan in an even tone.

The blue-lightning flapped its wings frantically, claws stroking its throat. Corlan saw the dragon was trying to tear open its own throat, making deep grooves, trying to get at the first iron bolt. It managed to flick the second bolt out of its throat and orange blood sludged from the wound. The dragon continued digging into its throat, losing its strength as it tripped like a drunken dancer trying to stay upright.

The dragon collapsed, flipping onto its side as it fell, the crunch of broken wing beneath its body, its eyes open and its mouth agape, the long blue tongue rolling out like a living snake, flittering in the air as though searching for answers to how it had come to this fate in the Valley of Death.

"Great kill!" shouted Tam, certain the dragon was dead.

"Wait."

"It's dead, isn't it?"

"It should be, yet don't tempt the dragon gods. Some can rise again after a brief visit to hell."

"Is it true?"

"It's always true."

Corlan watched the dragon, counting the rising and falling of its belly. Measuring the intensity of the glow from its throat. The breaths lessened, the glow diminishing. Eventually the beast lay completely still. Its inner fire had dulled and sparked out.

"Now?" asked the boy.

"Not yet."

"It's dead, isn't it? Now it is — isn't it?"

Corlan kept the dragonslinger aimed at the blue-lightning's silent carcass lest it rise again.

"I've had them return to life within as long as an hour of certain death. Never accept they are vanquished."

The boy sighed. He went back and sat on his bedroll.

"Don't be so impatient. We can always return to the city. I'm sure the lifter is repaired by now."

The boy grumbled but accepted the lesson.

They waited, watching the carcass for movement. Thin lines of steam rose from the pores of the beast's body, the breeze teasing them, drawing them down the valley.

"Other dragons may get a whiff of this one and come for dinner," said Corlan, his eyes on the carcass. "Better pack up the camp."

The blue-lightning lay heavy and unmoving against the riverbed, so Corlan lowered his attention and helped pack. Every other breath, though, he glanced at the carcass. He stared a while up and down the valley, listening to the wind.

The boy was quick and efficient. He understood they were still in a dangerous situation. Corlan liked he obeyed without complaint.

"What's that?" Corlan muttered.

Dawn was cutting across the eastern horizon, an orange glow painting the valley. And in that distant glow Corlan spotted a trio of black silhouettes: long wings waving up and down, ferrying taloned bodies toward them.

"I hate being right," he mumbled.

Tam turned. "What?"

"Here they come!"

Tam looked toward the horizon. "Dragons?"

"What else?" He hurried to finish clearing the camp. "They are coming for the blue-lightning!"

"Can we outrun them?"

Corlan paused a heartbeat. "We must!"

He swung the boy up onto the back of Elo and grabbed the reins of Pex, tugging him forward. The heavy dragonslinger, hanging from the saddle, banged against the girafor. Corlan ran as fast as the girafor would allow itself to be led. Tam had better luck on the other girafor, giving free rein to his mount, and moved quickly ahead of Corlan pulling Pex.

The valley bent, dropping sharply, and Corlan recognized it as the border that marked the furthest he had ever gone. Now he needed to go much farther, find some place to hide. Otherwise, none of them would ever return. In the Valley of Death, there was no room for error, no moment of hesitation.

"Come on!" Corlan shouted at the girafor.

Tam, riding Elo, was a half-mile ahead, almost out of sight.

Three tri-wings descended like arrows. Besides the two wings, a spine-supported sail rose behind their heads and peaked over their backs, tapering just past the half-way point of their tails, acting as a third wing.

The first tri-wing swooped down, hooked the belly flesh of the blue-lightning in its teeth and stripped it off in a single motion, never alighting. The other two tri-wings touched down on either side of the carcass and immediately began pecking at the scales, tearing them away and clawing at the meat that lay beneath. The first tri-wing spun around in the air, tossing the meat up and gulping it down, then landed and partook of more.

Corlan dared not stop to watch the carnage. He ran as fast as he could and Pex seemed to get the idea after seeing the tri-wings drop from the sky, ready for dinner. After a few steps, Pex was pulling Corlan by the reins and he could not keep up.

Corlan fell as the reins were ripped from his hands.

The girafor ran ahead, catching up to the others.

Corlan sat up, realized he had no weapon with him except his sideblade. It was only for defense against drunkards and palace guards, not dragons. He scanned the valley for a place to hide: any crevasse or cleft or shadow beneath a cliff. In this section of the valley there was nothing but the flat riverbed and shallow shorelines that offered nothing more safe than a boulder.

He dove behind one of the larger rocks there as the lead tri-wing spied him and grunted for him to keep away from their meal.

More than an hour later, Corlan no longer heard the tri-wings' cawing. He looked over the top of the rock. Only bones remained of the blue-lightning.

They should have thanked me better. He breathed deeply. *At least they didn't come looking for me as dessert.*

With the morning sun blazing down on him like dragon's breath, Corlan strode along the riverbed, sweat running down his body, until he saw the rest of his party huddled together in the shade of...a *tree!* In fact, there were several trees, growing out along the edge of the riverbed. More vegetation grew on the shorelines, too, and on the hills that rose beyond the shoreline. In the riverbed were small...

Puddles! *...of water!*

Corlan dropped to his knees, slapping his hands into the water and splashing his face. Although it was only a few inches deep, it was everything he wanted at that moment.

"Are you hurt?" Tam called to him.

Corlan sat back on the ground, shaking his head, water flinging off his hair and beard.

"Not at all. A man needs a good hard run every once in a while. Keeps a man healthy. Like a full night of joy."

He breathed deeply, sitting beside the pool of water, until he felt rested. Standing, he regarded the grove of trees where Tam and the girafors waited, safe in the shade, already refreshed by their own sips of water and grazing on tufts of grass.

"Come take a rest here," called Tam.

Corlan hated to move from his comfortable spot under the trees, his back supported by a bed of grass. He had drank as much water as he could hold, then pissed it out between a pair of rocks over by the side of the valley's ancient shoreline. Returning to the grassy bed, he told the boy a nap was required, his reward for dealing with the dragons the previous night.

"This is the farthest I ever ventured," Corlan mumbled, thinking aloud. "If I only knew there would've been pools of water and trees for shade, I would've kept going."

Tam had taken off the big shirt Corlan gave him after his pants became soiled, a shirt which had hung down on him like an ancient king's robe. He washed it in one of the pools along with his pants. After hanging them both over a rock to dry in the hot sunshine, he sat with his legs crossed under the same bunch of trees.

Tam sighed. "This is the life...."

"It is, isn't it?" Corlan responded.

"What kind of tree is this?" Tam asked, looking up. "I never saw any like this in the city."

Corlan gazed up at the long fronds that constituted branches and leaves, wondering himself. "I've never seen any like this, either. They look a bit like large bushes, like they have in the gardens of the palace, only much taller." Then he thought a moment. "Ferns! That's what they're called. So these must be fern-trees. Yes! We're entering the hot zone."

He kicked at his boots, set near his bare feet, pushing them out of the way. He wiggled his toes.

"From now on, we should expect to find more water and more of these trees. That will make our journey easier. We can hunt some food then, get fresh meat, and save our rations." He breathed deeply. "Makes me wonder why the upper valley is so barren."

"Maybe the dragons burned it," said Tam.

Corlan raised his head. "You might be correct."

"That's what I heard from people at the palace. They said the old dragons did it, burnt everything."

"Someone at the palace said that?"

"I was serving the dinner. They were talking. I listened."

"Who were these gentlemen? Dragonslayers or history scribers?"

"I don't know. Yet they seemed certain it was truth."

Corlan nodded. "Men full of dinner always believe themselves. It doesn't mean their truth is the real truth."

Tam agreed. "So I found a scroll where the story was recorded."

"A scroll?" Corlan laughed. "You know how to read scrolls?"

"My mother showed me some of the marks. The cook showed me more, especially the recipe scrolls."

"Then you're a boy with education."

"He tried to make me know a lot of things."

"All the better for life after your career in the kitchen."

Tam stood suddenly, crossed his arms over his bare chest. "I'm going to be a dragonslayer!"

Corlan grinned, nodded slowly. "There is much to learn for that, as well. Better to learn a recipe, eh?"

"No, I'll learn it! You'll see! If you teach me."

"Watch and learn, boy. Watch and learn."

Corlan closed his eyes.

"I'm watching you sleep," said Tam, "and I'm not learning very much."

Corlan grumbled. "You're learning how to conserve resources."

Once rested and refreshed, they dressed themselves and packed, then led the girafors away from the grove of fern trees and onward down the valley.

As they went, the valley narrowed and the vegetation thickened. In places it seemed it was never a river valley at all but, rather, a long-standing forest of ancient ferns and other tall plants, though Corlan did not recognize the kind of trees they were. He thought they were the result of the hot climate, more humid here than in the northern region of the valley. In other places, the sides of the valley were quite steep and the channel narrow. He felt vulnerable, as though a trap was being set to capture him. What nets were set to snag whatever animal or human stupidly stumbled into this gorge?

"I need to see where we're going," said Corlan, waving the others to halt. He gazed around, jutted his chin at a high hill just behind the south cliffs. "Wait here with the girafor. I'll climb up there and have a look around."

The boy was cooperative. He tied the girafors to a tree sprouting there and sat with the water bottle in his hands.

"The valley should not narrow like this. Remember how wide it was much closer to the city? It should continue widening all the way to the marshes."

Corlan searched for some hand holds in the face of the cliff. He began to climb up, unsteady and grasping the crumbling rocks of the cliff face. It was not high but it was sheer. He jumped down, went further along the cliffs.

"Here's a place," he called back to Tam, out of sight now.

What could have been called a trail led upward between the cliffs, a bit too close to a path made by men than by a rivulet trickling down to the river. Regardless, he needed to get up on top of the cliff. He followed the rocky trail as it wound back and forth, rising sharply.

From the top of the cliff, standing with the toes of his boots at the edge, Corlan saw they were heading into a side channel rather than the main valley. The increasing vegetation had obscured the way. He gazed back over his shoulder at the hill, wondering if he needed to go there. He still could not see the main channel. Where he was standing was likely only an island in the river long ago.

He jogged away from the cliff and down a slope leading into a small draw, then went up the other side. Bushes slapped at him as he scrambled up the rocky slope. Grass covered parts of the slope but loose rocks covered the path. He grabbed hold of a tree here, a bush there, to continue up until he mounted the crest of the hill and turned to get his bearings.

Far below, he saw the flora-choked canyon they had been about to enter. He saw the shifting shadows below that let him know where the girafors waited. To his right he could gaze far up the valley, until it faded into dust and haze. To his left, his eyes followed the line of flora marking the narrow channel. He calculated if they continued far enough, they would meet up with the main channel once more. A mile or two. If they backtracked a mile, they could reconnect with the main channel.

From the hilltop, Corlan scanned the landscape on the opposite shoreline. The earth was five shades of brown, streaked with green vegetation of many hues. His spirit lifted, believing that the hardest part of the journey was past them, the desert of the upper valley. Now there would be floral cover, water, and food to hunt.

Then his eyes caught something he did not expect to see.

His hands went to his forehead, shielding his eyes from the sun. He took a deep breath, focused.

Buildings.

They were brown like the land around them, so he did not notice them at first. Yet they were more than buildings. The central building was shaped like...like a palace! With spires, ramparts, and what appeared to be a grand staircase on the side facing him. The center of the palace held a huge dome as its roof.

He shook his head. The large structure stood on a similar hill, surrounded by lesser buildings, all the same color and style. Stone construction. No wood or metal that he could see. He could not see any person moving around. He waited, spying the area in front of the large building but saw no movement.

Perhaps it is only the ruins of a long ago city. He squinted. *Perhaps it remains standing because it is a temple. A temple could have treasure.*

Down Corlan went, locating the broken trail, and pouncing down between breaks in the cliffs to the channel where he left Tam and the girafors.

"I see something," he called, out of breath. "Buildings. And one is like a palace. Or a temple."

Tam jumped up. "Is it a city?"

"It used to be. I don't think anyone lives there now." He grabbed the water bottle, slammed down a few gulps. "We should take a look. There could be treasure there."

"Like jewels? And silver blocks? Like strings of those white balls from the deep sea? Those things?"

"Yes, like those."

Yet finding the way to the ruins proved difficult. They went back out of the narrow channel filled with trees and bushes and searched for a channel which would lead them up onto the north shore. Hours later, they had not found such a place.

"At least we found the main river bed," said Tam.

Corlan continued scanning the north shore for any cleft that might provide a way to climb up. Instead, they continued along the main channel, a wider canyon yet still too tight for Corlan's comfort. If they should meet a dragon there, they would have no extra space to escape or hide. However, the sky was clear and bright and nothing flew in it.

"Let's try this one," said Corlan, pointing ahead to what looked to be a break in the cliffs of the north shore.

The path they found led them up from the riverbed and fed them into a parallel valley at higher elevation, full of grass and low bushes. Corlan could see a trail wound through the flora, a path that seemed recently used. He checked his sideblade. Whenever his mind sensed danger, he would gaze across the sky, searching for demons from above. Yet the sky was bronze and clear, no clouds, no winged beasts. He needed to search for danger at his own eye level as they marched up the trail.

Corlan took the lead, sword in hand, followed by Tam pulling Elo and Pex trailing.

As they rose along the trail, they soon left the denser flora and had a wide view of the entire valley. Tam paused, amazed by the sight. Corlan let him take a moment, then they continued.

"Now here is what they call a road," said Corlan, halting with his boots just to the side of the wide, flat, smooth, stone pathway as wide as three wagons. He pointed to his right and then to his left. "I heard of large wagons, having no beasts to pull them, racing along paths such as these. The wagons moved from steam, I think. There was some kind of oven in the back that burned dragonfire. Long ago. The winners would be celebrated with wine, women, and song."

Tam gazed up and down the flat stone road, imagining the scene. "And the losers? What became of them?"

"I believe they were sacrificed on the altar of hasty judgment."

"They were killed?"

"Most likely, yes."

"Because they lost a race?"

Corlan nodded, his attention already directed at the next portion of the trail. He put away his sideblade.

"They had strange rules in those days. My grandfather spoke of it when I was a child. I was given some toys, wagons with no beasts to pull them, yet they moved on wheels across the floor. He said larger ones were used for racing, to see who was fastest. After they lost the last of the horses, and all of the birds called *osters*, too, they only could race in wagons."

Tam was clearly impressed. He ran up the road a ways, stopped, making sounds like a dragon was hot on his scent. Corlan thought he had a fantasy of being a racer. The boy ran back to the group, then ran off in the other direction, pretending to be a racer but only using his skinny legs.

Watching the boy, Corlan recalled running across battlefields carrying messages when he was about the boy's age.

"It was a long time ago, I said," called Corlan.

Tam returned to the group, breathing hard.

"I thought you wanted to be a dragonslayer."

"Or a racer," said Tam. "I could do that, too."

"Someday you will need to build such a thing."

From where they stood, Corlan could just make out the top of the spires that mounted the impressive temple structure. Calculating the direction, he led them down the flat stone road.

After almost a mile the road began a gentle curve, rising. Along the sides of the flat stone way were metal railings which seemed intended to hold in the wagons so they could not exit the road.

The road became steeper and Corlan paused to catch his breath as the girafors also complained.

"Give them some water," he said to Tam.

The boy reached for the limp water bag hanging on Elo's harness, slipped it loose and helped the girafors drink.

Corlan bent over, spit on the ground. He stood up straight and stretched. Past meal time, he knew. And how much longer to reach the temple? He gazed ahead, measuring the road, seeing it continue winding up the hill.

As Tam replaced the water bag on Elo's harness, the girafor jerked away. Pex also startled.

Corlan turned to see what had spooked them, reaching for his sideblade.

The bushes where the road curved were shaking. The leaves of the bushes flittered not from a breeze but from movement. The ground shook under his boots. Corlan ran to Pex, grabbed the dragonslinger and two iron bolts.

"What is it?" asked Tam.

"Something that will be quickly dead."

"Dead? Why?"

"Either it or us."

Corlan took his position on the roadway, kneeling against the hard stone, aiming at the upward curve of the road as the shaking of the bushes increased.

Suddenly, they broke from the bushes, stepping onto the stone road, and Corlan's finger weighed heavy on the launch spring. But he hesitated.

8

A Gathering of Drakes

TO TAM THEY LOOKED LIKE DRAGONS: reptilian, scaly, walking stiffly on thick legs, showing angry faces, as though they had always eaten poor food and never gotten dessert. Tam thought these must be baby dragons.

"They're called drakes," Corlan explained. "Related to dragons, yes, but no wings for flight. Also, no fire in their breath. They lack the glands in the throat. Yet they can and do attack anything to get their meal, though, so stand back."

The three drakes pushing through the brush were almost pink as the sunlight struck them. Otherwise, ruddy brown skin covered their bodies, with more red coloring on the line of short spines along their backs, the horns on their head, and the heart-shaped hammer at the end of their stubby tails. The larger one also had purple stripes on the cheeks and neck.

When the nearest one appeared to yawn, Corlan and Tam could see the long teeth, top and bottom, that would fit neatly inside the recessed sheaths in the upper and lower jaws, giving them a thick jawline and a wide snout.

"Are you going to shoot them?" asked Tam, fear in his voice.

"Probably no need. They won't hurt us if we don't hurt them."

They watched the trailing drakes step slowly out from the brush, crossing onto the flat stone of the road, gazing about, deciding where to go next. The shoulder-high bushes were full of flowering purple petals at the ends of black stems. The first drake to step on the road was the largest, possibly the mother of the other two, thought Corlan.

He backed away slowly, keeping the dragonslinger loaded and ready. There was no benefit to killing these three—a mother and two offspring. They did not usually harm people but were known to tear up crop fields and lumber into the sides of barns, causing them to collapse.

"We should let them be on their way," said Corlan, lowering the dragonslinger. "They are heading to their home, I would guess."

The three took their time, sauntering about as though they were already at home, ignoring the intruders.

However, the two girafors were unnerved by the presence of the drakes and Tam struggled to keep them calm.

The jittery girafors caught the attention of the drakes. The male offspring veered away from the mother, staring hard at Pex, the closer of the two girafors. Pex pulled at his ropes.

"Easy, Pex," said Tam spoke softly.

The drake took a few heavy, lumbering steps and reached out for the girafor with its forefoot claws. In one motion, Pex tripped away, backward from the drake's claws, and fell hard on his side. Supplies tumbled off the harness and spilled across the flat stone. The drake bounded forward, clawing at the girafor. This time, the claws landed and sank into Pex's hind leg. Girafors were mute but Pex let loose a feeble cry.

Corlan jumped into action, spinning on his heel and pulling the dragonslinger to his hip, the launch spring already screwed back, and released it.

The iron bolt went straight through the side of the drake's chest and poked out the other side. The beast whimpered a moment, then flopped over on its side.

The mother drake growled alarm and charged at them like an angry hippor. The female offspring followed slower.

Corlan whirled around, frantically trying to load another iron bolt into the dragonslinger.

The mother drake was quick, and butted Corlan with the horn on her nose, knocking him down. The forepaw hovered over him, claws drawn. Corlan unsheathed his sideblade and hacked at the paw above him as he scooted away across the stone road.

The mother drake followed, growling, spittle running from her extra large teeth.

Tam handed Corlan another bolt and together they got it inserted in the slinger and the launch spring screwed back.

Corlan fired the slinger and the bolt went into the mother's throat. She froze a moment, unsure what had happened, then tried to back up and turn away from them, withdrawing from the fight. She gazed back at her daughter, offering a low guttural sound, like a stomach rumble but sadder. With a final look at Corlan, she closed her eyes and collapsed belly down, her four legs bent under her heavy body, jaw and chin against the flat stone.

Tam had been tending to the wounded Pex as Corlan dealt with the drakes. The third drake, the daughter, remained in her place, watching them from a safe distance.

Corlan scrambled to his feet, catching his breath.

"That was unfortunate," he said with a grunt. "Both of them. Now that one is on its own."

He turned to check Pex, saw the deep cuts across his thigh.

"Will he live?" asked Tam, looking up sadly as he rubbed his hands over the fallen animal.

"If we had some balm...."

Tam hurriedly searched among the packs that had fallen from the girafor's harness. Checking and setting aside everything that was not what he was looking for, he found the bottle.

"Apply it to the wounds," Corlan instructed. "We will need to see if it heals by tomorrow. Otherwise, we should kill it, put him away from the pain. Of course, then we will suffer, not having the means of carrying all our supplies."

As Tam rubbed the balm into the claw wounds, Corlan took hold of the small male drake and, with effort, pulled the body into the field of purple-flowered bushes. The drake was as long as Corlan was tall, tail included, and had triple the weight. The mother, being triple the size of her son, something close to the hippor Corlan once rode, could not be moved.

He considered if drakes were edible.

"Let's try some tail," he said with a laugh.

He went to the male offspring's body and began cutting mid-way along the stubby tail. Some protruding barbs hampered his surgery, but he got a chunk of meat separated from the bones. The meat filled both his hands as he lifted it away.

He held it out for Tam. "Wrap this up. We'll dine on it tonight."

Corlan glared at the remaining drake and it gradually turned and stumbled away, moving across the flat stone and into the brush on the opposite, cutting a wide path through the purple flora until Corlan could no longer hear the noise or see the beast's back.

He spun around to locate the temple on the hill that had been their destination. The tops of the spires still rose above the fields of purple bushes. He estimated the distance: maybe a mile or two if they had a straight path to it. As it was, the stone road wound around the hill. It could take a few more miles to get to the top of the hill. He measured the sunlight, guessed at the hour. Evening was coming.

"I would prefer checking the temple in daylight, before we choose it as our camp for the night," he said to nobody in particular.

Tam and the girafors were silent, though Pex produced a steady, low moan.

"We can't stay here, not with the drake carcasses laying about. Others will surely come to dine on them." He gazed over at Tam, tending to Pex. "We must continue up the hill."

"I don't think Pex will be able to walk," said Tam.

"Try to get him up. Walk him a bit, let him get used to it. I know it hurts but it will mend. If he stays behind he will surely become food for some other creature."

"Up, Pex, up," Tam called, stroking the girafor's neck and gently tugging on the reins. The girafor resisted then sprang up all at once but favored its rear leg.

"If he can make it slowly, I won't need to put him down."

"Come on, Pex, you can go up the hill," said Tam, tugging more on the reins. "You don't want to be food, do you?"

Corlan jerked the reins of Elo, pulling the girafor.

"Get back!" he shouted suddenly.

Tam looked around, expecting a dragon to be alighting from the sky. Instead, Corlan pointed to his feet. The ground was churning like it was filling with water.

Tam pulled Pex off the ground and onto the stone road. The dirt was rippling, the bushes thrashing, and then long clefts formed in the soil and out of those clefts dozens of snake-like tubes arose, twisting and biting at the air with surprisingly sharp-looking teeth.

"Are they snakes?" asked Corlan, staring down. Unsheathing his sideblade, he rushed to Tam. "Get back! Stay on the stone road."

The creatures resembled snakes, just toothy eyeless faces at the ends of each long tentacle wriggling out of the ground. As Corlan watched, however, he saw they were part of the root system of the purple bushes they had been walking among. The purple flowers on the bushes had closed and the bushes themselves seemed to shrivel, shrinking down toward the soil, diminishing as the snake-like roots rose up from the soil, as if gathering power from the fading sunlight, then dropping to the ground again to bite at anything in reach.

What they caught were pieces of the fallen drake, both the mother, still mostly on the stone road but with two legs at the edge where the snake-roots could nibble, and the male offspring Corlan had pulled off the road and dumped among the bushes.

"I know now why we never find the bones of long dead animals up here off the riverbed," Corlan said, blade held ready. "Stand back. They are not after us."

Tam was scared, Corlan could see. He waved for the boy to come around him and wait behind.

"I've never been this far in the valley, so it is impossible to know what deadly creatures live here."

"They're eating the drakes!" cried the boy.

"Yes, because how often does fresh meat fall right at their feet?" He stared at the snake-roots wriggling over the carcass. "Though they have no feet. Fall at their hungry yaws...?"

"It's horrible!"

"Not an appetizing spectacle, for sure."

The girafors stood nervously at the very center of the stone road, away from either edge where snake-roots might grab at them.

"Come, we must leave this place now." Corlan backed away. "Watch your steps and keep to the center of this stone road. We will make our way up the hill."

Continuing up the road, Corlan took the lead, Tam and Pex next, and Elo following.

"I agree we should've stayed in the valley," said Corlan. "Down there we can see the danger coming at us. Leaving the shoreline we do not know what we will have to face. Like those damnable root-snakes or whatever they are called."

"They were frightening!" Tam cried. He sniffled back tears. "But I wasn't afraid."

"We need to get you a weapon. I won't always be with you when danger strikes. You ever use a blade before?"

"I cut up vegetables in the kitchen."

"That's a start. Now think of the vegetables as a dragon's talons.

Or a man's hands and arms."

"The cook showed me how to cut vegetables. You got slice, dice, julienne, diagonal, wavecut—"

"And I will show you how to cut dragons."

As the road neared the top of the hill, it split into three paths. The middle way was the wider so Corlan continued on straight. The stone road rose more and became a plaza at the top of the hill.

It was as wide and long as the entire palace grounds in the Burg. Flat stone tiles covered the space although some of them clearly were out of place, broken, tilted, and otherwise showed their age. In the center of the plaza was a recessed square, accessed by four square levels. In the center of that depressed square was a stone-ringed fire-pit. He thought it large enough to roast a dragon, or at least a drake. Perhaps it was designed for the people of this location to have their festivals.

"They must have great feasts here," said Corlan happily.

"Where are the people now?"

"Long gone."

At the far end of the plaza stood the gigantic building he had first spotted from the riverbed. He had never seen a single building so big as this one. Like a huge box a dozen levels high—with a gray domed roof as large as the building, from end to end. And at each corner of the building stood a tall tower, what he'd thought were spires. The tall towers were narrow and rose twice the height as the top of the huge dome. None of the towers flew flags nor did any banners wave from them.

"What is this place?" asked Tam, coming beside Corlan with Elo and Pex reluctantly tugged along with him.

"When I first saw it, I thought it was a palace." Corlan swept his arm across the empty plaza. "I expected to find a city here. I hoped we could get new supplies. Then I realized it must be a dead city. At least the ruins of a city might have some treasure. Yet now it's only this empty plaza and a temple. I suppose it's a temple. Why build something as large as this if not for the gods? Look at the high dome and the towers at the corners. See how the plaza is arranged? They intended many people to stand here."

Tam pointed to the center of the plaza. "What's that?"

Corlan saw that he meant the recessed square in the plaza and its fire-pit.

"Probably they lit a fire there when it was time for a celebration.

It may be they roasted drakes there."

"Truly?" Tam was excited. He ran to the edge of the steps and carefully jumped down level by level to the bottom and pressed up against the edge of the fire-pit, leaning on its enclosing wall.

Corlan hurried to grab the ropes of the girafors and maintain control of them.

"Watch it, boy! Don't forget your responsibilities! You're the one to mind the girafors."

Corlan tugged the ropes and led the girafors to the edge of the recession. He looped the ropes together and hooked the ropes around the edge of a broken tile. He descended into the square basin, a space larger than the Guild Hall in the Burg.

"It's not drakes they roasted here," said Tam as Corlan stepped up to the edge of the fire-pit.

They both gazed down into the pit, filled almost to the rim with black ash and assorted bones.

"No, not drakes," said Corlan. He looked up to catch his breath, and gazed again into the pit. "Those are the bones of men—humans. Yet I'll wager the ones who burned them were not humans, not like we know humans to be."

He backed off from the pit.

"I've fought in many a battle, boy, and none of us, as much as we hated each other, ever burned the bodies of our dead or any captured fighters of the other army. We kept some dignity about us."

"Then who did that?" Tam was still curiously studying the bones: skulls, jaw bones, arms and legs, vertebrae, broken pelvic bones. He saw smaller bones mixed in with them. "Are those children's bones?"

Corlan got up to look. "Yes."

"Why they burn children?"

"Look at the temple there. Maybe long ago a certain civilization lived in this land. Maybe they had customs to make sacrifices. I heard about that—about human sacrifices—when I was a child. It was common in the south lands, places like Rolina or Lanta. People were afraid. They likely believed the gods sought vengeance upon them. The gods needed to be given gifts, they thought. No better gift than to give your own kind, eh? Maybe from your own family."

"Their own kind?"

"Yes, either they chose someone special for it, or whoever was the administrator took someone and nobody could say anything against it or else they would be sacrificed, too."

"That's horrible!" said Tam, his face pale.

"Long, long ago, boy. Nothing to worry about now. None of them live now. We are alone here."

Corlan gazed around the plaza, pausing to study the temple, noting how grand the entrance was, an opening nearly as wide as the temple's front façade. Hundreds could enter at once.

"I would've expected other buildings. Unless they were all made of wood or straw. They would have faded away. Only this one stone structure remains. The most important one." He shook his head. "It's difficult to imagine a people who would build such a grand thing yet lived in straw huts. And sacrificed humans."

He waved his arm behind himself, the direction they had come. "And that hill, all those snake bushes, and the drakes — it's all come from evil."

"Evil?" asked Tam, turning away from the fire-pit.

"Evil is what man does to man, especially without reason, just to be cruel. You see, if I had just shot those drakes when I first saw them, knowing they shouldn't care about us, that would've been evil. I would be killing on whim. Dragons are different. Dragons are evil. They'll kill a man at first sight whether or not they are hungry, even if the man does not attack them first. Dragons come from evil, so they have no spirit."

"What's spirit?" asked the boy.

"Did they teach you nothing in that kitchen?"

"Only how to cut vegetables and serve the food without dropping it. If I did drop it, I put it back on the plates. I brushed off the dirt. The cook said never to waste the food. He said if I dropped the food to be sure I served that plate to the prince."

Corlan grinned. "Clever boy!"

"I only got to eat what was left on the plates after dinner."

"Now I see why you're so skinny. If you want to grow into a man, you must eat — and eat meat to build your muscles."

"I'm only twelve."

"Time enough to start becoming a man. We start tomorrow!"

"What will we do?"

"First, I should train you to fight, to defend yourself. You'll learn how to use a blade. Second, you train to build up your muscles."

"Here? In this place?"

"It's a good spot for training. Look around. You could stand half an army on this plaza. Lots of flat, open space to move around."

"But the...the bones...."

Corlan chuckled, spit into the fire-pit. "The first lesson is to never be afraid of anything. Concerned, yes—but only as much as needed to prepare yourself."

"I will." He thought a moment. "I am."

"Good," said Corlan with a wry grin. "You have mastered the first lesson: never be afraid. And never be afraid of the dead."

"Are we staying here tonight?"

The sky was darkening, the sun hanging on the western horizon providing only enough light for them to see what was in the fire-pit. The entrance to the temple was dark. Corlan hesitated. Exploration could wait until morning.

"Nothing will harm us here. None of those strange bushes about on this stone plaza. No drakes, either. And all of these murderers are long gone from this place. Bones won't hurt you." He pointed to the temple's entrance. "Or we could make camp in there."

Tam shook his head vigorously.

"Afraid to go inside?" asked Corlan. "I agree. I'd prefer to wait until morning, when we have more light. And yet...it could still be quite dark inside the temple. I don't know if they have any way for light to enter it. We have to go in to see what's there."

"Is it safer in there than out here?"

Corlan scratched his beard.

"Out here we can see danger coming at us. In there, the danger might not even see us. Maybe you're right. In the temple would be safer. Look how long it has stood. None would harm it, I suspect."

"But should we go in?"

"It's abandoned. Probably only some broken furniture and a lot of dust. Maybe more bones."

"You said there would be treasure."

"Yes, I hope there is. That's the reason for coming up here. For a camp tonight, we only need to go just inside, just out of the range of any dragons." He glanced at the fire-pit. "No dragon bones were in there. Only humans."

"I guess being inside the temple would be safer," said Tam. "Then nobody would see we were here at all."

"Now you're thinking like a man."

They gathered the girafors and led them slowly across the plaza toward the front of the temple, hooves clapping against the plaza's tiles.

Standing before the huge edifice, Corlan cranked his head back to spy the top of the temple's gray dome until he could no longer see its top. The front side seemed to have once had doors that stretched from end to end. The doors had been torn away so the entire entrance was open. As they got up to the entrance, they had to step upon four large levels which stretched from one side to the other side of the temple's entrance.

"They certainly were expecting a lot of people to come here to this temple," said Corlan. "Their gods must've been kind at first. Then the gods became cruel and the sacrifices began. You never can tell about gods. All manner of strange behavior, like they are caught in a spell and don't know what they're doing."

They paused to gaze into the temple. All was dark inside and they could not make out what things might be in there. Long passages, like hallways in the palace, leading people from the entrance into the center of the temple.

Corlan went to one of the packs on Elo's back and pulled out a long knife and a torch. At one end of the torch was a small wire cage for holding a chip of dragonfire.

"Here," said Corlan, handing the knife to the boy. "Use it if you need to."

Corlan held the torch in one hand and fished for the dragonfire in his trouser pouch, retrieved it and pushed it into the top end of the torch, locking the cube into its wire cage. He scratched the cube of charred dragonflesh and it glowed with a faint orange hue. He blew on the cube and the glow expanded to engulf the entire end of the torch, making a suitable light.

"Now, let's find a good spot to put down our bedrolls and have our meal of drake tail."

Corlan went first, stepping carefully, expecting there to be broken objects he might trip over. Inside, by the glow of the torch, he saw an empty gallery. Ahead was a wide corridor leading deeper inside. That could wait for tomorrow, he decided. For tonight they needed only a small room where they could shut the door and feel safe.

Tam followed, pulling the girafors. "Mind your heads."

They fidgeted, did not want to lower their heads but with Tam's coaching, they did and moved inside, keeping their head lower than was comfortable. The entrance was not high enough for the girafors to stand tall, nor was the passage inside.

To the left and to the right were other doors. Corlan checked the one to their left, found it locked. Strange that the outer doors were gone but this small, insignificant door remained and was locked. He went to the door on the right end of the entrance hall. It, too, could not be opened.

"I suppose they locked them to keep people from stealing, eh?"

"I would," said Tam.

"People are thieves...everywhere you go."

Corlan looked as far down the big corridor as he could within the light of the torch. It seemed wide enough to accommodate a crowd of people just like in the palace in the Burg.

"We might as well go this way. Probably it leads to a great hall. It's where everyone would gather to worship their gods. The girafors can stretch their necks there."

"Is it safe?" asked Tam, nervously.

"Lesson one: never be afraid."

"I'm only concerned."

Corlan pretended to listen for danger. "I don't hear any dragons. Nor drakes." He grinned but Tam was not amused. "This is likely the safest place we could be. A huge building like this, strong walls, well-protected from dragons and drakes, far from carnivorous bushes. We can bed down in comfort here. Come."

The corridor opened into a huge arena, the great hall rising up to the dome above and spreading to the far walls — much larger than the Great Hall of the palace in the Burg. Along each of the four walls were raised levels, and some had on them what appeared to be chairs, most of them broken. Other broken chairs were strewn about, as though a great battle had taken place in the temple. In the center below, on the first level, was a flat, open area, like a ballroom, and when they arrived from the passage, it seemed to be made of wood. Some wooden tiles had been torn away, but half remained.

"It seems a strange arrangement for a temple," Corlan muttered, "yet I'm not aware of the religion here. I can only guess what they worshipped in this place. Maybe it is not a temple, though I cannot think what other purpose such a grand structure would be built for if not to impress a family of gods."

"It could be a palace," said Tam. He heard his voice echo in the great expanse, his words bouncing off the far walls. "What is that?"

What is that? came the echo.

"It's your echo," said Corlan.

...your echo....

"Greetings!" Tam called out.

Greetings....

"Quiet, boy. You'll wake the ghosts of this place."

"Ghosts?" he cried out, laughing.

Ghosts....

"Quiet," said Corlan.

Quiet....

He shoved the boy forward and tugged the ropes of the girafors as they stepped into the center of the great hall, necks held tall.

"Halt!" came a loud voice, deeply echoing. "Who enters here?"

INTERLUDE

The Lesson

PRINCESS ADORA STOOD ON THE HIGH BALCONY of the palace with her tutor beside her, gazing out across the wide blue strait at the distant shore of another land. She had long heard the other land was a place of danger to which she must never venture. The list of crimes was long and her mother always warned of particular acts which might befall a girl should she find herself there.

"Remember what happened to my great-grandmother," Queen Dorothea would remind her almost daily. Long ago, in ancient days, the story went, she was attacked by several men. She was badly hurt yet escaped. After she recovered, she went about the land searching for them and found each of them. First, she lopped off their manly things, then their heads. Her acts became a great legend that inspired other women.

Her tutor, a woman called Jabuli, born and raised in the port of Rament on the north bay of the mainland, also liked to tell stories of the olden days. Long before that legend, before the island of Sannan broke away from the mainland, there were constant wars and people suffered greatly. Adora learned it was the blessing of the goddesses that saved her people from a graceless fall. She knew the story well; in fact, it was a common children's game. For many years women prayed to the goddesses for relief. Then, one day the ground shook fiercely and the sea rose up and the mountains fell and everyone slipped into slumber for seventy days. When they awoke, the place called Sannan had become an island, separated from the mainland by a body of water that others could not cross. The current ran fast in the strait and protected them from most invaders.

Isolated and safe, the women of Sannan developed their own

customs. They made many laws marking who did what and who was disposable. It was better that way, according to the queen and echoed by Adora's tutors. After all, one day Adora would be the queen and be required to protect her folk. The writing of laws would help her do that. Until such time, she needed to learn the history of her world—even the bad things.

"I want to go there someday and have a look," said the innocent princess to Jabuli. "I want to know why people act badly."

"You don't want to go there, Your Little Majesty." With a hand over her mouth, Jabuli repressed a chuckle. The princess often spoke the most remarkable words without thinking what she was saying. "The many dangers there could prevent you from returning here. That would not be good."

"Oh, I would return. This is where I live, so I have to return. My slumber seat is here."

"And your play girls, too."

Adora tilted her head. "I suppose they will be here, too. And my dragons. And my pet boy."

Jabuli frowned. One of her assigned tasks was to discourage the princess from caring for the pet boy. Then the boy could be quietly sent away without the princess complaining. Perhaps the plan was going well: the princess named her dragons before her baby brother.

In fact, one night, while the princess slept, a maid was assigned to snatch away the basket bearing the brother yet the princess awoke in the dark and called out, "Who dares take my pet?" The maid halted, set the basket down, begged pardon of the sleepy princess, then snuck out. The maid was punished for failing her task but none dared try it again.

"How does your little pet eat and drink?" asked Jabuli, noticing how fat the boy was, approaching one year of age.

"I give him my food and drink, of course. Wouldn't you?"

"He takes milk?"

"Yes. I give him my milk."

"But—but you're only ten years old. How do you have milk?"

The princess was quite serious. "The maid brings it in a cup."

Jabuli laughed. "I see."

"He gets plenty of food and milk."

Jabuli frowned. "You use the word 'he'?"

"I looked on an old parch and found the word for male babes. I can use the word because I'm a princess. So 'he' is my pet brother.

For you, and the other maids and tutors, please call him the name I gave him, or you can say 'Your Little Majesty's pet' — like that!"

"Indeed, Your Little Majesty. You are so clever!"

"Now tell me about the mainland. If I cannot visit, I want to know everything. You lived there."

"I did live there, yet Rament is a dirty town. The seaports usually are. All manner of dirty people come to visit and they do not leave the town in a cleaner condition."

"Then you are lucky to come here to Sannan."

"Yes...I am." Jabuli did not seem happy to admit it. "I came here in a group of slaves, remember."

"I remember. Mama told me. She wanted you to teach me about all the bad places over there. So I would be afraid to visit them." She swung her hand out over the balcony wall, pointing to the distant shoreline. "She let all of you stay because you are women, you and your sisters. Mama loves women."

"That is correct. Queen Dorothea bought us from the merchants so we would be free. I welcome the opportunity to live in this palace and tutor you, Your Little Majesty."

"I like it, too. You are a good tutor. You know about everything. I want to know about everything, too. And you're not mean or teach too hard lessons." The princess nodded, thoughtfully. "You also give answers to my questions without complaint."

"I do try, Your Little Majesty."

The princess turned to regard Jabuli. "When we are alone, such as now, having a lesson, you can call me Adora. It takes so very long to say 'Your Little Majesty' every time you speak. It's annoying."

"I understand, Your Little —"

"Adora!"

"Yes, Princess Adora."

"Oh! Yes, *princess*! I like that. *Princess* Adora. That's good. Better than just Adora."

They proceeded with the lesson.

Once upon a time, the mainland had several armies that fought with each other. People watched the battles, even paying fair coin to see which army won the battle. They built grand arenas to contain the fighting so the town would be safe for common folk to walk about. Even so, the townsfolk often wore streamers or garments emblazoned with the symbols of the army for whom they cheered. Fights often occurred between the common folk who supported different armies. In those days there were demi-gods who could strike down the street fighters. It was a violent age.

"How about the women? Did they fight?" asked the princess.

"Some were fighters. Women in my family had to fight most days just to stay alive. It was not safe for a woman to be out on the streets. The demi-gods did not protect the ladies. Women had to hire guards or they had brothers to protect them."

"Brothers?"

"Yes, Princess Adora. Brothers are common on the mainland."

The girl seem to go into a trance, pondering the lesson.

"Brothers can be good, I suppose. If they protect you."

"Yes, it's true. Brothers will protect you." She frowned. "Unless a gang of men persuades the brother to give you up to them. Then the brother is not good. He stands there enjoying watching her hurt by the other men."

Adora did not get her harsh meaning. Perhaps that was for the best, thought Jabuli.

"It's so easy," said the princess. "Good or bad. Only two choices. That makes laws easy to write on parches." She had a happy lilt in her voice. "We should make a law. Only good brothers may stay on Sannan Island. Bad brothers should be sent to the mainland."

"Not punished?" asked Jabuli.

"Punished?" The princess made a strange face. "For what?"

"If they are bad they should be punished. Shouldn't they?" Jabuli stared at her charge and thought the girl didn't understand. "Here is an example. If someone called Wex hurts another person, someone called Butul, should Wex be hurt for hurting Butul? And if so, who will hurt Wex? Should Butul get the right to hurt Wex in exchange for Wex hurting Butul? Should that be the law?"

The princess pondered the situation. "No one should hurt. That should be the law. If someone hurts another person — like Wex hurts Butul — then that person, Wex, should be punished. The punishment should be no play time and no play pals. Maybe for as long as it takes for Wex to feel ashamed."

"And then? Set free?"

"I suppose. If Wex learned the lesson not to hurt other people."

"Yet suppose Wex hurt Butul so much that Butul no longer was alive. Would you make a more serious punishment then?"

"That seems fair. The more the hurt, the more the punishment." She nodded happily, problem solved. Her face changed. "Except if

Butul died. Then Wex should die, too. Except if it was done for an accident and not with a purpose. Except if Wex was trying to have it only look like it was an accident but truly planning it with a purpose. There should be punishment."

"Who would perform the punishment?"

The princess gave it much thought. "Me?"

"You, Princess Adora?"

"The queen is the head of all laws. If I am chosen to represent the law, it should be me that performs the punishment." She laughed suddenly. "Before all of that, everyone should be told the laws so they do not make any mistakes or get ideas to hurt anyone. I think that is fair. Don't you?"

"I do indeed, Princess Adora." Jabuli had to smile. "I think you will make an excellent queen some day."

"Mama doesn't think so. Not until I send away my brother. That's what I heard her say. No woman can care for a male and still be the queen. That's a law, she said. I suppose she made that law, so she knows it. Or my grandmother made the law, or before her, all the way back to the Split."

"When Sannan broke from the mainland?"

"Yes, since then. Vuti called it the Split. More and more laws! Too many." She shook her head. "Everyone should just be caring to each other. Everyone, even if one is a male." She paused, thinking, a blank expression on her face as she worked out a problem in her head. "I like my brother. I like how he is so happy when he sees me or when I hold him in my arms."

"You're wise, Princess Adora. And kind."

"That is what my other tutors say. Taroi and Erra, mostly. And Vuti once in a moon. It is just a word. It is written on the parches. Anyone can say it.... But I am not on the parches."

Jabuli grinned. "You will be one day." Her grin burst into a wide smile. "I know you will be."

"First, I need to protect my brother," said Princess Adora. "Then I will write a law. A new law."

Jabuli smiled at her charge. "A new law may indeed be a good thing, yet sometimes a new law can be worse for everyone."

"Then how do you know if it is good or bad?" The princess tilted her head to the right, thinking, then to the left. "Do the goddesses tell us? They could write a parch and give it to the queen and she could read it to everyone. Then the people would know."

Jabuli waved the princess over to the parches on the desk, chose one and pulled it to the top of the stack. She put her finger to the left margin, running her fingertip down to the passage she searched for.

"Here," she said. "Read this. It is one of our sacred texts. Perhaps you are ready to learn it now."

The princess stood close, stretching over the desk. She read the words her tutor marked: "It says 'I, Karl Kowalsky, do hereby make this law that nobody uncool can make a law that all the cool dudes gotta follow.'" The princess looked up, puzzled and frowning. "Who is Karl Ko-wal-sky?"

"Take care, Princess Adora. These are the words of a god from long ago and far away. The Kowalsky, *Blessed be His Name*, ruled over the entire eastern realm. After that age, the land was covered in fire. These words were written and passed down from generation to generation until a copy came all the way to Sannan. This is how we come to know about laws. Read more."

The princess found where she left off: "'The admins just declared martial law, the idiots, police blocking every street, saying nobody can go out the dorms or even get food at the snack shop. It's chaos, man, chaos!'" She looked up at Jabuli. "What does 'idiots' mean?"

"It means a person who makes bad laws."

"Oh. And what does 'chaos' mean?"

"It is the worst of everything."

"Oh."

She turned her eyes back to the sacred parch, reading slowly and checking with her tutor every few words to be sure she was saying them correctly: "'We ain't gonna stay here and just die. So me and my brothers are gonna grab some of the horses from the campus stables and just try to ride home. No gas here. TV is out, cells down, internet gone, so no news. It's freakin' anarchy here! The only way to survive now is for me and my frat brothers to ride north, try to make it back to you. Taking our girlfriends and supplies. My roommate's got a 45 & ammo so we got protection. There's no law now, so whatever we gotta do we're gonna do. We make the laws now, whatever works for us, as long as dudes are being cool. Hopefully, see you soon, Mom & Dad! Love ya! Karl.'"

"Blessed be His Name," Jabuli spoke after her.

The princess frowned. "It is difficult to understand. Such an old style of words. What do they mean?"

"The Kowalsky, *Blessed be His Name*, is the lawgiver. From this short document we learned about making laws. There was chaos in the world. Only laws could save them. They had to make laws, so the Kowalsky, *Blessed be His Name*, told us how to make them. Some of the people of that time had to fight and ride horses—"

"What are horses?" asked the princess. "Are they like dragons?"

"In some ways, yes. Four legs, but they did not have fire in their breath. No wings. Yet horses were more comfortable to sit upon for long periods of time. Soft fur on their backs. They rode the horses to return to their homes."

"Did they ever arrive at their homes?" The princess seemed quite concerned. "Where were their homes?"

"There is no other writing until much later, centuries later," said her tutor. "All we can know is they must have reached their homes eventually or there would not be any other writing such as what we have in the archive. We have other parches which tell of the distant ages, so we know about the Kowalsky, *Blessed be His Name*, and all His guardsmen and the women of His camp. They had children and grandchildren, and so on. They made a great empire from a high tower, set in a golden city called Cago. Until the goddesses sought to destroy it."

"Destroy it?" asked the princess. "But why?"

"It is said the goddesses were jealous. They feared a god having too much power. Yet it was a long time ago. You need not worry yourself about it now."

Adora gazed out from the balcony, realizing how high her palace tower was. "So was the high tower destroyed?"

"I believe it was," Jabuli replied with a sigh. "We all know that a goddess will always be stronger than a god."

Adora grinned. "That's the truth!"

At that remark, Jabuli wanted to pat her charge's little head. "So much lost writing from the eastern realm—"

"So they made the laws?" the princess spoke up.

"The law they wrote said that whoever survived could make the laws. What they said was: 'If you have forty-five people who agree with the law then it becomes the law for everybody.' The group of forty-five people are called the *ammo*, and everybody must be calm about it, not get angry and not feel hot. When people are cool they can agree about anything. Then you know everyone will obey that law. Very wise, don't you think?"

"It seems a good way to make a law," said the princess. "If you can have your brothers with you, and you have the ammo of forty-five, and they get together and everyone is cool, they can agree what to do. That is good. If they do it a different way, it is bad. True?"

"Yes, true. That is the reason for always having forty-five people in the room when the law is written. Then Her Majesty, the queen, puts a rubber stamp on it."

Adora's face shone with the glow of wonder, as though she had learned something truly amazing, perhaps life-changing.

Jabuli wanted to give the princess a pat on the shoulder in that moment, to show her admiration, yet she knew the princess should not be touched. Instead, she asked:

"What laws would you wish to make?"

"First, I do not know forty-five people," said Adora with a pout. "I also do not know how to make a dude cool. Or even what a 'dude' is. But I like that he told his mama he loved her. I say the words to my mama every day."

"I know she welcomes the words, Princess Adora."

The girl frowned. "What does 'dad' mean?"

"It is an ancient name for the man that a woman employs to help her make a babe. As your mother, Her Majesty, did to make you."

The princess nodded, thoughtfully. "It makes sense. I also like that the Kowalsky said—"

"Remember to always say 'Blessed be His Name' after you speak His name."

"I also like that Kowalsky, *Blessed be His Name,* told his dad he loved him, too."

"You are so kind, little princess," said Jabuli with a light touch of her hand to the girl's little head. If only life had turned differently and this girl could be her daughter, she thought, instead of only her pupil. "It is important to tell those we love that we love them. It is a duty many forget." She took a breath. "And that, Princess Adora, is how we come to know that our goddesses are good."

9

The Temple on the Hill

CORLAN GRABBED HIS SIDEBLADE, unsheathed it while holding the torch higher. The glow did not illuminate much more than his own travel party. Hearing a voice call out to them within the dark temple left him fully expecting an attack from all sides.

He waved the boy back and heard him turn the girafors around. Pex gave a guttural rumble as he stumbled across the uneven floor on his injured leg. Elo complied without complaint.

"We are only travelers," Corlan called out. His eyes searched for movement in the darkness beyond the torchlight that would tell him the location of the voice. "We come in peace, seeking a place to sleep for the night. That's all. Then we will travel onward."

He waited a moment for his words to settle, for the echo to fade.

"Who are you?" asked the voice.

"We are only travelers from the north."

"Do you have a name?"

"I am Corlan of the Burg."

Instead of words, the voice seemed to grumble dissatisfaction.

"And he is—the boy is my apprentice."

"What burg do you call home?"

"The only burg—*the* Burg. At the head of the long valley that runs below this hill. It is a fine city, a living community of people."

"It's a new idea to me. People living together in a large group like that, large enough they would call it a burg."

"It's the common name of the city."

"Tell me more," demanded the voice.

"It's an ancient city. That is, the city has been renewed many times going back thousands of years, always in the same location, or near to it, as the eras shape and reshape the land. It sits at the head of two narrow canyons—now canyons yet once filled with two rivers. Below the walls of the city, the rivers merged and flowed further. They flowed into this valley and all the way to the sea. At one time."

"You have seen the sea?"

"Not yet."

"When you see the sea, will you see the seashore, too?"

"I suppose I'll see the seashore, too, if I see the sea," said Corlan, puzzled by the question.

"How about seashells? Will you see them on the seashore, too?"

He squinted in the direction of the voice. "Yes, likely so."

"So when you see the seashore you'll see the seashells, too?"

"Yes!" Corlan coughed to cover his rage. "I've a long way to go before I see the damnable seashells on the seashore!"

"Yet you stop here to enter this temple...."

"It seemed a safe place to stay the night."

"Safe? Did you encounter dangers out there?"

Corlan cleared his throat, the echo rough as it returned to him.

"Some dangers, yes. Dragons from above and three drakes on the hillside coming up here."

"I see your beast is injured."

Corlan was surprised. Whoever spoke to them could see well enough in the torch's light, and from a distance within the temple, to notice the wounds on Pex.

"Clawed by a drake. We have put a balm to the wounds."

"And you?"

"Me? I am unhurt."

"Did you strike at the drake?"

He was not sure at that moment if the drakes were some special guardians of the temple or not.

"I acted to protect the girafor," said Corlan. "In the act, the drake was killed."

The silence after the echo unnerved Corlan. He knew someone in a magnificent temple like this might have magical powers he could not defend against. In the Burg, such a person was called a magus. Yet the ones who attended his grandfather's final moments were tame enough for talk. They seemed pleased to live simple lives without much responsibility save to chant to the clouds.

This fellow, however, had been here for who knew how long. He was due for some entertainment, perhaps at their expense—

"I tried to avoid confrontation," Corlan spoke, "but the drake attacked this animal that bears our supplies. The beast is important to our journey. We have a long journey.... It was unfortunate."

"Yet necessary."

Corlan nodded, keeping his eyes focused in the direction of the voice. Something moved. "Yes, it was either my *necessary* girafor or that vicious drake."

The magus stood stock still for a while. In the darkness, Corlan wondered if the figure was only an apparition, a trick of the faint light of his torch. He stepped forward.

"A choice...." The voice echoed around the space.

"Yes, a choice. Everything is a choice. And every other thing is a choice not taken. We are tired and wish to bed down. Please spare us the word games."

"You dare insult me?"

"I dare not. Fatigue dulls my memory of ceremonial protocols. If you will allow us to camp here, we can talk in the morning. I can give you full courtesy then."

"You assume my generosity. That is another insult."

"It's not an insult. We are from another realm. Maybe you and I have different customs. I don't believe I am insulting you by what I say, yet you take everything as an insult. So I choose — there's that word you enjoy! — I choose to believe you are a clear-headed person and sharp enough to determine our true intent. We mean you no ill will or insult."

"What is your true intent?"

"I said at the start: to camp for the night, then rise and be away in the morning. We have our own rations and supplies. We need only a portion of the floor."

A low groan started somewhere behind where the voice seemed to originate, and grew steadily for a minute, then faded to silence.

"Have you brought a sacrifice?" asked the voice.

Corlan shuffled, fidgeting with the blade. If only he knew exactly where the person stood. His heart beat quicker.

"Where are you?" he dared ask. "I can't see well in here."

There was a laugh, quick and dry. "I am before you."

He felt a breath on his face. "But I don't see you —"

"I am behind you."

"What?" He spun around.

"I am to the side of you. I am to the other side of you."

"Stop it!" he shouted.

"You have come into my place. It is you who must stop, not I."

When the echoes ended, Corlan stepped forward.

"And who are you?"

A whoosh of air seemed to fill the entire temple space.

"I am the magus of this temple, the last of a great Order, which has maintained this place for generations."

A noise like shuffling parchments or the fluttering of birds' wings filled the immense space. Corlan cringed, expecting to be engulfed by some menace, yet nothing came at him. He straightened.

"What happened to the people?" he asked. "Where did everyone go? Will they return—"

"Go?"

"Yes. Go." Corlan chuckled. "Just a giant temple set on a hilltop in the middle of nowhere. Was there a city around it? Were there people who lived here? We saw a great fire-pit outside—twenty feet across—with human bones and ash. Is that where the people went?"

"So many questions...."

Suddenly a golden light burst in front of Corlan, brighter than a hundred torches. Corlan shielded his eyes, clutching the hilt of his blade. Through his fingers he spied an old man standing on the third level of the dozen levels which ringed the great hall. He wore a long robe, dirty enough that its original white could only be guessed. Some ornamentation ran down the front panel of the robe—written marks not unlike those Corlan had seen on scrolls. The man also had an equally long gray beard. On his head sat a white cap, rounded on top and with a projection in the front which seemed to block the face from sunshine. On the front of the cap was an emblem of some kind. It all appeared to be an authentic costume of a magus.

Despite the distance between them, Corlan thought the man was grinning. *No doubt he has been bored so many years, not having anyone to talk with. Now I'll have to tell him my story. That's the damnable custom, after all.*

"Come forward," called the man posing as a magus.

"Do you have a name, sir?" asked Corlan.

"Joragus is how I am known."

"Is that a magi name? Or did you have another name before you became a magus?"

"No one *becomes* a magus. We are born into the Order."

"He looks safe," Tam whispered from behind Corlan.

"Maybe he is," Corlan responded quietly.

Joragus the magus raised his arms, the long, dirty sleeves still somehow hanging to his feet.

"I said come."

"How do you make so much light in here?" asked Corlan.

"It is the power of magic." The old magus pointed to the top of the great hall, at the underside of the dome overhead. "There are glow worms in the corroded plaster up there. They make their homes there. When the queens are alarmed, they glow. You need not worry about them."

"Why not? I've never seen a glow worm."

"If one should drop down upon you, do not kill it," said Joragus. "Though it may be as large as your arm, they will not bite or sting. You may gently brush them off of you."

Corlan nodded, then led the group forward to the center of the great hall, their steps unsteady crossing the wooden tiles.

"How do we come up there to you?" he asked.

"The beasts may not come up. You may leave them there. They will be safe. As for you, put away your weapons or surrender them to me. I have a dozen guards at my beck and call."

Corlan paused, then decided to sheathe his sideblade.

"Now you may come up."

"We only mean to set a camp and sleep, cook some dinner, then be on our way in the morning. Will you permit that?"

Joragus seemed amused. "You wish to use this temple as your overnight lodging? The idea is sacrilegious. Do you understand? Many before you have made such requests and suffered for it."

"Then I take back my words. We can leave this very minute. We won't bother you any more, sir."

Corlan turned to go, waving at Tam to go ahead of him with the girafors.

"Not able to bear my words, eh?" called Joragus. "They are only words. Utterances of an old throat."

Corlan stopped. "We are tired and hungry. I have no patience for old men like you. Too many old men in my life have caused me much trouble. Old men and young women —"

"You will one day be an old man!"

"That I know. You are quite the wise man. I am filled with awe at your wisdom, your insight, your special powers! Forgive my rear air!" Corlan let go a trio of noises that echoed around the great hall like hammers beating on drums. Tam giggled.

Before the echo of gas could fade, a mighty laughter rose that was louder than any other sound.

"Come, then, whatever your name was, man from a burg. Let us be friends! Stay and have your rest and eat your meal. Your foul air amuses me."

"It amuses me to let the air go out," said Corlan.

Tam held his fingers over his nose.

Joragus the magus moved to his right and descended a series of steps that delivered him to the floor at the center of the great hall. The long, dirty-white robe dragged on the floor, along with his long, gray beard. He paused every few steps to yank back his beard and tug his robe.

"Seems I've shrunk over the years," Joragus the magus muttered. He snapped the hem of his robe up from the floor. Seeing Corlan grinning, he spoke more deliberately: "I am three-hundred thirty-eight years of age, though you may not guess so by my appearance."

Corlan approached the magus. Standing close, Corlan was a head taller than the old man. He did look quite old, but certainly not more than three-hundred years.

"How can you be so old? Men of my city only manage eighty or a hundred. Is it because of your special powers?"

"I have no special powers," said Joragus, weariness in his voice. "Not now. They have faded. Once I could levitate great things. I could strike down enemies a mile away. I could create fire, and food, and a useful idiot from a few specks of dirt or a crumbled stone. I could turn lead into gold—well, good enough to fool any fool. I could spin cheap cloth into precious gemstones. I could walk across thin air and hold the entire sea in my two cheeks for an hour or more. Alas, it was a long time ago. Now I can barely empty my bowels without assistance. And I have no assistant now."

"That's a pity," said Tam, imitating Corlan.

"Yes...," said Corlan, glaring at the boy.

Joragus took a step, wavered, and Corlan held out his hand. "Let me help you."

"You are my assistant now?" asked the magus. He tried to laugh but lost his breath. "Let us go now, you and I, to empty my bowels and then to sigh," he sang out, "or else I shall die if I do not try."

The magus took hold of Corlan's arm and swung himself down onto the steps.

"I am not so used to walking so far. Your visit tasks me."

"You truly are an old man."

"Takes one to know one! What're you, fifteen?"

"Yet your mind is bleeding sharp," Corlan conceded. He studied the ancient figure, a map of wrinkles and spots and rashes. "How is it you are still alive?"

"I am a magus. Do you know what that means?"

"Apparently I don't." Corlan tried to put on a pleasant grin. "I've heard stories about magic. What the magi do. I'd always thought it a way to make children go to sleep."

"That is only one kind of magic: putting children to sleep."

"Then what do you do?" asked Corlan, genuinely interested.

"Magic. I told you I know about magic."

"You are alive so long because of magic?"

Joragus nodded, breathing deeply like his thinking had been hard work. "It is the Clona magic."

"I've heard of Clona." Corlan pointed to the girafors. "These two animals were made using that magic. I always thought it was much more than magic."

"Magic is everything. Things happen, you know, whether or not you understand how they happen. It is the same with Cama magic. It cuts through us in each of our days and leaves us with spots of magic here and there throughout our bodies. Some cause pain, some cause joy. Together they make the balance."

"I only know what I heard people in the Burg talk about."

"Clona magic is very simple. We grow a new living thing from the dust of a former living thing. I am an example of this magic."

"You?" Corlan's eyes widened.

"Yes. I used Clona magic to create the person you are speaking to now. Impressive, no? The former magus also used Clona magic to make himself — or to make *myself* again. And again. It's so confusing. Am I me? Or am I some other me? Or is he him and I only another him? Or is it he? You see how it gets confusing."

Corlan stared, his eyes searching against his will for some small clue that the man before him was not a real man.

"And again," said the magus.

"Is it true?" Tam whispered to Corlan.

"That is how you can say you are three-hundred and thirty-eight years of age. You are counting all of your lives. True?"

"It is a single life. I am the same person, the same magus, who was born from a living womb three-hundred and thirty-eight years ago. That mother's name was Thala, and she had white-gold hair and very large breasts. That's what I recall. Only that. At several intervals, I claimed again my body and I was born again."

"Here? In this large room?"

"Oh, no! It must be done in a special room. Such a room is hidden away under this arena. We cannot mix the games of people with the magic of magi. They are two different sports. No magic will occur with uninitiated people getting involved. I could not allow even you, who comes to brighten my day, into the rooms where I perform the Clona magic. It must remain completely clean."

Corlan waved him off. "I have no interest in seeing the room. It is enough I have two girafors to bear my supplies on this trek."

Joragus pointed at Tam. "And the boy? Is he real or a creature of Clona?"

"He is quite real." Corlan called to Tam. "Say hello."

"Hello," called Tam, stepping away from Corlan.

"Such a lovely sight! A young person not yet consumed by lust and vengeance. He is so beautiful."

"Yes, he's been a good helper on this trek."

"And you—I can sense your pains when I took your arm. Much lust and much vengeance in you. How do you endure it? Such a life you have led. The killings of many people. And many dragons."

"That is my occupation."

"Such an occupation suits one so filled with hate as you—"

"There is no hatred in me."

"—and you hide it well. I should be grateful you have not slain me as soon as you approached me. My declaration of magical power was what stopped your blade, was it not? You became curious."

Corlan laughed. "You're an old man. It's not my custom to harm old people. Or children. Or even drakes that happen by. I am trained to kill men in battle and dragons in the skies. The gods called me to this task. The training I have completed is for this occupation, and I am proficient at my skills."

"Yes...yes...proficient."

"Now we require food," said Corlan. "We cut some tail meat from the drake that died on the hillside. Where may we build a fire?"

Joragus shook his head, crossed his arms in front of his chest.

"Not in here. No fire should burn here."

"It would be small."

"No, you must go out if you want to make a fire."

Corlan pursed his lips, nodded. "Then we shall go out to cook our dinner." He called to Tam. "Feed the girafors—half ration. Give me the drake tail and some dragonfire. I'll go outside and cook it and bring it you." He glared at the magus. "Then I'll be happy to serve you some delicious drake tail."

Corlan carried the wrapped drake tail meat in one hand and a sheet of silver metal he grabbed off the floor inside the temple as he exited. The metal seemed like it had been a small door ripped away from the box it closed over. It would make a suitable cooking surface.

He arrived at the fire-pit, juggling the meat, the metal sheet, and the torch. Stabbing the butt of the torch into the mound of ash in the pit, he dared gaze again at the broken, burnt bones in it. He thought of the people who were burned—executed?—sacrificed? He knew he was far from home now.

Placing the metal sheet on top of the debris, he set the tough yet moist chunk of drake tail on the rim of the fire-pit and reached into his trouser pouch for another chip of dragonfire. The night was dark and he heard far-off noises like a herd of animals planning an attack. He continued to feel movement at the edges of the plaza as he lit the dragonfire cube and placed it on the metal sheet.

Perhaps the ghosts of the dead are still here. Perhaps they are jealous I'm still alive.

When the metal was glowing white, he stabbed the drake tail with his sideblade and dropped it onto the sheet. It sizzled immediately.

So far away from the city now, he mused, and so far away from his destination. He had to be careful. There was no help out here, no place to go if he got any injury. Only the magus.

Magus! And the old man who claimed to be a magus. He had to be watched closely, too. If he did have any magic powers, they could be in danger. *Maybe he is a trickster!*

Corlan stared off at the entrance to the temple, a faint flicker of the light within making its way out through the corridor to the plaza. An old man living alone in such a forlorn place, for so many years, he surely must be lame in the head. Of what use was he? Why did he stay in this lonely place? How did he survive?

He thought more on the old man, using the unfamiliar name of Joragus, and sought whatever conspiracies he could conjure, until the meat seemed cooked. When it was smelling like something he would gladly eat and not the sour-bitter odor of most other dragon flesh, he speared it with his sideblade and wrapped it again.

As Corlan made his way into the temple and down the corridor with the torch tucked under his arm. The sweet-smelling meat he carried teased his nose.

When he entered what the magus called the arena, he saw Joragus seated on the steps that rose to each level. Tam sat on the floor at his feet. The two girafors were at the opposite end of the floor, munching on the pellets put in a bowl for their dinner.

"...and that was when the plague visited," Joragus was telling the boy, "and that is the reason for so many bodies to be burned. Awful, yes! Yet the people soon made a ceremony of it, singing praises to them, marking their faces with the purple essence of the *hyaga* bushes, the same as you passed on the hill coming up here. They wrapped the ravaged bodies in precious golden cloth. By the final days, there were too few remaining to light the fires or finish disposing of the bodies. The last of them wandered off, I suppose. I was young then so I did what I could to clean up the plaza. I saw that I was safe from the plague so it did not affect me carrying the remaining bodies to the fire-pit and burning them. At its worst, they tore down all their homes, burned everything. That was the only way to rid themselves of the plague. Then the plague was done. Now you see no city exists around this stone edifice. All gone, but for me."

The boy was enamored by the old man's stories.

"Here is dinner, your majesties," Corlan announced.

Joragus looked up and the boy turned in place.

"It smells better than I would have expected," said the magus.

"Let's hope it tastes good enough we don't become sick," Corlan said with a grunt.

He arranged the metal sheet with the roasted meat on it between them. Tam had pushed a broken seat over to them to serve as a table.

"I've got some greens back there," said the magus. He thumbed down the corridor behind them, passing between the levels. "Perhaps your kitchen boy could throw a salad together."

"I can do that! Chef showed me how to do it. Cutting vegetables is my specialty."

"Then go off to my kitchen," said Joragus. "In the cabinets to the left you will find the vegetables I have, put away in bins. I grow them in the garden I keep under a glass roof. Choose as you like and make us a delightful dish. There's a bottle of oil on the table, too, that can be used as a dressing. Add some vinegar and peppers if you wish."

Tam hurried away.

Joragus turned to Corlan. "I've been telling him the history of this place. I tried to keep it light but the truth is much darker."

"How so?"

"They became cannibals. People eating people. Neighbors killing neighbors just for food. The bones you saw out there in the plaza were the last of them, fighting each other *for food*. And the food was each other." He stroked his beard. "I didn't want to frighten the boy."

"He's witnessed terrible things on this trek already." Corlan gave a glance in the direction Tam had gone. "I'm sure he can stand strong while hearing the truth about this place."

The magus gazed across the arena, as though seeing ghosts playing a game. "I, too, consumed the flesh of the people who lived here," he said in a low voice. "I knew it was wrong. Everyone knew it was against the tenets of our religion, yet there was no other food when the Great Fire came upon us. Crops burned. The ground went dry. People starved. First they ate the animals they husbanded, next the pets. Then the older people were eaten, then the sickly and the deformed, the lame and the crazed. Finally, the mothers ate their children. Fathers ate their wives. Then it was man against man. Some gave themselves up for the good of the crowd. Others fought to the death to dine on the vanquished. I saw all that—and I took my place at the table, too. I pretended to pray for them, asking the gods to send food, so they thought me of value and did not threaten to eat me. In the end it was just a show I gave to them to save myself. Since then, I vowed to only eat vegetables, flowers, roots. And there was precious little of those for many years. So I used the Clona magic to remake myself and live on until the plant life was reborn."

Corlan scratched his whiskers, keeping an eye on the corridor where the boy went.

"It's a sad tale, old man. If everything is the truth that you say it is, I would not judge you for what you did. Maybe I would have done the same. It is a matter of survival. It is a primal instinct to seek food and find it wherever it exists—even in despicable places."

"I didn't want the boy to fear me. I'm not going to eat him—or you. Be not afraid. I said I only eat plants now." He inhaled deeply. "I do believe it's been long enough for penitence. And that roast has such a delicious fragrance."

"Join us, then," Corlan offered.

They heard the boy's footsteps and watched him emerge from the corridor with a large bowl in his hands. The bowl was filled with leafy plants and chunks of roots. A moist gleam covered the top.

"Well done!" Joragus exclaimed, clapping his hands.

"It was easy," said Tam. "I learned all about cutting vegetables so I can make salads better than any boy in the kitchen."

"We should put you to work in your own lodge," Corlan added. "If we ever return to the Burg."

They began eating, having both meat and salad. They took from the communal bowl and plate using their own knives or their greasy fingers. Conversation resumed after the first minutes of chewing.

Joragus turned to Tam. "I was telling your master here about—"

"He's not my master," said the boy with a grin. "He's my teacher. I'm his apprentice. I'm going to be a dragonslayer, just like Corlan!"

"Yes, I'm sure you will be a fine dragonslayer—if you don't get eaten by one first." Joragus laughed. "Watch well and practice your craft. Swing a sword much?"

"He uses the dragonslinger!"

"Yes, a spring-loaded bolt flinger. Most original."

"It does the task," said Corlan, stabbing another cube of meat.

"I was telling Corlan here about the Great Fire." Joragus waved his hand in the air like he was conjuring flames. "You may be too young to have read a scroll about that event."

"I heard of a fire in the Burg," said Tam.

"That fire was started in the merchant quarter, going on ten years now," said Corlan. "Not the same as the Great Fire, boy."

"Yes, indeed, young one. This was much more serious. Long ago the Great Fire came upon us, even here in Metta. Yes, Metta was a great city at one time, largest on the entire river. This city controlled all trade up and down the river. After the War of the Five Princes, all power fell to Metta and the city grew to double the size of Cago, where the winning prince held his audience."

"That was...Darus?" asked Corlan, trying to pull his childhood lessons from deep within his head. He dared not appear uneducated in front of the boy.

"No, it was Nilas." The magus chuckled. "Darus was the brother who was executed after the final siege."

"The siege of Inati?" Corlan checked.

"Yes, that's right. You remember as well as I do."

"Who were the other princes?" asked the boy.

"There was Teran, the eldest, a half-brother only. And Urix, and Agor. Teran was the poet, the artist. Urix was the power broker, the mediator—alas, unsuccessful in the end. Agor was the general of the army of Nilas. Agor escaped from Inati during the trials. They all died in the end. Nilas lived the longest yet always in pain."

"Oh." Tam frowned.

"My grandfather and *his* grandfather were both named Urix after that ancient prince," said Corlan automatically.

"I'm named after my mother's grandfather!" sang the boy.

"Tam is a good name," said Corlan.

"No, it's really Tamondarus!"

Corlan laughed at the boy's boisterous declaration. "You're right. Tam is much better."

"You can call me Tamondarus if you want to."

"No, I'll call you Tam. Or just *boy*."

"It's like that other Darus, the prince who died."

"He was the evil one, you know," said Joragus. "That's the story. Stole Nilas' betrothed, he did, then made a union with her, the poor maiden. That'll start a war, all right!"

"Then what happened?" asked Tam.

"Nilas asked for her back. Darus refused."

Corlan was ready to stop yet the glow on the boy's face said he wanted to hear more.

"So Nilas threatened war and Darus laughed. So Nilas gathered his army, put Agor at the head, and marched them from Cago to Inati and lay siege there for many months. In the end, some treaty or such brought Prince Friden of Salou and his army to Inati. Neither side knew which one Friden's army would join so the five princes met to negotiate a peace. Darus was never one to give in, no matter how Urix tried to persuade him. When the parlay failed, Urix returned to Danapo and killed himself. Friden joined Nilas and they broke the siege."

Corlan stared at the boy, frozen in his amazement. He could see the boy imagining the scene.

"They put on a trial for Darus, accused him of many crimes, then hanged him by the neck. So, in the end, Nilas became the king. And he lived a long and miserable life, his brothers all gone."

"Everybody?" asked the boy.

Suddenly Corlan recalled more, his school lessons returning. "Oh, there's part of the tale where his betrothed returns, late in his life, and so he dies in her arms. Still, a wasted life. It's uncertain if that truly happened or some scriber added it to a scroll."

"So, *anyway*," Joragus jumped in, "it was one day at the height of our city's power that the whole western sky turned especially bright and the sunset, bold strokes of orange and crimson, never faded but burned all night. And all day. And many more nights and days. The sunset bled into the sunrise and we all knew something was not right with the world. Even the ground shook under us, and we believed the giant earth-wyrms were turning over in their daily combat."

"Earth-wyrms?" asked the boy.

Corlan gave a smirk. "We talked about them. Dragons without wings. They live below the surface in large tunnels. Scramble around on stubby feet. Some are as long as this temple."

"Longer than that!" Joragus barked. "I've heard the largest are as long as a mile." The magus winked at Corlan. "And thicker than this temple."

"Are they?" the boy asked of Corlan.

"A magus ought to know. I've never hunted earth-wyrms."

"So one day the sun never set and the fire started in the western realms, burned straight across to our lands here in the east. A range of fire as high as the towers of this temple, as wide as the horizon, burning mile upon mile, coming closer and closer to us. Flowing ahead of the mountains of fire were rivers of fire—molten rock that turned into searing liquid that turned everything in its path to steam."

"That's horrible!" said Tam. "How did you escape?"

"We didn't escape." Joragus gazed around the arena. "However, we built a new city on this hilltop. The rivers of liquid fire flooded the valley below. We were safe up here."

"That's good!" exclaimed Tam.

"From that day forth, everyone called out to the gods to save them and few ever heard an answer. Meantime, huge rocks were dropping from the sky and the clouds rained droplets of fire and ash. It covered everything, even us here on the hilltop. When we opened our eyes and crawled out of our burrows we could not believe what we saw. Not a single living thing remained here except the few of us who hid away."

Corlan frowned. "So you began again...."

"Yes—again. We built a new city—made a new civilization!"

"And eventually this new city invented a new game to pass the long resting hours."

"That is what they did after the Great Fire."

"When was the Great Fire?" asked Tam.

The light in the arena had dimmed. The magus gazed up at the ceiling, saw glow worms bumbling about, the light flickering. He clapped his hands loudly and the glow brightened.

"More than a thousand years ago."

The boy was amazed. He turned to Corlan. "When was the Burg built?"

"Well, the Burg was not hurt by the Great Fire. The Burg is in the mountains. The fire started far away and didn't reach the Burg. The city you know is the same as what my grandfather's grandfather knew. It goes all the way back to the War of the Five Princes. You may not know it from the school lessons they teach now, but back then, in those ancient days, the Burg sent half a brigade to aid Darus in the siege."

"But it was Darus that lost the war," said Tam, disappointment in his voice.

"True. Not many soldiers returned to the Burg after the siege."

Joragus waved five fingers at Tam, then pointed one at him.

"So, young dragonslayer, learn your history. The War of the Five Princes was almost two-thousand years ago. Hmm, I think. After that was the rise of Metta, this city, which lasted for five-hundred years. Or so it seems. Then came the Great Fire from the west, about one-thousand years ago. Probably. Then came the rebuilding of this city of Metta on this hill. Then I was born—the first time. Then the plague came. The plague ended about one-hundred years ago when the last people wandered off. And then I awoke many, many days after—until you two travelers disturbed my peace."

"And then dragons came," Corlan added. "The first dragon seen in the Burg was about two-hundred years ago, coming in from the west. It's common lore in the Guild Hall. We've seven generations of dragonslayers."

"Yes, the rise of dragons!" Joragus stared sternly at Tam, causing the boy to fidget. "Some say they came following the Great Fire, that they were born from it. The world tore open and they arose, flying into the skies. Who can say with any truth how they came to be? Yet they rule the skies now."

Corlan waved his hand, dismissing the idea. "When the gods mean to punish you, they make great sport of it, and send you all they can imagine." He remembered his awful day back in the Burg.

"Including dragons?" asked Tam.

"And we are headed to their nesting ground to stop them."

Tam's eyes widened.

"All that history! And so many horrible things happening!" said Joragus. "Now you two visit, from far up the valley. And I do not know what I shall do after you leave. Shall I return to my garden and make salads every day? Shall I sleep as often as I like, to make the days fall as quickly as possible? Shall I use Clona magic once more to continue living another long life? Shall I write another scroll?"

Tam's face brightened, a grin spreading from ear to ear. "Why don't you come with us?"

10

The Reckoning

CORLAN LAID OUT HIS BEDROLL and Tam doubled the blanket he used as a mat on the second level near the steps. They did not want to be down on the center floor where the girafors slept in their standing position. The first level was quite dirty but the second one was not as bad and a few clenched bunches of straw from the magus swept away the debris down onto the first level.

"I'm not sure it's a good idea for the magus to come with us," said Corlan as they lay still so the glow worms wouldn't light up at the top of the dome. "We don't know where we're going, or what'll happen next. It's already dangerous. Besides, an old man would slow us. If dragons came upon us — and that is likely — it would take extra effort to protect him."

"But he's an old man," said Tam. "We can't just leave him here for another hundred years."

"Another hundred years likely wouldn't be any worse than the past three-hundred years he's been here."

After they ate the last bite of drake tail they could fit into their bellies and the final leaves and roots of the salad, Tam had taken the dishes away to the kitchen. He was instructed to leave the remaining meat to dry so they could take it as rations for the trek. Meanwhile, the two adults continued discussing the reign of King Hubor and the conflicts the city of Metta had with a warrior cult of women.

Returning, Tam had helped the magus to his feet and Corlan had escorted him along the corridor, back into the living quarters he had fashioned in rooms under the seating levels.

It was a small apartment, clean and spare. A cot and a stand full of scrolls filled one side of the room. Against the other walls were shelves overflowing with more scrolls, many of them in cases. Some of the scrolls were maps and Joragus showed them to Corlan. They searched a bit and found a map of the valley before the river dried up. At one time it was called the River Oh.

The magus had begun picking items he thought might be useful and placed them into an open trunk.

"We won't be able to carry a trunk," said Corlan. "The girafors can barely carry our supplies as it is. And the male struggles to carry the two quivers of bolts."

"Never a worry, I told you." The magus continued scanning the room, selecting items to take. "I have my own transport."

"You do? Is it another beast made with the Clona magic?"

"Why would you assume that?"

"Because no other animals but dragons exist here."

"And drakes," Tam added.

"There are plenty of animals." The magus pointed to the floor and the ceiling as though expecting animals to be hiding in each location. "The animal I have is made with Clona magic, yes, and it will serve me well on the journey."

"What is it?"

"Magi before me, who used the Clona arts, named them *donkor*. It is the name of the original animal plus a special identification code. I named the ones I have Ika and Gum. They are male and female — like the two girafors you have."

"Our girafors are Pex and Elo," said Tam.

"You have two of them?" Corlan asked the magus.

"Yes. It takes two to pull the cart."

Corlan's eyes widened. "You have a cart?"

"Yes." Joragus had looked askance at Corlan. "That is what I said. You heard me say it. So it is so. Do not be such a fool."

Corlan had grimaced, wondering then whether or not he would welcome the old man on their journey. Joragus just might make the journey seem much longer.

"At least he has a cart," said Corlan, flat on his back upon the bedroll. "That will lighten our burden. But it will slow us."

"I can ride on the cart, too," said Tam, happily.

"And I walk? Is that the plan?"

"You like to walk."

"I can't ride a girafor. They are still youth, no more than nine feet tall. So I must walk."

"We can all ride the cart."

"Might be too heavy for a pair of donkors to pull it. We will see how strong they are."

"We could take turns riding the cart," said Tam.

"You're a generous boy."

Corlan stared up at the ceiling a while, nervous at the possibility of glow worms dropping down upon him as he slept. The boy did not seem to have any such fears. The old man had retired to his quarters under the seating levels. All was quiet inside the temple.

Outside, a rough grating sound gradually awoke Corlan. He lay still, listening, too tired to awaken further, wishing to fall again into the slumber he needed. There had been images of Petula lazing beside a stream, pretty flowers about, her beautiful eyes gazing into his eyes, a few words of affection passing from her lips. Her hand touching him.

The noise increased and Corlan snapped fully awake. He sat up, listening. The sounds were outside and he heard the noise bouncing through the corridor leading in from the entrance. Corlan knew there was nothing to keep a curious animal or a human from wandering inside. If he and Tam had come upon this edifice, then another human seeking shelter might also.

Grabbing his sideblade, Corlan got up in the darkness and faced where the corridor opened into the arena. His movement startled the glow worms and they produced light that filtered down. He waited a minute more, expecting to see a huge shadowy figure approach.

The sound was multiplied: several instances of the same kind of rough, gravelly noises, but from more than one or two sources. He decided it had to be a gathering of beasts, likely drakes, attracted by something.

With a glance at the boy, even though he couldn't see him clearly in the dim light, Corlan stepped lightly to the end of the level and went down the steps, crossed the center floor where the girafors stood asleep, and headed to the entrance. As he stepped past them, the girafors awakened, turning their heads to follow him.

Before he was even half-way along the corridor, he could see movement outside on the plaza. Shadows splashed back and forth across the walls. Faint moonlight filtering through clouds showed him what he feared.

The wide plaza had filled with a convention of drakes!

Corlan stood at the entrance, blade in hand beside his hip, hiding in the shadows. The plaza undulated with shadowy motion. He tried to count them...twenty, no, twenty-six...thirty-one of them. They stood in small groups, like families, large and small bodies, different colors but all of dark hues. The largest group huddled near the square depression at the center of the plaza. The drakes there were nosing at the wall that ringed the fire-pit, as though they were searching for something.

Dinner! Corlan's stomach tightened. *They smell the roasted meat. They know their kin was cooked there. Now they've come to mourn.*

He dared not show himself. Although drakes were usually calm and harmless when unprovoked, he worried that they might trace the scent of their kin to the entrance of the temple and then inside it. They might think to avenge the death of their kin.

Then came the cries of greeting. Four dragons descended out of the moonlight-streaked sky—two grey-bellies, the first tree-eater he had seen in ages, and a juvenile mountain-master. He had not been able to see what direction each of them had come.

The dragons alighted among the herd of drakes, who moved to make space for them on the plaza. They seemed to share an affinity. The drakes showed no fear of the dragons and the dragons did not seem eager to snatch a drake as a meal. As Corlan watched, the two groups seemed to be communicating with each other through an assortment of growls and cries and grumbles.

A gathering of beasts from above. Never a good thing.

Corlan wished he'd been able to bring an army with him. The trek he had proposed was certain to end in death. He should have accepted the prison option. Petula could visit him, at least.

Some forty beasts now occupied the plaza.

Corlan retreated inside the temple, moving quickly but quietly up the corridor, into the center of the arena.

"Tam, wake up," he called in a hushed voice, standing on the lower level and reaching up to shake the boy.

Tam opened his eyes, started to speak but Corlan clapped his hand over the boy's mouth.

"Outside is a convention of dragons. We must be very quiet. We don't want them to hear us and come in here."

Tam nodded. Corlan released his hand and the boy sat up. Both of them knew what to do: pack quickly, be ready to flee, and be ready to defend. They had practiced it too often. Corlan took the dragonslinger from where it leaned against the next higher seating level, checked that it was loaded. There were two more iron bolts resting beside it.

The girafors sensed something was amiss and stirred, their hooves clicking against the center floor's wooden tiles.

Corlan pointed to the corridor leading under the levels, the way to Joragus's quarters. Tam nodded and continued gathering their belongings as Corlan hurried to get the magus.

"What is this outrage?" grunted the magus, roused from his sleep.

"There's a gathering of beasts in the plaza."

"Again?"

"What do you mean *again*?"

Joragus yawned. "They congregate there from time to time."

"Why didn't you tell me?"

"It didn't seem important. They gather once in maybe six months. To what purpose I do not know. They do not eat or fight."

"They seem to be communicating among each other."

"Talking? You think so?"

"I watched them. The drakes and the dragons—four varieties. The sounds they made seemed in patterns. One makes sounds, another responds with similar sounds."

"Probably they are discussing the weather. It has been unusually warm this autumn."

"It's likely more serious than the weather!"

"Yes, I once considered they could communicate with each other, much like any animal species, I suppose. All creatures communicate with their own."

"But they are drakes and dragons."

"Cousins."

Corlan grunted his impatience. "Will they depart without incident or do we need to find a way to escape? We cannot cross the plaza. There are forty or so beasts out there now."

"Yes...."

"Yes to which?"

"They should depart soon."

Corlan watched the magus stare at his trunk, the lid opened, its contents fully packed. He wondered if they could still use the donkors and the cart to escape. And the girafors, too. Would they be too slow?

"Is there a back way?" asked Corlan. "Another exit?"

"Oh, yes." The magus pointed past the kitchen area. "It leads out to my garden. Through that passage is a large room. It once contained several ancient wagons. Then people pulled them out and destroyed them. They thought they were evil."

"Where does that direction go?"

"The road winds down the hill, of course."

"Does it turn back to the valley?"

"Eventually—"

Suddenly they heard the boy shouting, calling for Corlan.

He rushed out through the corridor and into the center floor area. Tam was standing with the girafors, pulling on the ropes to keep them under control. They were scared.

Corlan saw the reason for their alarm. In the narrow opening of the corridor leading in from the entrance stood a medium-sized drake and a small two-feet just behind it. The drake seemed an adult and barely fit through the narrow space. The two-feet, mostly green with brown stripes along its back and tail, its two wings open and flapping behind its shoulders, squawked its surprise at finding a boy and his girafors inside.

Corlan rushed to Tam with sideblade drawn.

The two-feet stumbled forward, pushing up and over the drake, standing tall on its large webbed feet, squawking louder.

Corlan charged ahead and in the same swift motion swung his sideblade at the two-feet, catching the blade across its throat and opening a long crevasse. The wound unleashed an orange fountain of blood. As the two-feet turned to retreat, the blood sprayed over the drake's head. The drake stepped back, shaking its head to avoid the blood and battered the side wall of the corridor.

The drake let go a ferocious roar, a sound Corlan had never heard any dragon make. Fangs were shown. Teal eyes became red. The drake bounded forward at Corlan and he was forced to retreat.

"Take the girafors up a level," Corlan shouted to Tam.

The boy struggled to get the girafors to climb the steps.

Corlan circled around the center floor as the drake pursued him on thick legs and lumbering gait—faster than a hippor.

The two-feet collapsed, boney chest down on the floor. Orange blood pooled on the wooden tiles, running out to the center area. The drake stepped in it as it chased him and Corlan saw the liquid was becoming sticky as it dried. The drake found its feet hard to move; each step required effort to lift its stubby foot up and shake itself loose from the blood. More roars from the drake.

Corlan measured the angles, counted the steps over to where the dragonslinger leaned, always loaded and ready to fire.

The drake kept its eyes on Corlan, roaring its displeasure.

A new dragon appeared from the entrance corridor—a grey-belly with reddish horns on its forehead and nose.

Corlan feigned a step left and the grey-belly looked that way. Then Corlan rushed to the right and dove for the dragonslinger.

"Shoot!" Tam screamed, pulling the girafors away.

Corlan swung the dragonslinger into his lap and checked that the launch spring was screwed back to the first position of three: the one for short-range use. It was. He launched the bolt, hitting the drake behind its shoulder, penetrating to half the bolt's length.

He quickly loaded another bolt and set himself against the steps to take on the grey-belly.

"Take the girafors back through the passage to the old man," he shouted to Tam. "We have to escape out the back."

Corlan fired the next iron bolt at the grey-belly, striking it in the throat directly under the lower jaw. It did not cut deep enough into the throat to hold there. The bolt slipped loose, hung down, and the grey-belly's foreclaws flicked it out. A thin line of reddish-pink blood ran down the grey-belly's chest as it plodded awkwardly to the center floor where the drake's body lay.

Corlan slapped his sideblade against the stone of the level beside the stairs, wiping off the two-feet's sticky orange blood.

The grey-belly wavered, rose tall over him, opened its full-sized wings in the great hall, guarding itself with foreclaws drawn.

Instead of squawking at him, the grey-belly took deep breaths, each deeper than the previous, stoking itself for what Corlan knew was coming next.

"Back! Back!" Corlan cried out to Tam. He did not see them, did not know they had already escaped down the corridor leading to the magus's quarters.

The grey-belly raised its wings, forming a shield around its head, shoulders, and chest. Its eyes brightened, flickered as though it was entering a trance. Then came the tell-tale hiccup, followed by the blast of fire straight at Corlan.

He timed his dive perfectly, dropping into the narrow recessed trough between the center floor and the first level. His shirt sleeve caught fire. He slapped at it until the flames went out. Black smoke rose from his arm. He had two heartbeats to get up and run before the grey-belly could conjure another fire-breath.

At the opening of the corridor into the arena, two more drakes appeared. Behind them, another grey-belly appeared, head bobbing, sniffing the air, excited by the scent of fire-breath.

Corlan jumped up and dove over the broken metal railing, falling down into the corridor leading to the magus's quarters. He scrambled up, the dangerous end of the dragonslinger clasped in one hand, the last bolt in the other hand, and ran down that dark corridor.

He burst into the apartment. "Run! Run!"

Turning in every direction, he saw no one, nor the girafors.

Another door was open beyond the kitchen. He saw the dark sky outside, just enough sunrise illumination to notice the silhouette of a cart waiting there.

"Corlan!" called Tam. "We're here!"

Fire stormed through the corridor.

Corlan heard the roar, then felt the heat coming up behind him as he ran out of the apartment, exiting through the kitchen and the door that led into the large room the magus said once had housed ancient vehicles. It was empty now, but he saw the wooden cart with two donkors hitched, waiting for him. The two large outer doors had been raised.

The magus sat on the cart's bench, Tam beside him. The two girafors were tethered behind the cart.

Corlan ran toward them, the weight of the dragonslinger causing him to stumble.

"Let's go! Hurry!" he cried. "They're breaking into the temple! They're stoked and firing!"

"Patience, slayer," said Joragus. "Donkors have their own pace."

"They better learn to quick-march if they want to live. I seriously recommend the donkors learn to gallop!"

"They do not know the gallop," said the magus. "Is that the latest dance in your burg?"

Corlan wanted to grab the man and throw him from the cart. He wanted to take the reins himself and urge the donkors to hurry, but the magus snapped the reins and the donkors started off, pulling the cart reluctantly.

Corlan hefted the dragonslinger onto the back of the cart as he ran after it. As they moved off, he then tried to swing himself around and hop backwards onto the rear of the cart but it was moving away and he did not time his leap well. The back of his head struck the trailing edge. He felt himself crash to the ground.

On his back, Corlan gazed up and saw new dragons winging their way to the hilltop. The sky was melting into fire, sunrise mixed with dragon's fire. Black silhouettes spotted the sky.

"We're all going to die!" screamed Tam.

"Patience, good fellows," said Joragus.

Corlan saw one particular dragon above, a true mountain-master, the largest kind of dragon, focusing on the puny folk in the cart. It pulled up, hovering in the air with its giant wings calmly waving back and forth like mighty flags, maintaining its position above them.

"That's not very polite," said Joragus, standing up in the front of the cart where it had rolled to a halt a few feet away. He called back to Corlan, still on the ground.

The dragonslayer recognized the stoking of fire in the dragon's mighty belly, knowing they were all about to be burned to death. As he called to the gods, the mountain-master threw back its thick, ridged neck, giving a hot cough and a terse gagging noise as a half-hearted warning. Then the beast unleashed its great stream of fire straight down upon them.

Corlan was slow to open his eyes. He sensed his condition, his mind checking through his body, searching for injuries, expecting to be dead, burnt to a crisp. Yet he was not.

Then he turned and saw the magus standing behind the cart, his arms raised as his beard blew back over his shoulder. The sleeves still reached almost to the ground. His gaze met the last of the fading stars as the bright sunrise spread toward them, then covered them.

"You see, dragonslayer," Joragus spoke, maintaining his gaze skyward, "the powers of an old man remain. I had thought them lost forever. Yet now we are safe."

Corlan lifted his head, found himself on the back of the cart. The donkors had pulled at their slow, steady pace so they were about to descend the hill. The temple on the hilltop was behind them.

"Surprised?" asked the magus, turning and walking aside the slow cart.

"Yes, surprised." Corlan took a deep breath. "I thought we were done. How did—"

"He called forth a spell," said Tam excitedly.

"A spell, eh?" Corlan was pleasantly convinced.

"One does not live through three iterations of Clona magic without learning a few spells. The invisibility cloud is most useful when under attack. The dragons no longer see you and they turn away."

"But it was about to fire."

The magus climbed aboard the cart, taking a seat on the riding bench next to Tam. He took the reins from the boy.

"The first spell provided a shield over us. I was able to harden the specks of minerals in the air, to turn them into a fortress over us. The fire-breath was sent away, splitting to either side of us, raging over the ground. It was lucky the boy called me, told me you had fallen off the cart. We got you into the cart. The ground was scorched then, yet we were all safe."

"Then the dragons all flew away!" Tam exclaimed, clapping.

"Flew away? All of them?"

"Yes, all."

"How do you know this? Did you count them?"

"The sky was scattered with them," said Joragus, maintaining his pose as the mighty magus. "Dozens of dragons. Many varieties. Just as you said. Their meeting was adjourned and so they departed."

Corlan rubbed the back of his head, felt the bump.

"Was that your doing? Or they gave up once we were invisible?"

"Hard to say. We do not speak the same language."

Joragus shook the reins, urging the donkor to quicken their pace. He expelled a sigh. "We should be well beyond their attention now."

"They are gone now?" asked Corlan.

"If they had gathered in order to forge a plan against us, then we were no longer present to be the subject of their conspiracy. Their dragonly king dismissed them, or so it seemed from my vantage point."

"A king of dragons?" asked Corlan, shaking his head.

"A dragon king!" Tam exclaimed.

"They must have a king, as surely as humans are led by kings," said the magus.

"They are mere beasts, not men," said Corlan.

The magus scoffed, rubbed his weary arms. "You think so much of your kind. All you humans...."

"I'm a human, too," cried Tam.

Corlan gave Joragus a smirk. "You are my kind, also."

"Not quite. I am a magus." Joragus grinned like he'd said a joke. "I am a magus who is in his fourth iteration. I know much more than you ever will. You and your boy, together, know only as much as my middle finger knows. And I'm not counting the fingernail."

That shut up Corlan for a while.

The donkors pulled the cart down the hillside, passed the purple *hyaga* bushes that liked eating meat. The roots had disappeared and the blossoms were open to the sunshine. The cart descended further down the hillside, winding around the hill, all the way to the shore of the riverbed. They left the old road of flat stone and rolled onto the dirt and sand.

"I cannot maintain a spell for long," said Joragus with a sigh. "I become weak, and that's not what I seek. That effort was quite a test. Yet no more a bothersome pest. Now I must rest." He chuckled. "It is fortunate that I had no need to exert myself that way for a long time. For years! So I had the strength to shield us, then to hide us. And I receive no thanks from you!"

Corlan roused. "Thanks."

"I should think a proper courtly thanks would be due."

"Thank you, Your Majesty!"

"Not much honesty in your voice."

"Thank you, Your Magus-ty!"

"Somewhat better...."

"Well, I did hit my head on the end of the cart, remember. I need time to recover, too."

"I must rest, as well. You take the reins, dragonslayer. Keep to the straight path. Do not waken me till we reach our camp—or if dragons return overhead."

"I'll wake you after the dragons have been slain."

"That's perfect!"

11

An Unsteady History

AS THE DAY CRUMBLED AWAY, the sun burned lower and redder, casting ominous shadows along the rough shoreline of the ancient riverbed. Corlan guessed the channel was a mile across at that point. The cart held steady, creaking as the donkors kept to a regular pace and the tethered girafors followed.

"I have the faintest flicker of memory from my first iteration," said Joragus, thinking aloud as he held the reins. "I was a prince, I feel. Or my father was a king, at any rate. Someone of high repute, certainly. I recall the silver stars on his shoulders. Then I think I was a soldier, rejecting my inheritance and accepted stripes of service on the sleeves of my uniform. I proved myself skilled at combat and gained some notoriety. Yet that was not enough for me, so I exiled myself. It all seems so clear to me now —"

"That's not your story," Corlan grumbled, swaying as the cart rolled on. "It's my story. I told you before."

"Ah! That must be where I heard it. So it's not my story?"

"I said it all before, when we first met," said Corlan. "Your story is very different. You said you became a magus when you lifted a lady of the Court off a broken chair before she could sit on it and become injured. The broken ironwork frame would have — how did you put it? — it would have skewered her lovely bottom."

Joragus tugged on his beard. "I told you that story?"

"Yes, you did. This is the third time."

The old man cocked his head. "I suppose it's true, then. Just by the power of my mind I levitated her just high enough above the errant ironwork to avoid the skewering. She thought she appeared graceful. None knew it was me, of course, holding her up. I was only a youth lost in a crowd of diners. Sadly, she never suspected it was me. We might have had lovely children."

"You never told her?" asked Corlan.

"I was a servant." He glanced at Tam. "Little more than a kitchen boy. How could I ever speak directly to such a person? It would have been...inappropriate."

"Corlan's got a lady, too," said Tam, happy to spill a secret.

He glared at the boy. "She remains in the Burg."

They rode on a while.

"Likely I'll never see her again," Corlan muttered.

They rode further.

"She'll meet some other dragonslayer, have three or four or five children with him, and die a miserable old woman on the day when I finally return to the Burg."

A few more miles passed.

"That's a gloomy story," said Joragus. "I knew it would be. You have all your secrets embroidered on your jerkin. You have the look of a man possessed by demons. I saw it the first instant I lay my eyes on you. You are running away from your demons yet they are inside you and so you cannot run from them."

"He's got demons?" asked Tam.

"He knows it," Joragus responded, "yet he refuses to believe it. Or to do anything to remove them."

"Enough of that dream talk!" Corlan grunted. "You're talking magic spells, not any true thing."

"If you got demons, you need to get them out," said Tam.

He grinned, curious. "How to do that?"

"You must frighten them," Joragus answered. "They will flee you when you face death. It's the only way."

"That's a hard way to do it," said Tam.

Corlan kept his eyes on the horizon ahead, wishing the donkors could pick up the pace. He didn't know where they were going, but he wanted to arrive as soon as they could, just to have the excuse of setting up the camp and shut down talk of his *demons*.

"They'll be gone...soon enough," said Corlan.

As the last of the sunset faded to black, they set up the camp. Tam shared some vegetables from a bin he saved from the old man's kitchen. The rest of the meal was dried drake meat. Corlan thought of their rations. Now, with the magus, they had another mouth to feed. With all the dragons that had gathered around the temple, it would have been good to get more fresh meat, even if it was a bitter portion. With the right sauce....

The old man lay back after the final bite of dinner, complaining of not having anything to smoke. He talked about the weeds they used to dry and roll up in a large leaf. They set it to fire and breathed in the smoke—yes, just like a dragon! Tam was interested, asking many questions.

Corlan sat back against the cart wheel, thinking back to his final tryst with Petula.

"...and it was somewhere in my first iteration," the magus was saying as Corlan's attention returned, "I think I had a different name. Joragus. I know my name was different in my first iteration. It's hard to delve so deep into my mind's stores these days. It is nearly without bottom. Dangerous." He pretended to blow smoke from his lips. "Joragus.... Jorge...Uss. Or perhaps: Jorge Yoo'ess. Hmm. Yes! That may be it. I distinctly recall being called *Hor-hay*, not Jorge. So my family name must have been Yoo'ess."

"What's that mean?" asked the boy.

"Yoo'ess? It must be the name of a place. My family's homeland. The place they came from. So I was Jorge of Yoo'ess. Just like Corlan here is Corlan of the Burg. Jorge of the Yoo'ess. I like that name. Not a cloud-head magi name like possibly Ovu or Thetas or Mbowi, not like those. It's a proper name, a name for a man."

Tam smiled. "Do you want us to call you that name?"

"Certainly, young man." He pursed his lips. "If you wish. Call me Jorge of the Yoo'ess."

"I will!"

"Now I recall another name," the magus said with a long draw of breath, as though he was preparing another speech. "It must be who I was before the first iteration—before any of the Clona magic was used on me. Someone must have wished me to live on."

"When was that?" asked the boy.

"Oh, long before anything around here became like it is now." The magus grinned at the boy, enjoying the admiration. "You can never imagine the way the world was before the Great Fire. It was all green and covered with all manner of plants—flowers and trees, grass and bushes, everywhere. Lots of water, too. Everyone was well fed and happy. It was an easy life. They did not need to work so much, so they invented games to play." He swung his arm back in the direction they had come.

Tam turned to have a look. "They did?"

"You saw the place they built for one kind of game. They used to throw a ball to each other. Between members of their team, that is. The other team tried to stop them, to knock it down or catch it. I'm not sure of the rules, but if they took the ball over a line on the floor they got some numbers. The team with the highest number at the end of the night was the winner. They had a great feast and could mate with the most beautiful of the maidens who cheered for them. The losing team got nothing. In fact, they were usually executed the next day. That's what I always heard."

"They never got another chance to play and win?"

"I suppose they were the best they could be. How would they win a second game if they lost the first game?"

"Because men are cruel," Corlan spoke up.

"Not all men," said the magus, giving a reassuring glance to the boy. "There are all kinds of men. Just as many good ones as the bad. Every so often they would meet in what they called a *war*, to see who was stronger. In some wars, they only wanted to know whose ideas were best. Yet in other wars, they wanted some land or a city or all the things in the city, or they wanted the women."

"They fought for women?" asked Tam, puzzled.

"Oh, men always want women. The gods arranged the world that way."

"Some wars are fought over food," Corlan growled.

"That may be true in your fighting days," said the magus, "yet you managed to survive. Did you get your food?"

"I meant food for the people. All people." Corlan turned to Tam. "Don't let him convince you wars are for glory. I led an army into battle to take back a great swath of land stolen a decade earlier from my lord's kingdom. Prime cropland. We needed it to grow food."

"And did you get the land back?" asked the magus.

"Yes, we did. And we grew crops on the land. And we harvested what we grew. And we ate the food."

"And then what happened?" asked the magus, a sly tone in his voice, as though he spoke just for Corlan's ears.

"They returned to take back the land. And the crops we grew."

"And the people starved."

"And they starved, yes."

"So wars make no sense...."

"Unless you have vastly superior forces and can hold what you take. The Prince of Bany didn't have a large enough army. Too many boys instead of men."

"Boys got to fight?" asked Tam.

"Not *got to*—had to!"

The magus waved his hand, dismissing Corlan's harsh words.

"Don't mind this slayer, boy. Everything was different before the Great Fire."

"They sent children into battle!" Corlan slapped his thigh. "They sent legions of children to a quick death! All the while the old men and arrogant princes watched from the safety of their balloons."

"And then came the Great Fire!" sang the magus.

"The Great Fire was long before I led an army into battle," said Corlan, calmer. "Your iterations are mixed up in your head."

"So it seems," replied Joragus with a nod. "In four iterations, one tends to confuse the dates. So you led children into battle.... Better a cleansing fire than a cleansing army."

"Yes, the Great Fire cleansed everything, made everything pure again. A fresh start. Is that it? Is that the blessing we deserved?"

"You have many demons within you," said the magus, calmly.

Tam seemed frightened so Joragus patted the boy's head.

"Instead, what we got—what we *deserved*," said Corlan, "were all these dragons to terrorize us."

"There have always been dragons," Joragus responded. "Within us and above us."

Tam stared at Corlan: a frown crossed his tired face as he looked away, lost in his thoughts. "Is it true?"

Rather than answer, Corlan moved to his bedroll, dropped down and stretched out.

"Leave him be," said the magus.

They traveled three days without seeing any dragons, rising before dawn and stopping just after dusk. They made camps at night and ate their meals. They talked less and less. When they did talk, it was only to complain. Joragus complained about having to leave all of his magic potions behind. He might not be able to use the Clona arts to regrow himself and he was already so old that this iteration might be his last. Corlan complained about Joragus's complaining. Corlan also complained about the slow pace of the donkors, even though it was faster than they had gone by foot with girafors carrying everything. Tam complained about the two adults sounding like the crew of kitchen boys arguing over the instructions for dinner the cook had left for them. To make the trip even worse, the donkors complained about having to pull a cart of complainers. The girafors were content to be led along the path, free of the burdens of quivers and bundles, yet they probably had complaints, too; however, being mute, they kept their complaints to themselves. Overhead, there seemed to be no complaints from any dragons.

And the cart rolled on.

On the fourth morning, an hour after they were on the road, a pair of red-bulls descended to the sand of the long-empty channel of the River Oh.

"Quick! Into that grove," Corlan shouted.

The humans jumped off the cart and together push it under the cover of the trees growing along the riverbed. The girafors followed without hesitation, ducking their heads under the tree branches. The donkors refused to budge, however. Tam coaxed them into the shade of the trees just in time.

The dragons appeared to be interested in mating, Corlan saw. They nipped at each other's faces, clawed at each other's backs, and growled their flirtations. Their wings opened and closed, curled over each other, blocking anyone's view of their intimate activity.

"What are they doing?" asked Tam.

"Those two seem to be in love," said the magus.

"It's true?" Tam asked Corlan.

"Yes." He watched the boy staring at the spectacle. "Maybe you best not look."

"The boy needs to learn about the ritual," said the magus.

"Time enough for that," Corlan said with a grunt. "We could be here, waiting on them, for another hour or so. Yet do not take a nap. They may require a snack when they finish, and if they detect us here, we become the snack."

The red-bulls, about twenty feet from nose to the base of a ten-foot tail, wingspan of fifty feet, were loud, trumpeting their pleasure, roaring their efforts. Fire was stoked and launched yet each was well armored and not harmed by the flames. The fire-breath seemed as random and unintentional as a pair of humans letting out rear air during vigorous exercise. The mostly red aerial beasts with black throat stripes were not kind to each other, however; they appeared more to battle each other, the winner having his/her way with the other. The ground shook beneath their antics. When the ground no longer shook, Corlan gave them a glance.

"They seem done now," said Corlan.

The dragons lay beside each other, wings folded, bellies pressed against the sand and dirt, legs and feet bent beneath their bodies.

"Give them another hour to sleep it off."

"Another hour?" Tam complained.

"I was about to nap for myself," said Joragus.

"Patience," said Corlan, trying to imitate the old man. "Tasty snacks await them."

Joragus waved his hand. "They will be too tired to hunt for us."

"After they rest, they'll be hungry?" asked the boy.

"Oh, yes," Corlan responded.

"I'm surprised they don't mate in the air," said Joragus, blinking. "I have seen many an aerial battle that was not fighting but actually their mating."

"Different species have different rituals. These red-bulls grapple in the air, then pull each other down to finish it." Corlan scratched his beard a while. "Red-bulls are usually in the north. These are the first I've seen in the valley." He sat up suddenly. "After they mate, they will certainly fly on to the nesting ground. The female will lay her eggs there. So we must follow their route."

"Is that true?" asked the boy.

"Everything I say is true," Corlan sneered.

"Is it?" asked the boy.

Joragus laughed and Corlan cautioned him to keep quiet. The red-bulls were still close by, sleeping off their exercise.

"Perhaps we should be away as they sleep," Joragus suggested.

"They could hear us leaving," said Corlan. "I would feel better if they left first."

After a few minutes, their casual conversation was interrupted by the mighty roar from the male red-bull as he rose to his feet, stretched out his wide red wings, and tilted his pointy head upward as if to call to the sun for more power.

"Here we go!" Corlan grunted.

The male red-bull danced around in a semi-circle, hopping back and forth from one foot to the other, shaking its wings. As he danced, the female squatted in appreciation, crying out and waving her head on its long neck. The bull-like set of horns on each of them clanged together many times as part of their ritual. Then the female arose and opened her wings to their fullest extent, in fact, wider than the male's wings. She seemed the larger of the two dragons. With that dominance, she launched herself into the sky and circled the spot where the mating had occurred. She sounded her call and broke from the circle to streak off to the southwest.

Corlan's eyes followed her trail, a string of black puffs of smoke.

Meanwhile, the male strutted in his own circle, shaking his horns and grunting.

Corlan saw the discharge in the sand. This fellow was rejected again. She toyed with him, made him think he was going to be the sire of her offspring, then tricked him into leaving his seed on the ground.

The male red-bull stalked down the riverbed, away from Corlan hiding under the trees, and threw himself into the air, flapping his wings as he gained altitude, heading north.

"We can go now," Corlan announced.

As they checked the donkors' hitches on the cart and the tethers of the girafors, Corlan thought of Petula. In a flash he regretted going on this trek. Even if he had been put into the prison, he would have been granted conjugal visits. Maybe. In time he would be pardoned. Then he would be free and with her.

"Thoughts of home?" asked Joragus, climbing onto the cart.

"Thoughts of something I left behind."

"We have all left something behind."

Corlan nodded, kept nodding as the cart jerked, started ahead. They rode out from under the trees, found themselves in more trees, a row of them on each side of the sand that marked where the main channel had flowed in ancient times. He was glad of the cover, hiding from the hot sun when it broke through the clouds, and hiding from dragons that might pass overhead.

"I sense you have regrets," said the magus. "I can feel irregular waves of energy burning off you."

Corlan glanced at the old man. "Strange powers you have."

"Perhaps it is not magic but ordinary empathy. You appear as a man who wishes he hadn't done something."

"True. I wish I hadn't done...." He thought a moment. "Many things."

"That is clear to anyone looking at you."

Corlan coughed, spit. "It is not easy being a dragonslayer."

"I doubt your dragonslaying is the cause of your regrets."

"Are you going to keep haranguing me with your head talk?"

Joragus chuckled. "Is it a woman problem?"

"Problem?"

"It must be a problem."

"Who's got a problem?" asked Tam, waking from his nap in the back of the cart.

"My dear fellow here has a woman problem. He has regrets. He is not happy being on this trek. He—"

"I certainly didn't expect to be taking a kitchen boy and an old wizard with me!"

Joragus waved his hand in the air. A cool breeze encircled the cart and the donkors snorted yet continued.

"Another magic trick?" asked Corlan.

"To calm your demons. They hate cool air."

"I hate hot air. Both this desert valley and your hard words."

"Very well," said Joragus, waving his hand again. "I'll talk with the boy about your problems. You may listen if you choose. Please do not interrupt our conversation, however. That would be rude."

"Me? Be rude?" He sneered, his frown pulling in most of his face. Then his face snapped free, popping back to its normal shape.

"Yes, you."

"He isn't rude," said Tam. "He just thinks about everything all the time. No time to rest."

"That is very astute of you," said Joragus.

"I've been watching him for so many days I lost the count."

"Thirty-nine," said Corlan in a low voice.

"That is a long journey," said Joragus.

"A thousand days yet to travel," Corlan added.

"Will we ever reach the nesting ground?" asked Tam.

Corlan nodded.

"I hope I live that long," said Joragus. "We have many places to visit along the way. Metta is high up the valley. As I recall, there was a city downstream called Unting. It also had a large temple. Not a word from there in many years. I wonder if they managed to rebuild after the Great Fire."

"Unting?" Corlan perked up. "I've heard of it. A nest of red-bulls were discovered near there. A team of dragonslayers cleaned it out. That was about twenty years ago. I was not a dragonslayer then, but seeing the drawings of the red-bull carcasses paraded through the streets impressed me. That made me want to try it."

"And you did!" shouted Tam. "Now it's my turn."

"You will learn day by day, boy, and not sooner."

Joragus waved his hands again, producing a cool breeze. "I sense someday the boy will save your life. So be gentle with him now or the moment may pass without success."

"So you must be kind!" sang Tam.

"Yes, Your Majesty!" Corlan said with a lilt in his voice.

"That's the spirit." Joragus clapped his hands. "We must play nice when we visit Unting—if anyone remains there."

"Why is that?"

"Why, everyone should be nice everywhere. We need each other. In the case of Unting, when I last did hear of people living there, they tended to eat visitors. Or was that Covin? I've forgotten."

Corlan sat up. "Eat? Even people?"

"Anyone not from Unting."

"Even boys?" asked Tam.

"Especially boys!" said the magus, glancing back at Tam.

"That is not acting nice, as you recommend."

"We will pass by Unting. There is no way to avoid it if you stay in this valley."

"Then we should pass it in the night."

Joragus stared ahead a while. "If you wish to have some comfort, you will wish to pause there."

"Why is that?"

"There are women...."

"You think I need women? ...a woman?"

"You're a man. I'm a man—used to be a young man."

"I have a lady back in the Burg. And I have a mission to complete so no time for dalliance with a stranger."

Joragus frowned. "You must have been put under a powerful spell by some witch. You bear all the traits of a man whose head has been filled with poison. The only cure is to get it out of you. Only then will you return to being a true man."

Corlan laughed. "I'm immune from poison. And magic spells."

12

Warrior Women

THE DONKORS' PACE was regular and the old man and the boy had slipped into slumber, but Corlan remained alert. There were always dragons that might spy them from above and swoop down for an easy meal. There might be drakes blocking their path. Or there would be a fork in the channel. He would need to determine which way was best to go. He was not concerned with encountering a city of cannibals or a village full of women desperate for a man, as the magus suggested.

That old man fills my head with so many tales!

He thought of the two days he'd spent in the Burg, and all the impossible things that had happened, how he had not considered everything very well before he boldly declared his plan. He wanted to go, sure, to prove them all wrong, yet he might have been too quick with his brashness.

And Petula....

I have to let her go. I might never return to her, anyway. I wish she hadn't pledged to wait for me.

The donkors balked at a rough patch of terrain ahead. Despite Corlan's urging, they halted before a small drop in the riverbed. The cart definitely could not go down it safely, Corlan saw. He reined them in and hopped down to study the situation.

The riverbed was cracked and the portion ahead was much lower than where the cart waited.

"What is this outrage?" the magus roared, coming to life in the back of the cart.

Tam looked over the top of the cart's riding bench.

"The way drops," said Corlan without emotion.

Tam jumped down, stood beside Corlan. "It's too deep."

Corlan glanced around, searching the red and brown shore, now spotted with trees and grass and bushes. Hard to see any path while covered by so much flora. He climbed up onto the cart, stretching tall, again surveying the area.

"Stay here," he said, jumping down.

"What are you going to do?" asked Tam.

"Find a way around this drop."

Corlan set his sideblade on his belt and grabbed a spear Tam had made by sharpening a long branch he found. He gave it a quick look, then handed it back to the boy.

"You know how to load the dragonslinger, right?" he asked Tam.

The boy nodded excitedly. "It's already loaded."

"And launch the bolt?"

More nods. "Just pull the trigger thing."

"Use it only if the dragon's mouth is open and you can see inside its gullet. Only launch it then. Otherwise, run and hide."

Corlan turned and ran across the reddish sand and brown soil to the riverbank, climbed up onto the short cliff there and walked along a path through stubby bushes until he was out of sight from the cart.

Tam turned to Joragus, flashing a big smile.

"You heard Corlan. I get to be in charge of the dragonslinger. I'm the apprentice. I get to launch the iron bolt."

"Calm yourself, boy. Your eagerness may yet summon a dragon. I do not wish to test your skills so soon."

"I will protect you. Don't worry."

"It is not in my disposition to worry. I have concerns, however. It is not for magic that I have lived so long."

"So how do you get to live so long?"

"First I was lucky, then I was smart. After that, I learned the Clona arts. I learned how to make animals from a handful of dust. Many people feared the dust. They thought it was evil, thought it was filled with tiny shards of evil, or was poisonous to them. There was much fear in the days of my youth—in my first iteration. The world in that age was alive with dangers. As I grew old, I decided to live again, and so I made myself."

Tam laughed. "That's a long time ago."

"Very long ago. I am in my fourth iteration, as I told you—my last, because of the dragons' breath that burned out my quarters. The problem with making myself again is that every time I am reborn, there must be someone to care for me. Born again means being a babe again. I will need a nurse. Until I finally grow enough to care for myself, say to my tenth or twelfth year."

"I'm twelve."

"And you have Corlan to care for you."

"Corlan's a dragonslayer, not a nurse."

"Indeed, he is. A strong man. A good man to take after."

"He doesn't beat me when I do something wrong. Not like Chef always did."

"Well, that's good."

"I will be a dragonslayer like Corlan."

"If you wish it.... You don't need to decide so young. Have a life of pleasure first. Let yourself grow bitter and slightly mad. Then you will be better suited for going out to kill dragons. It is an older man's occupation."

"But not as old as you?" asked Tam.

"Not as old as me, no." Joragus smiled as though remembering a happy day in his past. "And yet there are so many days I would wish to live again, over and over."

"But you lived a lot of days already."

"Yes, however, not those wonderful days I lived only once. If I could live those particular days over and over...."

"But you can still live a long time."

"A few years more, perhaps. Or months. On this trek it could be only a few days. Everything depends on the color of the sky, how full of dragons it might be."

"Then I will shoot them down!" Tam shouted.

"Easy, young prince. Do not be so eager for conflict."

"I'm not a prince. Why did you call me that?"

Joragus pursed his lips. "You remind me of a prince I once knew. In my third iteration. That's all. Slip of the tongue, kitchen boy. Slip of the tongue, all it was."

Corlan wandered up the rough slope, farther from the riverbank. To the north he saw a range of mountains. To the south, the same kind of view. Both ranges were covered with dark green forests. Down the valley, ahead in the direction they were going, he saw thicker vegetation. Those channels were choked with trees and he could not discern the riverbed.

He searched the skies every few minutes, which had gotten to be his habit. Nothing beat its wings in any direction. What used to be the venue of birds had been taken over by dragons. Not many birds remained; those that did remain were most successful by keeping to the ground. The flyers eventually succumbed to the reptilian aerials and vanished —

Just like the small dusty birds he found crossing his path, a line of plump, small-winged, ground nibblers. The lead bird, gray and white, wings too small for flight, studied him. The others in the line followed without any attention to him. Once they passed, he thought they could have made a good dinner.

Further along the trail, a natural cut through the brush, he saw a red- and gold-striped snake slither across his path. Later, a small, furry brown creature with a long, naked tail, ran before him. The land teemed with life!

As he strode parallel to the riverbank, he rose higher. Eventually he came to the end of the trail and met a sharp drop-off. From that precipice Corlan could see far in every direction. Behind him was the line of mountains running away. Ahead, the land sloped lower and the riverbed widened, its flora thinning. The main channel went to the left, to the south, he saw, while the former islands of the river had become hills along the north shore.

If only Petula could see this view.

For only a few times in his life had he ever paused to admire the beauty of a scene. The way the sunlight shone on the reddish soil of the riverbed, with the green flora and the blue sky impressed him.

We keep to the left.

Satisfied, he retraced his path back through the brush. Again, a few animals crossed his path. This time, he chased the ground birds and caught one. He held it by its feet in one hand and wrung its neck with the other. Dinner. He pulled out a net sack from his trouser pouch, shook it open, and slipped his catch inside.

Later he stepped on another snake, let it try to bite into his boot, then cut off its head with his sideblade. Its fangs were caught in the leather. He kicked the head off his boot and added the long body to the sack. Further on, he cupped a small furry animal in his two hands and suffocated it. He added it to his dinner sack.

Carrying dinner back to the shore, Corlan was feeling hungry, eager to have the food cooked.

His feet ached inside his boots, unused to hiking over uneven ground for so long.

Just a little more, he thought, taking a breath. Then he could ride on the cart, take off his boots, and let the breeze cool his feet. A few miles down the riverbed and they would camp for the night under the trees, have a good dinner, and sleep deeply.

He broke through the last clump of brush and halted.

Ahead of him were two humans—obviously female to Corlan's eyes, though they seemed to disguise themselves as birds, covering themselves with feathers, mostly brown but also a few that were red and blue. They seemed as surprised to see him as he was to find them. With brown skin and golden-brown hair, garments of dun leather decorated with blue and yellow feathers, they blended into the landscape. The women carried spears, though, and that caused him to reach for his sideblade.

Dropping the bag of dinner items, he measured the angles. In an instant he counted the odds of defending himself against both of them. Their spears were long enough they could skewer him before he could cut them with his sword. He decided it might be better to gain their trust, and so he did not draw his blade.

The woman closest to him spoke but her words meant nothing to him, all whistley and high-pitched like bird calls. The second woman pointed to the bag he dropped. The first woman spoke to the second and the second moved to inspect the bag.

"You can have them, if you wish," said Corlan.

The second woman, crouched over the bag, saw animal carcasses through the netting. She gazed up at him and a grin spread across her face. She spoke to him but again her words were merely bird calls to his ears. She seemed amused.

"I'm just going to continue on my way," said Corlan. He took a step backwards. "I'll leave you to continue whatever you were doing before I happened by. You can have the meat, too. Let's pretend we never crossed paths, shall we?"

He had taken five steps backing away, hands held up, as the two women watched him. They held their spears waist-high, more in a defensive posture than preparing to attack. He didn't notice the women coming behind him—not until he backed into the speartips.

"Ow!"

He halted, glancing back over his shoulder. Five women formed a semi-circle around him. As he turned to face them, the first two women moved closer to guard the rear.

"Now, now, ladies," said Corlan in as soft a voice as he could speak, "let's not be quick. I haven't done anything. And I sure do not plan anything, either. I simply wish to be on my way...far away...and out of your territory as quickly as possible. That's a fair deal, isn't it?"

One woman with red feathers hanging from her hair seemed to be in charge. She spoke immediately, cursing at him, it seemed, then gave instructions to the others. They rushed him and tied leather straps around his wrists, binding his hands to the strap they tied around his waist. Speartips were set against his belly and back, and he was led away.

It was becoming too dark to make out any details of even the flora closest to them. Even so, Tam would stand up in the cart and look around every few minutes, squinting. Then he would plop down beside the magus and let out an angry huff.

"He will return soon," said the old man.

"Maybe he forgot the way."

"I'm certain a man like him can find his way back to us."

"Then maybe he got killed by something."

"Killed? Let us hope not. Only he knows where our little army is going."

"It's not an army."

"I only said that as a joke. Sometimes you say something is more than it really is, just for the laugh. For example, if I say this is a simple journey we are taking, you know there is a lot at stake, a lot about which we must be careful. You laugh because you understand the difference."

"I don't feel like laughing."

Joragus nodded slowly, then climbed down from the cart.

"It's dusk. I doubt we will travel any more today, so let us set up the camp. Corlan will be pleased when he returns."

Tam was in agreement. Better to proceed as usual. Corlan knew what he was doing. He would be safe. He just got lost or maybe he walked too far to return so soon. At worst, he would join them by morning.

"Come, let's make a camp," said Joragus.

They moved the cart a hundred paces up the riverbed, angled to the side to avoid the drop. They rolled the cart beneath a grove of trees. The donkors and girafors were let loose. The donkors grazed on grass around the trees and the girafors grazed on the leaves up in the trees. Beneath the branches, Tam unloaded the bags of supplies and Joragus arranged them.

"I don't think he will return tonight," said the magus.

They chewed on rations from the pack: dried meat and dried fruit of two kinds, pinkish-red and dark green.

"It's too dangerous to move about in the dark."

"Maybe he ran away," said the boy.

Joragus could see how Tam was worried. "I am certain he will join us at the first cracking of dawn. Probably found a lovely pool to bathe in and lost track of the hour. Perhaps he got some fresh food and is enjoying himself a lot more than he deserves. We will scold him for it when he returns. He might even have crossed paths with a woman and had to spend some time getting to know her. Men do that, you know."

"Corlan has a lady back in the Burg," said Tam as though it was an explanation for everything. "He's going to return to her someday. He said so."

"Then I'm certain he will."

They spread out the bedroll and blankets as usual and turned low the dragonfire in the lamp.

Joragus awoke three times during the night, unsure what had startled him. Tam awoke twice, expecting Corlan to be strolling into the campsite as though nothing was wrong. When the sunrise broke the horizon, they awoke assuming Corlan would be there, asleep on a bedroll beside them, yet he was not.

"I suppose we should wait longer," said Joragus, helping Tam put together a meal.

"I don't know where to go, not without Corlan to lead the way," said Tam. "It's an accident I'm on the trek with him."

And the day wore on.

"Take a look at this," Joragus called from the rear of the cart.

He thought he would distract the boy a while. He had opened a case that contained many separate sections. In each section was a small glass bottle with a cork plugging the opening. He examined each of them.

"What's that?" asked Tam, coming up beside him.

"This is my magic. Each bottle has the powder of a different beast. I can grow them in a kitchen if the right devices are available." He pulled out one bottle, showed it to Tam. "See? This is the essence of an animal called *sheep*. Many of them were created. In fact, for tens of thousands of years. They provide hair for making clothing and then provide meat." He returned the bottle to its section, retrieved another. "This is *emu*. It's a large bird. It cannot fly. Yet it provides oils and meat. All animals provide meat, of course." He handed the bottle to the boy. "One of its eggs can feed a whole family."

Tam held it gingerly, staring at the purple powder inside.

"It sparkles," said Tam.

"Some of them do." He accepted back the bottle, handed another to the boy. "These are seeds. For making plants. This is called *melon*. It grows on the ground in long vines."

The boy seemed amazed by the collection of three dozen animal and plant powder bottles.

"You could start a farm with these," said Tam.

"Yes, we could. If we had good soil, good water, some rain, and a steady growing season."

"When we get to the end of the valley, maybe we can see if it's good for a farm."

"I believe Corlan said the end of the valley is where the dragons have their nursery."

"After we kill all the dragons, we can make a farm there."

"Yes...indeed." The magus scratched underneath his beard. "It may be possible. However, I wouldn't think it such good ground for making a farmstead. Didn't he say it was marsh?"

"Some of it is," said the boy. "But there is also dry land."

"So you've thought this through thoroughly?"

"Yes. We kill all the dragons. Then we plant the seeds you have. And we make the animals. We can build a house and live there and sleep in it. And I will grow up and be a farmer."

"I thought you wanted to be a dragonslayer."

"After all the dragons are gone, there won't be any dragonslayers needed. So I'll be a farmer."

"It's an excellent plan. I wish I'd thought of that long ago."

Joragus closed the case, resettled it on the back of the cart. The hard edge of the box hit a long canvas bag on the cart. A metallic rattling made him pause.

"Those are his swords," said the boy. "And other weapons."

He showed them to the magus: swords, knives, two axes, a short lance, a hammer, a halberd, clubs, an unstrung bow and dozens of arrows. Together it was much too heavy for the boy to lift.

"He is well-prepared," said the magus. "Perhaps we should keep a couple of those out. Never know when a nasty beast may happen upon us. I'll take one of those swords."

Tam agreed and selected two blades. He gave the longer one to Joragus and kept the other for himself, slipping it under his belt. He swaggered through the evening, pretending he was a soldier.

Two days passed. With no particular reason to get up, Tam slept late and Joragus had to awaken him.

"Another day," said the magus. "Better to be up and ready to run if a dragon comes."

Tam rubbed his eyes, sat up. "I just want Corlan to come back."

"Yes, yes.... Me, too."

They sat under the shade of the trees, like previous days. They talked about many things. They reviewed each other's histories again, each recounting requiring the adding of details glossed over in earlier tellings.

The day slipped into afternoon.

"I say we turn around and head back up the valley," said Joragus after a series of long strokes of his beard. He almost stepped on it, hitched it up onto his shoulder instead. "We will return to the temple and see what can be salvaged. That is the best plan, I think. If Corlan has not returned by tomorrow morning."

"Maybe he got killed," the boy lamented, pouting.

"It is always a possibility."

"Now I'll never learn to be a dragonslayer."

"Who's to say it wasn't a dragon that got to him?"

"He didn't take the slinger with him...."

"With only a sword he likely couldn't fight off the beast—"

"Let's leave here," Tam said, anger in his voice.

They packed everything not needed for the night, then resumed resting under the trees. The donkors were content to graze, as were the girafors, not comprehending the change of plans.

In the morning, they packed Corlan's unused bedroll and their blankets and tied everything securely on the cart, ready for a hard day's march. Tam hitched the donkors to the cart, telling Ika and Gum the new plan, then tethered the girafors, repeating the plan to Elo and Pex. Joragus walked around the grove of trees, leaning on his staff, searching for anything that may not have been packed. Tam waited on the back of the cart, sitting atop the pile of bags and boxes.

The morning sun burned orange, almost blinding Tam as he faced east. He thought he heard something and looked up, stared ahead, shielding his eyes against the sunlight—

A reddish cloud of dust boiled above the distant brush.

Suddenly a man broke through the bushes, running as fast as he could. Another person broke from the brush right after him, running just as fast. The man didn't have any clothes on and the other runner appeared to be a woman, long brown hair flowing behind her as she ran. The man grabbed the woman's arm, pulled her along—

Behind them a group of people erupted from the brush in quick pursuit, spears raised. They were all women, long hair and feathers flowing from shoulders. One woman launched a spear ahead at the man and woman running from them. The spear fell short—

"Corlan!" shouted Tam, jumping up on the cart.

Joragus heard the cry, turned to see what he could. He rushed to the cart, holding his staff to steady himself.

"It is him!" said the magus.

The man was running hard, grasping the woman by her wrist.

"Who is following them?" asked Tam.

"No one friendly to us!"

The women in pursuit flung more spears, falling short. One had the distance but fell off-line.

Corlan veered away, jerking the woman with him.

"Tam!" shouted Corlan as he raced toward the cart. "Prepare the slinger!"

"Already loaded!" But Tam checked it again anyway, pulling it heavily into his lap.

"What happened to him?" Joragus muttered.

Then he realized that the band of women pursuing Corlan would not simply stop at the cart. He and the boy were in danger, too. He needed to do something. He thought for an instant, then took a stand between the rear of the cart and the couple running toward the cart.

Corlan and the woman were barely a dragon's wingspan from

the cart when the magus dropped his staff and raised his hands over his head. He thrust his open palms forward at the warrior band in the distance. The strength of his magic flung the warriors back. They tripped over themselves then scrambled to their feet. They seemed dazed for a moment, wondering what had happened. Two women came forward through the line and released arrows from bows.

One arrow clipped Corlan's bare arm just below the point of his shoulder. The other hit the dirt at the girl's feet, nicking her heel. They ran on, reaching the cart, out of breath.

"You got no clothes on!" Tam snickered.

"The least of our problems," Corlan grunted, breathing hard as he grabbed the dragonslinger.

With a quick check, he braced it against his hip, aiming at the center of the group.

The warriors stopped their pursuit, staring at him, seeing he was ready to launch the weapon at them.

"I'm aiming at your queen!" he shouted. "At this range she will be cut into thirds."

Corlan lowered the slinger a bit and grabbed the girl who had run with him. He took her by the wrist and spun her around behind him, out of the line of fire.

The magus stood between the cart and the warrior women.

"We need to go!" Tam shouted, sitting atop the supplies. At his shout, the donkors startled and the cart rocked forward. Tam went flying head over heels off the cart and landed face down in the dirt.

"Tam!" called Corlan, dropping the slinger and rushing to him.

The warrior women regained their fortitude. They ran toward him once more but slower. The girl frantically called his attention to their advance in her language, a series of caws and tweets, but he did not look up.

Joragus stood tall, hands raised. He took a mighty breath and expelled it with such a force that the front row of women were thrown down. Those behind them crashed into the front line. They all tried to run forward again but once more the magus blew his heavy breath at them, stopping them.

Corlan had dropped to his knees beside Tam. He saw the boy was not injured, just had the breath knocked from him.

The warrior queen saw how Corlan had rushed to help the boy. He was protecting the boy who had fallen off the cart. The queen waved one of her sisters forward and that woman launched a spear at Corlan.

The magus saw the spear launched. Corlan glanced up, saw with great clarity the razor edge of the speartip coming at him. The magus stepped forward at the same time Corlan stood. The magus put his right hand on Corlan's shoulder to brace himself, and wrapped his left arm around Corlan, palm out as if to stop the spear's trajectory.

Instead, the spear seemed to halt in the air, its sharp tip cutting into the palm of the magus's open hand. The shaft stood straight out as if still in flight. Then the spear dropped, the tip pulling from the magus's hand, bouncing off Corlan's shoulder, hitting the ground.

"I never tried that before," Joragus muttered, stepping back from Corlan. "An older magic. First iteration stuff. I thought I'd forgotten all of that." He chuckled, slapping his hands together.

Corlan turned to check on Joragus, who nodded he was fine.

The queen waved her arms over her head and the warriors halted. They watched Corlan lift the boy and carry him in his arms to the rear of the cart. He lay the boy there gently. He was no longer concerned with their attack, the warrior women could see. He was focused on caring for the boy.

The warrior queen knelt and the others followed.

After a moment she stood and called to Corlan. It was a stream of sing-songy words which sounded sad, like a surrender declaration. The other women joined in the song. They were ending their attack, it seemed. The queen waved her arms like she was performing some ritual. Then the women spun around to show him their backsides. The queen looked back over her shoulder at Corlan.

The girl who had run with Corlan tapped his shoulder and he glanced back at the warrior women lined up across the riverbed, their backs to him, their bottoms exposed to him. They could have continued, but they chose to stand down. If not for the magic of Joragus and the show of the dragonslinger, the warrior women could easily have caught up to them and killed them.

Corlan stood up straight, staring at the women as they turned to face him again. He pointed at the girl standing beside him, then threw his hand over at the cart. He repeated the gesture, letting them know she was going with them on the cart.

The girl wrapped her arms tightly around Corlan, hugging him, her head against his chest, as the warrior women slowly backed away. When they were far enough, they turned as one and jogged out of sight, lost in the brush.

"Now you're safe," said Corlan in a low voice.

As they parted, she studied the cut on his shoulder.

"Seems our hero found himself a woman, after all," Joragus said to Tam. "I told you he might."

"And he forgot to put on his clothes." Tam grabbed Corlan's clothing bag from the cart and dropped it at his feet. "Here you go."

"Thanks," said the dragonslayer. He regarded his dirty bare feet. "I need boots most of all. My feet are too tender."

He dug in the bag, retrieved trousers and a shirt. He found a long strip of cloth in the bag and wrapped it around himself. Soon he stood properly dressed once more, except for his bare feet.

"I hope this doesn't happen too often. I don't have a wardrobe full of clothes to spare."

"You can have my second set of sandals," said Joragus.

"Then I'll look like a magus."

"And that is so bad?" Joragus laughed. "Besides, your beard isn't long enough or gray enough for anyone to think you a magus."

"I don't have the magic to back it up, either." He clapped the old man on the shoulder. "Thanks for your magic today."

Joragus blinked, his eyes moist. "What's an old magus to do?"

"Use his magic," said Tam.

"You did well," said Corlan. "Don't tire yourself. There may be more situations ahead we'll need your help."

"Let us hope not," said Joragus, patting Corlan's uninjured shoulder, "yet I sense you may be correct in that prediction."

Corlan helped the girl up onto the cart. She adjusted her short leather skirt and leather vest, tugging at the laces in front.

Joragus stared at the girl, noting her age, sensing something familiar about her.

"So we have a new member?" He watched intently how Corlan treated the girl. "Will she go with us?"

"There's no other place for her."

"She have a name?"

"Likely."

"And what is her name?"

He glanced at the girl. "I don't know."

Joragus laughed. "It must have been a good night!"

"Think the donkors can pull all of us?" asked Corlan, ignoring the magus's remark.

"We shall see in about one heartbeat," replied the magus.

Tam called the donkors to start. They pulled hard, voiced their difficulty with loud baying. Tam urged them to put their shoulders into it and the cart slowly rolled. With a few turns more, the motion was steady and the donkors could manage to move the cart.

The steep slope came up fast—before any of them could recall it was there. The cart rolled over the edge, shaking back and forth then tilting dangerously to the right, spilling a few bags of supplies. The donkors protested, slipped and fell onto their sides as the cart turned over. The remaining supplies spilled off and the passengers were thrown. Corlan jumped free of the cart and caught the girl, easing her to the ground, protecting her in his arms.

Tam got up and untethered the girafors, the ropes pulling tightly at their necks as the cart slid on its side. The girafors fought to keep from being upended. Keeping the tethers taut, Tam helped them down the slope, eventually leaping down to the lower ground.

The cart slid downward on its side, wheel spinning.

"Not the best way to go, after all," Corlan grumbled. "I meant to find us a better way. Then I got captured. I forgot all about this drop. Too busy escaping."

"Is this the true way?" asked Joragus.

"It may look clogged with vegetation yet it is the main channel. I saw it from the hillside. All the channels are full of flora. What is not a channel is dry and only red dirt. Ahead, we keep left."

They righted the cart and gathered the bags and other supplies, put them on the cart. The donkors were afraid and wouldn't be calm. Tam spoke to them. Corlan took the tethers of the girafors, inspected their legs for injuries. The wound on Pex's thigh was healing well.

The girl stood to the side, watching. She started to grab a bag to put on the cart, then hesitated and dropped it, too heavy for her.

Finally the cart was returned to traveling condition. One wheel had become a bit wobbly but still would carry the cart. They hitched the donkors and Tam walked with them, talking them through the next few turns of the cart wheels. Corlan walked the girafors behind the cart. The old man and the girl sat on the bench as the cart moved along the river channel, through the groves of trees.

After an hour of everyone riding on the cart, they broke free of the forest and the riverbed widened, vegetation thinning. By then, it was dusk. Joragus asked if they should stop and make camp. Corlan thought it best to continue a while longer, to get farther away from the warrior band that had been after them.

"Who knows? They could catch us in the night," said Corlan. "It is easy now. There is only one way here. Let the donkors keep us on the path."

"Yes, certainly." Joragus gave an anxious sigh. "As long as we keep moving, we will arrive...somewhere." He turned to Corlan, winking. "And who is our new member? How did you meet her?"

Corlan was no longer breathing hard from lifting the cart on his back to set it aright but he grinned.

"This is...I think her name is...Madi."

The girl smiled, hearing the word, knowing she was the subject of the discussion. She moved her hand in a circle over her chest.

"Madi," she spoke.

"Yes, her name is Madi." Corlan smiled. "Must be her name."

"Welcome to our humble cart," said Joragus.

"Welcome, Madi," said Tam.

"*Madi*.... Like the cult of women warriors," said the magus. "They act like birds. Could she be one of them?"

"That, or it's her own name," said Corlan. "Doesn't matter."

"You've a story to tell, obviously," said Joragus, waving a finger at Corlan. "We've waited almost four days for you. You owe us a tale of adventure."

"I know, I know."

"Yes?" The magus studied Corlan as he stretched out on the back of the cart, his feet dangling off the rear. "Are you going to tell us how you happened to find this girl to bring along with you? After being gone so long?"

Corlan sighed. "Let me rest first."

The girl cradled his head in her lap. After a minute he was loudly snoring as the girl stroked his hair.

INTERLUDE

A Thicker Plot

THE NOISE WAS UNMISTAKABLE. Adora rushed into the chamber and saw her baby brother on the floor pressed against the corner of the room, facing a small dragon twice his size. The dragon hissed and steamed, baring its teeth, flapping its immature wings. The boy cried out loudly, holding his hands in front of his face.

Adora heard the frightened cries and left her lesson. She came running into the nursery. In an instant, she charged to the corner and grabbed the dragon by its swishing tail and swung the beast over the balcony wall as hard as she could. The dragon sailed into the air yet with immature wings could not fly and so crashed on the hard street below, a scattering of blood and flesh that provided a quick meal for some of the town's street canines.

She scooped up her baby brother and held him against her chest, patting his head, his locks starting to grow out. She soothed his tears with soft words spoken into his ear. Soon his whimpering faded.

"Princess!" cried Jabuli, hurrying into the room after her. "What happened?"

The princess shushed her tutor, turning where she sat on the floor to show her that the baby brother was safe in her arms.

"A dragon came," she said in a low voice, "but I threw it out."

Jabuli showed shock on her face. "You threw it out?"

"Yes. Over the balcony wall."

"How brave!" Jabuli's cheer slowly gave way to a frown. "More dragons...."

"Some people like them," said the princess. "Me, too. They keep bugs away. And they keep the room warm during winter weeks." She let her face twist into a scowl. "But I won't have dragons hurting my baby brother. Never that!"

Jabuli praised her courage, offered to hold the boy for her but the princess waved her off. It was not courage. It was love that made her act. Her mother likely would let the dragon attack the babe, she told her tutor, who nodded agreement.

"I must keep him with me every moment from now on," said the princess. "I wonder if Mama sent the dragon to hurt him. She wants me to send him away. But she promised he would have a good life, maybe be a games player. She said I could write parches and they would be delivered to him, no matter where he played." She tried to hide a grimace. "See? I say 'he' and 'him' like they are real words. It cannot be true that males are animals good for only one thing. Mama is wrong." Tears ran from her eyes.

"Shhh, Your Little Majesty. Don't let anyone hear you speak that way about your mother, the queen." She pulled a cloth from her pocket and dabbed at the princess's cheeks. "I've never seen you cry before."

"I never was afraid before." She sniffled back her tears. "I worry about my baby brother."

"You are a good sister," said Jabuli.

Adora lowered her eyes, smiling at her brother held in her arms. "Who could think a law is needed to protect these little pets? This one is so sweet and always smiles at me."

"Like the little dragon," Jabuli said, then paused to choose her words carefully, "when they grow to adult size they can be difficult to control and might be violent. Many people are hurt—"

"You mean women when you say people," the princess cut in.

"Yes, Princess, women, ladies, females. We can be hurt by adult males. It has been proven throughout our long history. Even when a male reaches nine or ten years it can be so dangerous. Your mother, the queen, is wise to warn you."

Jabuli watched her charge a while, unable to speak. The sight of the two siblings together was so innocent and beautiful. She could only shake her head. If only she could make the princess understand the need for such laws. The princess was wise for her age.

"I know there is a law," said Jabuli, "so we must obey it. As the royal daughter, you may be excused from some laws, if your mother, the queen, so commands."

Princess Adora looked up at her. "Is it true?"

"Her Majesty allows you to keep your brother as a pet, doesn't she? That was a law that she allowed you to not obey. It is written that a male child must be sent out of the city within seven days of its birth, then to be deposited away or given over to training for suitable work. The male must never again see its birther or any other family members, nor be given a name — except by the training master."

"I call him Puki." Adora presented a stern face. "I know I'm not supposed to give him a name. It's only for ladies. But I grew tired of calling 'Brother, come here' and say 'he' and 'him' so much. So I call him Puki."

Jabuli repressed a grin. "Puki? What is the meaning?"

"It has no meaning." She regarded the babe in her arms. "One day I gave him the food and he spit it up. The food went all over my gown. I was angry at the first. Then I remembered a nursing maid talking about Princess Lumina. The maid said it is usual for a babe to spit up food. Maybe the food is not good or it is too much for the babe to swallow, or something else is amiss. So I forgave him for making my gown dirty." She gazed up at her tutor. "So I call him Puki. I like the name so I always call him Puki."

Jabuli was laughing before the princess finished her explanation. "Then it's a good name for a food-spitter," she said. "Shall I call him Puki, too?"

"If you wish." Adora kissed her brother's forehead. "Yet I will give him a better name when he grows older. By then, a new law will be written and he can stay in the palace forever. I'm sure of it. Maybe he can be a queen with me. And have a real name, such as Durol or Pashal or Kuroth."

Jabuli hushed the princess, glancing behind her for any spies that would hear their words. She lowered her voice: "You must not say such things. Not loudly. Speak not the male names from our history. Her Majesty forbids them." She smiled to show the princess that she understood, then continued in her normal voice: "There is no law that allows a male to be a queen. Also, you cannot have someone else be the queen with you. It is another law. There has always been only one queen."

"So many laws!" The princess seemed ready to cry. "I hate laws! I want laws to go away! No more laws!"

"We need laws," said Jabuli, placing her hand gently on the royal shoulder, then realized the touch of a royal person was against the laws, as well. She quickly removed her hand. "They tell us how best to behave, how to treat each other, what to do and not do. Laws keep our lives simple and straight. And you know it is the responsibility of the queen—and you will be the queen one day—to make sure everyone obeys the laws that are written."

"I will write a law ending all laws!"

"You don't mean that, do you, Princess Adora?"

She nodded, frowning. "I do."

Jabuli sighed. She was drawn to take her charge's side yet she knew full well her duties as a tutor to the princess. To say what was not approved by the head tutor would cause her to be sent out of the palace, perhaps be sent back to the mainland where life would be impossible. Or she would need to flee to some other land where no one would know her or care what she did.

"Princess...."

"Speak." The babe was asleep on her shoulder now.

"If you do not like the laws, and you cannot write new laws, then you must leave this palace, leave this city, leave this island, and find a new place where you...and *him*...will be safe, free from...the woman who is your queen."

The silence that filled the chamber seemed full of knives. Jabuli almost expected blades to thrust into her body at that very moment. She glanced behind her, then returned her gaze to the princess. The girl had narrowed her eyes.

Jabuli knelt down to be eye to eye with the princess.

"I regret my words, Princess Adora. Please forgive me. I went into a strange world for that instant. Only for a moment was I lost. I am from the mainland, as you know. I had a memory flash of those days. Frightening days. Sad days. I spoke not correctly or properly to you. That life is not for you, nor for...*him*."

Adora smiled, as though she had not listened to Jabuli's words, while gently rocking her brother on her shoulder as he napped. "You said *him*. Like a true mama. I like that." She studied her tutor's face. "Your words didn't hurt me. I wasn't offended. I like that you speak to me always with a straight voice, without any masks to hide the meaning. It is a serious idea."

Jabuli bowed her head. "I apologize, Your Little Majesty."

"No more 'little majesty'—as I said long ago."

"Yes, Princess Adora."

Jabuli stood, took a step back, regaining proper distance, clasping her hands in front of herself, once more the demure tutor.

"Your words make me think deeper than before." Adora gazed

at the cloudless blue sky. A gray dragon winged past in the distance. "Look! Dragons can fly wherever they wish. Who knows where they live? where they come from? where they go? They are free. As I want to be." Her expression boiled into something serious. "If another day comes where someone is sent to hurt my brother or take him away, then I must leave this palace. And this city. And this island." She blinked, watching her tutor's eyes. "As you said. Every day is more dangerous for him. Though I have no destination, I must go away to save my brother."

Jabuli bowed again. "Forgive me, Princess Adora. Please. I never thought to give you any ideas which would put you under a hand of harm."

Adora nodded, still rocking her brother on her shoulder.

"I was wrong to speak that way to you," said Jabuli. "By my words, I have betrayed your mother, the queen. Please forget what I said. I fell into a strange world, as I told you. I shall never speak such ideas ever again."

"No, it's not a strange world. It was a window of clear sunshine. The clouds in the sky broke open. Now I see the blue. There are only storms ahead if I would keep my brother safe." The princess glanced down from the balcony, staring off in each direction at other towers of the palace. "If the day comes, as I said, and I must leave, will you come with us?"

Jabuli knelt once more, keeping her head bowed.

"Your mother, the queen, once saved me from a terrible life, and for that act I will forever be grateful. I have pledged to educate you, Princess Adora, about the world beyond this island, and I believe it is an important responsibility."

"You do it well," said Adora, keeping her face serious.

"Yet it is you, Princess Adora, who I ultimately serve. I visit you each day, work with you each day, talk with you each day, and so it is to you I truly dedicate my life. From this day forward, whatever you may decide, Your Little Majesty, if I may counsel you, I will do my best and obey your commands."

"I will ask for and receive your counsel. That's the reason I ask you to come with us. Not to be a nursing maid. Or even a tutor. I need an advisor. My mother has a hundred advisors. I probably should have one. At least one. You see, I'm not in adult age yet, so I know I don't know everything I need to know. Yet you know a lot. You are thirty years? Close?"

"Thirty-three, Princess Adora."

"A good age for giving counsel. You must also remember how it was to be my age. Not too old for remembering how it is to be a child. Please remember your child years when you give me counsel."

From her kneeling position, Jabuli reached out and hugged the princess, a daring act of familiarity that would be cause for severe discipline if noticed by members of the palace staff. Yet the princess did not agree with that law. So she allowed the woman's arms to encircle her and not cry out in alarm.

Jabuli released her. "Forgive me, Princess Adora, for my intimate touch. I did not think clearly. My head is cloudy."

"Another strange world you visited?" The princess grinned.

"No, Princess Adora. I was in the right world. I know it now."

"I wish you could be my mama," said the princess. A pair of tears dropped from her eyes. "You hug me well."

"I wish you were my daughter," said Jabuli, feeling a tear roll down her cheek. "I never got to have any children."

"I feel sad. It must be terrible to have your insides torn."

The babe awoke at that moment and gurgled for attention. Both the woman and the girl gazed upon his bright, smiling face, a big yawn bursting forth. Glancing at each other, they seemed to share the same thought: how wonderful was this innocent babe and, more importantly, how much he should be saved from harm.

"There are two festivals each year," said Jabuli quietly. "Only then are visitors allowed into the city. And after, the visitors leave this city. They sail away from this island, returning to the mainland. That is the only chance we have to leave. The water current is too strong for us to take a boat by ourselves. We need to go on one of the visitor ships." She blinked twice. "If you ever wish to go to some distant land where you and your brother can be safe."

"We will be ready," said the princess, holding her baby brother tightly in her arms. "You tell me the day."

13

Birdsong

TAM ENJOYED INTRODUCING the new member to the rest of the team. He pointed to the donkors. "That one is Ika, and the other is Gum." He had her turn around to gaze at the girafors trailing the cart. "He is Pex and she is Elo. They are girafors. You ever see such animals? Pex carries the quivers. That's because they are very heavy." Tam gestured at the old man. "He is Joragus. He is a magus. That's someone who can use magic. He's very, very old." And he threw a thumb back at Corlan, sitting on the riding bench, reins in his hands. "You know Corlan already."

"Cooorlaaan!" the girl cried out in a high-pitched voice. The words that followed were gibberish to Tam, but he saw that she seemed happy to say his name.

"My name is Tam, remember."

The girl grinned. "Tamremember."

"No, it's only Tam."

"Onlytam."

"No. Just say Tam."

She watched his lips carefully. "Tam."

"Yes, just Tam."

"Justam."

"No. Tam. Only Tam."

She smiled like she understood.

"Good."

The girl was clearly older than the boy although not close to an adult. She smiled at him, then pointed to herself.

"Madi." She pointed to Tam's chest. "Tam."

"Yes, that's right," he said brightly, pleased with his student's progress. "Actually, my name is Tamondarus. My mama named me after her grandfather, Datamond, and one of the princes of Cago from legend, Prince Darus. But you can call me just Tam. Or...Tam."

Again she pointed to him. "Tam."

Joragus cleared his throat. "Now that that's all straight, we must learn the fate of our dear hero, Corlan of the Burg." He held up his hand, palm open. "You see my wound has healed, so it must be time enough."

"It was barely a scratch," Corlan said with a snort.

"A scratch that saved your life!"

"Saved all of us—"

"And Madi, too!" Tam added.

"Tell us, old man, how did you perform such...magic?" Corlan asked with a sideways glance at Tam. "Is that what you call it?"

Joragus scoffed. "You would never be able to understand. It takes many, many years of training."

"Start a lesson for this boy here," Corlan challenged the magus.

"You must understand the workings of everything—everything seen and unseen in the world—before you can learn magic."

"Teach me, Joragus!" the boy shouted.

"As you wish." The magus gave an annoyed glance at Corlan who was happy to grin like a thief. "Everything is made of dust—very tiny dust, so small you cannot see it. The dust of the earth is solid so you can see it when it comes together in large enough piles. The dust of the air is thin so you can see through it even when it comes together in large piles. It is these tiny particles of dust which magic can move."

"How does playing with dust stop a spear that's thrown at you?" Corlan asked, a little more curious.

"Ah! I see your plan. You also want to know how to stop a sharp spear amidst the air."

"That would be a good thing to know," said Corlan with a nod at the boy. "Wouldn't it?"

"Oh, yes," said Tam.

"Have you ever seen lightning strike down from the sky?" asked Joragus. "That is the same fire-root that runs through every living thing. People, too."

"If that's true, how are we not destroyed by it?" asked Corlan.

"What is inside us is much smaller, not enough to hurt us. And yet, some people—a trained magus, for example—can draw together all of that fire within him and send it out just like lightning."

"But I didn't see anything like lightning when you held up your hand to stop the spear."

"No, it is still invisible. Just as the air is invisible."

"I think your magic is all in your words, old man," said Corlan.

"I told you there is an ocean of tiny particles, like dust, that make up all the air around us. When I use my magic power to gather all the fire within me, I charge those particles with the fire. It's like black and white. Everything is either black or white. The particles in the air are white—you can see through them and throw spears through them. When I send my inner fire out to those particles, they turn black—although they are still invisible to our eyes."

"So these tiny dust specks turn colors...."

"No, it is merely a tale to explain to you what happens, to show you. A magic lesson for the boy...as you suggested." He turned to Tam. "You follow my tale, don't you?"

Tam nodded eagerly.

"When those particles turn black," the magus continued, "they become tight to each other and nothing can come through them. They become like a shield, even though you cannot see it with your eyes. You must remember that our eyes do not see most of the things in the world—and what we do see is most often a mere trick of light. There is much more we do not see than what we do see."

"So that's what you did back there to stop the spear?"

"Yes, in brief."

"Though not quick enough to keep the speartip from cutting your palm, eh?"

"As we say in magus school, it is better to be late than to never be ready at all."

"Then we thank you again for being late," said Corlan, breaking into a hearty laughter.

Tam joined in, but the girl seemed confused and did not share their humor. She stared at Joragus, hoping for an explanation.

"And what is your tale, young woman?" the old man asked her.

"Madi," was all she said.

She knew he was addressing her but she did not understand his words. Nor did she have words of her own for a reply that he could understand. Her face turned golden, her eyes widened, owl-like, and suddenly her mouth opened. The sweet sounds of birdsong wafted out. It was a beautiful song, like something she had practiced many times, the tune pleasant to hear.

"That was lovely," said Joragus when she finished.

"Can't understand a word of it," Corlan said.

"It's pretty," said Tam, clapping his hands.

"Now how did we come to have her join our little army?" asked Joragus. He glared at Corlan. "Are you going to tell us?"

Corlan yawned. "All your magic spells have exhausted me."

"I haven't used any spells today," Joragus insisted.

"Talking about your magic tires me." He yawned again. "I must get a nap so I'm ready when the next dragon alights near us."

He closed his eyes and tucked his arms back behind his head and took several deep breaths.

"You won't get by so easily this time," the magus spoke.

After a while, Corlan stretched out his arms, yawning loudly as the cart rolled along and the sun began to wane.

"Tell us what happened," Tam urged.

"I went to have a look at our location," said Corlan, eyes closed. "I climbed high up the hill and that is where I met the warriors — those women you saw chasing us. The bird clan, I call them."

"That explains the feathers they were wearing," said Joragus.

"And Madi singing like a bird," Tam added.

"The feathers are from dragons — featherbacks, you know. Their huts were framed with dragon bones, the ribs especially. I suppose they hunt dragons — wait for them to ground, then trap them, kill them. The whole village was full of feathers and dragon bones."

"Wow," said Tam.

"They put spears on me, led me to their village." Corlan opened his eyes, gazed at Madi, her owl-eyes following him, understanding he was telling about her and her village. "They likely would've killed me right there if they simply hated foreign men who trespassed in their territory. Or maybe they didn't like that I killed three of their animals for dinner. I managed to get us a bird, a snake, and a rat. The three basic meats."

He chuckled. Alone.

"Like you, they were not easily amused. They led me away. So I thought there must be a reason to take me to their leader. Possibly I would be questioned, found to be harmless, and set free. I would have to promise never to return. Like that."

"I would guess that is not what happened," said the magus.

"I was questioned by the lady in charge. She wore very large feathers, looking like great wings. The owl lady. You saw her leading the chase."

"Were you scared?" asked Tam.

"It is permitted to be scared when you are in a scary situation," he answered calmly. "I was tied up. They had spears all around me. I didn't know what was going to happen next." He leaned over to Tam, darkening his voice. "They might have been planning how to *cook me!*"

Tam shrank back in fright.

"I'm sure an old dragonslayer wouldn't taste any better than an old dragon," the magus said with a snort.

"You're one to talk. Drake tail. You dined on drake tail not so long ago, and here you are: alive and well."

The magus drew a circle in the air over Corlan's head. "And here you are, alive and well, with the help of my magic!"

Corlan gazed around the cart. "It was all singing, everything spoken to me—like what Madi sang for us. All tweets and caws, and squawks and cries, and singing, just like being in a nest of birds. I didn't know what they were telling me. In fact, they had several giant birds in the village, as tall as me, strutting about. Some of them would jump into the air and fly. They would return later with food in their talons."

"So how did you escape?" asked Tam.

"By my wits!" He grinned at the boy. "By my guile...."

"What's *guile*?" Tam asked the old man.

"It's a word from the scrolls. It means trickery."

"Oh." It was clear by Tam's expression that trickery seemed less interesting than bravery. "Did you fight them?"

"Just wait. So they took me to a hut, something made of straw and brush, like a bird's nest I saw once drawn on some scrolls, only larger. As I said, the frame was made of dragon ribs."

"Was it a prison?" asked the boy.

"Not exactly a prison." Corlan turned to the magus. "There are many kinds of prisons. Some are cold and damp. Some are warm and smell like burned flesh. Others are full of feathers like you are meant to be comfortable. Even then, such comfort is deceptive."

"How so?" asked Joragus.

Corlan dipped his head in the direction of the boy. "It can often be too comfortable." He tilted his head toward the girl. "If you know what I mean...."

"Indeed." Joragus studied the girl. "Yes, she is almost of the age when birds must leave the nest."

"Too young for me," Corlan said with a cough. He coughed more, clearing his throat, and spit off the cart. "I thought she was probably not ready, no matter how much her mother insisted. I'm not a beast, you know. The next dragonslayer they capture might not be so kind."

"You refused the mother?" asked Joragus.

"Yes, of course."

"And you were set upon and punished?"

"Neither that."

"So you ran away?"

"Yes. Well...." He glanced at the girl. He raised his hand to her as though he was inviting her to accompany him. "I suggested she could flee with me and not have to go through whatever rituals they had planned for her. I told her I'd protect her from her evil mother."

"Evil mother, eh?" Joragus narrowed his eyes. "Your name for the mother, or *her* name for the mother?"

"It was all birdsong to me."

Suddenly Madi spoke—whistling a tune that seemed to explain exactly what happened. There were no words, of course, so Corlan pretended to narrate the song:

"The handsome man from the Burg woke me in the middle of the night and told me it was time to escape. I went with him because I did not wish my evil mother to make me do the things all the sisters had to do whenever they found a man. He was a very handsome man, did I mention? So it was easy to run away with him. Someday I will be mature enough to consider a true man as my partner."

Corlan grinned and Tam laughed.

"It's because dear Corlan will be dead, many years gone, by then, or simply he would be too old for a woman like me."

Madi's singing ceased just as Corlan's final words faded in the air.

"That is the story?" asked Tam.

"Yes, so don't be so curious next time." Corlan slapped at his head, missed purposely. "Think of her as your dear cousin."

"My cousin?" Tam frowned.

"Yes. Now you must teach her how to speak our language."

Joragus raised his hand. "Not so quick."

"What?" asked Corlan.

"As I listen to these *communications* of hers, I notice there are some patterns. It has been many years yet I recall the language. We encountered some of these birds in my third iteration. I had doubted whether or not the knowledge would transfer." Joragus tapped the side of his head with his finger. "Yes, I think it may be possible. If we understand the patterns, then we may communicate with her. I'm finding the patterns in my head now. For example, when she tweets like this—" He put his lips together and whistled a string of notes. "—I think she refers to her village and the women living there. Or those large birds living there."

The girl stared at the magus, clearly surprised by his tweeting. She seemed to understand his sounds, though.

"Is it correct?" he asked her.

She gave a high-pitched *caw*. They practiced together for a while, each whistling and tweeting to the other, correcting, repeating, until Joragus decided he had learned the language well enough.

"I'm not going to learn how to sing like a bird," said Corlan with a grunt. "She should learn to speak like people speak. No matter what they taught her back there, she is not a bird. She's certainly a human girl."

"My point, dear Corlan, is that your narration may not have been entirely accurate. Let me practice—"

"Not accurate? But that's what happened."

"I think, if she were to sing it again, I could follow the patterns of the song and we might find a different explanation."

"You calling me a liar?"

"Oh, not me. Never. You described what happened exactly as you believe it happened. That's not lying. It's just that your...umm, *perception* may be rather different from hers."

Joragus turned to Madi and with gestures he urged her to tell the story again. After some confusion, she got the idea and started her song.

The magus raised his hand. "Now listen...."

Madi began her story again, all tweets, caws, and cries. She added gestures when it helped emphasize certain details. She waved her arms as though flapping wings. She flicked her long fingers— like she was playing a flute, Tam remarked.

"And so our story goes that Corlan was captured and brought to the village. At first he was questioned by their queen, or whatever the title was they gave to her. This girl, our Madi, was her daughter. Our dragonslayer friend here acted arrogantly—my word, not hers—so he was put inside a hut, the nest, and guarded. 'He was fed to the nest' is how she tweets it."

"You're lame in the head, old man," said Corlan, waving his hand as if dismissing a pest.

"In the night a woman went to him, made him remove his clothes, and began to...umm, how to translate? To see to his comfort, let's say." He listened to more. "At first, he enjoyed it. Then he became alarmed at whatever she was doing and threw her off him— which caused a great alarm in the village." The tweeting went on. "Others arrived and he was taken out of the hut and . . ." He put his hand on Madi's arm. "Sing that last part again, will you, dear?" He tried to whistle the last few notes that he recalled. "That part."

Madi batted her eyes, resumed her birdsong.

"Yes, that's what I thought. He was tied to a stake in the center of the village. And the warrior queen threatened him—I say threatened, she said 'spoke with anger'—suggested harm to his manly parts if he did not submit to their...umm, customs." He waited for more notes. "There were no men in the village, so they use the men they capture to populate their tribe." He glanced at Corlan. "Makes a lot of sense."

"There was more to it than that," said Corlan angrily.

Madi paused, seeing him speaking to Corlan. When he returned his gaze to her, she resumed her singing.

"She—this one—knew what would happen." Joragus laughed. "Use him well, then off with his parts. The rest becomes food." He glared at Madi. "Just as I thought: a band of cannibal witches. There are several of their tribes along the valley. Each has made its own customs, seeking food and sex as it becomes available. This group is the bird tribe."

Madi stopped again, her face screwed up like she hated being interrupted by the magus's asides.

"Sorry, my dear. Proceed."

More birdsong. Joragus smiled as he listened, nodding his head as he followed the melody. She finished on a high note.

"And thus...this lovely one did you a kindness, true?"

"I suppose," Corlan mumbled.

"She persuaded her evil mother to let you rest, all the better to be ready for a great festival of nest indulgence. Then, before dawn, she released you and insisted you hurry away. But no! You had to be sure she meant for you to leave. You had to ask questions. You had to have your clothes returned to you. With...an apology?" Joragus glared at Corlan. "Truly? That was bold."

Madi clapped her hands to regain their attention, then continued.

"Yes, well, you ran. And to be sure you would leave the village, this girl went with you, to be certain you passed beyond the border of their territory. By then, the tribe's warriors were in pursuit and you had no choice but to run. And she ran with you, to keep you safe — if I dare to understand that last series of tweets."

"I was keeping *her* safe," Corlan said. "She wanted to get away from her mother, too. Like all daughters do."

Madi whistled frantically.

"See? She knows you're lying." Joragus smiled at the girl. "Pay no attention to the dragonslayer in the cart."

"It's not like that," said Corlan, sitting up, stretching his arms. "It was an escape. You saw how much we took with us. Me: nothing. Her: only the skirt and vest she's wearing now. I think she was intended to be a sacrifice. No, not actually a sacrifice. More like a formal firstnight, to gain her womanhood. Like they do in Rolina." Corlan slapped his knee. "I wouldn't do it, so her mother thought to punish me."

"That makes a better story," said Joragus.

"It's the truth."

"So Corlan was going to have to kiss the girl?" asked Tam. "And he didn't want to so they were going to kill him?"

"That's almost correct," said Corlan.

"Then just kiss the girl!" Tam exclaimed.

Joragus burst out laughing.

"I should have." Corlan glanced at Joragus and the magus gave him a knowing wink. "Instead, she came along with me, to join us. On the way, she fell. I stopped to help her. She could have refused my help and stayed with those bird women, but she got up and ran with me. It was her choice. But don't think she's any kind of wife or lover of mine." He pursed his lips, whiskers catching between them. "I don't know what we'll do with her. What can she do? We've little enough rations as it is."

"I can eat less," said Joragus.

"Me, too," said Tam. "I can share with her."

Corlan scratched his beard. "At least until we come to the next speck of civilization in this vast wilderness."

He pointed to the old crate in the back of the cart, the one that contained the map scrolls, directed Tam to retrieve one of them. Juggling the reins, Corlan unrolled the parchment, turned it to orient directions to match the valley they rode through. It was an old map but further along the valley in the direction they were going, he saw the small drawing of a city with a wall and towers.

"What's this?"

Joragus leaned over to gaze at the map. "That would be Unting. A city without humor, as I recall."

"Humor or not, we'd better gain fresh supplies there."

"If it still exists." The magus cleared his throat. "Perhaps it fared no better than Metta."

Corlan grumbled. "Perhaps somewhere along this valley there is a true city, a place to gather supplies, not just the old scraps from a temple of ghosts."

Joragus stared at the girl. She lowered her eyes. He turned his eyes on Tam, who was watching the girafors trailing the cart. Then he faced forward again, giving a glance to Corlan.

"The Valley of Death holds many ghosts, Corlan. And we may yet join them."

14

When Dragons Attack

THE FIRST DRAGON SWEPT IN LOW, inches above the rocky cliffs, gliding on its outstretched wings so as to be as quiet as possible in the darkness. Its ruddy wings did not beat and its rough, pocked face, long cheek barbs, and prominent horns under the jaw identified it as a hornchin. There were singles and doubles in the pantheon of dragons. This was a double-hornchin: the two horns projected down from the front corners of the lower jaw, like two staves of a donkor-drawn cart.

Opening his eyes from a dream of Petula, Corlan spun up off his bedroll and grabbed the dragonslinger that was always beside him, loaded. He buttressed the slinger against the ground, screwed back the spring, and aimed at the dragon.

With its fifty-foot wingspan cutting the approaching twilight, the hornchin spotted them in their camp circle, laid out between the cart and the grove of trees. Targeting them, the aerial beast dove in with mouth agape and eyes red with anger or vengeance — or both. Mere hunger and a hunt for food did not cause their eyes to change colors, Corlan knew. Yet he had met few hornchins, double and single, in his years of dragonslaying. The difference did not matter now.

The mouth agape was perfect. Corlan launched the iron bolt. It struck the rear wall of the dragon's throat, the barbs catching. That usually prevented the dragon from conjuring a fire-breath. Dealing with an iron bolt in the gullet took priority and might also injury the glands that provided the igniting fluid.

Corlan reloaded, screwed back the spring to its tightest setting for distant targets. He needed the extra power for its stronger thrust and deeper puncture. He aimed at the dragon's throat. Between the neck ribs hornchins possessed was a soft spot where a well-placed bolt could puncture the main passage for blood between the heart and head.

The iron bolt hit home and the dragon fell back. Its short forefeet clawed at the protruding shaft as the poison drained into the blood tube. The dragon roared weakly, stumbling back and forth in a half-circle, crushing one wing against the ground, bones breaking loudly. The tail slung around like a wild snake, slapping the cart, knocking it on its side, spilling everything. The double horns protruding from the chin scraped across the sandy soil of the riverbed as the dragon fought to stay alive.

At last it swayed on its hindfeet, neck stretching tall into the air and gurgles falling from its maw. The hulking mass tumbled back, crashing spines-first into the dirt and gravel, one wing crushed beneath its body, the other half-opened and swinging weakly.

"You got it!" cried Tam.

Corlan had not spent a second to notice if any of the others were awake. He sprang into action instantly, taking care of the disruption. That was his job, his training.

With his eyes fixed on the dragon's corpse, he called back to the boy. "How many bolts remain?"

After a moment, the boy said, "Twenty-six."

"Give me three. Keep the others ready."

Corlan saw the next dragon lining up a diving run about a mile away, another double-hornchin.

As he watched it approach, he saw others not far behind.

"Get everyone under the trees, out of sight," he commanded when Tam brought him the three bolts.

The others were already awake and rushing to hide. All except the magus, still asleep despite the noise and earth-shaking collapse of the hornchin's great body.

"What is this outrage?" roared the magus, roused from his sleep by Tam's hand.

"Dragons!" shouted the boy. The girl was pulling the donkors under the trees. Tam ran to gather the girafors.

Corlan rushed to a pile of rocks twenty yards from the camp and set the dragonslinger there, hoping to draw off the incoming aerials. He braced the slinger against the largest boulder on the ground, resting its long barrel against the other rocks. He could get better aim that way. He adjusted the slinger and used its sighting pegs for once, screwing back the spring to its tightest setting.

"Come on...." he spoke, teeth gritted, "Come on...."

The leading hornchin swooped low, targeting the camp.

As it came in, Corlan launched the bolt and it struck the hornchin on the side of its neck, a good wound yet not in a location that would halt it. The hornchin swore off the attack, tried to regain altitude, struggling and flapping its wings hard. With wild cries, it gave urgency to the others. They would be wary as they attacked.

Corlan reloaded.

The hornchin he had shot could not make it back into the air and crashed on its four feet on the ground right before him, almost on top of him, face to face. The dragon clawed at the bolt ticking back and forth from its neck, finally flicked it out. Corlan thought he saw only the shaft fall away, meaning the trident barbs were still lodged in the flesh. If it had gone in deep enough, the poison capsule would burst and flood the beast with deadly toxins.

The hornchin did not seem to weary from its wounding yet it was distracted enough that the others held up, circled in the air.

Seven of them!

"Run to the shadows!" Corlan shouted, keeping his eyes on the grounded dragon before him.

The beast stomped forward, its weight shaking the ground. The cairn of rocks where Corlan had set up his defense tumbled away in front of him from the quaking. He pushed fallen rocks off the slinger, pulled it up to his hip.

Already loaded, the spring set, he launched the iron bolt, striking the dragon in the eye. He didn't aim for the eye but the beast turned its head at the last instant. High-pitched screams erupted from the beast as it reared on its hindfeet then lunged forward, foreclaws scraping the soil around Corlan, tossing him a few feet to the side. The dragon turned and swung its chin horns down at him, the two points stabbing the earth on either side of Corlan.

He scrambled up, realizing he had lost the slinger. It lay under the claws of the dragon's forefoot.

Two more double-hornchins alighted far behind the wounded dragon, one of them on Corlan's side of the first slain beast, the other beyond the silent carcass. They knew what was happening, Corlan realized. The dragons were not dumb brutes that only knew how to kill. They could communicate and organize. Now they had found a dragonslayer pinned in this narrow canyon.

Corlan unsheathed his sideblade. Though not enough to take on a dragon, it could cut well enough. He leaped at the forefoot holding down the dragonslinger and stabbed the blade into the beast's foot. He hoped to get the dragon to lift its foot.

Stepping back, the dragon exposed the weapon. Corlan jerked the slinger away, then jumped up and ran as fast as the heavy weapon would let him.

Corlan detoured to snatch the other two bolts Tam had given him. He drag them over the dirt until he was beneath a trio of trees. He could see the three dragons through the branches and leaves but he doubted they could detect him, not the way the breeze made the leaves flutter and the branches wave.

The beasts still knew he was there, he realized. Just as he decided to flee, the too-familiar sound filled the camp: the guttural rumbling, raspy cough, the deep sky-sucking inhalation, then—

Fire!

The leafy crowns of the trees burst into flames above Corlan and his fleeing shadow was singed.

He was several steps away, glancing back over his shoulder as he dragged the weapon with one hand, the bolts with the other. No time to set up and load, then aim and launch. And his sideblade was still stuck in the dragon's foot.

Looking left and right he could not locate the others, did not see the cart or the animals.

"Tam! Where are you?" he called out, running and dragging the weaponry.

"We're here!" Tam called back.

Corlan wasn't sure the direction. "Safe? Are you all safe?"

"We found a cave!"

He wanted to scan the side of the valley but knew to keep his eyes on the dragon.

"Stay there!"

He saw another cairn of rocks, taking only a heartbeat to wonder who had constructed it, before he slid feet-first behind it. He spun himself upright and loaded the slinger, seeing the grove of trees where they had camped now reduced to charred trunks. He screwed back the spring, aligned the weapon on the hornchin with the fire-cough and launched the bolt, hoping it would dive straight down the dragon's gullet.

Close —

It hit inside its mouth, striking the rough, scaly tongue. Its massive molars crunched the bolt but could not snap it. Probably the poison capsule had burst but on the surface of the tongue the toxin could do little to disable the beast.

Corlan gazed cautiously over the top of the cairn at the dragon. A couple dozen rocks deliberately stacked into a tower as high as his shoulders, it made a perfect support for the dragonslinger. Then he noticed bones protruding from between the rocks. The two bones of the forearm. Human.

This is the place. The killing field for these dragons. Those who died were buried in cairns.

Extending along the riverbed Corlan could see twelve dragons, all double-hornchins. The two he had killed lay on their sides. The others milled around them as two others pursued him. Then dinner began. The late-arrivals dined on the first two killed. Except for the two who were stalking him.

The dragon he had hit on the tongue kept after him, its heavy head swaying left and right, searching for him, its twin jaw horns scraping the soil. He knew their eyesight was not sharp in the dark that now covered the valley; fire helped them focus on their prey. The next dragon seemed to simply follow the first, not knowing there was a dragonslayer ahead.

Corlan glanced about, seeking a better hiding place. He could not out-shoot them. He had one bolt remaining with him. There was no contest to be won between his iron bolts and their fire-breaths. Still, the slinger was all he had—

"Out of my way, fool!"

The white robes swung around Corlan like giant bird wings and he instinctively ducked. It was Joragus coming up behind him, arms raised, long sleeves flapping and gray beard trailing in the wind.

"You've done all you can! Stand back!"

Corlan crouched low as the magus climbed up the cairn until he balanced himself on the top rock, his arms raised as though he were holding up the entire sky.

"The dust folds...*now!*"

The magus threw his hands forward with all his might like he believed he could push the world back a hundred years.

The first dragon felt the punch, turned away, then came back with a roar.

Again the magus threw the weight of the dust at the beast and again it was halted only to resume its forward steps.

Then the raspy cough, the dry throat-clearing sound.

"It's getting ready to fire!" Corlan cried out.

Joragus did not seem fazed, standing firm atop the cairn.

"I shall not die in a bed!"

The dragon reared back, neck curling up into the air, then threw its head forward and down with its mouth open. The flame blazed out of its mouth like a dozen lightning strikes —

Instead of being burned alive, the magus caught the fire against the shield he had made by compressing the dust of the air. His two palms turned toward each other, containing the fire, collecting it into a large flaming sphere as wide as a man's height. The magus threw the ball of fire back at the dragon with the same force he had sent the shield wave at the beast.

The fiery sphere crashed against the dragon's face, bursting like a balloon over its nose and burning its eyes as the lower portion of flame spilled into its mouth and ran down the outside of its throat.

The beast reared backwards, off-balance, then fell over, landing on its spine. It immediately rolled to its feet again, though with effort. The back spines were broken, bent.

"Not so good when *you* have to eat it, eh?" the magus laughed.

Corlan could see its eyes were glassy, blinded. He jumped to his feet, slinger ready to launch.

"Wait! Save the bolt," said the magus.

"Tam!" Corlan shouted. "My battle axe!"

The second dragon stood glaring at the two humans: one atop the pile of rocks, the other standing to its side. Corlan watched it glance at the injured dragon in front then at the humans beyond. Eyes blinked, choices calculated. Wings folded against its ribs.

Corlan felt footsteps rushing up behind him. With a slight turn he saw the boy dragging the long-handled axe across the ground.

"Easy with that," Corlan growled.

He took the handle from Tam, swung the heavy weapon up to his shoulder. The weapon was shaped like an anvil, wide blade in the front, long spike behind the wooden clasp and iron rivets. It was only a little lighter than the dragonslinger.

"Get back, boy!"

Corlan took the axe in his two hands, raised it off his shoulder, in position to swing it.

"Ready!" he shouted. "Are you ready? Number two is agitated."

"I hope not," said Joragus. "I'm spent. The dust falls apart."

The second dragon plodded forward, mouth open wide, throat glowing with irritation.

There's the target! Come on, keep your ugly maw open!

Corlan dropped the axe at his feet, picked up the dragonslinger, laying it over the rocks as the magus climbed down.

"I'll use the slinger for this one!"

The second dragon stepped ahead, one forefoot pushing against the fallen comrade there, jostling the body. Though still alive, ribs rising and falling with each labored breath, it was too wounded to fight, its face and throat seriously burned despite the scaling.

After giving a nose tap to its comrade, the second dragon rushed forward and met the iron bolt of Corlan's dragonslinger —

It was a perfect shot: straight into the gullet!

Yet before the dragon could choke on the poison, it pushed ahead and with one clumsy forefoot smashed the cairn of rocks.

Joragus was thrown to the side and Corlan was knocked over, rocks falling over him.

He stared up at the dragon. Its red eyes seemed to know him, as if from memory. It must have a plan to kill him and in that instant calculating its next move. The dragon's head hovered over the two humans, its mouth closed but eyes examining them.

Suddenly the iron bolt was spit out, dropping beside Corlan.

He scrambled up, gained his balance, tossing the rocks aside and reached for the slinger, now unloaded. He pulled it free from the fallen cairn and tried to drag it away with him as he forced himself to move faster. He felt his knee crying in pain. He did not care; he had to get away.

The dragon roared, stomped forward. The long middle claw of the forefoot stabbed the soil behind Corlan. He fell, tripping over the handle of the battle axe on the ground. He picked it up as the twin spikes protruding from the dragon's chin stabbed down over him, marking the boundary of his prison.

Another step, another claw piercing into the earth. Corlan felt his leg stung. The claw had sliced open his pants, cut into the flesh of his thigh. A line of blood appeared.

He balanced the axe handle in his hands, took aim.

The forefoot claw struck again and Corlan swung the heavy axe down across the dragon's forefoot, breaking the tendon attached to that awful middle claw. The beast roared. Corlan hacked at the base of the claw again and again, as hard as he could, as the dragon lifted its foot and tried to shake the blade free.

The axe blade caught in the flesh of the forefoot. The middle claw was loose, hanging half-attached. Corlan swung up at the dangling claw, hit the last string of tendon and severed it. The huge curved talon dropped to the soil in front of him.

The dragon was screaming, stomping against the earth. Claws dug into the gravel where Corlan stood — right, then left, right again, then in front of him — as the two chin horns struck at him, stabbing at the earth. One caught his hip, grazing his skin.

Corlan danced among the claw strikes, swinging the axe as best he could against the chin horns and the other claws of the forefoot. Yet the dragon did not cease its attack. It brought the other forefoot into the battle, jabbing it at Corlan, pressing its claws into the soil around the pesky human.

Corlan was trapped, his blood soaking into his clothing, the axe heavy in his tired hands.

"Dive left!" called Joragus.

He dove.

"More left!"

Corlan dove again, losing his grip on the axe.

The dragon fell back like it had hit a wall as the magus stood tall once more, holding his arms aloft with his hands open, palms gathering the dust of the air and transforming it into a shield then thrusting it back at the dragon.

"Be gone!" cried the magus. "Be gone now!"

The dragon pulled its head away as though it smelled something vile. The magus pushed his hands forward. The dragon extended its head and neck, the first sign of impending fire.

"I can't hold him!" cried the magus, forced to step back.

"I have no weapon!" Corlan shouted, seeing the axe flat on the ground under the dragon's forefoot.

"Then it has been good to know you!"

"Likewise, old man!"

"See you in the Beyond!"

"I'll look for you!"

Suddenly a high-pitched shriek filled the valley, a siren as loud as a thunderclap. It startled the dragon, made it halt in place. But the shriek was not a shriek, the more Joragus listened. Corlan cocked his head, listening, though the noise was almost too loud to endure.

It was a bird call.

Corlan dared not turn to look but guessed it was the girl, Madi.

She stepped up behind him, singing as loud as she could.

And the dragon tilted its head, curious perhaps, eyes changing from deep red to soft teal then to dull gray, its claws curled back, its hulking body moving away, spiny tail curling around its retreating hindfeet.

Then the hornchin turned completely around as if embarrassed and lumbered away, wounded, off to join the other dragons feasting on their fallen comrades.

The girl continued to sing. Gradually her notes softened until at last they faded away and only the silence of the night could be heard alongside the chewing of the dragons farther down the riverbed.

"I suggest we get away while we can," said Corlan, limping over to the girl. He grabbed her arm and ushered her away, dragging the battle axe and the slinger.

"Amazing!" shouted Joragus, following them. "Your music is more powerful than my magic." He called to Corlan. "Or that one's weaponry. We could have used that trick about forty minutes ago. Now you've splattered your blood on my robe."

Corlan glanced back. "It's not my blood, old man."

15

City of Salvation

CORLAN WAS CERTAIN OF IT. His senses were never wrong when it came to dragons. He had felt it when one of them got close to him. He knew it without any doubt when the last dragon stared at him, eye to eye, waiting three heartbeats, as if deciding whether to kill him or for some reason spare his life. He was convinced the dragon knew him, had plotted to kill him, had sought him—and found him. They certainly knew his path; he was easy to locate, being limited to the valley. He didn't dare tell the others, unwilling to worry them.

"We need better defense," said Corlan as the cart creaked along the dry riverbed.

They passed under a few trees here and there. The two donkors were reliable yet slow, plodding at a steady pace. The girafors were unconcerned and happy to follow. Elo was tasked with carrying the quivers of iron bolts, saving Pex the weight. The wheels rumbled, one slightly broken yet holding together. The cart tilted from side to side as it rolled over uneven ground, Corlan pulling on the reins as the magus urged the donkors onto a smoother path.

"Besides the dragonslinger," Corlan continued, "we don't have much weaponry to handle an attack like that last one. A sideblade won't help much."

He glanced at the sheath on his hip, patted the hilt of his favorite short sword which he had ripped out of the dragon's foot after it lay dead on the riverbed and the others had flown away.

"I have magic," said Joragus, lifting his bandaged arm, "yet I am old and cannot perform it for long."

"As well you're not quick enough to keep away from a slicing dragon talon," said Corlan.

Somewhere in the final confrontation, the forefoot claw of the leading hornchin had clipped the old man's sleeve, tearing a hole in the fabric, scoring his arm. Corlan never saw it, switching weapons. It was not a fatal wound. Tam was able to apply the balm and wrap cloth tightly around the old man's arm.

"Hardly worth the bother, now that my robe's been soiled," he had said, patting his bandaged limb. Tam had stitched up the torn robe. "I thank you again for your skills. Every band of travelers has need of a kitchen boy, I say!"

Despite the wounding, the old man was able to join Tam and the girl in helping Corlan lift onto the rear of the cart the huge claw he had cut from the dragon's forefoot. The thing was as large as half the cart; curled as it was, it was longer than Corlan's arm. It would be the proof Corlan said he needed in order to return to the Burg. Or it could be sold as a souvenir in the next town, the proceeds used to purchase more supplies.

"I could not move away," Joragus protested. "I was keeping the beast from killing you!"

"Thanks for that," said Corlan. "Next time we might not have the same luck. Weapons...magic...."

"A worthy combination," Joragus sang.

"And Madi's song," Tam added.

Corlan smiled. "The song to soothe the savage beast. Yet how well will that trick work next time? Is it for only certain species? Or for certain situations? What if she sings off-key or out-of-tune? Or sings a wrong note?"

"I can fight, too," Tam offered. "Just give me a sword."

"You know how?" asked Corlan.

"Joragus taught me."

Corlan laughed, then reached back and lunged finger-first at the boy. Tam parried with his hand.

"I was a swordsman in my first life, yet you may not believe," said Joragus. "Quite handy with a blade. Then I died, of course—yet not before my essence was reformed in the kitchens of the Clona artisans in Danapo. Great kitchens there. Just need for remaking body parts after the wars. Once remade, I plied my trade with the arts, not a blade. And my glory did not fade!"

"You remember your training after these many years?" Corlan challenged. "At least you remember your songs."

"A master swordsman never forgets his moves."

"Where is Dian...apa...?"asked Tam.

"Danapo. A large city far west of here—west and much to the north, away from the River Oh. It was noted in those days as the city of Prince Urix during the legendary age."

"Oh."

Joragus chuckled. "I only came to Metta at the invitation of the prince. Gellas was his name, as I recall. Huge man, bald and toothy. He had need of a magus. He didn't live long after I arrived. I made my next iteration there. Then this present iteration. Or else I would have been gone long ago, long before the plague, before the Great Fire, before many things people have now forgotten."

"You got your history mixed up again," Corlan snorted.

"You should write a scroll about everything," said Tam.

"Don't think I haven't." Joragus waved his arm back at the bag of tubes. "There is the history of the realm in nine scrolls. I have written up to the final days of the plague. The fire-pit story."

"Then you can write about meeting us," Tam suggested. "And the drakes. And the temple on fire. And us running away...."

"Yes, indeed, that would make a lovely scroll."

"And you can write about how we found Madi."

The girl heard her name, turned and squawked.

"I'm not quite certain how that happened, despite two versions."

"And the attack last night!"

"I'm not quite certain I can relive that using only my stylus." The magus yawned. "I'm still agitated by the event."

"Then you should relax...."

"A great idea!"

The cart rolled along, the magus slipping into a nap. Talk of the legendary days had made them feel sorrow. The idea of recording events seemed frivolous and futile. If their party were vanquished, it would all be lost.

Corlan cleared his throat to send away the morbid mood.

"And in your swordsman days, did you fight for a prince?"

Joragus awoke, laughed. "Indeed, I did."

"No dragons in those days?"

"Rare. They were not such a problem in those days. Kept to the west lands mainly."

"And their origins?"

"None knew."

"Were they made with Clona art?"

"That's only gossip. We argued over that before. No more! What reason would any magus have for creating them? It's a ridiculous claim. And where came the dust from living beasts to use for the procedure?"

"You said they all flew up out of the earth during the Great Fire," said Tam.

"I said that? Was I drunk then?" Joragus shook his head. "I must have said it in jest. Pure jest."

Corlan scratched his beard. "Now they rule the Valley of Death."

"Indeed, they do."

Corlan pursed his lips. He cleared his throat, coughing loudly and spitting. "I think they know me."

Joragus turned his head to gaze at Corlan. "Know you?"

"The way that last hornchin stared at me.... It could've burned me in an instant yet it hesitated, like it was deciding my fate."

"Deciding your fate?" The magus chuckled. "You took a clap to the head, didn't you?"

"That delay gave us the extra moment we needed."

"Extra moments are gifts of the gods, not a dragon's whim."

Corlan nodded but he was still concerned. He replayed the battle in his head as the cart rolled on.

"The road ahead will become worse, I fear."

Joragus sighed. "Yet you do not fear it."

"I don't."

He let the cart roll on a while.

"The three of you don't belong on this trek," Corlan grunted, then spoke up louder: "I was meant to go alone. How many attacks could we survive? Any one of them could destroy us."

The girl tweeted loudly.

"I thought you were teaching her our words," Corlan addressed the boy.

"We got distracted."

Corlan laughed. "Dragons, eh?"

He pulled up his pant leg to check the cuts he had gotten from the jagged rocks of the cairn and the dragon's claw.

"Just a scratch," he had told them. Yet the boy applied the same balm used for Pex's thigh. Pulling off his shirt, they could see the streak across his back made by one of the dragon's chin horns. More downward pressure on him and the wound would have been fatal. As it was, only a long curved slice remained, a half-inch deep at the lower end over his hip. At the opposite end, the lower edge of his shoulder blade, it was barely a scratch. Corlan had laughed it off, compared it to the curved scar across his chest, told them how the ladies liked to trace the scar with their fingers before they made joy. Unamused, the magus had sewn up the deeper part of the cut and the boy applied the balm.

"Yes, dragons," said Tam with a frown as Madi began singing.

"What's she saying now?" asked Corlan. "She's taking credit for singing away the dragons, I suppose."

More tweeting from the girl, caws and cries as she became more agitated.

"She means to let you know how she feels," said Joragus. "She has an understanding with dragons. Her people, that is. They guard her village. They care for her and her tribe. When an old dragon dies, they use its parts to build the village. They don't hunt them."

"Is that so?" Corlan grumbled. "Then I suppose she hates me for killing them."

"No, of course not." Joragus smiled at the girl. "She knows they tried to kill us and we had to defend ourselves. She only wishes the entire episode had gone differently."

More tweets, sad in tone.

"She fears she will never be taken back to her tribe. The dragons know her now as an enemy."

"We are all the enemy of dragons," said Corlan roughly. "And the dragons are the enemy of all people. I can't understand what she means by having an understanding with them."

"They talk to each other," Tam blurted.

"I guessed as much," said Corlan. "Yet she clearly wanted to flee the village, escape from her mother, the evil queen or whatever they called her. She wanted to run. I never forced her to come along."

"Don't tease her, Corlan," cautioned Tam.

"Not teasing, boy. Speculating."

"She doesn't want to be here now," said Tam.

"A change of her heart," said the magus. "Happens the further from home one goes."

"Maybe she thinks she's a hostage now and dragons will come looking for her." Corlan stared at Madi. "Is that right?"

She shook her head fiercely, her brown hair fanning her face.

"No-oh go you ah you!" she spoke in her high-pitched voice.

"You don't want to go with us?" asked Joragus. "Do I get your meaning?"

She rolled her head around, eyes fluttering.

"She is afraid of us, of what dragons will do to her because she is with us," Tam explained.

"How can you two understand her?" Corlan cursed.

"*Fralio potee vasoz,*" said Madi solemnly, careful to pronounce the words correctly.

"Ah! The ancient tongue of Metta," said Joragus, then added a winsome sigh. "The sacred words: *Fralio,* the name of hornchins, and *potee,* meaning 'to go', and *vasoz,* 'to carry'. To carry like a mother carries a baby. Hence, the hornchins care for them."

Madi spoke more of the strange language of Metta and Joragus translated.

"It is too late," Corlan countered. "We are many miles from her village now. Besides, I doubt her mother will take her back. We have corrupted her, poor girl. She can only go forward. That means with us. It would be dangerous for a girl, a girl of her age, to be alone in the wilderness." He shook his head. "Or in a city. That would be much worse."

More of the strange tongue with translation.

"If she is so certain about leaving us," said Corlan, "she can go her own way when we get to a city. Wherever that might be." He shook his head. "What else can a girl do here in the Valley of Death? Share our precious rations?"

"She can protect us," said Tam. "She sings to dragons."

Joragus spoke up: "Every creature has worth and value—"

"I'm not saying she has no worth!" Corlan exclaimed.

"*Fralio...Hunio...Lertio...Saromio...Wegio...beo ti vasa noi ilagia Corlanio!*"

"She names the dragons of her region," Joragus spoke. "And she calls you a dragon, too, Corlan."

"Corlanio!" Tam snickered.

"Quiet, boy!"

"She says you have fire-breath," said Joragus.

"My belly is full of hot air, eh? Ready to spit fire, eh?" Corlan did not enjoy the comparison. "We protect each other. We're like a very strange family. I never had a family—not a real family, anyway. Just my father, grandfather, a woman here and there for a few nights, a child or two. I had a mother, certainly. I remember her." He paused, ran his fingers through his hair, tugged at the ends, realizing how long it had grown. "And I left them all. All of them. Never could stay for long. I'm meant to be on a road."

"Why is that?" asked Tam.

Corlan shook his head, pursed his lips. "I don't know. It must be a form of dark magic. Those days sleep in my head. Dark magic has rubbed out my thoughts." He glared at Joragus. "You know about dark magic?"

"Not I," the magus replied.

Madi tweeted a soft song. It went on for a few minutes, rising and falling, then came a slow and somber ending.

"Thanks," said Corlan. "That's what I feel."

"It's all those demons you carry," said Joragus. "I told you to get rid of them. They steal your good memories, offer up only sorrow and regret."

"That may be so, old man."

"Madi can sing away the demons, can't she?" said Tam. "She is a music girl."

The girl grinned, knowing she had dome something good.

"Whatever demons hang on to me doesn't take me from the choices we face now. The Valley of Death. The dragons. Whatever other beasts or terrors we encounter. They strike at my head harder than any legion of demons. Each day takes us closer to death."

"We were lucky last night," said Joragus softly.

Corlan's face turned serious. "Yes. It took everything we had to give and then some luck." He ran through the inventory in his mind. "We have a good, sturdy bow with a hundred razor-tipped arrows. And we've plenty of blade weapons—yet who but I could use them? The slinger is for hunting. It's no defense against multiple attackers."

As the cart rolled on, he stared off at the landscape: the smooth dry hills spotted with short yellow grass and stubby green trees, as though they were newly grown from previous destruction. He did not think the Great Fire had burned this far to the east.

"It will be more dangerous each day." Corlan gazed at the boy, then at the girl. "I was planning to go alone on this journey. I was *forced* to go on this journey. The truth is that I was banished from the Burg—unfairly, mind you. Politics! Mere social squabbling. Again." He regarded Joragus. "Now you three have joined me. And I've put you in danger."

"It's not you," said Tam. "It's the dragons that put us in danger, that's who!"

"If not for you, I wouldn't be a few days older," said the magus.

"I'm alive, too!" Tam shouted. "And we saved Madi. And Madi saved us, too."

"The reason for this journey is dragons," Corlan said, grunting. "It has always been about destroying dragons."

"According to the map scroll, there is a city further on," Joragus told them. "Unting is the name. It is south of the valley."

"If it is still standing there today," said Corlan, "and not lost in the dust of centuries." He met the eyes of each traveling companion. Then he looked away. "When we do find that city...we should part ways there. You can find more suitable things to do with your lives. Better than going on a crazy journey with a madman—a madman seeking death."

"What is this outrage?" the magus exclaimed, turning in his seat.

"And I will continue on." Corlan returned his gaze. "On to my destiny, following my plan. No matter what I find, no matter what finds me."

"To kill all the dragons?" asked the magus in a skeptical voice.

"To kill their eggs," Corlan replied. "In the nesting ground. That will end them once and for all."

"If they do not kill you first."

Corlan glared at the old man. "They do seem to have a plan for that."

"What?" asked the boy.

"Last night...."

The girl tweeted a song. She waved her hands in front of her belly as she sat with her skinny legs crossed on the back of the cart.

Tam frowned. "She says she doesn't want to part from us."

"It's better if she does," said Corlan. He took a deep breath. "Last night, I could've sworn that last dragon was studying me. Then Madi sang her song and they calmed and went away. If they connect her with me, she will be in danger. She is right about that."

"You'll need an army if you expect to pass through the Valley of Death unharmed." Joragus rubbed his hands together. "More men like yourself. In the city, perhaps there is a younger magus who would go with you. Magic has saved you each time we have been attacked. The iron bolt is, as you say, a hunting tool."

Madi tweeted again, something serious it seemed.

"Can you translate?" Corlan asked the magus, staring at Tam.

"She says she cannot go along her own way."

"She's afraid," said Tam, looking not too pleased himself.

"You would leave us to fend for ourselves?" asked Joragus. "An old man, a young woman, and a boy? What shall we do for ourselves in whichever city we find?"

"I thought whatever we find there would be safer than what lies ahead."

"Is not a strange city more dangerous than a wild valley?" asked Joragus.

Corlan sighed, felt the wraps around his leg tighten and hurt. His shirt had stuck to the balm on his back, too. *Let no dragons pester us this day. I need time to recover.* He hadn't thought it out very well, he knew, but the idea was sound. None of them had any reason to be on such a trek with him. And yet, were it not for them, he very likely would be dead now, food for dragons.

"We still must find the town," said Corlan. "We need to get more supplies. That is, *I* need supplies."

"And thus *we* find a lovely park to take our rest in? Then wander about the streets begging for some food." The magus leaned over to Corlan. "And what do you think will happen to a young woman like her in a dirty city like Unting? And this boy...he'll be back in a kitchen, at best. Or much worse. What is worse is—"

"Enough!"

When a road crossed in front of them, cutting the riverbed from shore to shore, they knew civilization lay close. They turned onto the stone path and rolled south, leaving the valley. The donkors found the going easier and their pace quickened.

The landscape turned from scrubland and desert to crop fields and orchards, vast hillsides of plenty, then fenced pastures holding animals destined for dinner. The girafors reached up for snacks as they passed under dark groves. Other roads intersected their path. Farmsteads. Houses. Other buildings, more of them gathered around road intersections. Corlan had never suspected such beautiful land existed so far from the Burg.

In the distance a long hill rose, and on the hill, silhouetted by the afternoon sun, stood the ramparts and towers of a walled city.

"That must be Unting," said Joragus, "unless my eyes are dim."

The boy and the girl rose on the cart to have a better look. Corlan remained quiet. The magus waved his hand ahead. The boy and the girl chattered excitedly, half tweets, half words.

"We must be on guard at all times," Corlan finally spoke.

Gradually the road led up through forested hills, rising higher until the road broke onto a plateau. There the road went straight ahead to the main gate of the city. By then, other carts, wagons, and carriages had joined them on the way to and from the city. People riding on strange animals passed them, some on mounts that looked like donkors but were larger, some on mounts that were striped, others with horns or antlers. Other people rode large black birds with clipped wings. One fellow scooted past the cart on the back of a long reddish wyrm.

Corlan pointed to the snake-like beast running on stubby legs with its flickering tail following. "That's a wyrm for you, Tam."

The boy was impressed, expressing his desire to ride one himself.

They passed a sign announcing the city of Unting.

At the gate, the line of travelers slowed and halted. Guards spoke with each traveling party. One wagon full of a kind of round green fruit was turned away. Another cart, with an elderly couple hunched atop stacks of some kind of golden plant stalks, was also sent away.

"Let me do the talking," said Corlan. He pointed at each of his companions. "If they ask any questions, you are my grandfather, you are my daughter, and you are my son. Remember."

"Your grandfather?" asked Joragus. "Not...father?"

"Not with a beard like that."

They nodded their understanding. Madi added a whistle.

"May they speak the same words as us," said Corlan.

When the way ahead was clear, Corlan shook the reins to urge the donkors forward, then reined them back to halt them beside the guards. The three guards wore red uniforms head to boot-tops, black leather braces and loin panels, and bore sideblades. One guard at the rear of the guard stand wielded a shiny halberd. The captain wore additional decorations on his shoulders and a red cap crossed with a shiny silver X pinned to it.

"Who wishes to enter?" asked the guard as the captain watched a few steps behind.

"We have been on a journey for two months...my family and me," said Corlan in humble tone. "We are weary and wounded and wish to rest a bit, purchase some supplies, and find our way again."

"Whence come?"

Corlan was about to say 'the Burg' but thought a moment. That would place them from far afield, possibly from a place these guards had not heard of, putting them at risk of being considered merely vagabonds. If he told them they were from Metta, that could also be a black mark to the guards, especially if they knew that the city had been abandoned following the plague.

"Whence come?" asked the guard again.

Corlan grinned. "I have forgotten."

"Forgotten?" asked the guard. The captain stepped forward.

"I took a hit to my head. I still cannot recall anything from more than a week ago. That was when we were attacked."

"Attacked?" asked the captain.

"By dragons," Joragus spoke, waving off Corlan. "My grandson here did his best to fight them." He turned and gestured at the lump behind him on the cart, rising between the boy and the girl. The tip of the dragon's claw poked out from under the tarp. "He managed to harm the beast. We have proof of it. Poor lad got hit on the head, however. He will be able to recover if we can rest a few days in your fine city."

The guards expressed surprise, even admiration at the sight of the claw cut from the forefoot of a dragon.

"True it appears," said the captain. "Intend you here to sell it?"

"Yes," said Corlan suddenly, acting as though he was breaking out of a stupor. "We hope to sell it for supplies to journey home."

"Know not your home? How there go you?"

"My mind will recover after a few days," said Corlan, putting his palm to his forehead.

"My grandson is a strong man," said Joragus, "yet who among us can receive a knock from a hornchin and not be lame for some time?"

"Speak you a commonplace," said the captain. "Hornchin? Mean you the duo-spike blackranger? From ancient days?"

"Not ancient days, a week ago. Likely the same beast." Joragus quickly picked up the local vernacular. "Know you a fine lodge for simple folk having little coin?"

"Many here are. West go you, past the gate, three turns then find you a good stayover."

"And know you good storage for beasts?"

"Beasts?" He studied the two donkors, not so unfamiliar, then stared at the tall girafors. He cocked his head. "What they be?"

"They are called *girafor*. From the south they come. Sturdy beasts of burden."

"Uncommon here."

"Have you an animal park in the city?" asked Joragus.

"None for strange beasts such as those."

"Then we shall mind them ourselves."

The captain nodded curtly and waved them on through the gate.

"The tall beasts! Mind their heads and necks!" he shouted.

Tam jumped off the cart and pulled at the tethers of the girafors, coaxing them to lower their long necks until they could pass under the archway. Even so, Pex bumped his head—rather, the two knobs on his head caught the ceiling bricks and he panicked. Tam grabbed the tether tighter, pulling his head lower, and spoke calming words to Pex while Elo seemed to glance with amusement at her twin.

"To the right your vehicle should turn," the captain called. "In the office, register you must your arrival, and all weapons for the duration of your stay put aside."

Joragus pointed to the office and they pulled up the cart. Corlan entered and when the parchments seemed too strange, he called for the boy to assist.

"Write your name there," said Tam, pointing. "Write your city on that line and your destination and business in this city on those lines."

"How about you write all of that?" Corlan suggested.

"Weapons have you?" asked the uniformed official.

"I have plenty."

"In a vault here all of them you should deposit. A small item for personal protection allowed shall be. Harsh penalties if found you be in fault of more than personal defense."

"I understand," said Corlan. He went out and retrieved the long bag of weapons, all the blades and the bow and arrows. Cataloging them took an hour.

"What about the dragonslinger?" asked Tam too innocently.

"What's that?" asked the official.

"It's not a weapon. It's a tool I use. It's not for people, at least. It's for hunting dragons."

"Dragons?" The official laughed and Corlan felt offended.

"Yes, dragons. We were attacked by dragons not a week past."

"Where that be?"

"North — in the ancient river valley."

"What a fine storyteller!" The official stood smug. "The old tales of the scrolls, I remember. Dragons from ancient days a myth be."

"It's true!" Tam spoke up.

"No dragons ever trouble this city?" asked Corlan.

"Not in my life." The official was not going to be someone Corlan ever had a drink with. "If true it ever be, not taught in schools be it."

"At any case, it's not a weapon. It's a tool of my occupation. I'm a dragonslayer." Corlan frowned at the official. "I won't be using it in the city, that's for certain."

The official was satisfied when the bag of assorted weaponry was hefted into a bin and locked, and sent them on. Corlan got to keep his dragonslinger.

"Keep to safe conduct in your stayover."

"We aren't going to get into trouble so don't worry," Tam called back as they stepped out of the registration office. The swinging door tapped his backside.

With all aboard the cart, Joragus took the reins and urged the two donkors to move on, the girafors trailing. The cart rolled into a large open square full of people walking every direction and animals strolling without purpose, and sales kiosks standing among small crowds of shoppers. Dust blew back and forth and the chaotic noise assaulted their ears.

"Keep to the left," said Corlan, glancing at everyone they passed, regarding each person as possible trouble.

People paused to watch the long-necked animals stroll through the marketplace behind the cart of foreigners. Children called their excitement at seeing such strange creatures. A few younger children ran alongside the cart, asking what the animals were called.

"They are girafors," Tam called back, proudly.

Their tall necks lifted the girafors' heads well above the crowds. The girafors became nervous in the noisy crowd and Corlan worried they might panic and kick out at anyone coming too close.

"Tam, get down and walk with them."

The boy hopped down. He walked between the girafors, patting their throats, speaking to them: "Be calm, Pex. Calm now, Elo. You're both safe with me."

The cart rolled slowly through the streets and the crowds fell away. As they went along each street, people paused to note their passage, the girafors' heads bobbing above the roofs and the trees.

Tam got back on the cart and they continued without any trouble.

Eventually they found a lodge, the third choice, in a quiet quarter of the city. Corlan pulled the reins and the donkors halted.

"THE DEWLAP SQUATTER," spoke Corlan, gazing up at the sign over the entrance. "Looks like the sort of place to spend our coin."

Tam questioned the meaning of the name and Corlan only shook his head. The girl tweeted something but seemed glad to be stopped and able to get off the cart. She reached behind herself and squeezed her backside several times, then waved her arms several times as though they were wings. Joragus needed help climbing down from the cart and, standing unsteadily, leaned on his staff.

"This will do for a few days," said Corlan, climbing off the cart.

Madi jumped off the rear of the cart, fell on her small knees. Tam helped her up. Her sparse garments twisted around her body when she fell and Tam's gaze lingered. She straightened her skirt and vest.

Corlan tossed a blanket from the back of the cart to her and she wrapped it around her shoulders. "We're in a city now. Different customs."

"Tan-gu," she spoke with a sharp nod.

"*Thanks*, Madi," said Tam. "It's Thank You."

"Tang yooth...."

Corlan examined the street in each direction. The buildings were three-level, stone and brick, with small windows high up, none on the ground level. Maybe thieves ruled the night, he considered. The late afternoon light filtered down like rain between the buildings, turning the intersection at the end of the lane into a bright golden fountain.

A few doors down the slope was a carriage house, Corlan saw by the sign protruding from the wall. At that moment, a stablehand escorted two beautiful beasts by their harnesses out the open doors. Both animals were black as night, bearing long heavy manes and wide-fanning tails, prancing dutifully on the stone street.

"Is that a...horse?" Corlan asked in raised tone.

"Quite so," said Joragus. "It has been a hundred years since last I put my eyes on a real one."

"Beautiful," Corlan muttered. "Too beautiful for pulling a cart. I'd still use the donkors." He grabbed Tam. "See those? Men used to ride them more than two hundred years ago in the Burg." Turning back to Joragus: "They must be expensive."

"You're not interested in them, are you?" asked the magus.

The youth led the horses down the slope where they turned and trotted out of sight.

"If I were traveling alone, I would," Corlan responded. "One for myself, one for supplies. Worthy of a prince, eh? Yet I know I'm but a dreamer. Our fresh supplies could include a wagon, large enough for the supplies needed for four people, not only for a banished dragonslayer"

Joragus chuckled. "Now is not the time for dreaming."

"I'll be dreaming tonight, that's for certain! After a supper! After a long soaking bath. And you shouldn't wake me for a long time."

The magus tapped the end of his staff toward the lodge.

"I wouldn't dream of it, dragonslayer!"

16

Exotic Trinkets

AFTER ARRANGING FOR THE CART and the animals to be cared for overnight in the carriage house — with an extra fee for the girafors to cover their special food and a youth to watch them — they entered the lodge and Corlan spoke with the innkeeper who gave them two rooms: one for the men, one for the girl. Corlan introduced them as his family members. They had been on the road for several weeks, he explained, which matched their sorry condition. However, he did have coin.

The innkeeper's grown daughter, a chubby-faced woman with muscular arms, came out of the kitchen to greet them. Their fare included supper, the innkeeper told them, and that hour was soon approaching.

Corlan dug deep in his trouser pouch and produced a few coins, stamped with the face of his cousin, Prince Vilmer.

"I'll be glad to part with these," he said with a strained smile.

Tam tugged on Corlan's shirt. "I got two coins. The stable master gave them to me. It's for helping with the girafors. I was supposed to give one to the other boy."

"But you never went back, did you?" said Corlan accusingly.

Tam hung his head down. "No, I didn't."

Corlan put his hand on the boy's shoulder. "Don't feel bad. That boy never had to face dragons. You've earned both coins."

He let the boy contribute a coin. Of course the girl had no money and the old man hinted that he had saved a box of valuables from the temple but he did not offer anything to their expense.

"Enough for a few nights?" Corlan asked the innkeeper.

"Gold is always accepted, no matter whose face is stamped on it." The innkeeper looked them over again. "And how many nights your stayover be?"

"Three, I think."

Corlan flipped a couple more coins onto the desk.

"Very good, sir."

"No need to call me *sir*."

"Very good, traveler."

They gathered up the belongings they had carried in from the cart, which they had set on the floor by the desk, and carried them up the stairs.

Entering the room, Corlan dropped the supplies he was carrying and threw himself on the bed. Tam set down beside the door what he held in his arms. Joragus sauntered in with staff in hand, leaning on it for balance, and set his large canvas bag at the foot of the bed. Madi entered and set down her share of the supplies from the cart, tweeting something.

"You have a room for yourself," said Tam, waving her back to the door. He took her out.

"You have no doubt noticed, at first look, my dear Corlan," said Joragus, standing stiffly in the center of the room, "that we've only one bed, though it is double-width, as for a wedded couple."

"What's that?" asked Corlan, not moving from his spot.

"I said we have only one bed."

Corlan sat up, looking about the room. "The boy can use the mat on the floor. And...you and I will have to share. I know you snore, but I let go the air, so we are bound to annoy each other equally."

"No worse than a campsite on hard ground, I suppose," said the magus with a snort. "I presume you will bathe tonight?"

"I must!" He sniffed himself.

"Then I shall be satisfied tonight."

"You must bathe, as well, though after me."

"I'm the old man, the poor sacred soul who needs gentleness."

"I am the dragonslayer who keeps us safe."

"My magic is what keeps us safe!"

Tam returned just in time. "She got her room now. She took off her clothes right away and started washing them. She looks strange."

"Good you left, boy," said Corlan. "A lady needs her privacy."

"And the cart? The dragon claw?" asked Joragus.

"The stable master promised us security."

"Is he trustworthy? A dragon claw is a mighty tempting item."

Corlan chuckled. "No thief could carry it away by himself."

"Two could. Or three. It is not hard to do." Joragus thought for a moment. "Perhaps you should guard it. If it is truly so valuable. The cart itself would not strike anyone's fancy and the donkors are safe in the pens with the girafors."

"I wouldn't put it past someone to be interested in our girafors," said Corlan. "They're exotic beasts here."

"Can I guard them?" asked Tam.

Corlan shook his head. "No, Tam. If someone wanted to take them, you're not big enough to stop them." He glared at Joragus. "I see what you're doing, old man."

"What's he doing?" asked Tam, glancing between the magus and Corlan. "A trick?"

"Yes, a trick. Our friend Joragus conspires to send me out to the stable tonight, so he can have the bed to himself. That's it, isn't it?"

Joragus bowed his head solemnly. "I only suggest that as you went through some difficulty obtaining that dragon claw, it would be a disaster to find it stolen by morning."

Corlan made fists, kept them at his sides. "We'll sell it tomorrow. I'll have this bed tomorrow night, old man. So you enjoy it tonight."

"Where do I sleep?" asked the boy.

Corlan pointed to the mat rolled on the floor. "That will do well, eh? It's not on the ground."

"A mat?" He frowned.

"Unroll it. Still better than out on the rough ground, eh?"

"I suppose."

Corlan studied the boy. "You can lay on the bed until the old man is ready to sleep. How's that?"

Tam nodded, pouting.

Corlan clapped. "Now, let's get the supper they promised."

Beans, they called it — a big bowl of them: round and brown, the size of the coins that paid for their room and dinner. The pile of beans in the large bowl was topped with a lot of green stalks, softened by cooking, and several oval-shaped yellow leaves. Another dish served to them and the other guests of the lodge was a red porridge with black speckles sprinkled over it. Another plate had cubes of yellow cheese; Corlan started popping the cubes into his mouth. There were lengths of black bread that had been cut and lay on a communal plate, and a bowl of hard-milk to spoon and slather over the bread.

The innkeeper's daughter muttered to her father how strange the strangers were.

Corlan laughed off the insult. It was a fresh meal for once and it was satisfying. But there did not seem to be any meat. To drink, there was a weak golden brew for the adults—Corlan still asked where the nearest tavern was—and small cups of yellowish fruit juice for the young ones.

"Not the same as drake tail, eh?" Corlan offered.

"Much better than drake tail," mumbled the magus, chomping on a mouthful of food. "A delicious flavoring I've not tasted before."

"It's yummy," said Tam.

Madi stared at her plate, her hands in her lap.

"You don't like it?" asked the innkeeper's daughter. "Go on, try it. Nobody's ever died from my cooking."

Madi dipped her finger into the red porridge on her plate, raised her finger and licked it. She made an awful face and pushed the plate away.

"She has special tastes," said Corlan. "Do you have any seeds? Or nuts? Or maybe some insects?" He turned to Tam. "She liked eating the girafor food, didn't she? Leaves ground into pellets."

"Yes, she likes those."

"I'll see what I can find in back," said the innkeeper's daughter, and stalked off to the kitchen. She returned after several minutes with a bowl of seeds, ready to plant in a garden. "Here you go: bird food," she sneered, setting down the bowl in front of the girl.

"Than-kuz," the girl spoke.

"Thank you," Tam corrected. Madi repeated after him.

She was delighted with the new dish and quickly began picking up the seeds and pushing them one at a time into her mouth. She bent her face down after a minute and licked up the seeds from the bowl.

"Youth these days," said the magus, "always so picky!"

By then, Corlan had sat back, patting his belly and sighing quite contentedly.

Everyone had fallen quiet—no small talk with the other guests. So they adjourned to their rooms to discuss the plan for the next day. There they agreed Corlan would sell the dragon claw while Joragus took Madi and Tam to the clothier for some new garments. They would all meet again at the lodge for supper.

Corlan tossed the blanket roll off his shoulder and onto the emptied rear of the cart. Everything had been taken up to the room in the lodge except the dragon claw. It rested on the floor of the carriage house in a pile of straw, mostly beneath the cart, covered with a tarp. The sharp tip still curved upward, making a dangerous obstacle for anyone climbing onto the cart.

"You're going to stay here, sir?" asked the stable boy, a youth of about eighteen years, tall and thin with short-cropped yellow hair.

"I am."

"That is not allowed. My master will beat me for allowing it."

"Then I will beat your master."

The stable boy looked scared.

"I won't steal anything, if that's your concern." Corlan hopped onto the rear of the cart, his foot just missing the claw's sharp point. "In fact, I am staying here to guard my own property until tomorrow when I can sell this thing."

"What thing is that?"

"Take a look." Corlan lifted the covering by the corner.

The youth bent down, gazing at the smooth, yellowish thing that curled upward. As they traveled, Corlan had cut away the meat and sinew so that only the bone and the enamel of the talon remained, clean and smooth. The youth seemed in awe.

"Ever see a dragon claw?" asked Corlan, puffing his chest.

"No, sir. Is that really what it is?"

"Truly." Corlan admired his trophy. "I did not kill the dragon it's from but I took this for a souvenir. I got the scars to prove it. Back and leg."

"How did you come to be attacked by dragons?"

Corlan smiled, wondering how much he should tell. The youth's tone was suspicious, unimpressed.

"They came upon us in the eve, and we awoke just in time to defend ourselves. About a week ago. There were a dozen of them but because the valley is long and narrow we only had to defend against one at a time."

"A dozen dragons?"

"Yes. A dozen that I counted. All had landed. Some dined on the first dragon I slew."

The youth maintained a calm facade, as though he was trying to hold his tongue in front of the customer.

"You don't have dragons here?" asked Corlan.

"I never did see one."

Corlan shrugged. "None fly over?"

"I hear of encounters when people go north," said the youth, tilting his head and fingering his chin. "We are safe here and have no difficulty with them." He laughed. "I almost didn't believe they still existed."

"Ah, but they do! Here is proof."

Corlan swung his hand at the claw.

"Not many folks go north from Unting. Our territory spreads to the south and east, not the north. You likely entered from the back gate if you came from the north. On the south side the river flows west from the hills—"

"River, you say?"

"Yes, the River Kana. It flows down from Carlet. In the east."

"Carlet?"

"The town upstream. The River Kana flows eventually down into the River Oh to the west."

"The River Oh? It flows still?" Corlan smiled. "I thought it dried up ages ago."

"North, perhaps." The youth seemed annoyed at the questions. "Here it flows west...as it always has."

Corlan sat back, grinning. "Are there boats that travel the river?"

The youth thought a moment. "I suppose they do. I never did go that way. We send horses that way from time to time. They might be taken by boat somewhere."

"To where? There are more cities that direction?"

"Oh, yes. Several. You never looked at a map?"

"Where I'm from we don't have maps of places that far west."

"Covin is the largest city on the river. Beyond there is Luval, then Evanal...and then you're into the marshes."

"The marshes!" Corlan's eyes lit up. "So it's true?"

"What is?"

"You said there are marshes."

"I know what I said." The youth seemed angry. "Yes, marshes."

"The river flows into the marshes then?"

"Yes. Stop repeating what I say." He stopped himself, lowered his head. "Sorry, sir. I misspoke."

"I was happy to hear the information, is all," said Corlan. "I only heard of the marshes from travelers. I wasn't sure they were telling the truth. You've been that way?"

"No, but I talk with travelers, too. Like you. People visit here and I care for their animals. Mostly horses. Not those long-necked things you brought in."

"The girafors. Special animals from another land." Corlan shook his head to clear his thoughts. "Tell me more about the rivers and the boats. Can a boat be hired?"

"You can hire anyone for anything in Unting. Be careful you get a fair deal, though. The rivermen are cutthroats. You might be put on a boat, then go the wrong way or sent off before your destination. I heard that happening. Or they kill you on the boat, just to get hold of your valuables, and throw the body over the side."

"Is that true?" Corlan stared at the dragon claw, thinking about his plan for the next day. He remembered the way people of Unting spoke. "Know you where a man could sell the talon from a dragon's forefoot?"

The youth smiled at the customer's imitation of the local speech. "Not so many shops deal in dragon parts. You could try down the Sundry Lane on the south side, near the main gate. They buy all sorts of things from people that visit. Mostly people that's needing money. So visiting people sell whatever they got. But I did see some weird items in the shops."

"Thanks. I'll try there. I may need assistance with this large item. If I could hire you for half a day.... Would your master allow it?"

"You better be speaking with him. I cannot ask for myself. That wouldn't be polite."

Corlan slept fitfully, his shoulders and hips not aligning well with the cart's slats. The occasional noise from the animals in the pens often nudged him out of sleep.

Then something soft and furry hopped up onto him and curled into the crook of his elbow. He petted it, listened to its purr, and for a few minutes thought he was a little boy again in the farmstead house at Stacol that he and his mother occupied before the family moved to the Burg after his father died. He'd had a pet there.

When he realized it was only a dream this time, he sprang awake in the dark, picking up the ball of fur, making sure it was real. Its golden eyes blinked in the dark as it let out a melodious exhale of contentment that glided over Corlan's face. He returned the animal to his elbow and tried to rejoin his dream-twin.

Before dawn, two young men entered the carriage house to begin cleaning it before the master arrived.

Corlan decided he could sleep no more. He gazed down, saw the sharp point of the claw still there. He smiled. This was going to be a great day! He got himself up and straightened his clothes, then went to find the stable master.

"I spoke with your master," Corlan told the youth as soon as he arrived. They had talked about the rivers and the cities to the west, somehow slipped into a debate about the gods until the youth had to excuse himself for the night. "For a small fee he will let you go free today. If you help me today, I will pay you double that wage."

The youth nodded. "I'm grateful, sir."

"What's your name?"

"Master calls me Deven."

"Is that the name you want me to call you?"

"I answer to that."

Deven pulled off his green stable jacket and put on a sleeveless leather vest. He shook his arms as though they had been tied up.

"Comfortable?" Corlan teased.

"If we are going about the city, I don't want to appear as a stable hand. I'm working for you today."

Together they set the dragon claw on the rear of the cart, tied it securely and covered it again with the tarp. Deven brought the two donkors from the pen outside and helped Corlan hitch them to the cart. The girafors remained in their own pen, stretching up to nibble on the leaves of trees in the next yard.

Following Deven's block by block directions, they made their way through the busy morning streets, to the main gate on the south side of the walled city. The stone walls were higher there, it seemed, the stone buildings taller and grander, yet the streets were older and narrower. It was the original district of the city, Deven explained.

They passed the palace with its towers and balconies, flags and rows of yellow-uniformed guards. No prince ruled this city, Deven told him. Instead, a council of eight administrators jointly governed. The palace was now only the council's headquarters. Some people complained how lavishly the families of the administrators lived there, as though they were the new princes.

"Palaces breed lavish living," Corlan muttered. He almost said more, decided in an instant not to talk about himself.

Finally they came to Sundry Lane. The storefronts there looked old and unused, quite plain, a few worn down and dingy. Corlan was not impressed. He asked Deven whether they were in the right location.

"FURLO'S ODDITIES is the one I went inside before," said Deven, pointing to the blue and white façade directly beside the cart.

"You know the proprietor?" Corlan tried to stare in through the foggy windows. "Is the shop open?"

"I've met him, though he may not remember me. It has been a few years. Orth is his name, I recall."

Corlan stared at Deven. "Is he in the market for dragon parts?"

"Go in and ask him," said Deven, not amused.

Corlan hopped down from the cart. He took a step, then stopped. In one swift sweep of his hand, he grabbed the brake handle on the side of the cart and clicked it back into the locked position. Now the cart could not be ridden away just as soon as he turned his back. Suddenly he did not trust the youth. He took the pin out of the pivot so the lock could not be unlocked.

"Good morn! Good morn!" called the stout man with the thick black moustache from the desk in the back corner. All around him were tall shelves overflowing with many assorted sundries, all of them old and dusty. "Fine you are?"

"Fine as best I can be." Corlan nodded, scanning the shop. "Are you Orth?"

"Why, yes, I am." He seemed suddenly happier. "What can I sell to you today?"

"I'm more in a selling mood myself." He waved his arm toward the door. "I've got an item you might be interested in obtaining for a rich client."

"Rich client? Is that so?" The man got up, pushed the chair aside. "That person is not you?"

"I'm hardly a rich client. This is only my second set of garments." He ran his hands over his shirt. "I'm a dragonslayer, truth be known, and I have a piece of dragonware to offer you."

"Dragon, you say? Really!"

Everyone seemed to doubt him, Corlan noticed. They hadn't had any battles with aerial beasts for a while. How then could they be impressed when they saw a souvenir like what he had brought?

"True." Corlan thumbed outside. "I hacked at it myself and took a beating for it." He pointed over his shoulder to his back. "Want to see the scar?"

The shopkeeper hesitated, waving off the scar inspection.

"What part is it?"

"The middle claw from the forefoot of a male double-hornchin."

The shopkeeper seemed skeptical. "What kind of dragon is that?"

"It's a common species. I heard someone here call it a duo-spike blackranger. Two spikes descending from the underside of the chin. One of them nearly ended me. That's the scar I'm telling you about."

The shopkeeper squinted, studying Corlan.

"Where did that happen?"

"North," Corlan replied. "In the ancient riverbed...."

"You came from the north? That must've been a foul voyage. I've never had anyone come from the north. It's a wasteland, isn't it?"

"Quite so. Then we found the road which led us to this city."

"All the way to Unting? You are so lucky."

"Yes, lucky in many ways." Corlan nodded toward the door. "You will be lucky, too, if you offer a fair price to match how much I risked my life. I will use the profit to purchase more supplies so I may continue my journey."

"And where go you?"

"I continue west." He rubbed his chin. "My entire family and me, we're traveling west to find a new home. We were attacked by those dragons along the way. In fact, too many dragons back there where we used to live."

"Those...dragons? There was more than one?"

"On that night, there were a dozen of them. Thankfully the valley was narrow with steep sides so only one at a time could attack us. I killed two of them. The third I only got the claw wrested from its forefoot."

"I have to see this!" sang Orth.

Corlan led him out the door and they stood at the rear of the cart. He tore back the tarp. There, gleaming in the sun, was the polished enamel of the dragon's talon. In the sunlight it seemed golden.

"May the gods have mercy on us all!" said Orth.

Corlan smiled. "You like it?"

"Oh, yes!"

"What's a fair price for a piece of dragonware such as this?"

"I can't imagine." Orth's eyes narrowed. "None here in Unting have ever bought or sold such a thing."

"Then what is a man's life worth? I saved mine by cutting that thing out from its foot."

"A hundred...two hundred...."

Corlan grinned wide enough that his teeth showed.

"Sounds like the price of a man's life. A man who could slay more than a hundred dragons would be worth more, true?"

"A fair account that might be. Yet who could pay such a price? Only the rich folk of the city. That's who!"

"I have more than three hundred kills," said Corlan in a low yet firm voice. "That's true."

"And here you are to tell of it!"

"Yes—and offer you proof for a price."

Orth frowned, glanced up at Deven sitting on the cart's bench. "I am not one of the rich folks of the city, you must be guessing. In truth, I'm a poor man. Do you know the reason?"

He returned his gaze to Corlan, who pushed his fists to his hips.

"Am I about to know it?"

"You see my fine shop filled with many exotic items. I do have much to offer the rich folks of the city. Yet they do not need what I offer. It's a strange arrangement. Nothing I offer is of necessity to anyone. The people here are too...*practical*. Although the rich folks can always afford to have meaningless items about their residences, they are unfortunately practical folks, too."

"I heard they live lavishly and people complain." He glanced up at Deven. "Right? You said so."

"I did hear that, yes," Deven confirmed.

"Then perhaps their lavish lifestyle does not include the dusty old things I have in my shop. You are the first customer this week. And I thank you for giving me a chance to sell you something even if you don't buy anything."

"And you?" asked Corlan.

"I have no money to purchase such a fine specimen of dragon claw as what you bring today. I wish I could but...."

Corlan shook his head slowly. He clapped his hand on Orth's fat shoulder. "I should offer this to the rich folks, you say?"

Orth tried to smile, took it back. "If you can get into the palace and meet any of them."

"How do I meet with any of them?"

"You have to know one of them."

"That's a puzzle! How can I know one of them in order to meet one of them?"

Orth laughed and could not stop.

"They keep to themselves in the palace," Deven spoke. "Never come out in public unless it is the annual festival or an emergency."

"They seem like the perfect family," said Corlan.

"In many ways they are," said Orth, patting his belly.

"What kind of emergency draws them out in public?"

"The usual events." Orth glanced up and down the lane. "People fighting or a fire." He glared at Deven. "You know it's true."

"There was a fire last year," said Deven. "They closed the city and hunted every house for the fire-starters. When they found them, they set fire to them outside the walls —"

"In the ancient rite grounds," Orth jumped in. "That place had not been used for a generation."

"Why was there a fire?" asked Corlan.

"Complaints about the administrators. Complaints about their laws. People are suspicious here, and neighbors speak of neighbors. Things happen. People can go missing in the night."

Corlan pursed his lips. "This city sounds much like the city I left a couple months ago."

"So you see my situation?" asked Orth, hands out to his sides.

"Can you help me meet one of the rich folks?"

"I can't just take you there and introduce you to anyone."

"And I can't keep carrying this dragon claw all over the realm. And it's too heavy to keep removing it into a lodge or other place where it would be safe from thieves."

"From thieves?" asked Orth with a hearty guffaw. "Are you sure someone wants such a thing?"

"Nobody has a dragon claw in this city? I'm sure someone wants to have it. Such a person could say, 'Look here at what I purchased from a true dragonslayer!' Everyone would be impressed and adore him for his good taste. Maybe some bravado will rub off on him and his admirers."

"You have a big imagination." Orth frowned. "We are a practical people. We do not clamor after exotic trinkets. Or the parts of dead animals." He screwed up his face in anger, sought to lock his eyes on Deven's for confirmation. "I don't want your business now. Be gone! Take your dead claw and from my lane wheel away!"

Corlan felt like punching the fat man but he told himself he was a better man than the savage he once had been. He had a reputation to keep up, even if there were none in this city who knew him. He knew who he was.

"So be it," said Corlan. "I'll take my precious souvenir elsewhere and sell it. Then you'll wish you had the coin to put this in your shop window for citizens to admire."

"So be it, as you say!" Orth cursed.

Corlan climbed up onto the cart beside Deven. Leaning down to the side, Corlan replaced the locking pin and unlocked the brake handle so the cart could move. By then, Orth had retreated inside his shop. He did not even watch from the window, Corlan noticed.

"Where else is a good place to sell this claw?"

Deven shook his head, then looked up and glanced down each lane. "If we take it to the main market, someone will see it and offer to purchase it," he said. "Perhaps."

"Perhaps?" Corlan felt regret spilling over him.

"Or," Deven continued, "if you are set on simply getting rid of it, we could take it to the palace and see if anyone there wants it."

Corlan sneered. "You think it has no value? I risked my life to get that claw. I might be dead now instead of trying to sell that claw. It is worth a lot!"

"Orth told you truly: the people of Unting are not interested in exotic trinkets."

Corlan shook his head as the cart started down the lane.

"Exotic trinkets...."

INTERLUDE

The Festival of Montra

FROM THE HIGH BALCONY Adora could see the ships approaching for the autumn festival. It was during her art lesson. She was taught to draw ships and praised for it, as though it was a masterpiece suitable for a museum. The ships arriving today were real, watching them glide across the strait. Ten of them, she counted. More might arrive the next day and the next.

Every autumn since before anyone could remember, the Festival of Montra was held, named for the village at the southernmost end of Sannan Island. In ancient days, it had its own port but after the Split the coast was rough and unsuitable. Thus, ships transporting people from the mainland had to arrive at the port of Sannan and then visitors went by carriages to the southern town. Over time, the festival was moved north to Sannan itself, although everywhere on the island the people celebrated the arts together.

In her next lesson, her tutor, Jabuli, told her Sannan Island was known on the mainland for its glorious seaside views, its tropical fruits and the delicious dishes made from them, its exotic crafts and tapestries which reflected the seaside, and its fabulous women, most of whom wore little covering during the hotter half of the year. With few men living on Sannan Island, and even fewer in the port of Sannan, ladies were free to go as they pleased, wearing as much or as little as they chose. They could lay wherever they wished, and to enjoy what pleasures with each other as they agreed. It was more than custom, Jabuli explained. It was a law in Sannan: formal unions were allowed only between women, and every woman was required to pair with some woman for official purposes by the age of thirty. If the woman birthed a babe, she must make a union with another woman within one year of the birth—if the babe were a girl. No such rule if the babe were male, of course. This helped social cohesion, Jabuli told the princess. With such a union, each woman would be assured of having someone to care for her in sickness as well as in health, thereby relieving the royal vault of the need to pay for care by hired nurses. In some cases, the royal vault still needed to care for a woman, said Jabuli, for example if a woman had lost her partner in older age.

"It is a good plan," the princess agreed. "I cannot yet dream of the girl I shall make a union with. The Nadal twins are friendly yet they have such strange tastes. Not like mine. And they do not like to learn, only play. And I could never choose between them. My girl should be like me, though not have auburn hair. She must be tall and I would like if she had skin like you, Jabuli. Perhaps she will play the lyre and sing wonderful songs, like a bird. Of course, she must care for my brother, as well. That is required. I shall care for her brother, too, if she has one."

"That is a kind thought, Princess Adora."

"I think everyone should care for brothers."

"I agree, Princess Adora."

"You can call me Adora. We are more like friends now, don't you think? You have taught me for three years. You are like my sister."

Jabuli bowed her head. "Many thanks, Princess Adora." She looked up from her cross-legged position on the floor mat. Her pupil stood before her, slightly taller. "You will always be my princess, even if you insist I call you by your common name."

"'Princess' is only a word written on parches. I did not choose it. I did not choose my name, either, yet I like it. So people may call it."

"Adora is the perfect name for you."

"Yes, everyone says so." A frown flashed across her face.

As the lesson continued, Jabuli described the Festival of Montra. In olden days, many artists and crafts people came together to enjoy being with each other. They ate and drank and sucked smoke. They swore they could draw inspiration from each other. So they made it a special event. Artists and crafts people from near and far gathered at Montra once a year to share their arts and crafts and have much joy. Ordinary people took the chance to visit Montra to have a look at the arts and crafts, purchase whatever wares they liked. Some people purchased the arts and crafts to sell them again on the mainland.

"Look there. And there." Jabuli pointed to the art works on the classroom walls. "All these came from Montra."

Because so many gathered at festival time, other people came to perform there, hoping to earn fair coin: singers, dancers, actors and comics. Those events brought other people to Montra just to watch performances. And that caused other people to go to Montra to sell everyday items to the people who visited. They needed all kinds of items to make their stay comfortable. It also meant that some women went to Montra to get some coin...

"...by using their bodies as entertainment," said Jabuli. She hesitated trying to describe to the princess what those women did. "They would recline with people who visited Montra. In time it became a problem."

"Why would it be a problem?" asked Adora. "If a lady wants to recline with a lady, they should share a mat. Or a slumber seat, or whatever they have to recline on."

"Some people say *recline* but they actually mean to make union."

"Why would they say one thing yet mean another thing?"

"Because some words, and some ideas, are too strong for a little girl's ears. That's why."

Adora gave a smirk. "I know what making union means. It's how I was put together inside my mama. It's written on the parches."

"Of course it is."

At the time of the twelve-day festival, people from the mainland were allowed to visit. Law enforcers of the city were on high alert to prevent trouble by foreigners — and by any local women who chose to make trouble with them. Mostly foreigners took up with Sannan ladies, enjoyed dancing and drinking with them, and in the night making union with them. It was one of the two times during the year that Sannan women could meet with men from the mainland.

It was no secret that several months after the festival, many babes came to be born. Some of the babes born were male, so they could be harvested and prepared to tend the farmlands. Also, the guardians of Sannan Island could form new patrols. A few males might aspire to the annual games, part of the spring Festival of Carm. A champion in those games would be well-taken by high-born ladies during the union season. A few champions might also win their freedom and go to the mainland. So it was common to see a Sannan woman recline with a foreign man upon mats along the beaches of Sannan Island's western coast during festival times.

"Shall I recline on a beach with a foreign man?"

The princess could be so innocent, thought Jabuli. "Her Majesty, the queen, would not approve of that."

"Oh."

Her baby brother babbled in his basket. His happy vocalizations were more like he was trying to make words but there was no sense to them. Everyone knew it took males longer to grasp the language, longer still to be able to communicate anything intelligent. Males were considered educated if they could follow basic commands in the performance of their tasks in the fields or on the farms.

Adora went to the basket and lifted the babe, straining with his weight. "Are you well, Puki?"

"He grows fast, doesn't he?" said Jabuli.

"I feed him half my food and most of my milk. I have a new goat keeper to bring us milk without Mama seeing."

"Oh, you must be careful."

"It will not matter now. The Festival of Montra keeps everyone in pleasure. No one notices what I do. Mama is busy showing my sister Lumina to everyone. She is arranging unions left and right for her. Yet no arrangements for me. She won't arrange anything for me until I give away my brother."

Jabuli frowned. "I think she might believe you are unsuitable for a union. It may be that Her Majesty believes your interest in your pet brother makes you unsuitable for becoming a queen."

Adora pouted, then turned red, anger filling her face. "Did you hear it? Could she say such a thing?"

Jabuli bowed her head, lowered her voice. "Yes, I did. She piles much praise upon Princess Lumina while singing laments for you. She prays to the goddesses that you will be rid of this brother. She says no good girl in Sannan will want to make a union with you because you have a pet brother."

Adora frowned, holding her anger. Her brother tried to speak the talk that had no meaning, and her attention switched to him. As she gazed upon him, her face softened. She cooed at him and he babbled back at her.

"Is it time for us to leave?" she asked, keeping her eyes locked on her brother's chubby face and his bright eyes. She twisted his locks between her fingers.

"Your Little Majesty...."

"You may call me Adora. We agreed."

"Yes, *Adora.*" She took a deep breath. "It may be time to leave. It becomes more dangerous for him each day."

Adora turned in place, holding her brother in her arms.

"Tell me a plan."

"The only way is to take a returning ship to the mainland," said Jabuli. "To go aboard we will need to pay for passage. We must be hidden as a man and a boy."

"And a babe."

"Yes, three of us to make passage."

The princess regarded her tutor, eyes focused sharply, her hand stroking her brother's head. "Can you arrange for it?"

Jabuli's face turned serious, eyebrows pinched, chin jutting.

"Are you certain this is what you wish? Are you ready to go off this island? You might never be able to return."

Adora was nonplussed. She smiled only when her eyes met her brother's eyes. Her face was solemn whenever she addressed her tutor. She regarded Jabuli with the aura of an adult.

"I have gathered enough coin for passage. A little each day. It is against the written law, and also the laws of the goddesses, to take coin without handslapping. Yet if a large good thing can be brought from a small bad thing, it is considered fully good by the goddesses. It is written on Sacred Parch thirty-two, the nineteenth block of the second column. I read it many times."

Jabuli dared smile. "What a wonderful pupil!"

"I study as you showed me. Read and think, read and think. So it fits with a plan. I take some coin to make a new life on the mainland. There we will not need to be ready for harm by Mama's maids or any other palace staff. No more chance of little dragons slipping into the nursery, or someone poisoning his milk. I will not allow any harm to come to him."

Jabuli was surprised by her charge's confidence. If only she could be paid wages according to how strong her pupil was, how well she achieved her examinations. Then she might be able to afford her own passage back to the mainland. But no matter the coin she could earn, she would never want to return to the life she had there before she was sold to the merchant in Olan who eventually sold her on Sannan Island, allowing her into the palace staff.

"The mainland is a wild place," said Jabuli. "I was a child there, I've told you many times. We cannot stop only on the far side of the strait. No, we must go farther. Olan is a dangerous place, a city ruled by men. There is much that is bad there. I am from Rament, not a much better city for women. In those places, women are the property of men. In fact, men can do whatever they wish to a woman without one consequence."

"Bad things?" asked the princess.

"Yes, very bad things."

"I shall make a law forbidding that."

Jabuli tried to smile. "That would be good. However, in Olan, you do not have any power to make laws. Until such time, we must go farther, perhaps stay away from all the cities. We can hide in the mountains. I know some people there. My training sister from my years in the fighting pits can help us. She knows the way. There are many high peaks beyond Olan. The highest is called Yozma and it is covered with snow all the year."

Adora tried to smile. "Then we should go to Yozma. I never want to be in a city where any harm happens to anyone. I don't care about a palace, or a city, or even a house."

"But you have no experience living in a house, a simple hut, or a tent, or with nothing over your head, Adora, my princess. I worry you will go to a new land and be unhappy. It will not be an easy life for you...and your brother."

"He will grow to adult age, become a man, and I will teach him how to protect me."

"That is a good dream, yet it will be some years before he is able to protect you in the ways you protect him now."

Adora frowned at her tutor. "I have thought of many paths I can take. I have seen all the many choices. The pictures come into my head when I sleep, like parches that turn over and over. I know what will happen. I should not share them with you." She looked away. Jabuli only sighed, so she spoke more: "I have seen you fall, Jabuli, and I don't want that to happen. I must go away, but I don't want you to come to harm, either. I need your help but I don't want you ever to die."

"Die? How? Why?" Her hands hid her face. She stared through her fingers. "Is it punishment for helping you?"

"No, not that. The picture is cloudy but I think it is a dragon that makes your end."

Jabuli stood up straighter, held her hands as though preparing to defend herself from an attack.

"If we know what will happen, then we can prepare for it. We can prevent it. So say the goddesses on one of those parches, on a parch somewhere, I'm sure of it."

"Passage forty-five on Sacred Parch thirteen, right column," said the princess. "In the second block. It has a dark smudge from a lazy scriber."

Jabuli was ready to cry. "It is written then."

"Yes." The princess pursed her lips, thinking. "I like reading the parches. All the things people say there on every sheet. Just turn the sheet over and read the next sheet. You can read until the parch ends and then get another parch, and you can read it, too, no matter how many sheets there are to turn over—"

Jabuli put her hands together, interlocked her fingers. She made sure the princess saw her gesture, then bowed her head three times.

"I will help you escape—*flee*—from here...no matter what the cost may be. Princess Adora, little majesty, you must be free to live the life you wish to live, that you deserve to live. That is all that matters. I agree with you. Your mother, the queen, will not allow you that freedom. Or else she will plot to harm you because you do not follow her rules. That is what I fear. Already there is talk...."

Adora held up her brother, enjoying his bright smile. "Talk?"

"I said too much."

The princess frowned. "You said too little. What is the talk?"

Jabuli glanced behind herself. "Her Majesty, the queen, said she wonders if you wouldn't better serve Sannan as a scriber of parches than as a queen."

"Oh." The news did not seem to connect. "Is that so bad?"

Jabuli shook her head. "Scribers are sworn to two things: Truth and Duty. The work requires them to be dedicated each and every day and night to the writing of law and the reading of law and history and science. There is no time remaining for a leisure life. That means no family for you, and no children, no lovers, and no pets."

"So no brother...."

"That is what I mean. If they send you to Scriber school, you will need to be cut, also. That is the custom. The law. Before your first blood arrives."

"Cut?" She batted her eyes. "Cut what?"

"They would cut out the egg bags inside you so you will never have a child come from you. Ever. No children for you, not from your body."

"But I have a brother. Do I need my own child?"

Jabuli repressed a grin. Her charge was both wise and innocent in the same words. Yet she knew how serious her situation was.

"Please listen carefully, Adora, my princess. That choice should be yours. Yours alone. And yet, the life of a scriber is an indoor life, hunched over a long table, stylus always in hand, and seldom you get a moment's rest. I think you are destined for greater things, more than writing parches. No, it's not for you. *They* should be writing about *you*! And you should have the choice to make a babe or not."

Adora set her brother down in his basket.

"Thank you for your counsel, Jabuli. I have counted everything, and the time for us to leave has arrived. Before I get bags of eggs cut out, or whatever you said. Before I bleed, too. If you do not wish to come with me, I will not think sad or mad thoughts of you. You are always kind to me. I ask only that you help us go aboard a ship away from here when the festival ends."

"You truly want to leave?" Jabuli's eyes were never more stern.

Adora closed her eyes. "We can be the children of artists. We are returning to the mainland. It is a plan."

Jabuli nodded. "Then I will go and make arrangements for three. A woman, her daughter, and her son. Or, perhaps we should be disguised as a man and two sons. Passage to Olan...and beyond."

The princess opened her eyes. "Then my dream shall be true."

17

The Backside of Society

DEVEN SUGGESTED ANOTHER SHOP on another street but this time Corlan waved him off. They had visited too many. Corlan made his usual proposal, was rejected, and they rode on to the next shop on the next street. After most of the day was done with no sale, Corlan decided they might as well return to the carriage house.

"We'll try again tomorrow," said Corlan. "We'll go to the palace itself! Some rich person there will want it."

Deven shook his head. "I'm not free tomorrow. Master has tasks for me."

"Does he? Is there another youth that can help me?"

"I will ask the others."

Deven seemed glad to be rid of the annoying dragonslayer.

Corlan watched the youth saunter out the carriage house doors as though he had just been freed from hard labor. He would have given the young man part of the profits for guiding him around the city.

Nobody wants a dragon claw, so therefore nobody will steal it, thought Corlan as he left the carriage house and trudged up the lane to the lodge.

"What is this outrage?" Joragus cried when the door to the room creaked open. The magus was stretched out on the bed without a robe to cover his body. His long beard served that purpose, covering him down to his ankles — until he sat up.

"It's me, returned from a day of slaying dragon-haters," Corlan grumbled, closing the door. He stared at the naked man on the bed. "I trust you had a good sleep. Tonight it's my turn. If you wish, the cart is free in the carriage house. Just move the dragon claw to the side and rest easy."

"My back may not agree," grumbled the magus, moving to the side of the bed.

Corlan explained his day. Nobody wanted to purchase the exotic souvenir. Nobody had the coin such a prize would be worth. And he could not meet any rich folk who had the means to purchase it.

"What would someone use it for?" asked Joragus.

"Use it?" Corlan's face turned red. "It's a sign—a great symbol—humanity's triumph over the aerial beasts! It's something you want to display...to impress others...to make them admire you."

"To show off...?"

"Yes! That. If I were in my home back in the Burg, I'd put it in the front window for everyone to see. And each person that walked by would think: There lives a great dragonslayer, that Corlan fellow of the Burg, that's who!"

Joragus stood, grabbing the wall for support, and stepped to the chair where his once white robe lay neatly folded.

"The maid did the laundry. Mine looks good as new. Pure white. She even removed the blood stains. Yours are over there," he said, pointing to the opposite corner. "That's another coin spent."

"You aren't interested in how difficult it is to sell a dragon claw in this city?"

"I only tell you about the laundry because it is a fact. The three of us went to the clothiers. You know that girl has only one outfit and it hardly suits her here in the city. So many stares, so many whistles—and she thought they were communicating with her by birdsong! So often she whistled back at them. I had to steer her away from the curs." Joragus cleared his throat. "The boy had need of clothes. You took him with only what he wore that first day, he said. And then you gave him your extra shirt. So I purchased three sets of garments for each. I would not take offense if you replenish my coin." He paused for effect, but Corlan seemed not to pay attention. "You likely need another outfit but I leave it to you. I don't know your sizes. Nevertheless, I got you a pair of boots."

Corlan regarded the shiny black boots on the floor at the foot of the bed. He could not continue wearing sandals like a peasant.

"Thanks for that, for leaving my clothing to me, old man."

Joragus coughed. "It seemed the right thing to do."

"Thanks for the boots. It's good you could set everything aright for us." He kicked off the sandals and paced the room, too anxious to be still. "We need to sell that damnable dragon claw. We need to get more supplies. Or I go alone and you three remain here."

"What good would that do?" asked Joragus, checking the fit of his robe. It seemed a bit short after the laundry. "There is no employ here for a magus. And do you know? Today someone dared call me a *mage*. A mage! The insult! I had to set him straight. I am a member of a long and distinguished line of magicians: the magi. Thus, I am a magus—not one of those fakes they call a mage!"

"You are the real wizard."

"Wizard? That's much worse. Might as well call me a sorcerer, if you're going to be disrespectful."

"Sorry," said Corlan. "I've seen your power in action. Next time you should give them a demonstration."

Joragus waved his hand to dismiss the suggestion.

"That is against the code. It takes so much of my strength for a simple power transfer—setting the motes of dust in the air into an impenetrable shield, like you saw. I would not use it for a simple trick to impress ignorant savages. If I wanted to, I could seize their breath and stop it in their throats! There's a simple trick. Even a mage could do that! But, no, I am a *magus* of the magi. I do not do simple tricks for the amusement of fools."

Now they both were worked up, shaking their fists, pacing.

"They said it's time for the supper," Tam called, barging into the room. "It's not going to be drake tail, they said."

Madi looked perfectly elegant sitting at the table, like a lady better fit for a palace in her pale yellow gown with emerald ribbing down the front and back and delicate blue lace around the collar and wrists. Corlan told her so. She smiled and tweeted a lilting response which everyone understood meant she was happy. The leather clothes she had worn were no more, the feathers set aside for another day. Tam called them souvenirs, memories of a life lived in strange places with customs that seemed so foreign now.

Tears dropped from her large, round eyes as she listened.

"Now you have no reason for that," said Joragus.

"Than ksoo alyoo," she managed to say, voice strained. "Dura slik dis vera moo cha."

"She likes the dress very much," Tam translated.

"We understood," said Joragus. "You're a good teacher, Tam."

The dinner set before them consisted of a plate of the same black bread, chunks of hard-milk, a bowl of sliced red root vegetables with a white sauce, a plate of long green leaves covered in yellow flower petals. The only meat was a skewer of some animal cut into cubes. They passed the skewer around, each person sliding off a cube or two. The innkeeper's daughter assured them the meat was from a farmed animal, slaughtered properly, not wild game. The other lodge guests had complained, questioned the meat. They would only eat farmed meat.

"We can't stay long in this city," said Corlan half-way through the meal, "or we'll run out of coin. Already we've spent half what we brought. I expected to sell that dragon claw for a high price but nothing gained so far. I'll try again tomorrow...at the palace. Care to help me, boy?"

Tam looked up from his plate. "Oh, yes!"

"I'll be needing an assistant. That young fellow from the carriage house...not so helpful."

"I'll help you, Corlan."

"Thank you, Tam."

"And I shall visit the gallery of scrolls in the archive house and read about the realm over which this city rules." Joragus glanced at Madi. "I'll take the girl with me. She can learn more of our ways."

When the table was cleared and Corlan sat back with a stein of ale, he turned to Joragus. "We could sell the girafors. Or the donkors. Or maybe all of them."

"Ah, you wish for a team of horses, real horses, I know." Joragus wiped his mouth with his sleeve. "I hear it in your words."

"And a proper carriage, not an old magus cart."

"There you go again: insulting me to my beard!"

"No insult, old man. We did the best we could. Much thanks we give to you. But you see how the once valuable girafors are now just following along. All our supplies fit on the cart."

"Yes, I agree they are now redundant. So sell them. Who would purchase such a pair of strange animals? The same folks that will be interested in your dragon claw?" He laughed.

"Now you insult *me*. We must have something of value to sell to get more coin. We need more supplies if we are to continue on our journey."

Tam asked if he and Madi could leave the dining table.

"What is the hurry?" asked Corlan. "Other youth to play games with? Oh, be off then!"

"No need to growl at your family," Joragus cautioned him as the innkeeper's daughter returned to finish clearing away the dinner.

"Will there be anything else?" she asked.

Corlan raised the stein and finished the ale. "No more."

After the table was cleared and Corlan went up to the room, he realized he needed more ale. He combed out his beard and brushed his new black boots with a soft cloth. He slipped off the sandals and tried on the boots.

"Good fit." Corlan stood and walked around the room. "Let me take a walk in them." He stepped out, closed the door behind, then called: "I'll be in a tavern somewhere. Fetch me in the morning."

"And you call yourself a dragonslayer!" said the big, balding man with the short black beard. He wore a burgundy vest with straps across the chest, black shirt and trousers, as though he was planning to visit a brothel — or already had. Although he stood no taller than Corlan and was larger at the shoulders, Corlan thought he could take him in a fair fight.

"I do! Because I am."

Corlan expected a fist to come flying at his jaw but none did. He held fast to the tavern bar, fresh stein on the counter. That was what usually happened in taverns in the Burg.

"Leave him be, Gorral," said the man's shorter companion. They could have been twins by the way they were dressed, one big and one small. The small one's dark blond hair was long and tied back like the tail of a donkor. The long hair helped hide his bent back, Corlan saw.

"Shut your spout, Rupas!" said Gorral, the taller man.

"All I said was that a city like this should be a prime target for any dragons that might pass overhead." Corlan tried to smile. "Yet there is no such thing here."

"There's no dragon trouble in Unting," said Gorral. "I know it and he knows it." He pointed around the tavern. "And he knows, and those people over there know, and all the people outside know it, too. No sighting of a dragon for fifty years."

"You have the favor of the gods."

"Not gods," said Gorral, "magic."

"Magic, eh?" Corlan raised an eyebrow.

"Now you come along asking questions nobody oughta be asking, like you're some kind of mage." Rupas turned to see Gorral's reaction to what he said. "True?"

Gorral nodded, his face like stone. He had nodded a lot as Rupas chatted away when Corlan first entered the tavern, sidling up to the far end of the bar. He asked for whatever local brew was good but not the most expensive. Then Gorral noticed him and asked who he was. Corlan had stepped along the wooden counter down to the pair of gruff-looking men and introduced himself. The two of them had been complaining about the city administrators and Corlan found common ground with them in that. Now they differed.

"Not an accusation," said Corlan. "I only meant, where I come from, dragons are a constant problem. Not a day goes by when one isn't seen and not a week goes without some kind of trouble. They go for the farmsteads, snatch animals away. Sometimes people. And when they don't actually attack, there's always the waste they drop."

Gorral made a nasty face. "Waste?"

"Heaping mounds of ashen mess."

"That's a northern problem," said Rupas with a chuckle.

"We have no such trouble here," said Gorral.

"I wonder how it is dragons pass by without threat. Do they fear you? Are the dragonslayers out of employ?"

"There are no dragonslayers in Unting."

"When I told my fellow slayers in my city the same thing, they did not like the idea. No dragons meant no dragonslayers. So they called on the prince to banish me."

"Is that true?" asked Gorral, his face showing amusement.

"He's another banned man, like I said," Rupas sneered. "He has the look. As soon as he came in I saw it. I said 'there's a man looking for a new home' — didn't I?"

"There are others?" asked Corlan.

"Were — not *are*. Last year."

"Last year? What happened?"

Rupas pointed his finger at Corlan. "Same as you. A man arrives from another place, talking about dragons. Nobody cared to listen. Said he was sent to warn us." Rupas turned to Gorral. "From where did he hail?"

Gorral had to think. "It was north.... Velan, maybe?"

"Somewhere in that direction. Up on the northern sea, anyways. I remember the map he showed us. Said the dragons take up fish from that sea. Attack ships, too."

"Sea serpents." Corlan was interested. "I've heard of them."

"You know a lot about them, eh?"

"I've been on the slaying trail for many years. I've talked with a few slayers from the northern sea. They told of sea serpents crushing boats, snatching people off the shores. I never went there or saw them myself, but I could slay them, I'm certain."

Rupas screwed up his face. "He wants to be our dragonslayer."

"But we ain't got no dragon trouble here," said Gorral with a slap of his hand to the bar. "I keep saying."

"I have no plan for that." Corlan glanced at the door, thinking of how far the carriage house was from this tavern. Four blocks? "I'm only passing through this city. I'll need to buy more supplies. If you want to see proof, I can show you something I'm sure you've never seen before."

"And what's that?"

Corlan tried to hold back his grin. "A dragon's claw."

"A dragon claw...." Gorral sounded skeptical.

Rupas laughed, more like a horse's whiny. "Yes?"

"Come with me and I'll show you."

Corlan led the two men to the tavern door and the barkeep called after them for payment.

Gorral shouted back over his shoulder: "Worry not, sir. We will return after we call on this stranger's bluff."

"No, first you pay," the barkeep demanded.

"You don't trust us? We are regular drinkers here," said Rupas.

"I don't trust anyone who walks out without paying."

Gorral dug a coin from his trouser pouch and flipped it on the bar counter. Corlan added one of his own.

Inside the carriage house, the two young men sleeping there to guard everything awoke in foul moods and cursed at the intruders.

"Be at ease," Corlan told the youths, "I'm just showing these two doubters my wares."

He strode between the wagons and carriages and over to the cart, threw back the tarp. The shadows continued to hide the prize there, so Corlan called for a lamp. One youth brought over something that burned the fat of birds instead of a chip of dragonfire. He studied the device a moment before turning his attention to the cart.

"You see?" He waved his hand over the upturned point, shiny and yellow in the lamplight. "I hacked it off the forefoot of a double-hornchin up north in the dry valley of the River Oh a week ago. I got a scar down my back for the effort."

The two men looked amazed though they said nothing, leaning over to inspect the item.

"It's real?" asked Rupas after a while.

Corlan tore back the tarp more and exposed the root end of the claw. "See that knuckle? The tendons had to be cut to separate it from the foot. I used a battle axe—two hands for that—hack, hack, hack, and the dragon screaming all the while!"

"Certainly appears real," said Gorral to his companion.

"Certainly it's real!" Corlan told them the story of the attack in inventive detail. They were impressed. They accepted he was truly a dragonslayer. "I've lost count by now yet it must be more than three hundred I've slain in my life. And I only started a few years ago."

"What did you do before that? Hunt hares?"

Corlan laughed. "I fought in the battles of princes, there in the far northeast. Useless conflicts, of course. Nothing settled. Many people killed for no good reason. I tired of that life."

"So you took up slaying dragons...."

"It needed to be done, so I did it. I was the best—still am, though you know how politics gets in front of everything. Even though I'm the best, the jealous ones persuaded the prince to send me away. So I traveled down the Valley of Death." He thought for a moment, details to be added or not. "With my family. We are seeking a new home."

"Unting's a fine place to settle, if you ask me," said Rupas.

"He has no employ," said Gorral, shoving Rupas who seemed to hurt when his humped back twisted.

"If you have no dragon problem, then I should keep traveling, find a place that does have problems." Corlan was measuring the tone of his voice. "But I need supplies. We hope to get some here. Alas, nobody wants to purchase this fine souvenir of daring. I would think the rich folks of this city would take much delight having this at their doorstep to warn visitors of the dragonslaying prowess of its occupants—"

"Indeed they would!" Rupas barked. He turned to Gorral and the hunch of his back was more noticeable. "Urix would buy it, I'm sure.

He thinks himself a strong man like that."

"Urix?" asked Corlan.

"One of the administrators of this city," Gorral explained. "He's a bit of a dandy but likes to boast of his manliness. I guarded him for six years."

"You have an administrator named Urix?" Corlan narrowed his eyes, felt the weight of his sideblade on his hip. He might be engaged in a fight depending on the relationship.

"Yes, from the line going back to legendary Urix," said Rupas. "Why so tight about it?"

"Oh, I have—*had* poor relations with that name. No matter now. I'm sure there's no relation to your Urix. It's a popular name. As you said, from legendary times."

"He would buy it," Rupas insisted. "Urix fancies himself a strong kind of creature and would show off such a thing."

"And we would surely gain his favor for finding such a thing and presenting it to him," Gorral thought aloud. He patted Rupas on the shoulder. "You might regain your employ."

"That is what I hope for."

The story they had told Corlan in the tavern was both of them had worked in the palace, Gorral as the personal guard for one administrator, the one named Urix, and Rupas was an accountant for a different administrator. Each managed to seduce the daughter of a third administrator. They did not know about the other suitor. When they discovered the truth, both accused the girl of cheating. That was the end of the affairs. That was the end of their employ, as well. They had remained friends, however.

Gorral turned to Corlan, setting a hand on the smooth curve of the claw, caressing it. "How much are you asking for such a prize?"

Corlan grinned. He brought his hand up to scratch his moustache to hide his grin. "Whatever it's worth, of course."

"Urix can pay a lot," Rupas jumped in. "He's in charge of the city treasury. Or, most of it."

Gorral nodded at Rupas. "We could introduce you to him. Bring the claw and he will surely be impressed."

"He likes foreign things. Likes to show them off," Rupas added. "Everyone will be impressed that he knows all of these foreigners and has all of these foreign things—these exotic trinkets."

"Exotic trinkets, eh?" Corlan feigned surprise.

"Urix loves exotic trinkets," said Gorral. "The fool."

"He surely does," Rupas confirmed.

"Yes, I see." It had the makings of a plan. "Tomorrow then. We'll take the cart to the palace and show off this dragon claw."

"Not this cart," Gorral grumbled. "Even our peasants ride better contraptions than this."

"It was all that was available at the place where we last rested," said Corlan. "We had to hurry on when dragons came, so only this cart was available. Before that, we only had the girafors."

Gorral squinted. "You keep saying that word—*Jee-raw-fourz*—and I don't know what it means. It's a kind of machine?"

"I don't think it means what you think it means," said Rupas.

"It's a giraffe. These two have been remade using the Clona arts." He watched their eyes searching for meaning in his words. "Giraffe is an animal from far away lands." Corlan grinned, then explained about the Clona arts. "The donkors, too. They are remade."

"I recognize those. But we ride horses here."

"Bring the girafors, too. Urix will like them—if you can part from them at a fair price."

Corlan stared at the two tall animals. Elo was looking back at him, Pex nibbling at leaves on a high branch. He felt something heavy in his gut. They represented his last ties to the Burg.

"I can part with them. They are only pack animals, not for riding. Actually, I'd like to trade them for horses. And the cart for a wagon."

"With your family," Rupas added.

There was a moment of silence.

"Yes, uh, with my family. All of us. Heading west, like before."

"We can arrange that," said Gorral. "Urix will buy the dragon claw and the girafor beasts, then you use the money for whatever you desire. We get a cut, naturally."

Corlan nodded. "Certainly you both get a cut."

Gorral raised his hand, spit into it, held it out to Corlan.

"That's how to close a deal?" asked Corlan.

Rupas spit into his own hand, held it up. "Yes, in Unting it's how we close a deal."

So Corlan spit into his hand and clasped hands with each of them.

"We meet at first light," said Gorral. "Don't be late, even if your whoring goes long."

18

Rites and Privileges

WHEN CORLAN RETURNED TO THE DEWLAP SQUATTER, excited to tell everyone about his new dragon claw deal, he found the innkeeper bruised and agitated, bent over the desk. His daughter was hugging Tam, who was in tears.

Before Corlan could ask what had happened, Joragus called out to him from the top of the stairs, then came stumbling down—as quickly as an old man in a long robe and beard could come down stairs with the aid of a staff.

"She's gone!" the magus cried out.

"What?" said Corlan from the front desk.

"Madi is gone!"

"Some men came and took her," said the innkeeper, his hand pressed against his cheek. "They knew where she was, just came in and demanded which room."

"They hit him when he refused to say," said the daughter.

"Then they rushed up the stairs and pounded on every door!"

"They wrapped her in a blanket and carried her out—not five minutes ago!"

Corlan rushed outside, looking in both directions, up and down the dark lane. He ran to the bottom of the slope and looked in each direction there but saw no one moving about. He ran to the top of the slope, past the lodge and saw no one.

"Come with me," said Joragus, appearing on the front stoop.

"Where?" asked Corlan.

The magus stood with his eyes closed, arms extended to each side, slowly twirling the staff before him.

"I see her in my mind...."

"You know where she is?"

"Keep your sword ready." Joragus lowered his arms and opened his eyes. "Come quick."

The dark green brick structure was the only building on the lane with a lit window. The light flickered and Corlan guessed it was an oil lamp like in the carriage house. He could not see any shadows or movement behind the illuminated curtains.

"Here?" he asked of Joragus.

The magus nodded slowly, as though waiting to be certain.

"How do we enter?" asked Corlan, stepping up to the veranda. He tested the door handle.

"Away from the door," moaned Joragus.

The magus closed his eyes and held out his arms, palms up. The door rattled, then broke open as though someone were exiting, the panels flung to the sides and the way clear.

Inside, the room was completely dark but Corlan rushed in with his sideblade drawn.

Up the stairs he went, not worried about making noise. He got to the second level landing and glanced around. To his left, at the end, he spied the room with light leaking under the door. He listened, heard men talking. Stepping lightly to that door, he kept his ears tuned to catch anything that might be a warning.

He took a deep breath, grasped his sideblade tightly. Just as he was about to crash through the door, leading with his shoulder, the floor creaked. Joragus had stepped on a weak spot.

Noisy rumbling came from the room ahead and the door opened. A bearded man poked his head out to investigate the creak.

Corlan rushed him, pinning the man's head between the door and the door frame. Then he kicked the door open and the man fell backwards, tumbling on the floor.

Inside the room two other men stood shirtless on each side of the bed. Flat on the bed was Madi, her thin body stripped to her skin and her belly painted with strange symbols in red and blue. She hadn't possessed them when they had first fled the women's village, Corlan knew, so the men must have put them on her. She looked scared, her owl-like eyes calling for help.

Corlan swung his sword at the first man who came at him, cut the man's upper arm and stepped aside, swinging the blade again at the man's back as he fell past and crashed into the half-open door. The second man dove for a scabbard hanging over a chair, retrieved the sword there. He lunged at Corlan, who stood a step too far for the man's swordtip to reach so the man fell to his knees. Corlan swung the blade down at him, catching the man's shoulder; then up, nicking his throat. The man's hand went to his throat as he rolled onto his back.

"Madi!" called Corlan, going to the bed.

He tore up the sheet under her and flung the ends across her body. She tried to sit up but seemed in pain. He pulled her up to a sitting position. She grabbed the other end of the sheet and wrapped it around herself.

"You hurt?" asked Corlan.

She tried to tweet but couldn't make a sound. Tears ran down her face, her large eyes darting about.

"Lets get you out of here," he said, about to pick her up.

The first man, who had his head caught in the door, got to his feet. With no weapon, he held up his hands to beg Corlan not to strike him. Corlan raised his sideblade anyway and was about to slice it down at the man when the room filled with a squad of men bearing lances and wearing yellow uniforms.

"Stay your hand!" cried the leader of the squad, the man with the red cap and red epaulets.

Corlan froze—the man on the floor could have stabbed a blade up into his belly at that moment if the man had a weapon. But he did not, so Corlan lowered his sideblade. At a gesture from the squad leader, he dropped the blade on the floor.

"Those men took this girl by force from our room in our lodge," said Corlan. "I came to rescue her, to save her from whatever they planned to do with her. That's all. I have no trouble with you, only them. They are the criminals."

"All violence is a crime in Unting," said the swarthy sergeant. He motioned for the patrol to tend to the wounded trio, then ordered that their hands be tied.

Joragus stood in the doorway behind the patrol. One patrol man sensed his presence and turned to him.

"What is this outrage?" cried the magus.

The sergeant turned, surprised, and fell back at the sight of the old man with the long beard in the doorway. Behind Joragus were other tenants of the house, curious at the disturbance and quick to voice their complaints to the patrol.

"Peacekeeping here. Depart to your private areas."

"I am related to the victim," said Joragus, breathlessly.

Madi, wrapped in the sheet stepped through the patrol on thin, wobbly legs. When she came beside the magus, he put his robed arm around her shoulders and she leaned weakly against him.

"She is my granddaughter." He waved at Corlan. "And he is her father. A man has a right to defend his daughter, I should think! How would you keep such a man from protecting his daughter? That is the crime. And those three: what manner of deviancy had they in their dark minds to do to such a young girl, eh? Look how they marked her! What kind of magic is that?"

"We know she is one of those bird girls," said the one who was uncut, rubbing his neck as he sat on the floor. The imprint of the door's edge showed on his neck. "Everyone knows bird girls are free to take by anyone. They are worth nothing. Everyone knows that. So we took her, as is our right."

"Your right?" shouted Corlan. Two patrol officers held him back. "No one is free to take! No one!"

"The right of any free man to take what also is free," said one of the men tied on the floor. "They belong to nobody."

"They belong to themselves! She belongs to herself," Corlan called before a guard slapped his face.

"You have no such rights," said Joragus, raising his hand as if to cast a spell on the man. "Everyone—every man, woman, boy, and girl, all who are human, as well as those persons who might be in a second or third iteration, all who are human are equal! None has more rights or less rights than any other human except by the fact of physical strength or advanced education. That is the truth as the gods know it!"

"You're not from here, old man," growled the man on the floor. "You know not our customs. A right to take her we have, and use her and sell her for others to use. You can't keep her to yourselves."

"You damnable deviants!" Corlan exclaimed. He broke from the patrol officer's grasp and punched the man across the jaw.

The sergeant warned him, then announced they were all going to speak with the magister. He would settle everything in the morning. Until then, they would be locked up.

"Please, I beg you," said Joragus, "let the girl go home. Let her go to the lodge and refresh herself, at least. It has been an ordeal for her."

"She must give her statement, as well," said the sergeant. "There is a place there for her to wash. She will not be locked up, but she must stay in the court until the magister speaks with her."

"And me? I saw those criminals take her from the lodge."

The sergeant frowned at Joragus. "You may depart. You are not a part of this matter."

"I am certainly a part of this matter. We are the same family."

"Then you may accompany us to the court."

The stone cell was too warm and damp for Corlan. Across the aisle from him, the three criminals waited together in their own cell. They talked among themselves in a language Corlan did not know. He decided they were planning what to say to the magister, to try to make their stories the same.

A bunch of low-life rapists was all they were, as far as Corlan was concerned. When he had been in one army or another, he had slit the throats of men he found atop a woman after a battle. And he hadn't known those women. If only he'd been quicker tonight—

If I had just stayed in, instead of going to that tavern....

Corlan had only one story: he was responsible for the girl. She had left her mother, her village, to be free—to whatever end, he did not know. As long as she accompanied him, he was responsible for her. Besides, no deviant vagabonds were going to steal a girl from her room and use her for their rituals—or worse!

He remembered a time long in the past when he had walked on by, had heard a girl screaming but kept walking. It was none of his concern, he'd told himself. Later, he learned the girl was his cousin, Talina. She was left badly wounded by the attacker and months later had jumped from a high window to escape from her dark dreams. Suddenly, he could hear her screams in his mind.

"Time to meet the magister," said the guard, rattling the keys to the cell doors. A squad of eight guards waited to escort all of them.

Corlan thought back to his last day in the palace, answering all the questions of Prince Vilmer and how ridiculous it all had been. There, he had only to defend himself. Now he had to protect a girl and an old man, too.

Must keep calm, must be polite, must stand firm.

"Charges?" asked the white-haired man in the dark brown robe. His red skull cap tilted to the side as he sat behind the long wooden desk overcrowded with scrolls.

"Violence in maintaining rights of personhood," the younger man in the purple robe with white fluting announced.

"Name and status?" asked the magister, yawning.

"Corlan Tang, visitor in Unting."

"Visitor?" The magister looked up from the writing pad and the parchment threatened to roll up.

"He is from a city called the Burg. In the northeast region. He travels to the west with family, in Unting for recuperation."

"Reasonable accord." The magister scribbled on the parchment a minute. Without looking up, he continued: "What occurred?"

"The man here standing," spoke the purple-robed man, some kind of court chamberlain, Corlan supposed, "followed close after the girl standing here, she who is named Madi, with intent to encounter the three men standing here. those who took her by force, witnesses confirm, from out her lodging for purpose of performing a ritual of encumbrance upon her. Such action is argued unwanted and not with the girl's approval. The man standing here, Corlan Tang, went to the place and interrupted the ritual, thus causing violence. A civil patrol did intervene. Code fifteen-nine, section ten."

The magister was writing throughout the description and did not look up until he had finished.

"Confession?" asked the magister.

"All standing here confess the truth of the description."

"Code?"

"For the three men standing here, code six-twelve, sections one, two, and four. Proven."

"And him?" The magister pointed his pen at Corlan.

"Code six-fifteen, sections two, four, and eight. Proven."

The magister reached for a scroll and unfurled it, read it, set it aside. He wrote more on the parchment before him, then looked up.

"Hear you the truth stated here before you?" the magister spoke to Madi.

She startled, not following the proceedings. Still wrapped in the sheet, she stood forlornly, her head and shoulders hunched.

"May I speak for her?" Joragus called out, stepping forward from the crowd at the back of the room. "I am her grandfather. The girl often falls mute. It is not her wish to be rude to the court."

"Speak then."

"She was taken by force, without her consent, for whatever evil acts those three flagrant oafs wished to do upon her, and this man hurried to save her. Mind those words I use: *save her*. Yes, from the evil plans of those three men. We have no violation." He turned to Madi and whistled a lovely tune.

Madi smiled a bit, responded with her own song.

"She agrees with the statements made," said Joragus.

"I did not understand her language," said the magister in rough tone. "I cannot confirm to what she agrees."

Joragus stated the case once more. Corlan tried to add to the facts but was waved off by the court chamberlain. The magister turned to the three criminals and asked them the truth of the old man's statement. They accepted as true the statement that had been made.

The magister spoke again to Madi and an older woman in a yellow uniform led her away.

"She will be let free?" asked Joragus.

"The girl standing here may depart," said the court chamberlain.

"And me?"

"You may depart."

"And my *son*?"

"We await the disposition order."

Joragus glanced over at Corlan, found him staring back: his eyes seemed to suggest some drastic action was in order. Joragus gave a slight nod, then turned to the court chamberlain.

"How soon will be the disposition order?"

The court chamberlain, face as glum as a statue, said, "There will need to be an investigation. The time it takes to read a few scrolls and talk with witnesses. It could be tomorrow before a decision is made."

"And the disposition?"

"In a case such as this, with violence occurring, there would be a severe penalty."

"Violence punished with violence...." Joragus sighed.

"Yes."

"There is no provision for payment of a fine?"

"Not when violence is involved."

"Not even when the violence is in one's defense?"

"All violence is abhorred in Unting."

"Even if a dragon should visit?" asked the magus.

"There are no dragons that pass here."

"None at all?"

"Not in fifty years."

"So you say." Joragus stroked his beard. "I should return to my accommodations and prepare for tomorrow. I may bring a witness. That's allowed?"

"You may bring the witness but only the magister may allow the witness to speak."

Joragus studied Corlan: standing for so long in the chamber after a night in a damp cell, following a swordfight, which came after a run through the streets of the city, preceded by a few drinks in a tavern. Before all of that was a full day going about the shops trying to sell a dragon's claw.

"He is not in any danger for now, is he?" asked Joragus.

"It will be a several hours before any disposition order."

"Then I shall return forthwith."

The magus swept his robe around his ankles, made a big, winged motion that caught everyone's attention. There almost seemed to be an eruption of smoke around him, but it was more likely the dust his feet kicked up as he turned and stalked out of the chamber.

The magister entered at the start of a fresh day and sat heavily on the big oaken chair behind the long, long desk. He straightened the piles of scrolls and found the parchment he wanted, read through it, then looked up at the people assembled in the chamber.

"It is this court's determination that, of the first order, the girl standing here is, in truth, of the Madi clan, said called the tribe of the bird women. Proven. As such, an unwelcome class of person here. She is thus free to be taken by anyone who finds her. Therefore, no crime exists. Of the second—"

"What is this outrage?" exclaimed Joragus. With a firm hand to Tam's shoulder to indicate he should stay put, the magus stepped forward from the group of possible witnesses standing to the side, holding onto his staff. "She certainly is *not* an unwelcome person. She is my granddaughter, not a creature from the wilderness."

The magister waved a female guard over to Madi, gestured for the guard to lower the girl's gown. In a flash her shoulders and upper back were exposed to everyone there.

"Look you there upon," said the magister. "See the fine features bearing witness thereon her body. It is proven."

Everyone standing behind her could see it clearly as she stood hunched over. At first it appeared to be a tattoo or some other painted pattern like what the three men who had taken her had drawn on her belly. As the stale air of the chamber moved, however, the crowd could see the pattern on her skin wave.

Feathers! A patchwork of growth spread from one shoulder to the other, from the back of her neck down along her narrow spine to the middle of her back. Small feathers of blue, teal, and brown.

"You declare she is your granddaughter?" asked the magister, jutting his chin at Joragus. "I ask you now with whom have you been mating?"

The magus frowned, spied Corlan from the corner of his eye.

"This girl standing here is clearly a member of the Madi clan, the bird women," said the magister. "According to the Unting civil code, she is a non-person, and so is free to anyone who takes her. It is the same as if they took a rat from the gutter and did with it as they please. So the three men standing here were within their rights to take her in any manner they chose. It is therefore this man standing here, this visitor, who did intrude upon them and disturbed their permitted and private activity, using violence sought to take her for himself. It is this man standing here who is now under charge."

"What an outrage!" cried Joragus. When the magister waved for guards to move toward him, he bowed his head in submission. "If this girl is free to be taken by anyone, and those three oafs took her, then would not this man standing here also be within his rights to take her? To take her back?"

Corlan listened to the debate, glad that the magus could hold up his side of the argument. He and Joragus knew where the girl came from, but they'd had no idea she would change into...something—a bird? How did that happen? When he'd been in the village he had seen large birds stalking about, some flying away and returning. He hadn't seen any women with feathers growing from their bodies but some of them did wear wing-like coverings.

"These three men standing here are citizens of Unting," said the magister. "They stand in contrast to this man standing here, a visitor allowed into the city by a gate captain's decision. It is charitable to allow your group to stay here for a short time, and for that you have no rights under the civil code. Thus, the man standing here had no right to take the girl standing here back for himself. She belonged to the three men who took her first."

"Your word play is superb today, dear magister! Yet mere words do not the truth make, nor is justice served."

Joragus railed against the indecency of the code. He demanded to know how the men knew about her, and for what corrupt purpose they decided to take her out of her room by force. He insisted there be some form of punishment for causing injury to the innkeeper and his daughter during the abduction.

"I saw her when you and her were going about the city," said the man who had his head caught in the door of the room when Corlan arrived there. "She was dressed as they do. Had the hair of those women. Had the look in her face of those women. The big eyes. I knew she was a Madi then and there." He gazed at the magister. "She sat on the cart they rode, as a perch, looking out of place. So I made a plan with my brother and his friend to take her."

The man spoke boldly, as though certain of his release.

"As many may know, when a man goes together with a bird girl, the act causes her to begin the transformation. She will sprout her feathers soon after. Not until that union will she transform from a girl to a woman—a bird woman, that is."

He turned to Corlan: "You did not know that about her, did you? I see a mask of surprise cover your face. Maybe you wish it'd been you to make her change, to initiate her transformation. The first blush starts the change. It can be a thrill for a man, the way it feels for him. The Madi *girls* are better than any human woman."

"Speak not of your personal fetish in this court," the magister growled.

Corlan suddenly realized what his predicament in the village had been. Once he was captured, they decided to make use of him, commanding him to perform the rite which would cause the girl— another girl, not the one he called Madi—to become feathered. It was a normal ritual to be performed by a human man. *A human?* Then what were these bird women? Some weird combination of human and bird? A trick of the Clona arts?

He glanced at Joragus.

"She could not be your daughter," said the man to Corlan. "Then we just had to find your lodging. We could take her without charge." The man laughed. "For ordinary pleasure. That's the reason. Like any normal man would choose for an evening's entertainment." He turned his gaze to Corlan. "We don't care if she sprouts feathers. It's only an effect of our union. In time, she'll be completely covered with feathers. All the Madi are that way."

"But I saw no women with feathers growing on their bodies in her village," Corlan spoke.

"Only some have this feature, I've heard. They will grow wings. They will fly in the sky, hunting as hawks. They feed the others."

Corlan nodded, understanding. *What a fool I've been!* The girl had freed him, urged him to run. Then she ran with him. She also wanted to escape, he believed. To get away from her evil mother? To escape the feathering? He had to gaze over at Madi—and realized then it was not her personal name but the name of whatever kind of creature she was. He saw she had lowered her head in shame.

"What will be the choice for her now?" asked Corlan.

"She must depart the city," said the magister. "No charges are put upon her. She would not have been allowed into the city had we known the truth—if the gate captain had known what she was."

The court chamberlain motioned for the female guard to pull up the gown, covering Madi's back and shoulders.

"Of the first order," the magister spoke, "the girl standing here is dismissed. She must depart the city this day, before the dark falls"

"Thank you," said Joragus.

"We are not unkind in Unting," said the magister. He cleared his throat. "Of the second order, the three men standing here were within their rights when they took the girl standing here. No charges are put upon them. They, too, are dismissed."

The people gathered in the chamber let out spontaneous bursts of approval. The local boys were saved.

Corlan frowned, sensing he was about to be disappointed.

"Of the third order, the man standing here is found worthy of the punishment prescribe by code after the charge of violence against an innocent person, by three counts."

The court audience's boisterous response showed they thought it was a good judgment. The foreigner who committed a crime would be properly punished and the local men would be set free. The noise rose as the magister waved the chamberlain up to the desk. The two men spoke a few moments, their words covered by the murmuring of the crowd in the chamber.

When they finished their discussion, the chamberlain returned to his place beside Corlan and unrolled the parchment. He faced Corlan and read from the scroll:

"For the charge of violence, there will be violence put upon your person. The choice is yours. Choose of the staff or the whip. As there was no death or severe injury in the crime, the count shall be only twelve."

Joragus stepped forward, coughing loudly. "He does not deserve that kind of punishment for trying to rescue a girl—even though he didn't know the laws here or that she was one of the bird women. It's not at all a fair outcome."

"It is entirely fair," said the chamberlain.

"Twelve strikes of a staff is all he must endure? Or twelve lashes of a whip?"

"That is correct."

Joragus glanced at Corlan. The dragonslayer, once strong and virile, stood defeated, exhausted and awaiting his fate.

"May I speak with the man standing here? At close distance?"

The chamberlain petitioned the magister, received a nod.

Joragus stepped over to Corlan, raised a hand to clap upon his shoulder for encouragement but held it in the air instead, unsure if he would be allowed to touch the prisoner.

"Corlan, dear fellow," spoke Joragus softly, his lips to Corlan's ear, "it has been a pleasure to travel with you these several weeks. I'm very impressed with all that you are able to do. And yet, it seems we have come to an end of one kind, which may yet be a beginning of another kind."

Corlan turned to regard the magus. "What?"

"They mean to punish you," Joragus continued with a peek at the magister hunched over the desk. "I do not see a way around it. Therefore, I recommend the whip for twelve lashes. It seems the least harmful to your body. The staff might break bone. Then you will be free. It is entirely unfair, I agree. I am in my fourth iteration; if there were a way for me to take it for you, I would. I am old and will not live much longer anyway. You are yet young—young enough to have a mission to complete. You must take care of that boy. You know how he looks up to you. He wants to be a dragonslayer like you. That is a reason to live—and get past this day."

Corlan blinked. His breathing was slow and steady, as though he was preparing himself to spring into action.

"I will do what I can do to help you," said Joragus. "Yet do not grieve if my plan fails."

"You have a plan?" Corlan asked in a low voice.

"There are many plans. The difficulty is matching the right plan to the situation. One of them is always ready, always at hand, always perfect for some situation but, alas, not for others. That is what I have learned in my three-hundred and thirty-eight years in this world."

The corner of Corlan's mouth pinched. He was about to grin but the magister called for them to continue the proceedings.

"I spoke with my grandson," said the magus, standing straight and strong. "He accepts the whip for twelve lashes. Then he will be free to depart the city, true?"

The chamberlain stepped up to Joragus as if to halt his words, his hand waving for him to stop speaking.

"It is those who were attacked who dispense the punishment. The men you attacked, the men you cut with the sword, they will be handling the whip. Each of them shall give twelve lashes."

Corlan grimaced. "I can endure that."

"You did not explain that previously," Joragus complained.

"You are foreigners. The code specifies each gets his satisfaction. If you harm ten all ten would get a turn."

"That is mathematically ridiculous—when the man did no actual crime, only tried to—"

"Silence!" cried the magister from the desk. He stood so his voice would be heard better.

Joragus stroked his beard a moment. "Is there a fine we might pay instead?"

"A fine?" asked the chamberlain as the magister lowered himself on the great chair.

"Where we come from, we may give something of value in exchange for punishment. It is often just as harmful as a physical injury. Coin or treasure, something rare and precious. For example, the claw of a dragon that was hacked off a foot during a vicious attack. There is perhaps nothing more rare. It has great value."

Corlan heard the tenor of the proposal and spoke up. "I've heard that your administrator Urix would pay much for such a gift. I would give it over as a penalty payment."

"So many questions!" the magister cried out. "Whip this man

and be done with it!"

"Send guards with me," Joragus called. "I will retrieve the claw from where it is stored and bring it here immediately."

"There is no time for playing games!" shouted the magister.

"Please don't hurt my papa!" Tam cried.

The chamberlain turned with hands raised to stop the foreigners from suggesting other ways to change the dispensation. Everything had already been decided, he explained.

"Don't hurt Corlan!" Tam shouted. A guard grabbed the boy's shirt collar.

"Enough!" cried the magister.

Joragus stamped the foot of his staff against the chamber floor.

"I must speak!" He stared at the magister who already appeared weary of the day's events. "This man standing here is a good man. He has saved his city from the terror of dragons. He has saved me from countless dragon attacks on our way here. He saved this girl standing here from the vengeance of her mother and others of that tribe. He rescued this orphan boy from a life of bondage. And the night last he tried to rescue this girl. He has only good intentions in every matter. He is not a rogue, nor a cheat, nor a thief, a brawler, vagabond, seducer, nor cruel master. There is nothing he has done which deserves punishment! He should be immediately dismissed. That is the only just outcome of these ridiculous proceedings!"

The magister pointed a crooked finger at Corlan.

"Prepare him."

19

Executive Action

A CROWD GATHERED IN THE PALACE riding range, its four stone walls providing a sturdy framework for the spectacle inside. In days past, the king's personal platoon rode their elaborate formations within the walls, impressing their liege. At the south wall rose the towers where the families of the administrators had their apartments. A few members watched from their balconies. To the north were the lower, stouter buildings used for public purposes. The court chambers were in one of them. At each corner, and at intervals along the walls of the square fortress guard parapets hung, standing out somewhat from those stone walls.

"Looks like a training field for cavalry," Joragus said to Tam as they walked to the center of the grassless field. "You can see how they would ride in formation from one end to the other, back and forth, like toy soldiers on parade. It could have been a marvelous spectacle. If only that were the entertainment today."

Tam was not interested in that kind of pomposity. He looked around anxiously for Corlan. The innkeeper and his daughter had joined them. It seemed half the city had come there.

At the center of the plaza was a low platform. Rather than a stage for actors to perform, it was the setting for public punishment. Older and newer blood stains spotted the wooden floor. On the platform already was a man in dark red suit, from collar to boots, a white beard covering his chest. He stood much bigger than Corlan. To the side of the giant stood the magister in his usual brown robe, carrying a scroll in one hand, straightening his red skull cap with the other.

Corlan was brought out, hands tied, and was made to stand beside the platform. The spectators stood in a tight square around the platform as though they knew what to do and had done it many times. Corlan recognized that it was much as the Court members in the Burg had stood around him while he was questioned by the prince. This crowd gave the platform a wide, respectful interval.

"The citizenry apparently take much delight in the punishment of foreigners," Joragus spoke, more to himself than to Tam. "It is likely they haven't seen much magic."

"I don't want to see anything," said Tam, mournfully. "He didn't do anything wrong, just rescue Madi from the bad men."

The boy took hold of the magus's robe, clutched the folds in his hand, holding it as securely as if he were holding the old man's hand.

"This is a lesson for you, boy," said the magus. "Life is innately unfair. Yet we go on."

Joragus held the staff firmly but did not lean against it. It was not a support for a crippled old man, after all. It was an important tool.

"Come, boy," said the magus. "Go stay with the innkeeper now. I have important work to do." He pointed to where they stood in the crowd.

"How long should I stay with them?"

Joragus thought a moment, staring at the platform in the center of the plaza.

"Corlan will collect you later."

A court crier in a tight-fitting purple uniform with tall, purple cap marched out to the platform, claimed his position, and shouted the announcement. The audience fell silent.

The magister handed the scroll over to the crier who opened it with dramatic flourish. He then read in a loud, dramatic voice the full order assigning punishment to the foreign criminal standing there.

Corlan tried to smile, impressed with the absurdity of this turn. He stood stiffly, his hands tied. He regarded the four stone walls surrounding the grounds and the crowd of spectators within them who had come to watch him receive the whip. For that prescribed act, he had been dressed only in a poor man's dingy white gown, nothing more. He imagined the blood would show better that way. Blood would drip, too. He regarded his bare feet.

Of course, he had been whipped before. His father had used a leather belt. He had not followed the man's instructions quickly enough. His mother tried to protect him, then fell victim to the man's rage herself so that Corlan had to protect her. Then his commander in the Nerk army, pot-bellied General Pellam Drumf, had used a proper whip on him when he refused to follow the order to charge into the line of child soldiers. That time was fifty lashes. Hard ones, but he did not pass out. He was young at the time. He still believed he could survive thirty-six lashes from three rather weak men.

Joragus stood unexpectedly at his side as Corlan broke from his dark memories.

"It is a good day for a spectacle," said the magus with a chuckle.

"I do not see the humor."

"Humor is not to be seen. It is to be felt."

"Then I don't feel it."

"Corlan, dear Corlan, dragonslayer extraordinaire, listen to my words. You will amaze yourself in the days to come. Perhaps today, as well. I'm certain of it."

"So you say...."

"It will come to be true."

Guards pushed Joragus away, grabbed each of Corlan's arms. He was led up onto the platform. The executioner stood taller than even Gefgar at the Guild Hall in the Burg. No mask for this fellow, only a scarred face and hardly any nose. The bushy white beard covered his mouth. He held a whip of nine strands laid across one outstretched hand.

The people who had gathered between the walls cheered as three men strutted through them, a path opening as they went. Once free of the crowd, they marched over to the platform, one of the men raising his arms as if in triumph.

Corlan knew them, hated them. He should have gone ahead and killed them in that room that night, then fled the city with Madi and the others.

The three weaklings stood proudly beside the burly executioner.

More vainglorious prattle from the crier, the stern old magister nodding pensively at each lofty clause.

The first man, the one whose head Corlan had pinned in the door that night, took the whip from the executioner's hand and chose a good position behind Corlan. He waited for the executioner to bid the victim kneel and lean against the wooden block set there. The executioner stretched Corlan's arms forward, past the block, holding on to the rope attached to his wrists.

The first man gave the whip a few easy snaps in the air, letting it crack, studying how it moved. Likely the man had never used such a device before, thought Corlan.

The first strike did not touch him. Corlan wondered if it counted. The man took a step forward and swung again. This time the nine strands struck Corlan's back; he felt them but did not wince. The next lash also did not hurt him. The fabric held together. This man simply did not have the strength.

As the man prepared to strike again, the sky seemed to darken. It was cloudy when the spectacle began, Faint sunlight had penetrated the milky clouds. It had seemed there was a storm coming, a darker horizon looming. Now it seemed the clouds had thickened, shutting out the sunlight. Some in the crowd looked up as the shadow extended over them.

Corlan hoped rain would fall.

Suddenly, the crowd screamed—almost in unison. A great roar exploded around him and Corlan turned his head upward, expecting to see the clouds break open with heavy rain.

Instead, he saw what everyone else saw: the shadow of a pair of dark brown wings spreading over the riding range, the wings of a double-hornchin dragon!

Its outstretched wingtips nearly touched both the west and east walls simultaneously, covering more than half the riding range. The dragon's wings swept back and forth in circular motion, keeping itself aloft as it hovered over the grounds.

People crashed into each other as they fled but the dragon turned its head one direction then the next, roaring at each stream of escapees—then changing to coughs, its raspy breath stinking of sulfur.

Corlan stood, searched for Joragus in the frantic crowd. He glanced around the platform. The three men assigned to whip him were no longer there. The giant executioner remained but cowered at the immensity of the dragon. The magister was absent. The crier was the first to run.

"Untie my hands," Corlan demanded of the executioner.

The giant glanced at him, nodded, then went to him and broke the ropes around Corlan's wrists.

"I need a weapon!" he cried.

The giant stood dumb-faced, then lumbered away—only to be crushed under the dragon's hindfoot when it landed, four clawed feet pressing into the soil.

The fire-breath was expected. First the exhalation of the noxious gas, then the hiccup to ignite it, forming a fireball as wide as a man's height. The fireball bounded across the bare ground, bowling over dozens of people as they ran, crashing against the east wall, splattering fire back into the fleeing crowd.

With another roar, the dragon turned its attention to the opposite direction and prepared another fire-breath.

"Weapon!" Corlan cried out to anyone who could hear him. "I need a weapon!"

At that moment, the weight of the dragonslinger landed on his shoulder from behind. His hand went to the barrel, recognized its feel. He turned to accept it, saw it already loaded with a barbed iron bolt.

Joragus smiled at him, then nodded at Gorral and Rupas also standing there. They pointed at the cart parked further behind, carrying the dragon claw.

"We thought you were coming to meet us," shouted Gorral over the screaming of the terrified crowd. "We waited two days. Then we hear you're to be whipped for some crime."

"This mage said we needed to bring the dragon claw right away," said Rupas.

"What is this outrage? I'm a *magus*, not a mage!"

Corlan swept the dragonslinger into position on his hip, screwed back the launch spring to the strongest position, the setting for long distance shots.

"Stand back!"

The dragon let go another fireball bouncing through the people running away from the west wall, then turned its attention forward.

Its forefeet had settled on either side of the platform, its double chin horns dropping in front of Corlan and his associates as if to block their escape. With one quick motion it could swing its spikes down at them, piercing their bodies like knives into sacks of grain.

Corlan saw something he didn't expect as he stared forward a moment too long, stunned by the sight: directly ahead, just seven feet in front of him, was the forefoot of the dragon — with its middle claw missing!

As Corlan gazed up at the dragon's lumpy black face and red eyes, the rumble in its throat grew louder, sounding strangely like a growl of satisfaction. The vibration ran down the dragon's legs into its feet, rippling through the ground, shaking the dirt under Corlan's bare feet.

The dragon reared its head up, its mouth now open, sucking in air, the inhalation cut by a raspy cough.

Corlan smelled the sulfur.

"Run! It's going to fire!"

He did not glance back at the others, expecting them to flee. He could not leave; he had a job to do.

Launching the slinger from beneath the dragon's chest, the iron bolt struck deep in the throat. But it was not the right spot, he knew, not the point of weakness he was aiming for.

The dragon lowered its head but did not exhale, merely glared at Corlan, eye to eye, as though recognizing him, pausing to wonder how best to deal with this one human.

Corlan had no time to reload the slinger. He fell back, tripping over the hem of the torn gown. He was flat on his back.

The dragon took a step toward Corlan, setting its forefoot down, shaking the ground as the missing claw left a gap for Corlan to fill. The other claws penned him in.

"Weapon! A blade! Axe! Anything!" he cried out.

"Here!" called Gorral from some distance away. He flung a long-handled axe into the air and it turned handle over blade twice before it fell a few steps from where Corlan was caught by the dragon's forefoot.

They both saw the axe had not gone all the way. Corlan needed to get free of the claws or Gorral would need to go closer to retrieve the axe for him — with the dragon standing right there.

Suddenly, there was a loud cry in the air that echoed between the walls and towers of the riding range.

Both Corlan and the dragon turned their heads skyward to locate the source of the cry. It was more of a screech than a cry. A bird call.

Something dark swept over the yard.

A bird?

"Madi!" Corlan shouted.

She was flying! Her arms waved like wings, her skin all covered with golden brown and blue feathers. Her feet moved as though she were swimming through a lake instead of the air. She gained height and circled the riding range, sailing above the walls, then turned back to Corlan.

The dragon was confused, its neck craning and head pointing to the bird-woman.

"Noooo!" cried Corlan. He feared the dragon would snatch her out of the air.

With the dragon distracted, Corlan scrambled free of the claws and dove across the dirt for the axe. Grabbing the handle with one hand, he rolled up to his knees and took proper hold with both his hands. He jumped to his feet, his gaze returning to the bird-girl flying above the dragon. The axe was firmly in his grip.

She looped twice and performed two back-flips, as though she were more interested in enjoying her new-found aerial talents than in distracting the dragon.

But the dragon had had enough of the curiosity and blew out a stream of gas. It did not ignite, but the breath was strong enough to knock her off her path. Unsteady, she dove awkwardly toward one of the guard parapets along the wall, but instead of crashing, she spun herself so her feet touched the stone wall, catching herself there with long feet that were more like talons now. She alighted like a bird perching on a branch.

The dragon returned its attention to Corlan just as he got the axe ready to hack at yet another claw.

"Come on!" grunted Corlan, raising the axe over his shoulder.

The dragon lifted the claw-less forefoot, stamped it down hard. The ground shook and Corlan fell. He was slow to get to his feet and the dragon stepped closer, trying to smash him with the same foot that had suffered the claw hacking.

The symbolism was not lost on Corlan. The dragon was thinking! It had intent—and that was certainly vengeance! He wondered if it had been searching for him all this time. Or was it summoned by...by a magus?

Corlan did not see Joragus, but he expected the old man would be somewhere safe.

"Joragus! Where are you?" he shouted.

A shadow flew in front of him, blocking his view of the dragon's forefoot rising and stamping again. The foot caught Corlan's leg and the axe slipped from his hands. The soft soil of the riding range kept the weight of the dragon's foot from crushing Corlan's leg.

The shadow was the shape of a man—a man with long sleeves and a long beard. The magus raised his hands, holding the staff over his head like a perch for a bird. The words he shouted were lost in Corlan's ears, something like a challenge, or a dare—or a curse—

Shaking his head, Corlan tried to pull his leg out from under the dragon's foot.

He heard the magus cursing and he looked up in time to see the dragon's open mouth full of glistening teeth, dripping with the teal fluid that swept its gullet. Then the mouth closed around the man with the wooden staff raised.

"I dare you to choke on me, foul beast!" the magus shouted.

The dragon tilted its head up, mouth half-open.

"Joragus!" cried Corlan, jumping up as the dragon stepped away.

The magus lay bent in the dragon's maw, one leg dangling out between two long teeth, an arm waving wildly between two other teeth.

"Remember what I told you!" Joragus called down.

Corlan could not give up. He raised the axe and swung it down as hard as he could against the same forefoot from which he had taken the claw. He swung the axe again and again. He swung again and the dragon's hard scales split open. Dark orange blood splashed out of the wound, streaking Corlan's dirty gown.

The dragon roared. Teal saliva dripped down on the man with the axe, staining the shredded gown and burning his flesh wherever it was exposed.

Corlan dropped the axe and rushed over to the dragonslinger, flat on the ground beside the platform. One quiver of bolts lay beside the cart, thirty feet away. He hurried to the cart, grabbed one of the iron bolts from the quiver and loaded it, screwed back the launch spring, and aimed at the throat of the dragon.

"It has been a good journey with you," Joragus called down.

"We're not done, old man!"

Corlan launched the bolt straight between the hanging spikes to the underside of the dragon's jaw, the point at the top of the throat. It seemed better to risk the old man falling from that height than be chewed up and swallowed!

With its forefoot wounded, the dragon still grabbed wildly at the bolt sticking under its jaw, trying to fling it away, but it was deep enough to stay. It folded its big wings half-closed then extended them sharply, pushing itself into the air. Its wings pumped the air, gaining altitude. It rose quickly, still fumbling with the iron bolt under its jaw with foreclaws. With its need to remove the bolt taking priority, it flicked out the squirming old man with its long, scaly, orange tongue.

The magus dropped to the ground with a thud.

As the dragon rose further into the air, Corlan rushed to Joragus.

"You shouldn't have done that," said Corlan, quickly checking the old man's body for injury. He had fallen from fifty feet. Corlan expected broken bones —

"Yes, I'm broken, if that's what concerns you," said Joragus. "You better be concerned what that aerial beast does next."

"Did you summon it?" Corlan glanced up at the dragon, seeing it turning in place in the air above them, still grappling with the bolt stuck in its throat. "It's the same dragon I cut the claw from, you know. Did you see its forefoot? It must have followed us here. Was that your plan?"

"It was one of many plans. Who can know which?"

"But how did you...?"

"I called for a dragon, yes. I confess it. However, I could not know which dragon would come. If any." Joragus tried to laugh, felt pain in his ribs. "They said there had been no dragons for fifty years. Now they must start the count again."

"Not now...." Corlan stared into Joragus's dull eyes. "Not you, old man."

"It is time. It has always been time." The magus closed his eyes as the sky seemed to lighten around them. The shadow of the dragon had left the riding range. "This is my fourth iteration. I have been troublesome to this world for long enough. Remember me to the gods."

"No, old man! It's not your time yet," said Corlan.

"Be sure to take something of me with you. Take a rib from my side. Cut off a finger, at the least. See that I am reborn — if you dare unleash me upon a fearful world once more. Then it will be on you to apologize to the world."

"We still have many adventures to go on. I need you to go with me. All the way to the marshes. We must complete the mission."

"My mission is complete, dear Corlan."

"Nooooo!"

Corlan turned his face skyward and no longer saw the dragon over them or blocking the sunlight. He scanned the walls for the bird-girl but did not see her. He could only hope Madi got away, flew off to some place where she would be able to live her life her own way, covered with feathers, her arms grown into wings, a new form of life in this very old world.

Returning his gaze to Joragus, he felt no more breath exiting from his nostrils. He placed his hand on the old man's chest and felt no beat of the heart. He felt the bones of his chest move, broken as they were.

"That was close," said Rupas as he and Gorral came beside them.

"So you really are a dragonslayer," the beefy Gorral conceded.

Behind them a squad of guards approached in soiled yellow uniforms. Beyond the guards, attendants in medical uniforms treated the wounded or took away the dead, many of them burned black.

"Would rather I never had to be a dragonslayer," Corlan grumbled, "yet here I am.... The truth we live with."

Corlan stood. His bloodied, stained gown in shreds, he regarded the silent body of Joragus, the magus, remembering him to the gods, wherever they might be. "Let him pass with no fee," he whispered.

20

Toll Road

THE ROAD TURNED NORTHWEST, the ancient riverbed filled with sand and gravel, and Corlan felt the comfort of familiarity once more. Overhead the sky was clear, on the horizon clouds boiled with storm warnings. Vegetation covered the shoreline, thick woods rising over the hills on each side of the narrow valley.

At intervals the ruins of various buildings rose, perhaps where a town had once stood, full of people going about their tasks. There were plenty of broken things, of metal and of something hard yet supple called *play-stix* by his new companions, Gorral and Rupas. There was play-stix in Unting, too: such amazing sculptures made of the material. It could only be made in a factory and there were no longer those kinds of places in the world.

Corlan was content to lay on his belly, stretched out across the back of the wagon, as Tam applied a fresh coat of the balm the boy had made. It worked well on the girafor after what they'd brought was all used. The injuries from both an unjust whipping and the corrosive dragon saliva were healing.

"It's no different than Chef telling me how to make the sauce for a dish," said the boy when Corlan had asked if he knew how to mix the ingredients. "I put everything in a bowl and take a spoon and mix it together, fast or slow, until it's all smooth and creamy. That's the way Chef wanted it."

"Thanks, Tam. You're a good boy."

Once in a while Corlan would raise up on his arms to have a look around, but the steady rocking of the wagon, pulled by two black draft horses, lulled him into a drowsy state. He stared from the rear of the wagon, studied the two horses following on tethers, one a piebald and the other a gray, both for riding. He did not know their breeds. No more girafors, though. Suddenly, he missed Pex and Elo. They had been reminders of his ties to the Burg and his life there. It was a fair deal, however. No more donkors, either. Although they were less strange to the citizens of Unting, he got a good price for Ika and Gum from the administration's procurement office.

And he had gotten a full pardon, too.

"You proved your worth," said a new magister when Corlan was brought from the infirmary. The previous old man who pronounced the charges against him had succumbed during the dragon attack, he had heard. "All is forgiven. Depart you may. Or, as another choice, in the city here stay. Protection we have need."

The matter of his belongings was settled rather laboriously by a team of four accountants who meticulously examined and valued each item, from his boots and loincloth to the cart and the animals. They counted each coin and put them into a newly-sewn pouch. For the dragon's claw, intended to be the centerpiece for a museum of ancient and dangerous souvenirs, Corlan was offered two-hundred-twenty-six *tuppance*. He didn't know exactly how much a *tuppance* was compared to a *regal*, but he was satisfied to be rid of the thing. He negotiated the price up to three-hundred-thirty-eight to match the age of Joragus. Coins were coins, after all; they held their value in the metal used to make them. The point was not to become wealthy but, rather, to gather fresh supplies and continue the journey.

Everything was collected from several shops and packed onto the new wagon—enough for a hundred days, he guessed.

Lying on the back of the wagon, Corlan gazed up at the pair of rogues he'd hesitantly welcomed in place of Joragus and Madi. He felt sad, like he had lost what was supposed to have been a good deal but had gotten instead an old sponge and a dirty brush in exchange for a trunk full of wisdom and a beautifully-framed mirror.

"We make a good team," he recalled telling them as they had arrived at the city of Unting. "I've got the swords and the slinger. You have your magical arms waving about. Tam is good at taking care of the animals. And the girl...she can whistle a happy tune."

Repressing a grin at the memory, Corlan opened the scroll and studied the map again. He noted the wriggling line that marked the river valley, the crude drawings of dragons on either side of the line, the rough city sketches. And the field of crosses representing marsh to the southwest.

Rupas, with the hunched back, glanced over his shoulder at

Corlan, saw him studying the map.

"How much farther to the next city, sir?"

Corlan shook his head. "It is an old map. Perhaps there is no city there now. And don't call me *sir*."

"Pardons, sir."

The three of them had been equals in the tavern. Then they were business partners. After seeing Corlan in action on the riding range, facing the dragon by himself without fear — without *showing* fear — the two rogues, unemployed and desperate, had begged to go with him.

"We have skills," said Rupas, who tended to speak for both himself and his larger companion, the stern-faced Gorral. "We can be helpful. And we have nowhere to go. The city is not for us."

"We want more dragon claws," Gorral had spoken up then.

"Not as easy to get as it looks," said Corlan.

More negotiation ensued, even as Corlan was distracted thinking about Joragus. Rather than keep arguing with them about how long and how dangerous his mission was, he eventually relented just to end their discussion. They were already proving useful, keeping the wagon rolling along the river road, heading toward whatever the next town might be, while he rested.

Corlan kept gazing at the sky, hoping to see something bird-like flittering past them. A bird-girl, perhaps. He felt certain Madi had survived, flying off and staying out of reach of that dragon. There was no indication she'd been harmed within the walls of the riding range. He just wished he could know for certain she was safe. And yet, how safe could the sky be with dragons about?

The citizenry gathered there in the riding range of the old palace had not fared as well. The mourning announcement had stated that sixty-four citizens had been killed and more than a hundred others injured to a lesser or greater degree. A few of the wounded had died in the days following the attack. It was a horrible event they would never forget. Corlan wondered how much blame he should take for a dragon visiting them. Or if it might be Joragus they should blame. He decided to blame the dragon that likely had followed them to seek its vengeance on him.

The administrators of Unting had offered him the official title of Dragon Master, with a suitably high wage, urging him to stay in case any dragon visited in the future. Meanwhile, with no dragons to deal with, he could have a life of leisure in the city, perhaps training others how to slay a dragon.

"I have my mission," Corlan had insisted. "When I succeed, that will solve the dragon problem once and for all time."

"What is that?" Chief Administrator Urix had asked as he stood beside the polished dragon claw, stroking its smooth surface like the mane of a champion stallion. He held his long, golden sleeve out of the way.

"I intend to travel to the western end of the Valley of Death."

"And there is your paradise?"

"No, there is where the dragons have their nesting ground. I will smash all of their eggs. There will be no more dragons. The old ones will die and not be replaced by young ones."

Urix regarded him. "It has the blare of a brilliant plan. You seem to be the best man for that task. And then you will return this way?"

"The Valley of Death has only one course," Corlan replied, "so I'm certain to pass this way again. Perhaps in a year or two."

"If you succeed...."

"*When* I succeed."

"If you are not killed by a dragon first. They do seem such nasty creatures. Who ever would have invented such things? Surely not the gods."

"Some people say the gods invented them to punish us."

"To punish us?"

Corlan remembered what Joragus had told him, not believing the magus at first.

"I've heard tales of sinister mages working late in the kitchens to make animals that have died away. You saw the girafors and our two donkors. They are remade animals."

"Yes, absolutely odd beings," said Urix with a funny face.

"They were remade from the dust of those animals that already died. It is a long process. Perhaps dragons were made the same way. It is only speculation."

"Speculation by who?"

"Who can say? People talk, share stories, and some begin to feel it's true because they hear people tell the stories so much."

"Ah, stories fly far on many wings while truth crawls through the dirt on half a leg!"

"Or, maybe, dragons have always lived among us. In far off times they may have hidden themselves in different lands. That, too, is a story. It is not important to understand the past. More important is to plan the future."

"Yes, the future." Urix strolled about the chamber, nodding and rubbing his throat, seemingly measuring the growth of his wattle. "It is of great importance that we send you off. You must go, Corlan of the Burg. Go onward to those nesting grounds and do your duty to humankind."

"I will."

"Tell us all that you need for your journey and we shall see that it all goes with you."

"Thank you."

Corlan turned to go, the attendant waving him toward the doors.

"Our sympathies for the loss of your...grandfather," said Urix, the Chief Administrator.

Corlan paused and gave a sharp nod, continued out the doors.

The magus had always laughed about his age, how he had not much time left anyway. He said he was in his fourth iteration—one life then three crafted lives, using the Clona arts. Yet who would have performed the art necessary to have him born again? Other magi? And where could that art be performed? It would require a large kitchen, he had told Corlan. There were special machines that were needed, not something that could be found easily.

Corlan turned on his side, facing the supplies on the wagon and dug into a bag. He retrieved a small ornately-carved box the size of his hand. He wanted to make certain it still existed and had not been misplaced during the packing. Lifting the lid he saw inside what he expected to find: a black cloth wrapped around memorabilia. He dared not unwrap it—not where others might see, not where the dry air of the valley could touch it. He knew what it was: the forefinger from the right hand of Joragus, the magus of Metta.

"It was not my fault," said Gorral with an angry grunt.

The journey was already becoming long for the new companions, so Rupas had been teasing Gorral about certain episodes from his sordid childhood. During their three-year friendship, they had come to learn almost everything about each other, it seemed, and neither of them liked that fact now.

"He thought you were the boy that stole the vegetables," said

Rupas. "That's what you told me. It doesn't matter now that it was your brother. You were the one punished for it."

"It had to be done," Gorral responded with smugness.

"You killed him? Your own brother? Just for laughing at you?" Corlan sat up in the back of the wagon.

"Yes." Gorral lowered his head. "He deserved it. And my father. He deserved to die, too. I killed my elder brother and my father was just as good as killed, not having an heir anymore."

"Then you ran away," Rupas added.

"They chased after me for a year." Gorral grumbled a moment. "I was born in the hills past War Basin." He glared at Corlan. "That's in the Lachan Hills, you know. An ancient forest of myth and troubles. No proper people ever dared enter."

"I've heard tales," said Corlan.

"More than tales," Gorral responded with a snarl.

"Why is it called War Basin?" asked Corlan.

"It's called—"

"Because of the battles fought there," Rupas cut in. "Brutal fights there between the tribes. The hill folk are naturally brutal, especially with each other. Outsiders can sometimes get by. Anyway, War Basin is where the land levels out in the forest, an open area perfect for fighting."

"It's the town there," grunted Gorral.

"You said the town owned the land, charged a fee to use it for any fights between tribes."

"That's true."

Tam was paying attention, Gorral noticed. He tried to grin at the boy but the effect was some kind of demonic mask. Tam looked away.

"It's really not so bad," said Gorral. "In that part of the world boys become men early. Those that don't, die quick. So every boy that lives is a tough bastard, for sure."

Tam snuck a peek at the stern-faced monster.

"I won't hurt you, boy," said Gorral.

Tam suddenly rose on his knees in the back of the wagon. "I'm training to be a dragonslayer, just like Corlan! He's killed three-hundred dragons!"

"Easy, Tam," said Corlan, pulling him down.

"He's got some fire in him," said Gorral, chuckling.

"Yes, the boy will make a fine dragonslayer someday."

"Not like you, eh, Rupas?" Gorral growled.

"What do you mean not like me?" Rupas responded. "I'm just not equipped to swing a sword or axe or anything like those weapons. I'm a schooled man, a scriber by trade, accountant in my last employ. I cannot do everything you big fellows can do, and yet you cannot do everything I can do with words and numbers. So you see, we need each other."

"And I can make salads," said Tam. He blinked. "After I practice for dragonslaying."

The men laughed. They stopped when they saw the boy looking glum, head down.

"Don't take our teasing seriously," said Rupas.

"What's the matter, Tam?" asked Corlan.

The boy wiped his eyes. "I miss Madi. I could talk to her. She understood everything."

Corlan sighed. "I miss her, too."

He instinctively gazed up into the sky, hoping to see a bird-girl winging her way after them, watching over them. But the sky was clear; only storm clouds on the horizon.

"We better find shelter," said Corlan. "Storm's going to overtake us, looks like."

They urged the horses to pick up the pace and, after about a mile more, they found a grove of trees and made camp there. Corlan pulled up the frame on the wagon and stretched the canvas cover over it to protect their supplies. The horses were tethered to the trees and given feed bags. The tent was erected quickly and they crawled inside as the first drops of rain hit the canvas.

"Hurry," Corlan called to Tam who had been tending to the meal for the horses. He raced to the tent, diving head-first inside.

"Fine looking contraption, this tent," said Gorral.

"I hope Madi finds a place to hide from the storm," said Tam to Corlan. The boy was still pouting.

"I'm sure she did."

"Is that your girlfriend?" asked Rupas.

Tam looked up. "No, just my friend."

"She was a girl, eh? So she's your girlfriend."

Tam protested and Rupas continued teasing him until Corlan had to intervene.

"She will be fine on her own. Let nature take over, I say."

Rupas cleared his throat. "You mean to let the gods watch over her."

Corlan frowned. "If you wish...."

"You don't believe in the gods?"

"I'm alive today thanks to the gods," said Corlan with a grin.

"What gods are those?"

"The gods.... Whoever they are.... I've heard they live in the clouds. They look down upon us, laughing or crying as we act our roles in life. I think that's the story."

"And Madi flies up there, too," said Tam.

"Seems like the gods hate us," Gorral spoke up. "Those dragons, always attacking, as you say. And we saw it ourselves!"

"Perhaps you call to the wrong gods," said Rupas.

"I doubt the gods send dragons to attack us," said Corlan. "They have their own intentions, the dragons do."

While they had ridden the wagon along the ancient riverbed, he had explained a little about their prior encounters with dragons. He did not know these men. He was not sure how much to say about dragons — or about his suspicions about that particular hornchin that seemed to have vowed to find him and kill him.

"Some of them...they think. Just like humans. They have hate, anger, vengeance. Like humans."

"Like humans, eh?" Rupas laughed. "There are good men and bad men everywhere."

Corlan grinned. "There are no good dragons."

"Tell him about Fluffy," Tam urged, clapping his hands.

Gorral and Rupas regarded each other.

"Who is Fluffy?" Rupas asked.

"Tam, that was a secret," said Corlan.

"Tell it, boy, now you've pulled it out of a bag like a cat."

"Go on," Gorral urged him.

Tam smiled, glad to have everyone's attention.

"Corlan said the dragon that attacked the city...the double-hornchin? It was the same dragon Corlan got the claw from. Did you see it? The front foot, missing a claw — the longer, middle claw. It was gone! Cut out!"

Rupas laughed. "Yeah, and that means...?"

"We was in the valley and got attacked by dragons. Lots of them. I hid in a cave but Corlan fought them all. The last one was that male double-hornchin. He cut off its claw!"

"We were trying to sell it in the city, the same claw," said Corlan.

"That was a prize!" Gorral shouted. "Urix got cheated by us, eh? Anything shiny and smooth he'll buy."

"It was a fair price," Rupas responded.

"But then the same dragon attacked the city," said Tam.

Gorral stared at the boy. "Are you sure it was the same?"

"Corlan said so," Tam replied.

They stared at the dragonslayer, who acted unconcerned.

"Tell them," Tam ordered.

"It was the same dragon," said Corlan, with no show of emotion. "Same missing claw. It stood over me right there. Stared me straight in the eyes, like it recognized me."

"But it did not kill you."

"No, it was readying a fire-breath but Joragus jumped in front of me and the dragon grabbed him."

"It was terrible," cried Tam.

Corlan patted the boy's shoulder. "I thought these dragons must be smarter than I could believe. That one, following me, attacking me again—and we'd better be careful; he could show up tonight! I swear he knew me, saw the same man just as I saw the same dragon."

"So you two should sign the scroll in the city office for an official union," Rupas suggested. He and Gorral burst into laughter.

"I hated always saying 'that male double-hornchin'—like I'm one of those scribers," said Corlan, his voice raised to be heard over their laughter. "I thought it would be better to give him a name. A name that fit his reputation, fit his appearance."

"And that's the name?"

"Yes: Fluffy."

"For a dark brown, scaly, ugly thing like that?"

"Exactly."

"He said that name dim-m-...what was the word?" asked Tam.

"Diminishes," said Corlan. "It's one of Joragus's words."

"That name *diminishes* the dragon's powers," Tam finished.

"You believe that?" asked Gorral.

"I would rather do battle with 'Fluffy' than 'that male double-hornchin dragon' if it drops in."

"Ah, I see!"

"You truly believe the dragon follows you?" asked Rupas.

"Joragus said he summoned a dragon and Fluffy is the one that arrived—and just in time, too."

"Yeah, a whipping is awful."

"A dragon attack is worse."

"And you got both!"

Corlan nodded, realizing how much punishment he had endured in the previous week.

"I'm used to it. All my life has been one pain after another. And deceit. Deceit and deception. And accusations and punishments. It started with my father. He was quick to beat me for anything I did wrong—or believed I did wrong, at least differently than what his idea was. When I was older, he took out his anger more upon my mother, so I had to stop him. Then he took me away, said I was old enough to fight in his army. Soon he was killed in a battle."

"That's like my father," said Gorral. "Like all those hill fathers. They all beat the sons. To make them tough, they say. Me, too. I took many a beating but I never learned anything from it. And the poor mothers, they weren't allowed to protect young boys. Older boys would not resist punishment or they'd be called girls. The girls were beaten, too. It's the way to train them, to make them submissive to the men."

"They beat girls, too?" asked Tam.

"Humans have ugly ways," said Corlan. "Tell them your story, Tam."

The boy shook his head. "No, I don't wanna."

"Orphan boy, this one," Corlan started. Tam shook his head for him to stop telling it. "You can guess the rest."

"Of course, I was punished by my father, too," Rupas said with a scowl. "And Mother protected me. Tried to. I was the youngest son so I saw more of it than I got myself. My two older brothers were always bloodied and aching. My sisters also abused. That was the reason I ran away when I was about twelve—about your age, Tam."

"Seems we've got a lot in common," said Corlan.

"So all boys are beaten by their fathers and saved by the mothers. At some time they run away. It's the way of the world. But does that make them men?" said Gorral. "Now we're on this journey to be men and do men things, that being killing and destroying and have some fun doing it. And take some women, too. Maybe our fathers did train us somehow. We still become violent bastards, after all."

"Not Corlan," Tam spoke up. "He protects me. He took me with him so Chef wouldn't hurt me."

"Like I said, humans are foul." Corlan coughed, spit into the dirt out the tent's entrance. "A man's got to stand for what is right—or he isn't a man. I always do what's right—what I *think* is the right way. There is no middle stand. And I got a lot of punishment for it. I'm on banishment right now, on this trek, and I must bring back a lot of dragonwares or I won't be allowed in the Burg, won't be able to see my lady again. I won't—"

"You've got a lady back home?" asked Rupas. "Her name?"

"Petula," Tam spoke out, getting back at Corlan.

He gave the boy a smirk. "Not a true lady, though. Not someone of the Court. But she's my lady."

"So what is she then, if she's not a true lady? A commoner?"

"She is a real woman. A woman like my mother. She comforts me. Also makes me feel strong. We met in the palace one eventide. She was serving the dinner there. After, we slipped away into the garden, got to know each other in the dark." He paused to recall it. "She also has employ in a tavern, The Toothless Knave. She takes mugs of brew from the bar to the tables."

"Ah hah! A true lady, after all!" Gorral laughed. "A garden wench and a bar maid. The best of both worlds."

"Probably she won't be waiting for you to return," said Rupas sadly, "if my experience is any indication. Those kind of *ladies* always enjoy their nights with any *prince* they happen to meet. They meet in the Court of last resort." He laughed.

Corlan pretended to laugh. "I advise you to stop with those kind of remarks. Those jokes. I'm sure they're only jokes, true?" He glared at Gorral and then Rupas. "They are only jokes, true?"

"Yes, sir," said Rupas with bowed head. "Pardons for a slip of my tongue."

"Between your lady's legs!" Gorral roared.

Corlan reached for his sideblade.

"Pardons," said Gorral seriously. "Part of my bad upbringing, you know. Father would beat me if I spoke like that to him—or any older person. It's the curse we have, eh? Nothing we can do now to change our ways, eh? So what's all that got to do with the price of dragon claws?"

INTERLUDE

The Passage

TWO WOMEN STEPPED INTO the slumber chamber well after dusk, tapping on the door and being granted entrance. The first was Jabuli, her tutor and friend. The other woman had black curly hair as wild as a washing brush. She stood shorter than Jabuli yet had broader shoulders. She wore common travel clothes.

"This is Rula," said Jabuli softly. "We trained together in Olan. She also was brought by Her Majesty, the queen, to Sannan. When I was appointed to be your tutor, Rula was sent to the laundry hall."

Adora studied the new woman, noting her stern face and the three long scars crossing her cheeks and nose. A black star had been burned into her forehead.

"Rula is from Yozma. She knows the way, so she will help us." Jabuli lifted a hand and wiggled her fingers at the woman. Rula moved her fingers, as well, nodding. "Also, she cannot speak," said Jabuli to the princess. "Though she can hear fine, she could not be anyone's tutor. Watch her face for answers. If she looks to the right, she means 'yes' and looking to the left means 'no'. She also speaks with her fingers but only if you know the code."

"She is going with us?" asked the princess. "All the way?"

"We need help to carry everything. I will carry your brother. He is heavy now, too much for you if we are to move fast. Rula will carry the bags—and her breasts. You carry yourself."

"Her breasts?" asked the princess.

"Yes, to feed your brother."

She gave Rula a long look. The layers of gowns hid her body.

"She has plenty of milk," said Jabuli. "She lost her babe not long ago. A male babe. Died soon after birthing. It's the law."

"Oh."

"So she will help us and go with us."

"Did you arrange passage?" asked the princess.

Jabuli turned to Rula, speaking to her by wriggling her fingers. More fingers for the answer.

"Yes. We are ready. Everything is arranged. Passage across the strait, then hiding with a friend, then a journey into the mountains. Now, Your Little Majesty, is it finally your wish to leave Sannan?"

The princess nodded solemnly. "Yes. I have put everything on the scale and it tips toward going."

"May the goddesses grant us safe passage, for your sake and for your brother's. Rula and I also hope to be safe. And free. We will be together again."

Past the middle of the night, when the corridor was dark and the torch extinguished, they exited the slumber chamber with a babe in a sling tight against Jabuli's chest and bags in their hands. Rula led the way, down the stone steps to the lower level. They passed the guard station there without being noticed, two guards asleep and the other looking away. Rula knew the best route and learned the guard schedule, collecting the laundry every night.

They crossed through the flower garden and hurried to a side gate, the one they expected to be unlocked. Rula had left it that way. Outside the gate stood a cart hitched to a drake that would take them to the wharf.

"The ship leaves at noon but we should be aboard before dawn, and hide in the bottom," Jabuli told the princess. "I know this ship captain. He's like a brother to me—a bad brother, though. But I have paid him well for the passage and keeping our secrets."

Rula spoke with her fingers, rather frantically.

Jabuli translated for the princess: "She is not certain we got away without being seen, she says. There was a torch following."

"There are many torches in the city," said the princess.

As they arrived, the wharf was dark yet noisy. Theirs was one of many carts, a snorting drake complaining to other hitched drakes, none of greater interest than the next. Torches lit a few spots where men were clustered, drinking and singing. A few women could be seen laying with them. Jabuli turned the princess away.

"Remember, we are a family from the mainland. Our home is Olan. I am the father, a craftsman, and you are my children," said Jabuli, pointing to Adora and her brother. "Rula is my wife. We sold all our wares at the festival so none to carry back with us."

Adora was dressed in shirt and trousers, a cap over her reddish locks, looking like a boy. Jabuli wore trousers and a jerkin, looking like a man. She had tied her hair up in a knot and pulled a cowl over her head. Rula wore a long rough-spun skirt and gray blouse with a flap in front that opened for nursing. Across her shoulders hung a ragged cape.

They found the ship, *Teflar's Serpent*, moored along the wharf and walked up the gangway to greet the ship's captain. He knew Jabuli by sight, dipping his head to her. Without words, he ushered the group aboard and showed them to the steps leading down into the ship's main hold. Jabuli, dressed in male clothes, got a wry grin from the captain as they descended.

In the hold, the stale air smelled like rotten fruit. The musty odor was overpowering. Jabuli wanted to let the princess go up and throw out her belly but she dared not risk being seen. Even now, she feared they might face betrayal. Someone saw them leave. Someone might have followed them to the harbor, perhaps already had marked this ship, perhaps knew they hid below deck. Perhaps the captain would take better pay from the palace for telling their secrets instead of the pouch of coin she offered him.

"Spill your belly here, if you must," Jabuli said after a while, and the princess let go a stream. "As you say, your brother is called Puki, for the reason you cannot endure the stench here."

The princess tried to laugh but her face was miserable.

"Rest, if you can," said Jabuli. "If there's trouble, I'll wake you. Rula will give your brother some milk to help him sleep."

Rula gathered the babe in her arms and opened her blouse. She pulled a breast free and pushed the nipple to his mouth. He fought it at first, then accepted.

"If he tries, he will get milk to flow," said Jabuli. "At least, he will be comforted and remain quiet. Her milk has not yet ceased."

The noise of the crew preparing for the voyage brought them to alertness. The boy had finished feeding and was asleep in Rula's arms. The princess lay flat against the beam, never falling asleep yet resting quietly. She did not complain but her face showed her belly was still tossing about.

Suddenly the captain appeared, descending half-way down the steps and swinging his head around the base of the mast to see them.

"There's guards on the wharf," he said with a grunt. "They query about you."

"Please protect us and you'll be paid well," Jabuli reminded him.

"Oh, I know I'll be paid well. Yep, just one more thing I require, and ya know what that is. Now's not a good time. Should I return when we're on the strait? Or after we make Olan? That's the only thing to decide."

"I prefer when we make Olan." Jabuli frowned. "Then I know we've gotten away. And arrived safely."

"That's fair. I'll be back when it's safe to dance."

He hurried up the steps.

"What's he mean by all that blabber?" asked the princess.

"He wants to do the ritual with me. It's part of his pay. Men like to make that act part of the deal. So I agreed and we slapped hands. To help us get away, it cannot be avoided."

"I will pay him more if he does not hurt you."

"Do not worry, Your Little Majesty. I don't think he'll hurt me. It's fair handslapping. Among ship captains, Teflar is considered one of the better men."

The calls of the crew above and the stamping of feet on the decks excited them. They were about to be underway. Passengers boarded, descending into the hold. More of the weary folk returning home after the festival. They brought crafts and art they had purchased. Others were taking back what they had not sold. The men seemed too tired to be dangerous, more interested in the festival than the poor family bedded down against the beam. What a forlorn family they seemed to be, buying passage in the lowest level of the ship, where it smelled like someone's bad stomach!

Finally the ship moved. They could feel it turning in the harbor and when it reached deeper water it rocked with each hard wave. The strait had a strong current and the ship had to go parallel to the coast for some time before it could turn and cross it. That route made the crossing take four hours. Eventually, they arrived at the opposite shore and turned up the coast to reach the harbor of Olan.

As the other passengers ascended to the deck, the princess and her companions remained below. It was late in the afternoon and the sun was strong. In the brightness they could not hide. So they waited until darkness fell before they exited the ship.

In the interim, Jabuli went to pay the captain additional coin. It seemed too much payment to the princess, and when Jabuli did not return soon enough, she became worried and turned to Rula.

"Will she be safe up there?" asked the princess.

Rula shook her head, eyes turning up toward the deck, hearing the noises of union. One after another, it seemed. Rula stood and climbed half-way up the steps to get a peek. She ducked down, then rushed to join the princess and her brother.

When Jabuli finally came down the steps, she was almost naked. Her skin was dirty and bruised, her face streaked with tears, and her hair matted. As she got to the bottom step, a bundle of clothes fell down upon her from above, covering her. She let them fall to her feet. Above her, the men cheered.

She picked up the clothing and sorted through them, then pulled each article on with deliberate motion.

As she ran her fingers through her dirty hair, she wore a grimace, as close to a smile as she could manage, solely for the benefit of the princess. Then, with stabs of pain, she sat down beside them.

"Did you pay them?" asked the princess in a serious tone.

Jabuli nodded.

"It seems they took more than was fair."

"The captain...." Jabuli had to take a breath. "He made a new deal. So I had to pay...more."

"Then I shall write a new law. I shall forbid it. No more making new deals. When you handslap, it's done."

Jabuli shook her head. Rula wrapped her arm around Jabuli's shoulders, held her close.

"This is not Sannan. The laws of Sannan are not followed here. In Olan, women are nothing. A toy at best. The men can change a deal as they like. And Teflar did." She gazed upon the sweet face of the princess. "You must forget this day, Princess Adora. What's done is done now. At dusk we will continue on our journey."

"Where shall we go?"

"I know a place, a woman who will hide us for a day. We will get some food there. And a good sleep. Then we will go south, then east. After many days we will go up into the mountains. To Yozma. Rula will show us the way."

They feared going on deck, even when the sunset faded and the night spread over the harbor. Jabuli tiptoed up the steps to have a look and returned with the news it was time for them to go. They gathered the babe and the bags and went up.

"Time to be off?" asked the captain, letting go a big yawn. Only he and his ugly, bearded first mate were on deck. "I've sent the crew into town. If you'd been a bit quicker, I could've sent you with them, you and your servant here. Two gals for the passage of one, eh?"

"Thanks for the dance," said the first mate, grinning.

"It's enough now," said Jabuli, anger in her voice. "You fulfilled your part and I did mine. Now let us be. Keep the secrets you agreed to keep. Have some honor."

"Will you dance with us on your return voyage?" Teflar asked with a chuckle.

"Do not bother us now and I promise to return to Sannan on your ship. I will pay for passage at that time."

"That's fair," said the captain. "So be off into town. And keep your dresses tight across your bottoms. Or your trousers, mister! The men of Olan are a wild and rough bunch."

Jabuli, carrying the babe in the sling against her chest, led the princess and Rula to the wooden walkway along the waterfront. With their footsteps slapping the boards, they passed taverns full of sailors and others who enjoyed drinking with men.

Soon they found a street leading to the main avenue where the open space of a market gave them some protection. They were less likely to be attacked in a public area. Most of the stalls were closed for the night, however. As they walked, they could still glance down the side alleys and see a couple here and there engaged in union, likely by force, Jabuli guessed from the women's cries.

They stopped in front of a forlorn building which seemed older than the Split.

"Here is the lodge," said Jabuli, knocking on a dark door. "I lived here a while when I was young. After my mother died."

Several questions were called out from within the lodge and Jabuli responded faithfully before the six locks came unlatched and the door swung open.

The woman who opened the door was old, bent almost down to the floor, her white-gray hair tied up in a big bun on the top of her head. Within her grinning mouth was only one tooth, there in front and to the left. She knew Jabuli instantly and her eyes widened.

Inside, the room was smoky, a fire in the brick bin sparking and snapping. Pieces of meat were on a skewer, turning over the fire, as the travelers took seats before the warmth.

Jabuli introduced everyone to the old woman, giving the princess the name Adolla.

"I never suspected you'd ever take a man for yourself," the old woman laughed at Jabuli. "Not the way they treated you. And this is how your son looks! White as cream. Hair red as curry. He must've been quite a pale man to overcome your tropic skin. But he's a lovely little boy. He's got handsome cheeks. Beautiful eyes, too. You've done well, girl."

"Thank you, Mema," said Jabuli with a soft chuckle. "It was a surprise to me, as well, when *she* appeared between my legs. She is truly my daughter, not a boy." She directed Adolla to take off the cap. "See? We dressed her as a male child just for the passage."

"So!" The woman seemed to lose her breath. "Then you must be carrying other secrets, eh? There is a night's worth of tales to tell."

They ate the meat from the fire and drank fresh goat milk as the tales were told. Rather than the princess feeding her brother, Jabuli took the role and offered him milk from a cup. He wouldn't take it, so Rula pulled out her breast and offered it to him.

"And what a joyful babe! I'm surprised you haven't sold him yet. As fat as he is, he would be a good farm worker. Or a smithy. I could see him wielding a hammer over an anvil. You make good children. I know you'd get a good price for this one."

"Thank you, Mema, but I intend to keep him and see him grow tall, not sell him."

"A woman from Sannan? With two childs? And not selling even the male?" Mema shook her head. "The only reason to birth two is to sell one and gain fair coin. How will you rise in status there?"

"In truth, I don't intend to return there." She pursed her lips. "It is the blessing of the goddesses I blame for a fortune such as mine. I could never find it in Rament. It's Sannan that has been good to me, but now I must leave there, as well, and find the path eastward. How is the road to Yozma these days?"

As Jabuli spoke, the woman noticed her uncomfortable posture. When she questioned her, Jabuli admitted to what she had suffered to cross the strait. The old woman put a kettle of water over the fire and helped Jabuli remove her clothing, then set about healing her wounds.

Adora watched closely, learning what women must endure in the world of men. She could read it on the parches or hear it from a tutor, yet now she understood. She glanced over at her brother, still bright-eyed on the rug on the floor, unconcerned with the workings of women. Whenever he cried, she would care for him. If she cried, he would do nothing.

"The way to Yozma is as clear as it's always been," said Mema as she worked on Jabuli. "The snows keep everyone away. I heard a few adventurers take a dragonflight up there but perhaps it's only gossip. But I don't see you riding a dragon any soon day, my love! You need to rest more than a day here. It's not good to pay them so much."

"I did it to save my...daughter. We needed passage. It was the only way to be safe. To be free."

"You give away your safety because you believe you'll be safe after?" Mema shook her head, continued swabbing her tender flesh. "At any moment everything you believe can be destroyed. At every step you take upon the street, you may come to the last step. Dangers are everywhere. What's this world becoming? There's no stopping evil these days! It grows and grows!"

"We have choices, Mema." Jabuli winced at the touch of the cloth. "I made a choice. If I am to be a sacrifice, let me be a sacrifice for the good that will come later."

"She is my tutor," the princess spoke up, "so she always protects me. No matter the danger."

"Tutor? That's a queer name for your mama."

Suddenly the princess realized her error. She blushed. "Yes, my mama is also my tutor on all kinds of things."

"Please, Mema. I've always respected you. You've helped me in so many ways. You saved me before, like getting me into the group of slaves that were sold in Sannan. I didn't have to go there. I didn't have to be a slave. But you had a plan for me to be free. How did you know the queen would be so kind to us?"

"Queen Dorothea is a kind woman. Too fat, by my eyes. She's got her quirks, as we all do, yet overall she's fair and just. She does not want women to be held as slaves by men. I knew she would buy your freedom and let you work for coin in the palace or else be hired by shopkeepers in the city. That's how she does it. So I've no reason to complain how much she eats. Have they built a new room yet to fit her in?"

"I am grateful to you." Jabuli started to cry. "And I'm ashamed for what I've done."

"What you've done? I think the shame goes to those who did to you, my love."

"My daughter...Adolla, and my son here...Puki."

"Beautiful children, I must say!'

"They are not truly my children," said Jabuli. "I can't have my own children. Not after the fighting pits. Some injury broke me."

Mema withdrew the swab, rubbed ointment into the flesh, then gazed at Jabuli's face. "I'm sorry to remember that episode. You won that fight, at least. Took that girl's head clean off."

"You cannot tell anyone. It is the greatest secret ever." By instinct she glanced in each direction, expecting spies even in the small room of a small lodge in the dirty backstreets, the fire crackling and smoke curling to the ceiling.

Mema leaned down. "Go on."

"This is not my daughter Adolla. She is truly Her Little Majesty, Princess Adora. Of Sannan. And her pet brother."

Mema's mouth fell open, her eyes wide, almost glowing. Her hand dropped the swab and her backside let out air.

"You've stolen the royal children?" Her voice was anxious yet deliberately hushed.

Jabuli bit her lip. "Not...*stolen*."

"I asked her to help me leave Sannan," the princess spoke, her voice filled with royal tone. "It is my plan. It is all my choice. I asked her to help me and she is. Yet already I see the plan is too harsh. Too much to be given up."

Adora, kneeling beside Jabuli, reached out and hugged her legs as she lay on the floor.

"My tutor is Jabuli, and my only friend. My brother is more than a pet to me. My mother frowns at me and gives away my life plan to my sister, Princess Lumina. My mother will hurt my brother, too, and possibly me. Already they let dragons into my chamber, hoping to kill my brother. It is more and more difficult to protect him. So I had to leave."

She removed her hands from Jabuli's legs, regarded her face.

"I did not want you to be hurt. I never expected that, nor did I wish it. I did not know that would happen."

Jabuli placed a hand on the princess's head. "I know, Your Little Majesty. We are on the right path. There will be obstacles on any path you take. I am willing to go with you, to take the punishment for you. Because you are innocent. And you must remain innocent. As innocent as a babe. I am already done with innocence."

"Then you best take this one far from Olan." Mema grunted. "The brother will be fine here. Easy to grow him, put him to work. This girl won't last a day on the street. She would be destroyed. You must go fast and go far. Even now there's talk of invading Sannan."

"We're going to Yozma."

"That may not be far enough. If the snows ever melt, there will be men finding the trail after you."

"Then we will go farther. Over the mountains."

"Is there a place beyond the mountains?" The princess pouted. "A place where women and their brothers can play together? Where they are happy together and they don't hurt each other? Is there such a place anywhere in this world? And can we go there?"

Mema grunted, shaking her head. "You talk of the dream lands, child. And only dragons will take you there. You best sleep and have your dreams there in the slumber land, not in your waking hours."

"Do you dream of dragons, Adora?" asked Jabuli. She pulled on a fresh gown from the drawer Mema had pointed to. "You told me of one dream—or was it a waking vision? You said I will fall? I would be attacked by a dragon. Is it true?"

"Aaa, nothing's true in dreams," Mema grumbled. "It's nothing but bubbles of mystery in a magic stew!"

The princess smiled warmly, as though she had some good news to give. "If you could see what I see in my dreams, you would know it is true. That it will become true. It is a special gift, Mama always told me. The goddesses blessed me—"

"More a curse, I say!" said Mema.

Adora made a face. "You are wrong. I can see things in my head, like I'm watching a bright stage full of actors, and they speak to me, just as though I'm on the stage with them, hiding among the trees, and they tell me what will happen. Or they act it out as I watch. It's rather entertaining."

"She's a clever one, this princess!"

Adora glanced cautiously at Mema then at Jabuli.

"I know this journey will succeed. For me...and my brother. It won't for you. I saw it already."

Jabuli bowed her head. "And yet...."

"I begged you not to come with me." Adora frowned. "You said I could not go alone, not with my brother to carry."

Jabuli threw her hands to her face. "In your dreams...did you see me raped?"

"No. Yet I saw you come down steps already hurt. I did not know what hurt you. Or where the steps were." Her face reddened. "I am just a girl—a child—and I did not know what I saw. I did not know what it meant." Tears burst from her eyes. "If I did, I would warn you! I swear! I would not let you come with me. I would have stayed in my slumber chamber, so silent. I would have been a good girl for everyone, especially for you, Jabuli! I never would let you be hurt because of me!"

The princess cried and the babe joined in. Jabuli embraced her charge, brushing her hair with her fingers.

"It's not your fault, little majesty," Jabuli whispered into her ear. "The things that happen are chosen by the goddesses. Or else they do not stop what will happen. Either way, I do not blame you. Nor would I let you go from Sannan by yourself with the babe."

Jabuli held the princess away, looking into her eyes.

"You are the closest I ever will have to my own child. And all mothers make sacrifices for their children. My mother attacked the men who wanted to take me away. She fought them as hard as she could, just so I had the chance to escape, to run away from them. I did run away. I never saw my mother again. I guess she died there but I never will know."

"I do not want you ever to die for me," the princess cried.

"I never will die for you, Adora." She hugged the girl, feeling tears against her chest. "But I will always *fight* for you. If the fight goes bad, I may die—if that's what the goddesses command. They seem to favor you, so perhaps the day will come when it is either you or me, and then the goddesses will choose me to fall. As you say, from the attack of a dragon. If you will be well, then I will not refuse to fall. I will know that you can go on, little majesty, and be a great leader in the world."

Mema waved her hand over their shadows. "You better get some rest if you intend to go in the morning. You best leave before dawn, when the roads are clear. I have kept your sword. Take it. It's the one you used in your final fight. I still have your fighting clothes, if you want them. And I have a small axe."

She opened the trunk beside her seat and lifted out the weapons.

Jabuli eyed the long, two-handed sword, its blade gleaming in the firelight. "You cleaned off the blood. Thank you, Mema."

"It looks better without the blood."

21

A Camp by a Lake

"THE PRICE OF A DRAGON'S CLAW is, in the end, two horses for draft, two horses for mount, one large wagon, and food and provisions enough for a hundred-day journey through the western wilderness. And also some fancy clothes for our great leader."

Corlan waved off Rupas. "Traveling clothes is all they are. Clean and fresh—at least when we left Unting. Not so clean and fresh now."

"I'll be the judge of that remark," said Gorral, pinching his nose between his fingers.

"That's more than we two got," said Rupas.

"Who cut the dragon's claw from the dragon's foot?"

"Uh...you did."

"Yes." Corlan scratched his beard. "I wish I could've replenished the iron bolts for the dragonslinger. I had the smithy make as many as he could in three days, but they don't possess the bulb of poison we like them to have."

"Then let us hope we don't see any more of those aerial beasts!"

"We are in the Valley of Death again." Corlan glanced around at each of them. "We have no hope of that now."

The valley had widened considerably once they returned to it from Unting, and a few miles west the shorelines had steepened. Roads crossed the riverbed in different directions. When they found one that led them to higher ground, they took it. The horses pulled the wagon up the slope to a road that paralleled the shoreline.

As they continued, they saw ruins of buildings on the opposite shore. Fallen structures of brick and stone. Burnt remains of wooden houses and shacks, the remains of old farmsteads. The fields had not been planted or harvested in many years, it appeared. Many fields were overgrown with wild flora, some with new trees.

Corlan told his companions the story of the Great Fire which had burned the land. That was likely the cause of so many abandoned cities and farmsteads and the sight of so many newly sprung trees and bushes. Rupas had heard it, but it was new to Gorral.

"Good it never reached Unting," grunted Gorral. "Or any place south of there."

"Civilization seems to have returned," said Rupas. He let go an annoying cheer. "I look forward to a long, hot bath."

The road dipped, rising on the other side and they looked down upon a large emerald lake. In all the journey through the Valley of Death there had never been a river or stream. At best the small oasis with a pond Corlan and Tam had found earlier. Now, the verdant hills surrounded a body of water which shimmered with inviting coolness.

"How do we get down to that?" asked Tam.

Corlan stood up on the seat and gazed in every direction.

"I see a road rising on the opposite hill, over there." He pointed. "This road must continue. It should drop down to the lake before climbing again."

Corlan sat, shaking the reins and the horses started.

Once by the shore of the lake, they made their camp. Actually, they made part of the camp. As soon as the main bundles were pulled from the wagon, the men stripped off their clothes and ran into the water, eager to refresh themselves. They began kicking and splashing in cool comfort.

Tam stayed on the shore, content to watch the adults acting like children.

"Aren't you coming in?" called Corlan from out in the lake.

"I don't know how to do it," Tam called back.

"What, swim?"

"I don't know swimming."

"It's easy. I'll teach you."

Corlan walked up the slope, out of the water, and stood before the boy. It was a startling sight to him. The man was covered in scars, a couple long ones and many short marks. Across his broad chest was a lot of hair and at the top of his legs was more hair. Tam looked away.

"Come now, boy. We're the same here. Men, boys, males. Don't be shy. You can swim in those clothes if you want to. They need some washing, too."

With a shrug of his small shoulders, Tam pulled off his sandals and joined them. He ran straight into the water with shirt and pants on, unafraid.

Then he slipped on rocks under the water and his head dunked below the surface. He came up frantic and screaming. Corlan caught his arm, held him so his head remained above the surface.

"Easy, boy."

Over the next hour Corlan taught Tam the basic arm motions and how to kick his feet to stay afloat and move through the water. He held Tam up, hands lifting the boy's belly as he practiced, then letting go so the boy could move across the water on his own. Tam was enjoying the swimming lesson, laughing and shouting. Finally, they decided they'd had enough fun and swam to the shore.

They lay on the sand and gravel along the shore, bare skin against the ground, late afternoon sun covering them with a golden glow. Corlan closed his eyes, his body soothed by a breeze crossing over his skin. He dreamed of Petula, wishing she could be here with him to enjoy the idyllic setting. He pulled his arms up and tucked his hands under his head.

"Time for a nap," he said with a sigh.

After a while he saw Petti reclining beside him and he invited her to take off that plain dress and apron she wore, to let down her hair from the two buns, to enjoy herself on the shore of this lake. She gently declined, saying she still had work to do.

"Is that...?" someone was saying outside of his dream.

"Come now, Petti, you always enjoy resting skin to skin with me," Corlan was saying, taking her hand and drawing it to his loins. "I've missed you so much these many months."

"By the gods, it surely is!" a man's voice cried out.

"Corlan!" someone was calling. Petti stood up and walked away along the shore of the lake, glancing back over her shoulder every few steps, waving her hand in farewell.

He opened his eyes.

"Corlan! Dragons!" It was Tam rushing up to him, shouting.

Corlan sat up, instantly scanning the sky. "Where?"

Tam pointed to the far horizon where three winged things were approaching just above the treetops.

"Grey-bellies," said Corlan, scrambling up and padding naked to the wagon. He shifted some bags over and hauled the dragonslinger out, reached for an iron bolt from one of the quivers, and returned to the spot on the shore where he had been napping.

"Are they going to attack?" asked Tam.

"You see them?" called Rupas from out in the lake.

Corlan nodded, then turned to the boy: "Likely not."

"They are flying low."

"You've a good eye, Tam, but that's a female and two younglings heading our way."

"You got the dragonslinger out."

"To be ready. Just to be ready." He loaded the bolt, screwed back the spring to the tightest setting. "Likely they'll take no notice of us."

Out in the lake, Gorral and Rupas were trying to swim back to shore. The narrow arm of the lake, extending to the north, was a ten minute swim and the main area of the lake, spreading west, would take much longer to cross. Rupas was closer; he waved his arms frantically at his friend to hurry.

The grey-bellies soared lower once they cleared the trees and were above the lake. The mother led the way, her offspring following in tandem. They swooped down over the lake, slowing enough to appear to hover. He wondered if the dragons saw the men in the lake and were about to catch dinner.

Gorral was anxious, splashing loudly, swimming wildly to shore as Rupas shouted at him to dive under the water.

Corlan knelt on the shore with the dragonslinger braced against the ground, aiming at the mother as she slid over the surface. The rumble from her belly told him she had no interest in the humans. Maybe it was a flying lesson for her two offspring.

Then something plopped into the lake. Followed by other plops, and more, as the three dragons cut across the water straight toward Corlan and Tam. Great globs of ashen feces were dropping into the lake—and then on the shore as Corlan sprang up and ran with Tam under the cover of the trees. One dropping hit the wagon, falling down its side and dissipating, smelly ash blown by the breeze into a cloud of gray soot. Where each drop splashed into the lake, the water sizzled, boiled a moment before the ash broke up and settled to the bottom.

"I really want to kill that mother for dropping on us but I don't want to waste the bolts," said Corlan to Tam, cowering behind him.

After a minute they left the woods and returned to the shore.

Corlan gazed out over the lake's surface for Gorral and Rupas.

He saw nobody in the water. He turned to stare in each direction along the shore. There they were: laying on the ground like they had been injured in an attack. Rupas waved his hand and Corlan waved back, then jogged down the shore to them.

"You hurt?" he asked them.

"No, just exhausted," said Rupas. "I never swam so hard in my whole life."

"You, too?" he asked Gorral. The man seemed embarrassed to be out of breath and so fatigued.

"Yeah."

"We were lucky, no attack. Just a mother and younglings."

"Who will soon learn to kill men, eh?" said Rupas.

"Someday." He glared at Gorral, pointed at him. "You got some dragon waste in your hair, looks like."

Rupas laughed. "Tell him," he urged his friend.

"No." Gorral frowned, reached up to touch whatever was in his hair. It felt like a mix of mud and ash, sticky yet only smelling of burnt wood and sulfur. He tried to flick it out of his hair.

"The mother dropped some waste on the wagon," said Corlan. "We better clean it off." He sighed, turning and regarding the lake. "We should have filled our water jugs before we swam. Now the lake is polluted."

"That's what I told him," said Rupas, gesturing. "Our friend here," meaning Gorral, who looked away, "he got so frightened when those dragons came low that he couldn't keep his belly tight."

"What do you mean?" asked Corlan.

"He shat in the lake!"

Corlan shook his head, not believing how this day was going.

"And pissed," Gorral confessed. "It's a large lake. Too far to the shore, so.... It'll stay over there, I'm sure. The water here's clean."

Corlan stood, hands on hips. The other men were covered in dirt and sand, and the dragon waste that had dropped on them.

"You men better clean yourselves before you return to camp."

"We will," Rupas offered.

"Meantime, I'll set up the camp."

Tam was hard at work when Corlan arrived at the wagon. The boy had already scrubbed off the dragon waste from the side and was finishing cleaning the bags that had gotten soiled. Corlan praised his effort.

"You'll get the first portion of dinner tonight," said Corlan.

After pulling on a fresh outfit, unwilling to return to the well-worn clothes he had been glad to shed before going into the lake, Corlan unfolded the tent and with Tam's assistance set it up. They moved the bedrolls and some provisions inside, then made ready the evening's cooking gear.

"Are those men really going with us all the way to the marshes?" Tam asked suddenly.

Corlan grinned. He knew what the boy meant. "They may be of some help." He chuckled. "They will be the first eaten by dragons — as I load the slinger. But don't say that to them."

"I won't."

Finally the two men returned, looking cleaner than before. They stood in only their skin as they dug through bags for fresh clothes. Dressed once more, they beamed with joy at being alive.

"Tam gets the first portion tonight," said Corlan. "He's earned it, cleaning off dragon waste and helping me set up the camp."

"I understand he's your favorite," said Gorral. "Yet he's just a boy. Men need a proper meal."

"You'll get yours. I said the boy goes first tonight."

"He's only a boy. He doesn't eat much anyway."

Corlan turned to the big man. "Are you challenging me?"

Gorral's gaze held strong. "He's just a boy."

"Then there will be plenty left for you."

"Let's relax, fellows," Rupas cut in. "So the boy goes first.... It's not as though he will eat all of the ration, is it?"

Gorral waved off Rupas, swung a shoulder at Corlan, stepping away from the campfire.

"What's his complaint?" Corlan asked Rupas.

"Hah! His pride's been wounded. Don't you see?"

"Pride? In what? A man's got to do something to have some pride. You don't get pride from pissing and shitting in a lake when a dragon flies overhead."

"That's what I mean. He was scared, even a big man like him."

"I don't blame him for being scared. The first time I saw a dragon up close, I nearly loosed my bowels, too. Yet I didn't. And this boy wet his pants the first time up close with a dragon."

"Don't tell them that!" Tam snapped.

Rupas giggled as only a full-grown man can. "He thinks you favor your son too much, but that's quite proper. He feels he's third-class citizen on this journey."

"Third...after you?" Corlan grinned.

"I suppose. He doesn't think the boy is really your son, so that is a wound for him, too."

"Not my son?" He regarded Tam across from them.

"Look at the boy," said Rupas. "He doesn't look like you at all. You have that reddish hair and that light skin and the boy is brown with a mop of curly black hair. It can't all be from his mother's side of the bed."

"It's no matter who the boy is," said Corlan with a frown. "He is under my protection. So it's no matter if he is not my true son. We've been together longer now than either of you two rogues have been with us."

"Who do you call rogues?"

"A simple word for vagabonds with minor skills."

"Who do you call vagabonds?"

"You and your large cousin."

"Cousins? Gorral and I had properly employ. It was only a fix of bad luck made us available to go on this journey with you to who knows where. I still don't know where we're going. You said some magical place where dragons lay their eggs, yet it might only be a place in your imagination. Once we arrive wherever you see as this magic egg place, you might just slit our throats to get all the eggs for yourself."

"Clearly you are raving mad now." Corlan turned as if to dismiss him. "Please take a rest and forget what you have said. It has been a day of strain, I know. We are all on edge. Tomorrow everything will be right again."

Rupas realized at that instant how close he had gotten to the edge, respecting Corlan's even-temperedness.

"Thank you, Corlan. You are correct. Tempers can flare under the strain of dragons ever in our midst."

"They do cause strain...."

When the dinner ration was prepared, Tam sauntered over to the communal bowl like he was the Prince of Lakeland—as Corlan teased him, even throwing a covering over his shoulders to affect a cape. He took the first portion of the lumpy gray gruel. One day's ration, prepared in one bowl. Usually, Corlan took the first portion. Then Gorral and Rupas, alternating each day who went first. Then the boy got to scrape up whatever remained in the bowl. Sometimes there was little left so Corlan, who always held back some of his own until the boy had eaten, would slip some to him.

"Ugh, this stuff is getting to be awful," Gorral dared grumble.

"If we stayed longer in one place," said Corlan, "we might go in search of local game."

"We got a drake one time a long time ago," Tam exclaimed.

"A drake?" asked Rupas.

Tam described the whole incident in great detail. The men were delighted at the story and how passionately he told it. Their bellies growled, unsatisfied, nevertheless.

"I wish we had some drake walk across our path tonight," said Gorral. "I need some meat. Real meat. Not this...this grandfather food, food for old men with no teeth...."

Corlan smiled at the boy.

"You need a magic bunny," said Tam.

"What's that?" asked Corlan. "A magic bunny?"

"Chef always said that. Whenever we would run out of food at the palace, he would pray for a bunny to appear in the garden. By magic."

"Did it work?"

"Sometimes a bunny arrived just in time for dinner."

Corlan laughed and licked his fingers. "That would be magic."

When the dragonfire was low in the lamp, Corlan stood and said it was time to sleep. A long day loomed ahead. They would need to find a path around the lake.

"Also, now that we are in dragon territory again, we'd better train you how to fight. How to use the dragonslinger, too. We can't know how things might go when dragons attack. You may be closer to the slinger than me and need to load it, launch it. Tomorrow, we'll have a lesson. I'll teach you the vulnerable places on a dragon for aiming the iron bolts. You need to know that now. We might not be hunting dragons but dragons will be hunting us."

22

City of Women

THE SOUND OF BIRDS in the trees awoke Corlan and for a moment he thought Madi had returned. He sat up, remembering where he was and the true state of his situation. He was back on the road, on the way to his doom somewhere over the next hill, or the next, with a couple of fools for dragon bait, and a boy who might as well be his son for all they had shared during the past few months, someone to make up for the children he had ignored, had harmed, had dared to treat as adults just because they were standing on a battlefield —

"Awake!" came a cry from outside the tent — a woman's voice.

The others opened their eyes. Tam looked afraid.

Spearpoints jabbed at the sides of the tent, pressing then cutting into the canvas. They were surrounded.

"Hey! It's a perfectly good tent!" cried Rupas.

Through the holes Corlan could see the women, dressed in dark leather with feathers as ornaments. He thought they were more of the warrior women of Madi's tribe, so he relaxed a bit, believing he could negotiate with them. He grabbed his sideblade and crawled out of the tent, clothed only in a loincloth, and stood before them.

Immediately, speartips struck close to his waist and at his throat.

"Be calm," he spoke in a gentle voice. "We are only travelers and mean you no harm. This morning we will continue our journey and be quickly out of your territory."

The woman wearing red feathers in her black hair gave orders to the others in some kind of coded language. It was not the bird calls and tweets of Madi's tribe, however. Other warriors ripped the tent down and cut out the men and boy inside the collapsed canvas. They were stood up in a line and the leader of the group inspected them one at a time, saving Corlan for last. She lingered before him and stared at his scars with a smile of admiration.

"The young one is yours?" she asked him in words he knew.

"He is my son."

She looked over the boy. "Age?"

"Twelve, I think."

"You think?" She grinned, like she had an evil thought.

"I wasn't present at his birth so I'm not sure of the date."

"It's no matter. He can be taught."

"Taught?"

"To serve."

The camp Corlan thought they were being taken to was far more than the bird-nest huts that Madi's tribe had as a village. He could see it in the distance when they reached a rise in the road that gave them a view over the lake and down the valley beyond. On the bluffs overlooking the far end of the lake stood a mighty city as large as Unting, filled with buildings of gray stone and other buildings that were mostly pale pink.

When they arrived at the main gate and entered, Corlan saw the houses were stacked on top of each other like children's nursery blocks. They seemed to be made of dried mud and straw, wooden beams as frames, so many of them that the city took on a pink hue. Even the fortress dominating the center of the city was pink though built of stone, not dried mud. The bustle of the square they passed through further showed them this was a major city. Corlan looked at Rupas for answers but received only a shrug of shoulders. Gorral had a wild grin on his face, like he had entered paradise. Tam stayed close to Corlan, sometimes grabbing the tail of his shirt to keep up.

"What is this city called?" Corlan asked.

The escort beside him smacked his cheek with her hand. "It is Covin, the Queen City." Then she had a smile for him.

They were led without ropes, keeping spears at the ready. They marched through the crowded market, citizens staring at them, a few daring to touch them. One woman that slapped at Corlan's arm was shoved back by one of their escorts. Winding through the crowd, they exited the market and continued down a wide avenue, arriving at a smaller fortress.

Their escorts spoke a moment with the guards at the gate. The business settled, in through the gate they went, prisoners ushered over to one of several doors along the side wall. The captives were pushed into the room and the door swung shut.

Behind them as they were led through the streets, some of the women led their four horses by the reins while others had pulled the wagon. The women did not seem to understand that the horses were meant to pull the wagon; they had been free of the wagon overnight, grazing near the tent when the women came upon the camp. Once in the city, Corlan saw that no animals were used as beasts of burden. People carried things themselves on shoulders or heads, or pulled their own carts. And he saw only women and girls. The only men he noticed were a scrawny pair struggling to carry a palette of pink bricks on their bent backs. He pitied them.

"I wonder what they have planned for us," Rupas mumbled once the women had left and the wooden door was locked with a support bar. "I very much wish to be on the road again."

"Me, too," said Tam.

"They want us to sire their children," Gorral said with a grunt. He regarded Corlan. "True?"

"Don't believe the tales of traveling rogues," said Corlan in a low voice. "Not all women's towns require men."

"Why else capture us?" asked the big oaf. "I'm ready to serve."

"Be careful what you ask for."

"I don't ask for a lot." He chuckled a moment. "It's been too long. I need to serve. And be served. I've got a lot to give."

"Be careful what you ask for," Corlan repeated.

"Why, I expect to be served by comely ladies, I do!"

Corlan ignored him, studying the door. He thought he could put a shoulder to it and break out. Certainly he and Gorral together could bust it open. But then where would they go? They were in some kind of prison with guards and a gate outside the cell. He had tried to memorize the route from the main gate of the city to this jail complex. He might be able to run away, escape from the city, but the boy would not be able to keep up. Because they had not been tied up or treated as criminals, perhaps all would be well.

"Many women's towns exist," Corlan explained in a teacherly tone to Gorral. "It's because men were too barbaric in days past, especially during the war era. Too many going where they wanted, taking what they wanted, being the worst they could be. So women banded together, formed their own towns and guarded themselves, stopped men that tried to enter. Sure, there was a need to replenish themselves so when a man was found, he was made to serve. After serving, he quickly disappeared. So I've heard. Travelers' tales."

"That's a good story," Gorral sneered. "That's maybe how I got to be born. My mother knew many men. One was my father. One of many men roving the country in search of women to enjoy. It's the way of the world. Men take what they want, discard what they're finished with. Nothing odd about that. It's natural."

"Natural, maybe, yet not so civilized," said Corlan.

"Civilized means you can't follow laws of nature? Rubbish! Laws of nature are higher than laws of government."

"It means we humans choose to honor a greater good, that being the idea of saving our kin by providing them benefits over a long time, rather than giving in to whatever animal instincts we have at the moment. This is what separates us from...dragons."

"You're all weepy and weak in the head, Corlan of the Burg. I'll take whatever I can and be happy with it. That's the world I live in. It's the strong that survive. The weak die."

Corlan glared at the oaf. "So you're a strong man. What good is it to you? It takes the same strength to protect as it does to attack."

"Attacking's got more pleasure to it."

"Not if you're protecting people you love."

"People I love?" He roared with laughter. "I love'em an hour or two, at best. If they're good at what I want."

Corlan narrowed his eyes, focusing more sharply in the dim light of the cell. Was this oaf challenging him again? in a jail cell? while captured? Truly Gorral was an oaf. *Do I fight him now or later?*

"I tell you what I know," said Corlan. "If you want to serve, you can go first when they come for us."

"Great! Finally taking my place among the men of nature. First in line for our ration! I have much seed to sow in this city." He glanced at Rupas, threw a thumb in his direction. "This poor fool he never wants a lady, so he can go last. But what woman would want a hunched back fellow like him?"

Rupas cowered in the corner, lost in the shadows. "You say that now? When we are fearing for our lives? I thought you and me were friends."

"Yeah, midnight friends...." Gorral waited for a reaction. "Ain't that true?" He set his eyes back on Corlan, laughing.

"How dare you!" said Rupas. He regarded Corlan, too, tried to see his reaction, but the dragonslayer had turned away, staring out the small window in the door. "Never again, Gorral. Never again."

"Ho! That's true. Never again!" The oaf sure knew how to laugh. "Let the sowing begin!"

Hours later, a squad of women warriors came to the cell. Marked by blue and yellow feathers fixed to their shoulders and neckline — feathers from birds rather than featherback dragons. The warriors or guards or soldiers, whatever they were, wielded spears and carried knives on their belts. These were larger and more muscled than the slender women of Madi's tribe or those women who led them to this city. Corlan wondered if he could fight any of these women one on one and win.

"Who is your leader?" asked the leader of the squad. In addition to the blue and yellow feathers, she also wore red feathers in her long black braided hair and at her elbows, so Corlan presumed she was their captain. "Who will speak for your tribe?"

He was about to step forward when Gorral grunted, cleared his dry throat, and spit on the dusty floor. "I'll go."

Corlan bit his lip, anxious to speak up. Rupas grabbed Corlan's arm but Corlan shook off his hand. Tam stood stock still in the darkest corner of the cell.

"Look at those lovely figures," said Gorral, leering. "Full chest, narrow waist, wide hips, long legs — they're perfect. And I'm in need of some perfection tonight."

He stepped out into the afternoon sunlight, blinded. He raised his hand. The women took his wrists and bound them together.

"So this is the way it's to be?" he asked playfully. "They like it rough, eh? I'm a master of this game, I am."

The beefy women pushed him forward.

"Easy now, ladies, I need to save my strength for tonight. I'm sure I can please several of you, so don't worry. No need to fight over me. I'll get to each of you in turn."

The squad surrounded Gorral, spears raised, then marched him away in tight formation.

"I'll be sleeping well tonight," he called back. "Or tomorrow, I mean. Tonight's not for sleeping! Enjoy your cold cell."

One of the guard women shoved him hard and he almost tripped but recovered, grinning back toward the cell window.

"Easy, ladies!" he barked. "Be lovely lasses or I won't be inviting you to dinner. I've got something special for you...." and his voice trailed away as they departed down the avenue.

The night was cool and the walls, fashioned from dried mud, along with its stone floor, did not hold any warmth. They huddled in the far corner to stay warm yet none of them slept well.

In the morning, a bowl of bread slices and a bottle of something more flavorful than water was given to them. There wasn't much to say that hadn't already been said, so they remained silent. However, Corlan would speak encouraging words to Tam every hour or so. Rupas kept in an angry mood, cursing under his breath.

Late in the afternoon, another squad of women came to collect all of them. The door was unlocked and half the squad entered, stood on either side of the door. The squad's leader pointed to Corlan, the obvious choice as this tribe's leader. He took two steps forward, then hesitated.

The leader waved him forward, held her hand up at the others.

"The boy?" Corlan asked when they seemed to only want him.

"He is yours?" asked the squad's leader.

"I'm responsible for him."

"He may come."

Corlan gestured at Rupas. "And my man-servant?"

"All men are servants here."

"He gets terribly afraid when he is left alone. I promise you he won't cause any trouble."

"Bring him," said the leader.

The women lined up the three males and the group marched off, passing out the gate and through the streets, catching the glances of women young and old who paused in their daily routines to stare at the fine looking male warrior, a man who might be destined to work for high-bred ladies—followed by his sniveling, broken squire who might tend a garden, and a handsome young man who might be good to have around a home for menial tasks—until he reached an age where he could not be controlled and needed to be put down. He could see their fate in the women's faces.

After a short walk, they entered a large gate. Corlan saw it was the main fortress that stood tall in the center of the city. Their next stop was a small room. They were stripped of their dirty clothes by a team of elderly women. Once naked, the women inspected each of them. Their gnarled hands worked meticulously on them, touching every part, poking everywhere, measuring everything. Tam felt ticklish and giggled through the procedure. Rupas was too nervous to comply and had to be admonished repeatedly. He became shy, trying to cover his loins with his hands. Corlan stood tall and strong without arrogance. At the end, each of them was cut on the finger to gain a spilling of blood and asked to spit into a bowl, both of which were taken away.

Next they were escorted, still naked, through a dark hallway to another room with a great basin set in the floor, large enough for perhaps twenty people. They were sent down into the foamy water. A team of five young women wearing thin white gowns already occupied the water. The bathing procedure began. Two younger ones were assigned to wash Tam, much to his chagrin. The women took sponges and cloths to the men's bodies, but the boy was too shy so the girl attendants splashed water over him until he turned away.

After the bathing, they were dried off with the gentle brushing of soft cloths, then dressed in fresh white robes that hung freely down to their knees. They found a robe in Tam's size, as well, and he was delighted to be treated like a prince.

"I wonder if this is what Gorral experienced yesterday," Rupas whispered as they waited to be taken to their next appointment.

"No doubt he enjoyed it," Corlan replied with a cautious grin.

"I hope I don't have to do anything with those girls," said Tam, his voice shaking. "I don't know what to do."

Corlan smiled. Maybe the girls would teach the boy what to do — if they truly wanted him to do anything. He was almost the age for his first tender moment. Yet it should not be under duress, Corlan decided. Not like his first time with a girl, the one his elders chose for him. He recalled how frightened she had been. His elders held her down and urged him to go ahead. It was difficult to do anything with them watching and her squirming — until they beat her into silence. He tried to show her a sympathetic face, like they both were being forced, but he knew she had no interest in how sorry he might be. Later, in the battle, those elders were killed and he had moved up in rank.

"I hope you will show them kindness when your time arrives," he told Tam.

When the time arrived, guards returned to escort them through several corridors, up a flight of wide, elegant stairs, and into a huge hall strung with ornate streamers of pink and white hanging from the ceiling, streams of curtains in pale green and teal crisscrossing the ceiling and draped over the polished wood floor. In the center of the great room sat a long, oval table. It sat low to the floor. Its surface was adorned with flowers standing in vases and silver goblets at each dining place. Women in pale pink skirts and slim vests which hid little of their bodies stood guard around the perimeter of the room, holding their lances ready. Swords hung in scabbards at their hips.

To one side of the great hall was a raised floor, much like in the palace back in the Burg where Prince Vilmer loved to prance. It had to be an audience room, Corlan guessed, yet it was prepared for a feast. He could smell the food roasting. If they were the guests, he wondered how they could rank high enough for such an invitation.

The three males were shown to their seats, instructed to sit upon the round cushions placed on woven mats alongside the low table. They had to cross their legs to sit, putting them at the proper height for the table. Corlan sat in the middle of their group, Rupas to his left, Tam to his right. The other seats around the large table had yet to be occupied.

"I can't believe Gorral was worthy of this kind of service," Rupas spoke, anger in his voice.

"Me neither," said Corlan.

"I wonder if we are being prepared for the women."

Corlan was not amused. "Don't wish for anything just yet."

"Truly."

"What are we wishing for?" asked Tam nervously.

"Not a thing."

Musicians started to play. Corlan heard the tune and thought of Madi. He could not see the players but he heard sweet sounds from a flute, the twang of a hammered dulcimer, and gentle plucking from either a lute or a harp.

After what felt like an hour, a rustling behind the curtains on the raised floor at the side of the hall got their attention. Four women appeared from a split in the curtain, all of them dressed in pastel-blue gowns of some filmy material. Corlan could almost see their lithe bodies through the gowns. He smiled.

Following the four women, a woman appeared, more regal in

bearing than any of the others. She wore the same kind of filmy gown yet hers was pure white, so white it seemed to glow. Around her waist a golden sash hung loosely, and over her narrow shoulders crossed glimmering metal braces of gold, as though she was ready for battle. On her head, rising from the mountain of black hair, a golden crown sparkled with white jewels.

The procession of women turned gracefully as they approached the long table, splitting and moving off in each direction until a line was formed across the room. The golden woman remained on the raised portion, overseeing the procession.

She smiled in a way that was both welcoming yet mysterious, as though she already knew what would happen to her guests.

Meeting her gaze, Corlan tried to return the smile.

"Greetings," the golden woman spoke in a strong yet pleasant tone. "You are welcome here. Please dine with me on this evening. I wish to know all about you and your travels."

Corlan was not sure if he should respond or not. They had not been urged to stand for her entrance. Maybe they preferred the men to remain seated as a way to assure they would not be able to attack. So he merely nodded to show his understanding.

The golden woman stepped down to the main floor and strolled to her seat at the table, directly opposite Corlan's. Her procession escorts took their positions along the table, all of them with almost identical appearances in both their garments and hair style as well as in their faces and figures.

The golden woman gazed down upon Corlan, her mouth locked in a half-grin. She was not gorgeous but certainly no man would ever turn away from her. What Corlan could see of her figure through the gown was voluptuous and reminded him of Petula. The golden woman carried herself like a goddess, her head held high. Her eyes were bright and he suspected gold dust had been painted around them to reflect the light. Her black hair, gathered in a long braid, had been wrapped in a spiral on the top of her head, fixed within the golden crown, then left to cascade down her back.

Corlan wished to know her name. He wondered how he should address her. Unlike in the palace where his cousin Vilmer reigned, he cared about protocol now. He wanted to know much more. Yet he dared not speak first.

The golden woman knelt upon the cushion, sitting on her heels, keeping her knees together inside her gown. That put her at a greater height than everyone else at the long table. She could look down on Corlan. He acknowledged that fact with a humble nod.

"Are you distressed, traveler?" asked the golden woman.

A grimace settled over his face, unsure whether he should smile or remain serious.

"Can you speak?" she asked.

He swallowed. "Yes, I can speak. I hesitate only because I do not know the proper ways of your city. We were not instructed."

"You may relax and be at ease." She held out her arms, turning her head to the right then the left. "We welcome you."

"Thank you." Corlan finally smiled. "May we know your name? How should we call you? We thank you for this hospitality."

Her eyes flickered as she gazed at him, her half-grin frozen.

"I am Hiro Ka."

She paused as if waiting to see if her name might be recognized. Corlan gave no indication of it, so she frowned, then glanced at the women to each side of her, as if sharing a joke.

"You have not heard my name?"

Corlan shook his head. "We're strangers here in this part of the realm."

"Realm?" A sweet laugh burst from her mouth. "You think this city is part of your realm?"

"I apologize. I have never been this far from my home so I don't know the boundaries of this land."

"You are in Covin, the Queen City."

"It is a lovely city. Very beautiful. Very pink. The pink buildings are so unlike what I've seen in the east."

"It is home to us...to all *wyma* who wish sanctuary."

Corlan noted her words, took a quick scan of the room, counted the women, counted the lances. He continued to smile.

"That is good, Hiro Ka," said Corlan. "Women need a sanctuary. Men can be so cruel. The past was a terrible time...."

"We say 'wyma' here." Again the sweet laugh. "You do not speak like most men."

"I speak my mind. That's all. I apologize if I speak too directly. I've seen a lot of cruelty in the places I've been. Yet I am a peaceful man now. If that counts for anything."

"Everything counts."

The golden woman, Hiro Ka, waved for the dinner to be served.

"Now tell me of your travels."

As various dishes were brought out and set before them, Corlan told of his journey down the Valley of Death, their visit to Unting and the way they had left that city. He held nothing back describing the dragon attack. He told her about Joragus and Hiro Ka seemed interested, asking questions about his iterations and his powers. Corlan eventually turned the conversation back to how he happened to be on this journey. He mentioned how Tam became part of his team, about the broken lifter, intending the anecdote only as a bit of merriment.

Hiro Ka waved a younger-looking serving girl over and she set down her tray and went to Tam. She sat beside him. The girl spoke in a soft voice and he replied to her questions in a shy voice.

"Go on. Tell more," said Hiro Ka to Corlan.

He told of his cousin, referring to him only as the prince, and of the unfairness of the judgment. He told how his grandfather had died in a poor house. He told her about the Guild Hall incident and other annoying events as his voice grew into an angry tenor.

"I hear how much those events stress you. Let us talk about pleasant trifles. You have a few joys in your life? You have a *wym*, perhaps, somewhere?"

He decided it was best to be completely honest—except about his youth and about dragons—so he replied: "I have a woman. However, I released her from any promise to wait for me. I do not know when or even if I shall be able to return to her. The chances of me dying on this journey are so great. First, there's dragons—"

He reached for the goblet which had just been refilled and took a long drink of what turned out to be a tart, smoky wine.

"Delicious!" he cheered, setting the goblet down.

"Enjoy," Hiro Ka urged. She waved for his goblet to be refilled.

They talked for what seemed like hours as they went through the dinner course by lavish course.

At one point, Corlan was chewing on what seemed to be meat yet it was too tough for him to continue. He did not want to simply spit it out, which would be rude, so he took the cloth next to his plate and held it to his mouth, passing the difficult morsel out and hid it in the cloth, which he pushed under the table.

"Not to your liking?" asked Hiro Ka, catching him.

"I apologize." He gave a sheepish grin. "It did not seem to agree with my tongue." He gestured at his plate, then at the previous plate still waiting to be taken away. "We have been on the road for so long, eating only travel food, mostly grain, dried fruits. We needed a meal like this, something with meat. I praise the chef who made this fine dinner. It is delicious. Except for that clump I couldn't chew. My teeth...I must be getting old."

"You are certainly not of an old age, dear guest." She smiled at him with great assurance and a sparkle in her eyes. "The report I was given ranks you high in many categories. This is the reason we dine together this evening."

"Is it?" As soon as he spoke, he knew it was too rough. "What I mean to say.... I was not aware there was a report. An old woman did check us, ran her fingers all over my body and took some blood from my finger. Was that for the report?"

Hiro Ka set down her eating sticks and intertwined her fingers, her elbows resting on the table.

"You may well wonder. I expect that. Men have always been a problem for us. We have to be careful. You may know wyma of what you call other realms. Here we are of one kind: Covin wyma. All who come here are Covin wyma—Covinas. They pledge to follow our laws and work together to maintain our city and make our land prosperous. We are all wyma here."

"And the men? What happens to them?" He'd heard tales, after all. "What about the boys when they are born?"

She laughed in a way that made her humor seem forbidden. The sweet sound was unnerving to Corlan.

"You must relax. You are guests. You will come to no harm. You have my protection."

"Thank you. We have no intention of causing harm, either."

She laughed again. "You, I can believe. Yet your other man, I heard, was among the worst. The kind of man we forbade when we built this city. A city for wyma. So he was taught a lesson."

"Gorral?" Corlan shook his head. "I told him to be polite. He is not one of my team, actually. We found him along our journey and didn't want to leave him on his own. We thought he might be helpful, but we never expected he would be so rude. Apologies."

"That poor sample of a man was very rude."

"I'm sorry for that."

"So we made a dinner of him."

Corlan was about to push another cube of meat through his lips. He took hold of the words sticking in his ears, played them again.

"Pardons, my ears must be clogged. You said you made dinner

for him? Like this one?"

"No, dear guest, we made a dinner *of* him." She pointed to the morsels on his plate, like the one he had spit out. "That's him there. Part of him. I would guess the morsels are made of those things that hang between the legs. What do you call them in your realm?"

Corlan dropped the cube of meat he held between the two sticks and it plopped into his lap, the sauce soiling his clean, white robe. His hand swept it away.

"Some people call them sweetmeats."

"And are they sweet?" she asked. She reached across the table for one of the morsels, snatching one with her sticks. She retrieved it and plopped it into her mouth. "I agree. Not so tasty."

Rupas had overheard their conversation. Suddenly, the sound of retching filled the room, then the stench of it.

"Gorral!" cried Rupas, catching his breath, gagging. He tried to get up but found his legs were numb from sitting in that position for so long. He tried to crawl from the table and two attendants rushed to him. Two women guards held him as other attendants came over to clean the mess.

"Take him to another room where he may be ill at his leisure," said Hiro Ka, flicking her hand at the attendants.

They picked up Rupas and escorted him out of the hall.

"Perhaps we should move on to the dessert," said Hiro Ka.

"Yes, yes," said Corlan, watching the man being dragged out of the hall. "Will he be all right?"

"Treated well enough," said his hostess with a tap of his hand. "Now what shall delight you next?"

Corlan tried to grin, shifting on the cushion.

Hiro Ka met his grin, her smile bright. "Dessert seems to be what is needed now."

23

Witch in a Bottle

CORLAN GAZED UP AT THE STARS and recognized the formation of lights that circumscribed the Virgin. They might have been virgins, also, those who had assisted him in changing his morsel-stained robe for something more comfortable: a short, pleated skirt in white that settled loosely around his hips, extending to just above his knees. He felt uncomfortable wearing it, called it girl's clothing, yet he could not refuse. That was all he was given: a skirt and sandals, his bare chest and back exposed for all to see, the scars and marks of battle.

He was led up to the private chambers of the queen.

"It's a beautiful night," said Hiro Ka, coming up beside him.

He rested his hands on the smooth edge of the pink wall made from dried mud and straw — what she'd called *doba*. The waist-high wall framed the balcony on three sides, hanging from one of the city's tallest towers — seven levels up from the ground, he counted. The tower rose higher but had no other balconies above. It seemed to be the tallest structure in the entire city. He gazed over the expanse of buildings, counting the lights, guessing this city of Covin was at least as large as the Burg.

Standing beside him, his hostess placed her hands on the wall. After a few breaths, she moved her hand over, on top of his hand.

"Don't you think?"

"Yes, a beautiful night," said Corlan after a moment to think.

She caught his unenthusiastic tone and turned to him, keeping her hand over his.

"Worry not about your friend. That person was a waste of flesh. Remember, you did not call him a friend. It is a small thing among many small things."

"I agree. The world is better without him."

"That is the mantra for healing," she spoke in a purr. "Now is the time for dessert, as you requested."

"I expected some kind of food."

"There are more variety of desserts than the kitchen can make."

"So what is this dessert?"

"I wonder how you might be as a dessert."

"I'm not so sweet, not as you likely crave."

"What I crave is a dessert we both can enjoy."

Her hand went from his hand to his arm, then up to his shoulder.

"Desserts are made carefully, you must understand. One must never rush to create something so full of delight. We must take as much time as we need...to be certain we both enjoy our dessert."

Her fingers ran over his chest, pausing at each scar. She leaned in to have a closer look. Her breath caressed his skin.

"You have many marks upon your body.... They remind you of adventures?"

"Yes, though I don't want to be reminded of most of them."

She moved around behind him and he froze. Her fingers danced down his naked spine, pausing at the fresh scar at the bottom of his back. "And this mark?"

"Dragon claw. I was lucky."

"So close to death," she purred.

"Too close." He sensed her mood. "That excites you?"

Corlan turned at that moment, found Hiro Ka had knelt down to examine the deeper wound that curled toward his hip. Their position was awkward, having her down there.

She lifted his skirt. "Shall we enjoy our dessert?"

"Will I become food tomorrow even if I please you tonight?"

She withdrew her hand from between his thighs.

"Or food if I don't please you?"

She stood. "That worries you...."

"Becoming food does, yes." He met her eyes. "I intend to leave this city soon and continue on my journey to the west."

"You surely shall."

"Do I have your word?"

"Words never mean much in this world," she sighed. "Deeds are better measures of truth."

"The deeds I've seen do not relax me."

She narrowed her eyes. "What deeds do you mean?"

"You butchered my comrade."

"I did nothing." She turned away, shaking her head.

"Then it was your staff."

"They did nothing either."

"Someone killed him."

She returned to him. "He was rude and ugly. He did not need to live. That was decided without consultation with me. I do not bother with trivial matters like those." She pursed her lips, as though hiding a lie. "However, you are much more than that stinky old rag. You are what we cherish. You are what we welcome. Your *maxa* is great. The tests confirm that."

"Maxa? What is that?"

"Your manliness. Your ability to sire."

He frowned. "Indeed...."

"That is why you are here tonight."

"To serve you?"

"Yes...if you wish to think in that way. I prefer to think I am serving you. In the end we serve each other, and both are better for the time spent together. That is what dessert means."

"That's charming," said Corlan, genuinely moved.

"There is nothing to think when we are together but sensual pleasure between a *wym* and a man. It is allowed, even for a queen, when a suitable specimen is found. It can be a delightful dessert."

"A specimen, eh?"

"You are a perfect specimen of the kind of men we welcome to sire our children. A city of *wyma* has no other way of continuing. So we have rules. We welcome a few men to visit for a while—"

"Then you eat them." He was not amused, even as she was on the verge of embracing him. Her hands played with his shoulders.

She turned away at his remark. "I explained about your servant. Unworthy. Unneeded. Now gone."

"And the boy?"

"What about the boy? Tonight is about us, you and me and us...a wym and a man, on the bed...joined in nature as we were meant to be. Tonight is the night for us, for my body to welcome what your body gives."

Corlan grinned. "I see now. You are on a schedule. You need me tonight or the time for seeding will pass."

She sighed impatiently. "The boy is fine. He is cared for by girls of his age."

Corlan grinned. "He'll enjoy that."

She swept her hands up around his neck, pulled him close.

"Now let us enjoy these hours of fruitfulness."

"Fruitfulness?" He chuckled. "I get it."

"I am the garden," Hiro Ka sighed. "You have the seed. Plant it."

Embraced at last, she walked them over to the bed, raised off the floor a few inches and soft with strewn furs. The candlelight in the corners of the open-air chamber illuminated the gleam of their moist skin as garments were shed and positions negotiated.

One candle blew out, then another, as their coupling created a breeze to draw the darkness upon them.

"It was a delightful dessert," Hiro Ka sang as she leaned back against the balcony wall. The sun shone brightly, made her skin glow, made her black hair seem darker. She raised her arms to the sun, stretching as if to hug it.

Corlan's eyes opened. Startled by the unfamiliar surroundings, he gazed down the bed, then across the floor to the naked woman standing by the balcony wall.

"Are you refreshed?" she called to him. "Did you see fire behind your eyes?"

He blinked, not fully awake, not understanding.

"Welcome to the second day. It is the most important day in the protocol."

He rubbed his eyes with one hand, rose up on the other.

"Uh...second day?" he spoke finally.

"Yes. According to legend, Queen Diatriva lay with the warrior Artok seventeen days and took him into her on each day. The second day of their union was filled with hourly desserts."

"More dessert?" Just saying the word was exhausting.

"I believe you enjoyed sharing dessert during the night." She went to the bed, climbed on it like a wild cat stalking prey. "Now you have rested, so the second day begins. We have only a little time before firstmeal arrives. We would not wish our dessert disrupted, would we?"

He shook his head, vaguely remembering the night. It started in the usual way, yet somewhere in the dark hours he was not himself.

He lost his memories, forgot who he was. Maybe there was some drug involved, he wondered, something that turned off his thinking yet left his body raging. He had felt exhausted when she told him it was finished. Then he slept like a stone.

Until now. Morning was beaming over the balcony wall, painting the bed in rosy hue. The warm breeze touched his bare skin, ruffled the sheet on the bed, and his hostess — his mistress — was demanding more of his *maxa*.

Hiro Ka embraced him, entwining her legs with his, her fingers massaging the long scar running down his back.

"In the end, Queen Diatriva birthed seventeen children. There were seven females and ten males. Each became a great queen or king in the lands south of here. One was in the north. I am from the line of Princess Iro Ha, one of the eleven granddaughters. I also have four brothers. They have already passed to the Great Beyond. It happened in the early years of their lives. Mother is so superstitious."

"Your mother? She is here?"

"Yes, in a manner of speaking." She kissed his lips, a suggestion to keep quiet and perform his duty. "We keep her in a bottle in the central chamber of the Temple of Womb. She tells the future."

A scowl spread across Corlan's face. Enough with the magic! The prophecies. All the strange spells and potions that old women like to make. He had no idea what he was given the previous night, but his mind had become a slave to whatever his body wanted to do. And his body seemed to want whatever she wanted. He could not resist.

"Do you believe what she says?" He blinked. "Does she actually speak? If she has passed already?"

"She...communicates." Another kiss, lingering, then: "It is not something you need concern yourself with. However, if the second day is delightful, I may take you to her and you may ask a question that she will answer."

He dared grin. "I'd like that." It might at least be a way to get out of the palace, he thought, a way to investigate possible routes for escaping the city.

She pressed forward again, locked him into a long kiss. Then the second day unfolded.

Dressed in a new leather outfit of cream and burgundy, much better suited to his role as the Queen's Consort, Corlan could barely walk through the crowded streets. His back was sore, his thigh muscles aching. The second day had exhausted his body. Behind him the queen rode a paladin carried by six muscular women. A pair of female guards made certain he did not abuse his privileged position by daring to run off.

They came at last to the massive pink building, built of the same *doba* as many others in the city. It was a giant pyramid with rounded edges and a flat top crowned with a statue of a rotund, pregnant woman with huge breasts. Corlan studied the temple's front wall, royal blue and emerald patterns upon the pink *doba* depicting the cosmos. It seemed to match his school lessons. He traced the orbits with his eyes and felt dizzy.

They halted among the throng of women worshippers waiting outside, hoping to get a turn inside the Temple of Womb. The crowd backed away, giving the paladin and the queen plenty of space. A few called out to her, begging for favors. Guards with lances raised held the crowd back.

Corlan stood beside her after she climbed out of the paladin, appearing like a husband, a protective warrior, and he felt pleased with his role. *Or was it merely a suggestion of my queen, cooed into my ear sometime during the night?* He wished he had a sword on his hip.

"Third day is a day of reflection," Hiro Ka spoke. "The only day a male may enter the Temple of Womb."

He nodded, understanding he still did not outrank most of the women gathered around them. Males were at the bottom of society in this city—except for the Queen's Consort, it seemed, but then only as long as he pleased her. He had never felt so weak or unimportant.

She led him firmly by the hand up the seventeen steps and across the narrow mezzanine at the top. The entrance was wide and oval-shaped, its encompassing frame curved to resemble a woman's entrance. Above it blinked a great silvery jewel that reflected the sunlight. The queen reached up and swept her palm over it before she stepped inside. She pulled him after her.

"Because you have entered the true temple of womb through the past night, you are permitted to enter this temple. Yet do not speak. Do not touch anything but my hand. After we communicate with her, upon our exit, you must go down to your knees before all the wyma gathered outside. I shall give you a blessing."

He nodded and her hand clasped his hand tighter. She stepped forward and he stumbled with her into the darkness and coolness of the Temple of Womb.

It was different than he expected. Never having explored in such detail the inner regions of a woman, he was amazed at the twisted path they walked, a lit candle at regular intervals to help guide their steps. When they came to the larger chamber, she stopped him and gestured for him to look right and left.

"Each doorway leads to an inner altar. No male is permitted in those rooms. Only here. And only when escorted by the queen."

"And that's you."

She slapped her hand over his mouth. "You must be silent."

Facing forward, Corlan saw the wall suddenly glow in an eerie pink hue just beyond the blackness of the wall's surface, as though a room behind it was lit and the illumination was leaking out to where the two visitors stood.

Hiro Ka casually released his hand and raised both her arms. As she did, the pink glow intensified. She spoke words which he did not understand. She repeated her phrases, adding a new word each time. Her voice grew louder and the pink glow burned brighter, until what actually were doors in the black wall burst open and a great cloud of pink smoke billowed out into the room, blocking his view of whatever was in front of him, almost choking him.

When the pink smoke settled, he dared open his eyes. In front of him was a large capsule, a bottle as tall as a man and twice as wide. All sides of the bottle were clear. Inside it was a pink liquid that was just thin enough to reveal the figure of a woman floating within. The woman was naked but her long, gray-streaked black hair covered most of her body. As she floated in the liquid, her eyes were closed.

At the final word from Hiro Ka, the eyes of the woman in the bottle popped opened. She immediately appeared angry.

"You!" came a voice.

"We meet again, Mother," spoke Hiro Ka in a loud, steady tone.

"How long has it been?" the woman inside the bottle responded. The voice echoed around the room. Corlan ducked to avoid it, then stood up, feeling silly.

"Almost a year, I suppose. I have not been counting the days."

"Have you birthed a child yet?"

"Oh, Mother, always the same demand!"

"You must birth children to continue our line."

"I know, I know. It's not that easy in a city with only wyma, you should know."

"I see a man beside you. Is he real? Or illusion?"

Hiro Ka gave a laugh. "Oh, this one is real, I assure you. He is so wonderfully real. In fact, we come to you on this the third day of the protocol. I promised him I'd introduce you if he delighted me on the second day. And he most certainly did! My Mother, I can hardly walk!"

"You came all the way across town and woke me from my sleep to tell me you finally got a man into your bed?"

"Well, yes, Mother. I thought that's what you wanted."

"It is."

"I told this man you would tell him his future. Can you do that?"

"What do I gain from this act?"

She pursed her lips. "My undying love?"

"I had that already. For fifteen years. Then you went crazy."

"I'm sorry, Mother. You know it wasn't my fault."

"Yet here I am."

"It was the only way to save you. Otherwise you would have died. Now you have the gift of prophecy."

"The difference between a life like this and death is so small."

"Will you prophesize for this man? Tell him his future?"

"Why should I?"

"If you do, he will continue the protocol. Then you will have a grandchild."

"Granddaughter!"

"Yes, a grand*daughter*."

"Tell me about the man. I will tell you what I see."

Hiro Ka glanced at Corlan, reached for his hand, clasped it.

"He comes from the east," she spoke, keeping her eyes on his face. "He was a warrior long ago and fought in many battles. He turned away from war and became a slayer of dragons. In this new venture, he has proven himself to be the top of the bottle. He is on a quest now. He seeks the way to the western marshes where dragons go to lay out their eggs, where draglings are born."

She gave Corlan's hand a squeeze and released it.

"He speaks with true words," Hiro Ka continued. "He cares for a boy who is not his son. He helps men even if they are stinky old rags.

His body has many scars yet his heart is pure. He is the best dessert I ever have had."

At that instant the pink liquid in the bottle boiled, rising until the entire bottle spun into a pink whirlpool. Pink smoke again spilled into the chamber, tumbling across the floor and rising to the height of Corlan's chest. Hiro Ka turned and embraced him as though she was afraid for him.

"I hope it was the right thing to do," she said to him.

The swirling pink liquid bubbled as though boiling the person inside—then abruptly ceased. The level of liquid dropped and the woman's head became visible, then her shoulders, then her belly, and on down until the liquid settled at a level below her knees.

The pink smoke floated away and the voice echoed through the chamber:

"He is the man from the family of Tang of the eastern city called Burg. A warrior, a rogue, a defiler of women, a—"

"What does she mean by that?" Corlan erupted.

"Silence, or she won't tell you your future."

"He is the man you seek.... The man of dragons who clears the sky for birds to sing.... The man who cleans dirt from the world. He is the man who walks without weight, who looks without seeing, the man who—"

"Oh, Mother, why are you always dramatic? Just tell him about his future. Will he stay with me and care for our children?"

The pink liquid boiled.

"Noooooooooooo," the voice wailed.

Corlan was unnerved at the response, the way the voice seemed to bounce around the walls of the pink chamber. He wished he had a sideblade with him, expecting to be attacked at any moment. He was still a man, therefore an enemy in this city, although he had bent to the queen's will.

Hiro Ka glanced at him.

"He will go west, there to meet an old man growing younger," said the woman in the bottle. "He will find an egg—many eggs—but they will not open for him. He will sing in a cloud and fall upon a mountain. He will speak to a child in harsh words yet the child will save him from death."

"Death? How? Where?" asked Hiro Ka.

"He will break a sword over a stone and bury the blade in the earth. He will sleep long and dream of you, Hiro Ka, and awaken with a new face. He will bathe in green waters and swim to the depths of the sea before rising."

"Will there be dragons? What about dragons, Mother?"

"There will be dragons. Many dragons. Led by one—the smallest of them.... He will kill many dragons. Until a dragon kills him."

The pink liquid broke into another boiling, the pinkness rising to fill the capsule, hiding the woman inside.

"What?" Corlan was not sure what he heard.

"What about a dragon, Mother? What did you say? Will a dragon kill this man? Are you sure?"

"Where will it happen?" asked Corlan, grabbing Hiro Ka's wrist.

"Where will it happen, Mother?"

"At the end of the Valley of Death.... In the night.... Where the dead gods watch."

"But—"

Hiro Ka clasped her hand over his mouth. The swirling pink liquid ceased its bubbling but the volume did not lessen, did not drain away. It remained opaque.

"Thank you, Mother. We will go now."

"You must bear daughters," the woman's voice echoed as the pink liquid thinned. Gradually they could see her figure, then her face, as gaunt as ever, eyes open yet turned up so only the whites showed.

"I will, Mother. Today is the third day. We have many more days of the protocol."

Hiro Ka took Corlan's hand. After a long time watching the black doors close and the pink illumination fade from bright to dull, she led him out of the central chamber of the Temple of Womb and back to the public entrance.

Stepping out into the sunlight, she shielded her eyes. Corlan held his hand up, as well. The crowd below cheered.

"The Great Mother has spoken," called Hiro Ka. "This man will be the Sire of your queen's daughters!"

Corlan glared at Hiro Ka. They had enjoyed a night and a long day together and another night, but he had no expectation of staying. He had a journey to complete.

"You need to bow now," she reminded him. "On your knees."

And he did.

24

The Protocol

SHE WAS STARTING TO GROW ON HIM, the mysterious queen of pink who welcomed him into her bed each night and lingered with him through the next morning, often into the afternoon, coaxing more and more from him. He was content to languish in her chamber and bathe in her pink aura. The long black hair that tickled his face, the smooth curves that rolled against his rough skin, the soft hands that guided him here and there were all so enticing. And her eyes. He gazed into those eyes for what seemed years as he obeyed her every wish, as he gave himself to her completely, without feeling like he was being controlled in any way, even if his mind wondered if he was being controlled. All was bliss, and became ever more blissful, as day three of the protocol extended into day ten.

"Are you still enjoying dessert?" Hiro Ka cooed beside him.

Her hand caressed his chest, her fingers outlining the long scar there. With the treatment given at the palace, the scar was less visible although it remained a target for her fingers. The more recent scar on his back, which began in the middle of his shoulder and curled to his spine, ran down it and crossed over to the opposite hip, was also less obvious now yet remained noticeable to the queen's loving touch.

She sensed his weakness. "You must drink the elixir every day if you are to heal." She rose on her elbow, gazing at her lover. "There is much left for us to do. This is only day ten of the protocol."

He tried to speak but the words did not come into his mouth.

"Be calm, my lover."

His hand went to her shoulder almost as if called, and pulled her down to him. They kissed. They parted. They kissed again but did not part. And everything seemed exactly as it was meant to be.

Eventually day fourteen of the protocol arrived. It came with the dawn, a morning full of storms, rain lashing the balcony, the wind blowing rain into the chamber and wetting the bed. Hiro Ka moved them to another chamber, closed to the outside. Corlan was carried on a litter to the Queen Suite by four strong women and placed gently on the new bed. His lover quickly joined him, shedding her gown and welcoming the dry towels from the attendants to wipe off the rain that had wet her. Other attendants cared for Corlan, drying his naked body and styling his hair exactly the way Hiro Ka wished.

"Our dessert may continue, dear one," she whispered into his ear, then kissed him quickly.

She gazed down the masculine length of his manly man's body, measuring her own feminine body against his, and smiled.

"You must drink the elixir," she reminded him. "It will give you strength. It will keep you alive. Then we shall continue to enjoy our desserts together."

His half-grin was enough to give permission for an attendant to come and present him with the long-necked bottle, to press the tip to his lips, and wait as he sipped from it.

"There you have it, dear one," said Hiro Ka. "You feel it down there? The burning? The engorging of your loins? You are ready for dessert now? I know you have much more to give."

He lay unmoving though able to move if commanded. His eyes stayed open yet he could not remain alert. His breath was shallow, relaxed, ready for a command. He no longer needed to tell his body what to do; it acted quite on its own, or by command of the queen. Further down his body, he felt ready to please her and awaited her command.

"I see you are ready!" She climbed over him, positioned herself, ready to command him as she wished. "Let us enjoy this hour, and the next."

Her hands caressed his chest, cradled his face. Her body moved up and down, back and forth, fast and slow, drawing out his last remaining essence.

It was the same protocol on each of the following days.

On the seventeenth day, he rested atop a bench on the balcony of the original protocol chamber, his breath shallow as he watched the clouds grinning at him. At the same time, a thick cloud of peace and harmony covered him, surrounding him like a mother's womb, like the queen's womb, like the Temple of Womb and all of its pinkness.

Hiro Ka needed to leave the chamber for some official business.

She would return later to finish the protocol, she explained. He could only smile in his cute, silly way, and blithely accept whatever she wished of him. His body would respond but not his mind. He knew he belonged completely to her now, but there was nothing he could do, no thought or action, to refuse her. Even the usually potent elixir failed to enliven him for this final day of the protocol.

"I know he's up there," said Tam, glancing at a certain balcony high on the main tower. "She keeps him locked in that room and nobody can see him."

"The dragonslayer must be enjoying himself immensely," said Rupas with a snort, straightening his aching back. He leaned the rake against his hip, staring at the garden plot before him.

Tam squatted beside the flower bed. "He forgot about us and about our journey."

They stood in the courtyard, a rectangle strewn with lush foliage and a few fountains, divided by curving stone walks. Working as staff members, they were not suspicious to any palace attendants. Rupas tended the garden and Tam took out the garbage from the palace kitchen. They managed to cross paths every day.

"I worry about him," said Tam.

"I also," said Rupas. "Maybe he will never come down from that tower, never continue his journey. Then what will we do? I'm not interested in gardening for the rest of my life."

"I don't like always taking out stinky stuff, neither."

"You know it's either accept our duties or accept our deaths."

"They wouldn't kill a boy," said Tam, "not a handsome, clever boy like me. Those girls tell me so."

"They're tricking you. Grooming you to be some kind of bed toy someday. When you're older. Like our Corlan is now for the queen, poor man."

"Maybe we should try to get him out."

"If he wants to escape." Rupas scratched at his knees, rough from his gardening work. "Maybe he likes being the queen's plaything."

"I wonder what kind of games they play."

"Not the kind of games children play, I can tell you that!"

"Then what? You mean like Army of Squares?"

"I doubt they spend their hours moving little soldiers across a board of squares. I'll tell you: it's adult games. The kind that adults play only in a bed."

"Oh. Like mamas and papas do."

"Yes, like that. So I don't think he would wish to give up that amusement for a hundred more miles of hard trekking down the Valley of Death."

"We got to help him," said Tam, his eyes filling with tears. "I miss him. And I know he wants to be with us again. He wants to be with men and boys, having fun with us, not playing those games with a woman."

"Are you sure of that?" Rupas grinned. "He is a grown man and grown men love to play games with the women—with the *wyma*, as they like to say here."

"But not Corlan. He likes slaying dragons! That's what's fun for him. He always said it."

"I suppose you're right about that." Rupas, bent over, rubbed his back. "I suppose we should do something to help our poor Corlan. Before he is all used up, as it were. Poor man." He glanced around the courtyard, decided the attendants by the wall were far enough away. "I suppose we could rescue Corlan from the throes of his lover. At least check with him, see if he wants to be rescued. We could do that."

"We need to do that."

"How?" Rupas checked their surroundings. "We can't get close to him. We can't get any message to him."

Tam scratched his chin like he'd grown a beard. His companion chuckled, seeing the imitation of Corlan thinking deeply.

"If I put on girl clothes," said Tam, "maybe I can take a meal up to them. I could drop a note or whisper to him."

"You'd wear a dress for Corlan?"

"I'll do anything to help him."

"I know you would, boy. We are all that's left to help him escape, now that poor Gorral has long been digested and pushed out."

Corlan's taut belly pressed against the straw mat that covered the low bench set on the balcony. His arms stretched forward and his hands made a pillow for his head. A small sheet was draped over his hips. Down his back the fingers of four young women massaged away the knots in his muscles. Another pair of attendants massaged his feet, giving particular attention to his toes.

In the corner of the room sat Hiro Ka, a cloth wrapped around her body. Her feet rested in a basin on the floor, washed by another attendant. She gazed across the room, out to the balcony, at her lover, naked on the bench, and sighed with contentment.

"You must enjoy all the sensations, dear one," she called. "After seventeen days you have earned a just dessert."

Of course, he could not move. Not simply for being too relaxed to call his body into action, to rise up and climb off the mat and then, perhaps, to scale the *doba* wall down from the balcony and run away across the courtyard, perhaps grab a horse and swing himself onto its back and charge out of the city with absolutely no care whether or not he had any provisions or any weapon, just glad to be free once more even if that meant he had no further pleasure. No, he could not do that at all, no matter how much he might want to do that.

As the girls worked on his body, making it ready for the final act of the seventeenth day, he heard something in the air that was little more than a bird call, only a faint line of words sailing up from the courtyard on a breeze. At first, he was not sure what he was hearing. Then he could not be certain he heard it correctly. Other sounds intruded. He tried to focus, even as the massage grew more vigorous and his body became more limp.

The words wafting on the breeze were brought by a voice that he recognized. He had forgotten it during the past many days but now he heard it again clearly: a boy's simple voice. There was a boy in his past, he recalled, someone who had joined him on the journey to Covin, who sat with him at a welcome dinner, who had wondered whether or not he should really go off with the queen after that dinner. The queen had told the boy he was being silly, that it was only dessert. Now that boy's voice was calling to him again. He listened. Another voice joined in and together made a message for him. Corlan blinked.

The queen arose from her padded seat and sauntered over to him, standing over him, preparing her command.

"Are you ready for the final dessert?"

The girls massaging him glanced up at the queen. She jerked her head to the right to dismiss them. Other girls took the cue and got up

345

from their tasks and departed.

Hiro Ka sat on the edge of the bench, took up massaging her lover's back, slowing each time she moved along the long scar. She leaned low, whispering in his ear that she was almost finished with him and when their final act was complete, he would be rewarded.

How will I be rewarded? As a main course?

He was surprised he was able to think his own thoughts again. It might be related to avoiding the elixir the past three nights, He only acted as though he was under her spell. There was no deception, he told himself, only a desire to experience everything without the filter of whatever ingredients were mixed into the drink.

That's a shame. I want to enjoy the woman, not be a woman's slave.

Were he to speak, she would know he was no longer drugged. He could only imagine what fate might befall him if his ruse was exposed. Dinner might come sooner than expected—with he as the main course. And yet, seventeen days was about to come to an end, anyway. Then what would happen to him? What had happened to his companions? Were they still alive? Had they been served to him as one of the meals he had eaten during the past sixteen days?

His stomach gurgled.

"My dear one, need you food before tonight's final act?"

The queen stood, remaining beside the bench, and clapped her hands. Two girls in pink gowns appeared.

"Bring us a plate of morsels, enough to pass the hour," she told them. She turned to Corlan. "We don't want to eat too much and be hindered in our pleasure, do we? Mother would be unhappy if we were not able to complete the protocol."

She stepped away from the bench, gazing up at the clouds. She hummed a lovely melody. Corlan had never heard her make music so she must be pleased with him.

"We might have already achieved our goal," she explained, "yet we must complete the protocol nevertheless. We want to be certain of success. We owe the Great Mother a full measure of truth. And I owe you the full range of desserts."

She spun on her foot and regarded Corlan, her eyes focusing on how perfectly round, how dearly tender his bare bottom appeared. She inhaled sharply, touching her fingertips to her lips.

"You love the Great Mother, don't you, dear? I know you must, for you honor her so vigorously, so, mmm, devoutly. I must admit, you are very proficient in pushing. I should hire you out to high-born ladies once the protocol is completed. Would you like that? Oh, of course, you would. You would have dessert every day."

Four girls in pretty pink gowns entered the chamber bearing platters of food and a tall beaker of drink. They stood awaiting instructions. One of the girls found her platter too heavy to hold up for so long and slipped, catching herself. The other girls glared at the imperfect girl; their punishment might depend on what she did.

Finally the queen arose from the bench on the balcony, standing upright in full shameless nudity, having no care how she appeared. Her guests were just four girls, members of the staff who had no cause to give opinion. If asked, they would all certainly declare the queen the most beautiful wym in the city, in the whole land, and for miles and miles beyond.

She waved them to set down their treasures on the low table at the foot of the bed. The platters and beaker were arranged over a pink cloth spread over the table. The platters overflowed with fruits and breads and cheeses, some merely decorative, most intended to be eaten. The girl who bore the heaviest platter, the one who had stumbled, continued being clumsy in her movements.

"Are you new to my staff," asked Hiro Ka of the clumsy girl.

The girl nodded, hesitantly then with more assurance.

"Be calm now," said Hiro Ka, sitting on the foot of the bed and leaning back on the support of her arms and hands. She crossed her legs, then uncrossed them, stretching them out toward the clumsy girl. "Every task takes full concentration. You will gain perfection in time. Even I took my turn in the staff line. Mother believed it would help make me a better leader if I did something humble."

The queen called to her lover, stretched out naked on the bench. The massage girls had departed and he rested without concern. He may have fallen asleep for all the queen could see. Her hand caressed his calf, then the back of his thigh. She pulled her legs up onto the bed, tucking them against him.

"Ah!" Hiro Ka grabbed her foot. "I broke a nail!"

She glanced about the chamber as if seeking the culprit. The four girls held their breaths.

"Perhaps my toe hit a hard surface somewhere in this chamber, or on the balcony. I shall call the repair staff to seek out the errant thing and smooth it." Her words seemed more to herself or her lover than to the serving girls. "We were so vigorous in our dessert a short while ago, so I might not have noticed the injury."

Grabbing her foot, she bent her leg so she could study the wound closely. The nail had ripped, a sliver of it hanging partially detached. A pedicure was needed.

She thought of calling for the official pedicurist who always did such lovely work. This seemed such a trifling matter, however. She did not wish to bother waiting for the official pedicurist to arrive.

"Clumsy one," she called to the girl who fit that name.

The girl stood at attention, the pink gown swishing around her knobby knees and gangly legs.

"You wish to gain experience serving your queen?"

She nodded slowly, uncertain.

"Come here."

Hiro Ka sat back, extending her leg, resting the calf over her other leg. Her foot bounced freely, the toenail elevated.

"I have no cutter in this chamber. This is a place of repose, not surgery. Be a dear one and snip off that dangling barb from my first toe, will you?"

The clumsy girl looked around, perhaps for assistance or advice, but the others waited nervously. She took a moment, apparently to think over what she was being asked to do. Then, feeling she had no choice, she knelt before the queen and cradled the royal foot in her two small hands.

"Go on now. Bite off that nail," said the queen with a little more irritation in her voice. "Make the edge smooth."

The girl bent low and took the sliver of toenail into her mouth, positioning her teeth around it. She bit. The nail was thick, being from the largest toe. Another bite was necessary, but the second bite did manage to sever the errant sliver from the remaining toenail.

The queen pulled back her toe.

"Now you must, of course, wipe off your mouth slobber."

The girl was not sure what to use, decided on her own pink gown. She lifted the hem of the gown and wrapped it tightly around the queen's toe, rubbing it back and forth for a minute, then releasing the hem of the gown, which fell to the floor where she knelt.

"Excellent," exclaimed the queen in a sour tone.

Sensing her next instruction, the girl rose and stood straight. She could see the other girls were fighting the urge to giggle. She knew she would get their teasing once they left the queen's chamber.

Hiro Ka waved them out and the girls turned to go.

"Clumsy one," the queen called. "Have you washed today? You carry the stink of garbage. I won't have you return if you do not take care of yourself. Be sure to go wash. Wyma must always be clean."

Tam was huffing and puffing by the time he arrived at the spot in the courtyard below the balcony where Corlan rested. He ducked under the trees where Rupas grinned at the boy's exercise.

"He's definitely there," said Tam. "He was napping on a bench, all naked. The queen was naked, too. Like there was nothing wrong about showing herself. I never saw any woman all naked like that."

Rupas chuckled. "You're just a boy. Who would care?"

"I was a girl, remember?"

"She didn't suspect anything? You played it well? I knew you could do it. Just slip into a fine pink gown and you're the same as any staff girl."

"But she made me bite off her toe nail!"

"She what...?"

"I think she did it to tease me. She also said I smelled bad."

"Well, frankly, my boy, you do have a scent about you which is not all that agreeable."

"It's my job to take out the garbage from the kitchen."

"You're lucky she didn't complain and send you for punishment. Then our plot would be exposed. You must be careful."

"When I bent down to wipe off her toe, I had to use the hem of the gown and...she almost.... She could've seen I was a boy"

"Then you'd be in trouble, eh?"

Rupas checked who was walking in the courtyard. No one of any importance at that hour. On the far side, along the wall, were a pair of scribers—women in brown robes carrying a few scrolls.

"Now, we need to decide a plan."

Tam nodded desperately.

"You can get into the chamber easy enough," said Rupas, "but how do we get Corlan out?"

"I heard her say it's the seventeenth day, so what they did is done. No more playing a game. Maybe they'll move to a different room now."

"That doesn't make our plot easier." Rupas shook his head. "You need to keep informed what room he goes to. And what guards are there. Some of these big women scare me. They're as big as Corlan!"

"I gotta drink something. I still taste her toe."

Rupas wanted to laugh. "Most men would kill for a taste of the queen's toe. You are privileged. Did Corlan see you?"

"No, he was asleep the whole time. I wanted to whisper to him but I couldn't get close at all. He was just laying on a bench with nothing covering him."

"You have to wonder if a man like Corlan wants to be rescued from that dire situation," said Rupas, hiding a smirk. "I think I might be willing to stay."

"But if he stays there, then we gotta stay here. You gotta stay in the gardens and I gotta keep taking out garbage. I don't want that. I want to keep going on our journey. I want to fight dragons again!"

"I can't say I want to fight dragons, but...it was a dragon that got us out of the last difficult situation."

"But Joragus is gone now. We don't know how to summon any dragon here."

"We only need to make Corlan aware of our need to be away from this city lest we become dinner for the next lucky man seduced by the queen." He let go a big sigh.

"You don't think she loves him?"

"Love? That's a tricky word. It comes and goes like the twinkle of stars in the night. Perhaps there is love in a moment or two but, for her, it's more about her legacy, I suspect. She wants to bear an heir."

"But Corlan already's got me!"

"And she will want him to stay and be the papa. Or she will be done with him and he can be sent to the kitchen — and I don't mean to help prepare the meal, I mean *as* the meal."

Tam's eyes widened. "They don't waste anything here!"

Rupas rubbed his eyes. "What to do.... What to do...." He blinked, stared up through the branches at the sun until he couldn't look any more. "Meet me here tomorrow, same time. I will have a plan. Be ready to leave the city. Even if we can't get Corlan to come with us. For our own safety, Tam, you and me had better go."

INTERLUDE

Dragoneers

THEY WERE NOT SO FAR UP the hillside from Olan when the first bell rang to call attention in the city.

"Now they have discovered you missing," said Jabuli, starting to breathe hard as she urged the princess to hurry up the slope ahead of her. "First, they would search the palace, perhaps believing you are hiding from them. Then they will search the city. Perhaps they would think you had been stolen. So they would question the people in the harbor and perhaps send patrols to Olan. They ring the bells, so they must be in the city now. They will question everyone. Some people, even though innocent, may be punished if they are suspected of giving help to us."

"You mean your granny?" suggested Adora.

Jabuli caught up to the princess. "It is only me who helped you, so I would take the punishment if they catch us. No one saw us with Mema."

Far below, the lights of the city glowed. They had been climbing all day, since before dawn when they stepped quickly through the mist-filled alleys to the end of the city and took the main road south. When travelers passed them at mid-morn they chose to go overland and took up a trail to the ridge that ran behind the city and stretched south to the bottom of the eastern bay. The town of Olan lay on the west coast of a peninsula that separated the wide, shallow bay to the east from the deep and quick Sannan strait. In some seasons the bay to the east, being so shallow, might turn into marshland.

"I can never blame you," said the princess, breathing hard from her climb. "May we rest now?"

From the heights they could view Sannan Island far across the strait. A great torch had been lit in the signal tower, an alarm to all.

"I feel great sadness in my belly," said Adora. "I know how angry Mama will be. I better not go back now or I will be punished forever."

"They will likely send dragoneers after us," said Jabuli.

"What are dragoneers?" asked the princess.

Jabuli shook her head, made an awful face. "You do not want to meet them, little majesty. They are warriors who ride dragons. I see them ride over land mostly, yet they can also fly short distances, like to cross a river. Both the dragons and the rider can attack. They were used in the Battle of Berk. Because of dragoneers, Olan now rules the peninsula."

Rula waved her hands, wiggling her fingers to give a message to Jabuli.

"She says she saw dragoneers, a squadron of them, when she was young. They swooped down from the hills and attacked her village. I think she means they punished her village for some reason. That is how she came to be sold as a slave in Sannan. We met in the training quarters." She grinned at Rula. "We are sisters now."

"I don't like slaves," said the princess roughly. "I mean I don't like that there are slaves. How should anyone decide who should work and who should not? I was born in a palace but it was not my choice. Yet my life was easy." She gazed down the slope at the city of Olan. "Yet others have a harsh life. Is it the goddesses who decide?"

"Indeed, little majesty, the goddesses are fickle." Jabuli glanced at Rula. "They do not make decisions with any regular pattern. For you, they chose an easy life. It is said an easy life is payment for hard work in the previous life. Now you choose a harsh life for yourself, being on the run."

"Previous life?" asked Adora. She stretched to gaze at her baby brother held in the sling around Jabuli's shoulders. The babe was whimpering. "He needs some milk, I think."

Jabuli pointed to a rock breaking out of the treeless turf and went to it, sat on it. Rula joined her, setting the bags down and putting her arm around Jabuli. Adora skipped over the grass as though she were trying out a new dance.

"Save your strength, little majesty," Jabuli called.

Unslinging the babe, Jabuli handed him to Rula, who held him against her chest and offered him a breast.

"He is growing so fast, he always wants to suck," said Jabuli with as much a laugh as she dared.

"He is going to be strong some day," the princess announced. "He can protect me then!"

Rula wiggled her fingers, pointing down the hillside they had just mounted.

"She warns of someone pursuing us, so we must be off soon," said Jabuli.

"You said previous life. How can anybody have a previous life?" asked the princess. "You are born then you die."

"Some people, especially in the north and the east, believe we are born and we die, yes, then we are born again in a different body. It's a great mystery. We say such people have twice-beating hearts. You could be one of them, little majesty. You are young in age yet much older inside. I have always felt that way about you, little majesty."

"Oh," was the princess's reply. "I always thought I was a bunny. I thought it was only a dream."

"Perhaps you were a bunny in a previous life," said Jabuli.

"If it's true, I don't remember it much. Vegetables is all. Lots and lots of vegetables."

"Do you still like vegetables?"

"Oh, yes!"

"Then perhaps it is true." She smiled. "Now you are a princess."

Adora pouted. "I think I prefer being a bunny."

"Unless a dragon comes to eat you," said Jabuli.

"No, not then." The princess watched the hillside, marked the city in the distance, the strait and the island beyond. "This is the farthest I have ever been from my slumber chamber. I never knew a world like this existed. It was only written on parches."

"The world is very large, and very dangerous. Not everything is written on parches."

With the babe satisfied, Rula put away her breast and handed the babe to Jabuli who placed him into the sling. They gathered their bags and continued up the mountain slope.

"He looks happy now," said the princess.

"We better keep on or they will catch us," said Jabuli. "They move faster than we do."

They marched onward, heading to the top of the ridge, with Jabuli carrying the babe and Rula carrying the bags. Adora carried the sword that was almost too heavy for her to bear, yet she had insisted on carrying something. As they went, she would take a swing at some tall plants, cutting them down as easily as if a strong wind bent them. The blade was sharp.

"Shall I be a swordswoman?" she called out, perhaps directed to no one. She waved the sword again and many blades of grass died. "When I am older I could be a guard in a city maybe. Or I could go to a battle, like the ones you've told me about. I could win prizes. I could do that. True?"

"Your Little Majesty," Jabuli breathlessly called up the slope to her, "you are not meant to swing swords. You are far better than that kind of person. You must lead people. I hope lead them in peace."

"I was just wondering. It seems a lovely thing to do."

They hiked farther. When they reached the top of the ridge, with each direction pointing down, they rested again. Jabuli stared down the trail they had ascended, searching for any pursuers. Rula gazed straight out across the sky.

"There!" cried Jabuli, marking the spot with a push of her chin. "I see riders. See how the brush moves? Someone is coming after us."

Jabuli lifted the babe in the sling over her head and handed him to Rula. She held him in her arms as Jabuli searched for a place to hide or make a defensive stand, but there was only the grassy slopes, no trees. A thick bank of clouds nearby might roll in, but not likely quick enough to save them.

Jabuli took the longsword from the princess and handed her the small axe.

"I'm ready to swing this," said the princess. "If they try to hurt any of us."

"No matter what happens, you run away. Do you hear me, little majesty? Will you obey me?"

"I will do as you say!"

They watched and after a minute the riders showed themselves: four persons in dark green uniforms, mounted on wydrakes. Rather than the slow, fat beasts used as beasts of burden in Sannan and Olan, these dull orange drakes were lean and fast, meant for riding. They galloped with quiet efficiency on their strong hindlegs. Their forelimbs were wings, yet too small for long flights. On the ends of their wings, however, were deadly foreclaws. In battle their armor plating protected them and their riders. Their horns and tail spikes were also weapons on the battlefield.

There seemed to be no place to hide, only the grassy moor and some rocks protruding from the turf here and there.

Jabuli glanced around them, spied a ravine far down the eastern slope and sent the princess and Rula to hide there with the babe as best they could. She cut some wild brush growing through the grass and told them to cover themselves with it. Then she found a rock to stand on to prepare for defense. She heard the babe start to cry as they slipped into the ravine.

When the riders cross over the ridge, Jabuli planned, they will find her waiting and her sword cutting them down.

They arrived—

Off went the head of the first rider, the wydrake faltering from the strike and scrambling to get its balance as it stumbled on. The second rider, seeing the cut, was ready for her and swung a sword down as the wydrake passed. She blocked the cut and swung behind him, striking his shoulder. He fell to the side of his saddle, trying to keep from dropping off the beast. The third and fourth riders pulled their reins, halting to take on the swordswoman.

The riders were men, likely come from Olan, eager to earn a reward for finding the princess. There were no dragoneers in Sannan. Or, she hoped, they happened to be crossing over the wind-swept ridge on their own business, quite uninterested in them. Their business turned to this woman who should not be standing on the top of the ridge overlooking Olan. Not swinging a sword.

Jabuli remembered her training as a pit fighter. She grabbed the sword from the sheath on the side of the second rider's wydrake and stood bearing two blades. As the last two riders came at her on their wydrakes, she took one sword and stabbed it into the nearest eye of the right-hand beast, causing it to rear up and its rider to fall from the saddle. The other rider charged hard at her and she swung the other blade up to meet his challenge. His blade caught her elbow as her blade severed his leather-wrapped wrist.

He turned away, tucking the handless end of his arm into the opposite armpit.

"It's done," he cried out. "Retreat!"

The three who remained, circled through the twisted brush clinging to the crest of the ridge and hurried down the slope they had come up. Behind, they left their headless partner and his confused wydrake. Jabuli strode over to the beast and stabbed the sword into its heart. The beast spit up its last meal along with its teal blood, and fell on its side.

"They know we are here," said Jabuli, waving the others out of the ravine. The babe still cried. "We stopped this group yet they will report they saw us and others will come."

The princess was shivering as she climbed out of the ravine. Rula took the babe and covered him, holding him under her cloak.

"You can fight!" said the princess, throwing her hands up in a gesture of victory. She gazed at the downed wydrake, steam rising from its skin. "How did you learn it?"

Jabuli shook her head, keeping her eyes down the trail.

"It's not a good thing to learn to fight, little majesty. When I was your age, I wanted to be a teacher—like my mother. I would teach children to read the scrolls. But we must learn what we need to learn in order to survive." She regarded the blood on the blade. "Men took away my dream, made me a fighter instead. When I fought in the pits for the entertainment of men, I usually wore claws on my hands. I was supposed to be a wildcat. They liked me fighting as a wildcat. I had to roar like a wildcat, too. But I trained with many weapons. The two-handed longsword was my specialty."

Satisfied the wydrake was dead, she turned to the princess.

"But I much prefer teaching you about the world beyond Sannan and being your tutor. I never wanted to fight. I wanted to learn of the world and do kind things for people. And yet, you never know what the goddesses have planned for you."

She let out a long sigh, wiped her face with the back of her hand.

"Are you hurt?" asked the princess.

Rula tended to the cut on her elbow. Not serious.

"Your mother, the queen, probably never knew I was a fighter. If she had known that, she wouldn't have let me into a chamber with you. I could be dangerous to you. I went through a year of training until they thought I was harmless."

"No, you protect me!" The princess rushed to her, hugged her. "I know you would protect me. You always say it. Now I see! Thank you, Jabuli. You are my bestest friend!"

"I just want you to be safe, little majesty, and to be free."

Rula waved her hand, pointing in the direction they were trying to go, down the eastern slope. Then up the next, higher slope. She gave some finger words.

"Yes, we must keep going," said Jabuli. "By the time they get back to the city and gather more dragoneers, then come up the trail again, we will have an hour advantage. But they will be riding and we only on foot. So we must keep a quick pace."

Jabuli led them, setting that quicker pace with the longsword resting against her shoulder. Adora followed next, a bag in her two arms, and Rula carried the babe in the sling while dragging one of the bags in her other hand. The trail ended and they strode along the top of the ridge for a while, then descended the other side. From the heights they could see the wide dark green east bay below, half of the expanse choked with reeds. Far across the bay, more mountains rose and many of the peaks were white with snow.

Rula shook her arm, pointing.

"That's her home," said Jabuli. "Where we are going. We will hide there for as long as necessary."

Overhead the sky shook with a roar. A dragon flapped its wings and glared down at them, deciding whether or not to grab a snack. The beast had a fat, gray belly, orange stripes along its throat, and bright blue eyes. As it swooped down toward them, Jabuli raised the sword.

The dragon came down in a smooth arc, its toothy yaw open, fangs ready to snatch up one of them.

Jabuli snapped the blade up and cut into the dragon's throat, just under its chin. Not a fatal wound, but enough to make it think twice about a meal. The beast pulled skyward, wings flapping hard.

"There are more dragons at these heights," said Jabuli. "We must always keep an eye to the sky now."

"That one was very large!" cried the princess.

"Not the largest of the dragons, either."

"I only know the little dragons of Sannan. They run around like a pet, or they grab food from a café or they have to be swept out from the gardens. Even I could ride one of those dragons. " She looked up, her eyes following the aerial beast as it was lost in the clouds. "I could never ride something as large as that one."

"Nor should you. We must stay away from dragons."

"I would be afraid it would let me ride just to trick me. Then it would eat me!"

Jabuli grumbled. "Don't think of such things."

She urged the princess ahead as they went down the slope.

"Mind your head out here, little majesty," she called. "Dragons are not to be dismissed. You know only the little beasts, but out there—" She pointed to the mountains. "—dragons rule the skies and much of the land. Humans are like furry dabblers to dragons."

The princess nodded several times. "I need to read the parches. I

357

will learn about dragons." She stopped to ponder. "Will there be parches where we are going?"

"I don't know. Perhaps some."

Jabuli caught up to her and passed her then, playing as though they were in a race.

"There is not much to learn. Dragons have their own minds, do what they wish, and always look for a quick bite. They will not bow to a little princess."

"I won't be a little princess much longer." Adora tugged on the back of Jabuli's shirt. "In fact, from today I am not a princess any longer. I declare I am only Adora, a girl from Sannan. I need a better name for my brother, too. I can't keep calling him Puki. When he is grown to adult age he will hate that name. People will ask him how he got that name and he will cry rather than tell them."

"Then you must give him a proper name. A name for a man."

Rula motioned again, and they all saw the pair of blue dragons emerging from behind the clouds. They seemed to be unaware of the humans on the hillside. Rula waved her arms as though dismissing them, sending them far away.

"There will always be dragons," said Jabuli.

Adora grabbed her, hugging her. "Thank you for protecting me," she said three times. "And my brother."

"It is my duty, little majesty."

Jabuli frowned, gazing at the pair of departing dragons. Not at all sure what might lay ahead, she knew it could not be easier than what they had already experienced.

"Though it will be harder and harder each day," she spoke, "I shall always protect you. Always, little majesty." She rubbed her elbow where she caught the dragoneer's blade. A cut to the cloth of her shirt, opened to her flesh, the cloth stained with blood. The wound was minor, little more than a kitchen mistake. "Until the day when I cannot."

25

Where the Girls Are

NAKA WU ADJUSTED THE LEATHER BRACES over her chest, straightened the short skirt, and grabbed her metal helmet and her sword. The blade, sharpened that very morning, glistened in the afternoon sunshine streaming through the open door. She flipped her long, black braid over her shoulder. With sandals strapped on her feet, she stepped out of the armory, lance in hand, and made her way to the west courtyard, a part of the palace grounds nearly filled with a fern grove and cut by a gurgling stream and a waterwheel. A pair of girls in pink loincloths keep the wheel operating, she saw as she passed. It was wet work, Naka Wu knew, having done that task in her youth. Wearing only a loincloth was welcomed.

She thought of all the menial tasks she had performed over her years of service. She could not remember a time when she had not served the queen in some way. Offered by her mother in exchange for taxes overdue, she had been trained to obey. And she had obeyed as much as she could. Each day, however, a simmering hatred grew in her heart and boiled in her belly. She knew one day the sun would rise on a new day when she was no longer a servant of Hiro Ka.

"It is today," she spoke to herself.

She noticed an old woman squatting in a gap between the thick clumps of ferns downstream from the wheelhouse. The woman hid her identity beneath a dingy ragged robe that had to be too warm for the season. She appeared to be a lowly toilet cleaner. She carried a brush. A pail of scrub water sat at her hairy feet.

"You are ready?" the old woman asked, knowing the answer by a glance at the uniform and weapons.

"I am." She gazed at the toilet scrubber. "You promise to leave the city if I help you and we succeed. There should be no men or boys in Covin. If the rebellion fails, then you will take me with you. Confirm it."

"I confirm it," said the old woman, on most other days known as Rupas of Unting.

The ferns rustled and a boy appeared. She guessed it was a boy. And yet, this youth was dressed in the pink gown of a palace servant and could have been mistaken for a girl. His hair was long enough and no whiskers had yet sprouted on his lip or chin.

"Who is she?" asked the young one.

"This is Naka Wu," said Rupas, the old woman, to Tam, the little serving girl. "She's a palace guard. She is going to help us."

"Can she be trusted?" asked Tam, narrowing his eyes.

"Ah, now, little Corlan, you must accept assistance where you can find it. Naka Wu does not like the queen, so she's been waiting for her chance to act, to do something about the queen's domineering reign. Now is the time. In exchange, she will leave the city with us."

"Only if we fail and I must escape," said Naka Wu.

"Then we must succeed," said Rupas with a nod. "We will claim our man and leave the city. You may continue with your rebellion as you like. And good luck to you and your sisters."

Tam grinned, rubbing his chin like Corlan always did. "I suppose it will be satisfactory."

"He's a smug troll, this one," grunted Naka Wu. She glared at Tam. "Listen, boy: I'm only helping you to get my revenge on her. Not to help you. I'm not your mother and I won't take care of you like your mother. Got it?"

Tam suddenly appeared frightened.

Naka Wu had a scowl. "Just like a little man: crying like a man!"

"Don't mind him," said Rupas. "He's swaggering like his father. A boy's got to grow up, eh?"

"There's plenty of labor for this one if we fail. And you. You'll be dinner, likely enough."

Rupas was nonplussed. "I was rather hoping to be dessert."

Tam studied the fierce woman. She was dressed for battle and stood as tall as Corlan. It would be difficult to say who would win a fair fight between them. Now, however, it was Corlan who was at a disadvantage, being under the spell of the queen.

"You apologize," Rupas demanded of Tam.

The boy bowed his head. "Sorry."

"I accept it." She did not smile. "Tell us what you know."

Tam recovered, glaring at Rupas. "It's the end of what they were doing in the tower chamber so they moved to a bigger chamber on the first level."

"The Queen Suite," Naka Wu spoke. "Her main quarters. There will be two guards outside the doors."

"The middle meal is always at the sixth bell," said Tam. "I'm in the team that serves them. I pretend to be a girl, but I only do it for Corlan, to help him. I don't really want to be a girl."

"What is so bad about being a girl?" the woman spoke, staring down at the boy.

"Ah, he means he was born as a boy so he is fine with being a boy," Rupas explained. "He meant no disrespect."

"I got to this city as a boy," said Tam, looking up from under his thick eyebrows, "but I can't get into the room except as a girl."

"Fair words. You will find, little man, that wyma are superior to men here. And most places. Speak no words otherwise."

He nodded vigorously. Looking up, he said: "I'll do anything to help Corlan."

"Understood," said Naka Wu.

"Now what is the plan?" asked Rupas of the woman.

She stared at Rupas, then at Tam, then returned her gaze to Rupas. "You do not have a plan?"

He regarded Tam, who rolled his eyes.

"All right, now listen," said Tam. "Here's the plan."

"Dear lover, you are ready to regain your strength," cooed Hiro Ka as she sat beside Corlan on the edge of the bed, her hand caressing his back. "Day eighteen, the first day after the protocol. And you have faithfully executed the protocol in ways I never could imagine. I never dreamed the protocol could be so...*intense*. I was exhausted after every session. I could hardly walk across the room."

She rose from the bed, still unclothed, and two young attendants stepped over to her, offering the queen a fresh gown folded across their four extended arms. The queen began to dress, working at a languorous pace. The gown was the same filmy fabric she always wore; this gown was pink, however, to show everyone that she had completed the protocol and could stand proudly pregnant before all.

The girls knelt to slip on the queen's pink sandals, then stood once more to await her next command.

"You are so empty now." The queen let loose a laugh, as though she was pleased with her trick. "And I am so full!"

She whirled about the room, dancing to a song only in her head. Delighting in the swaying of her gown around her legs, the pink of the fabric filled the room with streams of joy. Her hand went to her belly, lingered as though she already felt a new heartbeat.

"Can you see my belly? Can you?"

She studied the sleeping man for a moment, admiring his strong, scarred back and meaty buttocks.

"Look at my belly, dear lover! You must!"

She nudged the bed with her knee and the man stirred.

"Awaken, dear lover, and gaze at what you have created."

Corlan rolled absently onto his side, blinking weakly and taking deep breaths. After a moment, with his eyes settled, he gazed down the length of his body and saw a woman swathed in a pink gown twirling at the foot of the bed. She was clearly too excited for this time of the day.

His stomach gurgled, reminding him of the hour. Eat and sleep, eat and sleep. And serve the queen between. It was a simple life; he had lost all sense of time—and any memory of events before coming to Covin.

"I think it is larger this morning. What do you think?" she asked him. "I must have my belly measured."

Corlan cleared his throat, sought the words he knew were in his head somewhere, found a few: "Looks...same."

"Naturally it's the same as yesterday. The protocol only ended last night. Mother says—and the physician confirms—only fourteen days are required to start visibility. Three more days are simply to ensure that everything that can be done has been done."

He rolled onto his back with a loud sigh. "Yeah...done...."

"Lover, don't be so weary! We followed the protocol exactly so I have no doubt we have succeeded. Be happy! We could have twin daughters, perhaps a trio of girls. I have dreamed of that."

He nodded from the bed, slowly rubbing his eyes. Everything felt heavy: his arms, his breathing, his body, his head. The effects of the elixir, he figured, would take just as many days to fade away as the number of days he drank it. He had managed to skip a few days without her noticing.

Hiro Ka smiled at him, love in her eyes. "Will you be comfortable if I step out for a while to have my belly measured? I must go to the official measuring chamber. When I return we shall dine. Rest until then. Or perhaps.... Shall I order a bath for you?"

He blinked, unsure what a bath was. A big pot of boiling water? The girls with their baskets of wet towels? Small hands wiping cloths over his sweat-soaked body? Was that what she was referring to? He raised his hand off the sheet to signal his approval.

"Very well. I shall call attendants to bathe you."

With a wave of her hand the two girls departed.

She gave a glance to the tall, thin beaker on the low table that had previously contained the elixir. She smiled and gave a glance back over her shoulder as she stepped to the door of the chamber.

"Tonight we must have a feast," she called to him. "You surely have earned it. If you like, we can have more dessert."

Marching as the third of four girls, Tam carried a smaller platter than usual. The others did not suspect his true identity. He did not even have to raise his voice higher like Rupas did while pretending to be an old woman in ragged robe.

As the quartet moved down the corridor, Tam spied another quartet moving toward them from the opposite direction. Two of the four girls approaching carried pails of water. One girl carried a stack of towels. One carried a tall beaker.

The two quartets met at the door to the Queen Suite, guarded by two tall women guards bearing lances. Each quartet stared at the other a moment and Tam started to shake in his sandals.

"What is your task?" asked the tallest girl of the other quartet.

"We bring the middle meal to the queen and to Her Majesty's consort," said the leader of Tam's quartet, a girl named Bai Lo.

"We are here to bathe the queen's consort," said the other leader.

"We were called just now."

"Everyone knows bathing comes before eating."

"Then we will wait for you bathers to finish before we enter."

"That's stupid. You can't just stand out here waiting."

"You're right. The food will get old."

"You better return to the kitchen and wait there."

"Then we might be late and the queen will punish us."

"Better you than us."

"Hey," said Tam, "don't talk to her like that."

"Who are you?" asked the other quartet's leader.

"I'm Tamia," he replied with hesitation.

"Well, I'm Mazu Fa and I've been here a long time. You must be new. No wonder you don't know the rules."

"I am new," he said. "My mother sold me to the palace staff to pay her taxes. I'm trying to learn all the rules. Forgive me."

"You have a lot of rules to learn, new girl."

Another girl from the bathing quartet pointed at Tamia. "If you are on the palace staff, then why are you not wearing the necklace each of us wears?"

Tam blanched, his hand going to his throat to check. "It—it must have fallen off when I...when I was scrubbing the kitchen floor."

"We don't believe you."

"Don't be concerned with her," said Bai Lo. "She is clumsy and we laugh at her. Life would be dull if she were not on the staff."

"Maybe so," said Mazu Fa, "but it's probably more true that she isn't really on the staff."

"We should report her," said the second bathing quartet girl.

"No, wait," said Tam. "I—I admit I wasn't sold by my mother. The truth is...I—I just want to—to serve the queen so much that I snuck into the palace and and now I'm trying my best to be a good attendant, so someday I might be rewarded—*perhaps* be rewarded. I—I know I'm clumsy, but I don't have any other place to go."

"That sounds like a story," said Bai Lo with a giggle. "She always tells good stories. So who cares if she was sold or she wants to serve the queen. We all want to serve the queen, each of us in our own way. You bathe her and her guests. We serve them food."

"We should work together," said Tam.

"Wise words from the new girl," said the second bathing quartet girl. "What was your name? Tamia?"

"Yes, I'm called Tamia."

"Tamia what?"

"Tamia Tang," he said quickly.

"Tang?" asked Mazu Fa. "What a strange name."

"Is not!"

Bai Lo waved him back, then faced Mazu Fa.

"Forget her. We took too much time already. You better get the bathing started so we won't be late serving the meal."

"Yes, too much time wasted talking to a Tang."

"Isn't that a kind of *frog*?"

"An ugly frog, I know!"

Tam was boiling but he knew he had to stay calm.

Mazu Fa turned to the guards. "We come to bathe the queen's consort. Let us pass."

The two guards glanced at each other then nodded in unison. They took hold of the handle of each door and pulled the heavy wooden doors apart, opening the passage to the chamber. The bathing quartet entered.

Tam could see there was another passage from the double doors to the actual chamber, a short entryway separated from the chamber by a curtain made of long strings of beads and jewels that glittered as they swayed in the breeze wafting through the open doors.

"We bring the middle meal for the queen and her consort," said Bai Lo to the guards. "Let us also enter and wait for the bathing to be done."

"The queen is not here," said one guard.

"We have the order to bring the meal. The queen will return soon and expect the meal to be served."

The two guards regarded each other, unsure what to do.

"You don't want the queen to be hungry and there's no food here...do you?" asked Bai Lo.

Tam stepped forward. "Who would she blame for keeping her meal away?"

The guard who had spoken nodded. "You can wait inside."

"You serve the queen well," said Bai Lo.

The food quartet entered, passed through the bead-string curtain, and moved against the far wall, away from the entrance. The platters were set on the low table there. The beaker of drink placed on the stand next to the bed.

Already the bathing quartet was at work. With the man on his belly across the bed, the four girls swabbed his back and legs with wet towels, dabbed the washing liquid onto his skin, and rubbed the towels again. One set of towels for wetting, another set for drying.

Standing at the far end of the room, Tam didn't think the man was fully awake. The man did not seem like Corlan. He was like a doll, maneuvered by four girls who had only a hundredth of his strength if all four were combined.

"If you please, sir," said Mazu Fa, "we can go forward after you turn yourself over."

"What?" He moaned as if awakened abruptly from sleep.

"We need you to turn yourself over, sir. Then we can finish the task we have been assigned."

He groaned, half-turning on the bed. It seemed an effort, like he was in pain when he moved.

Tam stepped forward. Even though the bathing quartet's second girl stepped in front of him with her hands raised to stop him, he took a wet towel from the pile in one of the pails and flung it onto the man's back. The wet towel landed in the small of his back. The man reached behind for the cool irritant and, while stretching his body, tumbled on over so he was flat on his back, the wet towel bunched underneath his body.

"That's clever," said Mazu Fa with a sneer.

"Stand aside," said the second girl.

Tam stayed by the bed. As the four girls continued washing the man's front side in similar fashion as his back, Tam slid to the head of the bed. He gazed down upon Corlan, the dragonslayer's face smooth, beard gone. The scars on his body were so obvious now, naked on the bed. Tam's staring disturbed the man.

"Step away," said Mazu Fa, adding a sharp snap of her hand.

"I only want to help," said Tam. He noticed the man looking up at him. "What can I do?"

"You are a serving girl, not a bathing girl," the team's second girl grumbled. "Stand aside."

"If you want to help," said Mazu Fa. "If you *really* want to help, you can get a wet towel and clean between the mounds."

The second girl snickered. "Wipe the valley of dirt."

"What do you mean?" asked Tam, fearing a trick.

"Take the towel and wipe between the mounds. Clean the valley of dirt. Don't you know of those places? Do you wash yourself? Get down there and clean that area."

"And be gentle lifting the man-things out of the way," said Mazu Fa. "He gets fussy if you touch them too long."

The second girl handed Tam a wet towel. "Go on."

He frowned. He would do anything to help Corlan but this was too much. He glanced back at his own leader and Bai Lo shrugged. So he stretched over the foot of the bed and, using a dry towel, lifted what had to be lifted and dabbed the wet towel where it needed to go, sliding it up and down until the towel came back soiled.

"Now put it in the other pail," said the second girl. "Not the pail you got the clean water from. Don't be stupid that way."

Tam deposited the dirty towel in the correct pail and wanted to wash his hands. He returned to the bed. The girls were finishing their task by washing his feet. They worked the towels between his toes and scrubbed the soles.

Tam stood beside the bed, gazing down on Corlan's face.

"Who?" asked Corlan, his eyes blinking. "Look familiar...."

"They call me Tamia." He gave the man a big wink. "You can call me Tam, if you wish."

"Tam?"

"Yes, Tam of the Burg."

"Burg?" He scratched the back of his head.

"...of the Burg."

"Sure?" the man grunted.

"My mother sold me to the palace."

"She did?"

"She couldn't pay the taxes."

"She couldn't?"

"My mother's name is Rupassa. We are from *the valley...?*"

"The valley?"

"It's a long way from here. There was a man hunting *dragons* in the valley not long ago."

"Dragons?"

"Yes, dragons."

Corlan's eyes blinked faster and his pout transformed into a grin.

"What are you saying?" asked Bai Lo. "We are not supposed to speak to the queen's consort."

"Consort?" the man mumbled.

"You've been the queen's consort for seventeen days," said Tam.

The man seemed to be thinking about the information.

"Finished," Mazu Fa announced.

She stood back, admiring the team's work.

"Let us leave now."

She turned to Bai Lo. "You may serve the meal now."

"Thank you for telling us our task, Mazu Fa!"

"Kiss between my mounds!" growled the leader of the bathing quartet as they turned to exit. "Food slave!"

"Bath slave!"

"Girls, please," said Tam. "We each have a task to do."

"You can kiss my mounds, too, new girl!" Mazu Fa cried as she stomped toward the doors.

"She will go far here," said Tam to Bai Lo in a sour tone.

Corlan reached for the sheet, pulled it over his hips.

"What about dragons?" he asked Tam, still beside the bed.

The boy smiled at the man. "You used to *slay* them."

"Slay...?"

"Yes. With a dragonslinger."

"I did?"

"It shoots iron bolts."

"It does?"

"Tamia, come over here and help serve the meal. The queen will return very soon."

"I better wash my hands before serving food," said Tamia.

"What's your name, girl?" asked the man.

"Tamia. But you can call me Tam. I'm from the Burg. You know, the family of *Tang* that lived in the *Burg*? Now they live in the *valley* where the *dragons* fly over. It's on the way to the *marshes*."

"Tamia, get over here," called Bai Lo. "The queen approaches!"

26

Jemma of Danapo

THE QUEEN WAS CHATTING with the ambassador from Danapo, a wyma city northwest of Covin. Behind them followed the queen's four guards bearing lances. The two wyma strolled through the west courtyard, enjoying the lush flora and the autumn warmth. Being in no hurry, they shared details of each city.

"It was so long ago hardly anyone remembers," said Hiro Ka with a dismissive sigh. "You would find it difficult to read about it on a scroll. I tried and it was so dull. The big words and such! So there they were: an army of ten-thousand men coming upstream from Luval on boats, determined to—these were rabid, desperate men—determined to break into our city. Our walls held them back, of course, and whenever they tried to climb up them we sent down boiling oil."

"Amazing!" said Jemma of Danapo in her high, lilting voice. The buxom Danapoi ambassador was short and carried wavy blond hair that flowed over her shoulders. "How did you get enough oil?"

"We emptied all the kitchens, naturally. Boiled down all the fat we could find. We couldn't fry anything for weeks after."

"You had to grill all your food? That's a shame."

"They thought next to negotiate with us, to persuade us to open the gates and let them in. First, they insisted that we, as females, owed them all sorts of things, such as love and affection—that was the first week of negotiation, after a month of siege. Then it was simply the need for sex, they begged us—the second and third weeks. Then it was supposed to be *fair* for us to pair up with them, to make some children, then to make dinner, clean the house, wash everything while they laid about drunk. They called that the Natural Order, believe it or not—had it written out in a holy book, they claimed—a book older than the scrolls. They had a god, they said, who told some man what to write. That's believable! Hah! So I never liked words written by men."

"Me, too," said Jemma. "I can't believe they believed you would believe what they believe!"

"By the sixth week they were certain all the forces of nature were about to rebel against both them and us for our unnatural status. They called up to the clouds, claimed their god lived up there, and he was a cruel god. Only one god! That's all they had. They had gotten weak by then. Many had abandoned the fight. Others started eating each other in their camps. After the twelfth week, with the winter arriving in a heavy snowfall, only the sick and ragged remained. So we held out. We took in a few survivors at the end, nursed them back to health, and they helped us make children."

"Weren't you worried about disease?"

"Not after they were restored to health."

"What happened to those men," asked Jemma, "after children were born?"

"After they were born? Hah! They were sent to the kitchens as soon as pregnancy was confirmed."

"One and done?"

"Often they served more than one wym. The better men stayed longer, lasted longer in service, and I recall hearing that a few were sent away from Covin instead of to the kitchens. As a reward for good service."

"We pray for servants such as those in Danapo."

They passed under the stone arch, leaving the west courtyard and entering the corridor leading to the Queen Suite.

"So it's been this way ever since?" asked Jemma.

"Yes, ever since. A few generations." She waved her hand in the air as they strolled. "Oh, we find men still trying to enter the city from time to time. Or wandering the outer lands. We capture them and, if they are deemed worthy—you know what I mean?—we save them for some time and they serve us. Otherwise, they are disposed of as quickly as possible."

"And that is?"

Hiro Ka thought a moment, pausing along the corridor. "Usually it is to the stew pots. It takes a day or two. Or, if too boney, just a grilling on each side. That's a few hours."

"You eat the men? Aren't you worried about disease?"

"They are cooked thoroughly, of course. It's no different than the four-legged animals, really." She grinned as though she had shared a joke. "I know of no wyma here becoming ill from eating man-meat. And speaking of man-meat...."

"You do look quite healthy. Everyone I've seen here, in fact. In Danapo, we pay the men to serve us. Yet only what we need to be done. There are three ranks of wages: minimum, standard, and high. It depends what their skills are."

Hiro Ka started down the corridor. "In Covin, we just let them live."

"That seems rather wasteful," said the Danapoi ambassador with a sigh, "but I leave you to your customs."

They walked on. After a few steps, Hiro Ka gestured to turn at the next junction.

"Speaking of man-meat," said the queen, "let me show you what I have been dining on the past seventeen days. He is a specimen of manhood you do not find every day—hah, every year!"

"You have a man all to yourself?"

"For now. If he proves a good sire, I may lend him to other ladies. Now that he has completed the protocol. Perhaps, you would like to use him."

"You are so kind. In Danapo we must share them because there are so few of them. A good man is hard to find."

"And what do you do when they become useless—or they think to rebel, to claim the silly things they believe must be true, what they write in their so-called holy books? Or when they claim their god says they are superior to wyma and wyma must submit to them? What do you do with them?"

"If they grow weak or get old and die, then it's done. Otherwise, if they are violent, we remove them quickly. But we never eat them. We have plenty of hoven in Danapo so we've never thought of using men for food. We aren't like insects."

"They have a good flavor sometimes," said the queen, pausing to ponder her last dinner. "We cover the meat with sauces. I prefer a spicy sauce. Some parts can be chewy."

The queen resumed her walk and the ambassador followed.

"I can't imagine the taste," said Jemma.

"Shall I have a dish prepared for you to sample?"

"Oh, no need to trouble yourself with that."

"I would not trouble myself. I have a kitchen staff for that. They could prepare a dish within the hour, if you wish it."

"Thank you, Your Majesty, but I'm not hungry at the moment."

"As you like."

Hiro Ka gestured again and they halted before the double doors of the Queen Suite. Two guards stood at attention, lances flat against their shoulders. The quartet of guards following them took defensive positions.

"I went to have my belly measured. Today is day eighteen. The first day after completing the protocol. Already I have gained a half-inch around my belly. Can you see it?"

The queen swept a hand to her belly and Jemma gazed at the bare skin between her breasts and her hips.

"You can't see much advance, but the baby has begun already inside me. The royal physician confirms. I'm certain it's a daughter. Every wym in my line has born daughters."

"You have been blessed by the goddesses."

"It's a miracle. I can feel something inside of me, even if it is only a magic spell."

"Many people use magic spells in Danapo, all the time, like even for ordinary things. Like to make the grain ripen quicker."

"I meant a *wish*. Magic spells are old-days superstitions. Nobody believes in that now. We even had people to keep away the dragons long ago. The magic spells worked so well, all the dragonslayers went elsewhere for better hunting."

"You had trouble with dragons?"

"Not for fifty years."

"In our city people keep them as pets. Small ones, that is. I had one that I used to ride in the streets when I was a child. I have two drakes now."

"And none were harmed?"

"Some burns, as anyone might expect. Mine did eventually grow older, larger, so we had to let it go. A dragonmaster took her away and I cried."

"What a sad child!"

"I learned to communicate with her. To call her, give her some commands. I named her Tulip, like the flower. Ah, now you've made me feel sad." The blond woman laughed. "It has been such a long time since my child days and those pastimes."

"Everything good must pass," said the queen absently.

"I suppose it's true."

The queen paused and regarded the ambassador. A hand went to Jemma's bare arm, appearing to admire the soft skin.

Jemma smiled.

"You know it's true," said the queen.

"It is such an education talking with you," said Jemma, flipping her blond hair off her shoulder. "It is an honor to meet you, Queen Hiro Ka. I shall take your words with me back to Danapo and make everyone aware of how wonderful the city of Covin is and what it has to offer *wyma* of all classes."

"It is my pleasure, as well. If you wish to stay longer, you may. I have finished the protocol with this man, so I am free to give the man to you for a night. The choice is yours, whichever you like."

"Thank you so much! I feel truly honored."

The queen smiled warmly, then extended her hand to Jemma, who clasped it in her own hand. Hiro Ka pulled the coupled hands to her chest, resting them between her breasts for a moment.

"A quick look," said Hiro Ka, releasing her hand from Jemma's. "He is probably asleep still. So much has he labored in following the protocol. I ordered a washing for him."

"Thank you for this honor. I would certainly welcome any man you choose for me, or if you truly wish for it, I shall serve you as best I can, using all the lessons of my youth. I got high marks in my Pleasuring class."

Hiro Ka laughed. "It's an honor for *me*! I will let you play with the man if you find him worthy. I am finished with him today."

She faced the guards. At her blink they opened the doors.

"Pardons, my queen," called an old woman in tattered robe, a few steps down the corridor. The bent-over woman waddled up to the double doors. She dragged a pail and a short-handled mop.

The queen startled. One of the four guards moved to block the old woman's path but the queen waved the guard away.

"I won't be rude to an old wym," she said to the guard.

"Blessings upon thee," the woman spoke, arriving in front of her.

"What is it? What is your business?" asked Hiro Ka.

"I am the wym that cleans the toilets." She cackled a moment, the echo resonating eerily down the corridor. "I was told to hurry to the Queen Suite and prepare the toilet before your return." She bowed low, her knees on the stone floor of the corridor, her humped back showing prominently. "Forgive me for being late. I am an old wym and cannot move with ease."

"How lovely to see a mighty queen show such kindness to even the lowest member of the staff," said Jemma, ready to applaud.

Hiro Ka was about to rudely dismiss the old woman, but at the ambassador's words, she thought better to continue being kind. After all, the ambassador would report on this visit, and good relations between two cities of wyma were crucial to trade and security pacts.

"Worry not, old wym. I'm sure the toilet is adequate." Hiro Ka glared at Jemma, a smirk on her lips. "Unless the man has soiled the basin once more."

"I was told he did."

"I don't know how you have the patience for keeping a man for all seventeen days," said Jemma with a wide grin and several shakes of her head. "They are so dirty."

"It is the moment of ecstasy that pays for our patience," replied Hiro Ka. She turned to the servant. "What is your name?"

The woman looked up from under the dark cowl of her ragged robe, her face half-hidden in shadow.

"They call me many terrible names, my queen. My mother called me Rupassa, if you wish to know."

"Rupassa...." The queen thought a moment. "You have served us well. For how many years? Plenty, I'm sure. Let's give you a rest and announce that today begins your retirement. So, now, you may be off."

"How kind!" Jemma exclaimed, clapping her hands.

"My queen, I am delighted to serve you for so many years."

"How many years has it been?"

The woman hesitated. "Twenty...?"

"You're not sure?"

"An old wym loses her head first of all."

"I should think a wym loses her womb first of all," said Hiro Ka. She turned to Jemma. "Then, of course, every part has its collapse. The head last of all."

"You are wise, my queen," creaked the old woman.

"Go now and claim your wage, then be settled in a comfortable lodge...somewhere in the city."

The old woman bowed low again, reluctant to depart.

"If it please my queen, might I freshen the toilet one last time?"

Jemma giggled, threw her hand over her mouth. "How noble!"

"Very well," said Hiro Ka in a weary voice.

The queen glanced between Jemma and the door guards. They had already opened the door for the queen. As the group stood, the old woman was closer to the open doors—however, it would be rude for anyone but the queen to enter first.

"After you, my queen," the old woman offered, throwing her gloved hand forward.

"Certainly, after me!" Hiro Ka sneered. "You know the rules by now, old wym."

"Yes, my queen."

Hiro Ka stepped forward, a stately, elegant step. She entered the entryway at a determined pace, with her guest, Jemma of Danapo, a step behind. Next went the old woman, limping and scraping her foot as she went, dragging the hem of her robe, the pail and the mop.

Following them were the four personal guards who had escorted the queen back to her suite from the physician's chamber.

As the queen passed through the curtain of long cords strung with beads and gems, her eyes widened. She stopped suddenly with a couple cords still draped over her shoulder.

"Dear lover, you're all dressed now!"

The group of seven stepping through the short entryway crashed up against the queen when she halted, the crumple of people pushing her onward into the chamber. She almost tumbled to the floor but caught her balance as she kept her eyes fixed on Corlan.

The personal guards formed their squad behind her.

"My queen, let me do my last task in the toilet room," said the old woman, bent over and dragging her tattered robe on the floor. "Then I'll be away and leave you to your private pleasures."

The queen said nothing as the woman slunk away to the right, to the entrance of the toilet room.

In front of the queen stood the man who had been her faithful lover for seventeen days, who had hardly gotten off the bed during that time, who had barely worn any clothing, who had been ready to serve her in the morning, after the middle meal, and for most of each evening and sometimes during the night—several times during some nights at the beginning of the protocol. And yet he now seemed quite fit and vigorous standing boldly before her wearing a kind of leather uniform unfamiliar to her. There was a sword hanging from his hip.

"You must be rested by now," Hiro Ka spoke. She took a breath and turned slightly, gesturing at the blonde woman beside her. "I've brought a new wym here as my guest. I thought you would be able to serve her as delightfully as you have served me the past seventeen days. She being my guest, you only need serve her one night."

The queen's words did not seem to register on Corlan's face. He stood tall and broad-shouldered yet it appeared as though his mind struggled to grasp the situation. The sword at his side tempted his hand. He grabbed the hilt.

"You...," he tried to speak, frustration rippling across his face. "You...seventeen days...took from me...all that's...Corlan."

"What are you saying?" The queen laughed, a thin, rusty noise. "We enjoyed a lavish dessert together, as much yours as mine. We created new life together. The physician has confirmed our success. You see my belly? Already it is a half-inch more. Congratulate me, dear lover."

A girl in a pink gown rushed to Corlan from the quartet beside the serving table.

"Here," the girl said, extending her hand which was full of red-spotted yellow berries. "Eat more of these, Corlan."

The man opened his hand and the girl poured the berries into his palm. He raised his hand and slurped the berries into his mouth, a few at a time, until his hand was empty. Juice ran down his chin. He lowered his hand for a refill from the girl's supply.

"Yavo berries!" the queen exclaimed. "They are forbidden in the palace! They undo the effects of the elixir of love. Where did you get them, girl?"

Tam turned with eyes narrowed, glaring at the queen from under his dark, bushy eyebrows.

"I'm not a girl," he said.

"I knew it!" Bai Lo cried out.

"And Corlan is my father!" Tam shouted.

"No, he is my lover. He fulfilled the seventeen-day protocol."

"You poisoned him with that drink! Every day! I know all about potions," grunted Tam. "I worked in the palace kitchen in the Burg. I mixed them sometimes so Chef wouldn't get into trouble."

The queen was confused, turning in each direction to seek help, hoping for some kind of explanation. The three serving girls were frozen, unable to decide what to do. Jemma was puzzled, too, not sure what the procedure was. Corlan stood tall and strong but he was dull-headed.

Rupas, hiding for a moment in the toilet room, returned loudly dressed in men's clothing, having thrown off the disguise.

"Ah!" The queen fell back, startled by his transformation.

"It is time for you to sing to your gods—or goddesses, as you like," said Rupas in harsh tone. "Too long you have been cruel, too long you have kept men prisoners, too long forcing everyone to go swimming in the horror that is this city of Covin."

"What?" shrieked the queen. "How dare you!"

She spun around, expecting her guards to do something about the nasty intruders and the unexpected insubordination.

"Do something," she demanded.

The guard with the long black braid raised her lance to thrusting position. It was Naka Wu behind the queen and the ambassador.

"Today is your last day," spoke Naka Wu.

Corlan grunted, trying to find the word he needed: "Wait!"

"You're drugged, Corlan," said Rupas. "It's time to go home."

In one swift motion Naka Wu thrust the lance forward into the queen's lower back. Another sharp half-thrust forced the metal tip out through her belly, pushing a string of bowel, releasing a spray of blood.

The ambassador jumped aside, falling to the floor, cowering.

"You will not be harmed," said Naka Wu to the woman. "You are not part of Hiro Ka's reign of cruelty. Be silent and you will be freed at the end."

Two of the guards who had formed the quartet with Naka Wu moved to block the bead-string curtain entryway and the third guard had gone over to the serving girls to keep them in the corner.

Hunched over on bent knees, Hiro Ka held her belly as moans erupted from her—moans of pain and sorrow for the precious treasure inside her which she had just confirmed.

"Nooooo," she whimpered. "Not my babe...."

"One is the same, you and the next one, done. Your reign is over," Naka Wu declared. "As we speak, the Pink Lady is drowned, the bottle drained of the fluid that has kept her alive for all these years. In other corners of the palace, we have taken charge. In the city, we also command the streets. Now Fa Mei will rule in Covin!"

Corlan stepped forward, arms lowered to catch the queen, to help her. He glanced sideways at Tam, standing near the serving girls. The boy shook his head from side to side and Corlan stopped.

"I only know how to protect my wyma from harm," moaned the queen. "They worship me as their Great Mother. And I...now I am a mother, too. She is...this daughter of mine...she's the new hope for Co...vin." She lifted her head, tried to look at Naka Wu but the stretch of muscle and sinew was too painful. "Not me, but her...the babe. This child is supposed to be the new h-hope for C-Covin."

"There is no new hope, only generations of cruelty. My mother felt your cruelty. You fed her to drakes at the Eve of Eve celebration, as entertainment for your courtly sisters. Yet not before she endured the whipping. The lashes your jester snapped at her, flaming strands of coarse wire, were unspeakable cruelty!"

The queen wavered on her knees, struggling to breathe. "Your m-mother? I didn't know...who she was—"

"Because I was taken from her years before your soldiers brought her to the prison for a mere accident. Her last cow kicked one of your soldiers and broke her leg. They took my mother to a prison for that. When she was old, sick, trying to escape—she became your holiday entertainment!"

"The punishment was...fair," moaned the queen.

"And my elder sister...sent off to battle against the men-town of Inati—where she was captured and raped for months. And when she escaped back to Covin, you had her cut into pieces for desertion. I know more wyma who tell the same stories."

Naka Wu turned to the two guards behind her, then gestured at the guard standing by the serving girls.

"Uki Ma lost her mother to your warriors. I will not describe how they tortured her. Giko Song lost all three of her sisters to the cruelty of your soldiers. And Yuka Hei was tortured for seventeen days just because she dared look at a man—*some useless man!*—that you had brought to your chamber for the protocol. You see now she survived and has returned to meet you, to say farewell and send you into the Beyond. And me: sold by my mother because she could not pay your tax. So I grew up here, hating you each and every day. Now we take back this city!"

"And you are vanquished!" cried Uki Ma, rushing forward with arms raised, thrusting her lance down, piercing inside the queen's collarbone, forcing its metal point out through her belly.

"And me!" cried Giko Song, stabbing her lance into the left side of the queen, pushing the lance through her ribs and out the opposite side. Strings of flesh hung from the tip.

Yuka Hei, standing by the serving girls came forward slowly, then with a wide curl, slammed her lance down through the queen's bent back, forcing its tip out her breast. The force was so strong the lance continued through the queen's thigh and calf, penetrating the wooden floor beneath the queen.

Hiro Ka gasped, tried to cry out but had no breath. She could not collapse forward, held in place by the four lances. Locked in her pose, a pool of blood spreading out around her in a perfect circle.

The serving girls were crying. Tam spoke to them, telling them he had seen worse from dragons.

"Dragons?" asked Jemma, cowering against the wall.

Rupas coughed, swallowed. "I think we should start our plan to escape from this room now, then from this palace, and then from this city. I've prepared transportation—if we can reach it."

"What is this?" cried Jemma, pale as the pink walls. "What is happening?"

Rupas ignored the frantic woman, regarded Corlan, dumb-faced yet strong and improving. "Can you walk on your own? Standing is one thing, running is quite another."

Tam spoke to Corlan, repeating the words as though the boy was translating to him.

"Eat more of those berries," said Rupas.

Tam gathered more of the berries from the bowl on the table and fed them to Corlan, two or three at a time, as quickly as he could stuff them into his mouth. Some berries burst, yellow juice popping from his lips and staining his shirt.

"Quickly now!" Rupas ordered.

The sheet was ripped from the bed and placed on the floor. Posts from the bed were made to serve as both frame and handles.

"Now lie down there," said Rupas."

Naka Wu and the other guards took up their defensive positions, expecting other guards to enter the chamber.

"You and the girls must wait here after we exit," said Naka Wu to Jemma. "Tell them whatever you wish. Perhaps none will blame you for this."

"None blame me?" cried Jemma. "But I had nothing to do with this murder. I rather liked Hiro Ka. She was—"

Naka Wu rushed to the woman, sword drawn from her belt and held up to the ambassador's throat.

"You will be freed when we are away. Do as you like, say what you will, after that time. Or I'll kill you now."

"You said she was cruel to your relations. All of you? She seemed so lovely and kind. I can't believe—and you tricked her! The old wym was a...not an old maid but a hunched back man. And the girl, over there, is really a boy? And this man she loved for seventeen days is...a slayer of dragons?"

"How do you know that?" asked Tam.

Jemma glared at him. "The scars on his body."

Corlan had been fully dressed when they arrived.

"How do you know he bears scars from slaying dragons?"

Jemma frowned, disappointed she was not believed. "I sense the truth of his life. As soon as I set my eyes on him, I knew."

"Will you help us?" asked Rupas, positioning Corlan on the make-shift carrier. "We will claim an emergency and ferry him to the physician's office on the far end of the palace. Will you help us?"

"How? What can I do?" asked Jemma, holding out her hands. "I don't know if I should help. I'm innocent."

"Act frightened. You are worried about him. The queen sent you with him. She will meet you both there as soon as she can." Rupas turned to Naka Wu. "You four will escort us like any guard squad would." He called over to Tam: "Get that gown on again, boy."

"Me?" Corlan grunted from his position on the carrier.

"Just lie there. Act dumb. Like you're out of your mind."

"He *is* out of his mind," said Tam, breathlessly.

Jemma pointed to the serving girls. "And them?"

"They stay here and wait for someone to come for the queen," said Rupas. He glanced at the girls, frowning. "They likely will have dreams of horror for some time."

"You made them see this horror!" Jemma cursed.

"Perhaps someday," Rupas countered, "they will come to see it as the start of something better than the life they endured here."

"How can you say that?" asked Jemma.

"It's true," said Rupas. "How many girls were sold into service because their mothers could not pay the tax?"

"Can it be true?" Jemma cried, waving her hands as if trying to dismiss everything she had witnessed. "She seemed so nice."

27

Escapade

NAKA WU LED THEM through the bead-string curtain. Yuka Hei took hold of the front two handles of the litter. Uki Ma and Giko Song took hold of the rear handles and, being fit for guard duty, the three of them raised Corlan with little effort.

"Come with us, lady, or you will surely be blamed for this," said Rupas to a flustered Jemma. He glanced over at Tam, then down at Corlan, and ahead to the entryway. "Now let us try to escape from this palace!"

Naka Wu swept her black braid off her shoulder as she passed through the entryway, pushing open the double doors.

The two guards outside the doors stood at attention. Each of the outer guards grabbed a handle to help open the doors—and the warrior stormed out through the doors, sword in hand.

The guards stared at her, unsure what she was doing.

"Join us or die!" Naka Wu challenged. She glared at the right guard, short yellow hair and prominent chin.

"Sure, I'll join you," said that guard, "whatever it's about."

Naka Wu glared at the left guard, red-haired and green-eyed, as she held her sword raised to strike across the guard's belly.

"Join us or die!"

The red-haired guard stood firm. "I am loyal to the queen."

"The queen is dead," retorted Naka Wu, keeping her sword up.

"Are you certain?"

"Certain. Now join us or die!"

"Then I will join, as well," said the second guard. She jumped to the side as Rupas pushed his way out followed by the other guards carrying Corlan on the litter, one in front and two bringing up the rear.

"Step aside," grunted Rupas, unafraid in his full male outfit. He glared at Naka Wu. "Are they with us?"

"They say they are," she said with a snarl at each of the guards.

"We are," said the first guard. The second nodded.

After the litter came Jemma and Tam. The other three serving girls were ordered to stay in the room but the gruesome display frightened them and they ran out after Tam.

"I don't want to wear a gown anymore," Tam grumbled, dressed in the pink serving girl gown.

Jemma patted his shoulder. "You must fit in here or you'll be put in a bad place. Like the queen did. Apparently did. And she seemed so nice! She wanted to share her dessert with me."

"Tamia!" called one of the girls.

Tam turned. It was Bai Lo calling to him.

"What'll we do? Where do we go?"

"I'm going with Corlan," said the boy.

Bai Lo regarded the other girls, wiping tears from their faces. "I want to go with you."

"With me?" He shook his head, like he was head of the family. "I'm leaving this city, going far away."

"Take me with you! Please, Tamia!"

"I'm a boy. You know that now. Call me Tam, not Tamia."

"I will. Take me with you." The girl grabbed him, hugged him. "Please, Tam. I will only have more work if I stay here."

"All right," he said, releasing her. "Come with us."

At the same time, Jemma asked Naka Wu: "What is next? Where do we go?"

Naka Wu pointed down the corridor. The two serving girls were crying and swearing they would not report who did the terrible acts in the Queen Suite.

"You won't report this, will you?" asked Uki Ma.

"No, never," the girls swore.

"We never liked her," said one of them.

"She always complained no matter what we did," said the other.

"She was mean to everybody," said the first girl.

The two girls ran away down the corridor, the opposite direction Naka Wu had indicated.

"This way!" Naka Wu commanded.

The group hurried down the corridor but not a minute passed before they heard the cry echoing through the stone walls of the corridor that the Pink Lady had been found dead. Her bottle of pink life-preserving fluids had been broken, the fluids leaking out. Rebels were suspected. Staff members and guards were rushing to check the safety of the queen.

They crashed into a quartet of guards at the intersection.

"This is the queen's consort," Naka Wu announced, gesturing at Corlan on the litter carried by the other guards. "He's ill—could be he's been poisoned! We must get him to the physician immediately!"

The guards waved them by, then ran on down the corridor to the Queen Suite.

The group of insurgents hurried on in the opposite direction.

"Guards!" came the echo. "Halt!"

The guards they passed had discovered the crime and called back to them, Naka Wu realized.

"Stop! The queen is murdered! All of you halt!"

They shifted into a run, exiting the corridor into the courtyard. The jerking movements turning the corner threw Corlan off the litter. He struggled to get to his feet, his head aching. He pressed his hands to each side of his head.

"That's the drug fading from your head," said Rupas. "Can you run on your own?"

Corlan grimaced, nodded.

Tam grabbed his hand and pulled him ahead. "Come with me."

Bai Lo took Corlan's other hand.

As the group entered the courtyard, Jemma called that she saw through the trees there were guards ahead of them. While Corlan picked himself up, Rupas stared forward, saw the squad marching toward them.

"There is a side gate," said Jemma.

"We must get to the stables. There is our wagon," said Rupas. He looked up at the sky, startled by the shadow of clouds overhead. "Just don't think of dragons."

"I won't," said Jemma. "Although why shouldn't I? I did have a pet dragon when I was a little girl, a drake—"

"Stop it!"

They threw down the litter and everyone took to running along the path. They cut through the fern grove, hurrying over a small stone bridge and around a long flowerbed. The squad of guards spied the group, recognizing some of them were men.

"Men!" shouted one of the guards. "They have men!"

"They're the rebels," cried the squad's leader. "Members of Fa Mei's cult!"

Naka Wu grinned, hearing that. "Hurry!"

The guards turned and gave chase. Uki Ma and Giko Song slowed and swung their swords at the leading guards, cutting them down. Yuka Hei held her lance, threatening to spear the next guard who dared approach.

"The reign of Hiro Ka is now ended," Naka Wu announced. The guards stood frozen, unsure how to react. "Lay down your weapons and thank the twelve goddesses for your lives!"

Most did not. A swordfight ensued. After one minute of clanking metal, four warrior women were left standing, two guards were dead, and four others seriously wounded, one dragging herself to safety on wrist stumps, both hands cut off. Three had dropped their weapons and backed away.

"Now you have none of the freedom I promised you," said Naka Wu with some sadness in her voice. "Fa Mei rules in Covin now. If you continue to resist, you will be killed."

She turned to the others. "Let's go!"

They reached the west wall of the courtyard and slipped through the arched doorway there: Naka Wu and two of her comrades, then Corlan pulled by Tam and Bai Lo, then Rupas and Jemma, protected from the rear by the third woman, Yuka Hei.

Rupas waved his hand, as if pushing away a bad dream.

"No dragons in the courtyard this escape!"

"Stop talking about dragons," Tam shouted back at them.

"I'm trying not to think of them," Jemma yelled to Tam.

"Hurry!" Naka Wu called.

They entered another corridor which became a downward slope with a hairpin turn continuing down to the storage rooms under the courtyard.

"There!" Rupas cried, his arm extended, finger pointing.

Across the large, dimly lit garage was the wagon he meant. A stable girl stood there, tending to the horses, a quartet of beasts to pull the large wagon, half-full of supplies.

"We aim to go far," said Rupas to Corlan. "As you have planned. The journey continues. We've fresh horses."

Corlan nodded, smiling. "Thanks."

Tam helped Bai Lo climb onto the back of the wagon as Rupas got to the front bench and Corlan joined him there.

"How about me?" asked Jemma.

She and the four women warriors stood beside the wagon as the stable girl released the brake on the wagon and patted the horses one last time. Rupas tossed a small pouch of coin to the girl.

"You are free to go," said Rupas.

"You must take her," said Naka Wu, gesturing at Jemma. "She will be in danger if she stays. They will blame her for the queen's death."

"Blame me?" asked Jemma. "I did nothing."

"They could blame you because you were with her at the end."

"No, they wouldn't."

Naka Wu turned to Corlan. "Take her. Make certain she leaves the city."

Uki Ma and Giko Song picked up Jemma and set her hard on the back of the wagon as she batted their shoulders with her hands.

"I don't want to go," she argued. "But I can't stay either."

"See she gets out of the city," said Naka Wu to Rupas.

"And you?" asked Rupas. "What will you do?"

"We have a city to claim—"

A storm of shouting burst into the garage. The noise of guards running down the sloped corridor echoed into the room.

"They're coming!" said Yuka Hei.

"You must go!" cried Giko Song.

"Open the doors!" Naka Wu called to the stable girl.

She pushed on the heavy doors, moved them only slightly.

Uki Ma and Giko Song rushed to the doors and helped her push, their muscles flexing. The doors opened. They swung the heavy panels wider as the wagon rolled forward, the horses pulling hard.

Palace guards streamed into the garage, shouting for them to halt. Yuka Hei rushed to take down the first of the guards as they made their way through the narrow spaces between the wagons and carriages parked there.

Once the doors were opened, Uki Ma and Giko Song joined her and fought the guards spilling into the garage. They were like three demons holding a mountain pass against a single line of soldiers.

"Go!" Yuka Hei shouted to Naka Wu. "Protect them!"

"I will!" she called back, leaping onto the wagon as it rolled out the doors and up the outside slope.

Rupas guided the frightened horses through the turns exiting the palace grounds and into the streets of the city. He pulled his cowl up over his head, tried to look common.

"Stay low," he ordered Corlan. "I know the route. I have the map in my head."

"Go right," said Naka Wu, sitting behind him, up on her knees to look over his shoulder.

"I thought it's left," said Rupas.

"Right."

"Follow her directions," said Corlan. Rupas turned around to see the dragonslayer looking better, eyes clearer, voice stronger.

Naka Wu guided Rupas and they arrived in the market square by the western gate of the city.

The market was full of women and their wagons and carts, animals and baskets. They were packed among the stalls and kiosks. Dust rose from the ground, making the square fill with clouds. The wagon had to stop as they waited for women and their beasts to move out of the way. Rupas shouted at them, using a woman's voice to little success.

At the gate, a line of guards stood at attention, ready to check everyone entering or departing.

Despite it being a market with all the noises of haggling, a new noise cut through the crowd. News of the palace attack spread through the streets like fire, it seemed. News of the Pink Lady being destroyed followed. And the Queen, Hiro Ka, murdered in her suite! By her consort! And some other woman! The Danapoi ambassador!

Jemma crouched low, in shock, muttering "I didn't do anything" over and over.

"We know you didn't," said Tam. Bai Lo nodded to confirm.

The crowd seemed to recognize the people on the wagon all at the same time: a man trying to pass as a woman, another man, well-formed, and one of the queen's uniformed warriors riding with them. Suspicious! The wagon was limited to a few feet at a time, pushing through the crowd. The horses balked, whinnied, refused to trot forward into the mass of people. Rupas urged them on.

"We must go through the gate," he grunted. "It's the only way!"

"I will call my comrades to fight," said Naka Wu.

"They are in the palace, aren't they?"

She rose from her seat and gazed about the crowd. "I see none of my comrades here."

"Then we need a dragon to clear this square," Rupas grumbled.

"I thought you said to not mention dragons," Jemma called from the rear of the wagon.

"I did say that." He glanced over his shoulder at her. "Because at that moment it wouldn't have been the best solution to as simple a problem as exiting this city. Now, however...."

"Do you want me to think of dragons?" she asked in a serious tone.

"Think what you will. It is only Fate that we shall see today."

"I think I wouldn't welcome a dragon today," Corlan muttered.

"If we don't get through that gate...."

The crowd pressed against them, surrounding the wagon and the horses. A few reached out for the people on the wagon, as though they thought those on the wagon were some kind of treasure they could present to the palace staff in exchange for fair coin.

Naka Wu held up her sword, warning the crowd not to grab at the wagon. That aggressive act seemed to embolden those already trying to stop them. So she swung her blade down, cutting a woman's arm. The crowd shouted, cursing them, threatening them with death for the violent act.

"You don't know what freedom is!" she shouted at them. "Go on with your lives! Fear not the queen or her staff!"

Several women shouted back their love for the queen yet Naka Wu stood tall with her sword to silence them.

"Clear the way!" she shouted.

"This is not improving," Rupas snarled, trying to get the horses to keep moving forward — yards then feet, then inches.

Corlan felt a poke and turned to see Tam holding a sword. The boy had grabbed a sword from the bag of weaponry on the back of the wagon. Tam held it out, hilt toward Corlan, jutting his chin for him to take it. Corlan's hand remembered how it felt to curl around the leather grip, to feel the blade as an extension of his arm.

A shadow passed over the market square and few noticed it. The next shadow made most of them look up. The third shadow had everyone gazing skyward.

Wings! Three pairs! Dragons!

"You thought of dragons?" Rupas asked Jemma curtly.

"No, I—"

"Dragons!" Tam shouted, giving Corlan's back a shove.

"I only recalled my pet from years ago. A harmless drake."

"That's it!" Rupas turned to Corlan. "Are you ready?"

Corlan nodded, swung his blade in front of himself. Then, to

Tam: "Load the slinger, boy! It's dragon time!"

The first dragon, a flathead, the largest of the three, circled and swung low on the second approach. With a sloped forehead and long face, this species preferred snatching its food off the ground. As it dropped to the market square, its twelve-foot wings spread out, the crowd scattered in every direction. It landed, taloned feet crashing in the dirt just before their wagon.

The dragon tucked its wings against its sides and let loose a roar.

The horses startled, one rearing up, both trying to escape. Rupas pulled back on the reins. The horses snorted, pawing the air.

"Easy now!" cried Rupas. "It's only a dragon."

Corlan jumped off the wagon. Tam was in back, had the iron bolt out of the quiver, trying to stuff it into the tube of the dragonslinger but within the confines of the wagon it was difficult. Corlan pulled out the slinger with his free hand, eased it onto the ground, leaning it against the rear of the wagon.

"Can't do with only one hand," he said, setting down his sword.

The dragon noticed them not fleeing with the others but in full dinner display.

The raspy rumble from its throat caught Corlan's attention. A dry cough, a deep bellow — more noise than danger — and then the whiff of sulfur.

"This one's going to fire!" Corlan cried out. "Get back! Run to the walls!

"Give me that halberd," shouted Naka Wu, pointing to the bag as she stood tall on the back of the wagon.

Tam reached for it but she grabbed the long-bladed weapon from his grasp before he could hand it to her — and leaped from the wagon with her arms raised over her head, the halberd cocked behind her. Sailing over the ground, she arrived at the dragon, its four-foot thick neck extended in its fury and ready to blow fire. As her feet hit the ground, she brought the halberd down hard with all the strength of her arms, shoulders, and back, straight across the dragon's neck.

The strike cut deep into the neck — at the instant fire burst from its throat. The halberd opened a wide gap, exposing the inner throat tissue and more fire shot out through the cut than out its mouth.

"Impressive!" Corlan called.

Everyone in the square was aghast at the sight: the fire burned the opening in the throat, charring the dragon's flesh. The beast shrieked, a ragged, paltry cry, as it jerked its knobby head into the air, wings fluttering wildly, knocking down market stalls left and right.

Naka Wu swung the halberd again, finishing the cut, detaching the dragon's head fully from its thick neck. The head plopped in the market square, its toothy maw open and tongue aflame. Fire burned around the open end of the severed neck. The body slumped against the dirt.

She paused to admire her work, then turned and caught Corlan's welcoming grin. He pointed up.

The two other dragons circled, glaring at the first on the ground. At the sight of the dragon's still body, they descended quickly and rushed to take their first bites. One went for the neck, the other for the tail. The flathead dragon had rolled over on its side as it died and the other two dragons went for the belly next. The dining was noisy and messy, strings of flesh tossed randomly into the air, dark green blood splattering. Dragon blood stained everything, including any people who dared stay, hiding among the kiosks. They tried to flee but the narrow lanes could not accommodate the wild throng. Many learned for the first time how caustic dragon blood could be.

28

Flight

WHEN CORLAN HEARD A BIRD singing nearby, he thought that Madi had returned, yet when he slowly opened his eyes and saw Tam speaking to Bai Lo under the tree, holding hands, he simply smiled and knew he could return to sleep. All was well.

Later, when someone kicked his foot, sending a lightning bolt of pain up his leg and spine and into his head, he almost jumped up with his hand on the hilt of his sideblade.

"Time to eat."

Corlan focused and saw it was a tall woman with a long, black braid, dressed in black leather and wearing a sword on her hip.

"Who are you?" he asked, more as a joke.

"Naka Wu." She frowned. "You know who I am. I saved your life. The least you could do is give me respect worthy of your life."

Corlan pulled himself up to a sitting position. "Then I do thank you, Lady Wu."

"I'm a woman, but not a lady."

Corlan nodded. "That would have been my guess, but I gave you the doubt of my benefit."

She turned and marched away.

Dinner was something that looked like a deer yet having long horns rather than antlers. Jemma had shot it with the bow and arrow from the supplies on the wagon—to the cheering of Rupas. Tam and Rupas had cleaned the kill, then threw it on the spit they made and let it grill until the meat was dripping with flavor.

Naka Wu squatted, took the first portion, cutting a small chunk away with her dagger. Warriors eat first, she reminded all of them by her act. She did not even glance over her shoulder at Corlan to see what his reaction was.

"Go on," he said. "I'm not hungry. My head is still exploding."

"You need to eat," said Rupas. "Food will help wash out all the toxin in your body."

"So this warrior lieutenant is in charge now?" he asked, his hand on his head.

The woman stepped over to Corlan sitting on the bedroll. "If you want to be in charge, you may challenge me for that position. I do not think you are ready for that."

Corlan grunted. "Nothing truer has ever been said."

"Come now," said the tall woman, reaching a hand down to him.

He clasped her hand and allowed her to help him up to a wobbly standing position. Corlan stared straight into the chin of the woman. He raised his eyes to meet hers. She grinned.

Suddenly, he put his other hand to his head.

"Still full of clouds?" asked Rupas from beside the campfire.

Corlan dared not nod his head but the grimace let Rupas know the answer. "Storm clouds. With thunder...lightning...."

"It was seventeen days you were under her spell," said Rupas. "It will be seventeen days more to undo it. That's another thirteen days remaining. You better start following the protocol for recovery. Eat."

The woman took his arm and led him over to the campfire where the meat hung over the spit, flames still tickling the flesh.

"There are flowers I picked," said Tam, throwing a hand toward the wagon. "You can eat them. Chef taught me about plants you can eat. That's the reason for making a garden by the kitchen."

Bai Lo got up and fetched the flowers, brought them to Corlan.

He stumbled, dropping into a cross-legged sitting position, holding his head.

"Thanks," he said, wincing.

Bai Lo gave him the bowl of flowers. "You can eat these."

"Can I have meat instead?"

The woman squatted and sliced off some meat, then extended the dagger to him, a juicy cut dangling from the tip. He reached over and plucked it off the blade and plopped the morsel into his mouth.

"Thanks," he mumbled, chewing.

"We must work together now," she said. "Like a clan. Everyone to do a part, sharing." She shot a glance at Rupas across the spit from her. "We could call ourselves the Wu clan."

Rupas laughed. "Corlan might object to that. He started this clan—if that's what we should call it: a clan. He is a Tang by birth. It should be the Tang clan."

"That's right," Corlan muttered, chewing.

"Now I am in charge, you say. I wish to call us the Wu clan. There is a beautiful sound to the words."

"Why are you even riding with us?" asked Corlan in a sour voice. "What of your rebellion?"

"Fa Mei led the rebellion. She rules in Covin now," said Naka Wu. "I did my part, as you saw. I will return and be part of her reign. She has promised me a high command. With my sisters, we initiated the first step. Now I am bound by my code to escort the ambassador home." She regarded Jemma, sitting beside Rupas. "However long that may be."

"Another detour from our original journey," Corlan muttered.

"So many detours," Rupas mumbled. "It's a wonder we are not all dead. We'd better avoid cities from now on."

"The Wu clan is not afraid of cities," said Naka Wu boldly.

"The Tang clan is smart enough to avoid unnecessary dangers," Corlan countered.

"You two should work together," said Rupas. "It doesn't concern us what we call ourselves. Let it be the Tang-Wu clan and we will all be satisfied."

"Let us be the Wu-Tang clan," said Naka Wu. "And we will not be afraid of any city yet we shall not be so bold as to enter any city without caution."

"Danapo is a safe city," Jemma cut in.

"Fair enough," said Corlan, tightening his jaw.

"Then it's done: we are the Wu-Tang clan," said Rupas, clapping his hands. "Compromise!"

"Does that mean Corlan and Lady Wu are married?" asked Tam.

The boy's own young lady leaned against him, her head on his shoulder.

"That would be so good," said Bai Lo.

"Looks as though we have three couples in our clan," said Rupas with a chuckle. He gazed at Jemma, sitting beside him, and she blushed. "Even a hunched-back man can enjoy companionship with a pretty woman. Better if she can bring the dinner back from the woods, too."

Jemma raised her arm and rested it around Rupas's shoulders. "It does seem that way, doesn't it? One happy clan marching on the road to Danapo."

Corlan startled. "Danapo?"

"Yes, my home. I'm the ambassador. Don't you know?"

"Corlan is still lame in the head," said Rupas. "His faculties will return to him gradually. Until then, he has forgotten what happened for us to escape the city of Covin."

"He must remember the dragons," said Jemma. "They were there in the market, right above us."

"And Naka Wu cut off the dragon's head!" Tam cheered. "Just as it let go the fire! Fire came out the side of its neck! You shoulda seen it!"

Corlan chuckled, half at remembering and half being delighted at Tam's enthusiasm. "I recall grabbing the dragonslinger but she went ahead and used a halberd. Resourceful, indeed."

"You wouldn't have been quick enough," said Naka Wu. "I had to act. You do not need to thank me. I was saving myself, as well."

"Then the other dragons landed," said Tam, "and they started dining on the first dragon."

"I'm sorry," said Jemma, turning to Rupas. "About the dragons."

"Too late for apologies," said Rupas. "I somehow knew a dragon would arrive but I never imagined three. Your powers of persuasion are great, Jemma."

"I told you I had a pet when I was a little girl." Jemma regarded Corlan. "My mother has two drakes even now. I tried not to think of dragons." She looked around the circle. "My mother taught me a few spells. To call a dragon, you only need speak the words: *Draconus en Tafu—*"

"Not now!" Rupas exclaimed. "No dragons tonight."

"Apologies." She blushed again. "I can teach them to you."

"Better you teach them to Corlan."

Corlan chuckled. "I'm no magus. It should be you who summons dragons whenever we need a diversion. If they come to me, I'll have to take my axe to them."

Rupas turned to his lovely companion. "Such a pure face." He ran a finger along Jemma's cheek yet she did not slap his hand away. "And rosy cheeks. A delightfully small nose and wonderfully plump lips. A flat back, too. What a bonus! You are a treasure!"

"You make me blush even more," said Jemma.

Naka Wu stood. "The romancing has begun. I must go and make my evening vows, then take sleep." She stalked into the darkness of the woods.

"She's a stern woman," Corlan grumbled. "So there's one couple that's not a couple." He laughed but stopped immediately because it hurt his head. "At least Tam has a lady now."

The boy did not hear the remark, focused as he was on gazing into the eyes of his young lady.

When Corlan finished his last bite of venison and what remained was prepared for taking on the road, he wiped his mouth with his sleeve and stood, still feeling his head in a cloud. He knew it would pass after a moment and it did.

He stumbled back to his bedroll and was about to collapse on it for the night when he saw Naka Wu in the distance, kneeling under the trees. He decided to go talk to her.

She noticed him standing behind her but did not rise.

"Do you plan to join me in prayer?"

"You're praying?" he asked, surprised. "To a goddess?"

"To all the goddesses. That is the reason it takes some time."

"I'm sorry to disturb you. It's been a while so I was concerned."

"You needn't concern yourself. I am well trained in all military skills. You would be dead at my feet in the moment past if I had not wished to be disturbed by you."

Corlan repressed a chuckle. "I'm certain of that."

"I understand you are the leader of your little band of...males. I am tasked with returning Jemma to Danapo. Then I shall return to Covin, my city, to continue serving Fa Mei. It is not fated that you and I should have any more to do with each other than travel to Danapo. We shall go each our own way at Danapo."

"I understand."

"There is no need to speak to me except in dire circumstances."

"You mean if dragons attack."

"That is a good example, yes."

He knelt beside Naka Wu, his knees comfortable in the soft patch of grass under the cover of the trees and the gathering of the first autumn leaves. He bowed his head, more from being tired than for praying.

"I want to thank you for what you did to get me away from the city," said Corlan. "I'm still not sure what happened."

"It was simple," said Naka Wu. "As soon as the first dragon was slain and the others began to dine, we turned the wagon out the gate. The guards there only waved at us. Who would stop us for anything large or small after we had saved the city from the dragons?"

"I remember the captain saluting as we went under the arch and out the gate." Corlan smiled. "They might have stopped us for running from the palace, but at the moment the dragons were a more serious problem."

"They definitely were."

"And killing...the queen."

"It was appropriate."

"So you say."

Naka Wu glanced at Corlan but she could not see his face in the darkness.

"And I might've been under a spell," Corlan continued, "or else drunk on some elixir—"

"You were."

"—but I still wish you and your sisters had not been so quick to kill Hiro Ka. I—"

"You loved her." She looked forward again.

"I was going to say that I...." He took a breath. "Yes, I thought I loved her, was in love with her, wanted to be with her. I know now it was the elixir affecting me that way. And I enjoyed being with her, too, like any man who needs a woman. And no matter if I was part of some mystical protocol she was obsessed w—"

"That was all part of the spell, too, the drugging."

He sighed. "So none of it was real?"

She regarded him. "Who can say what is real, what is not, when you are in the throes of an elixir?"

He ran his fingers through his hair, breathing deeply. "Even so, I...we...she and I made a babe. That's what she said. And I.... It was true?"

"The boy tells me you have four children already, with four other women. One more child should not change you. The elixir still runs through your body. Go and rest."

He exhaled sharply. "You don't know me, madam, or what I have lived through. You don't know the reasons for what I've done."

"Each of us has done things for reasons both good and not good. I don't ask you what yours were. I only see what you do now. Forget

Hiro Ka. She was an evil person who tricked you. She deserved to die. The child was part of her mistakes, part of her cruelty. She would have killed you in a day or two. She was finished with you."

He rubbed his chin, scratching his whiskers, remembering how Hiro Ka had shaved his face so gently, how close the razor had been to his throat. He could not move, numb from the elixir.

"And the child, if male, would also have been killed?"

"So state the laws of Covin."

"So...only half a chance of my child living...."

"The boy said he thinks of you as his father, having none of his own. I cannot understand why he would think of you that way."

"We've been together on this trek for three months."

"Yet it's clear he is not of your body."

"True. Yet a boy needs a man to show him how to be a man. A woman can't do it. I don't believe in fate but maybe that's the reason he was made to accompany me. He told you the whole story?"

"I think he told the main events."

"What could I do? I couldn't leave him and I couldn't send him back. So I brought him with me. He's a good boy." He glanced back toward the camp. "Becoming a good man."

"Yet you worry about the babe you wanted to birth with Hiro Ka. Strange how the male mind works. Ignore those already born for the one not yet born. The wym you are finished using becomes a statue while the new wym is everything you wished for. And her child, as well, is the treasure you seek."

He thought over her words a moment. "I suppose it is as you say. If you have lived only with women, what you call *wyma*, how could you know so much and be so wise?"

"I lived with men in my youth. It was not a good time in my life. I fought with boys, then fought with men. It was better I left home and sought my fortune. I found it with Fa Mei in Covin. She is my goddess, as much of a goddess as any mortal wym can be. She took the name Fa Mei, which means 'tough' and 'beautiful' in old Covinese, although her birth name was Fanny Metzenbaum, or something like that, I once heard. Short names are popular these days. She impressed me. Her plans for the city made me want to follow her. I became one of her lieutenants."

"And Hiro Ka? Did she shorten her name, too?"

"Her birth name was Hillary Kavanaugh. A cursed name. A man's name. Given by a man. Symbol of ownership. So she made her own name from it, the only good thing she ever did."

Corlan watched her thinking dark thoughts.

"You said your mother...was killed by...?"

"The warriors of Covin came to my village. They wanted to bring the females to Covin, enslave the men. My mother resisted, fought back, demanding the men and boys be set free. So...."

"Terrible. That was Hiro Ka?"

"Not herself. A field marshal sent by Hiro Ka." She spit hard into the fallen leaves. "Tai Ro was her name. Like Fa Mei, she shortened her name from Talia Romanowski, trying to hide her evil. You need not fear her. She's dead now. She came from the ruins of Inati, across the valley from Covin."

"Yes, I've heard of Inati. The famous siege long ago, in ancient days. The War of the Five Princes."

"Princes!" She spit. "In ancient times it was the larger city. Then came the Great Fire. Or so I've heard. You, as well? After, the people who remained thought it better to build on the south shore. The river was no more. Only a dry valley. Then rain filled the valley and made a lake. Most of Inati sleeps under the lake now, all dead. Only water-ghosts that come up to the surface at night. Sometimes we can hear them wail for justice." Her breathing quickened. "If only Tai Ro had drowned there as a child."

Corlan glanced sideways at her. He knew there would be no tears on this woman's face, and yet he heard something.

"You?" he asked after a tense moment of silence.

"Me...?"

"You killed Tai Ro."

"Yes. Someone had to. Some wanted to cut her into four parts and be done. I thought she deserved more. We dug a pit and threw her into it with three hungry drakes. It did not take long."

Corlan shook his head, mumbled a curse.

"You do not approve."

"I didn't know her, this Tai Ro, so I'll take your description of it. A cruel person got what was due. I understand hatred. And revenge, justice. I've fought for all those."

"Warriors understand."

Corlan sighed, surprising himself. "It's difficult to compare such killings. Such deaths are like...like the twinkling of stars. From here it is something easily missed, a blink of light. Yet close, the star is a burning ball of fire, full of destruction. So say the scrolls. What is a death from afar compared to a death under your own hand?"

"You are either a poor scientist or a stubborn soldier," said Naka Wu with a slight tone of amusement. "I know you only as a statue we carried away, not as a man."

"I used to be a soldier. I fought in several battles in the northeast realm. I led armies, one after another, selling my services to princes who dared not face an enemy themselves."

"The weak ones...."

"I ceased that occupation when I was ordered to cut down an army of children. They were all that prince could send into battle. It was not worth the coin. I refused and I was punished for it."

"Then you became a slayer of dragons."

"You catch me quick. Yes, killing a dumb beast suited me better than killing soldiers, and widows, children, or any other of those standing before me. I'm not the immoral fool who would take an assassination for coin, either. Not me. I grin and I walk on."

"What I did was not for pay. It was for—"

"For vengeance."

"Only part. The rest was for the goddesses. They demanded the world be set right again."

"That's what soldiers do, isn't it? Set the world right whenever it tilts too far in one direction or another?"

"Yes." Naka Wu seemed to smile. "We are somewhat alike then. I have not killed a dragon before the day we fled the city."

"Now that you've killed a dragon, you're more like...a female me. The woman Corlan Tang."

"Stop your teasing. It is more that you are the male Naka Wu," she said in a serious voice. "Besides, I am from the Wu family and we do not keep time or space with Tangs."

"Do you know any Tang in your village?"

"None. Certainly not any with that red hair you have."

"It's the family curse. To have dark eyes yet red hair. Yet you are pure. Black hair and dark eyes. Perfect."

Naka Wu looked away. "Do not attempt flattery, Corlan Tang. You and I are not fated to be together, as I told you, no matter the shape of our eyes. No matter the color of our hair. No matter how we shorten our names."

"Tang is not a shortened name. It's always been the name of my family. Most have black hair but my mother had red and so do I. It's an old name, the name of kings, in fact. Is yours shortened?"

"Naka Wu is my name, now and before."

"Your mother did not shorten it?"

"I am not certain. Too much time has passed. I remember hearing her say a name, Nancy Kay Woolsey, or similar words. Does it have any meaning? I do not know the meaning of those words. Nothing was ever written. Mother spoke it a few times yet I was called Naka Wu when they took me away."

She lowered her eyes a moment as if waiting for the memory to pass, then returned her gaze to Corlan.

"Took you away?" he asked after the long pause.

"Each of us has a duty to something greater than ourselves. That is what's important. This is not the time to forget that."

It was Corlan's turn to lower his eyes. "I meant nothing."

"I forgive your words tonight."

"Thanks." He grinned. In the darkness, she likely did not notice. "How about tomorrow? Still forgiven?"

"Let us see how sharp my sword is tomorrow. Then you'll know my answer."

He liked her voice, the sweetness of the stab wounds her words cut into him. "Then I will be sure to mind my tongue."

"I wish for your tongue to be minded."

"Then it shall be."

"Good."

"Good, then."

Their eyes locked together in the darkness.

"Tongues are such fickle things," said Naka Wu, looking away. "So easy to cut out. In Covin they cut it out after the second lie."

Jemma's smile was like sunshine on a cold winter's day, according to Rupas. The sight of it warmed him as he sat enraptured by her tale:

"So there I was with nothing to feed them. Father quickly threw a pair of old hares into the yard and I offered them to the drakes. They were quite happy for the snack and fell in love with me at once. I think that was when I first realized I had some power to speak with them, some kind of communication. That's when I became interested in dragonaria. I didn't know then I had the ability to summon them. I know it seems strange. It's not something I wished for. Sometimes, it isn't really a good thing."

"In Covin it was a very good thing," said Rupas.

Jemma laughed. "That was an accident."

"A good accident!"

She dismissed his compliment with a wave of her hand. "It's more difficult to summon a dragon deliberately, by speaking a spell, than by my random thoughts."

"You certainly must keep your random thoughts tight," said Corlan, turning around from the front bench as the wagon rolled along the dirt road. Naka Wu rode one of the two lead horses, lance at the ready.

"Despite that talent, I was invited into political service. I was sent to learn how to be an ambassador. The program took two years and I endured many tests. Then I was granted my scroll and Mother was so proud of me. I only regret Father could not see the ceremony."

"What happened to him?" asked Corlan.

Rupas bid him be silent and not ask embarrassing questions. An argument ensued over what constituted an embarrassing question. The result was a period of conflict that Jemma hated listening to.

"He left Danapo," said Jemma just to stop the arguing. "He went to a men-folk town. Have you heard of Teraut? That's the town. To the west of Danapo. At the head of the Abaz River."

"I have heard of none of these places," said Corlan. "West of the Burg is nothing. Barren desert. The Valley of Death. I never imagined there would be cities and fertile land existing this far to the west. I thought the realm came to an end somewhere along the valley."

"Now you know there is more to a realm than your short view," said Jemma. "There is much that is good here and in Danapo. As an ambassador, I am privileged to see much of it. I also talk with people of different places. Sometimes I meet a queen."

She stopped for a moment, gazing at Rupas as though seeking his permission to continue. He grimaced instead.

"I'm sorry, Corlan. I know it must be difficult for you now when you think of that woman."

"It's no matter now," he said just over a muttering. "I know I did not love her. Not truly."

"It was pure chance I crossed paths with her," said Jemma. "I didn't plan to meet her. I visited with the Council of Elder Ladies in the Golden Room of the public keep. It was a dull meeting, all about numbers and quotas, and vegetables and grain deals. It's part of my duties, of course. But I was happy to see the talking come to an end and I could go outside and enjoy the sun."

"It is warmer than expected here in the south," said Corlan. "The winter days of my childhood have melted away in my memory."

"The northeast realm is known for its winters," said Rupas, as if he were reciting an ancient poem. "No more the snow-covered hills. Only brown grass and fallow fields here."

Jemma sighed. "Hiro Ka called to me, there in the courtyard, surrounded by her guards. I went to her. She invited me to speak as we walked. Such a lovely fern grove there. Very peaceful. I could relax there. If not for speaking with her, I would have liked to sit for a time. Then...."

The pause allowed the clopping of the horses to get the attention of the people on the wagon.

"Then all hell broke loose!" Corlan exclaimed; the horses startled.

The others concurred. They discussed how the events could have gone differently. They felt fate had been on their side. After a while they fell silent, realizing that Corlan was uncomfortable.

"Apologies, sir," said Rupas. "We forget how you were involved. The good and the bad."

"I said it doesn't matter now." Corlan sounded sad.

"You've gotten your maxa back, I see." Jemma tried to laugh. "No matter what happens in the night, a new dawn will arrive. Are you pleased to return to your man shell?"

"I am what I am," said Corlan, trying to smile.

His face turned sullen as he thought of the meaning behind her words, about *maxa* and what he had lost for several days. He thought about what it meant to be back to his usual self, his manly ways of dealing with the world. He had always been in charge, of himself and often of others. He had always made decisions for himself and others and he was usually correct in what he decided. He never cared much for receiving thanks or any kind of praise for being the man in charge; he had to do what had to be done. Like killing dragons—

Man shell! The shell and my body are one. I don't put on some mask as you women do.

The others were chatting happily about nothing of importance to him as he gave each of them a look. The pretty buxom blond Jemma, looking so like his Petula but having such a different head so full of words. Rupas, the man with the hunched back acting like a straight and tall man, winning the woman's affection with his words. And the children—youths, to be proper, both having twelve years perhaps—in the blossom of innocent first love. He envied them. And that cold warrior woman—always standing off to the side like she was too proud to sit with them, saying her prayers and watching over them. Suddenly, he worried she might try to kill him as he slept. She knew how to kill, he had seen clearly.

But there is good and evil in all things, he let himself muse, raising his hand slyly, as if to scratch the start of a new moustache, to hide his smirk.

People...good and evil.... And dragons....

Even if there were a few good dragons in the skies, he could not tell the difference; some innocents were always slaughtered to put down the evil ones. That was the thinking his general had had when he ordered Corlan to go into battle against an army of children.

Then came this Hiro Ka who seduced him and took away all that was Corlan—except certain parts of his body. He was still sore and aching in ways he never could have imagined. He might forgive her for all that injury in time, yet now there would never be that time. Ended by this warrior woman, Naka Wu, taking vengeance on her queen. Not without good reason, he accepted. If someone had done to his family what they had done to hers, he could never have held back his rage.

Still, it felt odd to be a man in a woman's world, in Covin, a world where he did not matter, where he could not be in charge of even himself, much less others. Helpless and vulnerable. Used and abused. He wondered if that was how a woman felt being in a man's world. Ordered about, expected to conform to some set of rules or the city's unwritten customs. He wondered if it was better to be the jailor or the one stuck inside a gilded cage. His homely cousin, Vorinna, lived in a gilded cage, kept there by her brother, Vilmer, perhaps to save her from the embarrassment of people's words. He would never wish to be either jailor or jailed, no matter how grand the cell.

He needed to get on the road again as fast as he could, a different road than this one. The road to the dragon nesting ground would lead him back to who he was, who he had always been. That road would restore him and at the end would redeem him. He was as certain of that as if one of the gods came down and spoke to him directly. He would earn all the praise he was due and the world would be grateful to him, maybe sing his name in a minstrel's song or write it on some scroll that youth would be required to memorize and recite. After his mighty deeds were done, he could finally take off his *man shell* and just be...himself.

Jemma was talking when he put his thoughts away: "And she seemed such a lovely lady."

"Never trust a well-made woman," said Rupas. An elbow hit his ribs, a warning from Jemma. "It's a saying. Only that. I'm repeating a saying. Doesn't mean I believe it."

"Like your warrior friend, Lady Wu," said Corlan. "Tough, sure. Skilled, perhaps. Yet beautiful. *And* beautiful, I mean."

"If you wish to keep your tongue, you will cease speaking of me," Naka Wu spoke out from her saddle on the lead horse of the quartet pulling the wagon.

"She warns you," Rupas laughed.

"He compliments you," Jemma called to her.

"Look!" said Tam, half-standing in the back of the wagon. Bai Lo also rose, her hand on his belt. He grabbed her hand, held it.

Ahead was a statue rising into the sky. It was easy to confuse it for a mountain, being so huge and the stone face gray. The figure of a person in long robes was neither clearly female nor male. It appeared to sit on the top of the mountain, holding a scroll with one hand in its lap while the other hand curled upward as if to scratch its head. One finger pointed skyward, the others curled into the palm. The face was blank, thoughtless, eyes like stars, mouth a flat line above a rounded chin. Stone hair carved on the head was long and straight, falling down over the shoulders and down one sleeve.

"What is it?" asked Tam.

"That is Sei Bo, the great goddess," Jemma announced. "We are almost to Danapo. Seven days has not been such trouble as I thought it would be."

"Who or what is Sei Bo?" asked Rupas.

"The great goddess. One of the goddesses. All wyma worship her. She is...the mother goddess who silences the male newborns. That is what I was taught. Wyma pray to her for strong daughters and stillborn sons."

Rupas let out a nervous chuckle. "And you Danapoi carved her image into a mountaintop?"

"The mountain was already there. It is said it sprang up during a single year. It is a firetop. It rises one-quarter of the way to heaven.

Maybe not truly so, yet it's how we think of it."

"More from the scrolls," Corlan grumbled.

"After the fire river ran dry, people took it as a sign that Sei Bo was watching over us. The people of Danapo constructed the image by carving the bare rock at the top of the mountain. The people of Danapo made it into a statue. It took a hundred years to finish carving it. Now she truly can see everything of the world from her seat on the mountaintop."

"How did they know she appears that way?" asked Rupas, in awe of the huge figure dominating the landscape ahead. "Seems to be someone who never had a good day in her entire life." He winked at Jemma. "Never made joy with a lover, either."

"Do not speak that way of our goddess." She frowned at Rupas. "She is formless. All of white: face, hair, clothing. She has no female features—and certainly no male features—because she represents all humanity. Yet because of the cruelty of men in ages past she turned her protection only to wyma."

"What a grim appearance," Corlan grumbled.

"She is not concerned with attracting men," chided Jemma. "She has much more important tasks, taking care of the world."

They rode onward a while as the statue stared down at them, waiting for them to arrive.

"Will she rumble at the sight of men?" asked Corlan.

"It's possible," said Jemma with a grin. "Unless you act humble."

Corlan blinked. "I have learned humility."

"He has," said Rupas. "He truly has."

"We should stop there and say our prayers." Jemma lay her hand upon Rupas's shoulder. "Remember: Sei Bo sees all, knows all, and punishes all."

Rupas tried to smile. "Then please say good words for me."

"And me," said Corlan.

INTERLUDE

The Sky Wardens

THE FOREST WAS QUITE DIFFERENT than the trees on Sannan Island, the princess remarked. Her homeland was warm and the trees had tall trunks with long fronds sprouting from their tops. On the high slopes of the mountains the trees were furry, full of green stickers that blocked the sunshine. When she grabbed at them, they cut her fingers and a drop of blood would leak out.

Rula waved her fingers frantically, an apparent warning for the princess not to touch the needles.

"You must be careful not to cut your skin. That way dirt can enter your body," said Jabuli. "And dirt will make you ill. Then you must rest on a mat for some time and hope the goddesses heal you."

"Unless you know an old woman who knows healing arts," said Adora with a laugh.

"Yes," Jabuli replied. "Like Mema."

Coming out of the forest, they soon reached the snow line. The woolens they got at Mema's lodge served them well in the colder elevation. A good tarp and bags of food to carry, plus the baby boy riding in his sling, were a burden. They stopped often once they were out of Olan and on the road east. They did not actually walk the road but parallel to it, keeping to the narrow hunter trails.

By day they hid in the forest. At dusk they took to the trail and by dawn they made camp and slept as well as they could.

Rula waved her hands again and the others turned to see what had gotten her attention.

A dragon cut the sky in the west, approaching the slope they were climbing. Adora had not studied dragonaria much and could not yet identify each species. She thought the one winging toward them was a green-horn. She recognized the nose horn that seemed to glow in an emerald hue. Green stripes stretched down its swarthy body and out to the end of its spike-laden tail.

The beast was impressive and she remarked on it.

"Let's get under the trees," Jabuli suggested. She gave the dragon a second look, remembering the princess's dream. "Hurry!"

They moved under the forest cover. The baby boy pointed up at the sky, as though wanting to warn them. Or wanting to play with the dragon. The princess crouched beside one of the larger trees, took the chance to hold her brother.

"Now you are not to call down dragons," Adora said to the babe, "even if you want a pet to play with, understand?"

The babe babbled back at her.

Rula knelt beside Adora and her brother, and both watched for the beast through the overhanging branches.

"It does not see us," said Jabuli. "From now we will see more dragons. They must rise here to pass over the mountains. On the other side they have the whole world as their play yard. Deserts and more mountains. The sheet of red rock laid out a thousand years ago. Nothing grows there. No humans there, either."

Rula added some hand signals.

"True," said Jabuli. "There are legends of humans living on the other side of the world, but we can never go there. It is much too far and the trek overland would be too long and harsh." She chuckled. "The way to go there, to go that far, would be to fly on a dragon."

"Yet a dragon would never let a person ride," said Adora. "The dragon would eat the person first."

"That is likely true," said Jabuli.

Rula got out the food packs and divided the meal among them, then offered her breast to the babe. He got excited at the sight of it, his fat hands waving, and gurgled happily as he took hold of her nipple like a favorite toy.

"He won't get much more milk," Jabuli said. "He sucks hard, but it has been a few weeks since Rula lost her babe. Her breasts are not ripe any longer. And mine have no milk. We need to find a farm and beg for milk. There are farms below." She pointed down the long slope at a few scattered huts dotting the green hillside. "I guess they have goats."

"We like goat milk, don't we, Puki?" said the princess, making a funny face at her brother.

When her supply was spent, Rula wiped her cheek, sniffling, and handed the babe to Adora. She held him on her shoulder, waiting for the air to come out. Then came the noise, like the grunt of a dragon.

"Where do dragons come from?" asked Adora so innocently, as though she expected the answer to be a tropical paradise full of happy children and endless fruit juice and warm milk.

Jabuli yawned. "Isn't it written on the parches?"

"I only read a little," said Adora.

Rula gave a terrified look, bending her fingers in crazy positions.

"She says there is a place on the mountain where dragons gather. She says that's their home. A mother dragon lays her eggs and they hatch and the young dragons fly out into the world and cause terror." Jabuli grinned. "I'm not sure I agree, but that's what Rula says. She's from Yozma so it may be true there."

"What did you learn from your tutor?" asked Adora.

"I did not have a tutor, not like me and you. I was taught how to fight by a woman called Guro. She had to teach me. We were slaves, so we had to do what we were commanded to do. She had to get me ready to fight. We never talked about dragons."

"But dragons like to fight. I think." She looked up as though she hoped to see one. "They always go around snapping at everyone. The little dragons in Sannan are mean. They can run fast but not fly. You know some have little wings on their shoulders. It must be quite sad to have wings but they are too small for flying. So they run on short legs and cause all kinds of trouble."

"That's better than having large dragons that can fly. Better than the large ones that can breath fire."

Adora laughed. "I couldn't imagine that!"

"You have read the parches. Or many of them. What do they say about where dragons come from?"

"I only read they live in mountains. They fly all the way down from the mountains when they are hungry. They eat every kind of animal. And people." She frowned. "But where did they come from? At the beginning, I mean."

"I think dragons have always been with us." Jabuli bit her lips, blinked at her pupil. "As long as I can remember they have flown overhead and attacked villages and eaten people. It's a terrible scourge sent by the goddesses, some say. To punish people."

"Wouldn't it be more fair if the goddesses never let them into the world at all?" Adora frowned, then shook her head. "Sometimes goddesses don't think very clearly! They might need tutors."

Rula made a rude noise with her mouth, fingers flickering wildly at the princess. Jabuli intervened. Nobody could say those words to the little princess. Jabuli's instincts kicked in but she caught herself and stood down, dropping her hand to her side.

"I know you lost your babe," said Jabuli to Rula, adding some finger talk, "lost him to the slavemaster's knife. I know you prayed every day to spare him and the goddesses did nothing. We can never know the plan the goddesses have for us. Yet there's no reason to get angry at this girl. She is a princess — *was* a princess."

Jabuli glared at Rula: sister or not, there was no need for such cursing at a little girl. She hugged Adora.

"The goddesses may be listening to us," she whispered into Adora's ear. "It may be best not to speak ill of them. That's what Rula was saying. She's had a difficult time."

"I'm sorry, Rula," said Adora, looking around Jabuli's shoulder. "I did not intend any cross words to you or to any goddess."

Rula bowed her head. Lifting her face, she wiped tears from her eyes. She spoke with her fingers to Jabuli.

"I am sure there are good reasons to have dragons in the world," said Jabuli, turning to Adora. "As you said, the little ones keep bugs away, and the larger ones can pull wagons. I hear in some places people eat dragons."

More fingering from Rula.

"She says in her village they often eat dragon meat. It's about the only meat they can have there, so high in the mountains. Dragons have chased away the birds."

"There are birds in Sannan."

"Yes, there are." Jabuli clapped her hands. "Enough rest."

They had wasted enough time discussing dragons, she decided, and yet she kept thinking about the princess's dream and could not keep from gazing around to be sure the sky was clear.

The trail turned steeper and they broke from the forest onto bare ground, rocks and scraggly shrubs. They had to go up slowly, step by step, and grab hold of the rocks to steady themselves. Passing the bags one by one, they each climbed up alone. The last was Jabuli, carrying the babe in the shoulder sling. She slipped on a rock and dropped on her knee. She let out a cry, but got up and tried again. Finally, she had to take the babe off her shoulders and hand him up to Rula, then continue up herself.

The winds were blowing hard by then, no forest to protect them. A looming storm darkened the sky in the west, moving quickly toward them. Jabuli looked around for shelter.

Suddenly, the dark clouds were lit with fire. It was not lightning they saw but orange puffs of flame igniting then fading, one after another within the dark storm clouds.

"I think dragons are coming," said Jabuli, repeating Rula's finger signs. "Never saw any come through storm clouds like that. Usually the storm is the only time we don't need to worry about dragons."

The orange bursts grew more intense, overlapping, and finally the beasts broke from the dark clouds into the clear sky ahead of the storm front. Seven of them, lighting their way through the clouds, flying in a V-formation.

"That's not normal," said Jabuli.

She scrambled up the embankment, loose rocks slipping under her sandaled feet. She stared hard at the dragons.

"Run!" shouted Jabuli. "Leave the babe. I'll get him!"

Adora and Rula hurried over the bare ridge, skipping around the rocks, then turned down the side of the mountain, seeing the grassy slope that seemed to roll gently down to the bottom where it met green pasturage.

Jabuli picked up the babe and pulled him close, hung the sling over her shoulder, pulled the strap tight, tucking him into the crux of her elbow, pinned against her armpit.

The downward slope of the mountain was steep and they half-ran, half-slid down it until it leveled out. By then the grass became a thick lawn. No fences marked the farmsteads but bearded animals with horns mingled about, some of them staring at the newcomers.

"See? Goats! I knew it!" cried Adora.

Jabuli caught up with them, glancing back at the upper reaches of the mountains. As she focused on the horizon, the line of dragons appeared again, filling the sky. Seven black beasts with blue stripes down their throats and red eyes piercing through her. She ducked out of instinct but she knew there was no place to hide.

"Get down!" she shouted to the others who were lower on the slope. The babe whimpered against her chest, threatening to bawl, as she tried to pull the sword loose from the scabbard on her back. "Easy now, Puki. Let me do the work."

She swung the long sword into her hands, letting the babe jiggle against her chest, as the formation of dragons descended.

"You!" cried the rider from the leading dragon, hovering in the air before her.

All the dragons had riders, uniformed men with helmets, sitting on saddles, guiding the beasts. They must be on a search for the princess—and the woman who stole her.

Jabuli held the sword steady, even as the babe cried.

The lead dragon dropped to the grass, touching down so lightly it did not shake the earth. The others circled the farmstead and two of them also settled on the ground while the others remained aloft.

"Run as fast as you can!" she shouted to Adora and Rula, and they did, racing for a small broken-down house at the bottom of the sloping pasture.

The man on the lead dragon climbed down, stepping along the beast's leg and jumping off onto the grass. He wore a dull orange uniform, a single garment with blue stripes down the legs and across the shoulders. His blue helmet had a dragon symbol on the front which marked him as a sky warden, the group of law officials who flew dragons. They had aided the Olan militia when the Anjoz army marched up the peninsula. They were halted by the dragon squadron. Jabuli had just arrived in Olan then to start her training.

"Stop there!" he commanded.

Jabuli was surrounded: two dragons landed on each side of her, one in front. And she with only a sword—protecting a crying babe hanging against her chest.

There was never a good plan, she realized, only the hope that the goddesses would favor them, guide them, and allow them to find freedom over the mountains. But that was not a plan; it was only a dream. How foolish she had been! Now she would pay a hard price for her boldness, for daring to listen to the musings of a child. Even a princess is not without error.

She lowered her sword, allowing its tip to touch the dirt at her feet. Her free arm cradled the babe. She spoke soothing words to him and he calmed.

"You look out of place on this mountain," called the man who had climbed down from the dragon. "Off to a mountain resort?"

"I'm a free woman, paid off long ago," Jabuli sneered. "I can go as I like, where I like."

"Here? The mountains? What seek you here?"

"A fresh breeze. If that is any of your concern."

He stepped toward her, aware of her sword.

"I'm Captain Martool of the Sky Wardens," he announced coolly. "We search for someone. Are you perhaps her? Or someone who knows where this person may be? Tell me your name and history."

She was nervous, worried for the babe.

"I have only me and my son here. I'm a free woman," she called to him as he stomped over the grass towards her. He paused to wipe goat droppings from his shiny boots. "I didn't know the dragons were yours. I was preparing to defend myself against wild dragons."

"Understandable," said Martool, standing stiffly before her, hands on his hips, examining her. "Your name?"

"Jamma," she spoke as confidently as she could.

"Your son's name?"

"Puki."

"Puki! What an odd name."

"It's an old Yozma name."

"You're from Yozma? You don't look like you're from Yozma. Too dark your skin. Not the Yozma hair, either."

"The babe's father is from Yozma. I'm from Rament. A long time ago. Times are difficult in Rament so we left. Yes, we are heading to Yozma. Before the winter comes on."

"That's a long walk over rough terrain." Martool looked around the farmstead, turning on his heel. "I saw others with you. Where did you send them?"

"Others...?"

"Don't lay tricks for me, woman. You have no rights or privileges here and can be punished in any way I choose. My fellow wardens can do anything here, as well. It's open territory."

"My daughter and a servant, that's all. I told you, we thought the dragons were wild. I told them to run because...who doesn't run when dragons are overhead? I certainly would."

"So we agree. The dragons scared you. The others ran. Perhaps to that old house down there. That's the only place to go among all this pasturage."

He signaled to the other wardens, then gestured for her to walk ahead. They would be going to that house.

The small building, little more than a hut, looked like it had no one living in it, and hadn't for some time. Boards were loose, the walls weathered, the roof in tatters. But it was the only building.

"Come out," she called. "It's Jamma, your mother. Everything is well. The Sky Warden is here. He wants to talk with you. Come out,

Avo, my dear daughter, and you, too, Ria, my helpmate. There is no danger now. The dragons are under control."

Instead of coming out the front door of the old house, there was silence. The Sky Warden knocked on the door. They waited but there was no sound within nor anyone exiting. He knocked on the door again—harder.

"Now you tease me," Martool growled. He put his boot to the door and kicked it in. "Let us see the truth!"

The wood splintered and fell to each side, the door breaking apart, revealing the dark interior—

A white robed figure stood in the center of the room, so white the figure seemed to light the room. Jabuli thought it was a woman. If the figure had a beard she could have called him a wizard or mage but this one had no beard or mustache. Her white hair went straight to the floor. She held out one arm, level and straight—defiantly—as if to halt the captain's invasion of her home.

In the open palm of her outstretched hand sat a large white stone as big as a person's head. The stone had the shape of an egg, small end at the top. Thin, watery blue veins streaked through its smooth, milky surface.

"What's this?" Martool cried, falling back in surprise.

Jabuli also stepped back, not expecting such a figure to confront them. But in the shadows behind the woman, she saw Rula cowering in the back corner, holding Adora in her arms.

"Who are you? Tell me. I'm a Sky Warden, Captain Martool. As you should know, we have the right of law to burn down your house if you do not cooperate."

The strange woman stepped forward—slid smoothly over the wooden floor without appearing to take a step. She kept her arm extended, her hand supporting the stone, unwavering.

The captain had to step back.

"Halt," said Martool. Another step back for him. He reached for his sideblade. Far behind, his dragon cried out, reminding anyone who dared threaten its rider that a dragon was close by, ready to aid its master.

"Are you all right?" Jabuli called into the dark house, ignoring the advancing steps of the white robed woman.

"Stop, I say!"

Martool continued backing away as the woman stepped forward, no expression on her face nor shift of her eyes or twist of her lips. She seemed like a statue, as much stone as the stone egg she carried in her one extended hand. Her other arm remained at her side. She halted when she stood about ten paces from the door.

"Good," said Martool with a victorious grin. "Now answer my questions." He took a breath. "First, your name. Then, your history. How is it you've come to live out here?"

He gazed at the egg-shaped stone, such a curious thing. Her arm had not tired of holding it up and, indeed, she had never flinched. The captain frowned, exasperated by the display.

"What is that thing you're holding?"

The white-robed woman brought up her other hand, laid it over the top of the egg so it was held between her hands.

Martool was irritated. "Answer my questions!"

In one swift motion, she twisted her arms, reversing her hands so the egg was flipped upside-down without ever leaving her hands.

Behind Martool, his dragon exploded. The beast became a cloud of fleshy shreds and splinters of bone that filled the air like pollen from a flower and rained down on the pasture.

Seeing the act, the other two grounded dragons jumped into the air, winging hard to escape. The woman adjusted her aim, flipped the stone upside-down again and another dragon exploded into a million pieces and its rider with it. The third dragon winged harder, trying to launch from the ground and gain lift quickly but the power of the stone again caused a dragon to explode. The dragons that had not landed were already hurrying away.

"What is that thing?" asked Martool from where he had fallen to his knees. His trousers were soiled from dirt and goat droppings as he tried to stand. As he had fallen, his knee bent awkwardly and he grabbed it, feeling pain, as he struggled to his feet.

His pale face showed the shock of seeing his mount explode into a cloud of pollen. He had no ride home, though that was now the least of his problems as he stared into the glowing white eyes of the white-robed woman holding the white stone egg.

"Please...please don't...."

Then she did.

He did not explode into a million bits like the dragons had. If he had, there would have been quite a mess to clean up, his body being so close to them.

Jabuli was not sure, but the Sky Warden seemed to have suffered a small explosion within his chest. Blood ran from his mouth, eyes, ears, and nostrils. He collapsed instantly on top of himself, dropping at his feet, onto his feet, like a wet towel slipping off a bather's body, crumpling on the floor. It was as though everything within his skin had been turned to liquid.

Jabuli bowed her head, then went to a knee in respect.

"Thank you for saving us."

Adora ran out of the house and hugged Jabuli and her brother. The babe still dangled from her shoulders, snug in the sling, Jabuli's arm protecting him. He fussed at his constriction. Rula came beside them, placed her hand on Jabuli's shoulder. She rose and stood with them in front of the strange white woman. The three of them, with the babe, hugged each other.

"How can we repay you?" asked Jabuli as they broke from their embrace.

For a moment the woman only stared ahead at the spot where the dragons had landed. It was the spot where two of them had sprayed the pasture with flakes of their bodies. Goats were feasting on the morsels, baying in delight.

She blinked and seemed to come to life, as though she previously had been under a trance she might have adopted to be able to use the stone egg's power.

"I have awaited you for some time," spoke the woman just above a whisper. She glanced out at the pasture. "Them, not so much."

29

A Band of Bandits

AS THEY MADE THEIR WAY toward the mountain topped by the great visage of the goddess Sei Bo, Rupas pursed his lips.

"Is it...dangerous?"

"Dangerous? You mean because Danapo is a wyma city?"

Jemma glanced ahead at Naka Wu, riding the lead horse.

"Not for you, dear Rupas."

"Why do you say not for me?"

"Because you're deformed. I don't mean it as an insult, dear. It's only a fact, isn't it? The wyma in Danapo would take pity on you. Because of your hunched back."

He cleared his throat loudly. "It's not a true hunchback. There is no hump. My spine is bent wrong. That is all."

"We would still not harm you. That is not our custom. Going back to the age of ancient princes, we have always welcomed visitors without any judgment. Urix was that way. You know the War of the Five Princes? Urix sided with Darus against the others, then he killed himself when the war turned bad for Darus. Urix was the prince of Danapo in those days. Perhaps that was when the custom of giving sympathy began."

Rupas glared at her a moment, then looked away. "I respect your customs and will abide by them, Jemma, if I were allowed to stay in Danapo."

"Do you truly wish to become a citizen of Danapo?" Her tone suggested skepticism about his success there, but her smile remained pleasant.

"I would be pleased to serve you," Rupas replied, "if you would have need of a gardener or...my true profession, accountant. I am also qualified as a scriber, if you should need someone to keep your confidences or compose your documents."

"But you are a man. How could you keep my confidence? I may need a scriber while in my private chambers. I often dictate forms and letters from my bathing basin. How would you be able to sit beside the basin and write what I speak?"

"I would turn away, of course. I would never gaze upon your form unless you wished it. Unless you wished me to look."

"Give it up," Corlan said with a snort.

Jemma repressed a laugh, hand over her mouth. "I am grateful you joined with Naka Wu to overthrow an evil queen, Rupas, but it was only by happenstance you crossed paths with Naka Wu and her sisters at the right moment. Didn't you say 'the enemy of my enemy is my friend'? Is that from a scroll? It fits that situation. I'm thankful Naka Wu accepted you into the plot."

"Actually, it was I who designed the plot," said Rupas, beaming.

"It was my plot!" Tam cried out.

Rupas grimaced. "True. He suggested how to get into the room. He would dress as a girl, the perfect disguise. Brave boy."

"I didn't like that!" grunted Tam.

Bai Lo stretched up and kissed his cheek. "I did."

"It all came together." Rupas took a quick breath. "So you see how resourceful I can be? We deformed folk must be clever. I would make an excellent advisor."

"Perhaps you would," said Jemma. "But you're still only a man."

Rupas sulked for the next few miles as the four horses labored to pull the wagon and its passengers up the side of the mountain. The road wound half way around the mountain, the high slope on their right, lower slope to the left. Naka Wu shifted to the right horse to help maintain the stability of the team, climbing from one to the other without touching the ground. Corlan watched her stretch across the horses, the leather of her trousers pulling taut.

As they turned around the mountain, a wooded grove covered the road. Shadows of the trees darkened the way forward.

Suddenly, two men jumped down from the trees, directly into the road. One held a sword ready to fight, the other with a halberd held in both hands.

"Halt!" shouted the swordsman.

It was not a man but a woman, Corlan heard. He jerked back on the reins to keep from running over the two people.

"Move away!" shouted Corlan.

The wagon rolled to a stop as Naka Wu climbed off the lead horse, unsheathed her blade.

Two more *persons* appeared from the shadows at each side of the wagon. Then two more moved out from the shadows of the trees and stood behind the wagon.

Jemma, Rupas, and the young ones, Tam and Bai Lo, sat up in alarm. Tam grabbed a knife and Rupas took hold of a sword. Jemma grabbed a lance. They took defensive positions along the three sides of the wagon. Corlan guarded the front.

"We will take your cargo," said the swordswoman in front of the wagon. More women bandits appeared, six in all. "You can get off now and walk back the way you came. All this is ours now. The wagon, whatever it carries, and your horses. Drop your weapons and you may leave with the clothes you are wearing."

Jemma rose up on her knees in the back of the wagon. "Stand aside, you vagabonds! This is an official transport."

"Is it? Then all the more good it does us."

"I am Jemma of Danapo, the Danapoi ambassador. These are my companions and guards."

"I see men among your group," said the halberd bearer. "How can you be an ambassador of Danapo and carry men folk with you? Who do you truly serve?"

"Because we are civilized in Danapo. We do not kill men on sight as in some places. They make useful servants and they fight tirelessly to protect us." She gestured at Corlan. "Like this one. He saved me from an attack in the city I have just visited. He is escorting me back to Danapo. Now stand aside and let us pass."

"Or what?"

"Or my escort will kill you."

The swordswoman laughed. "I am Wan Do, the high queen of this mountain. Nobody passes without paying!" She laughed more, glancing at the other bandits until they joined in.

"So you're nothing but a troll," said Jemma with authority.

Wan Do immediately frowned. "That hurts me."

"You should try a different line of work," Jemma suggested.

"We used to be musicians roving the countryside, playing at town fairs and weddings. Now people make their own music and none will hire us. So we put away our flutes and lyres, drums and trumpets, and have an easy life taking wares from travelers."

"What a sad tale of woe," said Jemma.

"Not so sad," said Wan Do. "We do well marking this road."

"I'm sorry to say your sad tale does not move my tears."

"Then we will need to strike harder at your tears."

"Let us pass and none will come to harm."

"There will be harm," said Wan Do.

"You should try again making some music in the city. Everyone likes songs. It's a better use of your lives than this...this foul rogue work, threatening to kill—"

"There is nothing foul about rogue kill." Wan Do taunted her. "It pays a fair wage."

"Don't be rogue kill," grunted the halberd woman. "Surrender."

"You have warned them enough," said Naka Wu.

"Let us pass," said Jemma one last time.

"Get them!" shouted one of the bandits at the rear of the wagon.

Naka Wu strode forward, in front of the horses. She held the blade level at her waist, two hands gripping the hilt. In one swift motion she took two steps forward and impaled Wan Do with her blade, center of mass, straight into the gut.

The woman holding the halberd next to Wan Do swung at Naka Wu but she easily stepped aside and the halberd hit the ground. A hard kick from Naka Wu separated the halberd bearer from the halberd. Withdrawing the blade from Wan Do's belly, Naka Wu swung the sword at the halberd woman, cleanly removing a forearm. The arm dropped to the ground and the woman bent over to grab it from the dirt while holding her gushing upper-arm against her body and screaming her pain.

As Naka Wu dispatched the two in front, three bandits struck at the rear of the wagon with their swords. Jemma thrust her lance into one of them, withdrew the lance and struck at another. The lance was longer than their swords so it was easy to hold them off. One bandit leaped onto the back of the wagon but Rupas swung his sword at her, the blade catching her collar. They heard the bone snap and the bandit fell off the wagon, shrieking.

Bai Lo clung to Tam, who held out his short knife but met with no attacker. When the attack ended, she kissed Tam's cheek and called him brave.

Corlan remained seated on the bench at the front of the wagon, reins in his hand, sideblade still in its scabbard. Gazing around at the carnage, he nodded, satisfied.

"Now we pass!" cried Jemma with a wave of her lance.

The only bandit unwounded stepped aside with a low bow as Corlan snapped the reins and the wagon rolled forward.

Naka Wu leaped onto the lead horse as it came beside her, not breaking the team's stride.

"I apologize for their poor manners," said Jemma, sitting down in the wagon again. "We are much better people in Danapo than that demonstration would indicate. After I return, I shall inform Lady Tarris, the governor, of our encounter with these vagabonds. She will send a platoon to clear the road of bandits. Danapo is not really a dangerous place." She smiled at Rupas. "Not even for men."

Rupas frowned. "With you and your warrior escort, I feel quite safe. Yes, indeed!" He turned to Corlan, studying his back. Muscles rippled under the tight shirt. His back was straight. "And our poor hero, Corlan, he had nothing to do. Oh, yes, he is still recovering from his ordeal, lost in the queen's bedroom, let us not forget. Poor fellow! Someday he will draw his blade again. I'm sure of it. When the right partner crosses his path. Then he shall stand *en garde* once more."

Corlan complained, insisting he was no longer interested in that sort of behavior. Rupas disagreed, challenging him. The argument escalated until both men were tired of talking and fell silent. Soon the only sound beside the creak of the wagon and the clopping of the horses' hooves was the romantic snickering of Tam and Bai Lo.

With the mountaintop figure of Sei Bo fading behind them, Rupas sat up, turned to Tam. The boy was snuggling with Bai Lo as though they had been lovers for years. Rupas smiled at the sight.

"On the subject of killing...," he spoke ominously.

Tam regarded Rupas. "What?"

"You must not hesitate." Rupas sighed. "When we are children we are taught to be kind, to act with politeness, and always to be gentle. That is not the way of the warrior."

"I know!" snapped Tam. "I was going to stab the bandit but...."

Corlan looked back over his shoulder. "He means you hesitated. You must not be afraid to use that knife if someone is attacking you. You have a lady to protect."

"I was ready to do that."

"Ready and doing it are different things," said Rupas.

"We are far from home—if even the Burg could be considered a safe place—and so we are set with danger at every turn," Corlan said. "You see how we do not cry or feel sad at the deaths of those who mean to hurt us, maybe kill us? There are two kinds of people in the world: those who wish to make trouble, and those who wish to stop or prevent trouble."

"I'm not sad for them," said Tam. "I'm a stopper."

"I'm not happy either," said Corlan. "At the right moment, Naka Wu acted. One moment sooner or one moment later and one of us could have been killed. It's the same with dragons. A dragon will not pause to decide whether or not you are a nice person. Neither should you pause to decide if you are a nice person who shouldn't act with violence to save yourself. You act or you are a victim. This is the law out here."

Tam pouted, looked away from Bai Lo. She put her hand on his shoulder.

"Don't be upset, Tam," said the girl. "I love that you were ready to defend me."

Tam returned his gaze to her. "I will always be ready to protect you. You are my lady. Aren't you? Corlan said so."

"Oh, yes! Yes, Tam!" She threw her arms around him.

"There's the beauty of young love," said Rupas, adding a sigh. "I have always missed it. Never had that experience in my youth. Too much running from the bully boys who wished to beat my back until I begged for mercy. So I never had a love meeting."

"Never?" asked Jemma. She shifted herself closer beside him in the back of the wagon.

"Look at me. I've got a bent back. I cannot stand tall. I'm not strong like a warrior. Who would want to experience young love with a hunched-back man like me? Or a hunched-back boy."

Jemma patted his back, then withdrew her hand. "Sorry."

"Your hand did not hurt me," said Rupas.

Her laugh was delightful to his ears. "Shall I touch your back and help you feel comfort?"

He nodded sheepishly. "Please."

As the sun reached its zenith, corralled by a herd of white clouds, Tam jumped up, his finger pointed forward.

"There it is! There's the city!"

Rupas raised his hand to shield his eyes. "Yes, it must be."

"It is!" Jemma burst into song, at first quick and lively then slow and stately. Her voice was pure and delicate, like a bird's. "We always sing the city anthem when we approach at the end of a long journey. Do you like it?"

"Oh, yes," said Tam. "It's a wonderful song."

Bai Lo tried to sing but missed the notes so Jemma practiced with her. They attempted to sing the song as the wagon rolled heavily across the plain toward the high, brown walls ahead. Ten towers rose and parapets marked the walls at regular intervals. Blue flags waved.

"It looks like a happy place," said Tam.

"A fabulous sight!" said Bai Lo. "I never believed I would ever travel so far. I never believed I would find a good boy to take me there. I thought I would stay in the palace forever."

"Looks from a distance can be deceiving," warned Rupas.

"But it's a city!" Tam shouted. "There will be kitchens there."

Rupas turned to Corlan. "The boy wants to share a fine meal with his young lady."

The men chuckled.

"Seventeen days! Seventeen days!" cried Corlan. "I'm tired of that number. Seventeen days in bed, seventeen days of recovery. Now seventeen days to go to Danapo. And there will be seventeen days to return to Covin."

"I will not require you to accompany me back to Covin," Naka Wu said, turning on her horse and gazing back at them. "I'm capable of riding alone. All I require is a fresh horse. Without a wagon to pull, I could make the trip in six days."

"Of course we will give you a fresh horse," said Jemma, "and our sincere thanks, as well, for escorting us safely back to Danapo. Please rest a few days before you set out. Enjoy the hospitality of Danapo."

Naka Wu nodded. "A day, then."

Danapo seemed larger than Covin though its buildings appeared built in a more ornate, older style, like those in the Burg, fashioned of hard gray stone hewn from quarries and timber-slat houses with thatched roofs.

Passage through the main gate was simple. Jemma of Danapo

handed over her red-ribboned diplomatic scroll. She signed an entry form and they were waved through. They did not need to place their weaponry into any locked container. As an official of the city, Jemma promised that her guests would not cause any trouble. She swore to monitor them.

The guard captain, a tall, thin woman with short brown hair, gave Naka Wu a warm, lingering gaze and the warrior returned a hard glare before the wagon rolled away.

"There's a love match," muttered Rupas to Corlan.

Jemma bid them be polite as they noticed a sorry sight.

"Sympathy to you," said Jemma with a low bow of her head to the old woman standing on one leg. The woman, poised beside the wagon as Jemma's group were examined by the guards, used a simple crutch made from a curved tree branch. When Jemma straightened, she called to the woman: "May the goddess ignore your calamity."

"You are kind, sister," said the old woman. "Yet the goddess always ignores my calamity, good or not so good." She shifted the gnarled walking stick to her other hand and tilted a moment before regaining her balance. "It is past for me, yet I still say 'May the goddess protect you from pouncing men-folk.'"

"Thank you," replied Jemma.

The men exchanged quizzical looks.

Several injured people stood or sat around the city's main gate, as if they hoped to garner sympathy, and perhaps some coin, from visitors who arrived.

Rupas watched them, curious about their unfortunate lives. He did not see any with hunched backs but many were missing a limb or two, standing on one leg or sitting on a cart or just a board with four small wheels because they had no legs. Others had one arm, and two had no arms—although one of those had fashioned a kind of pronged device from a dinner fork to act as fingers. Eye patches covered one or both eyes. Ears were missing. One person had her mouth sewn shut while another opened her mouth to prove to anyone who would give their sympathy to her that her tongue was indeed missing. And the line of the infirm went on.

"Why so many injured people?" Rupas asked Jemma as Corlan drove the wagon team slowly through the market square.

"Injured?" She seemed surprised—or offended. "No, no, they are ordinary citizens. They gather in these places to seek sympathy."

"I saw how you offered that woman sympathy. What happened to her to cause her to lose her leg?"

"I don't know her, so I cannot say." Jemma pursed her lips. "Perhaps she cut it off. That took a lot of courage."

"Cut it off? Herself? Why would she do that?"

"A lot of people do."

"But...why?"

"To get sympathy." She shook her head, realizing Rupas had no understanding of the customs. "Here in Danapo, we pride ourselves on being sympathetic, offering kindness and love to those who need it. Most who need it have some kind of deformity."

"Like me. With my bent back."

"Yes, like you." She offered him a smile. "I told you already that you would not be harmed in Danapo. Quite the opposite. You will be given sympathy for your deformity."

"So people here are deformed...just to get sympathy?"

She shook her head again, expelled a long sigh.

"Rupas, dear, here in Danapo long ago, soldiers returning from the wars against men-folk had many injuries. Naturally, we cared for them and treated them with respect. We gave them sympathy and kindness. There were so many wounded people that they became a class of citizenry. Little by little, having an injury became popular. Deformity from birth became more worthy of sympathy. When a mother birthed a deformed child, she garnered a great amount of sympathy. In fact, some mothers might create a deformity early on so everyone would recognize the child had a deformity and forever gain people's sympathy."

"That's mad," said Corlan.

Rupas waved him back. "But you have no deformity...."

"Yes, I do." She grinned like she was embarrassed.

"Apologies, but I don't see it," said Rupas.

She batted her eyes. She tilted her chin down to her chest.

Rupas frowned. "But you have all your limbs. And both eyes— lovely green eyes. So what is it you are ashamed of?"

"I'm not ashamed," she laughed. "Yet it is abnormal. You may not think it such an oddity but.... You may have noticed.... Don't you see it? It's right in front of you."

Rupas stared, looking up and down her. "I don't see whatever it is you're *ashamed* of having—or not having. You're very beautiful."

"Don't say that!"

"But it's true. I think you are very beautiful."

"What an unsympathetic thing to say!" she snapped. "Look! It's right in front of you!" She almost burst out laughing.

"What?"

"My chest. It is much too large. Do you see now?"

"Big breasts? That's your deformity?"

"It is a feature which makes people think I'm extra fertile. They have sympathy for me because they believe I will bear many babes one after another. Such a burden! They also believe I am one of those women who plays easy with men-folk even without earning coin."

"That's a deformity?"

"In Danapo, which is a wyma city, it is. We prefer wyma to have a slim figure—like someone who has not eaten for a while. A wym with large chest is considered abnormal—ugly to some. A large chest gathers unwanted attention from men. Such a wym is representative of nature's cruelty, which can gain her much sympathy."

"But you aren't doing anything naughty," Rupas insisted. "What is so awful about a woman being beautiful? Having men want you? That's what women are for, aren't they?"

"*Women*! Stop saying *women*! That's offensive," snorted Jemma. "*Women* comes from *men*: the property of men—and we need not be tied to another person as property like they did in ancient times. We are *wyma*, independent and separate. I am a wym, not a woman."

"That's a pity," Corlan muttered.

"It is," Rupas echoed. "But I'll submit to your lexicon."

"Rupas, I should be pitied because I'm burdened with protecting myself and defending against the aggression of men. Other wyma give me sympathy for that hardship."

"Hardship? More like courtship."

"The goddesses cursed me with large breasts."

"I would think you have been blessed."

"Because you're a man, Rupas. Now do you see how the world is upside-down?"

"In Danapo, perhaps."

Corlan burst out laughing, caught himself and fell silent.

Jemma frowned, tilting her head toward Corlan.

"My mother thought my deformity would harm me as I came to wombhood. She prayed in the temple day after day for me to be thin and sickly. She asked Sei Bo for me to have a ruddy complexion with boils—anything—just so I would not stand out. She did not want me to be raped."

"But you do stand out," said Rupas. "You're beautiful!"

"Don't say that. My mother would fall sick hearing me described that way. It's vanity and thus so rude."

"I'm sorry for that," he muttered.

"There! That is what you should say." She clapped her hands. "Give sympathy to all who have injuries or deformities."

"Then I shall applaud myself." Rupas let out a sigh, now that he had gotten the words right. "I certainly fit in here." He grinned, more a twisted smirk that Jemma did not see as irony. "Now I wonder if someone with the curse of beauty and a large chest could ever have sympathy for someone who has a bent back."

"Oh, in Danapo, anything is possible!"

"Then I must learn to like living among the infirm and destitute."

"Not everyone in Danapo is infirm or destitute." She repressed a chuckle, as though she'd thought the remark was a joke. "There are plenty of rude people here, too. They offer no sympathy to anyone." Jemma took his arm, held him close. "There may be a chance for you to work here. I will ask for you. We always need more people to earn some coin. Because so many citizens have an injury or deformity and cannot work, it takes more and more people to do the work that they cannot do."

"That's madness," said Corlan.

"Not madness," Jemma countered. "It's kindness. Sure, there are a few citizens who injure themselves with no thought to sympathy but only to avoid work. Those are the rude people. We still must be kind to them. We are happy to work and earn coin for those who truly need our help."

"So all you uninjured people must work because others refuse to work?" Corlan pondered aloud. "They injure themselves just to keep from working? And you still take care of them? That is madness."

"Some people are care-givers and some are care-needers," Jemma responded. She turned to Rupas. "After you gain some work, you may find someone who will give you all the sympathy you deserve."

Rupas met her gaze. "I think I already have."

"So soon? Have you someone here with which you've touched through correspondence?"

He frowned, shook his head. "Oh, no. Not that. I know none here save you, Jemma." His eyes lingered on her deformity. "If you will be sympathetic for a moment, I'm going to try to be bold now. Please forgive me if it should seem rude." He took a deep breath. "Jemma, ambassador of Danapo, would you give me the sympathy I need?"

"Me?" Suddenly she lost her smile. "Are you asking me to...to care for you?"

His eyes brightened. "Is that how you say it here?"

"Yes." She leaned over and kissed his bewhiskered cheek. Rupas blushed. "Instead of asking to join in a marriage union, we join in care of each other's deformities and pledge to nurse each other."

"And will you?"

She lowered her gaze. "I must have you meet Mother."

"Of course. That would be the protocol."

"No more protocols," Corlan grunted from the front bench. "I ban the word from the world."

Rupas dismissed him with a wave of his hand. "I would like to meet her." He smiled sincerely. "Is she...deformed?"

"Oh, no. She is a care-giver, not one in need of sympathy. We—my family—we are the other type of citizen. We care for others."

"That would suit me fine, as well."

"Dear Rupas, you already have a deformity. So I will care for you. You do not need to care for anyone. There are people who need help and people who do the helping. Some need and some care. That is how life is in Danapo. It makes a good balance." She gave him a long look, assessing his features. "It might be a good match: a hunched-back man and a busty woman. I will consult with Mother."

Jemma directed Corlan to drive the wagon through the streets of Danapo, past many a broken hovel and onward to a dark red brick structure of four levels. Through the arched gate with two female guards and past a flower garden, was a large canvas-roofed gazebo where a small gray woman rose and stood on one foot, reaching for a cane. She hobbled up the walk toward the gate, a smile in one hand and the stick of wood in the other.

"Jemma, my poor busty daughter, I've saved so much sympathy for you while you've been away!"

30

The Definition of Deformity

"MOTHER, I WOULD LIKE to introduce my new friend, Rupas of Unting, a scriber by trade."

The old woman struggled to stand on her one foot. "I've worried about you, so long away, though I gained some sympathy."

"You don't know what happened in Covin!" Jemma hugged her mother. "Let's go indoors. I'll tell you all about it. It was terrible — and I needed help from these people to return to Danapo."

They turned up the walk.

"How is your foot?" asked Jemma. "Still no better?"

"The pain comes and goes," said the woman. "Mostly stays."

"You have all my sympathy."

"You are a dear. So many have lost a foot that it doesn't seem very special any longer. I don't get much sympathy these days. So I've thought of losing this useless hand —"

Corlan spun around at a growling noise and saw two dark green drakes charging into the yard. He drew his sideblade automatically.

"No!" cried Jemma. "They're friendly."

"Yet dangerous," he shouted.

"They're my pets."

Corlan lowered his sword as the drakes approached Jemma.

"Here are my drakey-poos!" she called to them.

The drakes scrambled across the withered lawn as she knelt on the yellow grass to welcome them. The crests of their humped backs were chest-high on Jemma when she stood. The drake with the twin bands of orange stripes on its long black face was slightly larger than the other. It snuggled its mucus-dripping nose against her bosom, making happy grumbling sounds. The other drake, sporting a teal crescent moon-shaped spot on its brow, held back a bit. It had a larger nose horn than the orange-striped drake. When she released the first drake, the second pet lumbered in for its hug.

"This is Lulu," said Jemma, stroking the head of the drake with the orange stripes, "and this is Moon," referring to the one with the crescent moon. "They are the draglings of the pets I had when I was a little girl." She paused, staring at Lulu. "Ah! Looks like Lulu is going to have babies, too."

"How do you know?" asked Corlan. He sheathed his sideblade. "One looks as fat as the other."

"Not by looking," she said with a laugh. "I sense it in her mind. Moon has been enjoying the playtime, I think." She winked at Rupas.

"They remember you," said Rupas.

"Of course, they do."

"How old are they?"

"Drakes can live forty or fifty years. I didn't see my first drakes hatch, but I got them shortly after. We grew up together. We had to send them away when they got too large, at about ten years of age. And I was away on official business when Lulu hatched but I got to watch Moon break out of his shell."

"How old are these?" asked Corlan.

"Lulu is six years and Moon is four. Drakes are mature at three."

Jemma's mother reported on the mischief the drakes had gotten into during her absence: running through the garden plot, breaking a brick wall on the side of the house, eating the neighbor's lizard and a stray canine. They left a terrible mound of waste that she had to have carried off at some expense.

"They do have minds of their own, don't they?" said Jemma.

"One's large enough to make a dinner for all of us," muttered Corlan and Rupas slapped his arm.

"Jemma has her pets, don't you see?" said Rupas.

She straightened up, kept one hand on the head of Moon as she spoke to her mother: "This is Rupas...." She turned to him. "What is your family name? I can't recall you saying the name." And back to her mother: "He helped get me out of the palace when the rebellion began. And escorted me on this return trip. And you see he has a hunched back."

The mother held out her hand, only the thumb and forefinger remaining on it. He was not sure how to hold her hand so he just held out his own hand. She circled her thumb and forefinger around his thumb and gave his hand a shake.

430

"I'm so pleased to meet you, mother of Jemma. I am called Rupas Derwindel, of Unting, a city in the southeast, beyond Covin. Your daughter has become a wonderful friend to me. She suggested I could stay with her — and you, I suppose. I will look for a job here."

"Yet you need not seek employ," said the mother. "You already have a deformity. For you it is enough to suffer and gain sympathy."

"Mother, he wants to work," Jemma insisted.

"Like a fool, I say," said the mother.

Jemma turned to the others, one drake on each side of her.

"This is my guard, Naka Wu. And the children are Tam and Bai Lo. The man you see is called Corlan. He was the queen's consort for seventeen days. That was the protocol for conception. I told you they do that in Covin, Mother." She frowned. "Yet it didn't end well. He's not dangerous even though he routinely draws his blade. It's part of his training as a dragonslayer."

"A dragonslayer!" cried the mother. "Oh, dear...."

"He's told us that he's killed...how many? Two hundred?"

Corlan smiled. "In my career, more than three hundred."

"Shameful!" cried the mother.

"Where I come from," said Corlan, stepping forward, "dragons are only trouble. We don't keep them as pets, not even drakes. I'm on a quest to find the nesting ground and destroy all the eggs. Then we'll have no more trouble from them."

"What a cruel man, Jemma!" said the mother. "How dare you bring him into our city! He doesn't have any deformity, either, none that I can see. We don't want our neighbors teasing us about having a well-formed man here. We will hear no end to their complaints. I may need to remove an arm to satisfy them."

"Please don't do that, Mother." She gestured at Corlan. "He is a bit deformed in the head."

"Truly? I cannot see it."

"He was under a spell. He was given a poison, so his head is still lame. Sometimes he is not aware what he speaks."

"Ah, a head deformity! That will impress everyone...as long as we can explain it. Otherwise, one look at him and they will call us healthy and whole, too proud to give sympathy to others, too vain to go about our weekly passage without deformity."

"I could limp," said Corlan, "if that would make you feel better."

"Yes," said Jemma. "That is an excellent idea. You must always go with a limp in your step. Can you do that while you visit?"

Corlan grinned. "I wouldn't want your neighbors to have unkind thoughts."

Jemma smiled, then threw her hand toward Tam and Bai Lo.

"And these are—"

"The children," Rupas started, then stopped. "I'm sorry to say the children have no deformities. They are young and innocent."

The mother frowned. "There are shops in the city where a limb may be safely removed. They are licensed and the physician is good, follows all the rules. It will be a clean cut."

"We won't be staying long," said Corlan roughly, grabbing Tam by the arm and pulling him back. The boy was holding Bai Lo's hand and she stumbled at the sudden jerk. "I'll take them with me, so no need to cut off anything."

"So rude!" said the mother to Jemma.

"Well, they are strangers here, visitors, so they are not expected to know our customs."

"I suppose not."

Jemma and her mother turned and proceeded into the house.

"I see what you mean, Jemma. He does speak a lot of words he doesn't understand."

"Now, Mother, we must also be kind to those people who don't have any injury or deformity. After all, they get no sympathy."

Corlan let out a long groan, staring up at the sunset sky, wishing a dragon or two would pass by—something, anything to distract him, to get him back in fighting shape.

Once he had carried supplies in from the wagon to keep them safe from thieves, he pulled out the weapons and returned to the front yard. He took up the long sword and went through a series of exercises his mentor had taught him when he first trained as a soldier. Working up a thick sweat, he pulled off his soaked shirt and continued with the battle axe. The cool autumn breeze felt good. He trained with the halberd next, then tried the medium sword with a dagger in his other hand. In front of him at all times was a squad of soldiers, a fierce dragon, or a line of vagabonds and bandits in need of a lesson. As he cut the air with the blade, he imagined them falling away, one limb at a time, piles of heads, arms, legs—like the living people of the city of Danapo.

Several neighbors had come out to watch. Other people passing by on the street slowed then stopped to become an audience. Corlan gave them no attention, focused on maintaining correct form with each movement. He practiced each swing a hundred times, then a hundred more. A few of his audience clapped their hands in appreciation of his aggressive actions, joining him in his imaginary fight.

Rupas bolted out of the house.

"Corlan! Corlan, you must cease your exercising this minute. It is upsetting Jemma's mother."

Corlan halted, breathing hard, sweat glistening on his skin.

"You're causing a commotion," said Rupas in lowered voice, smiling innocently at the people gathered along the wall around the yard. Rupas waved to assure them that all was well. He leaned in to Corlan. "You know the custom here. There should be no display of normal, healthy, whole bodies. It is considered vain and prideful, which is considered rude."

"I need to get back into fighting shape. There's no other place I can swing weapons freely."

"But look: everyone is watching you."

"I know. I'd rather they didn't but they don't bother me."

"It's causing her mother to feel faint and then we must tend to her needs. Jemma is distraught. So please...please stop showing off. For my sake, at least. I need to get on with them."

Corlan grinned, glad he had caused Rupas to beg.

"Mister," someone called from the wall, "if you wouldn't mind, may I get a closer look at your scars?"

Corlan turned and saw an older man pointing at him. A woman slightly younger than the man smiled at him. Other people nodded in agreement: a closer look would be nice.

So Corlan sauntered over to the wall with the medium sword and dagger, letting his muscles shine. So many *oos* and *ahs* from the people at the wall. One woman reached out to touch his arm. She reported to the others how hard it felt. She licked her fingers, said how salty the sweat from his arm tasted.

"How did you get that scar?" asked one man, pointing to the long mark down his chest and over his belly.

"From a dragon," Corlan replied boldly.

"And your back?"

He twisted his body to show them his back. The more recent scar looked much uglier, he guessed.

"Another dragon." He surveyed the people staring at his back. "I took a claw away from his foot in exchange."

The audience was impressed. Suddenly someone broke through the crowd carrying flowers. The people along the wall each took a flower and tossed it into the yard. Corlan was soon showered with flowers. He didn't know what to do: pick them up or let them lay. It was some kind of ritual, he decided, so he didn't want to be rude.

"You have our sympathies," said the elderly man. "I once had to kill a rat that snuck into the house. It was a terrible experience. Poor me, that's all I have to boast of. And you have fought dragons!"

"Thanks, old man." He thought he sounded polite.

Many people there repeated the old man's words—"You have our sympathies"—and bowed their heads.

Corlan regarded the line of people along the wall. Many hung on the wall with one arm or a hand missing and the other gripping the bricks. Others had an eye sewn shut or an ear lopped off. One woman apparently had no nose and a square cloth had been sewn to her skin to hang over the opening. When he had gazed downward over the wall, he noted some of them had no foot or leg, and one lady was missing both legs yet she stood on wooden pegs that nevertheless had artistically carved wooden feet.

"I guess my scars are ugly enough to be interesting."

Rupas was amazed. "So you are now king of deformities!"

"Scars from dragons win the day," Corlan laughed.

"They honor you," said Rupas. "They envy you—for you are the definition of deformity."

"Then they dishonor themselves to think I deserve their envy."

Rupas frowned. "Please don't make things difficult for us while we are here."

Corlan stepped back from the wall, then turned his back to the audience. His muscles felt sore so he deemed his exercise done for the day and put away the weapons. He grabbed his wet shirt and was about to pull it on when a woman at the wall cried out for him to give it to her. With little thought, he flung it through the air. The damp shirt landed on the top of the wall and several people grabbed at it, tearing it into pieces.

He turned to Rupas with a scowl on his face.

"We are on a journey, let me remind you. I'm recovered now, it seems. We should leave this city of cripples as soon as we can and keep heading west. There are eggs to smash."

After a dinner of buckwheat noodles and cabbage, potato soup, and peppers stuffed with cheese, Corlan and Rupas strolled through the streets in search of a tavern. Rupas kept reminding Corlan to walk with a limp but he never did. As they went, the people they passed stared at the two odd figures: two men in a city of mostly women, one with a hunched back, the other tall and straight and without any apparent injury or deformity.

"You know what they're thinking, don't you?" asked Rupas.

"I can imagine."

"They're thinking: 'A man like that shouldn't be so prideful while others are in dire situations.' That's what I see them thinking, just by looking into their faces. They hate you, Corlan. 'He should at least cut off an ear or a finger or two just to show some sympathy to other residents.' They practically shout it the way they look at you."

"I've done my share of hurting. I won't injury myself so they won't feel strange."

"You're confusing the reality of this place with a fantasy of your mind." Rupas coughed. "It's all real to these people."

They pushed through a crowd standing outside a theater where a play was in progress. The doors stood wide open so people outside could watch what was happening inside. Corlan and Rupas saw two people dancing, each with only one leg. It was artful, the way they balanced each other again and again as they twirled. Yet there was a story to the performance, it seemed, and two others joined the first pair on stage, speaking lines in regular rhythm as another person to the side of the stage beat a drum.

As the two dancers came to a halt, two other actors appeared on stage pushing a large slicing device. They set the device on the stage and more lines were spoken. It was all in an ancient dialect Rupas barely understood and Corlan had no guess, but what they saw was clear: someone would lose a leg in that device and, through that dramatic act, would become worthy of sympathy.

Corlan turned away as the noise of the crowd inside rose to a boisterous climax and the clap of the blade resounded loudly. The audience applauded.

"That is no fantasy," Corlan growled. "It is all too real."

Rupas couldn't take his eyes off the players on stage. "Indeed, it is a fantasy to them. A fantasy of epic proportions, in fact."

"If only there were a dragon or two to alight," Corlan grumbled, "and waken them to reality."

"Yes, an epic fantasy...with dragons!"

"We must get out of this city," said Corlan. He grabbed Rupas by the collar, pulled him away from the theater. "This is a sick city. I don't know how they ever got to this state of madness but I won't be a part of it. They may not be as much against men living here as the women in Covin, but you see there is a different kind of evil here. If you stay, be careful you do not find yourself with the same fate as our friend Gorral."

Rupas gave a hollow laugh. "I'm sure they don't eat people here. I would think their innate obsession with deformity would preclude that outcome."

"And yet...."

Rupas placed his hand on Corlan's shoulder to halt him.

A tavern awaited them. The Broken Knee seemed to be exactly in the right place at the right moment. In they went, sidling up to the bar and tossing a couple coins on the counter to order mugs of ale.

The man behind the counter served them with one hand. The other arm had been removed just below the elbow, leaving a curious, miniature appendage bending at random. His face twisted into a scowl. He waited a moment, then held up his half-arm as if to remind them to offer a word of sympathy. But none came.

"You're not from around here, are you?" asked the barkeep. "So what brings you to Danapo? Come for a cheap lopping? They do it well here. I recommend Doctor Slice down on Footless Lane. He's the best. He took my arm off and left a bit of swagger."

Rupas gave the man a quick smile. "Thanks."

Ignoring the barkeep's questions about their origins and business in the city, Corlan and Rupas drank and talked.

"I intend to stay, I want you to know," said Rupas. "I feel a life here would suit me. I don't feel out of place here. In fact, I am better off than many. And there's also the lady. If Jemma wishes me for her aide, then I shall be happy to do so. It's time I do something proper with my life. Yet again. I can't keep running from employ to employ as the winds blow. I must settle down. I only needed to find the best location."

"Does she want you?" asked Corlan with a raise of his eyebrow.

"Yes." Rupas had to ponder a moment. "I have weighed all the signs and measured the quickening palpitations of her blessed heart. I conclude her feelings for me are the same as mine are for her."

"Seventeen days together can do that. I will congratulate you. At least one of us will be happy at the end of the day."

Rupas sighed. "Corlan, you will find happiness someday, too. I'm sure of it. You have that woman in the Burg, true?"

He laughed, tossed down the bottom of the mug.

"People make promises they cannot keep. I freed her from a promise to stay true. And I suppose I freed myself from staying true to her. We both knew how adventure would swiftly overtake us—"

"Overtake *you*! She would likely stay in the Burg doing her daily tasks as usual. In time she would meet another man, and there it is: the end of you. That's not adventure."

Corlan's grin transformed into a scowl.

"I was banished from the Burg. She knew I wouldn't likely ever return. Not the way life tends to turn. I still have my mission. Even though I got distracted going to these cities: Unting, then Covin, now Danapo—three awful places. I only need a resupply, then get out of this place of death and deformity!"

"How about that warrior woman?"

"Naka Wu?" He laughed. "Besides her being taller than me, she is a sexless soldier. I respect her training and her focus on duty. It is the reason also why she and I would never go along."

"You want a feminine partner, eh?"

Corlan frowned. "I don't want another *me*."

"As you continue west you will not likely find more choices. The way will be more like what you described of the Valley of Death: a barren landscape where you alone represent humans. With dragons passing overhead. There will be no love for you out there. So you best refresh yourself here before you go."

"Better I learn the spell of summoning dragons from your lady."

"Jemma is not my lady. Not yet. Perhaps tomorrow."

"So you've a plan to conquer her?"

"You see me. My body is deformed, as she is happy to observe. So I must be clever and woo her with guile. I will talk her onto a bench." He winked. "It will take some time, I know, but I do believe my plan is working...*has been* working all this way from Covin."

"Do not be so quick as poor Gorral thought to be."

"I would never be so bold."

Corlan laughed, then signaled for another mug.

"The queen ruined me," he said, accepting the fresh mug of ale. "Everyone knows that. I am drained. I don't feel love at all anymore. I need time—lots of time—more than seventeen days to recover. And the thought we made a child is...disturbing. I don't know what to think. I understand she was evil, and cruel, and not good to anyone. Except maybe me. She didn't hurt me like she did others, so I cannot blame them for killing her. That I didn't see the terrible things she did doesn't mean she wasn't a savage. Maybe I could have changed all that, if she had let me. Or maybe she'd send me to the kitchen. Who can say?"

He took a long draw of ale, long enough to think about what else needed to be said. He almost choked.

"It's still strange to think about it: that she and I made a babe. I feel an emptiness inside me. Oh, I have other children, maybe grown by now, yet I don't know them and they don't know me. The queen, certainly, was not a good match for me, even if we did see through the birth of a son. I'm too old for all that now. Love for me is just a passing pleasure. It's not for family making. It's not for ruling a land. It's only for a few hours of relief. Like eating or sleeping. Necessary, but you don't want to do it constantly."

"So, then, go talk to her. Perhaps she is interested also in having a few moments of relief."

Corlan scratched his head. "Who are you talking of?"

"Your good friend, Naka Wu."

"Good friend? Hah! She's a frightening figure of a woman."

"And yet, everyone needs a spot of relief now and then."

"You are mad, Rupas! Mad as a two-headed drake. There's your true deformity! And you have my sympathy."

Jemma looked up from her bathing basin, offering a gentle smile.

"You really don't need to watch over me here. I'm quite safe."

"There are hidden dangers everywhere," said Naka Wu sternly. She stood in the corner of the pink-tiled room, lance in hand, sword in a scabbard at her hip, black leather trousers to mid-calf, and laced black vest. "Until I know each corner of this place, you are not safe."

Jemma nodded, just for show. "I understand your need to fulfill a pledge to protect me, but I'm home now. You should go home, too, wherever that is." She swept some warm water up over her chest and rested her head against the end of the basin. "Where is your home, anyway?"

Naka Wu, grim-faced and narrow-eyed, stared at her charge. Was she joking? There is no home for a warrior.

A duty was a duty, no matter who she was guarding. It was more than the code of a warrior; this woman was special. She needed to be protected. She had seen everything that happened in the Queen Suite. She could identify all who participated in the assassination of Hiro Ka. For that reason alone, she needed to be guarded. Perhaps she was pretty by a man's standard of beauty—or a woman's—but she claimed deformity—a strange concept—for being *without* an injury or deformity. The people pitied her, it seemed, because she had no sign of harm upon her body. And she dared claim that her large breasts were her deformity.

Naka Wu stared at them a moment. Her own were no more than what that man, Corlan, had with his muscular body. Not that breasts mattered to a warrior. They got in the way of wielding weapons. Some of her sisters had them removed so they could fight better. She was blessed, if that was the right word, with a smaller frame—and it was no less muscular than an average man. She could easily defeat all men of that class. She could still defeat men of a larger class if she were clever enough to compensate for their greater natural strength.

She wanted to laugh but did not wish to disturb Jemma's bath, a time of relaxation, it seemed. The only bath warriors took was a quick shower to wash off the blood of their enemies. Then back they went, ready to fight again. There was no relief, no time for pointless amusement. What warrior would ever let down her guard for a brief moment of personal...what's the word? pleasure?

"I was born near Covin," she spoke after what felt like an hour. "It was not a happy childhood, yet there was no sympathy as you have here. Eventually I was given to the palace security regiment by my mother, as payment for unpaid taxes. Like many children were. Girls became servants, some boys became tanners or other unclean work, or else they were killed."

"So you never played games?" asked Jemma. She worked up suds and painted her chest with them, as her mother used to do when she was young. "You never had any fun in your childhood? Never fell in love?"

"No, none of those."

"I'm sorry. You definitely have my sympathy."

"Thanks. I know it is your custom to say those words, yet I do not need sympathy. My life is exactly what I want it to be."

"A rebel?"

Their eyes met when Naka Wu looked down.

"A rebel, yes. If that is the role I'm meant to play. I follow my leader, Fa Mei, who knows what is right. Hiro Ka was not the queen needed by Covin. She was weak, a gambler, a whore, a dragon in rabbit pelts, blind to the cruelty she tossed around herself."

Jemma pursed her lips, squeezing the sponge, letting the warm water run off her breasts, sweeping away the lather.

"So you killed her."

Naka Wu stared hard at the woman in the basin. "We have spoken of this many times on our journey here. You only happened to be in the room. You might not know about it if not for that fact. You would have left the city and only heard later what happened. Yet you were there, so we had to protect you."

"I'm not part of your rebellion. In fact, I'm opposed to all forms of killing. It was shocking to see someone so cruelly, brutally, and so boldly murdered."

"It was not murder but assassination."

"There's a difference?"

"Yes. Murder is for hate, for theft, for competition, for envy, for a love triad. Assassination is purely—*purely*—political. She had to be removed."

"Then send her to a prison for some time. Or send her to another land, never to return. Let her go out hunting dragons."

"She had no children, no relations but for her mother. You knew she kept her mother locked in a bottle, didn't you? You knew she had Corlan's companion killed and served as dinner, didn't you? That is cruelty. That is brutality. I told you how she treated my mother."

"I understand how terrible your life has been. So you wanted to get revenge. That is common in story scrolls. In real life, I shudder at the thought of someone deliberately trying to end someone else's life, no matter the reason."

Naka Wu grimaced, the first instance in a year. "Yet you tolerate the deliberate dismemberment of the people of your city. Because it is the fashion to garner sympathy by displaying a deformity."

Jemma shook her head. "No, it's not the same." She looked up. "Can you hand me a towel? I'm finished bathing."

Naka Wu set the lance in the corner and stepped barefoot over to the small table across the room, no dirty boots allowed in the bathing chamber. She carefully slid her hand under the top folded cloth and lifted it off the other towels. When she returned to the basin, Jemma was standing, water running down her body, her blond hair twisted and draining like a waterfall.

"Your towel," said Naka Wu with ironic tone. She extended her two hands to Jemma, the towel resting over them.

"No need to be so formal, Naky. We are all women here. You do not serve me except by your own choice."

"Until I believe you are safe, I will stand guard and watch you."

Jemma giggled. "I think you just want to watch me—watch me bathing."

"A person is most in danger when bathing."

"I don't feel any safer with you here. In fact, Naky, I feel quite a bit more in danger now. Why, I'm naked and wet and you are dressed in that horribly unattractive man-suit, looking so fierce and grim. It scares me. When was the last time you had a good bath? When did you last wear a gown?"

"Never." Naka Wu swallowed hard, staring at Jemma. Her eyes swept down Jemma's body, from her smile to her chest, across her belly, down to her feet with the little toe missing on each foot.

Noticing her gaze, Jemma wiggled her remaining toes.

"It's a small concession. Mother thought I would get sympathy. Something new for the start of my school years. To me, it matters not. Do you think my feet are ugly?"

She pushed the towel across her body, up her arms and down her legs, then tucked it between her legs.

"Feet are feet," said Naka Wu. "They are not ugly nor pretty."

Jemma lifted a foot to dry it with the towel.

"I didn't need those toes. But there's no sympathy if I cover them with shoes. I must wear sandals. I'm waiting for spring."

"Spring will come," Naka Wu intoned.

Jemma grinned, tossing the towel aside. "Until then, let's get you out of those leather things and into a hot bath. Relax for a while. Go off your duty. Let me serve you for a while. I can fetch some wine."

"I should not do that. It is against the code."

Jemma reached for the strings of Naka Wu's vest, began pulling them loose. "Oh, code schmode, Naky."

"I wish you would stop teasing me. You are endangering both of us. I need to stay alert."

"There is no one else in the house tonight. The men went out for drinking. And the children are with my mother, learning anatomy."

"All the more reason to remain guarded."

Jemma let the vest fall open, loose strings dangling. She slipped the vest off Naka Wu's shoulders and the warrior stood bare-chested. Jemma paused to admire the warrior's small chest, then reached for her belt, released the scabbard and let it drop to the floor. She reached next for strings at the front of her trousers, gazing into the warrior's dark eyes to reassure her.

As Jemma worked the strings loose, Naka Wu stood stock still, unblinking.

"Please make this easy for me," said Jemma. "I really want you to relax. Stop being a warrior for an hour. At least an hour."

Naka Wu frowned. "It is not something I consider safe."

Jemma knelt, her breasts almost blocking the view of her hands as she worked the leather trousers down the warrior's legs inch by inch. "So tight," she grumbled. She struggled maneuvering the trousers down. "How can you move so well in these?"

"They move with my skin, so they are one with my body."

"Now we can see how you look in your first skin."

Naka Wu stepped out of the trousers crumpled at her feet as Jemma rose. The two stood chest to chest. A small triangle of gray cloth covering the space between the warrior's legs. Jemma put her hand on the cloth, then immediately withdrew her hand.

"What's that?" asked Jemma, neither angry or pleased.

Naka Wu looked away yet did not move. Jemma decided it was an act of submission so she went ahead and pulled the cloth away.

"You do have a deformity," said Jemma. "I sensed something about you. Of course, it's not anything one would be able to know just by looking at you...in your uniform."

Naka Wu moved her hand to cover her private area.

"It was long ago. It was when I was a child. It made me suitable for training as a warrior. Now it's done and I am a warrior."

Jemma regarded her bath mate. "So are you still...a man?"

31

A Meeting of Minds

KNEELING IN THE BASIN, water covering her body up to her waist, Naka Wu considered Jemma's question and blinked.

"I am a warrior."

"But you don't have...anything there."

"There is an exit for the water. That is all a warrior needs."

"Yes, I can see that, but...how do you get any joy?"

"A warrior needs no joy. That is a distraction from duty."

"I'm sorry." Jemma threw her arms around Naka Wu. "I give you all my sympathy, all I have to give." She kissed Naka Wu's cheeks. "You had no choice. You were too young to know what you would be missing. It's such a pity!"

"I chose the warrior life when I took the oath at age six. Then my training began."

"Even so...." She released Naka Wu from the embrace. "You must take some time to rest, to recover, to relax so you can be ready to fight again."

"I sleep when I need to."

"You need more than sleep." She sat back. "Let's continue."

"Continue? What can be done now? You know my secret."

Jemma took her hand. "Let's wash away that secret. Let it never be remembered. We will leave it in the bathing basin."

"Are you certain this is for the best? How can I protect you?"

"I think I am safest when you are in the basin with me."

Naka Wu thought it over, nodded. She glanced at the scabbard and the lance, noting how far they were from her grasp.

"And don't worry, the water is clean. I poured a lot of soap into the basin. The bottle is nearly empty."

Naka Wu hesitated. "Soap?"

"Yes, soap." She grinned. "Come on, Naky."

The warrior blinked. "Perhaps that is best."

"Then I shall wash you. You want to be fresh and clean when you meet Corlan."

Naka Wu grimaced. "Corlan? Why?"

"Don't you know how much he wants you?"

"How can a man want me? I do nothing to call them."

They sank into the basin together, raising the water. It splashed over the side of the basin, then settled, a few islands of suds floating on the surface.

"He believes you are a woman."

"I am a warrior."

"Yes, yes, I understand, but he sees you *also* as a woman. I can tell when he looks at you. I sense his thoughts."

"It would be deception to continue letting him believe that," said Naka Wu. She glanced down as Jemma's hand swept suds over her chest. "In Danapo, no one gets sympathy if they act with deception. True?"

"Yes, that's true." Jemma grabbed the sponge from the stand at the end of the basin. She swathed the warm water over Naka Wu's slender body, letting the water run down her back, down her front.

"He is a warrior, too," said Jemma. "A soldier long ago, I heard. I suppose he never forgot his skills. Warrior should go with warrior, true? No matter what is under their clothing."

Naka Wu narrowed her eyes. "This is not true." She stood up so quickly that water splashed out of the basin onto the floor. "I cannot be some kind of play partner for a man. Or a woman, either. It is not good. Not because of my body, as you may believe, but because of my duty, my oath."

She stepped out of the basin, tossing water everywhere. Padding across the wet floor tiles, she slid as she grabbed her garments, then her scabbard.

As she turned to leave, Jemma called to her: "You cannot put on those clothes while you're wet. Not leather."

Naka Wu bundled her garments, and the belt with the scabbard and its sword, in her arms. She snatched the lance from the wall, and exited without a glance back.

The obvious topic for an evening's rest was the nature of dragons. Tam was happy to introduce the topic by comparing their too-mild, vegetable-heavy meal to the meal of bitter drake tail they'd had back in Metta. The boy told as much as he knew to Bai Lo, who hung on every word. Corlan answered any question Tam posed or injected corrections. Bai Lo seemed impressed that Tam was training to be a dragonslayer. He smiled. Of course, he was; that was the reason for accompanying Corlan on this long journey.

Naka Wu's straight black hair, undone from its usual braid, lay full upon her shoulders and flowed down her back to her waist. Wearing a simple white gown lent to her by Jemma, she appeared nothing like a warrior. She sat on a low bench near the wall, bare legs crossed at the ankles. She kept a sword resting across her knees as she listened to the others.

She watched Corlan closely, especially how he reacted to Tam's lively speech. They did seem like father and son. She searched her mind for a few minutes, trying to locate any memory or image of the man who became her father. She was not certain her mother knew which man it had been. Probably just an ordinary soldier passing through the battlefields, taking any woman he found.

There was a flash in her mind of a room, her mother in dirty rags standing with an empty bowl. A large man blocked their way out, she recalled. The next moment, the woman was handing her to the man and he gave her a scroll in exchange. Probably the scroll was a receipt for taxes paid. She could not remember what happened after leaving that room. All that remained in her head after so many years were images of training. Always training. When she was sufficiently advanced, she had been given leave to visit her mother.

Corlan was laughing and the noise broke her from the dungeon of memories.

"No, no, boy! That's not right at all. Think it through. If a dragon can make its fire within its body, there in its belly and its throat, then it would burn itself to death. They use the spirit air to float. Look how big they are yet they can fly with wings not large enough to lift a bird half their size. No, they hold the air within their bellies. Yet this air, the spirit air, is also what can be turned into fire. So the beast exhales the air it uses for buoyancy, then spits out an element from the glands in its throat. That's the igniting agent. That ignites the spirit air, its breath. The beast blows out the breath, adds the gland juice, and there is the fire! But it's outside its mouth. You never see dragons *shooting* a stream of fire all the way from out of their bellies. Then, as you've seen plenty of times, the beast exhales that breath, alight with flame, blows its breath at the target. It's a ball of flame. You've seen that. Remember how Joragus jumped in front of me and blocked the flame? If he hadn't done that—if he had no powers of magic that night, then I would not be sitting here in Danapo talking to you about dragons!"

"However," Jemma spoke, firmly holding the hand of Rupas, "drakes do not possess the gland that ignites the belly air. At least it's not fully developed. They can't make fire. That's one reason they are fine pets. They still have a hearty bite so they guard the house."

"Good for drakes," said Corlan, gesturing like he was blowing fire from his own mouth.

"Do you still remember the spells I taught you on the road?" asked Jemma. Her voice suggested she doubted his memory.

"I'm sure not going to recite them for you, if that's what you're going on about." Corlan looked around the circle of friends. "I'm not so stupid as to call down dragons for an after-dinner butchering. I'm not that desperate for a deformity."

"You can summon them for good as well as for evil. It's all in how you speak the spells. The shift of your voice. Speak the vowels higher than normal for good intents. Speak them in rhythm, too."

"I wrote them on a scroll," said Tam. "He can read them out if he forgets the words."

"Corlan doesn't know how to read," Rupas said with a laugh.

"Even I know how to read," said Bai Lo with a giggle.

"I can read what I need to read," Corlan said with a grunt. "If I need a dragon, say, for dinner meat, I'll have the boy read the spell to me and I'll speak the words after him to summon a dragon. Then we dine. I'll have him make a fine sauce, too. And a salad."

They all laughed.

Naka Wu observed the group: comfortable with each other, like a family. And yet she felt the distance between her and them. That was to be expected. Normal for a warrior. For a palace guard. For a rebel. She stood, tired of sitting, and the gown flowed down her body, soft against her skin. The folds waved about her legs. It felt strange to be dressed so. The sandals felt awkward after the boots she was used to wearing. The soles did not support her feet.

"That's enough talk of dragons for one night," said Jemma with a polite nod toward Naka Wu. "Let's talk about your travel plans."

Naka Wu returned the nod, then turned to the gate. She stepped lightly over the grass, wet with night-sweat and tickling her toes. She paused at the stone arch to admire its design, running her hand along the curve. A breeze made her gown quiver against her body and she wondered if she somehow was a different person.

Jemma was correct: they had no need of protection, being here in their yard, at their house, in their city. Corlan was there with a sword on his hip. He could handle any danger that appeared. And the two drakes slept in the yard, close at hand. So Naka Wu could step away and stroll the evening streets alone—a new pleasure.

As she had done each evening on their journey to Danapo, Naka Wu found a grove of trees to settle under for her nightly ritual. It was very different wearing a gown, her bare knees pressed into the cool, moist grass as she raised the hem. She put her hands together, bowed her head, and spoke her words to Sei Bo, the goddess of daughters. Finished, she whispered once more the warrior code she had pledged as a youth, she and her sisters-in-battle. This time she stumbled on the final line, as though she lost her breath and couldn't complete the sentence.

She gazed up through the branches of the trees, nearly devoid of leaves. She focused on the half-moon overhead lighting the night. As she regarded the moon, Corlan's hard words returned to her: 'Now that you've killed a dragon, you are more like a female me. The woman Corlan Tang.' She smiled to herself.

She remembered feeling sorrow at that moment, something like receiving a blade through the belly, the pain slow to register then suddenly exploding through her entire body. His words shook her more than she would have admitted that night. Instead, she had said what was expected: 'You and I are not fated to be together.' She knew it then as she knew it now. The only fate between warriors was when they met in battle—or some other duty while in garrison. 'Each of us has a duty to something greater than ourselves,' she had said to him, certain she believed it.

The thought made her cheek blush. She felt its warmth despite the cool breeze.

"There you are!" It was Corlan, following her down the lane and turning into the grove. He stood a few steps behind her.

She measured the distance instinctively, calculating the angle of the backswing needed to strike down the intruder with the short sword she carried in her left hand.

"Are you well tonight?" he asked, stepping beside her, shoulders bumping. "They sent me after you. Worried, I guess."

"No reason to worry about me. Jemma wanted me to relax, to go off my duty for a while. She does not know how that wounds me, to go off my duty."

"She also got you into a gown. You look lovely. I never could imagine how you would appear in such a feminine garment."

"It is not for your view," said Naka Wu in a stern voice. "I wear this to give my body a chance to breathe after so many days wearing leather. It was Jemma's suggestion."

"I agree. It's a good idea to give a body some air."

"As you did while training. I mean, showing the neighbors all your scars. And your physique. Very brave."

"Being a warrior, we must always stay in fighting condition."

"Yes, fighting condition."

They exchanged tales of training sessions, examples of fights they had participated in, victories taken. Naka Wu grinned at the friendly competition, each story an attempt to outdo the previous. Their voices settled into a lively banter—until the stories ended and the silence of the forest fell over them.

"It is a good life," said Corlan. "Though I prefer dragons now. You know my plans. I've sworn to kill them all. I must go on. So I and the children will leave tomorrow at first light. I don't know about the girl. Tam will watch out for her, I guess. And I'll watch out for him."

"You have all your supplies ready?" she asked hesitantly.

"Most of what we need. We will gather more on our way out of the city, then make camp whenever it gets dark. Now that we're in the late season the sun fades early."

"Yes, it's a mild winter in this clime. In Covin hardly ever is there snow. Here, not even a frosting. I can wear this gown."

"Back in the Burg we always get a few inches of snow in the deep part of the winter."

"Then you must need a fire to keep warm."

"Many of us use dragonfire. We make charcoal bricks from the burnt flesh of dragons. It glows when we set it to flame. Not much warmth, though. It's mostly for the light...as you know."

The talk paused as the moon above considered their words.

"I will ride with you," said Naka Wu to break the silence.

"You don't need to accompany us. We don't need an extra guard. Besides, we will go west, and you need to return to Covin to help your leader—Fa Mei, is it?—with your rebellion."

"I meant I will ride with you leaving the city. Yet only part of the way." She repressed a grin. "The road splits at the mountain of Sei Bo. I will turn southeast and make for Covin. You will need the west road if you wish to keep on your trek. That leads to Teraut."

"I see." Corlan seemed disappointed, she noted. "Anyway, it is a few days more of riding together."

She sensed him gazing at her. In the darkness he would be barely able to make out the features of her face. She stood where the branches would block the moonlight—for her, taking the defensive position and leaving an attacker to be blinded by the moonlight.

Corlan shifted his position.

"I said before we are not fated to be together, you and I."

"I remember," said Corlan with a nod.

She turned and set her eyes on him. "This is not a time to forget."

"Jemma thought you needed a friend tonight. That's all."

"So you are here...."

He swept back his tussled hair, pursed his lips. "Yes, I am."

The words slipped out of her mouth before she could stop them: "As am I."

Corlan leaned toward her, pausing as if waiting for her lips to meet his lips. It seemed to be what the moment required.

"I'm not going to kiss you, Corlan Tang—if that is what you are expecting."

"I—I wasn't expecting anything." He straightened.

"You expected that a woman would kiss you. That's your belief. What happens when a woman and a man stand together in the night. It's something that is normal and natural in your world. This time you are mistaken. Next time you expect so much, you may find a knife at your tongue."

He tried to smile. "Have you ever put a knife to the throat of a man who tried to kiss you?"

"Not that I can recall. I'm a warrior, not a foolish lover."

"Have you ever kissed a man at all?"

"No, never." She blinked. "I suppose a child would kiss a father on the cheek."

"How about a woman?"

She blushed. "Kiss a woman? I would, yes. Although it seems just as pointless as kissing a man. However, I have not."

"Never?"

"I have been engaged in my duties."

"It's a simple thing. You should try it," said Corlan. "Jemma said to mention it. Said you might be amused."

"Amused? By a kiss? With you? Is that what you're suggesting?"

"Yes, I suggest you kiss me. That we kiss."

"Why?"

"It's not painful. People enjoy it. It's a way to relax."

She frowned. "And if I dislike it?"

"Then I will apologize."

"That is not enough." She brushed her long hair off her shoulders as the breeze blew stronger. The hem of the gown wrapped around her hips. "You must offer more.... Something of value."

"I have nothing of value."

"The weapon you call a slinger?"

"My dragonslinger? I can't give that away. It's my livelihood. That is my *only* valuable."

"That is all you have?"

"That and...the finger of a magus I once knew."

"A finger?"

"It's a long story. I'll tell you another night."

"So the slinger, then."

"That's what you would bid me wager?"

"Yes, that."

"It is the only weapon that can take a dragon from the sky."

Naka Wu smiled in the darkness. "Teach me to use it."

"I guess you should learn to use it. We may encounter a dragon before we go our separate ways at the Sei Bo statue."

"Then a dragonslinger is the cost, and a lesson." She spit into her hand, held it up. "Deal?"

He spit into his hand and they clasped hands. "Deal."

"So we made the deal," said Naka Wu.

After a heartbeat of realization, surprised at what they had done, each of them leaned toward the other and pressed their lips together for a few heartbeats, then parted.

"It's really not worth a dragonslinger," said Naka Wu. She wiped her mouth with the back of her hand. "You can keep it."

The morning sun bathed the city of Danapo in pink and lavender as the remnants of the dragonslayer clan marched out the main gate and took the road south. Corlan, in the lead, rode one of the sleek black horses, the mare, and Naka Wu rode a fresh gelding while Tam held the reins of the two draft horses pulling the wagon. Bai Lo sat beside the boy, her hand always on his knee.

Jemma did not rise early enough to see them off but Rupas got up and hugged each of them. A few words were exchanged, the kind of pleasantries spoken between people who had shared traumas. And yet they would never again see each other, they knew.

"Don't get killed," he told Corlan, last of all.

"Stay whole," the dragonslayer responded.

Trotting down the road side by side, Corlan and Naka Wu dared share glances and an occasional grin. The young people on the wagon did the same. The road was clear and the day full of sun.

The next day, when they reached the statue of Sei Bo on the top of the fire mountain, they paused to whisper prayers for safety and good fortune on their journeys. The great statue of the goddess, staring at once down upon them and out across the land, seemed to pity them. The blank eyes appeared to challenge them to go on and live their silly fates with a stony smugness that left Corlan angry and Naka Wu puzzled.

"May we have daughters," Naka Wu spoke in a low voice.

Corlan winked deliberately but he guessed she did not see it.

The wood they had gone through before was without bandits this passage. Even so, Corlan and Naka Wu remained ready to fight. They rode on without any trouble and stopped to make camp just past the junction of the two roads. Tam and Bai Lo had dinner ready in no time.

"Good to be on the march once more," said Corlan, shoveling a big spoonful of meat and vegetables into his mouth. "I'm glad to be out of that mortuary town."

Naka Wu regarded Corlan, sitting across the campfire from her.

"Tomorrow you must take the road west and I to the south."

"Won't you come along with us?" asked Tam.

"Yes, come with us," Bai Lo echoed.

Naka Wu's lips moved: something close to a smile flashed there.

"And you, Corlan?"

He had just taken a mouthful of food. "You said you—uh—you must return to—umm—serve your leader—didn't you?"

"I did." It was difficult for her to smile but she was trying. "I still would like to know your call on the matter."

Corlan swallowed, cleared his mouth. "I want you to come with us to wherever we are going."

"That's rather ambiguous."

"I don't truly know where we are going."

"West, you said."

"We're going to the marshes," Tam cut in. "That's where all the dragons put their eggs."

"I see." Naka Wu seemed happy. "What will you do there?"

"Break them!" said Tam, acting surprised she could not guess. "Then no more dragons. No more trouble."

"There will always be trouble, little man." She glanced at Bai Lo. "I see a complicated future for you. More so if you stay with this boy. He will care for you, it seems. I believe that. And you must care for him. Sei Bo knows it. She told me. So make a pact, both of you to each other." Her eyes shifted to Corlan. "Be partners and help each other always. Take some time each day to tend to each other's needs, spiritual and physical. You will do well following that plan."

"Wise words," Corlan muttered. Then his eyes met Naka Wu's. "I never knew you to think in that fancy way. Are you sure you're not secretly a magus? Now I want you to come with us. That every day caring you mentioned...? I need that."

"Do you want that?" she asked softly.

"I think so."

She gazed at him a moment, then expelled a sigh. "I must return to my duties. You and I both know this. I cannot forget my training, or my allegiance, no matter what my feelings may be. No matter if I have feelings. Nor if I desire a different path."

Corlan pulled himself up from the ground and went to her, sat beside her and threw an arm around her shoulders.

"What are you doing?" she asked, startled.

"You're talking like a sad lover."

"I am a sad lover."

She reached for his scraggily beard, tugged his face close and kissed him long and deep.

32

Partings

IN THE MORNING, the ground was already cool where Naka Wu had slept, the dry leaves pressed into the soil where her bedroll had lain. There was no note. No final words.

Corlan stood, suddenly alert, and climbed up onto the back of the wagon, his hand across his brow, searching down the road for a distant silhouette of horse and rider. He lost sight where the road bent to the southeast. The sun poked through the eastern clouds like fingers through water, but he saw no figures on the road.

"Just as well," he grumbled. "Stupid words...."

They had said everything the night before.

Tam gazed at him, unable to find any words to say to Corlan, so he just threw together the breakfast, then packed up the camp with Bai Lo's help.

"Now your papa is mad," said the girl.

Tam glanced over at Corlan. "No, he's that way in the morning."

"I mean she left him. Not even goodbye. So he's mad."

"Maybe they said goodbye last night," said the boy.

She grabbed his hand. "Promise me you won't ever leave me."

He turned to her, his eyes serious. "I'm never going to leave you, Bai Lo. You're my lady."

Then they were off, taking the road west, the one that would lead to another city, Teraut, a town of men, after five days' ride. Jemma said they would meet a river there. The Abaz River flowed south and eventually met the River Oh, which flowed into the vast marshes Corlan was seeking. Going to Teraut seemed the best route to take. He could hire a boat there.

Corlan regarded Bai Lo, the girl sitting comfortably beside Tam. He wondered what to do with her when they arrived in Teraut.

Dress her as a boy? Except for her long brown hair, they could disguise her well enough for a short visit. Then again, they would not need much resupply by then so perhaps it would be best to skirt the town and continue to the southwest.

What lay beyond Teraut? A river that emptied into the marshes. No chance of resupply there. When they had left the Burg, he took all the supplies that could be packed on the backs of two girafors—which wasn't much. He expected to live off the land, hunting for food. But then he had a boy to feed. And dragons came—

"What's wrong, Corlan?" asked Tam when they made camp.

"Many thoughts of days now past," he responded. "They stack up like dragonfire bricks, ready to be lit and smoke away until they're nothing more than powder. Gone."

"You sound like Rupas. Fancy talk. Or like Naka Wu."

Corlan chuckled. "It must be the spell she put on me."

"She was a warrior, not a magus."

"Even ordinary people can cast spells sometimes."

Tam chuckled. "Will you recover?"

He sighed. "Maybe after seventeen days, I will."

Tam grinned. "I know you miss her."

"Naka Wu?"

"Yes, her. I saw you kiss each other so I know you love her."

Corlan laughed. "Sometimes people kiss before they love each other. Before they have a chance to know if they love each other. The kiss is only...like opening a door. Then you must step inside and see if you want to live there."

Tam took Bai Lo's hand, held up their two interlocked hands. "I know we want to live in a house together. We already decided."

"We did," said the girl.

"Ah, both of you are too young to be talking that way," he said with an obstinate laugh. "You're yet too young."

"We love each other!" Bai Lo exclaimed.

"Then hold that wish. Someday you may get to have a ceremony and make your partnership official. Yet not today. Nor this month. Or several months. Or a year or two more."

"A year or two?" asked Bai Lo, frowning.

"We can make it official at Teraut, can't we?" asked Tam. "We can find a magus and ask him to speak the words of union for me and Bai Lo. Then we will be a family."

"It sounds so simple. Snap your fingers. Make a wish. And you become husband and wife. And then children start popping out!"

"How long does that take?" asked the boy.

"Babes? Nine months, if the mother is healthy." He regarded Bai Lo. "What's your age?"

"I don't know for certain. I was sold by my mother when I was very young."

"Have you had your first bleeding yet?"

"What's that?" Tam asked with trepidation.

Corlan smiled. "When she's old enough to start thinking about being wed there is some blood that comes out. Down below. My lady back in the Burg said it didn't hurt much though it made a mess. There was no joy for us during those days." He gave Tam a stern look. "So you leave her alone until after that time. There's no reason to hurry all that."

"She has to bleed before we can have our union?"

"That's what I'm saying."

He got angry. "It's not fair!"

"We can still be together," said the girl calmly. She put her arm around him, rested her head against his shoulder.

"You've already waited nine months to find this girl, Tam, so you can wait another nine months more to wed her." He burst into laughter. "Then you have nine months more and maybe you are a father. Then life becomes chaos for you. How's that for a frightening scenario? No more a kitchen boy."

Tam pouted. "I don't like life becoming chaos."

Bai Lo patted his back, whispering into his ear.

"Nothing is fair," said Corlan, scratching his rough, whiskered cheek. "That's the reason we have weapons."

Corlan awoke before he opened his eyes, sensing danger was close. He listened hard for the approach of footsteps, the ring of metal, or, worse, the seething wind of an approaching dragon. His hand went to his sideblade, as he cracked his eyelids open.

Two rough-clothed men were stepping lightly into the campsite. They seemed to be common bandits. Maybe they knew the bandits Naka Wu had dispatched before. Maybe they recognized the wagon and thought to get revenge on him. Or they were determined to help themselves to what looked valuable on a wagon filled with supplies.

When the first one stood gazing down on him, Corlan sprang into action with an upward kick to the man's groin that sent him falling on his backside with a howl of pain. Corlan leaped up, sword in hand and the second bandit turned and ran. The first one rolled on the ground and tried to stand, failed.

"Who are you?" Corlan demanded.

"Just a thief, sir, nothing more."

Corlan glanced around the camp. The wagon was where it was set when they made camp and the horses were tethered as usual. Then he noticed the ground was empty where he remembered Tam and Bai Lo had put out their bedrolls. Sword in hand, pointing it at the fallen thief, he spun around to check each direction. The youths were not in sight.

They obviously had left. He thought for a moment. The bedrolls were gone so they were not snatched away by any bandits. They had snuck away! Like lovers escaping in the night. He felt both amused and alarmed at the situation.

"All right, up with you!" he commanded the bandit.

The man slowly got to his feet, holding his groin with one hand.

"Get away now!" Corlan shouted. "Go on! Be off or I'll take an arm off you so you'll fit in Danapo!"

The man got the idea, stumbled out of the camp, disappeared.

Corlan realized his problem. Go looking for the youths or stay and guard the supplies? He considered the children were testing him—or teasing him—and they did not truly intend to go on their own to Teraut. It would be crazy for them to face the road on their own.

He unloaded the bag of weapons, the quivers of iron bolts, and the long, heavy dragonslinger and found a ditch yards away from the campsite to hide them in. He swept dried leaves over the treasures, covered his tracks from the wagon to the ditch. He could not hide everything but the weapons were the most valuable items. He might lose the rest, the wagon and two horses, to bandits who might return, yet he had no other way.

The mare he had ridden from Danapo he called Breeze. The sleek black coat was beautiful yet he did not need a horse to be beautiful. He had once ridden a hippor, after all.

With a bow and quiver of arrows on his back and a sword at his side, he turned Breeze around and galloped down the road in the direction they were heading before the camp was made. If the two youths were intent on making for Teraut, that was the way they would go. He rode two miles, seeing no sign of them, before he wondered if they would have chosen instead to return to Danapo, which was closer.

The boy was tight with Rupas. Likely he wanted to return there.

He galloped back to the campsite, gave the wagon a long look. It appeared untouched so he rode north along the road. It was a day's ride to the statue of Sei Bo. If they went by foot they could not have gotten more than a couple miles. If they heard him coming after them, he thought, they might hide in the foliage.

Corlan reined in Breeze to slow the pace. He searched the woods on either side of the road. The road itself had no small footprints pressed into the dirt so he was not certain they had walked this way. If he called out, he might also notify bandits to attack him. He halted and rubbed his temples, furious at the boy for causing him trouble.

The boy wasn't meant to go with me, anyway. It's all by fate.

Sitting in the saddle, his horse standing in the middle of the road, Corlan listened to the wind rustling the last leaves of the season. He gazed as far as he could in each direction, penetrating deep through the branches and trunks, the fallen logs and ragged bushes. A proud buck pranced past him a few yards away from the road, unafraid.

He turned Breeze north and trotted toward Sei Bo. If only Naka Wu were with him, he thought. Someone could watch the wagon and supplies while he went on this senseless search for two unhappy children.

Children! Since when should children be so bold, leaving the safety of camp for the dangers of the road?

When he was Tam's age he never did anything so foolish. He had brothers and cousins to keep him from running off. He was near the Burg, on a farmstead his father operated when he was not involved in military campaigns. A tall, black-haired man who'd looked like his father had ridden onto the farmstead one day with a troop of soldiers and told his mother he was needed. The king was recruiting, the man told them. "You must go serve your grandfather now," his mother had said. "The king needs you — as does your father." She called after them for the man to treat him well. That was the end of childhood.

He heard the *whiz* only at the last instant, then felt the slice across his upper arm. Throwing himself off the horse, he landed on his unhurt arm, then rolled onto his wounded arm to pull free the bow he carried and grab the quiver. He notched an arrow.

Through the horse's legs he could see no archer in the woods. He checked his wound: a graze half-way between elbow and the point of his shoulder, a cut only. The arrowhead had nearly stuck, instead bit shallow and fell away. He saw it laying on the road.

"Come up, sir!" someone called. "We've got you. Come easy and no more harm we'll set upon you."

Corlan guessed they were bandits, possibly like the two he had encountered earlier come back with friends to get him.

Suddenly a plot hatched in his head. If he came this way and was attacked, then so might Tam and Bai Lo have been. They had taken off on their own, then were captured by bandits. They were likely being held by them somewhere in the forest. So Corlan would go with them, find the two youths, then they all would escape.

The horse was surrounded by five pairs of feet, two with boots, the others barefoot. Corlan stood beside the horse, holding the bow and notched arrow at the ready.

"Lower your bow, sir," said the one with the nicer-looking boots, a silver buckle on the side of each.

"Do it!" snapped the ragged man next to him.

Corlan relaxed the bowstring, turned the arrow to the ground. He let it fall free and it stuck in the moist soil. He held the empty bow out, hands raised.

"That's a gentleman," said Nice-Boots.

"Have you seen two children on this road?" asked Corlan warily.

"Two children?" Nice-Boots seemed amused. "I haven't. Have you?" he asked of his cohorts.

They laughed, which did not set well with Corlan.

"Are they yours?" asked Nice-Boots.

"They are under my protection."

"How you gonna protect anybody now you're captured?"

"I'm looking for them. If you have captured them, then I ask you to give them to me and we will be out of your territory as quickly as we can. Apologies for using your road without permission."

"Permission, eh?"

That made them laugh even more loudly.

"Please accept this fine bow and my quiver of arrows as payment for using your road."

Nice-Boots frowned. His hand shot up to slap Corlan's face but halted an inch from his cheek.

"We aim to take your horse—fine beast, this one—and then we're gonna find something for you to do." Nice-Boots glared at his cohorts. "Maybe we can sell this fellow to the meatcutter, eh? He's got some muscle on him, he does."

The bandits bundled him up with ropes and made him follow them as one man led Breeze away.

The camp was a collection of lean-tos made of branches and furs, a smoking fire at the center of the clearing. There were old women and young children at work there, sitting around the fire, cooking. A village, thought Corlan, so maybe he was not in as much danger as he believed. They were just family men—men who could be dealt with. They would understand his concern for the children.

"Over there," Nice-Boots directed one of his lieutenants, pointing at a canvas tent.

There was a loud squawk overhead and everyone turned their heads up to look. Corlan didn't see anything. He expected a dragon to pass by—hoped it would come to distract his captors.

Corlan was led over to the tent. His guard shoved him down on his knees at the entrance.

"Here's your lost children, old father!" said the man with a scowl and a ruffle of his long moustache. He stayed outside while Corlan crawled inside the tent. "Stay in there and be quiet."

The darkness initially kept him from seeing who else sat inside the tent. As his eyes adjusted, Corlan saw two small figures. Tam and Bai Lo sat huddled together, dirty faced and clothes torn.

"Corlan!" cried Tam. The boy moved to hug him.

"I don't know if I should be happy to see you again or spank your bottom for running away. I had to leave the wagon and our supplies unguarded to chase after you two. Now we are captured by bandits."

"They said they're gonna sell us," Tam exclaimed, "to Covinas or to Luvali, and Bai Lo's gotta wed somebody else, not me!"

"You're bleeding," said Bai Lo, pointing.

He checked his arm, blood running down it. "It's nothing, an arrow grazed me. It's nothing like the blood you'll see when these bandits get in front of my sword." He felt for his sideblade, found it missing. "I'll take a blade from one of them, then—"

"I'm sorry, Corlan." Tam bowed his head. "I didn't mean to cause trouble. We—" He turned to Bai Lo. "We wanted to go back to the city and get wedded."

"You're both too young for any of that. It's a great misfortune you're not too young to get into trouble."

"What're we going to do?" asked Tam.

"It's a village, not a band of thieves. They might steal for a living but they've got women and children here, too, so I expect they'll let us go and keep the horse I rode." He gave a quick glance outside. "We are about five miles from our camp. I hid the weapons but—"

"Quiet in there," grunted the man standing outside.

Corlan curled his finger for them to lean forward.

Before he could speak, the same loud noise screeched through the camp. He glanced at Tam, then Bai Lo, who cringed against the boy. Corlan scrambled to his knees, turned to the entrance. Not much could be seen through the gap in the door flap.

"What is that?" asked Tam.

"Have you heard it before?"

"No, only now."

"I wonder if a dragon is coming here to rescue us." He only joked a little. "But that sounds more like a bird. It could be a different kind of dragon than what we've seen before."

The screech cut through the village again.

"What *is* that?" Corlan wondered. "Maybe they have a captive bird tethered in this village. Village! It's more like a camp than any village." He focused on Tam. "You remember the way they brought you here?"

"I think so," replied the boy. "There was a trail in from the road."

"Can you find it? We're going to run out of here."

Another screech.

Corlan lifted the tent flap to peek out. The man guarding them carried a staff and promptly clapped Corlan on the side of his face with it. "Back you go!"

Corlan retreated, rubbing his cheek. "Oh, yes, we are going to run from here. We just need a distraction. I'll make a distraction and you both run as fast as you can. Head out to the road and five miles south you'll find our campsite but hide in the woods if you need to. I'll be right behind you but we may not meet again until the camp. If you're chased, don't wait for me. Take the horses and ride for

Danapo, if you can—or if that way is blocked, head for Covin."

Tam nodded, got to his feet with Bai Lo.

Corlan saw the red stain on her gown. "Did they hurt you?"

Bai Lo looked down at her gown. "What's that?"

"Blood," cried Tam.

Corlan shushed him. "Not a good day for that."

"For what?" she asked.

"You got first blood, looks to be. I still need you to run hard."

"So now we can get wedded?" asked Tam.

"Not until you run far from this damnable camp."

"And then?"

"I told you it's not for a while. We must escape before anything else. You understand?"

Corlan got up, stood bent over behind the tent flap.

"Ready to run?"

They both nodded.

Another screech rattled the camp. When Corlan lifted the tent flap the guard was turned away, staring up at the strange creature circling overhead, making the unholy noises. The man detected Corlan from the corner of his eye and spun around with the staff in both hands to clap him once more.

Corlan caught the staff and thrust the wooden pole up under the guard's chin. He ripped the staff away from the man and swung it hard twice against the man's face, then thrust the blunt end of it into the man's belly to drop him to his knees.

"Go!" he called to the youths.

They scrambled out of the tent and Tam led the way around the side and out the rear of the camp. It seemed to Corlan that nobody noticed. The people were gazing up at the large brown bird flying overhead.

Corlan had never seen anything like it. Though it appeared to be a bird, it was oddly formed. Golden brown wings full of feathers gave it flight but instead of a single tail, it had two feathery appendages that kicked the air like a frog would kick in water. Its head did not have the long beak he was expecting but a human face—

Madi!

Now she seemed to be seven feet long and her wingspan double that. At that moment of realization, he thought to wave his arms, to catch her attention and let her know he was on the ground below.

But he also knew his motion would attract his captors.

Glancing over his shoulder, he couldn't see Tam and Bai Lo. They had escaped through the woods and the brush hid their route.

With the wooden staff in his hands, Corlan surveyed the camp, looking for his horse. There were a few horses tethered at the far end of the camp but he did not see the coal-black Breeze among them.

So he also ran behind the tent and took off through the woods in the same direction Tam and Bai Lo had gone. Madi was providing the distraction, whether by design or happenstance.

"He's fleeing!" cried someone, but Corlan did not look back.

He ran among the tree trunks, around bushes, leaping over fallen logs and narrow leaf-choked streams, looking ahead for the youths and back at the men in pursuit. Four of them. Nice-Boots seemed to be one of them yet not the fastest.

The bird-creature continued to circle overhead, cawing loudly, not concerned with his escape.

Corlan broke from the woods onto the road. He saw footprints in the soil. Far down the road he saw two young people running.

Behind him were the men from the camp, so he crossed the road, breaking into the woods on the other side. He made a big show of crashing through the brush so the men would know which direction he had gone and follow him rather than the children.

The sky darkened. Corlan thought a storm had arrived. Clouds had been blocking the sun all day, so he did not think much of it. The evening was coming on. It would be easier to hide in the darkness.

The roar was unmistakable. A great rumble of thunder rushing into a mighty explosion of danger! It deafened him. He tripped at the shock and fell among the forest undergrowth.

Above him, above the treetops, swooped a dragon: a mature fang-master! Through the branches, Corlan saw the dark-gray beast, decorated with dull yellow stripes along its throat. The extra long fangs hung down outside its closed mouth. Its spiked tail waved seductively back and forth over what was—

The road!

He jumped up and turned for the road, running in the opposite direction he had been going. The children were on the road!

Corlan smashed through the brush and found the road, a little further down from where the men from the camp huddled in fright from the dragon. He bolted onto the dirt road and stared down it but did not see Tam and Bai Lo. He hoped they had slipped into the cover of the forest.

The dragon hovered over the trees, above the road, the steady flapping of its wings helping maintain its position, the bloated belly full of air for buoyancy—and fire.

Corlan possessed only the staff he took from the guard at the tent. There was no way to do battle without a slinger or at least a battle axe—or even a simple sword. If the staff were at least pointed, sharpened at one end, he might be able to hurl it like a spear and do some damage, enough to ward off the beast, at least.

The dragon turned to the clump of men on the margin of the road and roared at them. Just hot air and loud noise—and the raspy cough that told Corlan fire was being conjured.

The men were not ready for the fire. They had no thought to run away—as Corlan was doing at the first whiff of sulfur. Instead, they huddled together even tighter, forming the perfect kindling. The fire ball engulfed them and they burned bright. One man jumped up and ran—tried to run—but the dragon landed atop him, the weight of its hindfoot splitting the man into two halves. He was on fire anyway.

Corlan ran straight down the road. He saw ahead it would curve and he would be out of the dragon's line of sight. He dared not look back as he ran. Let the dragon be entertained with those men from the camp, not him. Not the children.

Dragons, being dragons, have an odd sense of humor. They often enjoy the sight of something they've set ablaze burning down to ash. At that point some will scoop up the ashes and swallow them. Others will stomp atop whatever they have burned, a way to mark territory. A few will abandon burning targets for the next interesting item—such as a man running down a dirt road.

Corlan felt the shaking of the ground and knew the beast was coming after him—lumbering on heavy feet, its neck and head much closer to him than the clawed feet under its body. The fire would come at any moment—or not. A foot might rise over him and drop hard upon him. Or not. Neither mattered if he did not run his fastest.

At least the children got away!

Then he heard another cry from Madi, echoing among the trees. He looked up, not sure if the bird-girl favored him or the dragon. He realized he was still in danger.

"Madi!" he shouted.

The bird-girl flapped her wings, gaining speed, overtaking the dragon, and reached Corlan. Squawking overhead made Corlan look up. Madi flapped her wings furiously to hold her position in the air. More squawks, but he did not understand. She dropped a bit, talons extended, clenching the air as if to indicate—

He understood and held up the staff in both hands as he slowed his running, held up like a perch. She clenched her talons around the wooden pole and Corlan held on as she rose in the air, wings pulling hard, gaining altitude as best she could with Corlan hanging below.

"Can you hold me?" he called up.

Corlan stared down at the dragon, now stomping on the same spot where he had stood an instant before.

He wanted to laugh, to flick his thumb at the beast below. But his grip on the staff slipped. He almost fell, managing to grab it tighter and concentrating on not falling, as Madi carried him away. She followed the road, rising to twice the treetop height.

"Take care! Not too high!"

Looking back, Corlan saw the dragon was watching them. They were far enough away that an ordinary breath of fire would not likely reach them. Farther behind the dragon the fire still burned on the side of the road where the bandits had huddled.

The dragon opened its wide yaw, the extra long fangs dripping with fluid from its throat glands. It seemed disappointed that a man had gotten away. It cocked its head to one side, as if making a plan.

Then it stepped forward, wings open and was airborne.

Corlan cursed as Madi swung into a sharp dive, turning right, following the road. She seemed to know what his cursing meant.

"Let me down," he cried.

Before Corlan could blink, the dragon was upon them, its open mouth only a few inches from his dangling legs and Madi's kicking tail-feet. She dropped sharply, released her grip on the staff, letting him fall to the ground—actually down into a small pond.

Madi launched herself higher into the sky as fast as her wings could pull, fleeing from the dragon.

But dragons, being dragons, have an odd sense of humor.

As Madi rose higher, the dragon slowed and hovered, watching the bird-girl ascend, appearing to calculate her direction. The dragon focused, eyes unblinking, on the small flying thing as its throat rumbled and the scent of sulfur cut through the air. A raspy cough followed—

INTERLUDE

The Birthstone

THE DOOR TO THE OLD HOUSE was broken apart and closing it as best they could still let the cold night air enter. Jabuli turned to ask advice from the strange woman in the white robe.

"You will never repair it, even if you had tools. Tomorrow I will conjure a new door," said the woman, standing in the center of the room as though she were yet another post to hold up the roof.

"Not tonight?" asked Jabuli. "We have a babe to keep warm. We will suffer from the cold."

"There is no cold. No hot, either."

"We feel the cold. We are humans," Jabuli countered, accepting that the woman was not like them.

"The stone must regain its power," said the woman plainly, as though she spoke to herself. "It takes much power to disarray a dragon. Even more to pull a door out of thin air."

Jabuli nodded. She didn't wish to be rude but the night would be cold. Only a few days trek from Sannan and her plan was failing. There never was a plan that had no weaknesses, she realized at that moment. They needed a new plan. They would decide everything in the morning – if they could just endure one night.

"We will sleep close together for warmth tonight," Jabuli said. She glanced at Adora and Rula, who was holding the babe, trying to get him to nurse. He kept batting her breast away.

The woman offered them soup. The big pot boiling over the iron rod in the fireplace was filled with roots and herbs. It had a strange, bitter taste but Adora thought it must be a new recipe. The woman did not know the recipes from the palace chef, after all. It was hot, at least, so she slurped it down. There was hard black bread and some pungent blue cheese, too. And a pitcher of goat's milk.

After the dinner, the strange woman went silently into the next room, her feet making no sound upon the wooden floor boards, even though they creaked when the others stepped on them. She pushed the door shut. It seemed as though the door was heavy or caught on some floor snag by the way the woman had to put her shoulder into closing it.

Jabuli stared at the closed door, feeling both angry and frustrated by the woman's treatment of them as well as thankful for her help. The woman would be warm enough in her room, Jabuli laughed to herself. More of this *fate* she had heard of from Rula. Things happen at random and only later make any sense. She understood Rula's idea but did not believe it.

They had half a door to protect them from the outside elements. So Jabuli arranged the room: Adora between Rula and her, the baby brother beside Adora. With Rula next to the babe, she could easily feed him if he awoke during the night.

The fireplace burned low as they closed their eyes to sleep.

"How did you get her to help?" Jabuli asked them in whispers. She hadn't wanted to ask such a question in front of their hostess.

"You said run and we did," said Adora. Jabuli cautioned her to keep her voice low. "We pushed the door open and ran inside."

"Just like that?" asked Jabuli.

Rula wiggled her fingers.

"Oh, she was just standing there? Did she say anything?"

"No, she looked at us and we were so afraid. She has a scary look about her. I cringed in fear. So did Rula."

Hearing her name, Rula, made signs rather frantically.

"You were afraid she would hurt you? But the dragons outside were more scary?"

Rula nodded, then wiped her eyes. Adora patted her shoulder as she had seen Jabuli do.

"She was scared," said Adora, referring to Rula. "But I was ready to protect her and my brother from the witch."

"Witch?" Jabuli put a finger to her lips. "You think she is?"

"She looks like a witch. Except she wears a clean white robe."

"Yes, it's dirty outside and in this hut," said Jabuli, "yet her robe is clean and white, spotless. And her hair, too: perfectly straight and white. There must be a magic comb somewhere." She snickered.

"And magic laundry, too," said Adora with a grin.

Rula was yawning. She signed that she would go on to sleep. The day had taken every last bit of energy from her. She was beginning to regret coming on the journey, she indicated. Jabuli frowned at her, then leaned across Adora to give Rula a kiss on her forehead.

"Sleep as well as you can, sister. I'll watch over you."

Falling back to her portion of the floor, Jabuli gazed at the babe, already asleep, tucked in against Adora's belly, her arm around him.

"I'll always protect my brother," said Adora at Jabuli's gaze.

"I know, little majesty."

"Just Adora. I'm not a princess any longer."

"What about the egg thing?" asked Jabuli suddenly. "Did she say what it is?"

Adora pouted. "She stared at us like she wondered why we ran into her house. I told her there were dragons outside. That's when she went to the side of the room and grabbed the stone off the shelf." She raised her hand, pointing to the board sticking out of the stone wall as a shelf above where they lay. "Right there."

"She never said a word? She just picked up the stone and stood there, stiff as a statue, ready to make the dragons explode?"

Adora nodded, the glow from the dying embers casting shadows over her face, giving her horns and wings.

"Amazing...."

"She must be a sorceress," said Adora with delight in her voice. "I can learn some spells from her. What do you think? Spells are always good to have in a purse for...for when you need them."

Jabuli smiled, reaching out to tussle the princess's hair. She wished her a good night and pleasant dreams. Then she hoped the wardens who escaped would not bring another squad down on them during the night. Or in the morning, either. She contemplated her charge's dream again, knowing she had encountered dragons but she did not fall, did not die. Perhaps that was all it was: a dream, just a jumble of images that meant nothing. A child could call them anything. Even so, horrible thoughts tormented her sleep.

They awoke early because the room had gotten cold. Adora shivered and Rula sat with her back to the stone wall, the babe under her cloak, feeding him, warming him. She looked around the room as though she were in a fog, remembering where she was. She signed to Jabuli, something about where they would go next.

Jabuli shook her head as she stared at the door to the other room, wondering if the strange woman also had awakened. She decided not to knock on the door. They would wait.

Digging through the bags they found the last of their food and put it on the table in equal portions for Adora, Jabuli, and Rula.

"Looks like I shall be hungry tomorrow," said Adora with an easy shrug. "And you two, as well."

Rula signed.

"She says we should kill a goat," Jabuli translated, grinning. "Maybe the sorceress can conjure some food as well as a new door."

"If she is a real sorceress," said Adora.

"I can't believe a sorceress would live out here on the wild range, in a hut this poor, and raise goats." Jabuli shook her head. "She looks like a sorceress. That's true. Maybe she is only a crazy woman."

"She used that stone egg to destroy the dragons," Adora spoke. "That's not what a crazy woman can do. She must be a sorceress."

"We shall speak with her before we continue on our journey. We need to know the way to Yozma. It doesn't matter if she is a witch or a sorceress or whatever she is. I thank her for saving us, but we have nothing to give her as thanks but our thanks."

"I have some coin," Adora offered.

"She wouldn't accept mere money. That has no true value. That's not how a sorceress thinks."

Jabuli shot a glance at Rula who seemed uninterested in learning the way to Yozma or what to give to the sorceress as reward for saving them. They should give the woman something of value, Jabuli signed. The two women exchanged finger signs, nods, and gestures. It did not go well.

"Are you ill?" asked Jabuli of Rula.

Only a cross-eyed stare in reply.

Jabuli turned to Adora. The girl was holding her brother in her lap, poking his cheeks to make him smile. But the babe was hungry and only pouted, on the verge of crying.

"We better see if she's awake yet."

Jabuli put her ear to the door, heard a faint whirring sound from the opposite side. Suddenly the door disappeared. It did not swing open but became instantly invisible — as though it no longer existed. The woman in the white robe stood in the center of the inner room, her white hair long and as perfectly straight as the previous day. Her arms were at her sides and the stone egg was nowhere to be seen. In fact, there was no bed in the room; no other furniture, either.

"Sorry to disturb you," said Jabuli, considering whether or not the woman had slept at all. She stared curiously into the room, then gave a bow. "We only wondered if you were awake yet."

With no expression on her face, the woman spoke: "I do not sleep. Over the long journey of time you will learn how much waste sleep is."

"I suppose you're right," said Jabuli, rising from her bow. "Truly, Madam. As long as you've lived, you must have learned quite a lot. Maybe you don't need as much sleep as I do, or as a child does. It was so cold last night we did not sleep well." She swung her hand around behind herself to indicate Adora and the babe. "We are about to finish the food we brought with us. There is not much left but we will share with you. Do you have more?"

"I know you require food every six to eight hours."

"Or sooner. The babe needs feeding more often." Jabuli frowned. "Don't you?"

"No. I never eat."

"But you made the soup. I saw you eat."

"I did not eat the soup. I gave it to you."

Jabuli nodded, knowing she was correct. After the sky wardens left, they had been so hungry they ate without noticing what the old woman did, or whether or not she ate any for herself.

"Who are you? May I ask?" asked Jabuli, then realized she spoke rudely. "I mean no disrespect. My daughter thought you might be a witch but I told her no. Are you a sorceress?"

"I am who I am. And you?"

"Who? Me? I'm...Bulo." The woman seemed unimpressed and Jabuli frowned. "Do you have a name?"

"Different people call me by different names."

"What should we call you?"

The woman remained stern. "Why should you call me?"

Jabuli never liked playing word games. "Suppose this little hut were about to burn down because of a dragon and we wanted to get your attention so you could destroy the dragon and save this poor little hut, what name should we call?"

The woman still did not show any emotion on her face. A stone or a statue was more expressive, thought Jabuli. She smiled to be encouraging.

"Bo," said the woman.

"Just Bo? What kind of name is that?"

"There are people who call me by that name, such as in the story you told. I am also known by other names: Bala, Vraya, Goush, Sei, Manaloumla, Wen, Ammor, Erra—"

"I see," said Jabuli to end the recitation of names. "We shall call you Bo. Are you a sorceress? The little girl thinks you are. We saw you use the power of that thing that looks like a stone egg. You saved us. We want to thank you."

"Not a sorceress."

"Then how do you have such power? How does that egg work?"

The woman lifted her hand and gave a minimal wave to dismiss Jabuli. "So many questions before the first meal."

"You said you do not need food," said Jabuli.

"You do."

Jabuli nodded. "Yes, food first." She looked around the outer room and saw nothing but the meager crumbs of their own meal on the table. "I think there is no more food. But you do not eat."

"I do not require food."

"So you *are* a sorceress!" Adora cried out. "I've read so many parches all my life. I read how sorceresses make fire and bend water and build mountains out of the hills of moles. And they can speak a hundred languages and count numbers higher than anyone. They can be beautiful or ugly as they choose and they never sleep or eat or do the union." She turned to her tutor. "I'm sorry but I read about that, too. Such a strange thing to do."

Jabuli shook her head, sweeping her hand in the air to forgive her infraction. "In time you will need to know it."

"The little one is partly correct. Yet I am not a sorceress."

"Then what are you?" asked Jabuli.

The woman narrowed her eyes. "I am a goddess."

Adora beamed with sudden interest. Jabuli squinted, suspicious. Rula got to her feet, smiling at the new information. She signed some message but Jabuli was not looking in her direction.

"Are you sure?" asked Jabuli, her head dipping slightly to the left. "Shouldn't you live in a great golden palace? Not this poor little wood and stone hut?"

"I do not live in this poor little hut, Jabuli Devry."

Jabuli was startled to hear her true name spoken by the strange woman. She had magical powers, no doubt, yet who the woman was and how they came to meet in such an odd, random place continued to baffle her. Her suspicions were mixed with fear for their safety. She marked the sword leaning beside the fireplace.

"...as a pit fighter from Rament turned into a child's tutor, now conspirator, a rogue and profiteer...."

"What?" Jabuli was alarmed. "Why are you saying that?"

"I am here now," said the woman, standing tall and white. "I am here because you are here."

"You said you were waiting for us...?"

Jabuli snapped a look at Rula who met her eyes with something disturbing. Her training sister had never seemed so cold. It was the same look they gave each other just before their master commanded them to fight. Did Rula sense danger?

"I remember you said that," Jabuli spoke, "after the sky wardens fled. What did you mean by that?"

"I have been waiting for you." The woman turned to gaze upon Adora, who stood beside the table. "For her."

Jabuli's face got serious. "For my daughter? Why her? We are just simple folk, on the way to Yozma, not destined for this place."

"You have many plans. Not all of them will succeed."

"How do you know?" Jabuli thought of Adora's dreams. "Do you see them in dreams?"

"I have lived for one-thousand one-hundred and ninety-nine years and many days—"

Jabuli blinked. "Yet you live in a hut on the side of a mountain, with goats and a stone egg. How strange!"

"You are not a believer."

"I believe what I can see," Jabuli snapped. The woman was an imposter, she felt certain, yet she could not explain the power of the stone egg. "I see you in your white robe playing with your magic egg, looking like a sorceress, yet this hut does not seem to match that role. It should be a tall castle, at least. Or in the clouds."

"I did not choose this place. I did not build this hut. It was built around me more than a hundred years ago. I stood here and people made it. They called me. They asked me to come and be the center of their home, small as it was."

"I suppose they died already or left for other reasons." Jabuli felt bad for being rude. An old woman was still worthy of respect, even a crazy woman. "So, you are alone. You decided to stay? Locked in some magic spell? Unable to depart? Is that it?"

"No," said the woman who called herself a goddess. "I come and I go. Wherever there is a home I am invited into, I visit. Where I am not invited, I cannot enter."

She picked up the stone egg from the shelf on the wall—where they suddenly noticed it sat. The shelf had remained empty during the night. The white woman held the egg balanced in the palm of her hand, her arm half-extended, elbow bent slightly.

"I was invited into this house long ago and as long as it remains I can visit. It was the best place to wait for you."

"To meet us?"

"Not you, Jabuli Devry. *Her.*" They looked over at Adora, who was following the conversation, eyes bright with attention. "She has been expected."

"Expected?" Jabuli studied Adora a moment. "For what?"

"For the future."

Even when Jabuli looked up, eyes fixing on the strange woman standing like a statue in the middle of the room, she still had no idea. Perhaps magic had led them to this mountain slope, after all. From the start, their path had been laid out and they could do nothing but follow it—if that were true. She wondered how Rula had decided on this route. She regarded her training sister—

At that instant, Rula jumped up, rushed forward, holding both her hands out.

"Here is the girl—as promised," Rula spoke in a strange, rough voice, deep like a man's guttural growl. "Let me keep the boy, for the one taken from me. He has little value anyway."

"You can speak!" Adora exclaimed just as Rula gave her a shove, hands flat against the shoulders of the princess.

Adora fell forward toward the sorceress and, as she fell, she put out her right hand intending to brace herself against the floor. At the same instant, feeling her knees about to crash against the floor, she stretched out her left hand, reaching for anything to catch herself, and that was the white robe of the sorceress. Adora's fingers clasped the fabric and the instant she touched it a sizzling pulse shot up her arm and crossed through her shoulders. Her right hand touched the floor, as did her knees, but her left hand began to glow as though it was aflame with white light—

"Not the left hand!" the sorceress cried out, trying to tear herself and her robe away from Adora's fingers.

But the girl's hand grasped the folds tightly, and her weight pulled the hem downward, threatening to topple the sorceress. It took all her energy to keep the stone egg steady in her hand.

"Now I want the gold," Rula growled in her deep voice. "As you promised. Gold for this girl—the one you wanted. And I can start a new life!"

As Adora fell, Jabuli glowered at Rula, not understanding why her training sister had turned traitor, in that instant unable to choose how to react. The words shot from Jabuli's mouth before she could think: "Gold? You betray us? For gold?"

In a flash, she saw that Adora was going to catch herself and get no more than a bump. The sorceress also would be unharmed. Rula, however, was holding out her hands, palms up, as if she expected gold to rain down upon them. Jabuli's eyes went to the sword leaning by the fireplace. She stretched awkwardly for it, grabbing the hilt and swung it up as she regained her footing.

"I prayed every night you would restore me!" Rula cried out in the gravelly voice. "We had a pact—"

Rula startled at the glint of steel, dropped back a step in horror as she felt the blade come slicing down across her extended hands. Off they came, plopping on the floor. The next swing of the blade sent Rula's head flying off her shoulders and over the table, crashing on the doorstep and bounding out the doorway into the grass of the pasture while a fountain of blood sprayed from her neck and wrists.

Jabuli stood still, stunned at what she'd done, the stained blade shaking in her hands.

Adora collapsed on the floor, her fall complete, as blood splashed over her clothes, over the white robe of the sorceress, upon the gray stone walls of the room. The sorceress bent over but did not fall, then stood straight again with the girl's hand firmly clenching her robe and glowing white as though she had dipped her hand in milk. The glow pulsed with her heartbeats.

The babe!

Jabuli spun around, dropping the sword to the floor, and saw the gurgling bundle fighting to get out of the sling where he had been put when Rula got up to shove the princess. He seemed unharmed.

"Adora!" cried Jabuli. She saw that the backswing of the sword had severed some of the long white hair of the sorceress. Every strand that had been cut hovered in the air, wriggling like white worms. She swept them aside as she reached for the girl, intending to lift her from the floor before the loose strands of magic hair could cover her.

"Do not touch her," called the sorceress, keeping the stone egg that sat in her hand level with her shoulder. "Not now. Not for a very long time. Let her be. Let her absorb the power first. Otherwise she will die."

"Die?" Jabuli cried out. "She can't die!"

"And she won't," said the white-robed woman, the sorceress, the goddess called Bo, whoever she was, "if you obey my instructions."

"Anything!"

"Leave her be. Let the glow cover her. There is nothing more that can be done for her. She will live a long time, so fear not."

"What will happen to her?"

The woman's face changed. "She will become me."

They watched Adora as the white illumination spread across her shoulders and down her other arm. The whiteness pulsed at the pace of her heartbeats, spreading down her back and over the top of her head. Her hair faded to white, glowing brightly. Her knees and feet, once pressed against the floor boards, pulsed with white light. Her legs glowed as she slowly got up, stood straight and tall. Her left hand still clenched the robe as she pushed herself up with her right hand. Her sleeve had turned white and glowed with white light. The stone egg pulsed in tandem with the white aura surrounding the girl's head and body, as though the two were connected through the body of the sorceress.

"Adora!" called Jabuli. She wiped her tears. "My Little Majesty! Poor little majesty —"

"Do not call to her. She cannot hear you. Not yet."

"Tell me what will happen!"

"The light will cover her. The light will consume her. Fill her. The light will be her power. The birthstone shall be hers."

"Will she ever recover from this accident?"

"It is no accident. Humans are so hard to convince." The woman showed no emotion. "I waited here for you — and her." She stared a moment at the fallen body of Rula. "She prayed to me night after night. She asked to be saved from her poor life. She offered a girl to me. In the end, it seemed she only wanted the minerals of the earth. She could have had much more." The woman shifted her hard gaze to Jabuli. "You ended that. Now it is all for your *daughter*. Everything is for her now. Although she is not your daughter. Is she?"

Fearful, Jabuli bowed. "No, she is not. She is Princess Adora of Sannan, daughter of Queen Dorothea. At the princess's request, I helped her flee her mother, who threatened to kill her infant brother. So we ran away." She lifted her head.

"And run away you did. Like any good tutor would do."

"You cannot judge me," Jabuli cried. "I have a pure heart, no matter the life I've had to live! I did not betray my charge. We must save lives, not cast some aside and welcome others. We must teach each other how to be one people together, not divided."

"Yet you took a life. Here in this house. Yet you cast one aside. You divided—"

"But she betrayed us!"

"She only prayed for a better life."

Jabuli was confused, her hands unable to be still. "Rula—she was supposed to help us, not lead us into danger."

"There is no danger. Only fear."

"Enough of your puzzles! I helped my princess! I did not betray her. I helped her do what *she* wanted to do. That's not betrayal!"

"And run away you shall. Again. There is nothing more for you here. Nor across these mountains. The desert stretches onward to the other side of the world and only dragons may cross it. You have come to the end of your journey, Jabuli Devry. Yozma is not your home, can never be your home. It is time to say farewell to your charge. Choose your words carefully."

Jabuli dropped to a knee, sobbing, her hand at her brow.

"I failed, my princess, little majesty. Forgive me."

With her head bowed, she mumbled the words she had learned as a child, a simple prayer her mama had taught her before she was killed by invading Olan soldiers and Jabuli was snatched away and taught to fight in the pits so long ago.

Before she could finish, she felt a hand over her shoulder.

"You did not fail me, Jabuli."

She looked up. Adora stood before her, engulfed in a glowing white aura.

"Are you alive?" asked Jabuli. She tried to smile, if only for the sake of a little girl's feelings. "You look just like a goddess come down from the clouds. A princess goddess."

Only then did Adora pause to look at herself, lifting one arm then the other. A puzzled expression fell over her face. Her mouth twisted into a puzzled grimace. Her white hair seemed to flutter in a breeze that Jabuli could not feel. Her garments had been burnt into a brilliant white gleam, and her hand, poised above Jabuli's shoulder, appeared almost transparent in the brightness that covered her skin.

"Where am I?" asked Adora, neither happy or sad. She turned in place, gazing around the room. "Can this be our palace? Is this my home now? Are you still my tutor?"

Jabuli could not speak.

"A true goddess does not live in a palace," said the woman, the goddess called Bo. "A true goddess needs no structures, although people sometimes make a house for her to rest in when she visits, whenever they call to her in their sorrow or their joy. Then she may visit."

The stone egg ceased its pulsing. The goddess Bo stared at it, resting steadily in her hand. She set the object down on the center of the table. The egg did not lean or tilt but remained perfectly upright.

"Am I a queen now?" asked the little girl, gazing at Jabuli.

"I...I don't know."

Turning from the table, the sorceress carefully examined Adora, circumscribing her white aura with nearly transparent hands, and seemed satisfied with her appearance.

"Yes...this is a good age. Although I had hoped to train her for several years first. When I was touched by the goddess Ushal, I had already lived seventy years. Look at me now: I still look seventy."

She lifted her empty hand and held it out, palm up. It seemed a gesture of welcome.

"This one will live a very long time. She will never grow older. Her body will always remain that of a child. What does she have? Ten years?"

"Why?" cried Jabuli. "Why must that be?"

"That is how the birthstone gives its power. 'Once chosen, frozen ye shall be.'"

"The birthstone?" She clenched her fists, shaking them in the air. "You mean the egg? The stone egg? Is that it?" She pointed defiantly at the object on the table. "*That?*"

"Yes. The birthstone is hers now."

Jabuli regarded the goddess Bo. "What is she supposed to do with it?"

"Use it for good. Or evil. Whatever she chooses."

"How can she choose? She's a little girl!"

"She is a goddess."

"A goddess? How?"

The goddess Bo smiled at long last. "You saw."

"That was an accident. We are meant to go to Yozma and raise this little boy. To save him from their cruel mother."

"That is a journey of a different direction, Jabuli Devry. Only you can take it. And take it you shall. I have seen it glow in the birthstone from the day of your birth."

"But—but what should I do now?"

"You must ask your goddess. Call to her. Send prayers."

"To Adora?"

"And she will answer you."

Jabuli regarded Adora, glowing as white as the winter moon, a smile on her pallid face, as though she had just gotten everything she had ever wished for and was still caught in the amazement of the moment.

"My Little Majesty...what will you have me do?"

Jabuli bowed low, her knees hard against the blood-stained floor, tears drowning her face, spilling off her chin.

"I don't know," said Goddess Adora. "Please protect my brother, I suppose. Keep him safe always."

"I swear I will do it!"

"And protect yourself, too."

"I will."

The sorceress took a step toward the open doorway, her feet not quite touching the floor. She paused as if fearing the next step, then spoke: "It is done."

Her next step brought a whirling wind with a tremendous roar, which came up the hillside and surrounded the hut. The walls shook then fell away, crumbling into dust and spinning into a dark maelstrom around them. The sorceress was likewise consumed. Day passed into night in the quickening of words. Above the swirling ring of storm, straight overhead, the black sky was full of twinkling stars. Once the storm faded, the ground was cool and moist at their feet, the grass matted and dirty. The low baying of goats became the only sound. The little hut was gone.

Jabuli collapsed, crumpled on the ground, holding the babe in her arms, afraid to open her eyes.

Soon the dawn broke over them.

"Adora," Jabuli called softly before she dared open her eyes. "My Little Goddess...."

"I am here," said a tiny voice. It sounded as though it had come from millions of miles away, the very last mote of dust left from an exploding nebulae, sailing forever to reach her ear.

Jabuli raised her face toward the voice, then opened her eyes and saw the princess, yet princess no more.

She was all aglow, as white as snow, holding the stone egg in her little left hand, her arm stiff and straight despite the weight of the stone. The egg seemed to sing, giving off a steady whine that Jabuli could barely hear, like the tap on a tin drum that echoes forever.

Jabuli gazed past Adora, staring over her white hair, seeing the dozens of dragons in mid-flight behind her. Thick waves of wings crossing the valley, soaring over the peaks, all of them coming to the hillside, she realized, all of them gathering above the little goddess.

33

Duty-Bound

"HEY! FANG-FACE! Here I am! Down here!" Corlan waved his arms frantically. "Here's what you want! Down here!"

The fang-master turned its head, lost its view of the bird-girl, and located the annoying noise on the ground. *That man,* it seemed to say with the next grumble. Then the fire burst out of its mouth, lighting the dusk, and Corlan dove into the pond.

In an instant the pond boiled until it was half-empty. He jumped up, his boots digging into the muddy bottom, and slogged to shore. He wiped off his boots on the grass.

From his hiding place in the brush, Corlan tried to find Madi in the sky but he did not see anything but the dragon. He hoped she got away while he distracted the dragon.

And the children were farther away and well-hidden by now.

The dragon descended, four taloned feet pressing into the soil of the road, wings folding against its sides—spanning the width of the road. Disliking tree branches poking the membranes of its wings, the dragon stood back on its hindlegs to shake its wings a bit, holding them half-open. It kept its wings above the treetops as it took several steps forward on its hind legs, searching for Corlan, the children, or that bird-girl. It was not amused.

Corlan found the wooden staff among the bushes where it fell as he dropped from Madi's grip. He sighed with regret that it was dull at each end. He looked for a sharp rock to shave off some of the wood to make it into a weapon, but he didn't find any suitable.

If the others were already safe, then Corlan need only wait out the dragon's boredom. Eventually it would fly away for something more amusing. Then he could catch up to the children and take them back to the wagon. He hoped nothing had been stolen while he was away. He worried about the horses he left tethered there—

"Cooorlaaaan!"

He turned, facing the road, recognizing the voice as Tam's.

"Here!" called Corlan down the road. He lifted his arm, waved it.

The dragon had ceased looking for him but the calling caught its attention.

"Keep down!" cried Corlan.

The dragon turned at his call, extended its head to the edge of the forest—a few yards from where Corlan crouched.

He guessed the children were on the opposite side of the road, hiding among the trees. But the dragon was focused on him now.

"No, run to your right! Up the road!" shouted Corlan. "I'll keep the dragon on me."

The light was failing and everything was transforming into black silhouettes against the orange sunset, but Corlan thought he saw two figures break from the treeline and run to his left. The dragon's face kept straight at him as he searched the road beyond the dragon for Tam and Bai Lo.

He held the staff up against his shoulder, felt its heft, and a plan came to him.

Corlan waited a moment to give the children a little more time to get away. Then he stood, staff in both hands, hiding it along his side. He stepped through the brush, loudly making his way to the road.

"Here I am!" he shouted. "Take me!"

The fang-master pulled back its huge head, pausing. Probably to see him better, thought Corlan. He knew the large dragon could not maneuver among the confining trees on each side of the road, so he was safe within its tangled bounds.

"Come on!" Corlan grunted. "Open that ugly gullet!"

The dragon seemed to understand his anger, his impudence, and growled. Its teal eyes brightened as its belly rumbled. Corlan knew what it was preparing to do—he hoped. At that instant, he couldn't tell the difference between the lingering scent of sulfur in the air from before and the fresh odor that emanated from the dragon's open mouth now. Bitter as its breath was, fire was coming—

Corlan dashed forward, breaking through the trees and brush, charging straight into the dragon's mouth, boots pounding up the coarse, pulsing tongue like the ramp onto a ship, entering between the two monstrous fangs, ducking under the upper teeth, kneeling at the top of the sloppy, mucus-coated gullet—where he planted the staff, pushing one end down against the base of the dragon's tongue and the top end pressed up against the roof of its throat, lodging it tightly there.

He somersaulted down the rough, undulating tongue and out of the dragon's mouth, his clothing soaked in dragon saliva, sticky and stinking.

The dragon choked, felt the object in its throat. Yet it was making fire already. Its breath billowed out, noxious to Corlan, who covered his face with his sleeve, nose pressed into the bend of his elbow. He rushed behind the trees at the side of the road.

The grunt which followed sounded like a plea for help, a final cry of apology. Then fire spilled out, yet not with any force. Flames leaked out the corners of its mouth. It cried out. The dragon twisted its neck back and forth as if trying to throw out the staff lodged in its throat. The gagging noise continued.

"Now if only I had a battle axe!" he growled.

Corlan knew he had only a few seconds until the dragon's throat muscles would snap the staff. Then the beast would either swallow the pieces of wood or spit them out. It would not be too wounded to continue pursuing him.

He jumped to his feet and ran up the road in the same direction he thought—*hoped*—Tam and Bai Lo had gone, back in the direction of the burning pile of men.

"Tam!" he called to the dark figures he saw ahead.

The two shadows stopped, turned toward him. One wore a gown that flapped in the breeze, so it had to be them. They were about three-hundred yards ahead as he ran to them.

Corlan did not have to look back to know he was being followed. He felt the earth move, knew the dragon was lumbering after him once more. It must have broken the staff—

A mighty roar shook the woods, the sound of hate.

In the darkness, Corlan could see the hulk moving down the road, its wings held aloft to avoid the trees on each side.

He stopped running toward the children and held his position.

There was nothing he could do without weapons but will away the dragon, make it turn around and go home by just the power of his mind. Like Joragus had done. Like Jemma said he could do with the right spell. But Tam had written the words on a scroll. He did not know them by heart.

"*Draconus en Tafu ae Luminarae....*" He searched his mind. *Was that the right spell?* He knew he should have paid better attention. "Or is it *Draconus raelana comptus lenius...?*" He didn't know the rest of the words. "*Draconus....* That much was right. *Draconus* go-away-from*us* now*æ!*"

The fang-master did not seem to get the message and continued stomping its way toward Corlan, half its steps on only its hindlegs, half on all four feet. It had indeed dispatched the errant staff and now grumbled with renewed vigor. Its belly was rumbling, and the air was thick with the odor of sulfur.

"Run!" Corlan shouted with all the capacity of his lungs. "Get into the woods!"

He saw the figures move, but not to the side, not off the road.

A raspy cough—

"Ruuuuuun!"

The fire breath burst out of the dragon's mouth at full strength— as straight a blast as he had ever seen. The spear of flame launched over him and lit up the road as he fell to the ground at the dragon's forefeet. Two figures ran far ahead, he could see. One fell. The other stopped and went back.

The flames shot down the road like a wagon pulled by a team of mad horses, streaming narrower and narrower the further away from the dragon they flickered—and faded out. The two figures were just out of reach.

The dragon stepped forward, ignoring Corlan who was on his back on the dirt between its forefeet.

More rumble from the dragon's belly, the cough, then—

The flame was thicker, filling the road from treeline to treeline. Branches caught fire. Dry leaves exploded into a conflagration.

Ahead, Corlan could only see fire. The entire road was aflame. He heard screaming. He got to his feet, just behind the tip of the dragon's swishing tail.

Breaking through the towering wall of fire down the road, a lone figure stumbled, arms raised, body streaming flames, shrieking—

The dragon, being a dragon, let out a long growl at the burning figure, then raised a forefoot and set it down hard.

Madi perched on the back of the wagon, now in full harpy mode, just as she once had done on an old donkor cart. She ruffled her tawny feathers every so often and craned her neck to gaze about, always wary of what might be preparing to attack her or her friends. She did not speak, not even the tweets and caws and cries as before. Yet she knew what Corlan was thinking, it seemed, and followed his movements with her large owl eyes as he went about his tasks.

With the horrors of the previous day and night, there had been no thieves to bother the wagon or the supplies. The two horses left there had spooked and one of them had come untied, possibly tore its bonds, to escape. One remained yet was not calm and pulled at the rope fixing it to a tree. It was good the wagon was not disturbed as Corlan needed certain items more than ever.

He rubbed the balm over the boy's skin, especially those places struck by fire. He was careful to apply the thick, pungent material around the boy's eyes. Gently lifting the boy's head, he placed his open hand over the crown and gently rubbed the balm there, from ear to ear and forehead to the back of his neck, all the places where curly black hair used to reign.

Corlan did not speak as he worked. It seemed words had no more meaning. If only he'd had a better weapon than a wooden staff. If only they had escaped in a different direction. If only they had not run away to begin it, he thought. If only he had humored them, gave in a little, encouraged them a bit more that their dream would be achieved soon enough. Then maybe they wouldn't have run away.

That dream would never become reality now, he sighed. A slow line of droplets dribbled down his whiskered cheeks as though they were parading from a mortician's hut to a cemetery. He wiped them away, would not give them any role in the drama.

I was meant to be alone on this journey. It was for me alone to take the risks, to bear the burden, to accept the consequences.

He gazed down at the boy, resting on the wagon under the watchful eyes of Madi. If not for the fate a handful of anonymous gods had bestowed upon the boy — that he should not be allowed to ride the lifter up — he would not be so disfigured. The gods were cruel — had no concerns for the lives of men and boys. And girls.

What he could gather from the dirt was barely enough to bury in a patch of land up the slope from the pond. Broken, charred remains, hardly distinguishable as a girl. Bones and leathery flesh. A girl who had just started to be a woman. He spoke words he remembered from long ago when soldiers died and he had to speak a few words over their torn bodies.

She was a delightful girl, too long abused, then saved by a boy who believed he was a man. That didn't sound right to him. He must keep the focus on her. *She had been forced into a long and miserable life which she did her best to endure. She escaped that life thinking a better one awaited her. And yet....*

He had broken down then, kneeling beside the mound, weeping. It was not until later he realized he had wept not only for a girl he hardly knew but for all the cruelties of the world he had tried to fight and failed. Years and years of fighting against the gods and their plans for him. And their plans for humankind!

The morning calm did nothing to assuage his feelings. As a soldier he was duty-bound to keep going, keep fighting, never withdraw into rage or explode in anger at the events of the day. Or slip into the dark pit of sorrow. He must always be ready for the next day, for the next fight. As a dragonslayer, he thought he'd gained the luxury of being a man alone who lived life completely, obeying only himself with no compromises, no turning back to whatever a mother or father had said, no general or sniveling prince had commanded, nor even what a woman might request him to do or say or think. He was supposed to be free of all that. Yet he realized that responsibility still had its claws deep in him.

Tam took a deeper breath and Corlan sat back from his work. He wiped the boy's brow again with a moist cloth.

The snorting of a horse caused him to look up. It was not his own horse calling, still tethered to the tree. It was a new rider entering the camp.

His eyes widened. He bounded up and stood with hands on his hips. The rider slowed and halted, the horse snorting at the thick odor of sulfur lingering in the air. The rider climbed down.

He regarded her only an instant before they rushed to embrace.

"I saw the fire last night," said Naka Wu, "and rode as fast as I could."

Corlan stormed back and forth across the campsite as Madi circled protectively overhead.

"It stared at me. Straight at me, the way a belligerent child looks at disbelieving parents. The child's happy to be bad but the parents can never believe the insolence. The same with that beast. It gave me the same look. As though it were making certain I witnessed its crime — and pleased with itself, pleased that it could curse me by harming my children."

He glared at Naka Wu, sitting with the boy on the wagon. She did not respond, brushing the boy's unhurt arm.

"After it blew fire the second time, it turned and stared straight at me. It knew it was hurting me. That seemed to be what it wanted, so it inflated its belly, launched itself into the sky. I had no chance to kill it. I had no weapon."

He paced as Naka Wu changed the moist cloth that lay over the boy's eyes. She set the bowl beside his shoulder and again applied the balm to his eyelids. The eye on the worst side of his body seemed injured, the glassy outer curve now flat and mottled.

"Just a boy and a girl," Corlan growled. "They never had anything to do with dragons. Completely innocent."

Her fingers worked lightly down Tam's burnt cheeks and over his singed nose. The boy did not move. His breathing was shallow but regular. He had yet to speak but winced at each touch.

"At least he's alive." Corlan joined her, sitting beside the boy. "It might not be the best outcome, though."

"You cannot blame yourself," she told him.

"I blame the dragon." He sniffled, looked away. "The sooner I can get to the marshes the sooner I can end this scourge. A few years after I destroy the nesting grounds there won't be any dragons."

She helped Corlan turn the boy on his side to wash his back and apply the balm there. Some of the skin was black, burnt through. The boy protested with a hand pushing against her arm.

After they left the boy to rest on his unscathed belly, Naka Wu went to Corlan, wrapped her arms around him from behind, and lay her cheek against the back of his head.

"I understand what you desire," she said. "To make him whole again. There is a better way."

He turned within her embrace. "What is that?"

"Instead of journeying west to Teraut, come back to Covin. Yet, before we arrive there, I will take you to a village on the river. You can hire a boat to take you downstream, and you will reach the marshes. Near the village there's —"

"There's a river?"

"It starts north of Luval and grows wide where it passes that city. I don't know what lies beyond."

"The river goes into the marshes?"

"I'm certain. I rode a boat some way down the river in my youth. My regiment attacked Luvali camps...." She brushed her hands over his chest, staying behind him. "If you wish, I can take the boy with me to Covin. Perhaps something can be done for the boy there. Many healers there."

"Not Covin. He's a boy. You know what happens to boys in a city like that. I won't abandon Tam there."

"It's not abandoning him. We have physicians, and we have people who would care for him."

Corlan broke from her grasp. "Better he return to Danapo and live among the deformities and disfigured folk there."

She pursed her lips. "We have what you would call wizards who can help him recover, make him whole again. The balm is only a quick solution. It's only for the pain. If you want his skin to grown again...."

He turned and gazed at her. "A wizard, eh?"

"I know her. She can be trusted. She lives near Covin."

His hands went to his head, as though holding in all the thoughts that were screaming to be heard. He dropped his hands, swaying.

"Look at this...."

Corlan took her arm, led her to the wagon. He dug in the bags and found what he was looking for: a small jeweled box. He showed it to her, then opened the lid.

"What's that?" Naka Wu cried in surprise.

"It is the last part of Joragus, the magus of Metta. He was killed by a dragon that attacked Unting. He saved my life that day."

"And you kept his finger?"

"You don't understand." He closed the lid, set the box down on the wagon's lowered rear panel. "He knew the Clona arts. To make again an animal from the parts of the previous animal. Or person. He made himself again four times. Each time he was born as a babe and grew into old age."

"That is certainly a wizard." She put her hand on his shoulder. "The woman near Covin is the same. She knows the arts, whatever they may be called, many of the arts. The boy will come to no harm there. She can repair him."

Corlan regarded her a long while, then nodded. "It may be the only way to save him. There is no mission now but to save the boy." He stared into the sky. "Then I'm coming for you, dragons!"

"I see how much he means to you, Corlan of the Burg."

"I'm responsible for him." *By the gods, I've been given this task! For what purpose, I cannot know. A test? A lesson?* "So say the gods."

Only after the boy was stable and prepared for the journey did Corlan think to search for and recover the bag of weapons he had hidden in a ditch near the campsite. It took a few minutes walking in the brush beyond the edge of the campsite but he located them and brushed off the bag. Under the bag was the dragonslinger, wrapped in cloth, with a quiver of iron bolts. His sideblade had been taken by the men of the bandit village. If not for their theft, he cursed, he would have been armed, able to fight the dragon.

He glanced at Tam, lying restlessly in the back of the wagon, his face and shoulders covered with moist cloths. Naka Wu sat with him, her hand on his hip.

The gods could be cruel, thought Corlan. They could put ideas in a young man's head and cause him to do crazy things, dangerous things. He knew it was not all Tam's fault. He had been a young man, too, a very long time ago, and fallen to the same distractions, the same temptations. Love is a strange poison, he considered, turning his eyes to Naka Wu.

"They are untouched," he announced, hefting the bag onto the wagon with a loud *harrumph*. The jangle of metal pleased him.

He opened the bag and pulled out a couple of medium swords, examined them, strapped the belt of one scabbard around his hips and set the other under the riding bench of the wagon as a spare. The dragonslinger he took in his hands and examined it for dirt, then loaded it with a trident barbed iron bolt.

He caught Naka Wu watching him. He remembered promising to give her a lesson on how to fire the weapon. After they see to the boy's healing then....

"There won't be another attack I'm caught without any weapons. Never again. I swear it."

Corlan studied the wagon, then the horses. The remaining horse was a dun mare with a shaggy brown mane. Zora, Corlan had heard Tam calling the horse. The boy was good with beasts. Leaving some supplies behind to lighten the load, Corlan hitched Zora and Naka Wu's sleek black gelding, Slate, to the yoke. Together they could pull the wagon down the road well enough.

Madi flew ahead. Corlan took the reins first yet as they turned to depart the campsite, he handed them to Naka Wu as he gazed back over his shoulder at the road they had traveled — the Road of Death, he thought to himself. Rage erupted through him for the girl who was lost, and for parents who would never know what became of a girl called Bai Lo.

34

Skin to Skin

THREE DAYS OF FREE ROAD, wind and rain, ancient trees watching them pass, and only a cart with an old man to give them any concern. They camped as they had done before, except with Tam on the wagon. Naka Wu slept beside him, half for warmth, half protection.

Mornings came fast and the days seemed to last long. One night snow fell over them, an inch or so, and they rushed to warm Tam, throwing their own blankets over him.

"In the Burg snow is common," Corlan told Naka Wu. He flicked flakes from her shoulders. She wore a black cloak and had pulled the cowl over her head, her braided hair hanging down her front. The white flakes spotting her garb, sparkling in the morning light.

"This is the second time I've seen this in all my life," she said. "Too warm in this southern land. It must be a horrible thing to be covered in this for many weeks and months."

"People learn to cover themselves with woolen clothes," he said with a grin. "They make clothing from the hair of remade animals called *alpor*. The beasts have long necks yet are fat with hair." He gazed at her, knowing how good it was that she had ridden back to them. "It's a time of beauty. We celebrate it: the end of the year, knowing that spring will come. We dance in the snow and give gifts to each other, light fires, and make joy together."

"Make joy? In the snow?"

"No, in a house. On a bed." She seemed to doubt him. "It's good to make joy beside a fireplace while the snow falls outside. You can watch it through the windows. I love getting up from a joyful bed, seeing the snow outside."

She blushed, and he was not sure if he had ever seen that rosy flush on her face.

"And no dragons fly while the snow falls," he added.

"Then snow is a blessing."

"Indeed it is." He turned back to Tam. "Now let's get this boy to your wizard."

Corlan saw the boy was shivering, even with the extra blankets on him. "You all right, Tam?"

"Cold...," he moaned.

"Yes, it's cold. Winter's come now. Remember winter back in the Burg?" He watched the boy's grimace come and go. "You play in the snow much?"

"Cold...."

Corlan glanced at Naka Wu. "At least he's speaking."

With a nod, she climbed onto the wagon and lay beside the boy, pulling the blankets over both of them. Corlan got up onto the bench and they started off for another long day's ride.

The bent woman in the ragged black robe who greeted them looked older than the world. Her wrinkled face seemed to show a map of all the rivers and streams of the realm, her reddish skin like the soil in the Valley of Death. Her gray hair was in tatters as it cascaded down her back and in her stoop dragged on the floor. On her scalp were perfectly round bald spots where it seemed a clump of hair had been yanked free. All about her hung a pungent scent of death, the moldy bitterness of bodies sewn up quickly for ceremony.

She lifted her gaze. "Naka, you've come home."

The warrior woman smiled in a way Corlan had never seen. So this is her wizard, he thought, comparing this dirty, broken, old woman to Joragus' relative spryness late in his fourth iteration. How long had this woman lived?

He shifted Tam in his arms, waiting.

"This was never my home, blessed Urma," said Naka Wu. "I only played in your garden."

"Your childish footsteps are still pressed into the ground. I will never garden over them."

The old woman took Naka Wu by the hand and led her from the snow-flecked stoop where they had stood to knock on the coarse, wooden door. Naka Wu had ducked her head to enter. So had Corlan. The woman led them into the sitting room and gestured to the large gray and yellow cushions that had been embroidered with scenes of birds and fish. The woman bade them sit on the cushions, crossed-legged beside the short wrought-iron table, its top made of polished glass—where a thick film of dust had collected.

Corlan gently laid the boy on the floor beside the table.

"I will make tea for you," said Urma. She glared at Corlan. "It is the custom here."

"I thank you, Urma," Naka Wu spoke up, "but there is no rush for that. We have urgent affairs. We need your help—your powers. Can you help this boy?"

Tam lay limp on the floor. With a nod from Naka Wu, Corlan carefully unwrapped the moist cloth covering the boy's face and shoulder. He was asleep, it seemed, his eyes closed and his breathing labored.

Urma pinched her thick eyebrows together at the sight of him.

"Alive yet?" she asked.

Naka Wu nodded.

"Just barely," said Corlan. "There was a girl, too, yet she did not survive. There wasn't enough of the body remaining to bring with us so I buried her."

"Can you help this boy?" asked Naka Wu.

Urma, already low to the floor in her hunched pose, proceeded to examine the boy. She touched her fingers to the skin of his face and head. That side of his face was the worst, where the dragon's fire had melted the skin. As it cooled, it set into a different configuration. She pulled open the wounded eye and stared.

"How old is he?" asked the old woman.

"I think he was twelve when we left the Burg. That's our city in the northeast," said Corlan. "We've been on this journey for...for months. He might be thirteen now."

"Then his recovery will require at least thirteen days."

"Only thirteen days?" asked Naka Wu.

"At least. Could be more."

"How long?" asked Corlan.

"The protocol is set. It must be judged each day. Only then will we know how long." Urma stared at Corlan. "I trust you, Naka, yet this man frightens me. Is the boy his son?"

"I've known this man for a month. The boy has always been with him. He treats the boy as his son. The injury was accidental and this man is not to blame. It was a dragon that did this."

"A dragon?" asked the woman. "That's a rare thing."

"It was up north, near that Sei Bo statue," said Corlan.

"A rare thing, still."

"I did not see it yet I saw the damage it caused," Naka Wu spoke. "The forest was aflame. There were large footsteps in the dirt of the road. People were burnt black."

"It was a dragon's fire that did this to the boy," said Corlan.

Urma frowned, fingering a length of her long hair. "I thought it might be from the rebellion. Just a boy getting in the way. Covin's not a good place for a boy." She narrowed her eyes at Naka Wu. "I heard you were involved in that rebellion. Now everything is much worse, I think."

"I'm on my way there. I thought you could help the boy. I don't see how the rebellion matters for saving the life of this boy. I rescued him from Covin, went with him to Danapo."

"Rescued? Is that what you call it? I heard people call it fleeing prosecution. Aaaa, I pay no mind to the happenings of that awful city yet when one of my own is named, I listen. You cannot go there now. They will kill you."

"Why? What have you heard? Fa Mei rules?"

The woman caught a laugh trying to fall from her mouth. "Dead. Hung by the neck. And her twelve conspirators, too. You are number thirteen." Urma glared at her. "What deeds have you done?"

Naka Wu blanched; Urma knew everything. She tried her best to explain what had happened but the old woman's stern expression never changed. Caught in the moment, she'd had to make choices, and only in the days that followed did she have time to reflect on those choices. One choice was to escort the Danapoi ambassador back to her home—which was how she had teamed up with this man who, by the nature of all men, must be an enemy.

"It's not that way, Urma. He is not my enemy, nor yours." She lay her hand on Corlan's knee as they sat on the cushions. "We have a connection between us. More than two fighters. I have a feeling for him." She regarded Corlan with dewy eyes. "I—I love him. Is that the right way to say it?" She paused, then gazed at the boy on the floor. "And I love this boy. Can you restore him to how he was before the dragon's fire caught him?"

Corlan regarded Naka Wu, clasped the hand that she had placed upon his knee. She squeezed his hand. He could not meet her eyes at that instant yet something powerful surged up his arm and struck his heart. It missed a beat, then resumed.

"I will help the boy," said Urma in a weary tone. "It is my nature to help all who need help. And I'll even use my powers for good not evil. That is the pledge we magi take when we enter apprenticeship. Yvella was my mentor. She was long passed before you were born, Naka. There was another girl with me, called...I think her name was Dreva. She went up in flames when she spoke the wrong words, trying to conjure fire just for some warmth one night. One slip of the tongue and she burst into flames herself. So only I remained to be taught by Yvella."

"I remember you talked about Yvella, but never said anything about Dreva. How are your powers now?"

"I haven't gone up in flames yet." Urma started to chuckle, then stopped herself. "Magic powers grow stronger as we count down the years. I have one-hundred-fifteen years now, with only fourteen more to live. So says the rabbit in my visions. I didn't listen at first—who would take a rabbit seriously?—so I didn't believe. Then she hopped ahead of me on a long trail and at each bend of the path sat a stone with my name on it, written in Luvali. Counting the stones, I came to the final number. The tally was complete. I knew then what day I shall be done with this life. That's both a blessing and a curse."

She screwed up her face like there was an unpleasant taste in her mouth and she wanted to spit something out.

"Unless I bend to my old scrolls and use the Clona arts to mend myself. It was forbidden by Yvella. In fact, the original words were written in a *book*. Do you know *book*? It's a flat type of scroll that turns page after page, something from the ancient days. She had me copy them all out onto scrolls because the paper of the book was crumbling away. I paid no mind of the words as I copied them lest I conjure a spell at random. So I do not know them now."

"Do you have those scrolls?" asked Naka Wu.

"Certainly!" The old woman cackled like a yard full of chickens. "It is the same for healing the boy. I have those scrolls, too. His head and shoulder can be restored by the same words we speak to remake ourselves."

"Excuse me," Corlan cut in. "I knew an old magus—"

"Old! Always putting 'old' with 'magus'! You know we were all young once, just as you are now. Do not pity us for our age, for we know much that you don't even know you don't know, nor would ever think to learn because your mind is so filled with adventure and thoughts of the violence you've done rather than the peace you can be spreading across the land!"

"Apologies, madam," said Corlan with a curt bow. "I said I knew a magus who *appeared* old to my eyes and he claimed to be in his fourth life, what he called an *iteration*. He said he also used the Clona arts yet it required much more than speaking words off a scroll. He said it required a well-stocked kitchen and many months of labor. And then it resulted in a babe, like any babe, and the child had to be raised like any child and taught everything all over again as he grew. He said he taught himself. He made another of himself and taught that child everything he knew until the child was a magus himself who appeared old to my eyes—and then saved my life several times. The last he gave his own life and begged me to remake him."

"Is that so?" Urma grinned like she had heard similar stories.

"I said *he said* that. I cannot prove it's true." He turned to Naka Wu. "Let me get it."

Corlan stood and went out to the wagon, returned with the jeweled box in his hands. He sat once more on the cushion and held the box in his lap. Carefully, he opened the lid, lifted out the item wrapped in black cloth.

"This is all that remains of Joragus, the magus of Metta."

He unwrapped the cloth and extended his hand out to Urma.

Her eyes widened. "A finger?"

"Yes, that's all I have of him."

"What a smelly thing," said Naka Wu.

"It is decaying now," Corlan admitted. "The damp weather has seeped into the box, molding it despite my wrapping."

"It is enough, I think," said Urma. "So you will have to choose."

"Choose?" asked Corlan.

"I can restore your boy's body or I can remake your magus. It is not possible to do both with only a finger."

Corlan shook his head. "You want me to give you the finger? To restore Tam? I thought you could make his skin grow clean. Replace the burnt and melted skin. This finger is only meant for remaking the magus Joragus."

"I need the flesh of a living being to use in the restoration."

"That finger is not quite living any longer."

"It is enough. Yet you must not delay even one more day."

"Then do it. Use the finger to restore this boy. I'm responsible for him. He needs to go on living and have a good life and become a man in time. Joragus lived three-hundred thirty-eight years over four iterations. I think he must've known this iteration would be his last when he stepped in front of that dragon. He told me to cut off his finger for another day."

Urma nodded all through Corlan's speech. When he fell silent, she only then gazed up at him.

"You people need to be at peace with the dragon folk," she spoke barely above a whisper.

"They are not dragon *folk*, they are dragons. Beasts," said Corlan, checking his angry tone. "Beasts of fire, and hate, and evil. We best be rid of them. That is my mission."

"Urma, please!" Naka Wu cut in. "We ask your help to save a boy. It goes beyond anything we did before or might do after. Save the boy. Please. That's all we ask of you. This is not about dragons."

Urma frowned. "Everything is about dragons when you are a...a dragonslayer. Am I right, Dragonslayer?"

"In any occupation it's always best to focus on the task you've trained for," said Corlan in serious tone. "Today I ask—we ask—for your help in restoring this boy, who I care for like my own son. I beg you to help him, for the love of Naka Wu who delighted you as a child."

Urma laughed openly. "Such etiquette given to an old woman!"

"Will you help us?" asked Naka Wu.

"Certainly." Urma nodded, stared at each of them. "They bring the bodies to me and I sew them together, make them look pretty so the families won't be too aggrieved. Those people in Madi's town never are kind to me, yet I do my *occupation* faithfully. I suppose I could restore one of their executed criminals. Wouldn't that be fun? Let the murderer return to Madi's town, walk the streets, restored to life...though his neck remains broken or his head teetering on his neck by the stitches I add to mend a lopped off head to a naked neck. I could certainly do that. Yet there's no want of the dead to walk the streets again. Is there?"

"No, definitely not," said Naka Wu.

"You said this town is...Madi's town?" asked Corlan.

"Yes, that's the name."

"It's named for Madi?"

"Yes, that's so."

"Who is Madi?"

"How do I know? Ancient times. All I ever heard was it's a place where great birds once gathered. The birds could carry people in their bellies then spit them out when they touched on the earth. Such trust people had in ancient days. No fear of the world. Harmony with nature! I don't understand how everyone went mad and started wars and now the world is divided between wyma cities and men cities. Or a town like this, of folk so poor they must share it. That is Madi's town. Mixed—both wyma and men. Yet they make it work somehow. Strange place. It's midway between Covin and Luval, a good place for a body-stitcher to gain some coin. They can send the bodies down the river or paddle them up. I work on all of them."

"You're really a magus, aren't you?" asked Corlan.

Naka Wu brightened. "Yes, she's the best—pardons to the magus you lost in Unting."

"She knows what I can do," said Urma, fingering her hair again. "I made her into the woman she is today. They would've butchered her but I made it clean. Now look at her: tough and strong as anyone born a boy and grown into manhood. She's taller than you! I'd put my wager on her to best you in fair combat. I surely would—and win that wager!"

Naka Wu hid her grin. "But I wouldn't fight this man."

Corlan glared at her, puzzled.

Naka Wu, perhaps sensing his thoughts, leaned over and took his arm, held it. Her hand clasped his hand. She dipped her head against his shoulder, let it rest there.

"First, let's restore the boy," she spoke.

Corlan and Naka Wu peered into the cramped room, a space filled with boxes large and small, bottles tall and short, vats and vials containing different colors of liquids. Some of them were boiling. A menagerie of curious metal tools hung on the wall or were strewn across a metal tray next to the long workbench. A pile of scrolls were stacked awkwardly on a shelf but one scroll was opened for reading, held open by fist-sized statues of dragons that grasped the corners of the parchment under their stony claws.

Urma worked on the boy, naked upon the table. It was the same table, Corlan thought, that she used when sewing up the dead bodies brought to her.

The boy winced at what she was doing and Corlan struggled to see.

"You mustn't distract me," the old woman grumbled upon noticing them. "You can watch from the door, if you must."

So they stood in the doorway, Corlan leaning against the wall. The magus kept her back to them. They could not see the procedure and she did not describe to them what she was doing. From time to time the sizzle of fire sparking alarmed them, the gurgle of fluids worried them. Corlan listened to Tam's murmurs, unable to discern words.

Standing beside Corlan, Naka Wu rose two inches taller. She saw his concern and wrapped her arm around his broad shoulders. He shook, surprised at her touch.

"You really love me?" he asked her, staring into the room.

"Does that surprise you?"

He turned to her. "Surprised to hear you say the words."

"They are only words. If you do not like them, forget them."

"I like the words."

She sensed a dark mood in his voice. "You are filled with the vile spittle of demons, Corlan of the Burg. If there were a potion I could give you, I would. Then you would be mine. Yet I have no potion so I dared speak the words."

He stared into the workroom, could only see the boy's legs stretched out on the table. Urma blocked his view of Tam's body and head.

"I know you care for the boy," said Naka Wu. "I don't know the reasons for caring so much for a boy that is not your true-born son. Yet I respect you for that. It must be a painful episode that drives you to be responsible for him and seek to heal him. Whatever it may be, I admire that. I never had any person to care for in my life—not since I was an infant."

"And what kind of babe were you?" he said coldly.

"Happy, I suppose. Like most babes."

"And then...?"

Her arm tightened around his shoulders, tight to the point of discomfort. "Do not fear my strange birth. What matters is now. I returned to you when I saw the fire, yet before then I rode slowly, constantly questioning myself, deciding if I should return to Covin or go with you—if you would allow me to go with you."

"Do you desire slaying dragons?" he asked, his tone lighter.

"No, Corlan. I desire being by your side, no matter what you do. If slaying dragons is what I shall witness, then I witness that. If you are merely traveling to the marsh to see what is there, then I witness that travel, also. If you lay on your bedroll and dream of your home, then I shall witness you tossing and turning in your sleep."

"My home...." He seemed to have forgotten it.

She let her arm drop from his shoulders.

"I know you have wounds, Corlan. I've seen your well-formed body, so wide your shoulders and many muscles. The scars on your skin tell many stories and I want you to tell them to me." A tiny laugh popped out of her throat. "Tell them as I touch your scars with my fingers. Gently, of course. Being a warrior, I know how precious the gentle touch is and I want to give that to you."

Corlan extended his arm and placed it heavily around her waist, pulled her closer, still watching the operation in the workroom.

"You said we are not fated—"

"A warrior has a code to obey. I also follow the goddesses of my mother. So my life is not my own. Yet at some point in every life there comes the greatest battle of all. We bring everything we have to this battle. I mean the battle for our hearts. We ask: Do I keep this heart for myself, or do I give it to another?"

He turned to her. Without either one meeting the other's eyes, they embraced. Their arms squeezed tightly around each other, as though determined to fuse their spirits.

"One day we must sleep together on the same bedroll," she said. "Then you may decide if we should stay together. Until that day, let us pray for the health of your boy—of *our* boy."

"Yes, the boy."

They released each other, both turning to check the procedure.

"I could do without the love chatter," said Urma in a rusty voice. "I must not be distracted."

More clinking of metal as she maneuvered her tools. The boy was not moving. The scent drifting from the room was thick with death. It made them scratch their noses.

"It goes well?" asked Naka Wu, covering her nose and mouth.

"The boy is asleep. I gave him a potion. Better to sleep through these steps. The scroll is clearly written yet I still needed to read it thrice. I'm short of Lerea cream, too, and could make more use of the *haline* if I had more. Do not worry. I made substitutions. He will be well soon."

"You said it takes thirteen days?" asked Corlan.

"Yes," said Urma. "Or more. Only the goddess knows."

"Which goddess is that?" he dared ask.

He waited for an answer, for more explanation. Yet she seemed to be concentrating on her work. Her elbow swung up, then down, as though she were sewing.

"Today is the first step," she spoke after a while. "Removing the burnt skin. Removing the melted, re-formed skin. I apply the haline to clean the underlayer. Next I will grow new skin. Then I shall sew the new skin on the underlayer. Much potion is needed so the body does not turn sour. Or feel the pain. After thirteen days we can see if my magic worked. Or not. Then we wait more."

"What happens if it does not work?" asked Corlan.

"You are the worrying one, I see." She cleared her throat. "He will remain unsightly, if my magic does not work. But he will be alive."

"Thank you," said Corlan. "Do your best work."

"All my work is my best. For almost a hundred years. Practice is the mother, the daughter is perfection."

Corlan frowned. He glanced at Naka Wu standing beside him.

"Come with me," she said, turning from the room. "Let us go out and clear our heads. Let us leave Urma to her work."

"The smell is rather strong."

He followed her out.

Once outdoors, they saw the yard and the hills and forest beyond were dusted with snow. The winds had fallen off and the gray skies painted the landscape in gloomy shades. He went to the wagon to be sure the supplies were secure.

"The world is full of death today," said Corlan, gazing at the cold, morbid sky.

"You have not trained in many days." She began unlacing her vest. "Not me, either. We warriors must always be ready for a fight. Agreed?" She slipped off her black leather vest and tossed it on top of a tree stump in the yard.

"I agree."

He watched her strip off the vest. Beneath, she wore a sleeveless tunic, also black. Her arms were lean yet muscular.

"So we are training now?" asked Corlan, going to the wagon. He grabbed the scabbard with the medium sword in it.

"Yes. Training will take your head away from the boy's surgery. You need to move about."

"So be it, then."

Corlan gave her a glance, smiling. He set down the scabbard on the ground and pulled his shirt off over his head. He tossed it to the front stoop of the house. The cold air felt good on his skin.

He breathed deeply as he examined Naka Wu. She was lean. Oh, she had muscles, he could see, yet they were lithe and taut, much like the slender legs of a horse, not bulky like the legs of a hippor.

She slid her two-handed sword out of its scabbard and began cutting the air with a fierce attack at invisible enemies. She spun effortlessly on each foot as she moved about the yard. Her muscles flexed, strength in each motion. Cuts to the left, gashes to the right. The sword rising over her head and the inevitable slash downward to sever an opponent in two halves.

She paused, glancing back over her shoulder at him.

"Will you not train with me?" She breathed deliberately. "Do I frighten you?"

"Not at all." He grinned. "I will join you."

Stepping around the yard, waving his medium sword, he went through his daily regimen like he had as an apprentice soldier.

"Shall we fight each other?" he called to her.

"It may be dangerous with edged blades," she replied.

"I have a staff. We can fight with sticks."

"We can."

Corlan strode to the wagon, returned the sword and scabbard. He pulled out two long sticks of about equal length, the longer one maybe six feet. He tossed the shorter one to Naka Wu.

"I think I should use the longer stick," she said.

Corlan gave her a smirk. "You have the reach on me already."

"Then it would be a fair fight, agreed?"

"Perhaps."

She nodded, set her sword in its sheath and leaned the scabbard against the tree stump. She stood and he stepped back, ready for her.

"Now it will be a fair fight," she said, grabbing her stick.

She swung herself into a defensive position. Corlan took up his position. Sensing the moment, both fighters attacked, swinging their sticks left and right, clapping stick to stick in perfect splendor, like a well-rehearsed dance. Neither could strike flesh or bone but only the other's stick.

"I don't want to hurt you," Corlan called out.

"Neither do I wish to harm you!"

"It's training."

"So fight me!"

"But you said you love me. How can I fight you now?"

"People who love each other often quarrel. They use words. We use sticks. That's the only difference."

She struck forward with the blunt end of the stick, punching Corlan in the gut. He fell back, lost his breath, almost losing his balance. He braced himself, recovered into a defensive posture.

"You had a weak point," said Naka Wu.

He stepped to the right, swung the stick at her shoulder. "Love. That's my weak point."

She caught the stick with her stick. "It is!"

He pushed her stick away with his and she swung back at him, aiming high for his head. He barely caught her stick before it could thump him on the temple. Slipping quickly to the left, he slid to a knee as she swung her stick laterally at his shoulder—where his shoulder should have been. Instead, Corlan's lower position put him in the right position to jab the stick upward at her ribs.

She took the strike but kept her balance. Her face switched to a grimace that caused him concern.

How can I fight the one who loves me? It was impossible. *Beat her and she no longer loves me. Lose to her and she no longer respects me.* He had to make her believe he was fighting his hardest yet not hurt her too much. He got one lucky strike on her; he regretted it.

"Come at me, sir!" she shouted.

He grinned, then charged at her. Swinging his stick toward her shoulder, she countered with her own strike to his hip. His strike missed as hers landed. He fell to a knee and she pushed him over with her foot and stood over him with the butt end of her stick at his throat.

"When an opponent challenges you to attack, you will always be the one who loses. Never accept the direct challenge. Mistress Kana Tei taught me. Did you learn nothing in your training? Ah! It must be a long time in the past. Then you got soft slaying dragons."

Corlan shook his head. "I'm being gentle with you, lady."

She held her stick away with one hand and reached down with the other hand to assist him in standing. Instead, he grabbed her hand and pulled her down. He wrapped his arms around her slim body and suddenly they were kissing. After a moment, with lips still locked, he rolled them over so Naka Wu was under him.

"Are you sure you wish to do this on the snow?" she asked.

He halted, pondering what he was doing.

"Would not a bed be better?" she asked, lips pursed.

"Yes, it would."

He threw himself off her and sat up. "My apologies. I lost control of myself."

"There's no shame in that," she responded. She rested her hand on his bare back, chose a scar to trace with her finger.

"Not shame in...*that*. I mean shame in letting my thoughts go there at all, rather than staying on the boy and his misery."

She frowned but nodded her understanding. "Even a warrior can divide her thoughts. In battle she thinks of the fight while she also thinks of the lives at home she is saving."

He turned where he sat and gazed into her eyes. "Where did you learn so much about fighting? More curiously, where did you learn so much about life? Your words.... How can you be so perfect?"

She gave a laugh that fell to the snow. "You heard what Urma said: practice is the mother and the daughter is perfection."

"You practice a lot, then."

"As much as I can."

Corlan grinned. "I meant fighting skills."

"So did I."

They stared at each other a moment before rising, again staring into each other's eyes, more as a challenge the second time.

"And the other? The loving skills?" he dared ask after a bundle of heartbeats had pulsed through him.

She closed her eyes, inhaling a frosty breath. "I am a novice."

Corlan held back a grin, unsure whether to speak kindly or tease her. "Then we must help you gain experience."

"You may train me." Her smile broke open his grin. "Only when you have earned that right. I pick my teachers with great care."

He nodded dutifully. "I would expect that of you."

She playfully pushed him away, started toward the stump upon which lay her vest. "I expect to learn a lot."

He went to his shirt. "As do I."

"Until the student surpasses the teacher."

35

Wounds

WITH A FRESH COVERING OF SNOW on the ground, Corlan awoke, alone on the bedroll, unlike in his dream. He arose, pulled on some clothing, and wandered absently to the front door. Outside, he saw that the footprints they had made the previous day were covered and he longed to mark the yard again with her. His body felt the fight of the previous day, especially as he stretched his arms out and cracked his back.

"Come quick," said the old woman appearing behind him. "The boy has awakened."

Urma took his hand and pulled him through the cluttered house to the workroom. Tam lay on the table, covered with a thick balm and wrapped in cloth from waist to head. His face was covered but he moved his lips, wiggling the fabric over them.

"Tam," called Corlan softly. "Can you hear me?"

The boy spoke but Corlan could not understand.

"How do you feel? Terrible pain, I imagine. Yet it will make you whole once more. As if the dragon never burned you."

"I...."

Corlan pressed his ear to the cloth over the boy's mouth. "What's that you say?"

"I...ha...."

"I can't understand you." He waited. "It's no bother. No need to speak now. You rest and heal."

"I hate...."

The boy shook his head, perhaps trying to knock the cloth from his face. He succeeded. The strip of cloth over his face dropped to the floor. He tried to stare up at Corlan but his eyes were nearly swollen shut. Around his eyes the skin was a deep red, but it was now closer to the correct configuration, no longer sagging sadly like melted wax on a candlestick.

"You look much better, Tam. I know it hurts, but in time you will return to normal. Then we'll be away to slay us some dragons, eh?"

"I hate...*you.*"

Corlan stood up straight. He gave a surprised look to Urma. She turned away to tend to her business.

Naka Wu appeared in the doorway, wearing a thin white gown that tied in front. Her long black hair flowed freely, released from its braid. She stepped barefoot into the room.

"I heard talking...."

"The boy is awake," said Corlan.

She stepped in and gazed down on Tam. "Is it better?"

Tam seemed to know her, closed his eyes after a moment.

"He is better now," said Urma. "This is a normal response at this stage of the procedure. We will know tomorrow whether or not the body accepts the new skin."

She leaned down and hugged the old woman. "Thank you for your help."

"Yes, thank you," said Corlan, stepping back from the table.

"I do it for you, daughter I never birthed. And the boy, innocent creature that he is. So long since I worked on such a young body. If you wish, you may believe I do it also for the man this boy hates."

"Hates?" Naka Wu's face was glass.

"He said that. He hates me," Corlan explained, turning away from them. He filled the doorway, ready to exit.

"I'm sure he meant he hates the pain."

Corlan paused, kept his back to the table. "No, I understand. He lost his lover. That's more painful. He blames me for that. And I must accept the blame for that."

"He's just a boy. It's his first wound—a wound to his heart." She pressed her hand down on Tam's chest. "I know that sensation. The first wound is the most painful because it's the first time we learn we are not invincible, not as we always thought. We know then that we can be hurt. The first wound to the heart stays with us."

Corlan stared at the sitting room floor, his back to the workroom.

"I tried my best to stop that dragon, but I had no weapons."

"What you told me...it's not your fault that happened. It was the dragon's fault."

"They ran away from the camp."

"So they are to blame? Children?"

"No...." He cleared his throat, turned to regard the old woman, his eyes narrowed. "I went after them. I found them captured, in a camp of thieves. We escaped."

"And that's your reason for taking the blame?"

"Everything is there for me...for me to accept the blame." He turned to face all of them but only Naka Wu met his eyes. "I'm here because of dragons. I swore to slay them—as many as I can. I'm on a journey to the marshes to destroy the nesting ground. Then dragons will die away and we will be free of their terror."

"A fool's mission," grunted Urma.

Naka Wu lay her hand on Tam's belly, stretched her other hand out to Corlan, but he did not take her hand.

Instead, he wrung his hands, anger flinging off his fingers like a magic spell to conjure fire.

"That fang-master...I could swear it knew me. It stared at me then let go the fire at the people it knew I was trying to save. It knew what it was doing, I swear. To punish me it struck at the children."

"You're putting pieces of a puzzle together, yet not seeing the picture," said Naka Wu. She lowered her hand.

"Leave him be," Urma snarled. "Men see what they wish to see."

Corlan wiped his brow. "I had the same feeling in the forest, on that road, as when the hornchin came upon us in Unting. It stared at me, too. It could have killed me right there in the riding range but, instead, it killed only people around me." He blinked. "And leaving Covin, too—that dragon, I had the same feeling. It almost seemed the dragon helped us escape by attacking the crowd in the market."

"And you believe they are following you? Hunting you?" Naka Wu responded. "Is that your story?"

"There is no other explanation. I thought they were dumb brutes, driven by hunger and hatred. Not like humans...."

"Are humans not driven by hunger and hatred?"

"Men are driven that way," snarled Urma.

"Some are driven so. The lower form of humans." He regarded the warrior woman a moment, remembering how they had fought in the yard. "Not like you and me."

"How are we so different?"

Corlan had to think a moment. He didn't wish to give an answer that she could easily parry.

"We make cities. We create things of beauty—art, music, all the damnable scrolls! We think of our actions before we engage them—usually. We...sometimes we feel guilt and shame for our actions. Or pride, joy. In the end, we talk to beings in the sky, ask for favors or beg forgiveness. We believe those rituals matter."

"How do you know dragons don't do the same?" Urma asked, seeing Naka Wu's grimace. "There could be cities. Perhaps in those marshes you seek. They could have some form of art you can never understand. And plenty of storytelling, too. How would we know?"

Corlan stood tall. "The fact remains that I am sworn to fulfill my mission."

"To kill the dragons?" asked Urma with a sneer.

"Yes, the nesting ground. Wipe them out as soon as possible and we will never be troubled by them."

"Suppose they have the same plan to wipe out us?" asked Urma, cocking her old head. "What then shall we do?"

Corlan gritted his teeth. "I'm doing it: striking first. That's my sworn mission. I was—and this boy—we were headed there before all these damnable detours got us into so much trouble."

Everyone stared at Tam's hand which had risen in the silence that followed Corlan's retort.

"You wish to speak?" asked Urma, going to the table. He did not seem worse, but a heated debate could upset anyone who was forced to listen.

"Tam?" called Corlan.

The boy lowered his hand. Urma leaned down over his face.

"What is it?" she asked him.

"I don't...."

"Yes, go on."

"Don't want to...to ride...with Corlan."

Urma straightened up, as much as a bent old woman could, and gave Corlan a hard stare.

He nodded, turned to go once more.

"The wound grows," said Urma to Naka Wu.

"Should I take him with me to Covin?" She searched for a sign from Corlan, found none. She turned to the old woman.

"That's no place for a boy to grow up," said Urma.

"It was a different place then."

"And now." Urma shuffled over to where Naka Wu stood. "You dare not return to Covin, either, dear Naka. Take the boy with you, if you must, but not to Covin. You must find a new home. For you and the boy. Teach him to be strong. Help him mend his wound."

Naka Wu glanced back over her shoulder, expecting Corlan to be in the doorway, but he had gone.

A new wave of morning snow blew across the yard as Naka Wu hurried to the door and stepped outside with a blanket wrapped around herself. Corlan was dressed and sorting the supplies on the wagon. He had set the dragonslinger on the ground near the stump and had gathered the most useful weapons beside it.

"Are you leaving?" she called to him.

He did not look up. "I suppose I should. Just need to decide what to take because one horse can't carry me and all of this. I'll live off the land as I go but I'll need the weapons."

She stepped off the stoop and walked barefoot across the snowy yard to him, the blanket wrapped around herself.

"You better say goodbye. You don't want to be rude after Urma did so much for your boy."

"You know he isn't my boy. It's by accident he is with me." His jaw clenched. "I'm responsible for him solely because a man should look after a child. Whether or not he wants to be with me or if he wishes to stay behind."

"You should stay until he is well." She put her hand on his arm to halt his work. "Let him recover. He may change his mind and want to go with you."

"You heard that woman: thirteen days it takes. Then only to see if the procedure had any effect. Thirteen days! How many dragons will be born? How many will attack? I cannot wait. My mission cannot delay further. Spring is coming. Eggs will hatch."

He gazed up at the two shadows that crossed the gray sky.

"There! You see them? They've been circling this area for the past hour. Featherbacks, by the look of them."

Naka Wu stared into the sky. The aerial beasts were too high for her to note any identifying features. Corlan described a featherback dragon for her as he continued sorting supplies.

"But it is winter now. I thought they sleep."

"Some do. Most live in areas where it never gets cold enough for hibernation. Besides, they know how to warm themselves, eh?"

"We are in strange times. I did not expect snow here. It comes only once in five years. Now dragons."

"Maybe that is the reason they fly, to escape the cold winds."

"Maybe that is the reason you want to escape."

He stopped his sorting and stared at her.

"The boy made his feelings clear. And I don't begrudge him the honesty he showed. He has a right to be angry. I did the best I could with him. Now I have to do what I entered the valley to do, what I swore to do when I left the Burg."

"At least wait until your magus is born again. The magus that died in Unting, as you said. Urma continues to work on your behalf. Be patient with her. She said that procedure would take longer."

"Longer! I don't have that time."

"A few weeks is all, she said."

Corlan paused his sorting. "She said one finger was not enough. She used some of it to grow fresh skin for the boy to wear."

"No, I heard her talking. Enough remains for her to try the Clona protocol. Then you get your magus back."

"Then I get a babe to raise." He shook his head slowly, resigned to his decision. "How would I care for him? How would I teach any magic to that child? I can't even read scrolls. That magus taught everything to himself—to a duplicate of himself." With hands on his hips, he glared at her. "I'm good for only one thing."

She went to wrap her arms around him. When she raised her arms to put them around his neck, the blanket slid off her shoulders and dropped to the ground. She held him close.

"Corlan of the Burg, what has so wounded you that you think so much about children?"

Caught in her arms, he tucked his chin beside her neck, curled his arms around her, his rough hands on her smooth back. His nose took in her smoky, flowery scent, like a fireplace where bouquets had been sacrificed.

"I've killed children," he said. "On my commander's orders. I've refused to kill children and taken the punishment for it. I've fathered children and know them not. Not their deeds nor their fates. I barely know their names. That is the wound. I've turned to a new life. But is it the right life for me? And I was a child myself, though I grew up too fast, pushed by the men in my life. I was a murderous child."

He took a deep breath, tried to hold it, couldn't.

"Tell me your wound," she whispered into his ear.

He breathed deeply. "One day I took a blade to a man who hurt me, cut him into pieces in my rage. That is a wound. Got judgment at the hands of my elders. Some of the marks on my back are from their whips."

She pulled her arms tighter around him, holding him with all her strength, as though she could squeeze out his pain.

"My dear...."

"I found a rough kind of redemption as a soldier. Yet my family would not claim me even though their relations ruled in the Burg. So I took my life to the north lands. I fought in the north for whichever prince needed a soldier. Lots of fighting there. Until I had enough of killing people."

"Corlan, my dear...."

"And what is your wounding?" he muttered. "What secrets do you put away at dawn?"

She kissed his cheek. "You know who I am. You know what I've done. I am an assassin. There is nothing lower than a guard who kills her queen. I will always believe I did right, but others will know it differently. I've lost my home. I could lose my life if I dare return there. For all I have done, now I am doomed."

His big arms surrounded her. "You killed my lover, yet it was only a ruse. You did what you had to do, and I had no choice in what I did. I was a doll led by magic. You freed me from that woman."

"We were both pushed into this...this fate." Her voice choked. "Both of us have been wounded by our fates. Yet even in our doom our wounds match."

He kissed her throat, made a line up to her chin.

"I was banished from the Burg. That makes me doomed, too. They thought I would die in the Valley of Death, but I found cities to the west. And I found you, Naka. You know what I've done, and yet you seem to forgive me of my faults."

"Every person has faults, some hidden and others in the open. They come with our hair, our blood, our skin. We cannot dismiss them." She kissed his mouth, softly, as though she feared his lips would be too hot. "Your faults match with mine, too. Sadly. I could easily say let's be assassins together, but you know that would be the end of us. You could just the same say let's go and be dragonslayers together. That also could be the end of us. We both are descending into a void we know not."

"The end...of us."

"We are falling into a whirlpool...."

He felt something wet coursing down his cheek. Her fingertip caught it, held it up for inspection.

"A tear," she said as though seeing one for the first time. "This is you, Corlan. This is who you truly are...when you set down your dragonslinger, when you forget the battlefields you trod, when you forgive the boy hiding inside you for all the foolish acts only a boy would do. You are all a teardrop." She licked her fingertip. "And this is who I am."

Breaking from his embrace, she took a step back. The blanket lay in a clump at her feet so she stood fully naked before him for the first time, her arms held out as though she were simply a bird standing in her nest.

Corlan gazed down her lithe figure, from her dark eyes to her thin lips, to her small breasts to her taut belly and narrow hips. He stared. He believed she wanted him to stare. When the moment had boiled hot enough, he closed his eyes and bowed his head.

"I am a woman," said Naka Wu. "Make no mistake. Now...I am a woman."

He opened his eyes, focusing on her face.

Pursing her lips, she reached for him, took his face in her hands and, standing two inches taller than him, pulled him close, chest to chest. In that position she could see into his soul.

"Although I was a boy for three years of my life."

Urma nodded repeatedly as Naka Wu knelt at her gnarly bare feet to apologize for leaving the boy before he completed his recovery.

"I swear I shall return as soon as possible." She rose and adjusted her leather vest. "It's only two days' ride each way. When the boy has recovered, I will take him to Danapo. We both can be safe there. They allow men and boys to be workers and servants, rather than making them into dinner, as the queen often commanded in Covin."

"It is a suitable plan, Naka. You are a good mother."

Naka Wu laughed, then placed her hands on the old woman's tiny shoulders. "Mother.... I never thought to be called such."

"There are all kinds of words that pass us every day. Some stick to us, like them or not."

"I cannot thank you enough for what you've done." She glanced back over her shoulder, searching for Corlan. "He thanks you, too. He is simply too distraught to find the best words. You know he appreciates your help. Both for the boy and...for the finger of his magus."

"I had enough work to do before he gave me the finger," Urma snapped. "Now only the goddess can know its fate."

"You are the only one who has the power to use magic."

"A finger is the last hope he has, eh?" The old woman chuckled. "I can only say the words and pour the fluids and stir the mixture. What lies beyond is for the goddess to decide." She winked at Naka Wu. "Have you given up nightly prayer for this man?"

She tried to repress a grin. "We pray together."

"You to the goddess, him to...a god?"

"I don't know. We speak no words."

The old woman nodded, her long stringy hair touching the floor. She almost tripped stepping on the hair. Grabbing Naka Wu's hand, she led the warrior to the door.

"I told him about a plan I found for him," said Naka Wu. "He wants to hire a boat to take him down the river, and I—"

"A fool's mission," said Urma, her face locked in a perpetual frown. "And it takes a fool to go on a fool's mission. So he is perfect. Lots of practice, I'm sure. He's ready for what he deserves."

"What he deserves? What does any wounded man deserve, dear Urma? A chance?"

Urma shook her hand free. "Dragons! That's what he deserves."

Naka Wu closed her eyes a moment, remembering a night from her dreams, when she and he were together on a bedroll, in joy.

"I shall care for him as best I can. You know that, don't you?"

"The man or the boy?"

Naka Wu tried to smile. "The man, first. Later, the boy."

Urma nodded. "I believe you. I can see that in your eyes."

"Thank you, dear Urma." She bent down to kiss the woman on her wrinkly cheek.

The old woman seemed to chuckle but rough, full of spittle.

"Now get you both away from here—before spring flowers come forth in the garden. The snow cannot last much longer. Once in five years it comes. An unlucky omen, a mark of defeat. Be careful."

"I told him so."

"Then you have learned well what cannot be taught. Same as the myth of dragon folk. He believes as he likes."

"We saw two dragons break the sky yestermorn. He is more set now on completing his journey. So I must let him go. I must let him or he will drown in regret forever."

"Regret is a marsh that cannot be crossed."

"Or a whirlpool...."

"Perhaps the regret is yours, I suspect."

Naka Wu turned to go out. "Perhaps. If only I'd known years ago what I would see today...."

In the yard Corlan had already mounted his horse, the dun mare. He held the reins of her black gelding. She could not meet his eyes as she marched across the yard to him.

"Remember the boy, and return for him," Urma called after her. "And remember the finger."

"I shall," she replied, not looking back.

Naka Wu joined Corlan, climbed onto her horse. She waved back at Urma, who had closed the door before Naka Wu could lower her hand. Somewhere far away a new door would open, she knew. That was what Urma always said.

36

The Boatman

CORLAN'S HAND CUT THROUGH the air, gesturing for Naka Wu to guide her horse off the road and beneath the cover of the trees, even though the branches had little foliage remaining. Corlan followed. Standing stirrup to stirrup with Naka Wu, he pointed up through the branches at the line of dragons in flight. Seven of them, soaring higher than usual. He could not call their kind at that height.

The next day they spied five more dragons in flight, heading due west, a line of three grey-bellies. A draper with emerald fins trailed a mile behind. A two-foot with dark red wings hurried after the others a few minutes later.

"Unusual for them to fly together," Corlan thought aloud.

"Horses of different breeds will herd together," said Naka Wu. "Canines of many kinds also run together."

"Dragons are different," he said coldly.

She thought to say more—"As are humans."—but saw he was concerned about the dragons so she decided to keep quiet. He was different now on the road, always aware of what flew overhead. She felt different, too, leather feeling less comfortable now than it had in past years. The saddle. The swords. Different now.

"The most I've seen since I left the Valley of Death," he muttered.

When the aerial beasts had passed, they rode on.

By nightfall a half-dozen more dragons had crossed the gray sky, as though fleeing the cold.

Alone together in the woods, words were unnecessary. Dinner was made, bedrolls laid, bodies collapsing on them with weapons close at hand. Dawn came late and cold, more flurries scattering over the landscape.

They rode a while, the steady clopping of the horses' hooves the loudest sound along the road. Once in a long while one of the riders would glance at the other; a grin would appear and just as quickly disappear.

"I should like to come along with you," said Naka Wu, looking ahead, nodding to herself as though she had thought over the best arrangement of words. "I could be of help to you."

Corlan gave a smirk. "I do not doubt you would be good to have on this journey. You're a fighter, skilled with many weapons. You are fearless, and bold. And when the fighting's done you're a fair sight for a weary dragonslayer."

"I mean to help you kill dragons, or mend your wounds if need be, not to only be some helpmate at the end of the day."

"Yes, I know." His laugh sounded forced. "At the end of the day every dragonslayer needs someone to comfort him."

"At the end of the day, a warrior needs someone to comfort her."

Corlan grinned. "It seems we're meant to comfort each other."

"It's a good idea. We both will be better after comforting."

"Better dragonslayers? Better warriors?"

"Yes, that." She gazed at him. "Better lovers, too."

"We've a long ride before any comfort time," Corlan responded, kicking his horse into a brisk trot.

By the next afternoon they first saw the village huddled down on the shore of the river. The whiteness of the slopes they rode over was already fading, the snow melting and turning the road into mud. The horses splattered it with each clop as the road wound back and forth down to the river.

At that point, the river was only twice the width of the wagon they had left with Urma.

"Around the next large bend of the river is Luval," said Naka Wu as they came alongside the shore. "A men folk city. Maybe twenty miles on. The river widens much more there. It's a port city. Boats ply the river downstream."

Corlan was happy to see the river, gazing upstream and down.

She smiled. "The village ahead is called Carel's town. The river is not wide here, nor deep, coming out of the hills west of Madi's town, but it is wide enough that you can hire a boat. I dare not go all the way to Luval."

He turned his eyes to her, seeing her serious face.

"Is it such a bad place?"

"I've heard stories.... They do not serve women for dinner in

Luval," she replied with a strained laugh, "but it's likely a gang of men would take me away, force me to serve them for a day and so. In Luval, they believe it is their right to take whatever they want, especially women. Unless she is protected by the men of her family. The women who live there do not go out alone. Some women do not survive the...the *gifting*, they call it. A woman must give herself to a man, any man who wants her. Unless she is protected by family men. That is what they believe in Luval. Such is the manner of men who live without many women. When one is found, she is set upon."

"Desperate men," Corlan said with a rough sigh. "They do not deserve women."

"If they do not value women, the women will leave."

He snorted. "And they did leave, made their own cities."

"That does not permit their actions! There is no law which allows rape. No law forbidding it, either. Not in Luval. So I carry a sword."

He nodded, then shook his head, thinking of her passing through the streets of the city, confronted by a group of men. She would probably unsheathe her sword and drop a few limbs and maybe a head there. No man could take her without her permission.

"You should not need to carry a sword to walk the streets," he said at last. "I would protect you there."

"It should not be your responsibility to protect me. I should never have need of protection. Yet that is the world we live in today. It is easier for you if I do not enter the city."

"Can the wild road be any safer than a city?"

"Most days, yes."

They rode a bit farther, passing the sign announcing the river port as Carel's town, where the forests gave way to coastal fields of long-harvested crops. The fields were muddy, spotted with frost.

"Carel's town is as far as I shall travel with you," said Naka Wu, slowing her gelding. "It is the village where I was born. Then I was taken away to Covin."

Entering the village, Naka Wu pointed to a small house, barely more than a hut, its walls broken and roof collapsed. The windows were shattered, the door ajar. Weeds had grown tall around it yet now lay withered in the winter chill. Other houses on the lane were in similar condition. She pulled rein on her gelding, halting and staring at the ruins.

"In there was I born," she said, her voice flat, cold. "The woman I called Mother lay on the floor and pulled me from between her legs. I remember she screamed in pain, loud and long, how she fought against me coming into the world. I thought she never wanted me. My father...a man who came by one day. That's all he was. So she didn't want me, yet I arrived."

"From humble beginnings, a great warrior comes...."

"None can know in that first hour what she may be called upon to do later in her life."

"Me, neither." He chuckled. "Dragonslayer! Pfft!"

"Certainly none have lived there for half a generation," she said. "It has long ceased to be my home. You recall hearing Urma call me the daughter she never bore? It's true. She raised me into my youth. When the patrol from Covin came for the taxes, Mother was glad to hand me over. The patrol took me to Urma, along with some bodies for her to stitch. They bid her care for me until I was old enough for training."

She stared hard at the house, breathing slowly as though she was preparing herself to receive torture.

"I have no more memories of this place, nor my mother who birthed me. Only that: the screaming when I came out of her. Rape was the reason I came into this world." She looked away. "Even now it does not appear to be the same place."

"I feel the same about my home," said Corlan. "My mother, she was good for a time. The man I remember as my father, he came and went. He fought with the army, an officer. Never knew if he was my true father or simply the man my mother welcomed into the house."

"We are so alike...."

"In the worst ways."

"This is not my home," she said with a loud sigh.

"We can only leave home once," he said. "That's why you feel nothing now."

She pressed her gelding against Corlan's mare.

"Shall we seek a boat for you now? Let us not waste more time being sad. I must hurry away...before you see me with tears. Must return for the boy."

"Don't have any tears," Corlan said with a grunt. "You're not a warrior? Warriors shed no tears."

"Until we fall in love with someone who is doomed."

"Yes...doomed."

"Apologies," she said softly.

"It's a fine word, *doomed*. I will remember it till the end."

Corlan pulled at the whiskers on his chin, past the threshold to call it a beard. He had so many feelings in that moment he could not choose only one. So he tugged on his beard, raked it with his fingers.

"To the wharf, then."

Naka Wu nodded, spurred her mount ahead.

There was only one wharf. It jutted into the stream from the main lane of shops, dropping down the slope from the village square. The lane was little more than a widening of the road that intersected the route from Madi's town. The cluster of buildings were worn and shabby yet alive. Shops were open. Only a few folk went about their daily affairs on this dismal day: women with baskets, men with tool boxes, children with their school scrolls. A canine barked after them, followed for a block. A second canine took over the chase, then perhaps realized there was no food to be tossed down and so it vanished.

At the head of the wharf was the boat house. The pair of wooden doors were thrown open despite the chill and inside, next to a forge, sat a man with a full gray beard, working on a repair to a small boat set on racks, hull up.

"Sir," Naka Wu addressed the man. "Could you tell about hiring a boat? This man wishes to go down the river to—" She turned awkwardly to Corlan, playing the role of stranger: "Where is your destination?"

"Luval," he replied.

"Then keep riding that horse of yours and you'll come to a bridge in less than a day's ride," said the man.

Naka Wu glared at the man. He wore the pin of a boatswain on his coat. "He wishes to go by river."

"Lost childhood, eh?" The man laughed.

"Yes, a lost childhood," Corlan spoke. "Only by sitting in a boat and drifting downstream may I recover it." He made a face.

"I sit here day after day waiting for someone to arrive wanting to hire a boat.... It's been half a year! Now you finally want a boat yet they are all out, all downstream and yet to return. It would be easier to go by horse."

Naka Wu stepped forward. "Is there no boat for hire?"

"None I know of."

"He doesn't need much, as long as it's water-tight. Not even sails are needed. Just for himself."

"And the horse?" asked the man.

"I can trade the horse for a boat," said Corlan.

"That old nag?" he sneered.

"She's not so old, just been through a long ride."

The man rubbed his nose, snorted a few times.

"There might be something from one of our townsfolk. I have none until that renegade Huver returns. Nasty fellow! Sailed upriver and got himself captured by a band of Covinas. You know what happens to men that get too close to Covin, don't you?" The man chuckled.

"They become pets of the queen?" Corlan said with sour laugh.

"No, they become dinner!" The man seemed cross that these two guests did not get his humor. He waved a gnarly finger at Naka Wu. "Say, gal, you have a look that pokes at my memory. I seen Covinas dressed like you. Long braid, too."

"Certainly you are too old to have such memories," said Naka Wu. "I lived here long ago. And now I return, but only for an hour to help this man get a boat. We crossed paths on the road."

"Thank you," said Corlan, playing the role. "I can probably find a boat on my own now. I appreciate you introducing me to this fine gentleman."

The man screwed up his face. "That's me! Fine gentleman!" He laughed, waved them away. "Go find a man on the lower shore, runs an inn, name of Brox or Brong. Ask him for a boat, if you really need it. And don't let them cheat you."

"Thanks to you, sir," said Naka Wu with a bow of her head.

"Thanks," said Corlan.

She turned to go. Corlan smiled at the old man and followed her out of the boathouse.

They mounted their horses and trotted up the road to the center of the village, the square. In the shops they passed, curtains waved as curious eyes snuck peeks, darting back into shadow when spied by the riders. Children stopped their play to stare at the statuesque woman and her husky brute of a companion on the two horses. Not the sort of travelers they usually saw, Corlan decided.

Taking the road west, following the riverbank, they came soon to a three-level wooden inn that had seen better days. It once had been painted in a bright yellow with red around the windows, it seemed, both colors faded now. The yard was overgrown yet withered. The tall trees that surrounded and filled the property likely had stood proud for a hundred years, thought Corlan.

They pulled up before the long veranda.

"Brox!" Naka Wu called out. "Brong!"

"Is there a living human here today?" Corlan added.

Naka Wu gave him a smirk.

The front doors creaked open and a middle-aged man with his left arm missing stepped out on the veranda. He did not seem well, or else he was upset by their presence. The moustache that hung down below his chin was spotted with blood. More blood dabbed his white shirt beneath a brown cloth vest.

"You hurt?" asked Corlan.

"Not me," said the man, holding up his stained hand. "I'm killing birds. Dinner, yeah. Hard to do with one hand. So I hold'em in my teeth. Better if the birds are bigger than these damn starlings."

"Yes, it would be," said Corlan.

Naka Wu sat up in the saddle. "We were told you might have a boat for hire."

The man studied them, rubbing the back of his head, not caring that his hand was blood-stained.

"I'd pay you well for a river-worthy craft," said Corlan.

"You got coin?" asked the man, scratching his belly like it had been empty too long, making his shirt redder.

"Enough to get you by a few weeks, I suspect," said Corlan. "Or a few months if you eat little."

He laughed. "I eat little, I do." He thought a moment. "I have a boat." He turned to close the two doors behind him. "River-worthy? I'm not convinced. See if you like it."

Naka Wu dismounted. Corlan followed, dropping off the mare and landing his boots in a puddle hidden by fallen leaves.

The man, Brox or Brong, led them around the side of the inn on a stone path. The stones were padded with moss. Thick patches of ferns grew in abundance beneath the moist cover of the ancient trees. They went down a slope and the brown river appeared before them.

"It's for lovers," said Brox or Brong, pointing to the craft tied up there. "In the summer they go out in the boat to share secrets." He glanced back at the two visitors. "I suppose you have the same plan? Some secret sharing?"

"No, sir," said Naka Wu. "We are not lovers. This man will be the only one to use the boat. I'm only helping him find a boat. We crossed paths on the road."

"That's all?" asked Brox or Brong with a wink.

"Yes, why shouldn't it be all?"

He grinned at Corlan. "I'd take a woman like her out on a boat. I got plenty of secrets to share. More of 'em after we go out there."

Corlan faked a grin. "She's not my type."

"Type?" The man chuckled. "One-armed men can't be picky."

"Maybe another day. This is a trading trip. I need to go far down the river. To meet with some traders. If I purchase this boat, I doubt you will get it returned to you."

"If you purchase the boat, it's yours. I don't want it returned." He gave a glance back in the direction of the horses. "And I suppose you won't be needed your horse.... Care to trade?"

"If the boat is sound," said Naka Wu.

The boat tied to a post at the riverbank was twice the length of the wagon they had used on their travels. The skiff seemed intact. A pair of oars lay across the three bench seats and a long trolling staff rose from the water, leaning against the side of the boat.

Corlan climbed down to the water's edge, slipping on some mud, wavelets rippled over the toes of his boots. He gazed inside the boat, staring at each corner and saw no water had gathered. It seemed water-tight.

"Not as old as I expected," said Corlan.

"It's a good boat," said Brox or Brong. "Maybe three seasons in use and only in the season. For lovers, as I said."

"May I give it a try?" asked Corlan.

"You might. The current's swift so you might not be able to return easy. Then you must hire a cart to haul it back on the road." He gave Corlan a glare. "You going downstream, you said?"

"Yes, to Luval."

"Then you best ride your horse. Take the bridge twenty miles southwest."

"Luval...and beyond." Corlan's face was grim.

"Beyond, eh?" He shot a glance at Naka Wu. "Eh, there's nothing beyond."

"Nothing?" asked Naka Wu, breaking out of her role playing. She regarded Corlan, who kept his eyes on the boat.

"No-thing," said Brox or Brong. "*Nothing*. The river goes down to the sea. And the sea has beasts." He glanced between them. "That's sea beasts. You know?"

"He means dragons," Corlan grunted.

"Yes, dragons! But in the sea." The man stared hard at Naka Wu, as though he were trying to persuade her to stop this foolish man from sailing down to the sea. "If you want the boat, it's yours. It's not worth what your fine horse is worth. I'd be cheating you." He held out his hand. "If you got five *lux*, the boat is yours."

Corlan turned to Naka Wu. She realized he didn't understand.

"All gold coins have equal value, do they not?" she spoke. "One *lux* is worth the same as a *regal*."

Corlan loosened his trouser pouch, pulled out five coins. "Enough for the boat? It's the currency of all men: gold. The name stamped on it doesn't matter."

"Yeah, enough," said Brox or Brong.

Corlan extended his hand, dropping the coins into the man's palm.

He held up one of the coins, staring at it. "Now who's this fine fellow?"

"Vilmer," said Corlan. "The prince of my city."

"Lovely profile, strong nose. But a weak chin—"

"So we have a deal?" Corlan asked.

Brox or Brong looked up from his coin examination. "The boat is yours." He grinned like he had successfully cheated the man. "May the sea beasts find you bitter in taste, tough to chew, and hard to swallow."

Corlan thanked him and they all went together up the slope and through the forest to the front of the inn.

"If I were you," said Brox or Brong, "I'd find a way to take her on the boat with you. Not a good season for boating but...a woman can warm you. Just don't go too far down the river. That'd be a poor way to end a lovely relationship. The men in Luval'd love to play with this one. Keep her close."

Corlan showed a grin. He knew the truth of his endeavor. Even so, that woman held fast to his heart. He thought of her as he carried his share of supplies from the back of his mare down to the boat and returned for more. The dragonslinger and a quiver of iron bolts were one load in themselves.

The man went inside the lodge to fetch parchment, saying he needed to write out a deed of sale to make it official.

"I'll take your horse with me," said Naka Wu. "Tam can ride it in a few weeks, perhaps. When he is recovered. I'll save this mare for him. And you...later. When you return."

Corlan caressed the horse's nose, patted its withers.

When he turned from the horse, the woman was staring at him, a broken smile struggling to stay straight. She desperately tried to hide her emotions. He went to her, standing against her horse, her hand brushing the gelding's croup.

"We cannot part in a simple moment such as this," he spoke.

Naka Wu shook her head. "Just lean over and kiss me, Corlan of the Burg, and wish me well. You and I have had our time together, it would seem. Fated, after all. Perhaps we shall meet again some day. In Danapo? I'll take the boy there. Come and find us." She wiped her eyes. "Find us after you kill your dragons."

He gazed into her eyes. "I will."

Turning away from the horse, she reached behind her head, one hand drawing out the long sword she carried on her back and the other hand swinging her long black braid over her shoulder. In one quick flip, the braid came loose from her head, severed by the blade.

"Here is something to remember me." She handed him the braid, about three feet in length. "I have grown it since the day I pledged to be a warrior and honor the code. I have dishonored the code several times since I met you, so it is proper I give this braid to you, Corlan. And start to grow a new braid. A new braid for a new life."

He held it in his two hands, the braid laying across his palms like a snake he should be wary of. Two tears ran down her cheeks but, holding the braid, he could not wipe them away.

Without clearing her eyes, she leaped upon her horse. Reaching back for the reins of the mare, she turned her gelding around, then galloped away as fast as she could urge the animals on, refusing to look back.

He watched her ride until the road bent and she passed out of view, only then realizing he had not kissed her.

"Now I know her!" exclaimed Brox or Brong, coming up behind him, a sheet of parchment in his blood-stained fingers.

Corlan turned to regard the man. "Who?"

He handed the deed to Corlan.

"She's...not sure the name...Nakel? Nakoo? Some name like that. She's known in Covin...one of the palace staff." He rubbed his head with his blood-stained hand. "Was she part of the rebellion? Report is sketchy. A man came by with a drawing of her."

"I just met her on the road and asked where I could hire a boat," said Corlan. "She offered to help."

The man nodded. "Just as well. People been looking for her. Yes, looking for all those women involved in the rebellion."

"Rebellion?" Corlan acted surprised.

"Yes, in Covin. The women's city. You didn't hear about it? The queen was killed right there in her chamber. They caught the leader, though. Hung her by the neck, then cut her body into pieces, fed them to canines. Women can be so cruel."

Corlan looked away, uninterested in the story. He climbed into the boat again, arranging his supplies. The man continued talking.

"Eh, I could be mistaken. All those warrior women look the same to me. Only wear black. All black. And leather trousers. Makes them look tough. Hah! Makes them look bed-worthy to me."

Corlan looked up from the boat. "And your name was...Brox? Or Brong?"

The man shook his head. "Wrong twice. I'm Alvo. The caretaker. My masters are dead. Brox and Brong were brothers, running this inn. Covinas killed them not a month past. I lost my arm, you see."

Corlan grinned uncomfortably. "Covinas?"

"Yeah, like that one you was with here."

"That's a Covina?"

"Someone from Covin. Evil women. Had a rebellion a little while ago. Everything was going to be better, we thought. Yet you know how Covinas are."

"How are they?"

"Betrayers. Deceivers. Witches. But they surely look beautiful."

Corlan pursed his lips. "I heard they hate men."

"Hate men! I thought you must be making secrets with that one."

Corlan shook his head. "Just met her today."

"Well, now it's Eun Hong ruling in Covin."

"Who?" That was not a name he'd heard. "What about Fa Mei?" He caught himself. "Is that the right name? I only heard—"

"You're a stranger here. Fa Mei was supposed to take over after the queen was assassinated, but Eun Hong—she was the queen's war marshal—Eun Hong accused Fa Mei of leading the rebellion and she was hanged."

Corlan winced at Alvo's descriptive gesturing.

"So it's true."

"Seems Eun Hong pushed Fa Mei into leading the rebellion, then took over what remained. Fa Mei did the dirty work, not knowing she was gonna get betrayed by Eun Hong. Anyway, Fa Mei was a religious leader. She never could've ruled there."

"You seem to favor this Eun Hong...."

"It's not about favor, sir. It's about trade. We need Covin to be a stable city. Or the whole river community is in chaos." He rubbed his chin a while, then spit to the ground. "I may be out of my class, sir, but I would support a strong woman over a weak man."

"I understand." Corlan nodded, ready to excuse himself. "I'll be glad to be away down the river." He pulled up the trolling pole and looked it over.

"Like that one come with you. She's a looker."

"I didn't notice."

"Then you're a blind man, I say."

"I've got business down the river."

Corlan shoved the trolling pole against the riverbank and pushed off.

She covered the road slowly, letting the gelding set its own pace, the mare following on a long, loose tether. The forest on either side of the road was quiet, dark. Not even birds cried. In the gray sky she saw more snow clouds building in the north. Cold, unlike most winters in the valley of the River Oh, cut through her leathers. Her mind was back in Carel's town, back at the edge of the river, as an old boat pushed off, the current tugging it downstream and around the next bend and becoming lost in the mists rising from the water. She felt glad to have missed that sight. She also regretted not seeing him fade into the mist.

Naka Wu wanted to go back, to sail with him on his journey, no matter if that meant slaying dragons. She had no future here in the river valley. She had done the right thing and left him, she knew. Warriors pledge loyalty, swear oaths, follow codes, and, in her case, make promises to return to old women who are healing boys. After a few more years she would turn a corner and no longer be able to hold up her warrior mission. She should be a captain by then, a leader of a regiment, not a rank and file soldier. If she had stayed in

Covin. Yet now she had none to command.

The trees rustled around her, a similar sound which Corlan had identified as the approach of a dragon. Their wings would change the air currents as they descended.

She paused to check the wind direction. Rain? The air did not smell like rain was coming. The clouds in the north would bring snow.

Ahead on the side of the road was a stump. For a moment she was confused, thinking she was back in the yard at Urma's house. She stared again. On the stump squatted a man who appeared old and hunched over. She thought of Rupas. He was a kindly person, so unlike most men. So she nodded at this man squatting on the stump, just to be polite as she passed.

"Good day to you," she called, not slowing.

"Is it?" said the man in a strange voice.

She paused to study him more. He seemed old at first but now she saw he was merely dirty and crouched low atop the stump.

Suddenly, the man sprang off the stump and grabbed the reins of her horse. From the forest on either side of her, other men rushed up, taking the second horse and pulling her from the saddle before she could draw her sword.

Falling to the ground on her back, she became a warrior, rolling under the legs of the gelding and jumping up straight with her sword unsheathed and marking them for butchery.

She backed away from the horses and the circle of men followed, keeping their distance as she held the sword at the ready.

"Take her!" shouted one of the men.

"She can't slice all of us," said another.

"I ain't gonna be first," cried one man.

She marked four who had blades: two knives, a medium sword, and a two-handed claymore. The men were all shorter than her; she measured the angle of her blade.

When the men holding knives attacked, it was easy to dispatch them, their knife-wielding hands severed and dropped in the dirt, handless fools retreating with screams.

The man with the medium sword charged in and quickly fell in two pieces, divided at the waist. She took a defensive stance, ready for any attack.

"I'm paying you good coin," called the man from the stump, now beside the horses. He held their reins, watching her. "Take her. We'll cut the reward into fewer portions."

The others pressed in on her and she swung the blade around the circle, striking heads and hands and shoulders—until she felt a pain shudder through her belly. She turned and saw that the man with the claymore stood weaponless, stepping back. She tried to take a swing at him but the pain in her belly stopped her. Looking down, she spied the tip of the blade protruding from above her navel, blood running down her belly. He had struck her from behind. The long blade and its hilt flapped behind her, scraping against her hip bone.

Before she could think of her next move, the man who wielded the claymore grabbed the hilt, twisted it sideways, then jerked it free from her body. She felt her insides torn out with the blade.

Collapsing to the ground, her knees crunched in the dirt as blood spilled out both front and back wounds. The men rushed her again, unafraid, stabbing with knives and farm tools until she lay helpless on her back, still alive yet unable to move.

"You fools!" cried the man from the stump.

The men got up, stood around her. She could see them staring down, half the faces grinning.

"What good is she now? There's no reward for us."

"No, master. They'll still pay five-hundred *lux* for her head."

"Will they?"

"It's proof who she is."

He turned to the fallen woman, amused she gazed up at them with such apparent disdain. He laughed, gesturing to the man with the claymore to come over.

"I told you it was her. I told you," said the bearded man from the boathouse. He had come out of hiding when the action was done. "I can take my share of the reward."

"You have to wait till we collect it. Same as us. You'll get your share. Plenty for each, now she's killed half our gang." He turned to the man with the claymore. "Finish it."

The man lifted the claymore, pushed the blade high over his head, arms fully extended, and with all his strength brought it down.

INTERLUDE

The Little Goddess

THE GATHERING OF DRAGONS overhead blocked the rising sun like a bank of storm clouds. The noise of the beasts' communal growling, cawing, screaming, and roaring covered the mountainside and the flapping of their unsteady wings must have conjured a new weather pattern for the villages below the mountain.

In the center of the gathering stood a little girl in a spotless white gown, pulled from the magical melding of her rough travel clothes. With her arms raised, she seemed to be welcoming the aerial beasts to her home. On the grass beside her knelt a woman in fighting leathers, bearing a longsword, her hair black and frazzled, ready for a fight yet wishing very much to escape.

"I think I am supposed to think my wishes while staring through the birthstone," said Adora. "Perhaps you cannot see it as I can but the stone really is transparent. I can see through it like it was clear glass. Except for the blue lines that curl around inside it. I can see those. It is rather like looking into a person's eye, through the hole in the front, and you can see all the lines in the back of the eye. Have you ever done that, Jabuli?"

The woman raised her head, not much, however, as the goddess was not so tall.

"No, I have not, my little goddess."

The girl snickered. "For you, Jabuli, be at ease. I shall let you call me Adora. It is my name, of course. I know you know I am now a goddess but I want us to still be good friends."

"Yes, my little god—I mean, Adora. You will always be 'little majesty' to me."

"You don't have to pray to me. Unless you need help."

"Thank you. I'm sure I will need help at some time in the years I have left."

"And I do not think I want any temples built, either. People need to do so many other things to have good lives, don't you think?"

"The people might take comfort in making a house for you."

"That is true. If it makes them happy then they should build it."

The goddess kept her arms raised, long after a normal child would grow tired and have to lower them. It seemed as though she was conducting a chorus of dragon verbalizations, waving to the right, waving to the left, raising up their wings, their tails, lowering their heads—making them do whatever she wished them to do. Even the birthstone did not grow heavy in her left hand as she held it up, testing each of her powers one by one.

"I think I am supposed to give people things, whatever they wish for. Is that true? When I was little—I mean more little than now—I remember Mama telling me to ask for things from the goddesses. If I whispered a prayer and I believed very much, I would get what I asked for."

"And what did you ask for, Adora, my little goddess?"

"Just toys and things like that. Pretty dresses. I had all of those as a princess yet still I wanted more. It seems strange now, the things I asked for. I did not truly need them. What sort of things would you ask for?"

Jabuli nodded, feeling once more that her charge was the simple little girl she adored, that everyone adored. Surely the great palace in Sannan was a sad place these days.

"I would ask for big things. Not a palace, not like that. Bigger than a palace. Not a whole island to rule, either. I would ask that all people think of good ideas and feel in their hearts all the goodness they can create when they are not so busy fighting over everything. That's what I mean by big things. Not things you can touch or see. Peace. Freedom. Love. Those things."

The goddess laughed, not at what Jabuli said, but how at that very moment she was able to manipulate the dragons to move this way and that way with only the smallest of gestures from her tiny hands. Once satisfied, she set down the birthstone in the grass between her little bare feet.

"You are right, Jabuli. Good thoughts. I shall try my best to give all people those things of which you spoke. It would be only fair."

"You've always been wise. A lot more than what anyone would

expect from a little girl. I've enjoyed being your tutor. If I can be of service to you any longer, please let me."

"Thank you, Jabuli. You are so kind to me. And protected me for so long. Yet I know everything now. It is all locked inside the stone. Like all the parches of the world have been wrapped together. I do not need a tutor any longer, yet I need a friend. People always need friends."

"Yes, they do. Always. If that is what you want, I'm happy to be your friend, Adora."

She waved her arms back and forth, watching the dragons dance.

"And I am happy to be your friend, too."

Jabuli stood, stepping around the basket where the babe napped. She felt that the little girl had full control of the dozens of dragons gathered on the mountainside and in the air above them. She kept the sword in her hand nevertheless but held the point down.

"What will you do with these dragons? I've never seen so many in one place. I'm very afraid now. Can you send them away?"

"Be not afraid, Jabuli. They are...well, not my *friends*, surely. I do not think dragons are suitable for being friends with humans, but they can serve a goddess. That is what Goddess Sei Bo told me. I also learned it from the birthstone. I could see my whole life there. From the day I was first made inside Mama—and *that* was a weird thing to see!—to the moment I touched the robe of Goddess Sei Bo."

Adora looked back over her shoulder at her tutor, the woman's wild hair blowing in the breeze. Sadness seemed to paint her face and the goddess smiled quickly at her.

"Someday you shall die. It happens to all humans. Then you can come and live with me. I see it in the birthstone."

"Your dream? The ones you have of me?" asked Jabuli. She kept her eyes on the dragons, all fifty or sixty of them.

"I do not wish to cause you harm or make you fear, so I better not tell you what I see."

"You said I will die from a dragon attack."

"I remember what I said. I was only a little girl then so I could not see it all clearly."

"Is it more clear now?" She glowered. "We are surrounded by all these dragons and you said I would die in a dragon attack. I'm rather nervous at this moment. I hope you can understand. I need to know if I die today or live on."

"Oh, you live on, lots more than today," said the goddess.

"Thank you. That's comforting to know."

"I need you to help me, so I cannot lose you to any attack, by men or dragons. I shall need to put a protective bubble around you to keep you safe. I know how to do it. I learned from the birthstone."

"It's good you have so much power now. You can protect your brother easily. You have no more need of me for that."

"I need you to be my friend, Jabuli. Don't ever forget. You have a friend who is a goddess. You can tell the people that, but they will not believe you. Perhaps they cannot see me if you were to introduce us to each other. Yet I can see them, and see all their lives, and the ends of their lives. It is all in the birthstone."

The dragons were getting restless, so long being made to obey the little goddess. They growled louder, fought against her random commands. She gave stricter instructions, forced them to obey.

"This is becoming so tiresome. Dragons! I shall continue training tomorrow," said Adora. "I think I shall take a nap now. First, I will send the dragons away. They only came here to welcome me. So now that I've been welcomed and I've listened to their songs, I shall bid them go home."

She waved her arms sharply twice. The dragons in the sky heaved as one, released from their spell. They turned and winged away in every direction. The dragons on the ground set their wings and launched themselves into the sky. The great fluttering caused Jabuli to cower, yet the little goddess merely waved her hand in farewell.

"I shall call a dragon tomorrow to take us east," she said when all the dragons were in flight, leaving the mountainside.

Jabuli tried to count them as they flew away: sixty...seventy...eighty before she lost count as they swung low or soared high and she began to confuse which dragons she had already counted.

"We only need two," said Adora, "not ninety-six as visited us today. One for me and one for you and my brother. We shall fly over the mountains and over the deserts to the other side of the world. Sei Bo said there is freedom there. Also safety. I want to see it."

Jabuli cringed. "We will ride on dragons?"

"You saw the sky wardens. They rode on dragons...some kind. What did you call them?"

"Wydrakes."

"Yes, those. Unnatural, made by men using the Clona arts. Those arts are forbidden in Sannan. No, we will fly on true dragons such as we saw today. Large dragons. Large enough for all of us to fly in comfort. They will have giant wings and long tails and they will cross the sky in half the time as the wind or the sunlight. We will find a new home there, in the east somewhere."

"A new home? For you?"

"And my brother."

"Is it suitable for your brother to live with you? Now that you are a goddess? Can he be comfortable?"

Adora regarded her tutor with benevolence, as a goddess should.

"Wherever I go, my brother should be safe and comfortable."

"I agree. I only thought—"

"I know what you thought. I know all your thoughts. It is part of my powers. The birthstone said so. You fear he will not be able to have a good life staying in a home like that old wood and stone hut that used to stand on this mountainside. So you think he should live among people."

"Yes, that is what I was thinking."

"And I knew your thoughts."

Jabuli bowed her head. "Will you consider it for him?"

"How can he be safe among people? We are fleeing people, are we not? Now you want him to be one of them?"

"He is a boy. He will become a man. He is not a god like you are a goddess, Adora. He cannot do what you can do."

"I only want to protect him. You said the same words, true? To save him from Mama's cruelty. We need to keep him close to us."

"Yes, I said that. Before...before all this happened. The plan now must change." She stoked her courage. "If you will trust me, I can care for him...as good as if he is my own son. I will raise him to adult age. You can visit him whenever you like. He will learn to be kind yet also how to act in the world of men. That is the best way for him."

"The best way for him...." Adora held her hand up, cradling her chin. "I do trust you, Jabuli. I know you will care for him with the same love and honor you give to me. Perhaps then he will also become a god someday. Or at least a king. It is possible, is it not?"

"It's possible, yet only if he grows into adult age among men. He will learn their ways, become the best of them, and then teach them our ways. From him will come a better world."

"Yes! I like the words you say!"

Jabuli smiled. "We will find a good place to live, he and I. My body was broken, so I welcome him as my son."

"Then I am your...niece? He is my...cousin? It's so confusing, even for a goddess."

"You are yet young as a goddess. Worry not. He will always be your brother, no matter where he goes or what age he is, or what happens to me."

Adora stepped over to the basket beside Jabuli, gazed down upon her brother, asleep there. He had slept through most of the dragon chorus. He had not been afraid. Even when the dragons began to arrive, he was more interested in seeing the strange beasts with his own eyes. She wanted to pick him up and bounce him in her arms once more, always enjoying the way he babbled and cheered, yet because her arms glowed so white she dared not.

Jabuli watched the goddess, felt her heart quiver joyfully. This beautiful child was chosen by Sei Bo to save the world. Never before had she believed that goddesses were real, yet now she was the friend of a goddess. A new goddess.

And she could not think of a thing to ask for. Except the chance to be a mother.

"I hear your thoughts, Jabuli." Adora gazed lovingly at her tutor. "I shall make it true. You can be my brother's mama, if you wish it."

"I wish it," replied Jabuli with a bow of her head. "For your sake and for his."

"And your sake, too, let us not forget." The goddess smiled. "I give you this task to thank you for everything you have done for me. The care you will give him will be the best. I know he will be happy and grow to adult age as a kind man who brings peace to the world. That is what I charge you to do, Jabuli Devry, daughter of Magre and Hortin, of the city of Rament on the north bay, devoted tutor of this Adora, the little majesty who is no more."

The little goddess grinned, a pretty bright light that seemed to shine throughout the world.

"It is a lot to ask of you. Yet, as a goddess, I only give my charges to those who can fulfill them. And that is you."

Jabuli bowed low to the little goddess. "How can I ever thank you for this honor?"

"It is a gift only. And only for a short time." Adora reached for her tutor, stopped her hand. An invisible bubble had formed around the woman, conjured by a twitch of the goddess's white eyebrow.

"Your time is not long, though I shall protect you as best I can."

"My time...?"

"I want to do more, dearest Jabuli. I want so much to do more, to do everything I can for you, yet the length of a human life is not a part of my powers."

Jabuli stood up slowly, as though wounded from battle, the clear bubble moving with her. "What are you saying?"

"I want you to be a mama, as you wish. Yet there is only a little time for you to enjoy that life."

"Then your dream will come true? The one about me?"

"I am sorry for it, but...yes, soon." She wanted to let some tears flow from her eyes yet there was nothing. She tried again. "I want to cry for you, Jabuli, yet my eyes will no longer make tears."

Jabuli wiped her own face. "I have enough of them for us."

"The day will come when you fall...so my brother will have no mama. It is best if we find a good home for him far, far away, where he will be safe and will be raised in the world of men, as you advise. I know that is what is best for him. Until that day, if you please, be his mama."

Jabuli sank to the grass, weeping for the count, the great measure of time, feeling the numbers marching closer.

37

A Gathering of Monsters

CORLAN SAT AT THE BAR, trying to enjoy the ale in the stein. Between long tips of the stein, he stared at himself in the mirror behind the counter. An older, haggard man greeted him with disdain; he almost thought it must be his father at first glance. With a grunt, he shook his head, raised the stein and drank again.

"Troubles?" asked a man sitting three stools down.

Corlan looked over at the man, who seemed to be worse off than him. In a thread-bare green coat and ragged scarf, the man hunched over the bar, his head almost resting on its wooden surface, thin gray hair falling over his face, a few strands dividing his face into good and evil.

"Missing your lady?" asked the man in a somber voice.

Corlan took another drink, thinking of his journey and all that he had been through just to get to a dirty tavern by the docks in Luval. The river had taken him from Carel's town with ease. He had lain back and watched the mottled gray sky overhead as the skiff drifted with the current. When he got within sight of the docks, he used the oars to angle across the river and tied up the boat. He flipped a coin to the dockhand to watch the skiff for him. He dared not leave the dragonslinger there, so he hung it from his shoulder, the quiver of iron bolts on the other shoulder, and walked into town.

"Not missing anyone," Corlan replied, not regarding the man.

The man got up, hobbled down the counter on one leg. The other had been replaced with a wooden substitute. Seeing that, Corlan thought of Danapo, where all the deformed and injured were given sympathy.

"You have the look of a man full of regrets," said the stranger, sidling up to the stool next to Corlan.

"I've nothing to say."

"Not one regret?" the stranger persisted. "Not even one simple choice gone wrong?"

Corlan didn't want to answer but the questions did prompt him to think through his list of bad results. The boy got stuck with him. Then dragons came. Girafors and a magus and donkors and a bird-girl came next. All were gone now. Then cities of cruelty. Men and women quick to kill. And dragons. Thieves and dragons.

"There was one," said Corlan. He was thinking of Naka Wu, the one good thing on this journey. "We went our separate ways."

"I knew it," said the stranger. "I can always tell a man who's full of regrets."

"Then you must be a magus." Corlan lifted the stein again.

"Not a magus." He wiped his hand on his coat, offered his hand to Corlan. "I'm called Frattle. Julan Frattle, man about town."

Corlan did not shake hands, kept to his drinking.

"I notice you bear a rather impressive device," said Frattle, his hand gesturing at the dragonslinger leaning against the bar. "Might I know its purpose?"

Corlan stared ahead into the mirror.

If everything went according to his plan, he would arrive in the marshes in a week. Another week smashing eggs, taking a lance to them, skewering the draglings. Maybe two weeks if the nests were spread out. Then a week padding up river back to Luval. He would trade the boat for a horse. Maybe sell dragon egg shells as souvenirs; that would bring some fresh coin. Then off to Danapo, the city of wounds to meet Naka Wu and Tam. What then? Make a family? Stay there or return to the Burg?

"I see a pouch of arrows," said Frattle. "They certainly appear to be arrows. Metal arrows. That's clever. So that long thing shoots those arrows, I take it. Must be for something mighty."

Corlan finally turned and glared at the stranger. "Yes."

"And what is it you shoot with such potent arrows?"

The stein was empty so he waved at the barkeep for another, then turned to the annoying man, intending to scare him off.

"Dragons."

Frattle's eyes widened. "Dragons?"

"Leave the man be," said the barkeep to the man about town, delivering a fresh stein.

"Yes," Corlan responded after a moment.

Not even drifting down the river could be as easy as he expected it to be. In a day's journey, thirteen dragons passed overhead. Two flew low enough they could have seen him and chosen to attack. Yet they flew on without incident. More dragons in one week than in the previous three months of travel, he calculated. He was getting closer to their nesting ground, he figured, so certainly there would be more.

"You have dragon troubles here?" he asked Frattle.

The man blinked. A few other men in the bar had turned in their chairs to face him. The word meant something. Corlan stared at each man. In their eyes he saw fear.

"I saw thirteen in flight yesterday. In a single day. Heading east by northeast. Is that usual?"

The men gave their attention to him, afraid to interrupt.

"I'm new in Luval, so I don't know what's normal for dragonflight here. How many usually pass each day? Any attacks? Any lost animals?" He scanned the tavern's patrons. "Any lost children?"

One hand went up. Corlan pointed at the man.

"My son was set ablaze last year."

"I had a daughter carried off."

"My farmstead was ravaged!"

"We lost five livestock in a single day!"

"Burnt twelve acres of rye month before last."

More jumped up with their complaints. Farm animals, children, a few buildings burned, crops destroyed.

"There are more now than in any other year I can recall."

"Three or more every week!"

"Every *day*! In the summer. Summer was the worst!"

"We've been lucky in Luval, though."

"Don't forget last summer. The attack in Nox. Four people killed and houses fired."

"Did you hear about the attack in Evanal? Seven killed!"

"Six in Hawz killed, two carried off, heads found later dropped on the ground. In piles of ashes!"

"And don't forget the lord-mayor of Oenal! He was lost to a dragon snatching. Carried away screaming in the jaws of a dragon!"

"The witches in Covin summon them, I hear."

Corlan held up his hands when he had heard enough.

"Are you here to kill them?" asked Frattle, taking his cue from the men in the tavern.

"I'm here," said Corlan, "because this is where I found a tavern." He grabbed the new stein and took a long drink. When he set it down on the bar, he spoke: "My destination is downriver. In the marshes."

"The marshes?" asked Frattle, echoed by others.

"What's there?" many asked.

"None of you know?" Corlan narrowed his eyes, gazing around the room. Most faces showed concern or interest. Some showed fear. "The marshes...where dragons lay their eggs."

By the looks on their faces, they either did not know that fact or they knew it all too well.

"I guess, to many folks, it's only a legend."

"A story we tell to frighten children."

"Is it real?"

"What do you know of marshes?"

Corlan climbed off the barstool, stood beside it. "It's my plan to go to the marshes and destroy as many eggs as I can find. That will end the dragons. We will still need to kill the adults as they come for us. But after a few years there won't be any more dragons to bother us. No more draglings growing into adult dragons. In a few years they will all be gone."

"All gone?" some questioned in hushed tone.

Corlan nodded. "That is my plan."

"Can you do it?" asked someone in the group of men which had swelled to fill the tavern. Men were pressing into the doorway from outside, eager to see what the discussion was about. The murmur was loud enough that Corlan had to raise his voice. The barkeep urged him to stand up on the counter. He did, and his dirty boots soiled the countertop.

"I am Corlan, from the northeast," he announced, "from a city we call the Burg. We have dragon attacks every week. We have so many that men there are dedicated to fighting dragons. We've formed a guild. I am of that guild. The Dragonslayer Guild."

The men in the tavern were surprised, disbelieving.

"I'm a dragonslayer! Though I started late in this career, I've already killed close to four-hundred of the aerials."

The men in the tavern gave a rousing cheer as though one of the gods had descended from Mount Zarg to bless them.

"He has the mighty weapon to kill the dragons!" Frattle shouted. He pointed to the dragonslinger as though he had practically invented it himself. "Look how big it is!"

The crowd turned its attention to the dragonslinger. Its black tube rested against the counter like a divine spear. Corlan told the crowd all about his weapon.

"Far to the east is the Valley of Death," he continued, "where there is no flora, no fauna. It's a canyon where dragons fly freely and any human who walks there must die. I traveled through the Valley of Death. I killed many dragons with this weapon: the dragonslinger. I took some wounds myself." He lifted his shirt and turned in place to show his scars. "Dragon fangs, dragon claws, dragon fire—I've faced it all. In the Valley of Death I hacked off the forefoot claw from a male double-hornchin, then sold it as a souvenir in a city called Unting!"

The crowd, now pressed shoulder to shoulder, stamped their feet, making a great noise.

"There is no longer any river in the Valley of Death, only desert. When I traveled west I found cities I never knew existed, like this one. Cities of men and cities of women, separate. In the Burg men and women live together. They respect each other. As the gods intended, men and women must work together as partners. Men and women have different strengths, different weaknesses, yet together we can stand against the dragons!"

The crowd seem puzzled by his diatribe against separation.

"If you want a woman tonight, I'll show you the marketplace," said Frattle. "If you can help rid us of the dragon terror, I'm sure the brokers will let you have a girl for cheap. The girls captured from Covin are cheapest though they will fight you—"

"I don't want a girl for cheap," Corlan sneered. "I don't care about women or girls. I only want—"

"There are boys, too, if you prefer."

"I only want to kill dragons and let our kind be free of their terror. That is my goal. That is the reason I came to Luval. I have no time for pleasures. Not until the world is safe for us once more!"

"To drink!" shouted someone in the crowd, followed by a great cheer. They raised their mugs and steins and bottles.

"To the dragonslayer!" another cried out. Others also shouted.

The barkeep could not fill vessels fast enough. Boys came out from the back room to assist. It was good for business to have this visitor ranting about dragons.

"Kill the dragons!" shouted others in the crowd.

A great chant arose that shook the floor and ceiling.

"Get your lances, men!"

"Can we go with you?"

"Let's all go to the marshes! Let's all destroy dragon eggs!"

"An army of Luval men!"

"The greatest fighting force dragons ever faced!"

The crowd was out of control, charged with civic duty. A civil patrol arrived at the entrance, concerned at the noise, at the violence that could erupt at any moment. They demanded to know who was causing trouble and some pointed to the man up on the counter.

"He's a dragonslayer!" they told the civil patrol.

"Corlan will lead us!" shouted a man there. Others agreed.

"Corlan the dragonslayer!" they cheered.

Morning came too early when the smell of smoke caused Corlan to awaken from the fitful sleep he'd had. His trained nose knew a house was on fire. He gazed out the third floor window of the inn to see a block of buildings ablaze. A glance skyward located the cause: two green-horns circled that quarter of the city, having dropped fire balls atop the roofs. Shouting arose from the streets.

Corlan heaved the dragonslinger to the window, loaded it with an iron bolt, screwed back the spring and aimed the weapon at the larger dragon.

The bolt barely made the distance yet snagged the throat of the green-horn, sticking in its flesh although not deep enough that the beast couldn't flick it out.

Taking no time to dress, Corlan pulled on his boots and dragged the slinger and one quiver down the stairs and out the front door. In the street, people were cowering. Or running away. No fire fighters brought water to put out the flames. He cried out for people to take action or the whole city might burn to the ground.

He spied higher ground a few blocks over and hurried to it. From between two warehouses, he loaded the dragonslinger again, launched the bolt, and saw it strike home in the upper belly of the same green-horn he snagged with the previous shot. It felt the bolt hit, Corlan could see. The dragon screamed and faltered in the air, beating its wings hard to maintain its position. The smaller green-horn came close to check its partner — its mate, it seemed.

Under the screaming of the dragon Corlan heard men rushing a wagon of water barrels to the burning buildings. The team sprayed water onto the roofs of the buildings.

The dragons circled twice more, screeching, then took a swoop over the burning buildings as if to claim their destruction. After another minute, they made a sharp turn and flew away.

"Another attack," said a man coming up to him. "Unprovoked. It's as though they enjoy harassing us."

Corlan, in loincloth and boots, turned to the man. "They are not the dumb brutes I always took them to be. They can think. They can communicate with each other. I fear there is a plot brewing among them." He gathered the slinger, laid it heavily against his shoulder. "All the more reason to destroy them. We must end their line!"

By dusk, the leaders of the city of Luval had formed squads of men to accompany The Dragonslayer on the mission downriver. Fifty-five men would take ten boats and all the arrows they could bear. The armory at Nox gave them four cannons they manufactured that could project iron balls. The six-foot cannons launched metal spheres that exploded on impact rather than bolts that pierced. They swore their weapon could blast a hole through a dragon's belly. Corlan liked that idea and said he was eager to witness it.

"May you go with bravery," called Regent Urix, another leader named after the legendary Prince Urix of Danapo. Corlan was given a crimson and bronze ceremonial stole to wear over his shoulders, indicating he was the person ultimately in charge of the expedition, a role he did not relish.

"We will go with bravery," he said, with a slight bow. Rising, he continued: "And if not, then we will perish. Therefore, remember us to the gods! Remember we did our best! To save humankind from the scourge of dragons!"

"From the scourge of dragons!" the crowd shouted.

With Corlan's words repeated throughout the city, his fame grew and within days plans had been finalized, contracts signed, and arms assigned. Dozens of men consulted with him about every little detail. He was in charge again, commander of a fighting force. It had been some time since the men of Luval had had such a worthy mission to complete. They felt proud and chanted how great it was to be men, men with a manly mission, men who would go out and do manly men things to demonstrate their manly masculinity! Those Covina women would never dare confront them now! Nor would dragons be so bold!

A massive crowd of men, youths, and boys had assembled to see them off on their dangerous journey. Flags waved, banners fluttered in the cool breeze, a brass band played heroic music and streams of crimson and bronze soldiers marched in close formation as the sun shone through the wintry clouds. Corlan had never seen such pomp in all his days, going back to his employ with the Prince of Nerk.

"May you all distinguish yourselves with your manly courage!" Regent Urix called over the assemblage. "Let the dragons know your full fury! Sing your rage! Let them know the determination of Luval men! The best men of the world! Let no dragon ever again harass this land! The reputation of Luval is in your hands, Corlan of the Burg! Bring back dragon blood!"

The assembled men, those in uniform and not, gathered on the docks and beside them, all saluted Regent Urix in unison.

Much of the talk was how they would return from the dangerous mission as nobility, as tall as kings, and women from far and wide would seek them and worship them for the risks they had willingly undertaken and the daring deeds they had done. The best of the men would be selected for mating. Women would desire a Luval man as a sire. Even Covinas would admire them, a few of the men suggested; if they could gain the eye of a Covina they must surely be the best of the men in Luval—of the world!—and thus be privileged to father many sons. And every son a dragonslayer!

The river widened considerably as it turned sharply south, flowing from the port of Luval, enough for four boats to sail abreast. As the river bent north again further along, the heroic men slipped into lethargy, singing songs and telling tales of what they had done in the past or what they planned to do in the future when they arrived in the marshes. Their slow pace on the lazy river lent a calmness that quickly sapped their determination. Corlan went among them, boat to boat, to encourage them to stay strong, stay on task.

Leaving his skiff behind in Luval, Corlan stood at the prow of the leading ship, the *Riverstallion*, the largest of the flotilla. It had a full complement of sails yet they did little to propel the ship downriver.

The current flowed strong and took the flotilla along its course.

They raised the battle flag to the top of the *Riverstallion*'s main mast. The dark green field had a white prancing horse silhouetted at its center and a red heart in the chest of the horse. The men of Luval were proud of their horses.

"There! Now we're officially at war," said the captain, a bald and bearded man named Bantun, dressed in tall brown boots and a long blue coat covered in brass buttons, bold yellow stripes crossing the cuffs. Shorter and older than Corlan, he came from the town of Lexin, to the southeast of Luval, where fine horses were the main trade. In his youth he had raced them in Luval. Then he became a river pilot.

"How long until we reach the marshes?" asked Corlan, standing beside him.

"I've never been there," Bantun replied. He stared far ahead at the river's next turn. "I've only spoken with travelers who described it. A vast sea of grass, shallow off the main channels. Everywhere is grass, though deep enough for a low-slung craft to pass."

"Like the skiff I used coming to Luval." He thought a moment. "How many days depends on how many miles."

Bantun pointed downriver, dropped his hand to the gunwale.

"Beyond Luval, the next town is Brandur, being of a thousand folks, a mixed town, men and women. Then comes Hawz, of perhaps eight-hundred folks. Between them is the great northern bend. There the river turns sharply to the north and later returns to the south. Beyond Hawz comes Oenal, a city of two-thousand. Then Evanal, a city of possibly five-thousand. After Evanal there is nothing much. Perhaps some scattered villages of a hundred or less. The marshes you seek are beyond Evanal. I heard of a village called Ducah, the farthest outpost of humankind, set on an island at the edge of the marshes. Maybe three-hundred folks there."

Corlan sighed. So much farther to go, and with these fanatics to keep in check. Which was worse, he wondered, to have a gang of loud brawlers to keep in order or to have a bunch of lazy louts he would need to urge to fight when the moment came? He did not trust any of them to watch his back or fight beside him when the dragon's fire came down. He would, as always, rely on himself.

"And the dragons?" asked Bantun.

"As many as the eyes can see, I suspect. In this winter season eggs would be common, which makes this the best time to destroy them. Then there will be no spring hatching."

"Can we truly match so well against such an array of beasts?"

Corlan turned to Bantun. "We must. Or else die fighting. Can the men of Luval return home with nothing to show for this fight?" He recalled their boastfulness. "Will women truly take them, men who fled? who slept through the fight?"

Bantun chuckled. "You're right. Luval men are full of vanity. They are the best of all men, they believe. Now me, I grew up in Lexin. We were a mixed town and every man had a woman and every woman had a man. Sometimes there were fights to decide who went with who, naturally. In the end every babe born was parented by the whole town. I can only guess who my father was—one of the horse breeders, I'm certain. My mother pointed to several men who could be him. I left and made my way to Luval, where there were no women to puzzle me."

Corlan smiled like he kept a secret. He thought of his life in the Burg and it seemed a lot better now that he was far from home. His mind settled on an image of him on a bed with a buxom woman named Petula. He could almost see her face in his head, smiling at him, calling to him. Rosy cheeks, full red lips —

"Thinking of dragons?" Bantun was asking when Corlan broke from his trance.

He grinned. "No, a woman actually. I knew her back in the Burg. Men and women treat each other equally in the Burg." He smiled to himself. "With equal consideration. With equal contempt sometimes. It's always a game. Say the right words. Give a gift. If she is right for you, she'll go to the bed with you. Then it's all about how you please each other."

"You Nor'easters have strange ideas!"

Corlan dared laugh. "You Westers have strange ideas, too."

Bantun broke into a roaring laughter that caught the attention of the men on the ship. He had to explain what the laughing was about. Then men joined in once they had been told the strange customs of Nor'easters.

"I'm glad they approve," Corlan said with a sneer.

The laughter died and they watched the river open for the ship like unraveling the threads on a bodice, shores sprouting thick with forest. So many seductive dangers hiding within its dark folds as the prow of the ship pushed ahead.

38

The River of Death

THE FLOTILLA PUT TO SHORE and the men made a camp, setting up lean-tos and building campfires. It was so innocent, thought Corlan, like they were on a training mission, just marching and camping, never having any threat of violence. They could train all day but without the possibility of a dragon attack, soldiers would never truly learn their tasks. Those days commanding regiments in the northeast haunted him. He could not sleep.

For days they sailed downriver, stopping to camp on the shore. One evening, they paused to seek a tavern in Brandur. The men filled the place and sang until dawn. It was difficult to gather them and herd them onto the boats. The drink reduced their fire. Some complained. Plenty of time to reach the marshes, they insisted. A few men did not return to the boats.

At Hawz, the order was given to stay on the boats. Only five men could go into the town each hour. The strict arrangement caused a day's delay as each man insisted on having his turn to visit a tavern. Corlan saw to resupplying the flotilla with help from Bantun and two other boat captains, Londrel and Durkin.

When the flotilla arrived at Oenal, the captains had to let the men have their rest or face mutiny. The large town provided taverns and whorehouses. It took three days to round up the men and get them back on the boats. Even then, more of the men disappeared and the flotilla had to set sail without them. Despite the loss, tales of dragon quests were told and when they left the town, two more boats of newly acquired men had joined them, desperate to make their mark in the world, dragons or not.

The river widened further between Oenal and Evanal, more like an inland sea that stretched a mile from shore to shore. Along the riverbanks reeds choked the water. Low isles barely rose above the surface, posing danger to the boats. Yet Corlan felt better, seeing more grass in the river, knowing they were closer to the marshes.

He took the captains aside and together they made a plan for a dragon attack. They assigned weapons and Corlan took some time in the evenings to train them. Many of them insisted they already knew how to shoot an arrow with a bow. The poor results with the targets hung on tree trunks, however, did not match their confidence.

"You've got to be ready!" Corlan shouted at them, realizing that was not going to be effective. "When dragons arrive is too late for training. You might have one shot. One shot! Then you are toast."

The men stared at him. He could see on their faces they could not connect the threat of dragons with the purpose of their journey. It was all a ruse for them to go sailing and drinking and whoring, not about saving humankind from dragons.

He took the bench in the first mate's cabin on the *Riverstallion*, but was too frustrated to get a good sleep.

"Evanal is coming soon," Bantun explained to Corlan on another morning. "We cannot keep the men away from it. They will abandon the boats for pleasures in the town. I recommend we let them have their play. Perhaps two days. In the interval we can plan our attack, maybe find a map of the marshes."

"You think someone has mapped that region?" asked Corlan.

Londrel, the tall, straw-haired river pilot with the hooked nose, grabbed Bantun's shoulder. "It's uncharted territory."

"They've a good archive in Evanal," said Durkin, scratching his thick brown moustache. "Or so I've heard."

The young man in scriber's robe and cap climbed up the ladder in the archive house and pulled out several scrolls from a high shelf. His elderly supervisor cautioned him only a heartbeat before the young scriber tumbled down off the ladder, crashing on the floor with scrolls held carefully in his arms.

"I do that about three times a day now," Pitir, the young scriber laughed, getting himself up. "Used to be six."

He took the scrolls over to a study table and spread out the first scroll, looked it over and rolled it up. He unrolled the second scroll;

not the right one, either. The third scroll presented the area they needed. Clamping the corners of the scroll down on the sloped table, he took a round glass disk that magnified the details and slid it over the scroll's surface.

"We are here." Pitir's finger pointed on the map, his beady eyes squinting at the small printing there. He slid the glass disk along the river's blue squiggle. "You'll keep to the northwest and you'll come to Evanal. Then follows five short turns with narrow breadth. Then four great turns with widening shores. The final bend brings you to the marshes. The last town is Ducah. It's on an island at the mouth of the river."

"How old is this map?" asked Londrel, craning his head to look over Pitir's shoulder. "I've been as far as Shaney and the river is quite wide there. Not the sharp precipices that map shows."

"There," Durkin exclaimed, his finger on a date in the lower corner. "This map is a hundred years old."

"I met a man from Ducah about five years ago. Not a river pilot but a merchant selling products from Ducah. Baskets and the like, things made from reeds. It's a mixed town, I think."

"That would explain the reed products," said Bantun.

"The reeds explains the marshes," Corlan spoke up.

"As you say," said Londrel with a nod.

They studied the map over Pitir's head and shoulders until he felt uncomfortable and stepped aside.

"It's marked as safe...here...and here," Durkin said, his finger marking two points where the map showed the river narrowing. "So someone was there and had no trouble."

"I'm not concerned with trouble from men folk or women folk," the tall pilot, Londrel, remarked.

"There are tales I've heard of women pirates on the lower river," said Durkin in a serious tone.

"Aren't they only some Covinas hoping to snare some men for bedding?" said Londrel with a nervous laugh.

"We've enough men to route any attack from river pirates, men or women," said Bantun. He slapped his hand down on the map just above Ducah, a clearly drawn island in the wide delta. "Here are all mixed cities. No chance of attacks from women warriors, nor from the men folk."

"Just dragons," said Durkin in an apprehensive voice.

"We would be blocked in, sitting on the river," said Bantun.

"The benefit we have is the water," said Corlan. "We might lose the boats to fire but the men can dive overboard."

"Then we're left swimming down to the marshes." Durkin glared at Corlan. "Weapons drowned, defenseless, bobbing vulnerable in the water. That's not a good plan."

"Plan? The only plan is to reach the marshes," said Corlan in an angry, impatient voice. "We'll divide the men into squads and send them in different directions, according to the terrain we find. Each squad will go about destroying whatever eggs they find. We'll meet up later at some designated point, count our egg souvenirs, and sail them home."

"I, for one, cannot wait to sail home," said Londrel with a cough. "I was pushed into this duty by my kinsmen. I was taken from my whoring appointments. They said I better join up, better earn my reputation. As though ten years of flawless river piloting were not enough to claim."

"Making the realm safe from dragons is a higher priority, I'd say," said Durkin, giving Londrel a stern frown. "Let us not forget the attacks last year. Your favorite whorehouse caught fire from two dragons."

"Yes, terrible. Lost a handful of good boys that night. And fewer good men, I'll say. Perhaps a good whore, too."

Durkin and Londrel continued to debate their roles as Corlan studied the map, tracing their intended path with his finger and pausing at the point where another river joined the River Oh. His finger ran up the twisting blue line and stopped at the square that marked the city of Teraut. That town had been his destination when he'd left Danapo, before they decided to return south to Covin.

Corlan rubbed his chin, beard growing fuller, his eyes fixed on the brown square. On the map, the square was a carefully drawn brick wall around a few towers. If they had followed that plan, they could have hired a boat in Teraut and sailed down this new river, the River Abaz, meeting the River Oh at what appeared on the map to be a tricky confluence of meandering streams.

"Is this likely to be difficult?" he asked the men, annoyed by their bickering. He kept his finger on the confluence.

Londrel and Durkin looked at the map, shook their heads. Corlan explained about his original plan and Bantun had nothing good to say about Teraut.

"You did better coming down to Luval and gaining an army of

dragonslayers," said Bantun proudly.

"Only I am a dragonslayer here," Corlan spoke in a low voice. He looked up when the silence was too loud. "I'm the only man on this journey a member of a dragonslayer guild. I'm trained to use a dragonslinger. I have nearly four-hundred dragon kills." He gave them a grin to reassure them. "Some men may yet earn the title. Or, maybe we could call it, instead of dragonslayer, dragonbait."

Londrel and Durkin chuckled uneasily.

"Or dragonfodder.... That sounds better," Corlan added.

"If you all are going beyond Ducah you better beware the Drid," said Pitir. The young scriber had moved to the side of the table to let the pilots peruse the map. Where he stood was the far western edge. Another river entered the marshes from the north, he showed them. "Here is the city of Salou. And this is the Issip River, coming from Nesota territory. It is very dangerous. Many rapids and whirlpools. The reason is the Drid."

"And what is this Drid thing?" asked Corlan.

Pitir smiled like he finally was the expert on something. "It is a place in the river where the bottom drops greatly. An abyss—"

"Greatly? Measure that in fathoms, boy!" grunted Durkin.

"I don't know fathoms," said Pitir. "Most of the upper river is twenty feet or less. It becomes ten feet in the marshes. Then comes the Drid and the bottom drops more than two-hundred feet. And it goes on like that for a hundred miles."

"You referred to this Issip River?" asked Bantun.

"Yes, the river coming from the north," Pitir replied. "Issip from the north, Oh from the east. They meet at the marshes."

"We need not go that far," said Corlan. "It's the marshes that are our destination, not some abyss beyond it."

"The marshes are vast," Bantun pointed on the map, "as wide as the whole of Luval territory."

Pitir nodded. "The Drid ends at the marshes. If you come from the north or west."

"How can there be such an abyss?" asked Corlan.

"Long ago," said the young scriber, "the nine dragons that live beneath us shook heavily in a mating orgy and the land fell down, crumbled into the sea. Mountains rose in the west and the river bottom dropped, sinking into the gates of Hell."

"That's a great tale!" mocked Londrel. "My grampy could spin a yarn thicker than that one."

"A watery hell?" asked Durkin.

"In the west," said Pitir, walking his fingers three inches over to the edge of the parchment, "is Mount Zarg. It is the highest peak in all the mountains west of the marshes and the Drid. It is known as a forbidden land, called by some Arkan. It's —"

"Arkan," said Bantun with a sneer, "another name for Hell."

"It's full of naked savages. If there are any humans there at all," Pitir continued. "Below there" — finger pointing south on the map — "the marshes eventually clear and meet the open sea. We just call it the Southern Sea. Some scribers have given it a name: the Olen Sea. I don't know the origin of that name. Perhaps a mythical underwater city. There you will find sea-dragons."

"By the gods!" said Bantun, staring at that corner of the map.

"We shouldn't need to go that far west," said Corlan. "Or south. This is not a sea voyage. The marshes are our only concern."

"But you see this drawing?" said Pitir, his ink-stained finger put to the sketch of Mount Zarg on the map.

Corlan looked. The drawing of that mountain, larger than all the others on the map that lay to the west of the marshes, featured a peak topped by a dragon with its mighty wings spread open, gazing over the marshes, a trickle of flame coming from its mouth.

"That's a mountain-master," said Corlan plainly. He turned to the others. "The largest of dragons. Wingspan enough to cover this town. It's a beast from a different world. I've encountered only two in my life. A juvenile on this journey, in fact. Yet I could not slay it. The other...was long ago, in my apprentice years. I had to hack my way into it with a battle axe, then hack my way out the other side to kill it. Using iron bolts from the dragonslinger was not enough."

The group stood silent, staring at Corlan.

"Eww," said Pitir. "You cut your way straight through it?"

"I was a novice," said Corlan with a sly grin. "I wasn't thinking clearly."

"Might we encounter such in the marshes?" asked Londrel.

"We might encounter any dragon in the marshes," said Corlan. "It's where they nest. Except the mountain-masters. They nest on the tops of mountains."

"That's obvious," said Durkin with an uneasy chuckle.

Corlan dismissed the dangers. "We will stay to the marshes only. Our mission is egg smashing and infant lancing. Small work."

"That's good to know," said Durkin with a louder laugh.

"Won't the dragons be guarding the nests?" asked Londrel. "As we would our own nursery?"

"Dragons are animals." Corlan sighed. "They drop the eggs and fly away. Whatever comes out of the egg is on its own. No love lost between parent and offspring." He thought then of his own parents, wondering how the gods had selected them. "The draglings may look upon us as their parents."

Bantun warned about dragons they had already spied passing overhead as they sailed down the river from Luval.

Corlan waved him off. "We are men, are we not?" He slapped his hand on the map, making the table rattle. "We do not fear dragons! Dragons fear us!"

"Do they?" asked Londrel.

"They fear me," said Corlan, his chest puffing. "There's a few dragons that know me by name. They tell their children about me, warn them never to go near me, not that Corlan fellow. Oh, no, not him! One dragon keeps following me about, trying to get revenge on me for hacking off its claw. I sold his claw upriver. Now it sits in a prince's gallery. I call that dragon Fluffy."

Pitir laughed. "True?"

"True." Corlan grinned. "Though he likely will not answer to it."

"And he truly knows you?" asked the scriber.

"I believe so."

"Dragons are smart enough," said Bantun with certainty.

"Dragons are dumb beasts," Corlan challenged. "They act only on instinct. What instincts? Hunger, mostly. Sex, second. Revenge, third. A distant third on the list, as I've noted. You have nothing to fear but dragon fire itself. Now let us gather our heroes and press onward to glory!"

"To glory!" cried Londrel and Durkin.

"At least to success," Bantun swore.

Pitir, the scriber, raised his fist. "May the gods be with you!"

News had somehow raced ahead of the flotilla, causing dozens of men to line the wharves at Evanal in anticipation of their arrival. An official delegation, the lord-mayor on his blue banner-draped white horse and seven gold carriages filled with high-ranking dignitaries, came to welcome the flotilla. Corlan was whisked off the flagship and escorted through the crowds and into the large community hall where he was urged to speak to the crowd about the mission they were on.

Corlan was not one for speeches so he fumbled for a while as the audience grew impatient. Finally, Bantun got up and spoke for him.

"Here is the man you've been waiting for: the dragonslayer from the east who'll lead our courageous men to victory over the dreaded aerials!" He continued and the crowd loved his rousing speech. He spoke words that excited the crowd. "To end this rage, we propose to destroy the dragons' nesting ground and forever after be rid of them!"

Cheers exploded in the hall.

"Corlan of the Burg, slayer of five-hundred dragons, leads this heroic expedition down the River Oh. Our destination is the marshes where they lay their eggs. We need many men to cover that vast region. Men with boats. All boats are welcome. And we need lances to pierce the eggs, hammers to crack their shells, and nets to capture the draglings. Any who dare join us are welcome—but you must bow to our commands, our directions, and follow our lead if you wish to become a dragonslayer like our brave leader, Corlan!"

The roar of the crowd deafened Corlan. He would have preferred to slink away to a quieter venue and down a few mugs of ale, yet he understood the need to stay on stage and play the role. There was no telling how many men would be needed. If the marshes spread for hundreds of miles and included hundreds of isles, then hundreds of men in boats would be needed to cover the territory. So he accepted the recruitment rally.

"Well done, Corlan of the Burg from the far eastern realm," said the lord-mayor, giving a hard clap to Corlan's shoulder. "I, Pontex, Mayor of Evanal, grant you safe passage down our river and award you as many men as are willing to take the risk. We grant you all the resources you may need. We shall gather our thoughts and present them to the gods to call for your safety in this mission. For you and your men, our men, and all men who fight dragons!"

Corlan thanked the stout, swarthy man in the blue robe, white moustache and beard worthy of a magus, and bowed at Bantun's quick, nervous gesture. Rising, Corlan was given a long scepter which might serve well as a battle club, he thought, but was, in its golden gleam, a purely ceremonial item.

The feasting went on through the night. Women captured from Covin were offered as entertainment. They danced naked around the men. An older woman in a thin pink gown and gray hair stood and sang. The singing and dancing seemed merely proficient, reminding Corlan of certain quarters in the Burg.

When the women finished with their entertainment, each woman took a seat beside one of the leaders of the expedition. The dark-haired woman sitting with Corlan introduced herself. Danissa seemed to know how to keep a man's attention. However, with Corlan, his mind focused on the mission, she had her work cut out for her. She kept at it, though, caressing his neck and massaging his shoulders, small talk that went nowhere, kisses and touches in places from which Corlan had to remove her hand.

"Not tonight," he told her several times.

"They will beat me if you look unpleased," she whispered into his ear, her fingers caressing his face and stroking his beard.

"I understand." Corlan leaned to his left, spoke to the Evanal official. "This one pleases me. Have her taken to my room."

A staff member escorted the woman out of the feasting hall.

Later, when he arrived at his room, Danissa was naked on the bed, ready for him.

"Too tired for any of that," he said in a weary voice.

"If they see me leave too soon, they'll know I have not pleased you and—"

"They'll beat you." He found some cushions and fashioned a bed on the floor. "Here. Stay here until you believe you have pleased me, then go."

Danissa took her place on the cushions, pouting. "If you change your mind during the night...."

Corlan nodded. "I once knew a Covina."

"Did you?" asked the woman.

"I miss her tonight."

"Let me be her for you."

Corlan chuckled and tossed one of the blankets down over her. "I doubt anyone could be her."

He slept alone in the bed, though he did not sleep deeply or for long. The woman started snoring after a while. He awoke her, told her that she had finally pleased him; it was time to leave. She did, sleepy and stumbling, bumping against the door.

He tried to return to sleep but thoughts of home bothered him.

At last he had arrived at his destination — or nearly so. With an army behind him he was certain to succeed. Then he would make his way home again. A journey of eight months to get to this point. Perhaps another six months to return home, if he could avoid all the detours and distractions of his westward trek. Then there would be Petula to wrap her arms around him. Unless she had found another in his absence.

Burning through the thoughts he had of Petula was the image of Naka Wu, supplanting what he remembered of the buxom Petula. They were different, he accepted, though he could not choose which one he should make his home with for his final years. Thoughts such as those were not allowed, he told himself, not until the mission was completed.

The next day, men who had volunteered for the mission stood in line, signing a register supervised by Londrel and Durkin. Corlan saw that another man had joined them, Arris Jankor, a colonel in the Evanal army, he was told. Three new river pilots were introduced to Corlan as well as a dozen captains, lieutenants, and sergeants assigned to companies and the boats they were using. He guessed, as he scanned them, there were more than a hundred men joining the expedition.

"What is our count now?" Corlan asked Bantun.

The *Riverstallion* captain examined the ledger in his hands. "From what we started with at Luval, adding and subtracting men along the way, plus these soldiers from Evanal...three-hundred-thirty-eight in total, including you and me and the other pilots and officers. A fine force to battle dragons."

"It should be less battling them and more searching for eggs and destroying them. As I've been explaining to the men."

"The Evanal men seem very eager to fight."

"Honestly, I hope we do not have to fight."

"Sounds like you have been too long from the battlefields," said Colonel Jankor, coming up behind them.

Corlan turned, and they clenched hands, Jankor offering his hand first. Jankor glanced at the ledger Bantun held, nodding approvingly.

"I sense the fury of our terror building," Jankor mugged proudly. "The men of Evanal await your orders. They are ready to kill."

"I was just saying I hoped we did not need to fight, just smash some eggs—"

"I'll warn you, friend, that's not the kind of effort these men are expecting. They've seen dragons in Evanal. They have grown to hate them. We all hate them. It is time for battle. Perhaps the start of the war. We need to end this scourge now."

Corlan nodded thoughtfully, wanted to look away but he thought the colonel would take it as some sign of weakness. So he came back with a hard stare.

"None of us truly knows what we will find in the marshes," said Corlan. "Only then can we decide which action is best to take. It will be good to have the backing of your soldiers...ready to kill."

"We are ready!" Colonel Jankor beamed. He saluted Corlan, who smiled and scratched his forehead as his return salute.

With the army lined up in the town square, a wooden stage had been erected and, with Jankor's insistence, Corlan stepped onto it, strutting to the center. Jankor introduced Corlan with great fanfare. Then he talked to the men about dragons. Although they knew about the aerial beasts, what they knew was the damage the dragons could inflict. Evanal had many buildings that appeared burnt from above. Several leaders from Evanal expressed their fear that dragons would continue to attack their city, igniting roofs at will.

"Dragons will attack. We expect that," said Corlan in a fierce voice. He puffed out his chest. "We are going into battle — as much of a battle as any I fought back in the east. Then, it was men against men. Now, with dragons, it's different, very different. We need to be ready to fight whenever they come. Though dragons are bigger than a man and they can fly and they can spit fire, they can also be killed. They can be defeated."

He surveyed the men as excited murmuring spread through the assembly.

"There are several ways to kill a dragon," Corlan spoke loudly. "First, you must have a weapon that can strike a dragon. I use a dragonslinger — one of the finest weapons ever made for taking a beast from the sky. Ordinary bow and arrows will suffice although you may find the dragon skin tough to pierce unless the arrowheads are made for that kind of target. Iron-tipped, the heads at least six inches long and heavy shafts. You are not hunting *elkor*."

He turned to Londrel, standing beside him. The man nodded.

"We do have the right kind of arrows, it seems. We'll see that each archer is assigned his portion."

He pulled Stepan, a chubby young man he had selected earlier to help him with the lesson, onto the stage. The youth took his position, pretending to be a dragon in flight as he faced the assembly, thick arms extended.

"If a dragon is coming straight at you," said Corlan, pointing at the youth's shoulders, "they provide only a narrow target, what with the wings in a flat line and the body trailing. So it's the head which is your best target. Aim for the eyes if the mouth is closed. A blinded dragon will usually abandon the attack if it's in flight. If the dragon has landed and you blind it, be prepared to run away to avoid its frantic dance that may yet cause you to be stomped into the ground."

Some men chuckled; most took the lecture seriously.

"If a dragon approaches with mouth open, two things are likely: either fire breath is coming, or it intends to scoop you off the ground and swallow you in one gulp. Neither is a very pleasant experience. I've seen both happen. So if the mouth is open, aim for the gullet. Straight down the tube. A good arrow stuck inside its throat will sufficiently annoy it to keep it from launching its fire. It will break the arrow eventually, throat muscles being strong, so it's not a final act. It can buy you a half-minute."

He was working his way around Stepan, poking the youth's thick neck. The youth seemed to be afraid already.

"If a dragon is above you, airborne, aim for the belly—especially if it seems bloated. If you can puncture the belly, you'll let out the spirit air that helps it float, which is also what it uses to make fire. That's a tough area to pierce, so you'll need more than a simple bow and arrow. The iron arrowheads we will issue you should be able to penetrate most belly flesh if you can put enough power behind your bow. Dragons with more scales on the belly won't be pierced except with a dragonslinger."

Londrel held up one of the iron-tipped arrowheads. The shaft was thicker yet made of wood. A machine-bow, with a mechanism like the dragonslinger, would have the strength to push one of them through a dragon's flesh.

"Fortunately, those tend to stay well to the south, where the days are hot and dry. In this region, they're mostly grey-bellies, red-bulls, green-horns, hornchins, and the like. In the east, where I'm from, there are featherbacks, flatheads, and blue-lightnings. A fair number of drapers, too. Not long ago, a few weeks past, I also fought a fang-master. I did not manage to kill the fang-master."

Corlan glanced around the assembly. All eyes were on him. He pushed the image of Bai Lo's burnt, crushed body out of his mind and continued. He had to go on.

"You can aim for the throat, too. There are two weak points on most dragons. At the base of the throat where neck joins shoulders, there is a weak point. Look for a V circumscribed by the musculature and collarbones. Aim there. A strong enough shot should pierce that spot and render the dragon unable to fire. If your arrow goes deep enough. Another weak point is under the lower jaw, where the jaw connects to the upper throat. Look for the U that sits there, within the underside of the lower jawline. Aim there and you could disable it, keep it from using its mouth to attack. It may also discourage the launching of fire."

Corlan had Stepan stand straight and pulled out his double-chin flaps, pointing to the place where the U would be on a dragon.

"Any wound to the mouth or throat should discourage a dragon from firing at all, because the wounds would become exposed to the burning agents from its own glands. If you smell sulfur, get ready for fire. Watch for the neck extension, too, as that indicates the dragon is bringing its throat glands into contact with the spirit air from its belly. It only takes a few seconds. Listen for a raspy cough. That will let you know it's about to fire. You have seconds to do something. Running is a good option. Dive into water, if you can. Be sure it's deep. I was in a shallow pond when that fang-master fired at me. One fire breath took most of the pond's water in a flash."

Corlan laughed. No one else did. He turned Stepan around, his backside to the audience.

"If you are behind the dragon, watch for the tail spikes. They often swing the tail without intending it as a weapon but you will be struck and killed anyway. If you find yourself beneath the dragon and it doesn't know you are there, certainly watch that you are not stepped on. You may be lucky to remain in a gap between its claws. Watch for the claws—the talons—because they will easily cut into you." He pulled his shirt collar down and away from his neck, exposing the upper end of several scars. "I've caught a few claws in my years of slaying dragons. They do not look pretty—except when you're in bed with a passionate woman!"

Fewer men laughed this time, half warily.

"You can aim at the dragon's wings, of course. Easy targets. The membranes most dragons have are thin, easily torn. With enough tearing the wing is useless. This will limit their ability to fly but it will not stop them from attacking. Torn membranes will heal in time, and the dragon will be able to return to battle another day."

Stepan stood with his back bent and his arms spread wide like dragon wings as Corlan pointed to the imaginary membranes.

"The best way to slay a dragon is to face it straight on. Get it to open its mouth. Yell at it. Make it react to you. Then, when it opens its mouth to roar, launch down its gullet a trident-barbed iron bolt from a dragonslinger and let the bulb of poison do its work. You have about two minutes until the dragon is dazed from the poison. When it is dazed in flight, it will fall and crash. If it is landed and dazed, you have a minute to strike the fatal blow with a good battle axe or, if you can, by launching another dragonslinger bolt. Aim for the heart. That's through the belly. Secondary kill zone is the head. But the head is well-armored in most species, so the position to take is from underneath the jaw. That weak spot I mentioned before? The U? That's the spot. A long sword or lance can strike all the way up into the brain and your dragon foe is rendered a heaping pile of canine dinner. I'm joking. Don't let your canine eat any dragon meat. It'll make the canine sick."

Corlan stood at the prow of the *Riverstallion* once more as the flotilla sailed away from Evanal with the blessing of the lord-mayor and all its officials and residents. The skies were dark gray, clouds laden with rain, yet their mood was bright. Men began singing drinking songs and the tunes spread from boat to boat until the whole river seemed to be one big chorus.

He hoped the men he'd acquired would remain serious about the mission. Perhaps Colonel Jankor would be able to keep them in line. He had doubts after his lesson on killing dragons. The men went out drinking to bolster their courage. Several men failed to make the morning call and were left behind. Even so, they gained about fifty men on one new ship and six more boats, causing the flotilla to extend up the river a few miles.

Corlan thought through his plan. He didn't mind the additional troops, each armed with blades and lances, bows and arrows, and several sharp farm tools, if needed. He was in command again, like the old days in the northeast, fighting for the Prince of Nerk. He gave orders and paced the deck of the flagship. Bantun was its captain, yet Corlan was clearly the general officer, planning the campaign, giving orders, leading all of them. He had the crimson and bronze longcoat with the brass buttons down the front, after all, a parting gift from Pontex, the lord-mayor, to signify his rank: River Marshal.

As they neared a village downriver called Veron, Corlan leaned forward against the prow, watching the river split before the ship. He heard a familiar cry and gazed up into the sky. Instead of a dragon about to attack, he saw a large bird. Yet not a bird.

It was golden-brown, larger than a person. The winged creature fluttered above him, descending.

"Sir!" warned one of the men behind him. "Should we kill it?"

Corlan spun around. "No! I know this one."

Madi landed on the gunwale, her talons grasping the wood panel, scoring it as her talons fought to keep her body erect. She folded her wings and smiled at him. The sight of such a huge bird-like creature with a woman's face alarmed the crew.

"Harpy!" cried the men fearfully.

"Stand back and she won't hurt any of you," cried Corlan.

He stepped over to her, held out his hand, palm up, a gesture of peace, to show he held no weapon, despite a sideblade on his hip.

"Cooooorlaaaan," Madi cawed to him.

"Maaaadiiii," he tried to imitate. He thought he was being kind. "How are you?"

The screeches and cries that answered his question did not sit well with the men. Many held their hands over their ears.

"I can't understand you," said Corlan. "But it's good to see you again. I thought you might've been killed by that fang-master on the road from Danapo. But you got away."

Her head bobbed as she listened, taking a moment to ruffle her feathers, refold them. Her face was that of a girl, yet a fine layer of beige down had grown over her cheeks, almost like a beard, as well as across her forehead. Her nose and mouth were the same although her chin had diminished. Her large, dark eyes watched him.

"Tam was hurt in that attack," he told her. "The girl we brought from Covin...she didn't survive."

He described what they had done to see to the boy's healing. It was a long report and he could see how the news affected her. She bowed her head. Tears spotted the wooden deck below her.

"When I left, he was doing well. The magus there grew new skin to put on his face and shoulder. To replace the burnt skin."

Madi nodded, spread her six-foot wings, and cawed to him for several minutes. It seemed to be an entire story.

"Thank you," he said.

She cried out, head raised, gazing up into the sky, wings ruffling.

"Be careful up there in the sky," said Corlan.

There was another cry above them and Corlan turned to see what it was. He spied another bird-like creature winging overhead.

"Another harpy!" cried one of the men, raising a bow and arrow.

"Don't you dare aim on that one," Corlan commanded.

The men seemed afraid.

Madi cried out to the airborne creature, then squawked at Corlan a bit before launching herself into the sky to join the other harpy. The two of them circled the ship twice in close formation before turning north and flying away.

"Sir, what was that being?" asked Bantun, daring to mount the foredeck once the harpy had left.

"A friend from afar," said Corlan, smiling.

"Is it bird or woman?"

"Both." Corlan turned to Bantun. "She warned that a large clan of dragons is heading our way. Mostly red-bulls and blue-lightnings, some grey-bellies and green-horns mixed in. And a stubborn double-hornchin."

"Then we should prepare for attack?" asked Bantun.

Corlan lost his smile, glaring at the ship captain. "I would."

39

Where Dragons Watch

THE VILLAGE OF VERON sat on one of the larger islands of the delta, all of the islands flat and low, clustered at the confluence of the River Oh and the smaller River Abaz coming from the north. The wide expanse of water where they met anticipated the marshes Corlan sought. The water along the shores was filled with grass and reeds. The thick forests which had lined each shore from Luval to Evanal had diminished, then disappeared, leaving only brush and scrub growing on either side of the widening river.

The ships and boats spread out to fill the channel from shore to shore as they arrived in the delta. A true naval fleet, thought Corlan, never a man for sea travel. He had ridden a ship off the coast of Nerk once, spent his time emptying his stomach. On this river, too, he had been on the verge of tossing his meals for days, yet he always fought the urge for the sake of a leader's appearance.

As they came upon Veron, everyone could see that the buildings had been burnt, blackened and fallen, a few still smoldering. They could see no people or animals moving, not even by peering through a glasstube.

Corlan ordered a few boats to land and search the village for any survivors.

"Dragons?" asked Bantun.

Corlan nodded. "A stray flame would not have taken down an entire village."

"Then it's dragons," said Colonel Jankor, his hand on the hilt of his sword.

"Your bird messenger said to expect dragons," said Bantun.

"Yes." Corlan stared across the water at the smoldering village. "They attacked here."

"Instead of us, it seems."

"Where are they now?" asked Jankor, gazing skyward.

"Long gone," said Corlan.

"But why?" It was Londrel who had come up to the foredeck to have a look. "Did the village so displease passing dragons they had to burn it down?"

"Dragons do as they wish," Jankor said with a grunt. He gave a nod to Corlan who had said the same thing the previous night.

"Dragons hate humans," Durkin offered, joining them. "We are not meant to exist on the same world."

"Perhaps they're not from this world," said Jankor.

"An old myth," said Corlan.

"With ordinary effects," Jankor added.

The flotilla waited half a day. The report from the shore party was that about sixty men, women, and children lay about, all burned and blackened. Corlan ordered the shore party to bury the bodies. They found a child unharmed, however, and a blind old man. Both hid in a waterwell and were spared from the flame.

"Wallan," said the old man when asked his name. "The boy is Ruk. Not my relation, though. I sat him on my shoulders in that well for two days."

"Unfortunate circumstances, indeed, but welcome to our flotilla," said Bantun. "We're on the way to destroy those dragons that burnt your village."

"Can you leave us here, then?" asked the old man.

Bantun frowned. "There's nothing in the village."

"There's less down the river," said Wallan. "Besides, the boy is frozen, locked in fear."

Bantun turned to Corlan, waving across the delta.

"We have a physician on one of the other ships."

"Send these two to the physician," Corlan ordered. "He's on the *Libertine,* I think."

"I'm a physician myself," said Wallan.

"But you're blind," said Bantun.

"The best kind of physician," Wallan responded.

"You need to be treated...for the fear-lock."

"I saw dragons before," said Wallan. "In my youth. The fire was what took my sight. I still administered to my fellow villagers. My other senses are sharper now."

"None remain but for this boy," reported one of the search party men, saluting Corlan. "And him," meaning the old physician.

"Ruk is only six, according to his mother," said Wallan. "He will likely forget this experience. I trust he will be in good health by next year." He turned his head around, eyes closed, as though he could see everything. "If you could take us to Evanal, we would be able to find comfort there. I have two nephews, almost grown, though my brother died a few years back."

"I don't think we can do that," said Corlan firmly. "Upriver takes some time and we are going downriver to the marshes."

"The marshes?" cried Wallan. "Are you mad?"

"Not mad," said Colonel Jankor, "angry."

"Furious," said Durkin.

"Enraged," said Londrel.

"Determined," said Bantun.

"We are on a sworn mission," said Corlan. "We will destroy the dragon nesting ground once and for all time. Within a few years no more dragons will fly the skies of our world."

The old man shook his head. "You really are mad."

"It is a sound plan," said Bantun, gesturing at Corlan, giving him credit for the plan.

"No, it's madness." Wallan turned his head up to the sky. "If you are sailing downriver, you can take me to Ducah. I'll make my next life there. I remember a certain woman there. Adai was her name, I think. Or Corra, perhaps. They were cousins. She won't remember me but where else have I to go? Take me to Ducah, if you please. Then you can go onward to your marshes. And the gods be with you, for you and yours will surely need their protection."

On the western horizon the early spring sun sat low, bleeding the sky a dull orange. Before that evening curtain, an even line of dark shapes split the sky from south to north.

The men were settling in for the evening, the fleet drifting slowly downstream, the pilots looking for a favorable shoreline to anchor for the night and make camp. To the starboard side rose high, jagged cliffs. To the port side spread only grassy shallows. It would soon be dark. Already men had begun drinking, singing their tavern songs, despite the order to leave the ale on shore.

Corlan stood on the foredeck of the *Riverstallion*, thinking how he would divide the men into squads, dropping each squad on an isle to do their duty, then reclaim them later. He counted the men: a little more than three-hundred. He did not expect his team of river pilots to do any of that work. And he himself would stand watch over their work, looking for dragons—

Like the line he suddenly noticed approaching the fleet.

"In coming!" cried Corlan at the top of his lungs, waving his arms frantically.

The men in the *Riverstallion* scrambled up, grabbing weapons, and stared ahead as the boats slipped downriver.

Flags were waved from the *Riverstallion* to the trailing ships and boats to pass on the warning and the commands. Other flags waved in response.

"Put to shore!" commanded Bantun, coming up beside Corlan.

The boats tried to make for the shoreline but there was nothing suitable. Given no good anchorage, the boats stayed in the center of the river. A little more to the grassy shallows, Corlan measured. The grassy water made it difficult to determine where solid ground lay. The vessels might run aground there.

Stepan brought the dragonslinger to Corlan, struggling to carry it with a quiver of iron bolts hanging from his shoulder.

"Well done, boy," said Corlan. "Load it. Just like I showed you."

"Sir, maybe it's best you prepare it properly for this attack."

"Dragons!" cried Corlan. "Hurry!"

The boy fumbled so badly Corlan had to take the weapon from him and load it himself, screwing the spring to its tightest setting, the one that would launch the iron bolt farthest.

The line of aerial beasts stretched from one side of his vision to the other. He counted twenty-two distinct silhouettes and detected more behind them. Slow wings, so no fire breaths yet. Perhaps they were merely venturing east with no intention to attack. Yet when did so many dragons of mixed breeds fly in one mass like that without it being an attack?

Stepan accepted a quiver of arrows and bow from a crewman. "Everyone must fight," said the man.

"Notch up!" Corlan grunted.

"But I'm—I'm only a squire!"

"You want to be a dead squire?" shouted Corlan.

As the line of dragons approached, Corlan saw at the center of the formation were red-bulls, the ones most quick to fire, with green-horns on either side. Behind them, he counted several grey-bellies. And a double-hornchin. He glanced at the quiver of bolts: twenty-seven but only nine were poison-tipped.

"Damn the armorers and smithies of Evanal!" They'd had no iron bolts to contribute to his arsenal.

The line of dragons came in fast, swinging low, flanks veering off to take on the trailing boats of the flotilla. Corlan was surprised how they coordinated. The main front swooped down on the *Riverstallion* with claws grappling at the masts, breaking off the beams, letting them crash to the deck. The second wave were coughing fire but the flames did not reach Corlan, instead struck at the middle boats of the fleet. Men shouted for help. Some screamed, engulfed in flames. Others dove overboard into the river to escape the fires.

Corlan launched the dragonslinger, sending a poison-tipped iron bolt straight down the gullet of a diving red-bull. It choked, lost its flight pattern and dropped into the river.

Quickly setting a fresh bolt into the slinger, Corlan screwed back the spring and launched it. Another hit in the gullet of a new red-bull—causing it to veer and leave the attack. The green-horns came at him in tandem. He launched another bolt at the right beast, struck it on the outside of its throat, a good hit, but not down its gullet. The green-horn on the left brought fire breath and Corlan dove aside and jumped up after the dragon had passed. The folded and wrapped mainsail of the ship was aflame, tongues spreading along the beam. Men below were spraying river water up to douse the fire with little success.

Corlan saw men on the other ships launching waves of arrows as the lines of dragons passed over them. The ships equipped with the cannons fired with good effect. The iron balls blasted holes through bellies, splattering flesh and blood through the air. The cannon balls ripped through wing membranes with deadly effect. Men cheered whenever a dragon failed. Others cried in fear or distress as they fought burning boats and their own wounds. One dragon, hit by a cannon ball, dropped down across several boats, its huge mass sinking all of them under its body.

The roar just behind his left shoulder threw Corlan to the deck. As he turned to look back, he saw his old friend: Fluffy. The dragon was hovering above the foredeck as though it was awaiting a proper greeting. Crumpled on the deck, Corlan loaded the slinger, screwed back the spring and swung the weapon on line, aiming for the gullet.

"So we meet again," Corlan intoned.

The beast coughed, the raspy noise that always unnerved Corlan. The odor of sulfur filled the air. The dragon scraped its chin horns across the foredeck, ripping away wooden planks and tearing off the railing, seemingly for its own amusement. Then the neck extended, the head thrown back and the fire breath was due.

Corlan launched the iron bolt—straight into the gullet, as perfect a shot as he'd ever made. From that short distance he could not fail!

"Eat my bolt! Eat it and die!"

Fluffy grumbled, realizing something was wrong, yet its fire had been made, neck extension bringing the throat glands in line with the spirit air rising from its belly—and ignited!

With the iron bolt stuck in its throat, the fire did not get expelled and burned within its throat. Seeking relief, the dragon tumbled into the river, gulping water. Its frantic motion set off huge waves that slapped at the boats upstream. Pressing its hindlegs into the river's bottom, the dragon stretched up out of the water and scraped its way onto the deck of the *Riverstallion*, tilting the ship dangerously to the port side.

Corlan loaded another bolt, took aim on the hornchin in the river. The water was not too deep, he guessed; the beast seemed to have its feet on the bottom, the water line rising half way up its body, as its forefeet grasped the deck. Its wings fluttered wildly, knocking boats aside, tumbling the mast of the next ship, Londrel's pride and joy.

All around him, Corlan saw flames. The brush along the shores was burning, too. Boats bobbing in the river were aflame. His own ship was on fire, men daring to put out the flames with no regard for their own protection from attacking dragons.

He arose on the foredeck, what remained of it, broken and burnt, and aimed the slinger at Fluffy once more.

The dragon lifted its massive forefoot, as wide as Corlan was tall, and the absence of the middle claw was apparent. The beast slapped its forefoot down on the prow of the ship and the vessel shook like the ancient earth wyrms were dancing under it. Planks popped from the frame with the nails and plugs, all flying into the air like cannon fodder, falling back to the deck and over Corlan.

He reached for the battle axe, found it was not at his side.

"Where's my battle axe?" he called out, expecting Stepan to be there to hand it to him. His squire was nowhere to be seen. Instead, bodies lay still on the deck, some bloody, others burnt.

Corlan rushed to the nearest one, thinking it was Stepan, and rolled the body over, saw it was not him. Whatever this young man's name was, his skull had been caved in. The point of a dragon's claw had struck his forehead, it appeared, pushing inward flesh and bone.

"You scaly bastard!" cried Corlan, grabbing an iron bolt from the quiver.

He grasped the bolt like a lance, using both hands, and despite its weight stabbed hard at the hornchin's forefoot, the one with a claw missing. His attack forced the dragon to withdraw.

With a roar, the beast sank back into the river, wings flapping above the surface, slapping the water. Its head rose suddenly, shot up like the launch of an iron bolt, its head high and glaring down at the ship and at Corlan—and dropped heavily against the deck of the ship, the chin horns stabbing through the deck, sticking there.

Corlan fell back, breathing hard, glaring at the mass of flames that flickered like a curtain across the river. The frantic cries of men were deafening. The roar of dragons filled the night air. The stink of sulfur cursed his nose and mouth. He knew then he had failed. A flotilla of jubilant men would attract attention. He should have sneaked into the marshes alone and done what he had planned.

Overhead, the sky moved like a snapped blanket over a soiled bed. Instead of clouds sailing gently by, the sky was a patchwork of dragons in flight. Never before had he seen so many aerial beasts in one formation, beasts of different kin flying together. They winged eastward in tandem. Those dragons were not bothering to attack the flotilla. Only a small contingent was needed to destroy these pitiful humans and their silly watercraft.

A shudder rang through him, settling deep in his gut as night fell over them. The dark river was lit by the burning wreckage of the flotilla, the crackling of flames all the noise that remained after the dragons had swiftly departed.

Corlan heard a cough and his eyes popped open, realizing suddenly that he lay upon the deck of the *Riverstallion* among a dozen dead bodies. The cough was not the sign of dragon breath about to fire but of an old man stumbling onto the deck from the hold below.

"Ah, I should've told you," said Wallan. He held the boy's hand as the two of them stood gazing about the damaged ship. Except that the old man could not gaze. Instead, he listened to the silence and sniffed the air.

Corlan sat up, found there was a sword in his hand, orange blood staining its cutting edge. The sword was not his sideblade but something longer and more deadly he must have grabbed during the night.

"He's frozen," said Corlan, staring at the wide eyes of the boy.

"Wouldn't you be? Dragon attack...twice in the same week."

Corlan got to his feet, felt a twinge of pain in his knee. Another sore spot on the back of his shoulder. There were cuts on his forearm that had stopped bleeding. His ribs hurt when he took a step.

"Now you know the fury of dragonkin scorned," said Wallan.

"I already knew it," Corlan sneered.

He gazed in every direction, taking stock of his navy. Boats still smoldered upriver, stuck in the shallows. Others had burnt until the flames met the waterline, then remained buoyed in the water. The ships that bore cannons on their decks had survived, it appeared, yet men were busy with repairs. His own ship was damaged by fire and dragonclaw. The dead on deck had yet to be removed.

"Bantun!" he cried out. No answer returned. "Jankor!" he called next and waited for a response.

"Seems your friends were the luckier of us," said Wallan.

"Unlucky, you mean."

"No, I meant to say lucky. They went quickly, without pain."

"How much pain must a man endure before he is lucky enough to welcome death?"

Wallan chuckled. "Only a man who's faced death before would say something like that."

"Only a man who's never faced death would make me say it."

Corlan went to the stern of the ship, gazing upriver. He took up a flag that had fallen there, a signal banner, and waved it at whoever might see it among the boats there. A flag arose on another boat, then another flag on another boat. He didn't know what he had signaled but it was enough to know there were survivors.

"What will we do now?" asked Wallan. When Corlan returned to the main deck, he was resting on a fallen beam.

"Continue the mission," said Corlan firmly.

He studied the huge dark green dragon head resting on the deck.

Its mouth was still agape, as though it had been frozen open at the moment of death. Only the head sat there, its dull orange eyes still open. The body was in the river, he supposed, although the flotilla had continued to drift down the river as the night passed.

"So you've come to see me off," said Corlan to the dragon's head. "That's very kind of you."

The two spikes that projected from under the chin were lodged in the wooden deck. The cut end of the throat was singed with fire, black charcoal now and stinking of death. The nostrils leaked blood that had turned black and thick as tar. He wondered how to remove the monstrosity from the deck.

Corlan went around the dragon head and found his battle axe embedded in the neck. He remembered hacking at the neck again and again until he could not swing the axe any more. Once the flesh was cut apart, he swung at the bones until they separated and the head alone lay on the deck as the body slipped into the dark waters. Fluffy was no more.

"I smell dragon," said blind Wallan.

Corlan knew what the man meant. The beasts had a certain odor at once moist and damp and pungent like a forest floor full of decay but also with a spice of distant lands. Combined, they made a unique scent that was only enhanced by sulfur when they became enraged. In death, the pungency took over, although it never smelled the same, or as awful, as a man's rotting body.

"There's a dragon head a few steps before you."

"Ah, that's what's gotten the boy so unnerved. He's squeezing my hand enough to close off the blood."

"It's staring straight at the boy. You best turn him around," said Corlan, "Its eyes are open. A frightful thing for a boy to see."

Wallan took the boy and spun him around, made him face the bow of the ship, told him to gaze down the river for any sign of a village. It was the first lesson for learning to be a river pilot, he told the boy. Always be looking ahead.

"I don't remember much," said Corlan. His voice was coarse from shouting all night. "I suppose I cut off its head sometime during the night. The body must be upriver. This one's been hunting me for months. I think I'll miss him."

"You're a credit to your blade, sir."

"No time for credit. There's work to be done."

Corlan didn't hear Wallan's words as his eyes fell upon the black, burnt figure of his squire, Stepan. The lad lay on his side, bow in one hand, arrow clasped in the other hand, ready to notch it. Fire had touched him, his front side rendered into charcoal from knees to head, arms and hands untouched. He could see that the youth had turned as if to glance back at the moment the dragon seared his front side with its fire breath—and the back of his turned head.

"So he fought bravery," Corlan acknowledged. "Let the gods and the mama he left at home be proud of him."

Corlan dropped to his knees and worked his arms under Stepan, hefted him up and half-carried, half-dragged him to the stern of the ship. Then he returned for another body. And another. He worked for an hour clearing the deck, piling the corpses at the stern. He would drop them overboard after speaking a few words. But he thought it best to wait until he could talk with the other officers.

A small boat drew alongside the *Riverstallion*, and Londrel climbed aboard.

"What a mess! What a tragedy!" he cried out, his voice shaking. Blood had stained the front of his river pilot coat along with mud but he seemed uninjured.

"You're well?" asked Corlan.

Londrel looked over Corlan's dirty clothes. "Not as bad as you." He pointed to the dragon's head on the deck. "Yours?"

"Apparently."

"Tear out the fangs. You can sell them in Evanal as souvenirs," said Londrel with a sneer. "People like those kind of things as gifts."

Corlan was in no mood for harvesting souvenirs. "You can have them, if you want them."

"Fine, I'll get some men to work on it."

"Have them toss the rest of it overboard. I'm tired of looking at it. Tired more of smelling it."

"It does have a peculiar odor."

Corlan nodded. "What do we have remaining?"

"Remaining? You mean the men? You intend to go on?" Londrel threw his hands up as he paced behind Corlan. "There's barely a humble church choir remaining to serve your vanity!"

"My vanity?" asked Corlan, hands on hips.

"You persuaded these fine men to go with you on a dragon hunt, did you not? Fine speech that."

Corlan nodded. "I was pressed to speak."

"And now we see what fate has brought them to. Death! So much death. And for what? Only nine dragons killed. Is that the count? Six others mortally wounded. Perhaps they will go home to their mamas and cry how the terrible humans hurt them. How does that measure against one-hundred and twenty-two men dead and more than a hundred horribly wounded?"

Corlan rubbed his chin, tugged on his beard. "So we have about a hundred men still able to fight."

"Able-bodied? Not one remains unhurt." Londrel swept his hair out of his face. "Durkin was scooped up and carried away, I was told. An arm dropped on one boat as the dragon departed. I saw several men missing limbs. A few boasted they had been carried by dragons then dropped into the river. I think they're lucky to be alive. Some of those men lost an arm or a leg, or both."

Corlan gestured at Wallan. "That one thinks those who died are the lucky ones."

"I did say that," Wallan called out, cocking his head toward the sound of Corlan's voice. "Because it's true."

Corlan turned to Londrel. "I haven't seen Bantun or Jankor yet. Have you seen them?"

"Jankor fought with his own men on the *Seahag*. I don't know their fate. Bantun...he was pilot of your ship. He's not aboard? But, then, you're the one in charge of this expedition. Aren't you?"

Corlan frowned at him, then looked around the deck once more.

"I've been clearing bodies off the deck the past hour. He is not among them."

Suddenly the reality of the morning washed over him.

"I fought as hard as I could, as hard as ever. I know I took down four dragons with the slinger. I hacked and cut other dragons. I took my own wounds. And you see my nemesis dead here on the deck, no doubt dreaming of home.... We didn't have a chance to set up a defense or prepare for the attack, being on these boats, limited to a river. We were locked in, unable to escape. And they—they seemed to plan their attack for here, in this bottleneck. They knew we were coming. But did you see the others?"

"What others?" asked Londrel, alarmed.

"The other dragons—passing over us, late in the battle. Dozens more. They didn't join the attack but carried on eastward."

Londrel's eyes scanned the sky from horizon to horizon. "Do you think they flew on to another attack?"

Corlan's eyes narrowed. "Another attack.... Evanal, maybe?"

Londrel spun on his boot heel and slapped at the stump of the main mast. "Evanal! We came on this vain junket because of Evanal being attacked so often. The men were excited to help save their city. We've left the city unprotected to sail on this river of death!"

"We need to finish this," said Corlan. "Now."

Londrel shook his head sternly. "Most are setting sail upriver. They aim to return to their homes. I, for one, have had enough of this hopeless venture."

"Let me speak with the men, see if any will join me."

"Join you for more? Of this? I doubt you'll see even the backside of a stupid boy if you suggest continuing with you."

Corlan took a deep breath. "You're right. I cannot ask anything of those that survived. Let them return to their homes. Maybe it was this large collection of boats the dragon scouts saw. If I had stuck with my original plan, I would have sneaked into the marshes alone and never been detected."

"So the blame is all yours."

Corlan stared hard at him. "Blame the dragons."

"You swore to attack them, to kill their offspring. You laughed when you were speaking of smashing eggs and lancing newborns. Why shouldn't they try to stop you?"

"The dragons didn't hear me!" He wanted to punch something.

Londrel frowned, shook his head. "They knew. Somehow they knew and they came to us first."

"How? There are no spies among us."

"What was that bird thing that visited you?"

"She warned us they were coming."

"Or did the harpy warn them *we* were coming?"

Corlan started to reply but Londrel turned and strode away, a final wave of his hand acting as his final thoughts.

"Take your cowards back to Evanal, Londrel!" Corlan shouted after him as he climbed down the side of the *Riverstallion* to his boat. "Let them tell tales of the past eve's battle. Tell it strong! Make them into heroes! Write of their bravado on scrolls for all time! The gods know what they really did here! And the gods will never forget!"

40

The Marshes

HOURS AFTER LONDREL DEPARTED, a small boat pulled beside the *Riverstallion*. It was Bantun who climbed aboard. His beard was caked with mud, his clothing wet and dirty. A cut crossed over his bald head. Half his thick moustache had been seared away. Corlan gave him a hand up. Two men climbed up after him while another remained on the boat.

"Mister Corlan," said Bantun in a weary voice.

"Captain Bantun," Corlan replied.

"Pardons for not being aboard when you awoke. I was taking stock of what remains."

"I worried about your fate," said Corlan.

Bantun stood straight and saluted but Corlan waved him off.

"It's a disaster," said Bantun, lowering his eyes. "Almost all the fleet is left in the shallows upriver. Thirty-nine boats and a ship in the shallows, burnt or broken or both. The river is littered with so many bodies. There are carcasses of dragons. I counted eleven. That would be a fair day's battle if not for the fact that so many attacked us and flew on unharmed." Bantun stared at the dragon head. "And this one. Only the head? Then its body must remain upriver with the others. The disaster trails ten miles along the river, boats and bodies. The water runs in teal and red up there."

"Thank you for your report," said Corlan. "Londrel visited some time ago. He also gave a report. Less encouraging than yours."

"Londrel! That coward." Bantun scowled and made a fist. "He dove off his own ship when the first dragon attacked it. Breathed fire and caught the bridge aflame. I could excuse a man for reacting like that to save his own life but he didn't return to the battle. Durkin's men had to pull him from the river...well after the last dragon had flow away."

"He said Durkin was killed."

"Aye, snatched away by a dragon. Bit off his arm, too! The poor fellow. The arm plopped right down on one boat, the rest carried off. He's been swallowed by now. That's no way to go to the Beyond—"

"We must press on," said Corlan. "Or, at least, I must go on. If I give up, then everything I've fought for up to now will be wasted. Those men will have died for nothing. We must finish this mission."

"Finish? I'd say we are done. There's nothing left to take into the marshes. All ships and boats are damaged beyond safe passage or they're lost completely. What craft would you use to take yourself there?"

Corlan glared at Bantun. "You came back to your ship on a skiff."

"I did." He glanced over his shoulder where the skiff had come alongside. "Two men to row it. The river's too deep here for trolling. You thinking of continuing to the marshes on just a skiff?"

"I started with a skiff," Corlan responded. He scratched at his beard, stained with dried dragon blood. He tried to scratch it out as he continued speaking. "I started on foot...with two girafors as my pack animals. Then I gained a cart and two donkors. Finally horses and a good wagon, and then only a horse, which I traded for a skiff."

"Out in those marshes? In only a skiff? You'd surely be dragon bait there, Corlan."

"Out in the marshes with my trusty dragonslinger."

"Then I wish you the best of the gods' luck." Bantun offered his hand and Corlan clasped it. "May the gods watch over you, Corlan of the Burg. I cannot say with certainty you are on the right path, yet I believe *you* believe it's the right path, and that makes it the right path for you."

"Spoken like a true river pilot," said Corlan and Bantun grinned.

"The men seem ready to return to Evanal. We will stow as much as we can on the river-worthy vessels and return. The *Riverstallion* is one of the river-worthy vessels, I'm sorry to tell you. Damaged yet it still floats."

"I said I would continue on the skiff."

Bantun frowned. "I wanted to tell you directly."

"There is still Ducah," said Corlan. He pointed to the old man sitting in a slump on the fallen beam. "The blind physician wishes to travel to Ducah. And I suppose the boy with him."

"Too many for a skiff, mind you." Bantun stared at the old man.

"You best take one of the boats. There's a jonboat that's not too bad off. It'll seat eight so if two more men wish to go with you, perhaps to handle the oars, you will all fit."

"Thanks," said Corlan. "If there are any men who wish to visit Ducah, see the sights, have a good dinner, and find a few pleasures for the night, then I welcome them to accompany us. Beyond Ducah, though, I must go alone." He smiled at Bantun. "That is what the gods wish for me. So that is what I must do. Or else I can never go home."

"Perhaps, friend, you will never go home again."

"Then I can say I met my fate without blinking."

Bantun clapped both Corlan's shoulders and saluted once more.

The jonboat was a larger skiff. The old blind physician, Wallan, and Ruk, the boy he'd saved, sat at the bow, all the better to look for the village of Ducah, set on the last inhabited land at the edge of civilization. Two young men from Bantun's ship, Hadley and Foyle, and a stout youth named Vandur, from Durkin's ship, volunteered to man the oars and handle the rudder. Corlan helped with an oar, too, and their progress downriver was steady and, with the gods' oversight, also uneventful.

The boat was veering to the side of the river. Corlan saw Foyle was weak in rowing, kept wincing with each stroke.

"What's wrong?" asked Corlan.

The man wouldn't answer, perhaps afraid to admit the problem. Corlan crawled over and saw the sleeve soiled with blood. He pulled up the sleeve and saw the wound on Foyle's upper arm, a deep cut that had opened and started bleeding again. He knew by the shape of the wound it had come from the tip of a dragon's claw.

"You shouldn't have come with us," said Corlan. "You should have gone back with Bantun and the others."

"I believe in the mission," said Foyle weakly.

"Take the rudder."

Foyle moved out of the rower's seat and Vandur took his place, grabbing the oar. Foyle dropped beside the rudder.

"You're of no use to us being wounded." He called to the blind physician. "Wallan, come take a look at this wound. What can be done?"

Wallan laughed. "You want me to take a *look*?"

"Feel!"

The old physician clambered up the boat, touching his way. Corlan took hold of his robe to halt him, pushed him down on the seat. He lifted Wallan's hand to Foyle's arm then he resumed rowing.

The river current did most of the work so rowing only kept the boat in the main current. To each side the river widened, as though it had overflowed its banks and flooded vast fields on either side. The shore had fallen away and grasses from the shallows spread almost to the center where the boat passed.

Above them, the clouds had thinned; some blue sky appeared.

"I can stitch the wound if I had needle and thread," said Wallan.

Corlan paused to grab his bag and hand it to the physician.

"Find it in my bag. I've stitched myself a few times on this journey to the marshes."

Wallan found the kit and went to work. Foyle cried out in pain with every poke of the needle.

"That's worse than the original cut?" Vandur teased him.

Foyle tried to laugh, then got the next needle puncture.

"Seems a lovely morning for catching some fish," Hadley spoke when Foyle's screams had stopped and the warm breeze calmed everyone. "I remember going out with my grandfather on a morning like this, just him and me, in a boat, smaller than this one, just listening to the birds tweeting and the fish splashing and we talked and talked—in low voices, of course—about how everything in the world had gone to shit, except for the pleasures of fishing, that is, said it was the only thing left to give a man pleasure in life, see, he lost his willy in a fight, a man cut him with a sword and that was that, so after that he only took pleasure in going out to catch fish, and he was rather good at it, too, bringing home lots of fish day in and day out, for his family—and mine, too—and neighbors, so everyone said he was a kind man who always thought of his fellow citizens— and I suppose people who weren't no citizen neither but they lived there nonetheless—that's just how he was, my grandfather, and I loved him for that, so now I can't help remembering those days, those mornings, going out fishing with my grandfather, may the gods rest his weary soul."

The boat hit something in the water and the men looked hard at each other. Corlan thought it might be a body that had drifted down the river.

"Couldn't be a body from our battle, not faster than us in a boat," said Hadley. "Unless it drifted as we was waiting to decide what to do. Remember how we had to take time taking stock of everything and getting our supplies together. Then we joined you on this boat, like a few hours, anyways, to start on down the river like we done now, like that—"

"Quiet," Corlan muttered, rising up on his knees on the bench, searching the water ahead for any obstacles. He grabbed the trolling pole and pressed it down into the water, finding the soft bottom half the length of the pole. He withdrew the pole and found the lower end muddy. "Eight feet," he announced.

"Could be a log," said Vandur as Corlan washed off the pole.

Suddenly, another thump hit the boat from the opposite side, the jolt almost knocking Corlan over and into the river. He stood up, holding the pole as a weapon.

"Look!" cried Foyle, pointing ahead of the boat. "Something in the water. There!"

Corlan narrowed his eyes. Straight ahead were smooth humps in the water, brown like stones, moving like a school of fish. Then one of the humps rose in the water, turned and opened its mouth to display a wide yaw and several huge teeth.

"Hippors!" cried Corlan. "Veer left—er, port!"

They paddled as hard as they could to avoid the beasts in the river but the current seemed to be pushing them right at the animals. Several of them turned, seeing the boat coming. They moved away, paddling to each side, making a path for the vessel.

The boat pressed through, the hull riding up on the backs of the beasts then settling down in the water. The boy sitting with Wallan was thrown aside. Corlan grabbed the boy's leg, jerked him back into the boat as the beasts jostled and slammed their huge bodies against the hull. The wood creaked. A side panel snapped and water leaked in.

Corlan stood and held an oar out to guide the boat through the mass of animals. They were not *hippors*, the beasts remade from the powder of dead hippos and renamed *hippor*. These were true hippos. Where the river widened and became marsh, more to the south than the cities of Evanal and Luval and Covin, the warm climate suited them. They gathered in a herd of a hundred or more. Even if the boat managed to pass through this first wave unscathed, there would be more ahead.

"Make for the shallows!" cried Corlan.

He touched his oar to the back of the beast beside the boat, urging it to move away. Then he swung the oar to the other side of the boat to suggest to the beast there that moving away would be a better choice than closing in on the boat. It seemed to work.

Until one of the beasts refused to budge and opened wide its huge mouth in protest — brushing its chin against the oarlock. Was it merely a yawn? Corlan pulled out his sideblade, stood ready to compel the beast to fear the boat.

The hippo's long shovel tusks grazed the gunwale, sheering off the top strip of wood. Apparently content with that warning, the beast closed its mouth and swam away, charging through two other beasts and becoming lost in the crowd.

The boat squirted through the bodies and found open water once more. Ahead, however, were more hippos lounging in the river. Corlan could hardly call it a river any longer. It was as wide as a sea and the shore on either side was nearly too distant to see. Most of the expanse was choked with grass and reeds — the marshes.

"That was close!" Vandur grunted.

"When I was out fishing with my grandfather," Hadley started, "we never saw nothing like those things in the water there, nothing at all, not even — "

"Quiet," said Corlan. His eyes were focused on the next crowd of hippos in the marsh. The river current was directing the boat toward them. "We are not yet finished with them."

"Horsies!" Ruk shouted, pointing ahead of the boat.

Corlan nodded. River horses. That's what they were called in the scrolls. They carried the ancient kings and princes. They provided the only steady meat supply for a starving population. They were worshipped as gifts of the gods. They were bred and set loose in the marshes, he recalled from a boyhood lesson. Now he faced them, faced the ancient myths.

As the boat pushed toward the next crowd of hippos, Corlan took the trolling pole and got into position. He would gently nudge them to the side, enough to give them the suggestion yet not enough pressure to anger them. He'd seen plenty of mouth from the hippo that had tried to bite the side of the boat.

The edge of the beasty wall came fast and they crashed into the backside of the first animal. It did not like the bump and tried to reverse itself among the throng of hippos, intent on retaliation, but it could not turn. It pushed to its right instead and another hippo slid into its place, blocking the boat's course. Corlan prodded them with the pole and one hippo, then another, got the idea to move. Working steadily and with great patience, Corlan guided the boat through the first hundred feet of the hippo herd.

"Look!" cried Foyle. He directed Corlan's gaze to the sky.

A familiar pattern appeared in the sky. Corlan watched their approach. Five dragons, grey-bellies, swooped down and snatched up whole hippos from the marsh and with single gulps swallowed them. Their bellies full, the dragons flew low.

The frantic response from the hippos that remained caused the water to boil and the boat rocked violently. Vandur almost fell overboard but Corlan grabbed his arm in time, yanked him back. The others were tossed back and forth as the hippos around the boat panicked.

One dragon returned for another bite, grabbing a fresh hippo from the marsh but not cleanly enough. The body was bitten in two, the head still in the dragon's mouth as it soared into the sky. The bulbous body of the hippo dropped, crashing onto the backs of the stampeding hippos—too near the boat—sending waves washing over the side of the boat.

The beasts in the marsh seemed to run away from the boat, away to the shallows, to escape the dragon attack.

"They're going," said Corlan, referring to the dragons winging to the east. He scanned the marsh. "River horses, too."

A path through the marsh opened, hippos and grasses bending away to each side.

"Let's row like there'll not be another day!" Corlan shouted, taking the oar and paddling as hard as he could. "We need to make it through the gap before the herd reforms."

They all paddled hard—Hadley, Foyle, Vandur, and Corlan—and only when they could not stroke the oar even one more time did they pause to check their progress.

"Where are we now?" asked Vandur, cautiously.

"I thought we were going to Ducah," said Hadley. "Never been there, o' course, but my grandfather he said he been there so many times, did the river trade back then because, well, see, Ducah's got basketwares made from the reeds of the marshes, and there's lots of reeds in this marsh, ya know, or that's what he always said, and I never dared to think he would go and be fibbing to me."

Corlan stood up in the boat, waited for the rocking to settle. He put his hand to his brow to block the sun and scanned the horizon.

"Could we have missed it? The marsh is so wide...."

He gazed across the grassy sea.

"You see anything looks like a village?" asked Hadley. "Maybe you can't see it from here because it's a low island, that's what my grandfather always said, can't see it from a low boat like this one, just gotta be up high on a crow's nest on a tall ship, then you could see maybe a tower or two they got there in Ducah, or so I've heard from time to time, but only two towers."

"Or just an island to set foot on?" added Vandur. "I'd be happy to set foot on anything solid about now."

Corlan sighed loudly. "It's on a good-size island, Bantun told me. Maybe the island is to the north of where we are. We rowed past it, I suppose, blocked from getting there by all these damnable hippos!"

"Corlan!" shouted Foyle, flinging up an oar.

A hippo had sprouted from the water suddenly, its mouth open, its yellow tusks aimed at the boat. With foul exhale, it clamped down on the side of the boat, then tore the wooden panels away. Water rushed in. The boat tilted toward the water and took in more.

Hadley held tight to the gunwale on the higher side of the boat. Foyle was swept into the river but dug his fingers into the broken gunwale. Wallan grasped the prow and the boy grabbed onto the physician's robe. Vandur was knocked backwards, flung over the gunwale into the water. He tried to swim to the boat but, desperately slapping the water, he slipped farther behind.

Corlan stood, boots flat on the boat's bottom, and took a blade to the hippo, hacking at its nose and drawing blood. The beast rose angrily in the water, its body as large and fat as any dragon. It roared and in that moment Corlan shoved his whole arm down its throat, lodging the blade in the hippo's pink gullet.

Pulling his arm out, Corlan fell back in the boat, swamped with water. He grabbed the gunwales on either side to keep from being swept away as the hippo sank into the water, a hefty wave rolling over all of them and filling the boat.

"Hold on," he cried out to everyone.

"To what?" shrieked Hadley.

"We're taking on water!" shouted Foyle.

"We all gonna die!" screamed the boy.

"We'll make it to the shore—somehow," Corlan called out. "Just. Hold. On. Tight."

The river wyrms attacked at dusk, smelling flesh in the water, racing through the marsh like ravenous snakes.

Corlan called for everyone to keep their hands and feet out of the water. They moved to the safety of the center of the soggy mound that rose just enough above the water to be called an isle. Despite its grassy muck, it counted as land in the vastness of the marshes. Even so, the isle was only double the size of the boat that lay broken in the surf.

When the damaged boat foundered, Corlan fought to hang on to the weapons bag. He saved most of it, swords and knives spilling out anyway, but he could not haul up the heavy dragonslinger and the quiver of iron bolts, which sank. From the cache he saved, he selected a two-handed sword and swung it mightily at each wyrm that tried to crawl from the water onto their isle.

The river wyrms had narrow, scaly bodies as long as a man, set on four stubby legs with webbed, clawed feet, a flat tail designed for swimming, and small, useless wings which sprouted from shoulders. Corlan had heard of them but never encountered one.

One river wyrm grabbed Foyle's foot. The wyrm, firmly clamped around an ankle, dragged him into the water but Corlan hacked at the wyrm's neck and severed its head. Other wyrms swarmed the fresh carcass. An orgy of blood stained the marsh as Foyle pulled back his foot with the wyrm's head still clasping his ankle.

The large-boned Vandur had gone under when the boat had capsized. He never rose. Corlan knew when the wyrms reached the youth's body below. A hand floated to the surface, then his head popped up. Both bobbed on the surface only a minute before wyrms shot up to grab them betwixt their fangs and retreated into the dark water.

Foyle sat back, frantic, screaming as he held his wounded foot. There were claw marks in his calf and shin. Deep puncture wounds bled on his ankle. He said the bone felt cracked, if not broken.

Hadley sat on the highest point of the isle, too frightened to move, knees bent up against his chest, making himself as small as possible to keep away from the shore.

Corlan stepped around the watery perimeter of the isle, watching the wyrms eyeing him, ready to swing the sword at them. Whenever a wyrm tried to mount the isle, Corlan chopped at it and it slunk away or died there, half on the isle and half in the marsh. The wyrms were quick to claim their dead brethren.

Several times wyrms tried to climb onto the isle from opposite sides and Corlan cried out for the others to fight them.

"Pick up the damn sword and stab the damn wyrm!" Corlan kept shouting, wildly swinging his sword down at them.

Hadley was frozen with fear. When two wyrms rose from the marsh and snapped at him, he could not move fast enough. They latched on to his ankles and dragged him into the water. Corlan spun and leaped over Wallan and the boy to save Hadley but he was pulled down into the water too fast for Corlan to get to him. Blood poured into the water. There was nothing for Corlan to grab hold of to pull away from the wyrms.

Foyle had a sword and tried to stab at the wyrm coming for the boy, striking the beast's nose and opening a wound. The wyrm slunk back into the water and was immediately set upon by other wyrms. Foyle stood, hobbling on his injured leg, took a step to the edge to have a look and lost his balance. His hand touched the water—just one hand to break his fall—and a wyrm closed its jaws around his wrist, snapping bones and jerking him down to his knees. Foyle tried to jerk his arm away as another wyrm rose from the marsh and bit his other hand. The two wyrms pulled Foyle, shrieking, hands first into the marsh. When his face entered the water, Foyle was done. Corlan swung his blade at the wyrms but Foyle's hands and head were already gone.

Exhausted, Corlan retreated to the high point of the isle, barely a body length from the water's edge in any direction. Wallan held the boy in his arms, on his lap, making themselves as small as possible, as Corlan stood over them, sword held at the ready.

INTERLUDE

The Forests of Kan, The Mountains of Miz

BELOW THE STEADY WINGS of the green-horn dragon she called Hidel, son of Gugil, father of Damor, the leafy emerald blanket stretched to the farthest horizons. From the birthstone she knew the way and sent her directions to Hidel in the dragon tongue she had mastered. With hardly a grumble, the lumpy-faced Hidel nudged his right shoulder higher, initiating a slight turn to catch the east by northeast thermal. As he did, the birthstone tilted in its bag, strapped to the carrier in which the goddess rode.

Behind them, the dun-brown draper she called Aerog, daughter of Umor, mother of Grano, winged cautiously, following the green-horn, bringing the goddess's helpers, obeying without any quarrel all the directions given to her.

Jabuli held fast to the leather straps and dared glimpse the babe in his carrier, the same kind as held the birthstone in Adora's carrier. Jabuli realized she had a paralyzing fear of high places. At least the mountains they had climbed were attached to the world. Not these dragons, who soared and swooped and cut the sky like rainbows.

From her perch, Adora could see no borders cutting through the lands below, only the occasional line of a river which men might call boundaries rather than passages. She knew from her lessons that once long ago there were a thousand-seventy-six nations spanning the world. After some time there were only fifty-five nations. Then there were only twenty, then eleven, then three. Then there were none as the great western mountain blew its golden crown into the sky and the fire river rushed over the land.

Still some people lived on, the birthstone told her. There were a lot of people who lived beyond the mountains of the western isles, across the rocky deserts, over the vast tree-filled concourse. In ten-thousand years all the seas of grass had become oceans of giant trees. Ahead were more mountains, and beyond them lay other lands, possibly new cities built by women and men, their hardy hands put together for the building of cities.

She knew that nations were made of cities, and worlds were made of nations. Furthermore, the worlds she knew and worlds she did not know were all wrapped around things called *planets*, and they all spun around things called *stars*, which all surged within a mighty maelstrom called *galaxies*, which floated in a thing called *universe*, which balanced on the tip of a thing called *O*, which was kept locked away inside a small treasure chest called...*what was it called?* She suddenly forgot, and Hidel shifted awkwardly beneath her as if he sensed her distress.

There were other goddesses, of course, so she did not have to do everything herself. Yet it was quite clear that this land over which she soared was meant to be cared for by her. The goddess Sei Bo had told her so, and when a goddess tells you something, you believe it and you remember it—

Ah! The treasure chest is called *Ah!* And every person carried a piece of it inside themselves, said the birthstone in a strange new language she was still learning, full of squiggles and dots and checks and lines cut into pieces. They filled her head, made her want to sleep, even though she knew there would never be any sleep for her. The days extended for ages and the nights even longer.

The great mountain ahead as they flew rose taller than the next world beyond, a mass of rock and ice that gleamed in the sunlight. The dragons and their charges circled twice as measurements were made. Adora gazed down on the massive blemish, as disturbing as any mountain she had seen since they flew away from Yozma. Surely it had the same dimensions of the great golden mountain that blew its crown off. How many ages until this heap also blew its top? She would need to watch it.

With a wave of her little hand, the pair of dragons broke from the circle and stormed straight on, passing over vast wetlands full of grass and water and birds and animals of all kinds, and passing over a new land that rose reborn from the ashes of the old, become fertile and giving life to death.

And there below she spied the collected grumblings of people, a ragged band of humans and the things they had built. A city! There!

She noted its location, measured the distance from Yozma, almost amazed at how far she had come and how far below the humans stood who spent their days working and singing and loving without at all noticing her or how her hand glided over their lives.

Adora commanded Hidel to follow the jagged line below, the one that was a river, and continue following it as the river ended and the riverbed became a desert highway for journeymen, twisting and turning to the north and the northeast, until all at once it ceased at the foot of a large city.

So many people there! Tall buildings full of tall people! And so many quarrels and scrabbles she heard and so much anger she felt. They hated each other there. Not a suitable place to raise a babe, even a male babe.

They flew on, the mighty wings making quick time of the travel.

Soon they found the thick greenery she loved and they set down among the forests and fields of a new land she did not know, even as she was supposed to know everything about everywhere. A pause in her notes. The birthstone had not yielded all its knowledge to her just yet, but she had plenty of time to finish the other ninety-four portions of its depths.

White moonlight shone upon the farmstead. As she gazed about, nodding thoughtfully, a smile graced her cherubic face.

"He will enjoy running through this forest," spoke Adora, "and those fields. It is suitable for a male babe."

"This is the place you choose?" asked Jabuli, standing beside her with the babe in the sling looped over her shoulders. The boy was getting heavy, so she pulled off the sling and set him gently down upon the grass. "He is awake now."

Adora bent down to gaze upon her brother. His eyes were bright, happy, not at all confused or distracted or upset at finding himself in a completely new world far, far away from that of his birth. The babe babbled to her, telling her his thoughts and for once she could clearly understand the sounds he made. He knew the language of O as well as she did, perhaps better than her. She replied to him in that same language and both grinned.

"Your Little Majesty," called Jabuli simply out of nostalgia for a distant time that was barely one year past. "Will he be safe here, in this place? What of the wild animals? What of the men?"

Adora straighten, her white gown glowing like a fire amidst the moonlight.

"He will not fear animals nor men. He told me so. As for women, he will love them, not fear them, though he agrees it is good to have caution and a healthy degree of doubt when speaking with women, and especially if they would have a union."

"That is wise," said Jabuli.

"Of course. I am supposed to be wise. The birthstone told me I have to be wise, so I am."

"You are also smart, especially for a little girl."

"Not a little girl, a goddess. You cannot judge me by my small size. I am filled with all that is and ever shall be. It is very filling, and a bit uncomfortable."

Jabuli grinned, like she dared not laugh at a goddess but could not restrain herself. "Bless you, little majesty."

Adora nodded. "Thanks, Jabuli, but I think I am supposed to bless you, not the other way around."

"Perhaps even a goddess needs blessing from time to time, don't you think? Even from a lowly human who once was a slave."

"And once a tutor to a princess. That is how I remember you."

The little girl wanted to grasp the woman's legs, to give her a hug that expressed all the love she felt for her, yet she knew it would not be safe to touch the woman, so she kept back, always three full steps, twenty-nine steps being optimal.

"We have come to find a family to care for my baby brother. There is a farm over there. It looks nice. Truly lovely. I can smell the animals and they are happy. I can hear the crops growing, also happy. It is full of life here. Now if the humans here can be kind, as well, this shall be the perfect place for his rebirth."

"His...rebirth?"

"Yes," said the goddess. "Once he goes off to the slumber land, he will awaken tomorrow in a new family, not knowing anything, and having to learn it all again. That is his rebirth. It is like magic. You call it magic, people call it that, yet it is the normal way the universe operates. It is more than clockwork, Jabuli. It is...a very big wave of dots, very tiny dots, that sparkle and twinkle and are so bright and full of many colors, and I simply rearrange them as I like, as seems best, and there are so many patterns to choose, too. You should have a look."

"But I cannot see anything," said Jabuli.

"Yes, it is a pity. You have human eyes and they have so many limits. Pity. Someday you will see more, and then we can meet and talk about what you have seen. Agreed?"

"Yes, agreed." Jabuli smiled, wishing to embrace her but the balance of everything depended on the goddess now and she would not wish to be the one to tip it. "I believe in you."

"We shall see each other again."

Jabuli gathered the babe and followed the glowing white gown with the white hair atop. The little goddess seemed to float through the forest, stout trees leaning away in both directions to provide a wide berth for her.

The morning light was breaking over a band of mist that melded the treetops together. Ahead was the farm's house, a lovely structure of stone and wood. Smoke curled from a stone tower. Three strange beasts stood nearby, behind a fence of crossed sticks, speaking their own language.

The little goddess went to them, the masters of the farm.

"Worry not, for you will not become their food. The people of this house like you. As long as you serve faithfully, you may go as you like and be at ease."

She glanced back at Jabuli, as though showing off that she could understand the animal's language. Then she continued to the front entrance of the house —

And passed straight through the heavy wooden door without even a polite knock.

Jabuli caught her breath, halting where she stood.

And she waited.

The sun rose higher, burning off the mist, and the forest became a magical place. The farmstead, too, seemed a place of mystery yet also filled with a calm Jabuli had seldom known. She squatted, held the babe in her arms. He rooted for a nipple so she whispered to him that a new breast would be forthcoming. He must be patient.

Suddenly the little goddess stood beside her, white and regal.

"Are you ready?" Adora asked her.

Jabuli stood, holding the babe gently as he grabbed at her hair.

"Ready? For what?" she asked. "Is it time to give him up?"

"We do not give him up, we pass him on, so others might share him. He is carrying all the love I could put into him. Enough to last a few years, I think. By then, he should be able to gather love from the people around him."

"And give it on to other people."

"Yes, that is correct. Did you see it in the birthstone? No, silly.

You cannot read the parches locked inside the birthstone. But no matter, love is nothing more and nothing less than love, and it floats all around and through O rather like huge clouds of pollen in the air, touching people quite at random."

"I feel it," said Jabuli with a calm sigh.

"I tried to give you enough love to carry you on." She glanced at the house. "This family has enough love for him."

"This is a good family?" asked Jabuli.

"They recently lost their babe. So they will be delighted to care for my brother, who has a similar appearance as the boy they lost. The mama is yet full of milk."

The little goddess smiled warmly, as though all the mathematics sparkling in the universe had finally come together to equal 1.

"Come."

Jabuli followed her.

The door was already opened a crack. On the front porch was a mat and a basket. At a look from the little goddess, she placed the babe down into the basket. She wiped her eyes.

Adora gazed down upon the basket, too, remembering the first moment she had gazed upon the babe, a snap of fingers away from death. Like everyone is, at every moment, she recalled from the birthstone.

"Be well, my baby brother. Grow strong and wise. And most of all, be good to all you meet, and they will be good to you. So it is written on the parches and in the birthstone. In everyone's birthstone. So never forget."

The goddess turned to go, her feet seeming to step a few motes of dust above the grass, never bending the blades, never spoiling the dew.

"Just like that?" called Jabuli after her.

The little goddess paused, looked back at her tutor.

"We just leave him on the doorstep?" asked Jabuli.

"No, of course not."

Jabuli was puzzled. "Then what?"

The little goddess smiled, as big as the universe, and Jabuli could see O as clear as day.

"You have to knock on the door."

41

Where the Gods Watch

WHEN THE FIRST SPARK of light startled Corlan to wakefulness, he did not give himself any slack for nodding off. He stood up, sword ready as an orange line cut across the horizon. Gazing at the sunrise, he saw the entire world was marsh, and he had no boat.

What have the gods decreed for me?

He searched the skies for a sign, an omen—anything to break the spell of hopelessness that stuck to him like the dried blood of a slain wyrm. Blue-gray clouds spread over the expanse while the brown-green sea of grass filled every inch below.

He had no more ideas, no other plan. Find dragon eggs? Was that even possible now? Here was the marsh. He found it. Where are the isles covered with eggs? The days were turning to spring in this southern clime and the eggs would hatch soon—

A lone cry sailed through the sky, the faintest of noises that found its way through the silence of the morning.

Corlan gazed up, searching for its source. In the distance a small dark figure glided on the breeze. As it approached, the caw the aerial creature let out calmed him. It was not a dragon; it was Madi, the harpy—his messenger, his savior!

She hovered over the isle, batting her wings to hold herself a moment while Corlan cleared a space for her to perch. The weapons bag made an acceptable perch, her talons digging into the canvas.

"I need you," said Corlan. He started to say more but Madi's cries stopped him. He had no idea what she was communicating. The last time she spoke was to warn of the dragons approaching. "I hope it's not a new warning. We can't face another attack. We have nothing left. We already lost three here." His proud face cracked. "In fact, we have no reason to go on."

She rustled her feathers, settled them, tweeted at him, turning her head to the old man and the boy sitting together.

"Yes, them," he said, somehow understanding. "They need to find solid land. There is a village on an island. It's called Ducah. It's to the north of here, I suspect. We tried to reach it—"

More tweets. The caws awoke Wallan who awoke Ruk. The boy took one glance at Madi, a bird-like being as large as Corlan but with the face of a woman, and became scared.

"What is it, boy?" asked Wallan, unable to see.

"This is Madi," said Corlan. "She's a...harpy. That's what the crew called her. She used to be a girl. Then she turned into a bird. It's a kind of magic. She's here to save us, I think."

"Fine thing, that saving business," said Wallan. "Are we able to be saved? What of the men?"

Corlan told him the fates of Vandur, Hadley, and Foyle. And the boat. The blind physician could only hold onto the boy and Corlan had fought most of the night to keep them safe.

"Can you take the boy with you?" he asked Madi. "As far as that village? He's already alone. His family was killed by dragons."

Madi squawked and cawed, glancing back and forth between the boy and Corlan. Then she dipped her head.

"You can?" He was surprised, thinking that the boy might be too heavy for her to carry. "How far is the village?"

"You've got a plan?" asked Wallan, not understanding.

"The plan is for my friend to carry the boy to the village. He can be safe in Ducah. At least, it's a better fate than another night on this isle with the river wyrms coming for dinner."

"Aye, that!"

"If she can carry him that far. Maybe five miles? Ten miles? No way to measure how far we are from Ducah."

"Here." Wallan stood the boy up. "Give him a lift and see what he weighs. A six-year old boy can't be much. He's undernourished, too. He sat on my shoulders for two days in that well."

Madi sprang from the weapons bag, got her balance and rose in the air. She turned and descended over Ruk. She lowered herself, talons open and closed them around the boy's arms. He began to cry, frightened.

"It's the only way, Ruk," said Wallan. "This creature will take you to the village. You'll be safe there."

"You must be brave," Corlan added. "You can't stay another

night on this isle."

Ruk seemed to understand. He gazed up at Madi's face. He saw a girl's face covered in fine down yet not so feathery that she didn't look like a girl. The boy calmed.

"Her name is Madi," Corlan told him.

"So that's it?" asked Wallan. He reached for the boy's leg, gave it a squeeze. "Be good, Ruk. And remember me when you're old. Make sure you become old. Fare thee well, my boy."

"Good luck," said Corlan to both Ruk and Madi. "When he is safe, come back for us. Bring some wood, maybe, too. Then we could repair the boat and sail away, maybe make the village ourselves that way. It's our only chance."

He watched Madi rise, lifting the boy from the isle.

"Then I can take a rest," he spoke louder, as though he continued to address her. "I can be alone, take a long sleep, and dream of all the days past."

With Ruk grasped securely in her talons, Madi winged her way north over the marsh. Corlan waved after them. Wallan waved, too, but faced the wrong way.

"I would dream of a certain Covina I knew not too long ago. And a boy from the Burg I was teaching to be a dragonslayer. I'll go to them." He fell quiet. "Then we'll go somewhere—some place that's safe. Up north, where it's cold. Too far north for dragons. I think we could make a family. She can't make children, sure, but we would have that boy as our son. And we'd be happy in that place."

"Ah, you have great dreams!" Wallan chuckled.

"It's possible."

"What of your grand scheme to rid the world of dragons?"

Corlan scoffed. "Dragons, wyverns, drakes, wyrms...the whole damnable lot of them! It is my calling, for sure. I'm a member of the dragonslayer's guild. Yet out here nobody knows what I do. You saw them: the ships, boats, the crew, and the army—all following me to the marshes of death."

"You must've been persuasive," said Wallan in a voice much too light for the situation.

"No, I'm not a speech-giver. I just talked about killing dragons. They got excited, thought they could do it, too."

"I did not actually see all that. I heard much. I smelled more. Death has a certain odor. It was not a good thing. But I understand your need to kill. It's your nature, a man like you. What is it? 'Kill or be killed.' I think that's how the scrolls say it. That was in a darker time, before the War of the Five Princes. These marshes were high ground in those ancient times, a rolling plain cut by forests. Long before dragons came."

Corlan nodded, wishing he had a mug of ale in his hand. It was easier to talk if he could drink also. "Before dragons came?"

He took a quick glance around the isle, checking for any threats, picking up a sword, before he sat down beside Wallan, the ground soggy under him.

"Before I lost my sight, I read the scrolls. More than five hundred of them, half in school lessons and half on my own. History, mainly." Wallan took a deep breath. "Dragons were not always with us. Only in the past, say, two-thousand years. Did you know that fact?"

"I heard they came here because of the evil men do to each other. A punishment from the gods."

Wallan laughed. "That is an old story. No, not a punishment. Not *intended* as punishment. People can believe what they want. I learned medicine because I wanted to make the world a better place than it was. My parents paid for that with their lives. As many people did in those days. Lawlessness. Anarchy. Clan fighting clan. Thievery. Assaults. Brutality like you never could imagine—brother against brother, sister against sister, parents against children. And plenty of disease. It was the way of life in my land, back when I was a child. Other than yesterday, they were the worst days of my life."

"Your land seems much like my land," said Corlan quietly.

"All lands were alike at that time. Long are our days on this world. Long.... And I am finished with this life, ready for the next. I'm bound for the Beyond, I am. Got my words fixed what I'm going to speak to the Boatman. Ah, but you wish to know how the dragons came to us, eh?"

"I'm sure it's a golden story."

Wallan reached out, found Corlan's thigh and gave it a slap. "We have some time, do we not? The wyrms will return later. When the sun goes off my face. For now, let us tell stories. When we are done, you can have your dream, and I...I've lived long enough and done everything I thought to do. I'll close my eyes—"

Corlan coughed. "The story?"

"Yes, the story. Once upon a time there was a dragon.... No, that's not a good way to begin."

"Just say it out!"

"So anxious to hear about dragons! They came from a mountain in the west. I never went there. Perhaps, nobody has, so it's only legend. It's called Mount Zarg. Some people worship it, chanting 'O Zarg' to awaken it, as though it was a stone god. It arose when the Drid was formed."

"The Drid." Corlan nodded, thoughtfully. "I have heard of this place. A bottomless sea west of the marshes. Go on."

"Mount Zarg arose when the Drid dropped. 'Twas well after the Five Princes. Perhaps two-thousand years after. It's been many years since I read those scrolls. My accounting may be wrong."

"The Drid is a whirlpool to the west of the marshes. True?"

"Yes. The land fell, sea rushed in. It's how the gods awakened us. The Drid was a hole—*is* a hole, a pit, an abyss—under the water. Out there." Wallan waved his arm in the wrong direction. "Some people say it goes down to Hell. At least a hundred miles down."

Corlan grunted. "Dragons came from the Drid? Out from a hole leading up from Hell?"

"No, not that way. Although I surely wouldn't bet against river wyrms being born there." Wallan chuckled uneasily. "No, dragons come from Mount Zarg. That's what the story says. From a cave in that mountain. It's a tunnel of some kind, so say the scrolls. From somewhere beyond death come these beasts. They come out from Mount Zarg and fill our world. That is the truth of the scrolls. Believe it, if you dare. It makes a good story for the last day of one's life. So I tell it to you."

"It's not the last day of your life, old man."

"Tell me that tomorrow."

Corlan sat in silence. It was starting to make sense. Everything he had heard from dragonslayers before, from distant travelers he'd encountered, and from the men who swore they'd read the scrolls. He remembered the map in Oenal. The scriber there had pointed to the edge of the map, said a tall mountain stood there, the tallest in all the land. On the edge of the map were also drawn dragons, as if to indicate their place of origin.

"So dragon eggs are not set in the nesting grounds? Not in these marshes?" He took a deep breath and held it. The sky started to spin around him and he finally exhaled. *"Are* there any eggs?"

Wallan exhaled loudly. "I cannot answer that."

Corlan could see as far as the horizon in every direction. Maybe he was not in the right part of the marshes. Maybe what he'd heard were only stories meant to entertain him. He shook his head. Maybe there was no dragon nesting ground. He asked Wallan.

"I told you what I know. But, then, I don't know everything. Nobody does. And what I know is old. You best go see for yourself."

"It seems so wrong now." Corlan kept shaking his head. "All this way. All these months of travel. And it has not been easy. How can I return home without proof of dragon eggs, without egg shells as souvenirs? None will believe I've come this far."

Wallan chuckled. "Your kin needs egg shells?"

"I promised." He coughed and spit. "I must return with dragonware if I wish to be let into the city." He launched into the story of Prince Vilmer, explaining his banishment. "I have no choice if I want to return. I once had a dragon claw. Hacked it off during a fight. I sold it to get supplies to continue on this journey. I could've had a huge pile of dragonware by now if I could just carry them with me. But I needed to travel light—light enough to make good time and always be ready to fight."

"And here you are in a marsh, ready to fight." Wallan tapped the blade laying across Corlan's knees. "Now...or tomorrow, if we can survive the night."

"We need food. How does river wyrm tail sound for dinner?"

"As good as an empty belly feels," said Wallan.

Corlan laughed. "If we can make a fire."

The morning waned, the sounds of the marsh rising to press upon their ears: insects humming, fish splashing, birds singing, the grasses rustling in the breeze—

And the sudden cry of something in the north.

Corlan jumped up, staring in the direction of the noise. Another cry cut through the air. He could not make out the figures in the sky, at the edge of his vision, but he could guess it was a dragon—

And Madi!

He squinted, held his hand to his brow. As the dark spots in the sky split, he could identify the larger form as a dragon. The smaller form faltered, struggling to rise then plummeted. He could not see more. A roar shook the marshes and the large form spread its wings.

"I'm going for it," Corlan grunted.

Before Wallan could ask what he was going for, Corlan kicked off his boots and dove into the water.

He swam down through the sea flora, scaring fish, pushing aside waving reeds and grass, and found the dragonslinger. With his arm hooked around it, he pushed with his legs, pulling with his free arm, dragging the heavy weapon to the surface.

"Here!" he shouted at Wallan, laying the weapon on the shore.

Then he went back under the water and found the quiver of iron bolts. It felt heavier than the weapon but he hung the leather strap over his shoulder and swam hard for the surface.

"Here!" Corlan grunted, shaking off his wet clothes, and stared north. The form approaching them appeared larger.

"What's the splashing about?" asked Wallan, flicking his hands to deflect the droplets of water flung from Corlan's clothing.

"I hate to turn a good morning into a dark noontide but we have a dragon flying toward us."

"So you got your dragonslinger!" Wallan laughed like he had no choice. "Will it work after being wet?"

"I will determine that in a moment."

Corlan unlocked the spring mechanism, pried it loose and shook it. He checked the launch tube and, despite objections, used Wallan's robe to dry the inside. He also took the robe to the first iron bolt he could reach. It had the bulb of poison—undamaged. The dull green liquid bobbed playfully within the glass sphere.

"The only thing that matters is the spring. If it rusts it won't work, but it's still wet. No trouble. I dried it off."

The roar of the dragon shook them out of their preparations.

"It sees us," said Corlan.

"What should I do?" Wallan stood, holding out his hands. "Give me something."

Corlan grabbed the sword he had lain across his knees before, and fitted it into Wallan's hand.

"Don't cut me," Corlan warned. "Swing it over your head. That'll be safe for me. By the gods, just stab upward!"

Reassembling the dragonslinger, Corlan screwed back the spring as tight as he could. He grabbed the iron bolt, slid it into the tube. He set his eyes on the target: a blue-lightning about three-hundred yards from the isle, swooping low, clearly intending to grab lunch from the only spot in the marshes hosting humans.

"Come on, beast!" Corlan shouted.

"Do I stab yet?" asked Wallan.

"No, not yet."

The dragon dropped lower, coming just above the surface.

"Open that foul mouth!" Corlan shouted.

As if understanding, the blue-lightning parted its fangs, grinning like a hungry man about to be served a feast.

"Now?" asked Wallan.

Fifty yards.

"Wait."

Thirty yards.

"Now?"

Corlan released the spring and the iron bolt shot directly into the dragon's open mouth. A rough choking noise replaced its roar, then a gasp, and the dragon lost its balance, attention put on its injury rather than on its flight.

"Get down!" Corlan dropped to his chest, flat on the wet ground.

The dragon dropped over them, crashing into the marsh on the other side of the isle, sending a huge wave of warm, murky water splashing over them, washing over the entire isle.

"It's down," said Corlan, soaked to the skin.

He turned to check the dragon. Was it dead? He grabbed another iron bolt, reached out for Wallan's robe to dry it off. But there was no robe. He glanced about the isle and did not see Wallan.

Corlan called to him.

His next call echoed across the marsh.

He went to the tail of the dragon, draped over the lower end of the isle. Walking barefoot along the spine of the dragon, up to its shoulders, he held the bolt ready to stab if the beast moved. The carcass remained still, though, its dark blue skin cloaked in steam, sulfur venting from its pores.

Covering his nose, Corlan jumped into the knee-deep water and waded to the dragon's mouth, clamped shut against the muddy bottom of the marsh. He bent over, staring at the dragon's head and saw what he did not want to see.

Golden-brown feathers had stuck there but now floated free in the water. A torn strip of cloth was caught in the craw of its mouth. Then a man's arm swung up from under the dragon's head, pushed by the current, attached to a body that was pressed into the mud beneath the bulk of the dragon's body.

42

The Way the World Works

IF A MAN WAITS LONG ENOUGH FOR DEATH, he will grow tired and become restless, and to break the monotony he will do something. And that something will often save him, pulling him away from the abyss, possibly sending him on his way, perhaps to the very place he is meant to go. And then, by reaching that place, everything will be decided once and for all. Or the wait begins again. That is the way the world works. And, as everyone knows and some have written on scrolls, the way the world works is controlled entirely by the gods.

The starboard side of the boat was marred with bite marks and two half-circles where wood had been snatched away. That made the craft take on water. The hull was intact otherwise, although Corlan was not sure the boards were still watertight after being thrashed with the pressure of hippos crowding together.

He waded into the shallows and with all his might pulled on the boat's port side. The vessel rocked in the surf. He could not get a strong foothold in the muddy bottom, so he worked his way around to the bow and shook it back and forth. The boat slid loose for a moment from the watery muck. He grabbed the gunwale and pulled until he was leaning backward into the water himself.

The current fought against him, tugging the boat, but with more effort, he got the bow onto the isle. With aching hands gripping it tightly, his palms bleeding, his sore back bending, he jerked the boat forward several times, as far up onto the mound as possible. Then he clambered aboard and on his hands and knees did a close inspection of every seam and rivet. Satisfied after a couple hours, he lay back, breathing hard, and looked at the blood on his hands.

The night came, noisy and frantic. With the dragon hulk lumped on one end of the isle, the river wyrms made meal of it and ignored the man. He kept his sword ready but only one of the wyrms dared test his verve, losing a foot to a quick slice. By first light, the dragon carcass had slipped into the marsh waters, collapsing on a skeleton chewed clean by the night's wyrms. Only the rough, dark back skin remained above the surface.

Corlan worked on the boat until he felt confident it would bear him further. In what direction he could only guess. With only a man and a few blades plus the slinger and a quiver of bolts weighing it down, it might be seaworthy. There was an oar remaining, jammed against the bottom boards.

After another night of thrashing as the river wyrms finished the remaining parts of the carcass, he got a few hours of sleep. He awoke ready to give the boat a try. However, his hunger the night before compelled him to cut into the dragon's tail and try to chew some of the flesh. He lay ill the next day.

The following morning, he tried the boat again.

The same current they had drifted on before ran to the south, he calculated, remembering the map he'd seen in Oenal. The village of Ducah lay to the north—straight north, if he could steer the boat against the current. With one oar, though, he didn't think it possible. He would try, however. He had to.

And if he failed, his second plan was there for the grabbing: to continue with the current wherever it took him. If he met up with the Drid and was lost in its whirlpool, so be it. That would be the gods' decision, not his. If he managed to skirt the great whirlpool and found himself on the far shore, so be it. That would also be the gods' decision. Then he would climb those mountains and maybe find his destiny there. So be that, as well. The gods knew everything, decided everything, then stood back to observe the play of their game pieces and be entertained.

"I'm still alive, you cloudy bastards!" he shouted to the sky.

Settling in the water, the boat listed to starboard yet did not take on water. Not for a while. He paddled lightly with the oar and made progress through the grassy sea as the sun shone bright and sweat ran down his body. He pulled off his ragged shirt, dirty as it was and stinking with marsh pungency. At regular intervals, he rested from paddling and swept out the water that had collected. Every hour he paused to clear the water.

By dusk, he found another isle to make his night's stop. He heard waves of river wyrms coming close, seeking dinner, yet he was not harmed. This new isle, twice the size of the previous mound, gave him adequate acreage for him to stay away from the water's edge. He pulled the boat safely up on the shore, too, and it remained ready in the morning.

The second plan seemed to be the one he was meant to follow. He could not steer the boat to the north against the current, so he went with the current, passing through the marsh at its whim, isle to isle. He visited eleven of them and not once found any dragon eggs. He felt stupid and angry. If the marshes were the dragons' nesting ground, they had long gotten wind of his plan and moved their eggs. Or the marshes never were their nesting ground.

Each day he paddled, he moved the boat a few precious feet with each stroke as the sun beat down on him. Soon he had stripped down to the loincloth to continue his back-breaking work.

Once in a while he had to stand up to use the oar to troll the boat through thicker marsh grass. Sometimes the marsh was not deep and the boat caught on a mound that did not rise above the water.

Each night, or whenever he was close, he paused on an isle for rest. On a few of the days he was able to catch a fish that swam by or snare a bird that came to examine him, perching on the gunwale without fear. In that way, he managed to eat and keep his strength, enough to keep going.

He saw few dragons winging overhead in his days of paddling. Every night river wyrms made noise but did not attack him. In the mornings marsh birds sang to each other and he thought of Madi. The gentle slap of waves against the boat lulled him into drowsiness but he kept paddling, as though his arms and back had been locked into perpetual motion. Once, after a particularly large meal of both fish and bird, he took a whole day to rest on the isle he found, the largest yet. He slept with his head in the shadow of the boat pulled onto the shore.

When he awoke at dawn, he went for a walk around the isle — Corlan's Isle, he proclaimed. After an hour circling the isle, finding fruit growing on the stubby trees, he also found what he had been looking for: a collection of sixteen pale blue eggs, each about the size as his head.

Being surprised, he almost fell backwards into a patch of eggs while staring hard at those in front of him. The isle was maybe an acre total, its high point four feet above the water, enough for a small grove of trees to take root. The largest tree was equal to Corlan's height if it had stood tall and straight, but it bent to provide shade for the eggs.

He carried a medium sword on his hip, in place of the sideblade he had left inside the hippo's gullet. For his walk about the isle, he had grabbed a lance, too. The staff had snapped sometime during previous struggles but he carried the two-thirds that remained.

Flipping the lance so the point was down, he pressed the metal tip against the nearest egg. He jabbed it, made a scratch on the shell. He pressed harder yet the shell refused to crack. He aimed at the middle of the egg and stabbed the lance. The shell did not crack.

He pinched his eyebrows together. *Had they turned to stone? Were these old eggs? Was he a hundred years too late?*

Stepping back, he took his sword in hand, swung hard at the top of the egg. His blade made a scratch but the shell did not break. The blade took a notch in its edge.

Corlan erupted in laughter, like a man possessed by the demons of mirth. He crashed onto his knees roaring great guffaws. How the gods had tricked him! How they had pushed, pulled, and prodded him to this final moment of realization! He had to appreciate their humor. He fell over and shook against the ground. Then he leaped up and kicked the nearest egg with his foot. Without boots, his toes crumpled against the hard shell and he howled in pain.

Alone and ragged, exhausted and wounded, he lay on his back, head braced against one of the eggs. The weeping tree covered him with shade even as the breeze tossed its fronds back and forth. Words filled his head, words from everyone he had spoken to on the long journey. He wondered how he could have missed the signs, the omens that his efforts would all be in vain.

"I've found my home among the eggs," he spoke to the clouds overhead. "I've a broken boat and a bent sword. I've a tree that bears fruit, an endless sea of grass. And I've my memories, both loving and cruel. I've stories and they'll comfort me in my final days, spent here on Corlan's Isle, the last refuge of humanity, the last spot of land where civilization reigns, the end of everything I began."

Corlan rested a few days on the isle, gathering all the fruit he could pick, adding some fish he had dried under the hot sun. He packed the boat and shoved off into the marshes.

The bottom was barely five feet, he calculated, plunging the oar into the water. Yet the marsh spread from horizon to horizon. The marsh eventually would give way to open sea, where the bottom would drop further. The Drid would give him whirlpools to fight. And yet, there was no choice but to go on and on and on until he could go on no more.

He stopped to rest each night on a new isle, more numerous the farther he paddled. The marsh grass was thinner. There were open channels, free of vegetation, and he assumed the bottom was deeper. He could see no land high enough to stand out against the horizon, so he kept paddling—and stopping every hour to scoop out water that collected in the boat.

And scanning ahead for the next isle.

Each isle where he stopped he found more eggs. They were pink, or dull red, mottled brown or smooth tan, light blue or dark green, all the same shape, most the same size. A few were twice the size of the others and dark red at the top, almost white at the bottom. He picked up a few of them, comparing their weight. The average egg was as heavy as the quiver of iron bolts with six bolts remaining. He sniffed them, put his ear to them, shook them gently then harder. There seemed to be no life inside any of them.

He felt even more foolish.

By the time he arrived at the edge of the marsh, with the boat once more in need of emptying, he saw the wide expanse of clear water before him. He panicked, never having been a sailor and not trusting the boat in deeper water.

Across the sea, on the far shore, Wallan had said there were mountains that would give him the answers to his questions. He squinted, sitting up in the boat—which pushed the boat lower. A wave of water washed over the gunwale, adding to the pool in the bottom. He thought he could see a line that might be a distant shore. He thought he saw something above that line which could have been mountains. Or maybe they were only clouds.

A triangle of beasts in flight cut across the sky, too high for them to care about him on his boat. They came from the west.

To the north, by the way the horizon wavered in the bright noon light, he thought he saw white, churning water. That would be the Drid, he guessed. As he thought of his situation, he began scooping out the water, feeling the boat rise again.

All roads lead to death, he suddenly recalled Naka Wu saying. It was part of the warrior's code, or another rule she was determined to follow. He felt words lining up in his head, whole stanzas of words. They came from Jemma, something she had taught him, perhaps a spell. He had tried one spell on the road from Danapo and saw it fail. The words were different.

"All streams lead to death," he muttered, dumping out the last scoop of water.

He had to go on — on to somewhere.

As the sun beat down on him and he paddled the broken boat out into the open sea, he knew his final days were at hand. He only cared that people back in the Burg wouldn't know his fate, would never imagine how his life came to an end. He didn't even have a scriber to record his deeds. He left some women and children behind, but they would never know him. Too dire to even imagine what he would do. Impossible to know how he would swear to make things right if only the gods allowed him to return. He would, he decided. If the gods would allow him.

The harder he paddled, the more he realized the boat was caught in a new current that was dragging the boat north. He held the oar steady but could no longer fight the swift current pulling him into the Drid. He didn't know how far it was, how long it would take for him to fall into the whirlpool, so he spoke out his private thoughts, clenching a fist and tapping it against his heart.

"To a glorious end!" he shouted as loud as he could.

The boat reached the whirlpool the next day and began the spin around its outer circuit, making the compete circle every few hours. As he and his boat fell further into the whirlpool, the time to make the circle lessened. Corlan lay in the boat, dizzy from the motion, sick in his stomach, his empty belly crying its pain. He bent over the side of the boat, tried to spit out whatever hated his belly so much. The boat rocked too far and he fell over the side but was able to hang on with his hands. He struggled to climb aboard and, after almost another full circuit of the whirlpool, managed to fling himself over the gunwale into the boat, breathing hard — as though saving himself at that moment truly mattered when he would soon be welcoming death down inside the dark abyss.

*Draconus raelana comptus lenius...*was how it began. *Prelæus aet fili corpio denexi uani sovo...*was how it ended. In the middle was more of the same. That was all he could remember.

When Corlan opened his eyes he saw the entire world spreading far below, the endless blue sea, the swirling white whirlpool to his right, the brown marshes further in the distance. Only high, gray mountains filled the sky to his left. Above all of it were pale pink clouds.

He turned his eyes closer at hand and realized he lay within the great maw of a mountain-master, the largest kind of dragon. His six-foot figure fit comfortably inside the dragon's mouth. Its teeth and fangs were parted enough that he could gaze out between them at the world as though he rode in a flying carriage.

Words had continued tumbling from his head, string after string of the strange words, chiseled from a language he did not know. Yet there they were! His mind spoke them, spoke them again and again, as his boat had washed into the innermost circuit of the whirlpool and was sucked down into the Drid —

And with the words mumbled in careful rhythm, a dragon came and snatched him from the boat, nimbly picked him up, and bore him in its mouth without succumbing to the desire to chomp down on him or swallow him in a single gulp, as mountain-masters were wont to do. Instead, he was carried westward across the sea — away from the whirlpool, toward the range of high mountains. To the lair of this mountain-master, he supposed, there to be offered as dinner to its younglings.

"Perfect...." The gods were always so perfect in their plans.

The peaks were lost in the clouds. As the dragon mounted the air current, they were hidden in the whiteness of heavens. He breathed deeply, finding it harder to get enough air in his chest, then lost consciousness.

When Corlan awoke, he lay on his back upon a flat stone. Beside him, and apart from him, were other stones in shades of gray, mostly smooth, some with crystal seams, some sparkling with minerals. A flat gray light filtered down from above. He was in a narrow gorge, he saw, somehow dropped into it without injury. His dulled head swam with fantastic images, his dreams merging with reality.

Climbing off the stone, he felt himself, checking for injuries. With only the loincloth covering him, his bare torso showed a multitude of scars. He felt no bones broken. His feet were cold without the boots. The loincloth was moist and uncomfortable, smelled of the dragon's saliva and from many days' effort paddling the boat. He shivered at the chill, feeling an intense cold for the first time.

So this is how the gods' home looks....

He stepped around the stone he'd slept on and saw what seemed to be a trail through the other rocks. On either side of the gorge the mountain rose straight up like the walls of a castle. Only this trail provided a passageway, so he took it.

He followed the trail, which seemed to lead upward rather than down, shivering as each footstep touched the cold pathway. He wrapped his arms around himself, knowing he had nothing left. First, it was to be death by dragon attack. Then death by all sorts of stupid means imposed by men and women. A short time ago he was supposed to drown. Then he was certain to be dinner for a brood of draglings. Now it seemed as though he was meant to freeze to death.

He was uncertain what he was looking for, walking along the gorge's trail. He blew out frosty breaths, uncertain what he expected to find. Every few steps he glanced about but saw only gray stone rising on either side of him. Gazing up, he saw only a patchwork of gray clouds. All was silent; the only sounds were the echoes of his feet slapping against the stone path, his shallow breathing, and the soft pulse of his heart.

When he had to step up onto a rock to continue along the path, and stepped down on the other side, he saw the first dragon.

43

The End of All Beginnings

CORLAN SHIVERED. His bare feet were frozen against the stone path, his weary arms wrapped tightly around himself.

Seeing the dragon emerge from between the rocks ahead of him, he fell back a few steps. The beast was smaller than he was used to seeing, the size of a donkor, so he took it to be a juvenile. The dark red body with black stripes along its ribs and down its tail stood out against the gray rocks looming around them. The beast hobbled on short gnarly legs. On its narrow shoulders short, red wings sprouted, flapping at random, completely useless for flight.

The small dragon waddled up to the gray stone between them. The wheezing noise from the beast alarmed Corlan, made him step back more. The beast's head rose and its neck elongated, and the whiff of sulfur stung his nose at the same instant the hiccup of fire erupted from the dragon's mouth, striking the stone.

Glowing bright orange for a moment, the stone soon faded back to gray. The dragon withdrew. Corlan stepped forward cautiously. He put his hand to the stone, felt its warmth, then hesitantly climbed onto it. Feeling comfortable, he pulled up his legs, placing his feet flat on the stone's surface.

He regarded the dragon, wondering if the stone-warming was a deliberate act. How could the beast know what he needed? He shook his head. Nothing made sense. He didn't need to concern himself with whatever dragons chose to do. It was part of his death march.

Noises above made him look up at the top of the cliffs that lined the gorge. Gathered on both sides were dragons similar to the one that helped him. Juvenile dragons, curious to gaze upon a human. One after another yawned, showing their teeth, flexing their wings, grunting and growling and hissing down at him.

Thinking he was being mocked, Corlan climbed off the stone and continued forward, staggering through the gorge, stepping carefully along the stone path that seemed prepared just for him.

Another dragon appeared on the path, emerging from a cave to the side. Like the first dragon, it had stunted wings and walked awkwardly on short legs, its thick tail flicking back and forth as though helping to keep its balance. The ugly beast faced him, showing a full set of jagged teeth, four rows deep, then turned abruptly away and scooted down the path.

Corlan took that as a sign to follow, so he did. There was no other path to choose. *This is the path to doom.* The words echoed through his head. He tried to will them away yet they persisted.

The path widened and the dragon circled around the open area, grinning at him, then turned to the side. As it flicked its tail, a deep rumble arose. He did not understand, so the dragon came up to him and snapped at the dangling end of his loincloth. The dragon continued tugging at the ragged end until Corlan moved forward.

Two more dragons arrived, both the same size and appearance as his toothy escort. They were both a somber green with no noticeable stripes or other coloring.

"Where to now?" he asked, staring at the two.

The previous escort had already slunk away. He watched the new pair of escorts flick their tails to call him, then waddle off around the corner of the open space.

"I'm certain to be dreaming all this. It must be a dream—it must be. I've died, and now the gods torment me with all these dragons."

Around that corner, the path widened more. On each side the cliffs stood lower but were mounted by more dragons: grey-bellies, red-bulls, green-horns, hornchins, drapers, blue-lightnings, and more. They squatted along the rim. Some cried out, others grumbled. A few stretched their heads out over the edge, showing him teeth. Others swept a set of talons down across his path, threatening him.

Corlan halted, thinking this was the end. Despite the luck he'd had leaving the marshes, the gods meant for him to face a jury of his enemies. That much was clear. They would toy with him, tease him, harry him, and at some point, surround him and shred him with talons and fangs. Only when he lay broken and bloody would they mercifully ignite him and roar at the flames.

His twin escorts paused. The air behind him warmed. He glanced back at the dragon following him. The draper had a body twelve feet long, wingspan thirty feet. Its wings were tucked against its body to fit through the gorge. When Corlan hesitated, the draper growled and lurched forward, urging him to continue.

The congregation of dragons cheered with cries and screams and roars. The draper again lurched at him and he fell ahead, tripping over the uneven path. His knee hit the stone and he cried out in pain. The draper stepped around him, its wing brushing his back, forcing him down against the stone, down on his hands and knees. The draper roughly pushed past him, cawing to the congregation. They responded with louder voices.

Corlan got to his feet slowly. No, they were not dumb brutes as he had always believed. He'd learned they could communicate. And they could plan an attack. And carry it out with deadly effectiveness. Now he had been captured, paraded through their sanctuary solely for the entertainment of the clans. As a lesson for the juveniles. This soft-skinned weakling, having neither talons nor fangs, is what they call a *dragonslayer*. The dragons above him seemed to laugh.

A surge of hot breath blew over him from behind. He turned and saw that a new dragon had taken up the rear. The brown mountain-master, even with its wings folded against its body, was huge and filled even this wider passage from cliff to cliff. It lowered its face to Corlan, nostrils flaring, saliva oozing off its fangs, its face twice as tall as Corlan.

He smelled sulfur and the mountain-master hissed the vile odor at him, made a performance of his belly rumbles and throat rasps. The dragon knew he would recognize the staging of a fire-breath kill and that it would be the final terror for this weak dragonslayer they had brought into their fortress of stone.

Corlan ran ahead with genuine fear, trying to get away from the mountain-master. In his hurry, he tripped and fell, splayed across the gray stone path. His knee was bleeding, ripped open against the stone. On his side, he gazed around; it was a temple forum now, a space at least sixty feet across. He stared up at the cliffs, marking the congregation gathered around him.

Ahead of him was the wall. In the wall was a dark opening — a cave! He considered whether he could make it to that entrance and dive inside before any dragon could launch fire at him. Could they follow him into the cave? Probably smaller dragons could. Maybe he was meant to be given some hope — just a moment of hope — all the better to make the final act more glorious, he thought.

The mountain-master nudged him forward with its steaming nose and stinking breath. Its nose spike tapped Corlan's backside, pushed him ahead. He took three more steps. *Why not kill me right now, right here in this arena?* The audience had already gathered.

"Let it end quick," he whispered to the gods, hoping they would hear him. "And let my relations live long and happy without me. Protect them from the fury of dragonkin."

The mountain-master could barely contain itself, nudging him to take another step. Then the nudge came to his shoulders, forcing him to his knees like some wayward slave that finally had been caught. He bowed his head and clasped his hands in his lap, breathing deeply despite the thick sulfur odor that filled the area.

The mountain-master let out a mighty roar and the sheer power of the air it expelled threw Corlan down, face flat against the stone, his chin hitting hard. He expected a foot with claws spread to drop over his outstretched body. Then it would be done.

"Stop playing," he grunted. "Get it over!"

The dragons assembled around the stony arena roared with the mountain-master, creating a cacophony that grew in ferocity, noise directed at him, the lowly human —

Until it all suddenly stopped.

The silence was complete, not even an echo.

Corlan dared not look to see the reason for so many dragons to be so quiet all at once. He turned his head, cheek pressed against the stone floor, and saw the mountain-master had squatted, lowering its head, eyes closed. As if praying.

He turned his head forward, focusing on the dark cave entrance. Two fang-masters crouched at each side of the opening, their six-foot fangs like the halberds palace guards might bear, their powerful shoulders like stone statues the gods themselves would fear.

Between the two dragons appeared a little girl dressed in a white gown. She stepped from the black of the cave and stood perfectly still, gazing down at him for what seemed like most of forever.

Then she spoke: "Let this one live."

In the front sitting room of their new residence on the northeast side of Danapo, overlooking the lake, the lady of the house, slipping into a pink robe, strolled out to the veranda where she saw her husband had prepared a light meal to break their fast.

"Good morn, Rupy darling," said Jemma.

She tossed back her curly blond locks and brushed her hands over her wide belly, certain that it had grown more during the night. Her husband gazed at her in delight.

"He calls you yet?" asked Rupas.

"He does not speak," Jemma replied, a smile breaking across her rosy-cheeks, "yet he kicks a strange code known only to him. I will learn it soon, I promise."

"Then he will be strong and healthy," said Rupas.

"Oh, don't say that!"

"Isn't strong and healthy what we want for him?"

"The goddesses will curse us with strength and health if we speak it so loud." She stepped up to him, took his hand, and placed it on her belly. "I wish him to have an easy deformity, like a bent foot, well enough to gain him the sympathy of his peers yet not keep him from doing whatever he wishes in life. Even if he is born in full health, I will love him anyway and be proud of him."

"I will love him, as well." Rupas gazed at his lovely spouse. "Yet, in this year we've been in union, I've always wished he would be born with no deformity. I've lived my whole life with this hunched back and always gotten teased for it."

"In Danapo, no person teases. You know that by now. None have teased you, have they? They give sympathy to you, don't they? We give sympathy here. Our son will be welcomed here, also."

"Unless he is perfect."

"I pray for imperfection. Imperfections give a boy character."

Rupas grinned, feeling the kick inside her belly. "I want most for him to be strong and healthy. If the people here will not accept him for it, then we will go to another city."

"Another city?" Jemma was perplexed. "What city could that be? To Covin, a wyma city? To Luval, a men city?"

"I had considered that city our friend Corlan hailed from. He only called it the Burg. It was a mixed city. And he described it as a place of harmony and care."

"Harmony and care? Then it must be similar to the great hall of the goddesses." She laughed.

Rupas sat back, and Jemma took her chair. They dined, gazing out at the lake, enjoying the summer morning with the birds singing and the sun warming them.

"I wish I could know of his fate," said Rupas suddenly, between bites of fruit. "Heading to the west, to the marshes, he always said, to the nesting ground of the dragons, to destroy them."

"We have not seen a dragon pass in many months," said Jemma, shaking her head. She knew her husband always regretted not going on with the dragonslayer. That was the one thing she disliked about him. "Perhaps he succeeded. No need to worry."

"We will never know." Rupas ate more. "Unless we see a dragon fly again. The news from Evanal was incomplete. A bunch of useless fools setting course for the marshes...then likely they fell off the edge of the world. Who would draw them to such a mission?"

"It's only gossip. Besides, men are such fools." Jemma snickered. "Except this man I have. He is smart and clever and pleases me."

"I'm pleased that I please you, Jemma, my queen."

"Oh, I'm not a queen!" She glanced suspiciously back over her shoulder. "Not yet."

"Not ever, if we can be blessed."

"You bring me so much sympathy, Rupy dearest. One day I may be raised to a higher position. With a deformed son, perhaps I could become a queen."

"So I've nothing to fear...."

"That would take a conquering army. So stop suggesting that! Danapo does not have a fighting force sufficient for that conquest. Besides...you really don't wish me to be a queen. Too much work, you keep saying. That should not matter. We would have plenty of servants to care for our son."

"Servants we trust."

"Yes, of course. Not like those Hiro Ka trusted. Not like those."

"No, no, of course not. Not like any of those rebels."

Rupas smiled at his wife, truly happy for the first time in his life.

"So what shall we do today, dearest?" Jemma asked with a sigh, gazing at the sunshine on the distant hills.

"Live well, my love. Live fully," he said. "And remember to sing and dance some every day, no matter your deformity."

Swinging the front door open with a bang, the old woman stepped onto the stoop and from her bent pose chastised the boy for the noise he was making. He didn't hear her complaints, too busy slicing the wooden sword through the air as though he was in a great battle. He chopped left and right, spun around and chopped at new enemies. When he turned in her direction, he saw her and froze.

"Sorry, Granny," said Tam. "I was training. I didn't think it was so much to bother you."

Urma hissed at him. "I have one-hundred and sixteen years, Tam. I need my rest. Rest! You can swing your sword without all the shouts and grunts. I'm sure real warriors do not waste so much spirit on such cries."

"You're right," said Tam, swinging the sword over his head and coming at her.

Urma fell back, almost lost her balance. "Boy! Stop that! Don't frighten an old magus!"

"I was only playing."

"You frightened me."

"I'll frighten anyone who comes at me. I'm going to be ready for anyone. Man or dragon, won't matter at all. Corlan taught me how to use a sword."

"Corlan...the man you swore to hate?"

Tam lowered his face. "I know. I did say that."

Urma, bent over, stood low enough for his eyes to meet hers even with his face lowered.

"When you get attacked by a dragon, you can't think clearly," said Tam. "He didn't believe I really loved Bai Lo. He didn't respect our love." He frowned. "I did love her. I'm gonna think of her all the rest of my life. She was my first love. I know what love feels like because of her. But Corlan wouldn't see that. He said I was too young to know what love is."

"He knows a good deal more than you, Tam. He was right. You were too young to know. But still you felt it, the greatest trick of the goddess. You fell into the trap."

Tam bowed his head. "Yes, Granny. I know that now." He took her gnarled old hand in his. "Thank you for everything you've done for me. My new face. My life, too. And raising me as your son." He released her hand.

"Someone had to." Urma sneered, spit on the ground. "I trusted Naka would return. I should've guessed what she'd do, run off with that man. I'm not suited for raising a boy. Too old for that. Every day

I curse her. Wanting to be with your Corlan hero! Vagabond, I say. Who knows what kind of life they've now? I know one thing: they won't ever be making children. That's for certain." She chuckled, like a creaky door swinging back and forth, catching a rat's tail with each swing. "Good luck to them both."

"Corlan had to finish his journey," said Tam in a softer voice. "We men understand that. Got to finish what we start. Got to finish the mission. Always. I'm going to finish what I started."

"And what's that, little man? You on a mission today?"

"Don't call me that!"

"You *are* a little man. Though soon you'll be a big man. Cannot keep that from happening, much as I may wish. Then it'll be your choice whether to do big man deeds or big man terrors. Both exist in this world, Tam. If Corlan taught you anything, it likely was to be a good man, honor other humans, keep to your promises, and act with strength and duty—"

"And be kind to everyone." He grinned, happy—then slipped into something darker. "Until they trick you!" He swung the wooden sword through the air again, its blade landing an inch from Urma's foot. "Or they betray you!"

"Stop that!" She swung her hand out to smack his face, just catching his chin. "You save your sword play for a real fight."

"I will. I'm going to Luval—the men's city. I'm going to join their army and fight for justice!"

Urma cracked a smile, her thick eyebrows pinched. "Justice?"

Tam nodded with a sincere smile, laying the wooden sword against his shoulder in the rest position. "Justice for all."

"And what do you think that is?"

"I want all cities to be mixed. I want to find my own lady. I want everyone to live in peace and harmony. I want everyone to be free from worrying about dragons or each other or mountain fire or rivers of rock or crashing stars."

"Ah! So you want to be a god. Is that it? Playing with stars!"

Tam gave her a smirk. "Is that so bad?"

"Well, I'll not worship a boy god. Nor a little man god."

"For you, I can make an exception, Granny."

"Thank you, Tam." She looked him over. "Now put on clothes and help me with laundry. And get the goat's milk in here. Gussie's gonna be hungry when he wakes and these teats of mine haven't seen milk in sixty years. There'll be a new body to sew up coming later today, too. You're helping with that. Another lesson for you. That, and the lesson of responsibility! No time for you to be playing swordsman or running around in a loincloth like your hero! There's work to be done. Besides, we can't expect a newborn babe to learn the arts of a magus, can we?"

Tam looked up. "Is he crying?"

Urma glanced back, shook her head. "I'm too old to hear him."

"I'll check on Baby Joragus." He stepped around the old woman. She grinned as he entered the house.

"He'll be a good papa," she muttered. "I know it like I know the soles of my feet and the wax in my ears. Though that Gussie is such a temperamental babe!" She raised her voice, calling to Tam: "If the wetcloth needs changing, save a sample for the fermentation bin!"

In the Great Hall of the palace in the Burg, Prince Vilmer solemnly sat upon his throne, wishing for the days when the hall had been filled with dancing and merriment, song and revelry, and everyone loved him, hanging on his every word. Instead, no one came at his invitations. So the musicians sat in silence and the guards stood as required. He squirmed against the throne, like he'd become stuck.

"I blame Braden Batiste," the prince muttered over and over. "Silly little man. Devious man. Seducer of princesses. Vile human waste. Dreg of the Valley of Death. May dragons burn him to ash."

He considered that place: the ancient river valley. He had not spoken of it in more than a year. *That lifeless spread of dried earth that touches the very walls of the palace.* And in the opposite direction it snaked across the realm like...*like a snake, a poisonous snake...like that Batiste snake!*

Tomorrow would be a great day, he told himself, rubbing his hands together. That snake would be killed, its head cut off. Already his favorite executioner was sharpening the mighty axe. Then he, Prince Vilmer of the Burg, would reign supreme once more. None of this contemptuousness, no more rebellious acts —'twould be the end of dismissiveness and rudeness and plain ignorance of his official *royal* position as head of the state. He would smash them all.

The dragonslayers' guild hall would burn, too, worse than if a dozen dragons set it aflame. Then the people would know who was their true leader. His guards would fan out through city streets and arrest every one of the rebels, lock them away forever. He would not be as kind as he was when he sent his brutish cousin into the Valley of Death to gather dragon eggs. Corlan was so stupid, he laughed. The only man who could ever challenge him! Yet he had gone off into the unknown so willingly.

He smiled, sitting up, feeling his mood lift.

The sound of a child crying distracted him. He turned to see his sister, Princess Vorinna, approaching with her little bastard. The child had her homely face. Its appearance was like a *girafor* whose head was ungainly large. Poor creature! And they named him Alfik, after some long-forgotten sage nobody ever liked.

"Brother," the princess called as she entered the hall wearing a golden gown with high collar and drooping sleeves. "Why do you sit here day after day? It's not as though you have called an audience. You expect people to arrive spontaneously just to gaze upon your magnificence?"

He turned to meet her eyes. "Yes. That is what I expect."

"Then you are a simple man." She frowned. "I pity you, Vilmer."

"You should pity yourself!" he roared like a dragon.

He realized how his outburst echoed through the hall. When his words returned to him, he felt embarrassed at losing his composure. The musicians were staring, so he dismissed them with a sharp wave. As they departed, he cocked his head, staring at Vorinna. She had not cringed at his rage.

He sharpened his stare. "Such a whore. Worthy of the dirtiest of streets. Letting that filthy Batiste lay with you! Disgusting. And now, the forlorn babe, with the appearance of all that is evil and vile. I shall not vacate the sentence on that pox-filled pustule of yours. Your *dear one* must remain in seclusion. And there's no better seclusion than our cold, damp dungeon."

Vorinna leveled her eyes at him. "I did not come here to ask you to vacate the sentence." She stepped onto the dais despite his sneering glare, a stern warning not to. "This is my hall, too. I have as much right to be here. As much right to sit on that throne as you. Father wanted us to rule together but I tire of courtly protocol."

"I'm the older child!" he barked. "I'm the male child!"

"You are correct. You are the older *child*. You've been acting like a child every day since you actually *were* a child. And being the male is hardly any great honor. I've just read a scroll about a city where only women live, and the few males they have are all slaves. Seems like a wonderful place. No, the Court life has not matured you at all. Instead, it's coddled you, kept you locked inside that child mind of yours."

"How dare you insult me!" He wanted to jump up—yet at that moment he felt he should not be compelled to expend the effort. He was the prince, after all. Let others do the jumping.

"The truth is not an insult." She stepped closer to him as he sat up straight in the throne. "I tell you the truth no one else will dare speak. Only I will be honest with you, for all the good it does me."

"You? Tell the truth?" He laughed, feigned surprise. "You have ambitions the same as others. I see that. Perhaps the ladies' quilting symposium? I shall appoint you the director. That should keep you away from boredom."

"I've never worried about boredom," said Vorinna. "I worry only about truth. It's a strange thing to have to keep focused on that thing we call truth, as though it comes only on a dragon's breath, even as some would try to put it out. Yet how can one cut a flame?"

"Flames are easily extinguished, Sister."

"Not if they burn hot enough."

Vilmer snickered. "What makes you so willing to fall on the knife for everyone, telling me the truth—the truth as you create it?"

Vorinna smiled, holding it until Vilmer lost his grin.

"You have no response?" the prince demanded.

The princess demurred. "Yes, Brother, I do indeed have ambitions. And yet I have hidden them all these years, tucked behind this elegant dress. I've kept them locked in the folds of my bed sheets, safe under my pillows. I have kept them from your sight by pretending to be a feeble-minded dolt. 'My crazy sister' or 'that stupid girl' I recall you calling me much too often. Not like Corlan, who always treated me with kindness." She pursed her lips. "But Corlan isn't here. I thought you'd ruin yourself in good time, but I grow impatient. Braden has grown impatient, too."

"What does that filthy lout have to do with our relationship?" asked the prince, stammering. "He is not at all part of the family."

"He is the father of my child. He is the man I love."

"Yet I've forbidden you from wedding him."

"I need not your approval for a love match."

"Is love possible with such a crumb of excrement?"

"I do so enjoy how you mince words."

"Do you?" He laughed.

"I do." She laughed back at him. "I shall miss your wordplay."

"My wordplay—?"

The words slipped from his lips at the same instant the knife slid between his ribs.

He stared at her face, saw a bizarre synthesis of pale delight and radiant glory. His gaze fell upon her shoulder, followed her arm, elbow bent, the golden sleeve tight around her wrist, the golden embroidery looking so detailed, excellent work. The white lace encircling her wrist was gorgeous. With the lace folded over her soft, fair hand, he could barely see the handle of the knife.

He wondered in the next instant whether he could perhaps turn back time and change his last words. They were not what he wished his final utterance to be. He should have said something bolder, like "I am known for my wordplay" or something sour: "How dare you disparage my clever wordplay!" That would be much better than the underwhelming retort he'd given. That really had no meaning in the context of assassination.

Glancing down at his elegant golden vest, he saw blood dripping there, confirming his suspicion about what had happened. Done by Vorinna! His stupid little sister! All these years playing dumb. Then the scandalous affair with Braden Batiste—

"Is he done yet?" asked a melodious voice the prince recognized as belonging to Braden Batiste. "The guards have released me from my cell, just as you said."

Vilmer would have preferred his brutish cousin Corlan be the one to drive the dagger home. Better him, a strong and violent man, than his little sister.

"Yes," Vorinna calmly replied. "He is done."

44

Apotheosis

THE GRAY STONE STOOD as tall as a man, flat and smooth, polished to a fine gleam. Standing before the stone, Corlan could see himself clearly. He saw his scars—the ugly marks of battle, the love pats of dragons. More important than those images of himself he saw on the stone were the images he saw of the world outside the cave where he was imprisoned.

There were no iron bars here, no wooden door with lock and key, only a pair of drakes or dragons standing watch in the entryway, blocking any escape. They never slept, and scarcely batted an eye or gave any attention to matters other than him. Their teal or orange or crimson eyes always watched him, as though they were awaiting permission to dine.

Sometimes, when he was at the edge of despair, a meal would be brought to him: usually flowers, stems, leaves, roots, berries, or fruit, and he wondered how far from the icy mountain they would need to fly to find such food. He had many questions yet no one to answer them.

He feared the one who brought the food, a tall, ghostly human—formerly human, now a hideous figure half skeleton and half rotten flesh, walking so stiffly and ungainly, staring at him with blank eyes, perhaps seeing nothing, and a neck that bent awkwardly to the left. The creature obeyed some force he could never understand, but he was glad for the food.

"She is called Jabuli," said a small voice.

Corlan looked up from his plate of plant food.

"I did everything I could do to protect her," the voice continued, "yet none can mend the severed cord that stretches from each person all the way to O. Everyone dies, of course. I warned her. In the end it was Aerog that was startled by the sudden flutter of a bird from the brush. She stepped back suddenly and her tail swished carelessly to the side, quite innocently. Jabuli fell—as I saw in my dreams—and at the bottom of the gorge her neck was broken. I had not yet learned how to mend such an error or undo the cycles of time. Before I could learn, the decay was too much. Some would say it was her fate. Yet 'fate' is just a word they write on the parches for people to read and make complaint—"

"Why did you show me those pictures?" he asked, staring up at the flat, polished stone as the images faded away.

He wondered whose voice he heard. Perhaps it was the strange little girl he often caught staring at him from between the stones, as though she were afraid to show herself. He was a man, frightening to a child, he knew, yet he was so weak it might not matter.

"Why—why did you have to show me the murder of Naka Wu?"

His wavering words echoed around the chamber, slapping him as they returned. He tossed the plate of food away as tears spilled from his eyes. He could not breathe.

"Because it happened," came the answer in the same tiny voice, seeping into the chamber from a crack between the stones. "Because they are part of who you are."

Corlan stopped his panting, thinking the voice was only inside his head. He grabbed his head to stop it.

"Part of who you have become," said the voice.

He thought the voice must be the little girl's, and he spun around searching for her face among the gray stones.

"But...why?" he called out.

"Because of everything you have done. You are the cause of what others have done. That is how the world of humans goes."

"I went on a journey," he spoke with more confidence. "Only that. It was my duty, not theirs. They are innocent."

"Not even a babe is innocent."

"Punish me then, if that is my fate. But not them. Not those people I met on my journey."

"It is done already," said the voice. "The wave has caught them, and carried them away."

Corlan glanced quickly about the chamber.

"Where are you?"

Out from between two stone walls stepped the little girl wearing a white gown once more, as calmly as though she had slipped out of bed without her parents knowledge and went to play with dragons and a strange man who wanted to kill them. He had expected a toy or doll to be dangling from her little hand; instead, she carried only a small hand mirror. It appeared to be made of stone, a small slice that had been polished the same as the great stone he despised.

Corlan stared at her, not intending to show a mean face. He was simply too weary, too distraught to smile. He focused on the mirror she carried.

"Is that your personal looking glass?"

She nodded ever so slightly.

"What do you see there? Me? My life? My journey? What?"

She remained without expression. "Everything."

Corlan shook his head, uncertain what to think or do, how to act before this little girl who seemed to hold his fate in her tiny hands.

"What do you feel?" said the girl in her small voice.

"Feel?" He was not sure what she meant. "I'm cold, and hungry, tired, and several injuries on my body pain me. I need more than a loincloth in this cold cave."

"What do you think?"

He was perplexed. She did not intend to help him, unconcerned with his condition, it seemed.

"What do I think? I wonder why I am here. How I got here. Why I am not dead yet."

"What do you want?"

He bowed his head. Nothing he said seemed to matter.

"I want...I wish I could go back. I wish I had the chance to start again and go on a different journey."

"How would you go?"

He shook his head, uncertain how to answer. "As the magi say, and scribers write, a journey has no good or evil. It is simply a road and anything can happen on a road."

"Have you found your road?"

"My road? I've been on a road for many months!" He realized his outburst and waved his hand to dismiss it. "My road has lasted all my life...it seems. I'm sorry. It has been a long journey, a long road. I'm too wounded to go on." He let out a long sigh. "Yes, I've found good as well as evil."

"What have you done?"

Maybe when he finished answering her questions she would help him, give him a robe to wear, and better food, maybe let him know what he had to do to be freed. Or else call in her dragons to end him.

"I walked where there was no road. I hunted for dragons, killed a few — or many — but I swear they attacked me first. I had to defend myself and my companions. Dragons are like any beast. They get hungry, they seek food, and sometimes humans are food. But I don't want to be dragon food."

The girl's eyes seemed to brighten at his remark.

"You can understand, can't you?" Corlan begged.

"There is much that can be understood." She observed him for a moment as he rubbed his eyes. "What do you understand?"

He bowed his head again. "If I was spared death only to answer a bunch of questions from a little girl, then I want to know who you are and how it is you are here. Both of us seem out of place among this dragon horde." He raised his face, met her eyes. "Please tell me."

"You cannot speak my name or terrible things will erupt in the world below. I must always be careful. If you need a name, say the word 'Adora' and I will know you call me."

He furrowed his brow. "Adora...?"

"The word surprises you."

"I remember a story...long ago, when I was just a boy, a story I heard. My mother told me. A story about a girl named Adora. I don't remember more. Except that...she said it had something to do with the day I was born. She said she had a dream and when she awoke I was there in her arms."

"There are many stories. Some are true, some not true. Not all of them make the world."

"I also heard a story about a princess who ran away, got lost in another world. It was a world where...where she was protected by dragons. I remember it was the first time I ever heard of dragons. I didn't believe they were real."

"They are real."

"Yes, yes, I know. All thirty-eight species of dragons, wyverns, wyrms, and drakes, and a few strange beasts I know not the names for. All of them. They are not of my world."

"They are of my world."

Corlan's breath caught in his throat.

"Your world?"

The girl glanced to the side, indicating the gap between the stones, he guessed.

"My world," she confirmed. "Your world is out there. Beyond the whirlpools, beyond the marsh, off in the lands of cities, where women and men fight each other. Your world is the place where the pictures come from."

The images flashed through his head again, quicker than before, landing like hard whacks from a wooden sword.

"What am I supposed to do?"

He could not bear the thought of Naka Wu dead. Nor could he endure the way his companions had gone on without him. He'd made promises and could not fulfill them. He'd left them thinking he was either dead or he had succeeded with his plan to destroy the dragons' nesting grounds. He laughed to himself.

"There are no nesting grounds, are there?"

"Not in your world."

"They exist in your world then?"

"Everywhere."

"Then how...why...do dragons attack in my world?"

The girl seemed to grin. Or perhaps it was only a trick of the light filtering through the cavern's gray rock, a ghostly illumination that wavered as though disturbed by passing clouds. He squinted: yes, the slightest of grins....

"The door has been open for some time," she said.

Corlan froze. He regarded the little girl a while before he dared ask his question: "Why?"

"A door is meant to be opened."

"And closed," he responded quickly.

"The reason for a door is to open and go through it," she said with a giggle.

"Then you close it to keep others out," he retorted.

"So be it. The door fell open, likely when your world shook apart more than two-thousand years ago. I cannot close it. I cannot keep them from entering your world. You see...I have a curse, as well as you. Not even a babe is innocent."

She stared at him as he struggled to comprehend her words.

"You are not pleased."

"A lot of terror has wounded my world," said Corlan in a solemn tone, close to launching into a lecture on the evils of dragons. "If you can see my history, if you can show those damnable pictures to me, then you know everything that has happened in my world."

The girl smiled, a genuine upturning of the corners of her dainty mouth. She seemed satisfied at his supposition.

"Yes, I have seen everything. All of the twenty-two-thousand eight-hundred and ninety-three years of your world's history. I see them in the birthstone. All of your thirty-nine years, as well. Yes, I have seen the rivers dry up and blow away. I have seen mountains explode and the red rock flow over the green lands. I have seen the stars fall and burst into millions of knives. I have seen the rise of the new people, yet so like the old ones, women and men, fighting each other, and welcoming death as relief. The years crumbling by the hundreds and still the killing, the dying goes on. All the stories of death collected on parches. I have seen the nights grow colder and the days burn hotter, and the seasons flip and turn and fade and die. And I have seen you, and men like you, take up arms against the dragons, and I have seen dragons fight for their lives, too. I have seen all of these things in my time in your world. I have seen them all in a blink of my eye."

Her face had become red as she talked. Suddenly she burst into tears, sobbing—as any child would, he supposed. He wondered if she truly was a little girl who had lost her way, or was wearing some kind of disguise and beneath it was a demon teasing him.

The tears he saw, however, told him he had touched a weakness.

"It has taken so many years of training," she spoke through her crying, "and seeing all the evil that has occurred, for me to be able to shed tears like a human does so easily."

"I'm sorry...Adora. I—I did not intend to upset you by asking a question. But I want to know. I am so confused. What is this place? How did you come here? Why are you here? Why am I here?"

Her sobbing grew louder and her dragon escorts grunted their concern. The fang-master on the left coughed, preparing to fire if the situation called for burning up the threat. The odor of sulfur curled into the chamber.

Corlan dropped to a knee, his loincloth coming loose. He pulled the end of the cloth, made it tighter. He felt a chilling draft.

The girl ceased her crying, wiped tears from her face with the back of her hand.

"Like you, there are many things I wish I could undo, moments in which I wish I could unwind time. Yet only the goddesses have such powers. I cannot use such power willy-nilly or other terrible things will happen."

"Oh, if men and women could do that...unwind time, do things differently...."

"I wanted to save my brother. That is the reason for everything. For me to be here. For you to be here. I fled from my home and took him with me. I ran and I hid. He was just a babe and knew nothing. Then I met a sorceress who gave me a stone. I thought I could use it and its powers to protect my baby brother from our mother."

"Your mother?"

She stared ahead, as though seeing right through him.

"Since that day, I have learned everything from the birthstone. I have seen everything happen. Awful things. I found this mountain, rising in the middle of your world, and I knew it, too, will blow off its crown someday. So I made it my fortress, to watch it—to watch over all of you. And the dragons followed after me."

Corlan gazed up at her from his bent knee.

"You came to my world from another world?"

"There are many worlds.... Yours and mine are but two of them. I told you: I fled my home. I hid from the people chasing me. I arrived here. And I brought the dragons to protect me. For that, I apologize. I did not think it would be so difficult for dragons to live among you and your kind, as they did in my world. Yet now my world is gone. War came, people died. Only dragons reign there today. Men of the Anjoz army came to my homeland and destroyed it. Dragons destroyed the armies. None recall the names: Westina, Lumina, Dorothea, Marvala, Jothea, Folina, Aloa...back to the first dew of time, all the queens of Sannan. Dragons used to be our pets and protectors there, and they might share their wisdom with us if they felt at ease. No more that. Yet in your world, dragons are—"

"Terror—sheer terror! Fire from the skies. Vile beasts that snatch children from their play-yards, swallowing them whole. That is the reason we fight them. And the reason we train men to slay them. We build weapons to kill them. And some of us get ideas how to destroy them forever, so we can be at peace in our world."

"I have seen that." Tears tumbled down her pale cheeks. "I could not save you every time. I tried. I sent a dragon...but...."

"You...*sent* a dragon?"

"Yes. The first I sent was Laxon, son of Rexor, father of Erax. With two horns under his chin."

"The hornchin? *That one?* You sent it to protect us?"

"As I said."

"Protecting us from what? ...other dragons?"

"Yes."

"And at Unting? That dragon? Also sent by you?"

"You needed help, so I sent Laxon again, though he loathed you."

"And at Covin, too? Escaping the rebellion?"

"I said I tried to help you."

"And the dragon on the road from Danapo? The fang-master?"

"He was supposed to protect you from the bandits. I saw —"

"No protection! It attacked us — and the bandits, too!"

"They do not always obey me."

"And the flotilla, down the river from Evanal?"

"I wanted to discourage you from continuing your pursuit."

"Forty dragons? Nearly two-hundred men dead?"

"Yet you continued."

"My mission!"

"To kill dragons? To destroy their eggs? To meet your destiny?"

"All that!"

The girl wiped her eyes. "I tried to protect you."

"I died a dozen times!"

The dragon grunted at him: *Do not threaten my mistress!*

It was the girl's turn to bow her head. Tears dropped like rain upon her feet, spotting the gray stone.

Corlan coughed, cleared his throat, took a long breath.

"I'm sorry, Adora. I didn't intend to speak harshly."

"It is I who am sorry." She looked up. "I am sorry for what I have done."

"What *you* have done?"

She wiped her wet face. "In my attempt to be free from the rules of my world, I set loose these creatures into your world." She brushed her cheek with the back of her hand. "If not for dragons, you would not have gone on this journey. You would not be a dragonslayer. You would not have taken up the dragonslinger and marched through the Valley of Death. There would not be any Valley of Death...if not for me being so selfish."

She burst onto sobbing once more.

"Be at ease, Adora. You're only a child."

"No," she muttered through her tears, "I am older than you. Time is different in my world, as it is throughout all that touches and is touched by O. The power of the birthstone keeps me appearing as a ten-year old girl, yet as white as an old woman. And I will live for a thousand years more, so I cannot be at ease. There is so very much to which I must attend."

A few sniffles ended her tears and it seemed to surprise her, as though she had forgotten about that effect.

"I only wanted to save my baby brother from death. He...he looked so *pretty* resting in my arms, straight out of my mother's womb. I could not let him be killed, not like the other male babes. So I ran away with him...and caused so much trouble in my world and in yours."

Corlan pinched his eyebrows together, staring at her.

"And did you save him, your baby brother?"

The fang-master grunted, holding its fire at the final threshold. She waved at the dragon, commanding it to reject the fire breath and the beast's belly rumbled sadly. It must hurt to conjure fire then have to swallow it, he thought.

"What happened to your brother?" he asked the girl.

She wiped her eyes again and regarded him.

"You tell me how he is...Corlan."

As their eyes locked, he felt a hand on his shoulder though none was actually there. He remembered the small arms that cradled him, the gentle eyes that gazed down upon him, sharing the babble language as though they had learned it together.

He took a hesitant step toward her but halted when she raised her hands in front of herself.

"How is he?" she repeated, lowering her hands. "Is he well? Has he learned all his lessons? Has his journey come to its end? Or is it only now beginning? How is my baby brother?"

Corlan's face softened, his eyes moist.

"He is dumbfounded. That's how he is...sister."

Bowing his head, he knew the histories he had been taught were lies, truths only as firm as the wavering ripples on the surface of a stormy lake. Or like the winter winds bending reeds in the marshes. Everything and nothing were suddenly wed. And yet, as he gazed once more upon the girl, he knew that union would finally bear a new world.

"Might I have some clothes now—"

Before he could finish his request, he found himself fully dressed in fresh garments exactly like those he had worn the day he left the Burg, clean and new: shirt, vest, trousers, belt, and boots. He noted there was no sideblade in a scabbard hanging on his belt.

"Thank you, Adora. They fit well."

The little goddess wiped her last tears, willed them never to return, and spoke to him:

"Now I know who you are, brother. I was not certain at first. Just a man from the marsh. With hate in him. I did not know if you were a man that could be trusted, a man who could do what needs to be done. Now I see you are that man. If you are ready, I will teach you."

Corlan grinned shyly, too tired for a lesson.

"What would that be about?"

The little goddess smiled and the chamber suddenly warmed.

"Everything."

Epilogue

ON THE COLDEST MORNING Mount Zarg had ever known, Corlan made his way to the snowy peak, wearing a black leather jerkin, black cape, and thick, gray woolens from a world he barely knew, dressed for his travel home. Instead of a mountain-master cradling him in its wet, stinking yaw, a trusted green-horn had been selected. The dragon would be large enough to bear him yet not so large he would have difficulty controlling it.

He climbed up its barbed tail, found the leather saddle mounted between the beast's shoulders, and strapped himself in. The dragon answered to the name Hidel, he learned the first day of his training, and Corlan had spent several months getting acquainted with the beast and learning to ride. Adora supervised the training, explaining everything. She taught him how to direct the dragon while in flight. She made Hidel promise not to eat Corlan, nor burn him, nor step on him, no matter the circumstances. In exchange, Corlan swore not to harm the dragon in any way, nor to allow other humans to harm the dragon. It was the start of a new pact between humans and dragons.

With a wave of her small hand, Adora sent them off, and the cry that echoed through the mountain peaks was the cry of a newborn world awakening.

No longer would dragons venture across the wide marshes into the realm of humans; no more would they cause alarm there. No more would humans dare cross the marshes nor mount the far shore above the Drid. It might be impossible to close the door once opened, Adora knew, yet she could limit contact between her world and the world of humans. Corlan was part of that plan.

"Spread the message far and wide," she had told him.

Corlan gazed down from Hidel's shoulders and tried to trace his route through the marshes below. He saw the firm land approaching and thought he could detect the wreckage of boats at the river's mouth, pushed downstream by the current. He called to his dragon to turn up that river, following the bends, staying high enough that no one below would see them or think to shoot an iron bolt in their direction.

They passed north of a city he thought must be Evanal, and they circled around to the southeast, dropping from the gray clouds onto an open field near an old wooden hut where a young man stood swinging a wooden sword.

The dragon gave a cry, setting its feet on the ground, then folded its wings against its body.

"Corlan!" shouted Tam, dropping the sword and running to him as Corlan climbed off the beast. They embraced. When they parted, Corlan gestured to his flying mount.

"This is my dragon. His name is Hidel. He's a green-horn."

"You ride dragons!" The boy was amazed.

"It seemed a better way to make a long journey."

"Can I ride, too?"

"Yes, you must. How else can we go home?"

They could not stay long or else the dragon and the neighbors might meet in an unfortunate encounter. So Corlan made his peace with Urma, told her what Adora had shown him of Naka Wu and the others who had accompanied him. They wept together.

"I dared not believe she cut apart a promise made," said the old woman. "Better death than dishonor, though I'm sorry to know her end. May she be at peace."

She motioned for Tam to go to the next room. She and Corlan drank their tea until he returned.

"This is yours, I believe," said Urma.

Tam set down the basket and Urma dragged it across the floor, pushed it up against Corlan's crossed legs.

"Here," she said. "He belongs to you now. I call him Gussie, but I think you'll call him Joragus the younger. Your choice. I measure his age at six months. Be sure he gets plenty of goat's milk."

Corlan grimaced. "Goat's milk?"

"You think these teats have any milk in them?" She cackled. "I surely know yours do not, mister."

She showed him her toothless grin as Tam broke into laughter.

"Take this boy with you, too. I'm done with him. Always causing a ruckus. He needs to learn a trade. I taught him some magi arts but he's a poor learner. He wants to be like you. I am close to my end, anyway. I'm too old to worry about both a boy and a babe. Teach him something that'll take him through his life in good order."

"I did return for him. It's part of the plan. A little goddess told me what to do. We'll return to the Burg and live our lives there. And raise this babe."

"With your dragon?" asked Tam.

"Yes, boy, you can share the saddle with me. We'll lash the baby behind us."

Corlan roared with laughter at Urma's cross face. With the hut full of laughter, the dragon outside roared in sympathy.

"Go now! Leave an old woman in peace."

Alarms sounded throughout the city and Corlan could hear the noise high in the sky as they circled over the palace. Squads of archers formed in the plaza before the main gate. Others stood ready within the palace compound and along the walls.

"Stand down!" Corlan shouted at them. "I'm Corlan! From the Burg! Do not shoot! I've returned from banishment, bringing back dragonware!"

He repeated his plea as his dragon hesitated, batting the air. With his forty-foot wingspan and twenty-foot head, neck, and body, Hidel made a good target. A ten-foot tail swung back and forth to keep his body in a steady position.

Corlan directed Hidel to descend, talons closed, showing them no threat. He waved a gold and black banner, the mark of the Burg, just to be certain people on the ground knew a man was aboard this dragon.

Hidel settled on the ground, claws digging into the groomed lawn of the courtyard, squashing a few bushes along one side. Wings flapped slowly, then folded against his body, tail wrapping around his rear feet, providing a way down for the man, the boy, and the babe in a basket.

A platoon of guards rushed to them, staying in formation, lances and bows aimed. The captain was ready to give the order. Archers on the walls had turned and set their targets.

"Greetings, guards of the palace!" Corlan shouted, as though he wanted everyone within the palace precincts to hear him. "I have returned, and only a year later than expected."

The guards stood nonplussed. More people came from the palace buildings to see the strange sight of a man riding a dragon.

"Have you forgotten?" Corlan smiled awkwardly, waving his hand. "I was banished from the city until I could return with dragonware. By order of Prince Vilmer—my little fart of a cousin." He let go a great guffaw. "Now you see, I've brought a whole dragon, a live beast, trained to bear me across the skies. What a prize!"

He swept his arm toward Tam, who gave a slight bow.

"I've returned the boy from the palace kitchen, also, as promised, though he is worth much more than a servant's wage. Yes, I speak of the great, the noble, Tamondarus! No more apprentice dragonslayer but forevermore a dragon*master*! And behold this: a baby magus, too, the fifth iteration of Joragus of Metta!"

Corlan gazed around the yard, smiling at the gathering.

"What a great day! Can anyone beat this return? I think not! Why is there no band playing? No trumpets blaring? We must have a fanfare! I am Corlan of the Burg! I am returned from the very gates of Mount Zarg, where I was taught everything by a goddess, and now am returned to these nor'eastern lands!"

He regarded the stunned crowd.

At the approach of an elegantly dressed woman, the guards lowered their weapons. She passed through them, her black hair waving and her golden gown flowing. She stalked right up to Corlan with no fear and hardly a glance at the dragon filling the courtyard. She embraced the man.

"Welcome home, Corlan, dear cousin," said Vorinna, releasing him. "Quite the surprise, indeed. Mmm, you smell like dragon—at once enticing and revolting. We'll prepare you a bath. Vilmer is, unfortunately, unavailable to greet you, but I doubt that disturbs your sleep much. Such a tragedy! Alas, a fatal illness overtook him. I am on the throne now. Yet there is conflict because I am, as you well know, *only* a woman. We never expected you would return. Yet now that you've returned...."

Following behind her was his old rival Bratiste, carrying a babe in his arms.

"I'd heard you were returned to us," said Braden Batiste, always one to affect airs. "I scarce could believe you weren't already long in some grave in the Valley of Death. Yet here you are, dragon-borne at that! Truly a divine spectacle! I must finally bow to your prowess in dragonmastery. It is an old occupation for me, I do confess. And so retirement comes easy. I'm lucky to be engaged as the plaything of Her Majesty, Vorinna, our lovely princess."

"If my cousin is pleased with you," said Corlan, "then I won't have any reason to engage you."

"Rightly so!" He handed the squirming babe over to its mother. "So let us put away our knives and work together to make this the place we would call home. All the hard labor has been done."

"The hard labor?" asked Corlan, narrowing his eyes.

"Cousin, now you've returned, I shall make use of your counsel," said Vorinna. She lay her hand on his arm as he extended his hand and Braden clasped it. "You must join me on the dais."

"I will agree," said Corlan. He looked Braden straight in the eye. "There is yet more hard labor, but let us make this a home worth living in. I have the plan...straight from a goddess."

A bustle of people on his left side caught his attention. A flurry of noise arose as guards tried to keep the crowd back. One woman shouted to him, calling his name, pushing her way through.

Corlan turned to see Petula sauntering toward him. She wore a blue work dress with white apron, her golden hair tied up in twin buns. She appeared as lovingly full-bodied as he remembered. They embraced instantly, then held each other's face through a rain of kisses.

"Corlan, my love!" Petula wept. "I never thought you'd ever be home. I never dared believe it. I prayed to the gods every night for your safe return. You told me not to wait...yet I did. I knew I had to wait for you when I—"

"I have come home, Petti, though not without too many wounds both long and deep. I have been through so much and I need you to mend me, make me whole again. Only you have that power."

Another woman arrived beside Petula. In the thin woman's arms squirmed an auburn-haired girl, her chubby arms grabbing at the woman's black braids. Petula gathered the child from the woman, handed the child to Corlan. He stared a moment before realization washed over him.

The child gurgled at him.

"She says 'Welcome home, Papa.' Your daughter wishes to give you a kiss. You want another kiss, don't you?"

He laughed. "There can never be enough kisses!"

His face lit up, accepting the child into his hands. He raised the child to his lips, kissed her forehead.

"Her name is Flora," said Petula. "I hope the name pleases you. Flora of the Burg. How is that?"

"It's perfect."

Corlan hugged his woman, kissed his daughter, and gestured for the boy named Tam to come and join them, bringing baby Gussie with him.

When he finished introductions, Corlan noticed a brown-haired girl standing at the edge of the crowd. She wore a blue dress with a white apron, the uniform of the palace staff. Corlan put his hand on Tam's shoulder, turned him around.

Tam grinned at her, dared to wave.

"You're a dragonslayer?" she asked shyly, stepping over to him.

"Not really," said Tam, fidgeting. "I'm a dragonmaster. We don't slay them anymore. It's a new law, Corlan said."

"Even so, I think that's so brave. And...you're so handsome, too. My name is Dixi."

"I'm Tam."

She blushed. "You—you want to see the garden?"

"I saw the garden already," he said innocently.

The girl frowned, bowed her head.

Corlan gave Tam's shoulder a pinch. "Go and see the damnable garden, boy. And be happy."

Tam handed baby Gussie to Petula and took the girl's hand. They ran off to see the garden. Petula gave Corlan a wink, wondering if something new would blossom there.

"And where's that old wizard? The one named Nilas," Corlan called out to any palace staff that could hear him. "I have need of his service."

In a matter of minutes, plenty of time for more kisses and hugs, an old wizard was ushered before Corlan.

"I heard you'd returned from your long adventure," said Nilas, holding his long beard off the ground. "I feared the world was about to end, sir, seeing that dragon alighting over the palace."

"I have a task for you. In the saddle bag of that dragon is a small piece of folded parchment. Unfold it and you will find some hair. Use your best Clona arts to remake that being. Can you do that?"

Nilas seemed surprised. "I shall try my best, sir. The kitchen has everything we need. What manner of creature is it?"

"Not a creature but a person."

"A person?"

"Yes. A woman. And when she is born again, call her Jabuli."

"As you wish, Your Majesty."

"What's this *Majesty* you speak?"

"Why, everyone knows you're Prince Corlan. Don't you rule the Burg now? Alongside your cousin? That is what she has decreed."

Corlan smiled like he had just invented the sun and summer had arrived. He held his daughter, the auburn-haired child wriggling in his arms and tugging his beard. Petula, with baby Gussie gazing out from her arms, rested her head on Corlan's shoulder. Above them, Hidel stretched out his neck and head to create some shade—just as the twenty-nine heralds finally let their trumpets blare throughout the palace precincts.

"You hear that? Now I know I'm home," said Corlan. "Trumpets always mean that. At least, that's what I heard a little goddess say."

He nodded thoughtfully, remembering all that he had learned, knowing all he needed to do.

"Now let us begin."

About the Author

Stephen Swartz grew up in Kansas City where he was an avid reader of science-fiction and quickly began emulating his favorite authors. Even after veering from science-fiction, his stories usually feature exotic lands, foreign languages, strangers lost in all-too familiar places, and the occasional breakfast menu.

Along the way, Stephen studied music in college and, like many writers, worked at a wide range of jobs: from French fry guy to soldier, tax clerk, TV station writer before heading to Japan for several years teaching English to whoever was willing to learn.

Stephen is now a Professor of Epic* English and has taught various kinds of writing in New York, Pennsylvania, Kansas, and Oklahoma. Today he lives in the center of tornado alley in Oklahoma. He can be found working on his next novel most evenings and weekends. He does not own any dragons; however, neighbors insist they have heard strange noises.

*without dragons